The Stars of Eger

A Historical Novel by Géza Gárdonyi

Egri Csillagok by Géza Gárdonyi
originally published in 1899

Translation © 2022, T. László Palotás
ISBN 9798829947033

HISTORIA
AZ EGER VARNAC
CZODA NAGY S'ERENTZES VI-
tatáſſáról, és à Törökektól valo meg mene-
:✠: kedéſſéról :✠:

EZ ÉNEKNEC ELÓL IÁRO BESÉDE.

Tu Magyároc már Iſtét imád-
iátoc, Es ónęki nagy hálá-
kat adiátoc, Ielesben Tiſſan
innét kic lakoſtoc, Egri vi
tęzeknec ſoc iót mondiátoc.
Im egy Cronikát mon-
doc, meg hallyátoc, Talám
máſſát ſoha nem hallotátoc, Magyaroc vég ház
ban ſem ſolgáliatoc, Eger várat mint meſt ól
talmaztátoc.

Nem emberi hatalom eſt induele, Mert czae
Wr iſten hatalmáe iclóñe, Ez világ hatalmáe ſem
-iat néut, Töröc Czáſſár eiciét ſégyenire.
R üi

Title page for the 1552 publication of Sebestyén Tinódi's chronicle,
"History of the Miraculously Successful Defense of Eger Castle
from the Turks ..." This chronicle provided much of the detailed source material
for Géza Gárdonyi's historical novel.

The Stars of Eger

**Historical Novel by
Géza Gárdonyi**

Géza Gárdonyi

Table of Contents

Introduction

The successful Hungarian defense of Eger in 1552 was celebrated throughout Europe immediately after the Ottoman Turks withdrew. It was the great Hungarian victory to avenge the Ottoman rout of the Hungarian army almost three decades earlier, at Mohács in 1526. Tinódi and others wrote poetic chronicles in praise of the Hungarian defenders. They are the Stars of Eger. The Captain of Eger, István Dobó (otherwise a rather disreputable character), became a national hero, and Eger became synonymous with national pride for Magyars.

Géza Gárdonyi, the author of the historical novel, *Egri Csillagok* ("Stars of Eger" or "Eger Stars"), made the primary character in his book the *deák*, Gergely (Gregory) Bornemissza. The Hungarian word *deák* has several shades of meaning. It means student as well as scholar. It was used to describe common folk who acquired an education and could read and write. They served as secretaries, stewards and accountants for the nobility.

In the records kept during the famous siege of Eger, Gergely Bornemissza is identified as a *deák*. Not much is known about him aside from his participation in the defense of Eger Castle. He was the son of a Pécs blacksmith. Somehow he acquired his education, became a Lutheran, and was appointed lieutenant of some 250 gunners sent by King Ferdinand to reinforce the defense of Eger. (The guns of those days were not rifles or even matchlocks. They were cumbersome arquebuses, muskets with a touch hole for igniting the gunpowder.)

We do have many details about Bornemissza's participation in the defense of Eger. One verse in Tinódi's poetic chronicles reads:

Serén vala Gergely deák dolgába,
Hordót, kereket ő hamar hozata,
Kerék küllőit deszkákval burítá,
Töltött puskákat beléje alkota.

Talám ily fortélt kevés embör látott,
Gergö deák mint szörzé ez bölcs dolgot,
Puskákkal, szakállasokkal nagy hordót
Tölte forgácsval, kénkőt, faggyút, szurkot.

Ezt nehezen az bástyára tolyatá,
Felgyújtatá, árokban taszíttatá,
Hordó, kerék fut széllel az árokba,
Az terekök vesznek, futnak az sáncba.

Scholar Gergely undertook his work industriously,
He had barrels, wheels quickly brought,
He covered the outsides of the wheels with boards,
And fixed loaded guns inside.

Perhaps such tricks few people had seen,
Scholar Gergö (Greg) cloaking this clever construction,
With guns, bearded cannons, and barrels
Filled with shavings, sulfur, tallow, pitch.

It was difficult to push this to the bastion,
He ignited it, aimed it towards the ditches,
Barrel, wheel run with the wind to the ditches,
The Turks are taken and run to the earth ramparts.

Géza Gárdonyi attended a teacher's college in Eger then earned his living as a school teacher in western Hungary. He wrote articles for local newspapers, began writing two novels, and studied foreign languages. He moved from Budapest — where he had published some short articles and contributed to an opposition newspaper — back to Eger in 1897. The old castle and the historical records of the 1552 siege must have inspired him.

He did research in Vienna for his historical novel, then in Istanbul where he not only witnessed the Shiite Day of Remembrance procession described in this novel, he also gained admittance to Seven Towers by making a sentry drunk, an incident he also adapted for the novel.

Gárdonyi invents a detailed childhood and adolescence for Bornemissza, details that bring us a fictional, delightful, and almost fairytale childhood romance with Éva Cecey. We do know that Bornemissza was married twice: to Erzsébet Fügedi who died in January of 1554, then Dorottya Sigér, and that he fathered six children.

The first draft of *Egri Csillagok* was completed in 1899 and published in serial form in the Budapest newspaper, *Pesti Hírlap*, over Christmas of that year. It immediately became popular. Gárdonyi edited and tightened that version and the novel was published in book form in 1901. That book has become one of the most recognized and widely read books in Hungarian literature.

Cover of volume 1 of the first edition of Egri Csillagok, *1901*

Some Notes on the Hungarian Language

The Magyar language, Hungarian, is not related to any other language in Europe except, very distantly, Finnish and Estonian. It is classified as a Finno-Ugric language and has borrowed many words from Turkish. No one is really sure about the origins of the Magyar people (if defined by language) or how they acquired their language. What is certain is that the Indo-European languages of Slavic, Germanic, Romance, Greek and Celtic neighbors are completely different, which helped isolate Hungary historically.

Although syntax and grammar are complex, spelling and pronunciation of Hungarian are consistent. The stress is always on the first syllable. Accent marks on vowels change the pronunciation, not the stress.

a — short, like the "o" in hot or pot.

á — long, like the "a" in father.

c — always soft, like the "t's" in it's. (The hard "c" sound, as in cat, is spelled with a "k".)

cs — considered a single letter, pronounced like the "ch" in check.

e — short, like the "a" in apple.

é — long, like the "e" in end.

g — always hard, like the "g" in goat.

h — always pronounced, never silent.

i, í — like the "i" in the word "in"; í is longer.

ly — considered a single letter, pronounced somewhat like a "y", as in yellow, only with a hint of "l" preceding the "y"..

j — pronounced like a "y", as in yellow.

o, ó — short, like the "o" in or; ó is slightly longer.

ö, ő — long, like the German ö, like the "ea" in early; ő is slightly longer.

s — always an "sh" sound, like sheep or, as my father used to say, the "s" in sugar.

sz — considered a single letter, pronounced like the "s" in salad.

ty — considered a single letter, pronounced like a soft "st" in stew or "T" in Tuesday, or the "t" and "y" together in "met you".

u, ú — short, like the "u" in Spanish or the "u" in put or "oo" in foot; ú is longer, like the "oo" in good.

ü, ű — long, like "ü" in German, or the "oo" in food; ű is longer.

zs — considered a single letter, pronounced like the "s" in pleasure or the "Zs" in Dr. Zhivago.

Maps of Hungary & Eger Castle

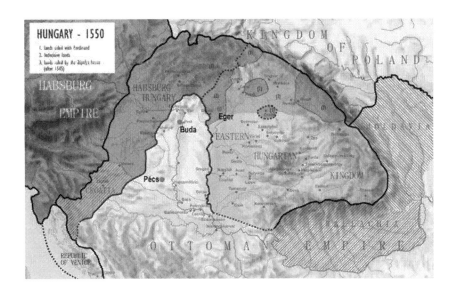

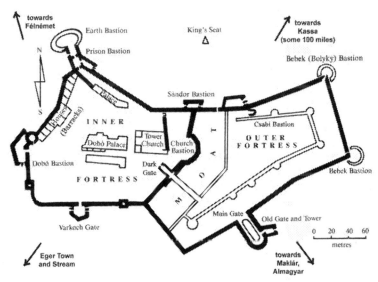

Eger Castle.
The "tortoise" faces east, the earth bastion being its tail.

Part I
From Where Come Hungarian Warriors

1

Two children are bathing in the stream: a boy and a girl. Perhaps it is inappropriate that they are bathing together, but they do not know that. The boy is hardly seven years of age and the girl is two years younger.

They were walking in the forest when they came upon the stream. The sun was blazing hot. The water appealed to them.

At first they only dangled their feet, then up to the knees. Gergely got water on his pants so he took them off. Then he threw off his shirt. Soon both were splashing about naked.

They could bathe. No one would see them there. The road to Pécs was far from there and the forest was endless. But if someone had seen them there, there would have been a ruckus! Not about the boy. He was not any nobility. But the little girl was the daughter of the honorable Lord Péter Cecey. She was a young lady who had disappeared from her house unseen.

It is visible on her naked body that she is a noble girl: chubby like a dove, and white like milk. As she jumps and splashes in the water, her two braids of blonde hair slap on her back.

"Derdő," she says to the boy, "Let's go."

The Gergő[1] named, skinny, brown skinned boy turns around. The little girl grabs onto his neck. Gergő starts heading towards the bank, the little girl still kicking and splashing the water with her feet.

As soon as they reach the bank, Gergő heads for a green tuft of reed bush and looks around worried.

"Oh, the grey!"

He steps out of the water and runs here and there, looking about among the trees.

"Wait, Vicuska[2]," he said to the little girl. "Just wait a bit. I am coming."

And with that, he gallops off naked.

---

[1]   Gergö (Greg) is a nickname for Gergely (Gregory). Derdö is a child's pronunciation.

[2]   Vicus, a nickname for Éva (Eve). The diminutive Vicuska means "little Vicus" and is a term of endearment and affection.

After some minutes, he returns sitting on an old, grey horse, a pitiful rope halter on its head. It had been tied around its legs but the knot had unraveled. As he reaches the bank where they had been bathing, he holds onto the horse's neck, slides and jumps off.

"Let's hide!" he says shivering. "Let's hide! I saw a Turk."

He ties the horse to a tree with one or two loops. He grabs his clothes off the ground. The two naked young children run to a hawthorn bush. They hide behind the bush, lying flat on the dry leaves.

In those days it was not unusual to see Turks on the road. And you, my dear reader, who might think that these two children were bathing in the stream this last summer, would be wrong. Where are these two children now? Where? And where are all those people who come living, move, act and speak in this book? They are all dust!

Well, just put aside your current calendar, dear reader, and bring to mind the year 1533. You are now living in May of that year and either King János is your lord, or a Turk, or Ferdinand I.[3]

This little village where the children belong was hiding in a forest on the Mecsek Hills. Altogether some twenty mud brick houses and one large stone house. Every house had oiled linen for window panes. Even on the lord's stone house. But otherwise, the houses were not that different from those today. The small village was surrounded by the dense vegetation of the forest and its residents believed that the Turks would never find their way there. How would they find it? The road was steep without any wagon ruts. The village had no tower. People lived and died concealed in that village, like forest insects.

The Gergő child's father at one time was a blacksmith in Pécs, but he had died. The mother returned to Keresztfalva with her father, an old, grey peasant who fought in the György Dózsa peasant uprising. Which is why he got shelter from the lord of the village, Cecey.

The old grandfather would occasionally cross the forest to Pécs in order to beg. That was how they lived, even in winter, from whatever the old man could beg. They also got whatever fell off the table from the lord's house.

Well, on that day also, the old man returned from the city.

---

[3] After the disaster at the Battle of Mohács, 1526, there were three competing rulers of Hungary: Hungarian nobles first elected János (John) Zápolya as king who controlled Transylvania and parts of Upper Hungary; then another party of Hungarian nobility elected Hapsburg Austrian Ferdinand as king who controlled parts of western Hungary; then the Ottoman Sultan Suleiman the Magnificent controlled much of central and southern Hungary.

"Take the grey out to graze," he said to his grandson. "The poor horse hasn't eaten anything since morning."

This was how Gergő set out with the horse to the forest. Along the way, as he passed by the lord's house, little Éva snuck out through the garden gates and pleaded with him, "Derdö, Derdö! Let me go with you!"

Gergő did not dare tell the little lady to stay at home. He got off the horse and led Éva in whatever direction she wanted to go. Éva wanted to go wherever the butterflies were. The butterflies were flying into the forest, so they also ran in that direction. Finally, when they saw the stream, Gergő set the horse grazing in some grass. This was how they ended up in that forest stream, and from the stream behind the hawthorn bush.

They lie low. They are shivering because of the Turk.

And it was no shadow that frightens them. After a few minutes, they hear the underbrush rustle, and then under the trees appears an ostrich-feathered, tall white Turkish fur hat and the brown head of a horse.

The Turk turns his head this way and that. He looks at the grey horse. He walks holding the reins and leading his own small, dark chestnut horse.

Now it can be seen that the Turk has a boney face and brown hair. He has a walnut-brown cloak over his shoulder. A tall white fur cap sits high on his head. A cloth is tied over one of his eyes. The other eye is studying the grey tethered by a tree. That he does not like the horse is revealed by the grimace on his face. Still, he unties the tether.

He would prefer the boy whom he had spotted sitting on the horse. The boy is worth more than the horse. He would fetch three times more than the horse at the Constantinople slave market. But the boy is nowhere to be found.

The Turk looks behind some trees and some branches.

Then he spoke in Hungarian, "Where are you, little boy? Come out, little buddy! If you don't come out, I will take your horse."

And indeed, he grabs the old gray by the rope and leads both horses away in the trees.

Until then, the two children, mute and pale, just listened to the Turk. The fig leaf offering did not loosen their terror-stricken paralysis. Many times at home they had heard hair-raising tales about the Turks and they had been scolded with, "May the Turks take you," so that no sweet words of friendship gave them any courage. But when the Turk said that he would take the grey, the Gergő child moved. He looked at little Éva as if he expected some advice from her, and with a face of a person whose foot was pierced by a thorn.

He is taking the grey! What are they going to say at home if he returns without the grey?

Little Éva did not respond to these worries. She cowered with him, deadly pale. Her blue eyes became wet from terror.

Nevertheless, the grey left. Gergő heard its steps. The grey has big, sluggish steps. The dry underbrush evenly rustled under its hooves. Well, the Turk is indeed taking it!

"The grey ..." stammers Gergő, his mouth and nose quivering from tears.

He raises his head.

The grey is leaving, leaving. The underbrush is crackling under its hooves.

By now Gergő has forgotten everything to do with the world. He jumps up, naked, and runs after the grey.

"Mister," he announces shaking, "Mister Turk!"

The Turk stops and smirks. Such an ugly man! He smirks as if he wants to bite!

"Sir, the grey," stutters Gergő in tears. "The grey is ours ...."

"Well come then, if it's yours," replies the Turk, "Take it." With that he drops the grey's rope from his hand.

Now the child sees only the grey. As the grey sluggishly starts, he runs to it and grabs the rope.

In that instant he is captured. The Turk's big strong fingers grab the weak little boy's naked arm and he flies onto the saddle of the other horse, the chestnut.

Gergő cries out. "Shh!" says the Turk, pulling out his dagger.

Gergő continues shouting, "Vicuska, Vicuska!"

The Turk, his hand on his dagger, turns his head in the direction where the boy is looking.

Of course, as the other naked child gets up from the grass, he puts his dagger back in its sheath and smiles. "Come, come," he says. "I won't hurt you." He starts moving towards the little girl with his two horses.

Gergő wants to wiggle down from the horse. The Turk gives him a big slap on the back. Gergő cries and remains sitting as the Turk leaves the two horses and runs after the little girl.

Sad little Vica would escape, but her legs are tiny and the grass is tall. She falls down. Within seconds, she is kicking and screaming in the lap of the Turk.

"Shh!" says the Turk slapping her chubby bottom. "Shh! I will eat you if you aren't quiet! Yum, yum!"

The little girl quiets down. Only her little heart is beating, like that of a sparrow caught in one's hand.

As soon as they reach the horses, she again begins screaming, "Daddy! Daddy!"

The Gergő child is also bawling, his fists wringing his tearful eyes, "I am going home. I want to go home."

"Quiet, you ragged bastard," yells the Turk, "or I will split you in two!" And he menacingly shakes his fist at Gergő.

The two children become quiet. The little girl almost faints from hopelessness. Gergő whimpers quietly as he sits on the back of the chestnut.

They leave.

They emerge from the forest. The Gergő child sees colorful Turkish people accompanying wagons and carts on the road headed up the Mecsek Hills: mounted *akinjis*, *azab* foot soldiers, and a band of colorfully dressed irregulars.[4] They ride nimble horses and they are carting plunder home.

This band of Turks accompanied some ten loaded wagons and carts. The carts were carelessly loaded with white bedding, cupboards, bed frames, barrels, leather hides, and sacks of grain. Prisoners walked sadly by the carts, their legs in chains and their hands tied behind their backs.

Our janissary has three carts and seven captives. There are five janissaries wearing blue pants, red boots, and tall white fur caps, and three *azab* foot soldiers with fur caps and large spears. The one-eyed's dusty, white ostrich feathers swing from the front and over his cap almost to the middle of his back.

---

[4] The *akinji* were irregular light cavalry raiders that served as scouts and an advance party. They were not paid; they lived by looting. An *azab* is an Ottoman infantryman.

While he was spending time in the forest, his three carts had pulled over to the side of the road to make way for the other homeward bound migrants. The janissaries laughingly accepted the two children and the grey.

What they babble in Turkish, Gergő does not understand. They look like they are talking about them and the grey horse. When they look at him or at Éva, they laugh. When they look at the horse, they gesture like someone chasing away a fly.

The Turk throws the two children onto a cart on top of some bedding. The two are entrusted to a plump-cheeked maiden sitting there, a captive girl with chained feet. Then one of the Turks with caps loosens a ragged sack and pulls out all manner of clothes. They are all children's clothes. Among them is a little dress, a little coat, a little metal-buttoned waistcoat, cap, hat, and little boots. The Turk choses two little shirts and a little coat and throws them up on the cart.

"Dress them," says the one-eyed to the prisoner girl.

The girl is about seventeen years old. She is a peasant girl. As she dresses the children she hugs and kisses them.

"What do they call you, my angels?"

"Vicuska."

"And you my little soul?"

"Gergő."

"Don't cry dears. I will be with you."

"But I want to go home," cried Gergely.

"Me, too," cries the girl.

The prisoner girl hugs them with both arms. "The Good Lord will guide us home. Just don't cry."

2

The village dogs bark angrily around a white bearded and long haired pilgrim. They surely would have pulled off his monk's cowl if he had not menaced them with his long, crucifix-capped walking stick.

Initially he walked in the middle of the road, but as the big, shaggy dogs multiplied, he carefully backed into an L-shaped hedge where he scornfully waited for someone to come and relieve him from the siege.

Those who initially had come out to see what all the barking was about turn towards five Hungarian warriors (*vitéz*) galloping into the village. A red jacketed, blonde cavalryman rides in front. A crane feather on his tall cap. In front across the saddle rests a gun. Mail glittered under a thin, dark cherry-colored jacket. Behind him the other warriors. As they enter the village, they turn their heads left and right as if there was something marvelous in each house in the village.

A peasant armed with a spear sat in front of Cecey's gate. He had been sitting on a rock, dozing. The commotion roused him from his reverie. He hurriedly opened the other door on the gate and the horses trotted across the bridge into the yard.

There Cecey crouched in the shade of the barn like an old eagle. Some serfs were shearing five sheep. Scissors in their hands, swords at their sides. This was the world in Hungary back then!

Cecey saw the warriors. He got up and ambled before them. The old lord had a strange walk: one leg did not bend at the knee, the other did not bend at the ankle. But how could they bend when both were made of wood? And his right hand was missing. The canvas jacket just dangled on his wrist.

The crane-feathered warrior dismounted and threw his horse's reins to the nearest warrior. He hurried towards Cecey.

"I am István Dobó," he said taking off his tall cap and snapping his heels together.

Tall, boney lad, but all strength in every movement. And his strong grey eyes piercing.

Cecey hid his missing hand behind him.

"In whose army do you serve?"

"Now, in that of Governor [Bán] Bálint Török."

"In that case you are a partisan of Ferdinand."

And he offered his hand to him. In an instant he sized up his mount, in another his sword.

"Well, what wind brings you here?"

"Sure, older brother. We come from the palace."

"From Móré's castle?"

"That is no longer Móré's castle."

"Well?"

"Just now it belongs to no one. It's not even a castle now, just a pile of stone."

The old wooden legged was stunned. "Did you tear it down?"

"To the ground."

"Praise God. Now, come inside where it's cooler, my younger brother, here under the porch. Just look, mother, at how many guests have arrived."

"They tore it down!" he repeated, stunned.

The little stout lady was already turning into the porch, moving the table into the shade with a servant. Another servant was already opening the door to the storeroom cellar.

"How do they call you, my younger brother, Bodó or Dobó?"

"István Dobó."

"Pista[5] Dobó," said Cecey, introducing the young man to his wife.

Then he arranged for wine and food to be brought to the soldiers, and also someone to get the priest.

"Before we would sit down, my older brother," said Dobó, "I have to ask you whether Móré is here because I am searching for him."

"I haven't seen that rascal's remains. I wouldn't want to, except hanging from a tree."

Dobó shook his head.

"Then we are on a bad trail." Then he asked for water.

"Well wait. They are bringing wine," said Cecey.

"If I am thirsty I drink water," replied Dobó. He picked up a large round jug and lifted it to his mouth.

"Will you permit, my older brother, that we rest here until evening?" he asked after a satisfying grunt from the good water.

"I won't let you go after a few days! What are you thinking?"

"Thank you. Now is no time for carnival. We move on at night. But I would like to take off my shirt of mail. It's beastly hot these days even if this shirt is all holes."

While Dobó dressed inside the room, the pilgrim arrived at the gate.

---

[5]   Pista (Steve) is a nickname for István (Stephen).

"You come from the friar!" said Cecey to him, his head lifted.

"From him," replied the pilgrim surprised. "How do you happen to know?"

"Not from a witch, you can trust me. Your beard is white from badger grease. I recognized it at first glance."

"True," replied the man.

"From that I can tell that you have come to me from afar."

"That is also true."

"I do not often get visitors from distant parts except the friar at Sajólád who is my cousin."

"But for a long time he has not been a friar, but a friend of the king."

"I also know. May lightning strike him and his master. What do they call you?"

"Imre Varsányi"

"How old are you?"

"Thirty"

"Well, let's see. What news have you brought?"

The pilgrim sat on the ground and he picked open the lining of his cloak. "It's ungodly hot in these parts," he mumbled in good spirits. "The Turks are all over like flies."

"We can thank your friar friend and your king. Now where in the hell did you sew that letter?"

Varsányi finally picked the stitches apart and pulled out a letter sealed in red wax and gave it over.

"Give something to this man to eat and drink, and lodging," said Cecey to his wife.

And he broke the wax seal and opened the letter.

"That," he said bent over looking at the letter, "is the friar's handwriting. Clear as if printed, but really tiny. I can't make it out to read."

The pilgrim was sitting in the shade of a nearby walnut tree.

"Certainly he wrote only good," he volunteered, "because he didn't tell me to hurry. When he uses a big seal, I always have to hurry. This is only a small seal. It's not a national matter." Having made this wise distinction between the types of letters, he pulled a swig from the pot of wine that had been placed before him with a satisfied face.

The wife took the letter into her hands. She looked at the top, then the bottom, and the broken seal. She turned towards the pilgrim, "Is uncle Gyuri[6] well?"

The pilgrim was eating cheese and swallowed a big chunk. "He is never sick."

A bull-headed, broad shouldered, and strong old priest came in the gate. The pilgrim stood up and wanted to kiss his hand.

"Are you a papist or protestant?" asked the priest. He stroked the white beard that reached his chest so the pilgrim could not kiss his hand.

"I am a papist," replied the pilgrim. Then the priest accepted the kiss on his hand.

They went into the room. There the priest stood by the window and read the Latin written letter in Hungarian:

"Dear brother-in-law ..."

The priest had an unusual hollow voice. One could barely make out the consonants as he spoke. But whoever got used to his speech had no trouble.

He continued, *"... and dear Juliska! I wish you all good health and untroubled life from God. I further inform you that there in your vicinity from day to day rages Móré here, the Turks there, so that now only the serfs tied to the land remain in place. Whoever is able runs, some to Upper Hungary, some to the Germans. How about you? If you are still alive, my dears, and if you are still there in Keresztes, you also should save yourselves. I spoke with Her Majesty to compensate you for whatever you lose."*

"Read no more," interrupted Cecey. "Only a dog needs a dog's mercy!"

"Quiet, my dear," pacified the lady. "György is clever. György knows that we will not accept anything from Zápolya. Listen respectfully to the rest of the letter."

The priest scrunched his bushy eyebrows and continued reading:

"The king cannot return your Sásod village to you, but there is a village near Nagyvárad ..."

---

[6] Gyuri is a nickname for György (George). The friar is George Martinuzzi, commonly referred to as Friar György (Hungarian, Fráter György).

"Stop it, stop it Bálint!" said Cecey, all fired up with anger.

"Now something else follows," answered the priest. He continued reading, *"But if your hatred for him has gone into your bones ..."*

"In me, in me," Cecey shouted at the table. "Both here and in the next world. And if there, well, with arms there also!"

The priest continued reading, *"Here in Buda my little house sits empty and we are soon relocating to Nagyvárad. Only a bow maker lives there in the lower house. The upper three rooms are empty."*

"I don't need it!" announced angered Cecey. "Friend, you bought it with Zápolya's money. Let it collapse in a heap if ever I enter it!"

"Do you know that is how he bought it?" said the priest vengefully. "What if through an inheritance?"

But Cecey was no longer listening to them. He stormed angrily out of the room, his wooden legs knocking all along the porch.

The pilgrim was munching under the walnut tree at the end of the porch. Cecey stopped before him and stood formally. "Tell the friar that I send him my respects. But as for what he writes, only this much. It's as if he wrote nothing."

"Well, do I go back with a reply letter?"

"No."

With that Cecey walked further, out to the barn. Up and down he paced in the sun. Right and left he beat the air with his walking stick, angrily muttering, "I do not have a wooden head."

The peasants zealously sheered the sheep. Even the dogs pulled father away. Even the house looked like it had slipped down the bank a little.

The lady stood on the porch with the priest. The priest shrugged his shoulders. "And if it's not an inheritance," he said, "then it's from your brother's earnings. He gives it to whomever he wants. He gives to Péter. Then it's within the Cecey house, and the king has no say in it at all."

Dobó stepped out of the room. The lady introduced him to the priest. Cecey also returned and snarled at the priest, "You priest, you've turned. You later will serve [King] János [Zápolya] as his standard bearer."

"And you in your old age will drop your Hungarian name!" replied the priest angrily.

"And you will serve as a hangman!" shrieked Cecey.

"And you will be a German!" said the priest angrily.

"Hangman!"

"German!"

"Dog catcher!"

"Traitor!"

The two grey haired men were blue in the face from anger as they shouted at each other. Dobó was waiting until he had to separate the two from fighting. "Don't fight. May God bless your graces," he said calmly. "Better yet, go fight the Turks."

"You don't understand this, my young brother," replied Cecey who had dropped into a chair. "Zápolya cut this priest's tongue and me my right hand. Well, isn't he mad who defends Zápolya with what's left of his tongue?"

"If he were my only enemy," replied the priest in a lowered voice, "I would have forgiven him a long time ago. But I will also add that I would rather he be lord for Hungarians than a German."

"But trust more in the German than in the Turk!" said Cecey in response.

Dobó interjected again to keep the two men from getting fired up again. "Neither is good, that is true. We have to wait whether the Germans will muster force against the Turks, and whether Zápolya wants to sell the country to the Turks."

"He gave it away a long time ago, my young brother!"

"I don't believe it," replied Dobó. "He never needed the Turks. He only wanted the crown."

The lady placed a platter of fried chicken on the table. The sight and smell of the fried brown chicken dissipated the anger from the faces of the two old men.

"Hey, when I was as young as you, my young brother …" said Cecey in good humor. "How old are you?"

"Thirty-one," replied Dobó. "Indeed, before long no one will call me young."

"Until a man marries, he is always young. But how the devil is it that you haven't married?"

"I've not had the time," replied Dobó. "I, my older brother, have been a soldier in war since I was a child."

"Well, in that way it's good. This is how the Magyar has lived since the beginning of the world. Perhaps you think I became lame in both legs from dancing? I certainly, my young brother, began with Kinizsi. King Mátyás called me by name. Then I ended with Dózsa who, believe me, was a hero among heroes."[7]

He picked up his own full cup and said in good humor, "May God love the Hungarian, and you, my young brother, exceptionally. May He give victory to your sword. A beautiful young wife would be good for you. Can you play chess?"

"No, I don't," replied Dobó, smiling at this line of thinking. He emptied his cup. It was good strong red wine. He thought to himself that he now understood the anger between the two old men.

"Well then, You won't become a good general," said Cecey.

"No, not if they are fighting in the eastern fashion, army against army. We only fight in the Hungarian fashion: man against man. A chess board doesn't teach this."

"Accordingly, you may still know."

"No, it's just the game I don't know."

"Well then, if you learn, you will judge differently. One hour of chess, my young brother, a man lives through all the turns and attacks of a real battle."

"Do your graces always play chess at home?"

"We? Never. Two fired up men should never sit together for chess. If they play chess, they will end up fighting each other. Now, however, my young brother, we are pushing up towards old age. We lived together. We fought together."

"We will also die together," finished the priest nodding.

The two old men gave each other a friendly look and clinked their cups together.

"But look here," said Cecey wiping his beard. "Still, Ferdinand is a worthy man, if he kicked that fox of a man Móré out of his castle."

"Not just Ferdinand. The two kings together. Both were in the battle. Móré had done too much evil. Most recently he even had graves turned upside down."[8]

---

[7]   Pál Kinizsi (1432–1494) was a general under Hungarian King Mátyás (Matthias). György (George) Dózsa (1470 - 20 July 1514) led the 1514 Peasant Revolt in Hungary against the landed nobility.

[8]   The reference is to László Móré and an incident during the two-week siege in 1533 of his Várpalota castle in Veszprém County. The captain of his castle, Gergely

"But still, it was Ferdinand who fought more?"

"No. Rather János. Ferdinand sent only Bálint Török with fifty sappers to help János."

"To mine the walls?"

"For that. There was a small Turkish force with us also."

"Of course, under János' flag."

"Under that. But the devil take such help. They go from house to house stealing."

"Those pig *akinji* raiders!"

"Them."

"Did you deal with that castle easily?"

"I can't say that. It was built with strong walls. None of the attackers brought siege artillery. Of what use is a light canon?"

"I have been there," the priest said. "It was a stone castle, not wooden piling. Didn't they surrender it?"

"No. We had to use the fifty sappers to mine the walls. I can say they had a long and difficult task. They attacked the rock with pickaxes, and even using iron pikes, only the occasional hit had any effect on the rock. But ultimately, with many hands even rock gives way."

"Did they blow it up?"

"At first we sent word to Móré that the shaft was full of powder. Then they replied and asked us to wait until morning. We waited. What was that evil fox doing? He called together the people in the castle and assured them that if they hold onto the fortress, he will sneak out and run for help. 'Good' they replied, 'but what assurance do we have that you will return?' 'Both my children will stay with you" replied the rascal, 'with all my gold and silver. What more do you want?' Like that, he climbed down the walls on a rope. He slipped away. In the darkness, of course, we did not see him. When the sun rose the next day, and no white flag, nor open gate, we blew up the mine. The walls fell and we rushed inside. Our warriors were so angry they killed every man in the castle."[9]

Nagy, was killed during the siege. Before his escape from that castle, described below in this novel, Móré hid some of his treasure under the buried body of his captain.

[9] Gárdonyi refers to the 1533 siege of Várpalota by King John Zápolya. Móré did not support King John, King Ferdinand or the Turks, attacking and plundering each as the opportunity presented itself, which it did again when war broke out in

"Children, too?"

"Those, no. We found them in a large vaulted room. Two small little brown boys. Since then they are with King János."

"So now you are searching for Móré?"

"Just now we wandered this way looking for Móré with these four men of mine. Along the way we were talking with a field guard. He had stayed in his cellar. He told us that Móré was headed towards Pécs."

"You, Magda," called the Lady Cecey turning around to the servant cleaning in the yard, "Where is Vicuska?"

"I haven't seen her," replied the girl. "She was playing in the garden after lunch."

"Run. Go find her!"

"She is my daughter," explained Cecey to Dobó. "God gifted me in my old age. You will see what a sweet little Fairy Helen she is."

"You have no son, my older brother?"

"None," replied Cecey sadly. "Because if I had a son, my young brother, my hand would grow out again, just like a lobster."

But the child is not to be found. Everyone had forgotten about little Vicuska during the great discussions and the letter reading. Neither did the girl servants pay attention. They all found work to do in the yard. The warriors twiddled their beards. The girls played with their skirts. They were enjoying themselves as if so many warriors had come to Cecey in order to eye the girls.

Immediately they searched the entire area around the house. They peered under every bush and in every play area in the village. Where is auntie Kató? She was looking after her. It could be that she fell asleep while the child left the village. Who saw her? No one saw her. A little boy talked with her behind the garden in the afternoon. Who went behind the garden in the afternoon? No one. Just the Gergő boy. He was taking his grandfather's horse to graze. He is also nowhere to be found. Definitely he went with the horse to the forest. Oh! Such childish thoughtlessness! How many times I have told him not to go beyond the blackberries with the horse!

1527 between the two rival claimants to the Hungarian throne. The rivals reached a cease-fire in 1533 which allowed Zápolya to turn his attention to Móré. Even the Hapsburg Ferdinand and the Ottoman Hussein Bey helped. Ferdinand contributed fifty sappers from Bohemia. The siege of Várpalota was the first siege of a fortress in Hungary using mines (digging tunnels under the walls, then planting and exploding gunpowder to breach the walls).

They searched in the forest around the village. Even Dobó's warriors joined in the search. They searched every tree, oak, ditch, gully and thicket. Gergely's mother also searched yelling out. They found old auntie Kató in the forest. She also joined the search, shouting until her voice was horse.

Finally, towards night, one of the servants stood up and shouted, "Found them."

"Well, thank God. Where are they?"

"Their clothes are here."

Their clothes, indeed only their clothes, the little shirt made of fine white linen, little red shoes, yellow taffeta skirt, and the Gergő child's shirt, pants and cap. It looks like they were bathing. On the banks of the stream they see footprints in the soft sand. The bigger foot, whose toes are more widely spread, is that of the Gergő child. The smaller footprints are Vicuska's.

Surely they drowned somehow in the water.

3

"My name is Margit. Just call me aunt Margit" said the prisoner girl sitting on the cart. "I will tell you a story. I know many stories. From where are you, my darlings?"

"From the village" replied Gergő with teary eyes.

"Which village?"

"It is in this forest."

"But what is the name of that village?"

"Its name? I don't know its name."

Margit was a girl with a round face and a mouth that always looked like it was kissing. Her face was freckled here and there and she wore a blue glass bead hanging from her neck. The Turks had captured her from the plains of Somogy County.

She wondered what she could do for the children, then she tied some rags together and fashioned a doll for Vicuska.

"This will be Vicuska's doll. She has a yellow scarf and a red skirt. We can dress her, rock her, dance with her, and put her to sleep."

The prisoner cart rolls on quietly.

A wide chested peasant boy is walking alongside the cart together with a pock-marked Gypsy. The Gypsy wears a heavily patched pair of blue pants and a similarly patched dolman robe. A filthy wooden pipe sticks out from its inside pocket. On the other side of the cart, a black robed priest trudges along with a big faced peasant man who could be some forty years of age. The priest is younger, a broad faced, tall man. He has no beard, no mustache, not even eyebrows. And he is red like a beetroot. Only the pupils of his eyes are black. Indeed, only a few days earlier, the Turks had repeatedly poured boiling water over him to make him reveal where the church treasures were hidden.

As if his church had any treasure.

Well, I tell you, all these poor prisoners. Chains on their legs. Their hands tied, some in front, others in back, also in irons. The lad with the Gypsy and the priest with the peasant chained together. The lad is barefoot, rags lining his ankles under the leg irons.

The rags are already bloody.

"Let's stop," he pleads, turning around. "Let me adjust my leg irons."

The janissaries do not take the slightest notice. They chatter in Turkish with each other. At most, their response is only an angry glance.

Gergely's eyes fixes upon the young peasant lad. How large are his hands! And how bloody are his legs! He is not afraid. If his two hands were not chained behind him, perhaps the Turks would run away from him.

The lad indeed was not afraid. He lifted his head and yelled at the horseman next to him, a crooked backed Turk.

"May fire swallow you up, you pagan wolves!"

"Gáspár, Gáspár," said Margit from the top of the cart. "Carry your fate peacefully as best as you can. Look, the sun is already resting low, so we will have to stop."

As she wiped her tears the two children also cried.

"I want to go home," blurted Gergő.

"To Daddy," cried little Éva.

The Turks indeed halted. They got off their horses and brought out some jugs. They washed their hands, feet and faces. Then they bowed down in a straight line towards sunrise direction. They kissed the ground and prayed.

With this there was silence.

The girl climbed off the cart and ripped a rag off the hem of her shirt. With it she wrapped the leg of the lad, then carefully pulled down the leg iron over it.

"God bless you, Margit," said the lad with a sigh.

"At night, if possible, we will put some bandage on it, Gáspár."

And her face wrinkled from crying. Every hour she cried a few minutes, but immediately she would sing for the children. Because when she cried, they would cry.

"Hey, how hungry I am," blurted the Gypsy as he sat by them in the dust. "I could eat three loaves of bread by myself as well as two sides of bacon."

The man driving the cart, his legs similarly chained, smiled at the Gypsy's sigh.

"I also am hungry," he replied with a scornful glance at the Turks. "But tonight I will cook such a paprika stew that it will all be left just for us."

"Well, thou art a cook?"

At the "thou"[10] word, the cart driver raised his eyebrows. But then he did reply.

"Just at night. By day these guys will pillage even for their lunch."

"Well, since when do you serve these tufted lords?"

"Three days."

"Can't we slip away somehow?"

"No, from these, never. Look at the boots on my feet."

He stretched his legs out from where he was sitting. Heavy, thick chains rattled with the motion.

"But what if you didn't cook?" the Gypsy anxiously wondered.

"Definitely I will cook. Yesterday I cooked them such a meal that afterwards they were licking their mouths like dogs."

"If only I could lick my mouth. But I no longer know if I have a mouth unless I say something every now and again."

"They also plundered wine in the south. Here it is on this rack."

---

[10] The Hungarian language has the formal "you" (*ön*) which the characters in the novel generally use with each other, and the familiar "thou" (*te*) which is directed only towards children, intimate friends, and subordinates. The Gypsy addressing the driver with "thou" (*te*) was insulting.

"But the Turk doesn't drink!"

"Not one of them is a Turk when he sees wine."

"Well, then I have a holiday," exalted the Gypsy. "I will play such notes on a flute for them that they will get up and dance."

The one-eyed janissary did not start the wagons or carts until after the prayers ended. In the grey of evening and from the top of the hill he could already see the palisaded city in valley. A Hungarian nest. Full of wasps.

The Turks consulted. Then the one-eyed janissary called out to the cart drivers.

"After me! Into the forest."

And for five minutes they drove the carts and wagons deep into the woods.

By now the sun had dropped behind the trees. Darkness clouded the forest. In the clear sky, the first stars twinkled.

The Turks tethered their horses in a suitable clearing. The janissary untied the priest's hands and shouted, "Make a fire!"

"I know how better," volunteered the Gypsy. "Your greatness, honorable lord, I kiss your hands and feet! Let me build the fire. That is my expertise!"

"Quiet!" barked the Turk.

They also untied three women to help with making the fire. The women and the priest gathered brush and dry branches from under nearby trees. With steel and tinder they quickly kindled a fire.

They also freed the cart driver from his seat.

"Make, like yesterday," said the one-eyed Turk to him.

"It will be done," replied the cart driver.

He put a large cauldron of water over the fire, and as the priest and the Gypsy skinned the sheep, with skillful hands he cut small pieces into the cauldron. He added red onion to the meat, and lots of paprika, and surely he would have added potato into the stock, but this he mainly did not add because there were no potatoes. In those days, they had no idea of potato! Only very rarely would a lord taste one. After a meal a potato was placed on a great lord's table as a dessert, and it had yet to be given a name!

Some twenty various Turks lay around the fire. They had set the carts and wagons in a circular fence. The horses were tethered outside the carts.

The gathered the prisoners together into a group. There were fourteen of them altogether: nine men and five women, counting the two little children. They just lied on the grass. Some of them immediately fell asleep.

Little Vica was already sleeping on top of the bedding. Her head was peacefully dreaming, resting on Margit's lap. Gergő was next to them lying on his stomach, his hands holding his head up, dreamily staring at the Turks. Periodically the one-eyed janissary would glance in their direction. He had left the two children on top of the cart.

Large flames leapt from the fire. Turks killed sheep, chicken and goose. The prisoners diligently worked to get the food prepared, and within a quarter of an hour the simmer of meat in the cauldron was already in full swing, and thighs were roasting on the spit. A Turk opened his sack of dried noodles.

An appetizing smell of food mingled with the forest air.

4

It didn't take an hour before the wagon driver András got such a slap that his hat fell a dozen feet away.

"How in the seventh hell can I digest this?" yelled the one-eyed janissary at him. "How much paprika did you put in this food?"

The prisoners ended up with the *paprikás*, to the great delight of the Gypsy. The Turks divided the roasted meat among themselves.

Meanwhile the barrels got tapped. The Turks drank Hungarian wine in their cups and horns. The Gypsy got up. He wiped his mouth with his hand and his hand on his pants, then twittered like this: "Your greatness, honorable Lord Guardian-zsák,[11] I kiss your hands and feet. Let me play my pipe for our honored guests!"

The Guardianzsák-named one-eye, in fact, Yumurjak, turned around and sarcastically said, "You would cockle-doodle-doo the Hungarians here, eh?"

---

[11] In Gárdonyi's writing, the Gypsy pronounces Hungarian with a thick accent. The Gypsy had heard the one-eyed Turk's name as "Gyamarzsák:, the word "gyám" meaning guardian or person in charge. The Turk's actual name is Yumurjak. Later explained in the novel, it is a nickname meaning "plague" or "pest".

The Gypsy, somewhat dejected, whimpered as he returned to his group where they were eating, and lost himself in thoughts holding his wooden spoon.

The Turks also ate and drank. They even bartered and argued. One gloomy *akinji* with a long hanging mustache pulled a small iron case off a wagon. They spread out its contents. Gold coins, rings, and earrings spilled out.

The argued by the fire.

Gergő was sleepy, but he could not take his eyes off of his Turk. He had a particularly fearsome leathery face. As he took off his tall cap, his bare face seemingly dissolved into his bald head. He laughed strangely. You could see his gums when he laughed.

He pulled a thick deerskin pouch from under his robe where he safeguarded his money. The purse was already swollen with coins. The Turk got up and went behind the carts where the horses were grazing.

Gergő kept watching him. He saw how the Turk pulled out a wooden pin from the saddle and stuffed money into a small opening.

"Well, aren't you eating?" said the priest to Gáspár.

The lad was sitting to the side of the group, gloomily staring.

"Don't need," he replied.

A little later he said to the priest, "If the honorable sir has finished, I would like a little talk, if you would listen."

The priest put down his wooden spoon and rattled over next to Gáspár. "Well, what do you want, my son?"

"My honorable sir," said the lad darkly, "give me confession."

"For what?"

"For that," replied the lad, "so I can go to the next world pure."

"You are a long way from that, Gáspár."

"Not as far as you think."

He glanced towards the Turks and continued. "When the prisoners finish eating, the Turk who captured me will come here. He will come here to bind our hands. I will kill him."

"Don't do this, my son."

"However, I will do it, reverend sir. When he comes here, I will grab one of his knives and stab him! In the dog's stomach! So just give me confession."

"My son," said the priest calmly, "I cannot give you confession because I am a Lutheran."

"The new religion?"

"It is called the new religion, but in truth, it is the true, old religion which Jesus the Nazarene left for us. We don't give confession. We only confess. We believe that God sees into our souls. But why would you lose yourself? See, here we are still on Hungarian land and Pécs is there below us. It has often happened that Hungarian slaves are freed."

"And if they don't free me?"

"God's goodness will accompany us on our road. There are those men, not just one, who on the Turk's land deserve the luck of God. He goes there in a slave's chains and becomes a lord. Then he finds his way home. Come, my son, eat. Eating will cheer you up."

The lad looked ahead gloomily.

The priest again spoke. "Why did you call me if you won't listen?"

At this, the lad got up and trudged to join the others.

The prisoners were mostly young and strong men. Among the women was a little, skinny Gypsy dressed in rags. Her hands and feet were reddened with Brazil nut dye, in Gypsy fashion, as was her hair.

Every now and again she threw her head back to get her hair away from her eyes. And she usually talked in the Gypsy language with Sárközi, the pock-marked Gypsy.

"Perhaps she is your wife?" asked the other prisoners.

"No," replied the Gypsy. "Until now, not even once."

"Well then, what are you saying in Gypsy?"

"This woman is saying that if I approach the fire she would tell me my fortune."

"The future is in the hands of God," said the priest. "Don't play any comedy in His name!"

Among the men sat two older men. One had a scarred face, didn't speak, and looked as if he were a nobleman. One could not determine whether he was noble or a Gypsy because he never responded to any question. That man smelled of burnt gunpowder. The other, a fleshy faced peasant, was chained together with the priest. He always stared intently as if he was astonished, and his head would always be hanging down, as if it were too heavy, like a son is to another man. What is true is that his head was big.

The prisoners, as they ate the *paprikás* mutton stew, spoke quietly.

During their rest they began, of course, talking about how they could escape from the Turks.

"No way," curtly said the large headed peasant. He swallowed a spoonful of meat and continued. "I know. I have already completed one service as a slave."

"In Constantinople?" three of them asked simultaneously.

"There," replied the peasant, digging his spoon deeply into the iron cauldron. "For ten years I swept Turkish ground."

"So how did you escape?"

"How? Well, for nothing. Under the cloak of Jesus. One time they brought me up to Belgrade. There I escaped. I swam across the Danube."

"And how was that slavery?" asked the pale-eyed sixteen-year-old.

"Indeed, my young brother," replied the peasant sorrowfully. "Not too many chickens were killed for my benefit."

"Did you serve a rich man?" asked a voice from under a cart.

"The emperor himself!"

"The emperor? What were you for the emperor?"

"Chief cleaner."

"What sort of chief cleaner? What were you cleaning?"

"His stables."

"Well, how do they treat women?" asked a black haired young woman.

The man shrugged his reply. "Those who are young, there also, she is a woman — only a Turkish woman. But mostly, she is only a servant.

"Do they beat women?"

"And how."

The priest got up. "Then you know the road?"

"Sure I know," replied the man.

The priest put one of his legs on the hub of a wagon wheel. Using light from the fire, his eyes focused on the locked, wide, smooth iron on his leg. Small scratches were visible on it. They were some prisoner's notes. Twenty words from someone's long suffering.

The priest read the words. "From Nándorfehérvár to *Hizarlik*, one day. Then *Baratina*."[12]

"No," replied the man. "There are five stations until there."

"Then the five crosses here mean five stations. Then five stations. After that comes *Alopnica*.

The man nodded.

"After *Nis*."

"That is already in Serbia," sighed the man and he crossed his legs. "That's where they start making rice."

"Rice?" marveled one of the women.

The man did not reply.

The priest continued reading his leg iron. "After that begins *Kuri-Kezme*."

"There are lots of scorpions there."

"*Sarkövi*."

"There three water mills grind. May their waters run dry!"

"*Czaribród*."

"That is where they gave me a thrashing."

"For what?" asked six of them all at once.

"Because I broke my leg irons."

"*Dragoman*," the priest continued reading.

"That is Bulgaria," said the man. From there we arrive in Sofia. There are many towers there. Big city. May it burn down to ashes!"

"*Iktimán*."

The man nodded.

"*Kapiderven*."

"There may be snow. Even in summer there is snow on the mountains."

---

[12] Nándorfehérvár is today's Belgrade in Serbia. Hizarlik and Baratina would be in Serbia and the final place names are in today's Bulgaria and European Turkey.

"*Pozárki* or something."

"That's it, Pozárki. May the ground swallow it! Lots of mosquitos."

"*Filippe.*"

"That also is a city. May it fall down!"

"*Kaladán.*"

"There they sold one of my mates. A plague on them all!"

"*Uzonkova.*"

"Many orchards. Good place."

"*Harmanli.*"

"There a Turk lord bought little Antal Dávid."

"*Musztafa-basa-Köpri.*"

"There is a large stone bridge there. May it collapse!"

"*Drinápoly.*"

"Big smelly city. That's where I saw an elephant."

"What's that?" asked several prisoners.

"That," replied the peasant, "is a big, living beast, like a loaded cart, but bigger than that. Hairless, like a buffalo. Its nose is so big that it wags it, like other animals wag their tails. When flies irritate it, it whisks back as far as its waist."

"*Corli.*"

"Starting there we can see the sea."

The prisoners sighed. Some buried faces in their hands. Others marveled with teary eyes.

5

The scar-faced, gunpowder smelling man spoke up. "My father's sons," he said with a soft, raspy sound, "If you could get me unchained, I can ransom all of you."

The prisoners looked at him.

The man glanced back at the Turks, then continued even more softly. "I am a lord. I have two castles. I have money. I have soldiers."

The former slave-peasant shrugged his soldiers. "Then you can escape anyway because they will ransom you."

"What is your name, brother?" asked the priest.

"Slave is my name," replied the scar face irritated.

And he got up. He hobbled a few steps towards the Turks. Then he sat down and carefully studied the faces in the light of the fire.

"He's no lord," said one prisoner, "but some sort of Gypsy, perhaps an executioner."

Gergő shivered at the word executioner. In his childlike mind, he thought the man really was a Gypsy executioner.

"If only there were some verbena plants!" said Gáspár beside a wheel with his bloodied legs.

The prisoners sat quietly musing sadly. Gáspár continued, "Verbena is such a plant that leg irons will drop off from it."

A loud cheering arose among the janissaries. They found some Tokay wine in one of the barrels. They were rejoicing. They rolled the barrel close to the fire and commenced slurping and sipping the fortified sweet wine.

"Long live Hungary!" yelled Yumurjak, lifting his cup towards the prisoners. "Long live Hungary so the Turk can drink until he dies!"

"How do you know Hungarian?" asked the scar-face lord who earlier had named himself Slave.

"What's it to you?" replied Yumurjak over his shoulder.

By then, stars and the moon shone in the sky. May bugs hummed among the dew laden tree leaves.

The prisoners laid down here and there in the grass and searched for their freedom in their dreams. The priest also fell asleep, his hand under his head. Surely he was used to sleeping with a pillow. The Gypsy slept on his back, his hands clasped together on his chest and his legs spread apart. They were all in deep sleep.

Only Gáspár sighed once more in his dreamy complaint. "I will never again see beautiful Eger city!"

Gergő also was already dozing. He had dozed off similarly when the sun was blazing, holding his little face in his hand. His head dropped lower on the folded corner of a quilt. He would have fallen deep asleep had the doors of his little ears not opened to the name of Cecey. The Gypsy executioner's raspy voice said this name, and the boy's Turk repeated it.

They were talking by the cart. "With him is Dózsa's treasure. For sure I know it," insisted the Hungarian.

"And what kinds of treasure are they?"

"Gold chalices, gold cups, bracelets studded with jewels, silver necklaces with precious stones. Everything that a lord's treasure would have. Unless they have already been melted down into ingots. But then, you will find the ingots with him."

"Here below the forest?"

"Here. That is why he fled in fear."

"Does he have arms?

"Beautiful swords and mail worked with silver. Possibly his entire attic is filed. I know that in his room there are some six large iron chests. The most precious items are probably in them."

"Cecey ... I have never heard the name."

"He is no longer fighting. He was Dózsa's treasurer."

The Turk shook his head. "We are few," he said thoughtfully. "We have to stay here until tomorrow night. We have to wait to gather a good force."

"Why do you need so many men? If you are many, you have many shares. He is an old man. He has a wooden hand and wooden legs."

"When were you last there?"

"Perhaps last year."

"A year is a long time. It's better if we go in numbers. If it's true, what you say, I will pardon you. More than that, I will reward you. If it's not true, I will have you hanged on Cecey's gate."

The Turk returned to the fire and certainly he shared the prisoner's words there because the soldiers listened quietly.

Gergő's head grew heavy. He fell asleep. But his dreams were all terrible. Finally he dreamed that Turks brandishing swords were running in their forest, caught his mother, and stabbed a knife into her chest.

He shook and woke up.

The dark of night and nightingales singing everywhere. A hundred nightingales! It was as if all the nightingales in the world had gathered in that forest in order to bring beauty to the prisoners' dreams.

Gergő looks up to the sky. Scattered clouds. Here and there in the breaks a few stars shine. In one place the moon's sickle shines through a cloud.

By now the fire has smoldered to ashes. Only in the middle is there a red glow the size of a fist. The janissaries are lying about, scattered on the grass around the fire.

Yumurjak also was lying there, some sort of satchel under his head; by him some cup or goblet. One could not see well in the dark.

I need to go home. That was Gergő's first thought.

It's not allowed. That was the second.

He looked around. All asleep. If only he could sneak through them! But he has to escape, otherwise he cannot get back to his village.

Little Éva was sleeping next to him. He gently shook her and whispered in her ear. "Vicuska! Vicuska!"

Évica woke up.

"Let's go home," whispered Gergő.

For a moment Vicuska pouted her mouth, but immediately she straightened it and sat up. She looked at Gergő astonished, like a cat that sees a stranger. She looked at the doll lying in her lap, picked it up, and looked at it with little cat eyes.

"Let's go," said Gergő.

He climbed down the far side of the cart and lifted the little girl down.

A soldier happened to be sitting by the cart. Spear on his lap. Head on the wheel hub. Canteen beside him.

He was sleeping so deeply that the entire camp could have left, excepting the wheel on which he was leaning.

Gergő held little Vicuska's hand and pulled her away.

As soon as he glimpsed the horses, he stopped.

"The grey," he mumbled. "We also have to take the grey home."

The grey was tethered together with a small Turkish horse and their reins were tied together. He could barely manage to undo the tethers on their legs. Untying their two reins was hopelessly beyond his ability.

"Damn this," he grumbled at the knot.

Angrily he scratched his head tearfully.

Again and again he tried, even with his teeth. But he just could not untie the knot. Finally he grabbed the grey and lead him.

There also was a guard by the horses. But he also was asleep. He slept sitting, leaning against a crooked tree. He snored with an open mouth. Gergő almost led the horse over him.

The sound of the horses' hooves were lost in the grass. They went like a shadow. Neither within the wagon circle nor without did anyone wake up.

Gergő stopped the horses at a suitable tree stump and climbed on back of the grey.

"You sit here, too," he said to the little girl.

The little girl was unable to get up on the stump. Gergő had to get down and help Éva up, first on the stump, then on the back of the horse.

They sat together on the grey. Gergely in front, little Éva behind him. The little girl was still holding the red skirted doll. It never occurred to them that the girl could sit in the saddle of the other horse. That horse wasn't theirs. Little Éva grabbed onto the boy's shoulders. The boy shook the reins and the grey started off and headed out from the forest, taking the Turkish horse with it.

Soon they were on the road. The grey already knew the way. It walked sluggishly and sleepily.

The road was not maintained. The dark shapes of huge tree branches hung over the road. Gergő was not afraid. They were all Hungarian trees.

6

No one slept in the village that night. They searched for the children until dark. At sunrise the next morning, they decided to search all along the stream. Only the warriors remained calm.

Father Bálint remained at Cecey's house and consoled the inconsolable parents.

The woman was like a madman. She lamented, wailed and fainted.

The wooden legged man only shook his head in response to the priest's encouragement, and bitterly shouted, "There is no God!"

"There is!" the priest shouted back.

"There isn't!" repeated Cecey.

"There is!"

"There isn't!"

The priest swallowed and continued, with a tone changed to mild. "What God gives, He can take. And what He takes, He can also return."

The old miserable man sobbed for his child.

The priest only said goodbye to them towards dawn.

As he stepped out the door, the pilgrim got up from the grass mat thrown on the porch. "My reverend lord," he said softly.

"What do you want, my son?"

"They are not drowned."

"Well, what do you know about them?"

"That the Turks took them."

The priest almost fell against the wall. "How do you know this?"

"As I was searching with the others by the side of the stream, I saw the Turk's footprint on a mole hill."

"A Turk's footprint?"

"A boot without a heel. A Hungarian doesn't have that."

"What if it was the print of a sandal?"

"That doesn't have a spur. My eyes are good. It was the footprint of a Turk. There were even hoof prints of a Turkish horse. Do you happen to know what Turkish hooves look like?"

"Why didn't you say anything?"

"I thought about it and decided that I would not talk. Who knows in what direction the Turk took them? The entire village would have run off in all directions. Of what use is that? There are many Turks, and they are all armed."

The priest abruptly looked up and down. He stepped towards the door but stopped before he put his hand on the door handle. Then he returned. "You speak the truth," he said, his hand pressed against his forehead. "But how can we be of help?"

"Do like me," replied Varsányi. "Be quiet."

"Terrible! Terrible!"

"Turks are riding on the roads everywhere. Which way would they have gone? To the east? West? Only fighting and death would have come of it."

"It might have been better had they died!" said the priest painfully.

"God only knows where those have gone, or where we should go searching for them."

The priest stood sadly on the porch. To the east the sky turned a pale pink. It was becoming dawn.

From the forest came loud shouting.

"People! People! They've come!"

The priest listened. What is this?

Movement in the distance. Mixed shouting. A few minutes later, thumping on the gate. "Let us in! Open up! The children have come!"

The priest rushed into the house.

"Péter! There is a God! Wake up because there is a God!"

The two children were waiting in front of the gate. They were sleepy and pale sitting on the grey.

7

The entire village crowded into the yard, some fifty men and an equal number of women. Some women had just put on their skirts; the men without caps. They came as they were dressed.

They reached for the Gergő child, passing him from hand to hand, as they also did with Vicuska. Whatever they could reach, they kissed.

"From today, Gergő is my son," said Cecey putting his hand on the boy's head.

The boy's mother, barefoot and in her underskirt, fell down at Cecey's feet.

Dóbo looked with astonishment at the little peasant boy who had brought a horse from the Turks.

"My older brother," he said stepping forward. "Give me this boy. Let me take him to the north. I will raise him to be a warrior."

And he lifted up Gergő. "Son, would you like to be a warrior?"

"I would," replied the child with eyes sparkling.

"You already have a horse," said Dobó. "We will also get a sword from the Turks."

"So the horse is mine?"

Dobó's warriors praised the Turkish horse as it was led cantering around the yard.

"Of course it's yours," replied Dobó. "You got it in battle."

"Then the money is also ours," boasted the child.

"What money?"

"What's in the saddle."

They untied the velvet decorated saddle. They shook it. It rattled. They found the peg in the saddle horn. Well, that is how gold falls from a tree.

"Phew, imagine that," announced astonished Cecey. "Now I won't be adopting you as son but you will be adopting me as father." He told the boy's mother, "Pick it up, woman."

The boy's mother looked at the glittering gold with dazzled eyes.

"That's mine?" she stuttered looking towards Cecey, then Dobó, then the priest.

"Yours," said the priest.

The woman would have held her skirt but she wasn't wearing it. A man gave her his tall cap. The woman picked up the gold with shaking hands.

Her son looked on. At the same time he spoke up. "Put it away carefully, mother, because tomorrow they are coming here."

"Who is coming here?" rattled Cecey.

"The Turks."

"The Turks?"

The boy nodded. "I was listening when the Turk told the executioner."

"The executioner?"

"The Gypsy executioner. An ugly man."

"How are they coming here?"

"They are coming here to steal your lordship's treasure." Saying this, he pointed towards Cecey.

"My treasure?" said Cecey astonished. "Have you gone mad? Well, have I any treasure?"

"They talked about iron boxes, that you have six."

Dobó spoke up, "This is something serious. Let's go inside the room."

He took the boy's hand and led him inside.

They questioned him, getting everything out of him that the child had observed in his slumber.

"Scarred, brown faced man. What is that scar like?"

"A red furrow from his mouth to his ear."

Dobó leapt up from his chair. "Móré!"

"Well, who else would it be! The scoundrel wants to escape and that's why he sets the Turks onto me."

"But who knows the way here?"

"He was here about six years ago. They turned everything upside down here, even my wife's little silver crucifix and my seven cows."

Dobó angrily paced back and forth across the room. "My older brother, how many men do you have who can bear arms?"

"Perhaps forty altogether. They too are mostly older."

"Few," replied Dobó. "What place is closest to here? Pécs, isn't it? But there, János Szerencsen is the lord. He belongs to the János party, our adversary."

"We have to run, to run!" exclaimed Cecey desperately. "But where can we run?"

"The whole village can't run away! How can you abandon the village? Ay, it's all the same. When it has to do with fighting the Turks, it's only Hungarian and Hungarian, regardless which party!"

And he went outside.

"Mount up, men!" he shouted from the yard.

"My lord, I am going to Szerencsen. Until then, work. Drench every roof with water until it runs off. The villagers must collect whatever cattle they have and bring them here into the yard. Put some barrels behind the gates. Put rocks and more barrels behind the walls. Arm the women with scythes and iron pitchforks. I will be back in two hours."

He mounted his horse and galloped away with his warriors at full speed.

8

The Cecey house was surrounded by a rectangular stone wall, but the wall was barely as high as a man, and indeed, it was already falling into ruin.

By noon, the entire village had moved into the enclosure. Cows, goats and pigs were wandering, geese were gaggling, ducks were waddling, and chickens running around bedding and piles of furniture. One man by the shed was sharpening swords, knives and scythes. The priest tied on a broad, rusty sword and cut the air with it some six times in the middle of the yard. The old man was testing whether he still knew how.

Some women were cooking food in a cauldron in a corner of the yard.

Cecey had some six, mouse-chewed sets of bows and arrows in his attic. He distributed them among some of the older men who had fought with him in the Dózsa war.

Dobó returned around noon. He brought only thirty mercenaries with him, but even so, the villagers happily welcomed them.

Dobó walked around the yard. Here and there he climbed onto the wall, placed platforms, and placed rocks. Then he called the armed villagers, numbering some fifty, and divided them into groups to man the walls.

He stationed himself with ten good guns by the gate on a platform.

He sent a bugler to each of the two village entrances with instructions to announce the arrival of the opposition.

They did not have to wait until nightfall.

At around three in the afternoon the bugle from the south entrance to the village sounded, and within a few minutes the two bugler soldiers galloped back.

"Are we all here?" asked Cecey.

Only Gergely's mother was missing. The poor woman went crazy from the gold. She was digging and burying it. She was afraid to leave it at Cecey's for fear the Turks would take it.

"By now it's all the same," said Cecey putting on his helmet. "Shut the gate! Bags and rocks behind it! Leave only an opening big enough for a horse to get through."

Meanwhile the soldiers arrived.

"They're coming!" shouted one from a distance.

"Are there many?" asked Dobó.

"Can't see from the trees, only the first ones."

"Well go back," shouted Dobó at him angrily. "See how many are coming! You will have time to run if they chase you."

The mercenary from Pécs blushed, turned his horse around, and galloped towards the enemy.

"What kind of soldiers are you?" asked Dobó of one of the other Pécs mercenaries standing near him.

"Not at all," he replied embarrassed. "He just joined us. He was a tailor. He hasn't seen battle."

A few minutes later the tailor galloped back, some fifteen red hatted *akinji* on his tail. They really were chasing him.

"Open the gate," said Dobó.

And he ordered the men with guns, "Fire!"

The ten gunners aimed. The shots fired with loud cracks. A janissary turned and fell off his horse into the shadows. The rest recoiled.

They turned around and trotted back.

The tailor galloped inside the gate.

"Well, how many are there?" asked Dobó with a smile.

"A thousand," replied the tailor sweating and panting. "Maybe more."

"That's nothing," replied Dobó. "If there is only a hundred, then we will have them dancing."

"I said a thousand, my lord."

"I understood correctly, " replied Dobó. "If you saw a thousand, then there are only a hundred, if that many."

Smoke billowed up from the village end.

The *akinjis* were already setting fires.

"Did you water the roofs well?" asked Dobó.

"It's hay and straw that's burning," replied Cecey. And he drummed his sword on top of the gate.

At that moment, the one-eyed janissary appeared on the road. Mail on his chest. Dagger and pistols in his belt. Beside him also on horseback the Hungarian whom Gergő had named the Gypsy executioner. Behind them a band of *akinjis* and by the side a few *azabs* on foot.

Burning firebrands in their hands.

"László Móré!" shouted Dobó, stomping his leg. "You shame of the country, you belong in hell."

The janissary looked at the horseman next to him with astonishment.

"Don't believe him" he said, his face pale. "I am not Móré. He wants to fool you."

The janissary stopped his horse so those following could group.

"I know you too, Yumurjak!" shouted Dobó. "So this is Turk honor, that you rob those with whom you battled alongside yesterday? You are a robber, a scoundrel, just like your accomplice."

The janissary glanced at him, but did not reply.

"Just come on! Come on, you fool!" shouted Dobó. "There is no gold here, only iron. Of that you can get a good portion."

And he aimed at him and fired his gun.[13]

Yumurjak leaned over on his horse. He turned and fell into the dust. At the same time the rest of the guns fired and Turk pistols returned fire.

Móré grabbed onto the fallen janissary, but he only managed to grab the dagger from the Turk's belt. The next second he slapped his mount with the flat of the dagger. The mount leapt and ran. Móré flogged his horse as best he could.

"There runs the gold!" shouted Dobó to the Turks.

They recoiled for a minute, then chased after Móré with angry shouting and cracking.

As they dashed by the front of the house, Dobó was reading them. "Ten … twenty … forty … fifty."

He waited a minute then jumped down from the platform. "On your horses, men! There's not even sixty of them!"

They mounted. From the gate Dobó turned and said to Cecey, "That Turk in the mail shirt. If he is still alive, keep him prisoner. Let the villagers kill the Turks who started the fires!"

And they rushed out the gate.

The villagers did not need much encouragement. Smoke billowed into the sky from some five places in the village. Several armed with scythes and axes rushed out the gate.

Cecey, the priest, and two peasants rushed out onto the road. Yumurjak was sitting up. He had only fainted. Dobó's bullet had hit his chain mail shirt just above his heart.

---

[13] Gárdonyi's note: The gun [what we now term "arquebus" which pre-dated even the flintlock and musket — TLP] and pistol were such unreliable weapons in those days that it was possible to get within fifty paces of them.

"Tie him up," instructed Cecey, "and take him into the yard." The Turk allowed himself to be tied up without a word.

"Can you play chess?" said Cecey to him.

The janissary nodded yes with his head but said, "No."

As they were tying his hands, another Turk lifted his bloodied face from a ditch. "Keep tying him," said one peasant, "While I beat that guy to death."

"Stop," yelled Cecey. He stumped over to the bloodied janissary, pushed his sword onto the man's chest, and asked, "Do you know how to play chess?"

"Kaplaman" replied the Turk weakly.

"Chess?"

"Chass, chess, check-mate?" groaned the Turk.

"Yes, that's it. May Muhammad kick you. Take this fellow also to the yard. He is my slave!"

9

Dobó and his warriors returned at night bringing many cloaks, mail shirts, and all kinds of weapons. And also a prisoner: László Móré, on a horse and tied up.

"A good hole for this fox!" said Dobó as he jumped off his horse.

Cecey almost jumped for joy. "How did you catch him?"

"The *akinji* caught him for us. They had enough brains to give him only a young horse. They caught up with him easily, and we in turn dealt with them."

"You cut them all down?"

"As many as we could."

"Quickly, my best steer," ordered Cecey to a servant. "On a spit. But first, bring wine here. Bring the barrel farthest in back from the cellar!"

"Not yet," said Dobó as he glanced back at Móré being escorted to the storeroom. "Where is that Gergő boy?"

"What do you want with him? He is out on the porch playing with my little girl." He continued in a lower voice, "Don't tell him that they killed his mother."

"They killed her?"

"Indeed. Some bastards happened upon her while setting fires and stabbed her."

"And the gold?"

"The woman is lying face down in the corner of the room. Probably she buried her gold there."

Dobó muttered angrily and turned towards the boy. "Gergő! Gergő Bornemissza! Come here, my little warrior. Quickly, mount your little steed, dear boy."

"Where are you going?"

"After the prisoners, my older brother, about whom the boy had talked."

"Well, at least have a little sip. Wine, quickly!" he shouted at the servants. "Your Turk is still living. He is inside the room."

"Yumurjak?"

"The devil only knows his name. The fellow you shot."

"That's him. He didn't die?"

"No. He only fainted. We grabbed another one from the ditch. I expect that he won't stay alive for long."

"You're waiting? Hang the bastard."

"Ho, ho," replied Cecey. "He is my captive."

"Well do with him what you want. But bring that Yumurjak here and a horse for him."

The warriors drank deeply from the wine jugs, then brought Yumurjak.

"Now, Yumurjak," said Dobó. "Did you really need all this?"

"Today me. Tomorrow you." grumbled the Turk. Then when he saw his horse and Gergő sitting in his saddle, he stared with his mouth agape.

Dobó gestured for the boy to follow and they galloped out the gate. Behind them galloped the Hungarian warriors with the Turk close by.

"Do you know where we are going, Gergő?" asked Dobó.

"I don't" replied the boy.

"Now we are going after the sword."

"To the Turks?"

"There."

"For me?"

"For you. Are you afraid?"

"No."

"That's the first thing, my boy, that a man should never be afraid. After that, everything else will come by itself."

Nothing more was said.

The horses' hooves kicked up white clouds on the Mecsek cart road, then the horses' canter became a clatter on the stones of the rocky hillside.

Within Gergő's ears, he heard the words ringing over and over, "That's the first thing, my boy, that a man should never be afraid."

10

They found the prisoners in the forest. Altogether six *azab* soldiers guarded them.

As the Hungarian warriors emerged from among the trees, the prisoners jumped up with shouts of joy, rattling their iron chains.

The six *azabs*, of course, ran away in six directions. The Hungarians did not chase them. Their attention was on the prisoners whom they freed from their chains.

Dobó first held out his hand to the priest. "I am István Dobó," he said.

"My name is Gábor Somogyi," replied the priest. "May God's grace be upon you."

The captives joyfully crowded around Dobó, giving thanks with teary eyes, kissing their liberators' hands and feet.

"Don't thank me," insisted Dobó. "It was this little boy who saved you." He pointed towards Gergő.

Of course, the Gergő boy had never gotten as many kisses or blessings in his life as he got that day. Oh well, he will not be getting so many afterwards. Not for a long time.

The booty included fifteen loaded carts and many weapons.

Dobó, before dividing up the plunder, asked the prisoners who among them had been captive the longest.

The young peasant lad stepped forward and took off his cap. "That would be me."

"What's your name?"

"Gáspár Kocsis, at your service."

"From where do you come?"

"From Eger, my lord."

"Where were you captured?"

"By Fehérvár, my lord."

"Do you know whose property is on these carts?"

"I know about a few barrels and some bedding. These thieves plundered everywhere."

Dobó turned towards the Turk. "Yumurjak, talk!"

"We gathered where Allah allowed us to gather. What belongs to an unbeliever, that is ours. Where we find, we take."

"Then spread everything out. I will divide it among you."

In one wagon was a heap of all kinds of shoddy weapons, mostly plundered from Móré's castle. But among them was a small sword in a dark cherry colored, silk sheath. Dobó picked it up.

"Gergely Bornemissza, come here. Hold this sword. It's yours. Be a loyal warrior for your country and a devout servant of God! Blessings and good fortune upon your weapons!" He girded the sword around the boy's waist and kissed the little warrior on his forehead.

The little boy accepted the decoration seriously. He almost turned pale. Perhaps for a moment a breeze from the future touched his soul. He felt that it was not just a sword that was tied onto him, but he to the sword.

After, what the soldiers did not want, Dobó gave to the prisoners. The warriors had no need for the harnessed, skinny peasant horses. Each prisoner got a wagon or a cart, a horse, and some weapons.

None was as happy as the Gypsy! He screamed loudly, running in circles around his allotted horse and cart. Then he rushed to the pile of weapons. Whatever rusty old weapons the soldiers had left behind, he grabbed like treasure. He tied a cloth around his waist in Turkish fashion and stuffed all manners of knives and daggers until he looked like a hedgehog.

A cheap, broken shield woven from sea canes was among the strewn items. He put it on his arm. He tied two large rusty spurs on his bare feet and pulled a helmet over his head. He had enough brains to keep his cap on underneath. Then he picked up a long spear off the ground and, as if walking on eggshells, he took dainty steps and danced towards the Turk.

"Well, Guardian-zsák," he said, poking a dagger under the Turk's nose. "How are you now, you blockhead Turk?"

As others burst out laughing, Dobó rebuked the Gypsy, "Stop your boasting. Where are you from?"

The Gypsy immediately bowed from his waist, adopting a gesture of servility. "From everywhere, I kiss your hands and feet, where music is played."

"Do you know how to repair guns?"

"Of course, my lord and great warrior. I repair the worst guns so that …"

"Well, these next few days, go to Szigetvár, to Lord Bálint Török's court. There you will find plenty of work."

The skinny little Gypsy woman pleaded with Dobó to be allowed to tell fortunes. "Your wife?" asked Dobó of the Gypsy man.

"Yes," replied the Gypsy. "We married this morning."

The Gypsy woman sat down by the fire, stirred up the embers, and sprinkled tiny black seeds on them.

"*Datura stramonium*,"[14] said the priest looking at the seeds.

Two columns of blue smoke rose up from the embers. The Gypsy woman sat on a rock and put her face in the smoke. The warriors and the former captives stood around her with curiosity.

"Your hand …," said the Gypsy woman to Dobó after a few minutes. Dobó held it out.

The Gypsy woman lifted her face towards the sky, showing the whites of her eyes. She spoke with a trembling voice. "I see red and black birds. They are flying after each other. Ten… Fifteen… Seventeen… Eighteen…"

"Those are my years."

"An angel is flying with the eighteenth bird. It flies down to you and stays with you. It puts a cloth around your forehead. Her name is Sára."

"According to this, Sára will be my wife. Well, I'll be an old man when I find Sára."

---

[14] Devil's snare or jimsonweed, a plant in the poisonous nightshade family. Even its seeds are poisonous.

"The nineteenth bird is red. It brings a dark cloud with lightning. On the ground three large columns fall down."

"Buda? Temesvár? Fehérvár?" mused Dobó.

"The fourth is already in flames. You are holding it up as fire falls on your hands and head."

"Szolnok? Eger?"

"The twentieth bird is gold colored. It is dressed in sun rays. A crown on its head. A jewel from that crown falls into your lap."

"This bodes well."

"After, again red and black birds are flying, one after the other, followed by darkness … I don't see anything else … I hear the sound of chains rattling … your groaning …"

She was shaking and dropped Dobó's hand.

"According to this, I will die in prison," said Dobó with a shiver.[15]

"There is no value in this," said the priest with disgust. "What good is this rubbish?"

The Gypsy woman held Gergely's hand. She put her face in the smoke and was quiet for a minute. Then again she looked up into the sky.

"A dove is with you throughout your life … a white dove, only its wings are pink. But fires surround you. Fiery wheels come out from your hands … After, the dove stays alone and searches for you sadly its entire life."

She remained silent for a minute. Her face distorted with serpentine twitching. She let go of the boy's hand, and with her palms held up towards the sky, she stammered, "Two stars rise in the sky. One from prison. The other from the seashore … They shine forever …"

Terrified, she covered her eyes with her hands.

"Stupid nonsense," said Dobó angrily. "Douse this woman with water." He pulled the Gergő boy away with him to the horses.

"What are we going to do with this thieving, murderous brigand?" shouted the Gypsy man after Dobó. He pointed towards the Turk.

"Hang him," responded Dobó without bothering to turn around. He mounted his horse.

---

[15] Not in prison, but soon after. See the Appendix on István Dobó.

— § —

"Well, you Turk mongrel," blurted Gáspár Kocsis. "You will die!"

The other former prisoners also shouted, "Die, die!" shaking their fists.

"You will croak!" said the Gypsy angrily, his eyes rolling with rage

And one of them untied a rope from one of the carriage harnesses.

"You broke my legs with iron!" shouted Gáspár.

"You killed my father!" shrieked one woman at the Turk.

"You stole our cattle and pulled down our house!"

They surrounded the Turk with angry faces and fists. Some wanted to stab him there and then, but a former prisoner, the large-headed peasant man, brandished his sword in front of the Turk. "What, kill him quickly? No, let us first put a fire under his feet."

"A fire under his feet!" shouted some others. "Let's burn the damned Turk!"

Vengeful thoughts transformed everyone into an executioner. Women gathered sticks, broke them into pieces, and kindled a fire under a tree.

"People," said the priest. "While you are entertaining a hanging here, another group of Turks can wander here and again take us prisoner." The people looked at him. The priest had a bone-handled Turkish lance in his hand. He continued, "You know what this evil man did to me. My body, from my head to my toes, is red like a boiled crab. Which of you has a better right to take this man's life?"

No one replied to his question. Most of them had seen the Turks tie the priest to a bench and pour boiling water over him.

The priest continued, "Just go with the protection of the warriors as long as you can, then disperse in different directions on little traveled, bad roads. May God bless you and lead you home." He held his hand up in a blessing.

The fire kindling was abandoned. The sour taste of prisoner's bread was still in their mouths. All of their thoughts turned towards returning home. One after the other they jumped onto the carts they had been given. "Giddy up, by God!"

The Gypsy also got on his cart and turned around to tell his woman, "Follow me, Beske!"

Gáspár tied his cart with Margit's. They sat next to each other. Perhaps they went like this for the rest of their lives: in the same cart.

"Torture him well!" he shouted back at the priest.

"Don't be stingy with the fire," added a woman.

They left in a line. The last was the cart driver whom the Turks had pressed into service as a cook.

"I am not leaving until I return the slap," he said. And he punched the Turk.

Finally, the priest remained alone with the Turk.

11

Gergely thought he must be dreaming. As he sat on his nimble little Turkish horse, trotting next to Dobó, he pondered how it was that he had come into such an honor.

He would look at his horse, then look at his sword. He would stroke his horse and pull out his sword. If they were to accidently run into some Turks, and Dobó would tell him, "*Cut them down, Gergő!*", well it is certain that Gergő would go after them, even an entire army!

Already the sun was setting. As the sun lit up the sky with golden colors, wispy clouds made the sky look as if the heavens were gilded with gold.

As they trotted down the windy road, Dobó's horse suddenly stopped. It lifted its head, snorted, and pawed the ground nervously.

Dobó looked back. "My horse senses Turks," he said shaking his head. "Let's stop here."

When they started out, he had positioned two soldiers to go in front. He was waiting for them. A few minutes later, they both returned at a gallop. "Down in the valley there's a band of Turks coming on the highway," said one to Dobó.

"They are coming in marching order," said the other.

"Are they far away?" asked Dobó.

"Very far. About two hours away."

"About how many of them?"

"Maybe two hundred."

"And they are coming on the highway?"

"On the highway."

"Do they have any prisoners?"

"Prisoners and many wagons."

"Then that's Kaszon's rearguard," replied Dobó. "No matter. We will attack them."

The highway makes broad curves as it climbs the Mecsek Hills. Dobó found a bend where a large rock could serve as a place for his band of warriors. There they could hide and ambush the Turks.

"Aren't we too few?" asked one freckled, blonde young soldier. You could tell from a glance that he had grown up in velvet.

"Not really, Gyurka," replied Dobó smiling. "When this blessing suddenly falls on them, they will not have time to count how many we are. Plus it will be dark then. After that, if we don't cut them all down, at least it will be enough to make them all scatter. Then, one by one, they will be taken care of in the surrounding villages."

That was when the long column of former prisoners showed up behind them on the highway.

Dobó sent a soldier to tell them to turn around and head towards Pécs, and from there head towards the east or the west, but not to the north or south. He could see the soldier reaching them, the carts halting, then the entire column turning around.

Dobó looked at Gergely. "Where the devil can I put this child?" he grumbled, irritated.

12

The priest remained alone with the Turk.

The Turk stood by an oak tree staring at the grass. The priest stood ten paces away leaning on his lance.

After a while the loud creaks of the wagons faded away and they stood in the midst of forest silence.

Then the Turk lifted up his head. "Before you kill me," he said with a pale face, "hear what I have to say. The belt around my waist is filled with gold. For this plunder you can do this. You can bury me."

The priest did not reply. He just angrily looked at the Turk.

"If you hang me," continued Yumurjak, "dig me a grave here under the oak tree and put me in it sitting. Turn my face towards Mecca. You can do this for my money."

He said no more. He waited for the priest and the rope.

"Yumurjak," the priest finally said. "I heard yesterday when you said that your mother was a Hungarian woman."

"True," replied the Turk with a little brighter expression on his face.

"In which case you are half Hungarian?"

"True," replied the Turk. He stared at the ground.

"Turks stole you as a child?"

"You have found me out, my lord."

"From where?"

"I have forgotten."

"How old were you?"

"Really very small."

"Do you have any memory of your father?"

"No."

"Not even what your name was?"

"Not even that."

"No name at all sticks in your mind from when you were a child?"

"None."

"Strange how you didn't forget the language."

"There were many Hungarian boys among the janissaries."

"Did you know a boy from Lak? His name was Imre, Imre Somogyi."

"I seem to recall this name."

"He was a small, stocky boy with a round head and black eyes. He was all of fifteen years of age when they stole him. He had a cloverleaf shaped birthmark on his right chest, just like mine."

The priest opened his shirt to reveal three round birthmarks grouped like a cloverleaf between his shoulder and nipple.

"I know that boy," said the Turk. "I often saw that birthmark when we were washing ourselves. It's just that he has another name now, a Turkish name like Ahmet or Kubat."

"So then, weren't you together?"

"Sometimes yes, sometimes no. He is now fighting in Persia."

The priest paced back and forth in front of the Turk. Suddenly he shouted, "Liar!" and stared at the Turk. The Turk lowered his eyes.

"No matter," said the priest in a clam voice. "I'm not going to kill you."

"Oh, my lord!" exclaimed the Turk falling on his knees. "Is that possible?"

"Possible, possible. But whether it's smart or foolish is another matter."

"Have mercy on me. Take everything I have and make me your slave. No dog is as loyal as I will be to you!"

"The only question is," said the priest, "whether you are human or a wild animal. If I free you, who will guarantee that you won't again murder and pillage my poor country?"

"May Allah beat me with every whip if I ever again hold a sword!"

The priest shook his head. The Turk continued, "I swear to you with the most terrible oath a Turk can give."

The priest folded his arms and looked into the eyes of his prisoner. "Yumurjak, here you are chatting with me on your knees at the threshold of death. Do you take me for a fool? You don't think I know what the Koran says about giving an oath to an infidel?"

Sweat poured out from the Turk's forehead. "Well then, tell me something, my lord. Ask me anything and I will do it."

The priest rested his chin on a hand and thought. Then he said this. "Every Turk has some sort of amulet which protects him in battle and brings him good luck."

The Turk hung his head.

"I don't need your money," said the priest. "I want that amulet from you."

"Reach under my vest," mumbled the Turk. "It's hanging around my neck."

He lifted his head. The priest found the amulet sewn in a little blue velvet pouch. He tore it off its gold chain necklace and put it in his pocket.

Then he stepped behind the Turk and cut the ropes tying his legs, hands and arms. The Turk shook off the ropes from his two hands and suddenly turned around. With the yellow eyes of a tiger he stared at Father Gábor.

But the priest had already pointed his lance at him and smiled. "Oh no, Yumurjak! Don't stick your nose in this."

Yumurjak was so angry he was almost breathing fire. He backed away from the priest. When he was about twenty steps away, he shouted derisively, "Do you know who you had in your grasp, you stupid infidel? I am the son of the famous pasha, Oglu Muhammad. You could have ransomed me for sacks of gold."

The priest did not reply. With a contemptuous glance, he tossed his lance onto the cart.

13

The sun was just setting below the horizon as Father Gábor sat on his cart and rumbled onto the highway. He could see the tail end of the line of wagons of his former fellow prisoners. They were headed downhill towards Pécs, but he realized that it was only some of them. The rest were headed north.

He knew the way home. There was no other highway that way, just the one from Pécs to Kaposvár, then across to Székesfehérvár, and from there to Buda. But he was going only as far as Laki, to the castle of Pál Bakics. There a narrow cart track turned west towards Lake Balaton. His village was there below a grove of poplar trees.

How his flock will marvel and rejoice when they see him and learn how he had escaped!

He climbed down and tied brakes on the wheels. He cheerfully slapped the faces of his two horses, then got back on his cart and headed downhill.

But Dobó's men were blocking the road.

"Why did you turn back?" asked one of the soldiers when he recognized him as one of the prisoners they had freed. "The Turks are coming," explained the soldier. "You just turn around and hurry towards Pécs with the others."

"Stop, my dear priest," said Dobó. He rode over to him. "Which is your village?"

"Kishida," answered the priest.

"By the Balaton?"

"There."

"I ask you to take this boy with you and, as soon as possible, send him to Bálint Török's castle in Szigetvár."

"With pleasure" replied the priest.

"I fear some harm will come to him," explained Dobó. "We are about to frighten off and scatter a considerable group of Turks. See, one of them might harm him."

The priest turned his cart around. "Will you sit up here?" he asked Gergő, "Or will you stay on your horse?"

"I'll go beside the cart," replied the boy sadly. Because even if a bloody fight awaited them, he would have felt safer next to Dobó. Will there be a slaughter? The Turks are not human, only wild beasts pillaging the country. In his child's heart, he already hated them.

Dobó leaned down from his horse to give Gergő a kiss. "God bless you, my little soldier," he said. "I know you want to be with us in battle, but you don't even have boots. You just go with this reverend, then in a few days we will meet again."

The priest released the wheel drags and shook the reins of the horses.

Gergő sadly trotted after the cart.

14

It was already dark when the cart passed by the castle of Pécs.

They did not stay. The priest wanted to arrive home before noon the following day.

They had to go all the way around the Mecsek Hills.

Towards midnight the moon came out and lit up the narrow, dirt cart tracks for them.

By then Gergő was riding ahead so he could warn the priest if they got to a bad bridge.

Around midnight they came to a white building that looked like an inn.

"Look inside, my son," said the priest. "See if it is an inn or some other house. We can feed our horses here!"

Gergő rode into the courtyard and returned a few minutes later. "It's an empty house," he said. "Its door isn't even closed."

"No matter," replied the priest. "We'll feed them here." And he turned the cart into the yard.

A shaggy little white dog barked in front of them. Apart from the dog, no one appeared.

The priest jumped off the cart and walked around the house. He shouted in doors and windows, "Praise God! Who is at home?"

The house was dark. No one replied. Doors were wide open. On a threshold lay a cupboard all broken apart. Definitely Turks had been there.

"Well then, we are here alone," said the priest as he returned. "But first, let's look at the well because my skin is still burning."

He dropped the bucket to pull up some water. Then he rummaged around his cart. All kinds of stuff were there: bedding, grain, boxes, a carved chair, a barrel of wine, and stuffed sacks. One sack was soft. He opened it. He found what he had been looking for: underwear and linen.

He wetted a cloth in the bucket of water and stripped down to his waist. He used it as a cold compress over his body.

Gergő also dismounted. He led his horse to water at the trough.

The priest then gave some fodder to the horses, and as he had found some bread in one of the sacks, he pulled it out. "Are you hungry, my son?"

"I'm hungry," answered the boy.

The priest pulled out his sword, but before he cut into the bread, he lifted his face to the sky. "Blessed be your name, oh Lord!" he said in a warm and grateful voice. "You freed us from our chains and have given us our daily bread."

The sky was clear and full of stars. The moon hung in the sky like a round lamp, lighting up their dinner.

They sat on the stones that lined the well as they ate their food. The priest even threw some to the dog. Gergő tore his share of the bread and gave half to his horse.

In the distance a faint sound of pattering could be heard. The two eaters listened carefully. Their mouths stopped moving.

"Horses are coming," he concluded.

"Just one," replied Gergely.

They continued eating.

The patter slowly became a loud pounding on the dry, hard cart tracks. In a few minutes the rider himself appeared. He slowed his horse in front of the inn and entered the yard.

"*Műbarek olsun!*" ["Be blessed!"] said the priest with his hoarse voice. The man looked like a Turk because he had a white, wet cloth on his head. "I am Hungarian," announced the priest getting up.

He recognized Móré.

Gergő also recognized him. He shuddered.

"Who is here?" asked Móré as he dismounted his sweaty horse. "Where is the owner?"

"No one else is here, just me and this small boy," replied the priest. "The house has no owner."

"I need a horse," said Móré roughly. "A fresh horse."

The priest shrugged his shoulders. "There is hardly anything here."

"I am in a hurry. It's urgent. I have no money. We are Christians. Give me your horse!"

With a glance he sized up the priest's two horses. The third horse, Gergely's, was grazing in the shade. It was a small horse and looked worthless. Móré didn't wait for a response but started untying the harness from the cart.

"Not so fast!" said the priest. "At least tell me why you are running."

Móré did not answer. He hoisted himself up on the peasant horse and ran away.

"Well," mumbled the priest. "He bargains quickly for a horse."

As he moved, he felt something slipping out of his pocket. He picked it up and marveled. Then, as he touched it, he remembered that it was the Turk's talisman.

Something hard was in the small silk pouch. He slit it with his sword and a ring fell out. The stone in the ring was unusually large. It was a rectangular black stone, either dark granite or black obsidian. He couldn't tell in the faint moonlight. But he could clearly see a smaller pale yellow stone in the shape of the moon and surrounded by five small diamond stars, all set into the black stone.

Inside the pouch glittered something else: Turkish words written with silver thread.

The priest knew some Turkish but he could not read Turkish writing.

He looked at Gergő. The boy was already sweetly sleeping on a sack filled with white clothing.

15

How cheerfully the sun shines down from the sky! But around Lake Balaton, it cannot see anything but blackened roofs, dead bodies scattered about, and trampled crops.

Oh, if the sun were the face of God instead of sunshine, then tears would be falling on the ground!

The priest already knew that his own village had been ravaged. Still, as they reached the crest of the hill, beyond the branches of garden trees, his eyes teared up to see a roofless, burned out tower.

The entire village had been razed. Nowhere did a roof remain standing. Not even a gate was left standing anywhere. There were broken furniture and barrels in the yards, piles of flour, dead people, and dead animals. Nowhere a living soul, just a few frightened dogs that had run away from the danger and later returned after the peril, and some poultry that could fly away from the hands of the thieves.

The priest got down off his cart and took off his cap. "You also take off your cap, my son. This village belongs to the dead, not the living."

He got off the cart and led the horses further into the village.

The broad face of a long haired, grey peasant stared into the sky, his body lying in the road. It was as if he was looking at his own blood dripping from his head to the ground where it had turned black. His pig was behind him, grazing in a yard strewn with mattress feathers. Turks do not bother pigs.

A naked infant boy lay there near the gate, a gaping wound in his little chest.

The priest held his horse's reins and led him on. He did not look to the right or to the left. He only stared at the road ahead of him, and its dust glittering in the sunshine.

— § —

Finally he arrived at the rectory. Its roof was also missing. Its charred, black rafters formed large "A" letters rising up from the smell of ashes. Above the windows facing the street, the walls were black from flames.

They had set his house on fire while they were pouring boiling water on him to make him reveal the church treasure.

The bench was still standing in the yard. Around it the wreckage of a large walnut chest, books, scattered grain, the remains of flowers from inside the house, chair legs, and broken dishes. By a table with broken legs, an old woman in a black dress lay on her back, her two arms spread apart, in a pool of blackened blood.

She was the priest's mother.

"We are at home," said the priest, turning towards Gergő with cheeks drenched in tears.

16

For two days they buried bodies without a break. The priest took off the sides of the cart to carry three or four bodies at a time to the cemetery.

Gergő always went in front of the cart, the sword he got from Dobó at his side, a burial crucifix in his hand. The priest drove the horses, now singing, now praying. He also wore his sword at his side.

Out there he covered the dead with rush mats so the ravens and crows could not pick at them until he returned.

In the afternoon of the third day, a peasant woman with a child showed up in the village. They had been hiding in the reeds of Lake Balaton. That nightfall two men came home. They joined the priest digging graves.

Only when the dead were buried did the priest begin to settle in his home as best he could. The house had three rooms, but the ceiling everywhere had collapsed in the fire.

The priest first covered the room by the street with boards as protection from the rain. Then he put together a cabinet and with Gergely, he collected the books strewn around the yard and put them inside.

After having done all that sad work, Gergely enjoyed the book gathering. He flipped the pages of one or the other book looking for pictures. Five were illustrated. One had pictures of all sorts of insects and another was full of drawings of flowers. Altogether, the priest's library consisted of some thirty parchment bound volumes.

Meanwhile the woman organized the kitchen and cooked. She made sweet peas without meat, and thin soup made with flour and scrambled egg. Two dishes for an entire village!

After lunch, the priest recovered a little from his deep sadness. He took Gergely to the garden where there was a small, chapel-like place where he kept bees. The Turks had torn off its doors as well, but because they saw nothing else but a bench, a small fireplace, a table and some tall glass jars, nothing was destroyed.

The glass bottles were for experimenting with chemicals. The priest marveled that they were left undamaged.

Then a woman came in the garden gate. In her apron she carried the body of a dead child, maybe one year old. Her face was red from crying.

"My little János," and she burst into tears.

"We will bury him," replied the priest, putting on his cap. Gergely picked up the crucifix and led the way.

"I hid him," she sobbed. "I hid him in the grain storage. Then I ran. I wanted to come back at night, but then we met another group of pagans. They were thrashing all around the reeds. God knows who they took, who they killed. When I was able to come back, I found my baby János like this. Oh, God, my God! Why did you take him away from me?"

"Don't ask God," replied the priest as he was digging. "God knows what He is doing. You don't."

"But why was he born if he had to die this way?"

"We don't know why we are born and we don't know why we die," said the priest as he continued digging. "Don't talk any more about God."

The woman untied her apron and with that she placed her child in the ground. "Not yet!" she said to the priest, her voice choking. She tore up some grass and picked some flowers and scattered them over her child as she cried and wailed.

"Oh! I have to give you to the earth. Never again will you hug me with your tiny arms! You will never again say the word, 'Mummy'. Oh how the red roses wilt on your weak little face! Oh, how I can never again stroke your beautiful blonde hair!"

Then turning towards the priest she continued lamenting. "He had such beautiful eyes. Didn't he have such beautiful brown eyes! How he could see with them so dearly! Oh my dear soul, you will never again look at me, never!"

Meanwhile the priest shoveled dirt into the grave, formed a mound on top and packed it down with his shovel. Then he tore a strong branch off an elder tree at the edge of the cemetery, a cross-shaped branch. He stuck it in the head of the mound.

"Oh how God took you away from me!" cried the woman. She fell down and hugged the mound.

"God took him and God will give him back," comforted the priest.

He put the shovel and hoe on his shoulder. He nodded and continued, "Some go ahead and wait for those who still have work to do on earth. Sometimes the child goes first, sometimes the parent. But the Creator has arranged that when someone ends up beyond the stars, someone else is there waiting for them."

They left for home.

The woman followed the priest silently crying, As the priest became quiet, she started sobbing again. "What beautiful eyes he had! Isn't it true, reverend sir, that he had such beautiful brown eyes!"

17

The next day they mounted their horses and set out towards the south, to Szigetvár.

It was a hot day, not a cloud in the sky. In each village people were burying their dead and repairing their houses. In some villages only one or two men loitered, just as in the priest's village. In such villages the Turks had carried away the population.

As they approached the reeds by Szigetvár, the priest looked up. "The lord is at home."

"At home?" asked the boy amazed. "How do you know that?"

"Don't you see the flag?"

"On the tower?"

"There."

"Red and blue."

"The colors of the lord. It means that the lord is at home."

They reached the reeds and continued riding side by side. The priest again spoke. "You son, do you not think that Dobó is dead?"

"In the battle?"

"There."

Gergely did not think that. To him, Dobó was invincible. Gergely would not be surprised if he had attacked the Turkish army alone.

"If he is dead," said the priest, "I would be happy to take you in as my son."

He galloped over to the first wooden bridge, built over the water on high piles, that led to the outer castle. They went through the new town, then reached another short wooden bridge. The wooden bridge led to the old town. Only here and there loitered a man. In front of the twin-towered church sat three fruit vendors, each one selling cherries. The doors of the church were barred with iron.

Then another bridge followed, but this was a broad and long bridge, and the water under it deep.

"Now we are getting to the castle," said the priest. "About time." He carefully wiped his face with a handkerchief.

The castle gates had been left wide open. Inside the spacious courtyard he spotted a man in armor madly galloping, a cloud of dust behind him. Then a second man galloping towards him.

The two suits of armor were similarly fashioned and the two horses were of the same breed. Only the two helmets were different. One was smooth and spherical, and the other had a glistening silver bear head on top.

"That's the lord," said the priest. "The one with the bear head."

The two horsemen charged each other with swords and as they crashed together, the two horses reared up. The two men in armor stuck each other with such force that their swords made sparks fly.

"Maces," yelled the bear-headed as the two horses separated.

Neither face could be seen because each wore a helmet that completely covered the head.

A page dressed in blue and blood-red ran out from the doorway and handed two identical copper-headed maces and two iron shields to the warriors. They turned with their horses and charged each other again in the middle of the yard.

The smooth helmeted fellow struck first. The bear-headed man held his shield above his head. It made a huge noise like a broken bell. At the same moment, the bear-headed man struck his adversary on the head with a blow hard enough to dent his helmet. At this, the smooth helmeted fellow wrenched the reins of his horse and threw away his weapon.

The bear-headed took off his helmet and laughed.

He was a full faced man with brown hair. His long, thick mustache had been flattened against both cheeks from the pressure of his helmet. One side of his mustache reached his eyebrows and the other dangled down to his neck.

"Lord Bálint," said the priest respectfully, then to the boy, "If he looks this way, take off your cap."

But Bálint Török did not look their way. He was looking at his adversary as servants were pulling the helmet off his head. The horseman, after they had pulled the helmet off with some difficulty, spat three teeth onto the gravel of the yard, then swore in Turkish.

From under the gate some eight Turkish slaves sneaked out. They helped take off his armor.

Well, the horseman himself was just another prisoner, like the others.

"Now, who else is up for a match?" challenged Bálint prancing his horse. "Whoever can beat me will be rewarded with freedom."

"Me," said a muscular, thin-bearded Turk. "Maybe today I will be more lucky."

He pulled the armor on himself. His companions strapped the armor behind his back, pressed the helmet on his head, and tied metal plates to guard his legs. The Turk had big legs. Then they worked a crane to lift ·him onto the horse and put a heavy broadsword in his hand.

"You are a fool, Ahmed!" shouted Bálint boldly. "A broadsword isn't suited for an armored man."

"Well, it's what I'm used to," replied the prisoner. "But if you *don't dare*, my lord, then I won't even try otherwise."

They spoke in Turkish.

Lord Bálint donned his helmet again. His mount pranced around the yard as he roughly brandished a light sword. "On it!" he shouted and charged towards the middle.

The Turk leaned forward in his saddle. He held the heavy broadsword with two hands and charged Lord Bálint. When they crashed together, the Turk lifted up and prepared to strike a terrible blow.

But Lord Bálint also understood this trade. He used his shield to block the Turk's heavy cut while in that same motion, he grabbed the Turk's arm and pulled him of his horse. The Turk fell on his side in a cloud of dust.

"That's enough," said Bálint Török as he removed his helmet. "Tomorrow, if I am at home, we can match up again."

"Not fair!" shouted the Turk as he struggled to sit up with one hand.

"Why isn't it fair?" asked Lord Bálint.

"It's not proper for a mounted knight to use a hand to pull his adversary off his horse."

"Well, you are no knight, pagan dog. I certainly am not taking lessons in chivalry from you people, thieves *ordinaire*."

The Turk remained silent and angry.

"If I challenge you to fight, don't think you are in a joust with a knight," continued Bálint Török shouting. "Look at yourselves, a bunch of rags!"

"My lord," said a skinny, grey bearded prisoner. "I will match with you again today."

Those standing in the yard burst out laughing.

"Of course. Now you are thinking I am tired. Well, have your fun." He picked up his helmet from his lap and pulled it over his head. "How many times have you fought with me, Parrot?"

"Seventeen times," replied the parrot-nosed Turk grimly.

Bálint Török took off his helmet and threw it down. "Well," he said, "I give up this much of my strength for your benefit. Let's see!"

There was an obvious, visible difference in strength between them. Lord Bálint was a well-built man in the prime of life, all muscle and agility. The Turk was about fifty years of age with no muscle and a curved back.

They charged each other with spears. In that first crash, Lord Bálint simply pulled the Turk out of his saddle with such force that he somersaulted in the air and crashed with a cloud of dust!

Lord Bálint took off his helmet

Lord Bálint dropped his shield, removed his iron gloves, and jumped off his horse so that the pages could remove its armor.

Parrot was getting up on his feet during this time. "My lord!" he cried, turning his bloody face towards Bálint Török, "Free me so I can return home! My widow, my orphan have been waiting for two years!"

"Then why didn't you stay at home, pagan!" Bálint Török said annoyed. He was always angry when prisoners pleaded for mercy.

"My lord!" shouted the prisoner wringing his hands, "Let your heart have pity on me! I have a beautiful little black-eyed son! I haven't seen him for two years."

And he slid on his knees and crawled in the dust to Lord Bálint's feet.

Lord Bálint wiped his face with a cloth. "Only if every villainous Turk were here in chains together with their emperor! Thieving, murdering beasts!" He stepped aside.

"Well, may Allah strike your rotten, cowardly heart! May you grow old in chains so you have widow and orphans before you die! May Allah teach you to cry three times as much as I have before your soul is pushed into hell!"

And as he cursed like this, the tears from his eyes mixed with blood from his wounded cheek.

The servants carried away the pagan foaming with anger. They took him to the well where he was washed mercilessly.

Bálint Török was already used to these scenes. They disturbed him. But neither cursing nor sweet words undid chains in his castle.

In the end, every prisoner at all times and in every place cries for freedom, some more loudly than others. Since he was a child, Bálint Török had lived with the begging of such prisoners. And in those days, prisoners were a valuable commodity in the local economy. Some were exchanged for money, others for Hungarian prisoners. So why would anyone think that an enemy prisoner would be released just for the sake of God's name?

He stood straight with his arms as his pages brushed him off. Then, angrily twisting his red mustache, he walked towards the priest.

"Dear priest, God has sent you!" he said holding out his hand. "I heard what a terrible boiling you went through. Don't worry, my little father, at least you will grow new skin, like a lobster."

"My noble lord," replied the priest holding his cap in his hands, "My skin is the least of my worries. My biggest misfortune is that they took or killed my congregation. They even murdered my poor mother."

"May dogs eat them!" said Bálint Török angrily as he turned around. "One curses me for not letting him go, the other wants to teach me chivalry."

The priest just listened.

"He comes at me with a broadsword," he continued turning back towards the priest, "like an executioner. The joust is a game to him. But when I pull him off his horse, he thinks he is standing honorably." He angrily pulled on one of his pant belts. It was red, like the bear on his coat of arms above the castle gates.

Then he looked at the boy.

"Well, who is this?" he asked somewhat surprised.

"Get down quickly," said the priest to Gergő. "Take off your cap."

The little barefoot boy with a sword turned on his stomach in the saddle and slid off the horse. He stood before Bálint Török.

"Is this the horse you captured?" he asked amazed.

"This," replied the boy proudly.

Bálint Török gabbed the boy's hand and took him so quickly to his wife that Father Gábor could barely keep up.

The woman — a fair faced, beautiful, blonde creature — was sitting in the garden inside the inner keep of the castle by a table made out of a millstone. She was sealing jars of preserves. A reverend priest with white hands was helping with the work. He was the vicar for the castle. Near them two boys were playing, a five-year-old and a three-year-old.

"My dear Kata, just look," said Bálint Török laughing. "Dobó's page."

Gergő kissed her hands. The blue eyed little Swabian lady looked at him with an astonished smile. Then she bent down and kissed his cheeks.

"This?" asked the castle vicar equally astonished. "I think he is still nursing."

"Yes, he is nursing: on Turkish blood" replied the lord of the castle.

"Are you hungry, my little soldier?" asked the lady.

"I am hungry," replied Gergő. "But first I would like to see Lord Dobó."

"Bah, my son. That's not possible," said Bálint turning serious. "Your lord is lying wounded ..."

He turned towards Father Gábor. "Do you not know? He attacked two hundred Turks with fifty men. One Turk's lance pierced his thigh so deeply that the iron stuck in the wood of his saddle."

"The iron of the lance?"

"That. It broke inside him."

"I pulled it out," boasted the castle vicar.

"Well then," said Bálint Török. "You pulled it out like a carrot."

"That's how I pulled it out. Well, how else would you pull it out?"

"Did he fall?" asked Father Gábor.

"The devil he fell," continued Lord Bálint. "He cut down that Turk and trotted back home stuck to the saddle."

Gergő was pale listening to this. He was bothered that he had not been by Dobó's side. He would have cut down that Turk.

"Go," said the castle vicar. "Play with the lord's sons." The two dark haired boys were already staring cautiously at Gergő standing by Lady Kata's skirt.

"Well, what are you afraid of?" said their mother. "He is a Hungarian boy. He likes you."

Then she said to Gergely, "The older one is Jancsi. The younger Feri."

"Come on," said Gergő. "I'll show you my sword."

The three boys quickly became friends.

"Well you, my dear priest," said Bálint Török as he sat on a bench . "What in God's name are you going to do without a congregation?"

"Well," said Father Gábor sadly, "I will just live there, if not otherwise, as the hermits used to do."

Bálint Török twisted his mustache thoughtfully.

"Do you understand Turkish?"

"I do."

"And German?"

"I studied for two years in Germany."

"Well, I'll tell you something, my dear priest. Get your belongings together and come here to Sziget. Well, not Sziget but Somogyvár because we will be moving there in a few days. You be there. My wife has a Catholic priest. Why shouldn't I have a protestant priest? After one or two years as the kids grow up, I will entrust them to you to teach them."

"My noble lord," said the vicar suddenly dropping his work sealing preserves. "What about me?"

"Well, you can also teach them. You teach them Latin and he will teach them Turkish. Believe me, my good vicar, that the Turkish language is needed for salvation as much as Latin."

He looked at his sons being chased around an apple tree by Gergely. Each had faces red from laughing.

"I will take this lad from Dobó," said Bálint Török. "It may happen that he becomes the third teacher."

Part II
On to Buda!

1

King János [Zápolya] has died. His son is still an infant. The nation has no leader. The country is like a coat of arms in which griffins on either side are angrily reaching for the crown floating between them.

The people's thinking is confused. No one knows whether it is better to submit to Turkish rule or that of the Germans.

The Austrian Ferdinand sent his old, decrepit general Roggendorf to Buda. The Turkish Emperor himself set out to fly his crescent moon flag over the royal Hungarian palace.

The year was 1541.

— § —

On the highway through the Mecsek Hills, on a moonlit August evening, two horsemen canter up the hill. One is a clean shaven, thin man in a black robe — definitely a priest. The other, hardly sixteen years of age, is a long haired nobleman.

A mounted servant follows behind them on the road. Instead of a saddle, the servant sits on two stuffed sacks. On his back is a large leather satchel, what today we would call a backpack. Three sticks of something poke out from the satchel. When one of them glints in the pale light, the metal of a gun barrel is recognizable.

There was an old, thick, wild pear tree in the dark by the road. They rode off the road to the tree.

"Well, is this it?" asked the priest as he studied the tree carefully.

"This is it," replied the young man. "When I was younger, an owl build a nest in its cavity. That cavity has grown wide enough so that at least one man can fit inside."

From horseback, he monkeyed up into the wild pear tree. With one jump he reached where two thick branches grew out from its huge old trunk. He used his sword to poke around the decaying wood. Nothing flew out.

He lowered himself into the cavity.

"The two of us will fit inside," he shouted cheerfully.

He climbed out and jumped down onto the grass.

"Well then, let's get to work," said the priest. And he tossed off his cloak.

It was Father Gábor. The scholar was Gergely Bornemissza.

Eight years have passed since we last saw them. The priest had not changed very much. His eyebrows had grown back. His beard and mustache remained scraggly from the boiling water, so he shaved. And he had gotten a little thinner.

By comparison, the boy had changed a lot. Eight years had almost turned him into a man. But only in form. His face was definitely neither attractive nor ugly but just like that of a typical fifteen-year-old boy. Only the color of his face remained, a pale reddish-brown. His shoulder length, wavy hair was fashionable for men in those times.

The servant pulled two shovels out from his satchel. The priest took one, the young man the other.

They went back to the highway and they started digging a pit in the middle of the road.

The servant dropped the two bags, the ones he had used as a saddle, by the pit and returned to the horses. He took off their bridles and tethered their legs. He let them graze in the good smelling grass of the forest.

Then he also went to work. He took everything out of the leather satchel and spread them out on the ground: bread, wine flask, weapons. He stuffed the satchel with the red soil that the other two were digging out, then scattered it in the roadside ditches. He would return with large rocks that he dropped beside the pit.

It wasn't an hour until the two men stood waist deep in the pit.

"That's enough," said the priest. "János, bring the bags here."

The servant picked up and carried the two bags to the pit.

"Don't put the gun on the wet grass," said the priest to him. Then he further instructed, "Take this shovel and dig a trench from the pit to the wild pear tree. The trench here on the road should be about a yard deep. Half that is enough in the grass. Dig up the grass so we can put it back. Nothing should be visible after we have finished our work."

While the servant dug the trench, the two noblemen lowered the two bags into the pit.

The bags were filled with gunpowder.

They pressed down the two bags and covered them with large rocks, then smaller rocks and dirt to fill the gaps.

Meanwhile, the servant finished the trench to the tree and lined it with rocks. The fuse was strung along the trench, then covered with flat rocks all the way so in case it rained, it would not get soaked.

"Now I know," said the servant, "what is going to happen here."

"What's that, János?"

"Someone is going to be flying from here into the sky."

"And who do you think that will be?"

"Who? That's easy to figure out. The Turkish emperor is coming this way tomorrow."

"Today," replied the priest looking up at the sky turning pink.

When the rising sun lit up the highway, nothing revealed the pit or the trench.

The priest wiped his brow.

"Now then, János my son, get on your horse and go to the top of the Mecsek Hills. Go as far as you need to be able to see the highway all the way to Pécs."

"I understand, my lord."

"The scholar and I will lie down behind the tree for a twenty-thirty minute nap. You keep a lookout for when the Turks are coming. When you see the first horseman, gallop back and wake us up."

With that, the priest turned around and went into the forest with the scholar. They found a nice grassy patch, laid down their cloaks, and immediately fell asleep.

2

Around noon the servant returned from the hilltop at a fast gallop.

"They are coming!" he shouted. "A huge army is coming! Like a sea!"

When he got closer, he continued, "They are all sitting in wagons, as if they are sick."

The priest turned towards the scholar.

"Well then. We can go to your second father for lunch."

"To my Lord Cecey?"

"There."

The scholar looked at the priest with puzzlement, as did the servant.

The priest smiled.

"We arrived a day early. Don't you understand? These are the men who make camp. They go ahead and pitch tents so that when the army arrives at Mohács, they find beds and dinner ready."

"Then let's go to my Lord Cecey's" said the scholar cheerfully.

They dismounted at a stream and washed themselves thoroughly. The scholar plucked a wildflower.

"Who's that for, Gergő?"

"For my wife," replied Gergő smiling.

"Your wife?"

"That how we talk about ourselves. Little Éva Cecey will be my wife. We were kids together; then, as her father adopted me as a son, each time I see her I always have to kiss her."

"I hope you do that kindly."

"Yes, indeed. She has a face like a white carnation."

"But it doesn't follow that you should consider her as your wife."

"The old priest told me that they want her for me. Cecey will give me the girl and the village."

"In that case, the old priest divulged a secret."

"No. He just warned me to be careful about hurrying to be worthy for such good fortune."

"But will you be happy with that girl?"

The boy smiled. "You just look at her, master. If you see her you won't be asking questions whether I will be happy with her."

The scholar swung onto his horse and cantered a few steps. The scholar stopped his horse.·His eyes sparkled as he said, "That girl is like some little white cat!"

The priest smiled and shook his head.

They reached a dense thicket. They had to dismount. Gergely went ahead. He knew the thicket hid the village.

When they descended into the valley, women ran out from the houses.

"Gergő! That's Gergő!" they shouted joyfully.

Gergely waved his tall cap left and right. "Good day, aunt Juci ... Mrs. Panni!"

"The lord and his family aren't home," announced one woman.

Gergely was taken aback. He stopped his horse. "What are you saying, auntie?"

"They are gone. They moved away."

"Where?"

"To Buda."

Gergely was stunned. "All of them?"

Silly childish hope! He thought they would answer. *No. the young lady stayed at home.* But it was predictable that they would straight away respond, "Indeed, all of them. Even the priest went with them."

"When?"

"After St. George's Day."

"Surely someone is at the house?"

"The Turk."

Disappointed, Gergely turned towards the priest. "They went to Buda. A long time ago Friar György gave them a house there. But I don't understand why they didn't tell me what they were planning. And here I ride here like to a carnival."

"Well then, we're not getting any lunch."

"Of course we will, because the Turk is here."

"What Turk?"

"Cecey's Turk, Tulipán. He does everything here. But here we are at the cemetery. Allow me to visit for a few minutes. My mother lives here."

A graveyard surrounded by lilac bushes was visible behind the house. It was not much bigger than the house. Nothing but wooden crosses, crusty and grey from age. No name on any of them.

He handed his reins to the servant and entered. He stopped at a crumbling brown wooden cross. He put the wildflower on the grave. And knelt down.

The priest also dismounted. He knelt by the boy, looked up into the sky and prayed out loud, "Lord of the living and the dead, oh God living in heaven, give peaceful dream to the sweet mother turning to dust here. Give a happy life to this orphaned boy on his knees here. Amen."

Then he hugged and kissed the boy.

Lord Cecey's house stood across from the graveyard. Its gates were already open and a thick set, red faced woman was smiling at the newcomers.

"Good day, Mrs. Tulipán," said the scholar. "Where is your husband?" Because it was Mr. Tulipán's job to open the gate.

"Drunk," replied the woman angrily.

"Drunk?"

"Indeed. Every day that scoundrel steals the cellar key even though every day I hide it in a different place. This morning I hid it under the clothes wringer. Even there he found it."

"Well, don't hide it. If he has a drink when he wants, he won't drink so much."

"Oh, but no. He drinks like a pelican. All he does is drink and sing. That damned fellow has no desire to work."

A brown peasant was sitting in the cool of a mulberry tree. Under him a grass mat, in front of him a glazed green jug. He was not that drunk that the key could have been taken from him. He drank with his son, a six-year-old barefoot kid whose eyes were as black as his father's.

That Turk got mercy from Cecey because he said he could play chess. Later it came to light that playing chess with him was worthless, but he was useful for all kinds of work around the house. He was particularly good at cooking. His father used to be a cook for some pasha. The women liked him because he showed them how to make pilaf, *börek* stuffed pastries, polenta, and sorbets, and he liked to joke with them. Cecey grew to like him because he carved him a wooden hand with detailed fingers. If he wore gloves, no one could tell his hand was made of wood. For the first time the old man tried shooting arrows. He fetched a bow from the attic that was as long as he was tall. He could string it with his wooden hand. For that, he would do anything for the Turk.

About that time, the husband of one of the Hungarian girls was killed. Well, the Turk warmed up to her, then married her. Of course, he was baptized first. He turned into such a good Magyar that he could have been born one.

When he saw the scholar and the priest, he got up and crossed his hands over his chest in the Turkish manner. He also wanted to bow low, but before he was able to bend over for his bowing, he completed his respectful greeting by stumbling forward.

"Well, Tulipán," said Gergely shaking his head. "Are you always drinking?"

"I have to drink," replied Tulipán seriously. "I was a Turk for twenty-five years without drink. I have to catch up."

"But if you're drunk, how will you make lunch for us?"

"My wife will cook," replied Tulipán, pointing his thumb towards the woman. "She will make cottage cheese pancakes. They are really good."

"But we'd like some pilaf."

"She cooks that, too. She knows."

"Well, where is your lord?"

"In Buda. A letter came. The lord's family has gone. He got a house. The beautiful young lady sits in that house like a rose in a garden."

The scholar turned towards the priest with a look of worry on his face. "What happens to us if the Turks manage to occupy the castle?"

"Oh no!" replied the priest. "The entire country will be lost before they can take Buda Castle." Because Gergely continued to look worried, he continued. "The nation protects the country. God Himself protects Buda Castle."

Tulipán opened the doors to the house. A stale smell of lavender came out of the rooms. He also opened the windows.

The priest stepped inside. His sight fixed upon portraits hanging on a wall. "Perhaps this is Cecey?" he asked pointing towards a figure with a helmet.

"Yes," replied Gergely. "It's just that his brown hair is now white."

"And this woman with a squint?"

"That's his wife. I don't know whether she had a squint when the portrait was painted. She doesn't have one now."

"She must be a bitter woman."

"No, rather sweet. I address her as my mother."

The boy, as he felt like he was at home, gave the priest a chair to sit on and proudly showed off the various pieces of cheap furniture.

"Look master. This is where little Vicuska would sit when she was waiting. She puts her feet on this stool. From here she would gaze out the window at the sunset, her shadow cast on that wall. She drew this picture. A weeping willow and a grave. I painted the butterflies in it. Then, you see, she would sit here on this chair. She used to sit here, leaning on her elbows, her head half turned, smiling so mischievously, so mischievously, that no man has yet seen such a smile!"

"Good, good," said the priest fatigued. "But hurry with lunch, my son."

3

They went to sleep late at night.

The priest said that he had to write several letters so he did not sleep in the same room as the scholar.

The scholar also sat down to write a letter. He wrote to his little pussycat how surprised he was at the empty house. He asked why he had not gotten any letter about them moving away. If they did send word, it must have gotten lost.

Because in those days there was no postal service on Hungarian lands. Only great lords could exchange letters with each other. Whoever wanted to send a letter from Buda to their old home also had to find someone willing to deliver it.

Afterwards, sleep weighed heavy on the scholar. He laid down on a wolfskin covered bench and fell asleep.

And perhaps he would have slept until the sun shone brightly in the morning had not a cow mooed under his window at dawn.

He was unaccustomed to that sound. Neither in Somogyvár nor in Szigetvár nor in any of Bálint Török's other castles did a cow moo under his window. Valets always woke Lord Bálint and his children, and the priest would already be waiting in the garden with books.

The scholar sat up and rubbed his eyes. It occurred to him that today's lesson would be different. The Turkish emperor had to be blown to paradise.

He got up and knocked on the neighboring door. "Master!" he called. "The sun's coming up. We need to get going."

No answer. The room was dark.

The scholar opened one of the window shutters and its window made of oiled linen.

The priest's bed was empty.

Some white letters were lying on the table.

Gergely was stunned.

"What the devil?" he mumbled. "The bed hasn't been touched since it was made."

He hurried out the room. In the yard Mrs. Tulipán, barefoot and wearing her underskirt, was driving her pig.

"Mrs. Tulipán. Where is my master?"

"He left at midnight under moonlight."

"Did János go with him?"

"No. He's still here. The priest left on foot, alone."

Puzzled, the scholar went back inside. He feared that he knew what the priest intended. He went straight to the table. Among the letters was one that was open. On it, written in bold, thick letters: "*My dear son, Gergely!*"

It was addressed to him. He held it by the window. The ink on the paper was still damp.

Gergely read:

"*It is your idea and your merit if that crowned beast flies to hell today. But there is also danger in your plans. You hand that over to me, my son.*"

"*You live in love and you are young. Your ingenuity, your knowledge and your courage can be of great benefit to the nation.*"

"*Next to my letter you will find a pouch. There is a Turkish ring inside. It is my only treasure. I leave it for the person I love the most. It is yours, my son.*"

"*In addition, my cabinet of books is also yours. Read them, once the clouds have dispersed from over the house. A Magyar needs a sword now, not a book!*"

"*Give Bálint Török my weapons, my collection of stones to János, and my flower collection to Feri. Let them chose one or two of my books for memories' sake, and tell them to be heroic patriots like their father, and never support the pagans, but rather stand with you to restore and strengthen the national kingdom. Otherwise, I will also write to them, and what I write, let that stay among you three. My soul is divided among you three.*"

"*When I left, you were sleeping, my son. I kissed you.*"

"*Father Gábor.*"

Gergely turned to stone staring at the letter.

Death? A fifteen year old boy does not understand the word. In his mind, all he can see is flames and smoke and the Turkish emperor blown to bits.

And to be deprived of this sight?

He stuffed the pouch with its ring and the letter into a pocket and stepped outside. He hurried across the yard to the Tulipáns.

"Tulipán," he said to the man lying under the eaves. "Do you still have your Turkish clothes" he asked in Turkish.

"No," replied Tulipán. "The lady used it to sew a vest for herself and another for her child."

"You don't even have your turban?"

"From that, the lady made a small shirt. It was fine linen."

The scholar angrily paced up and down under the eave. "Well what can I do? You advise me. The Turkish army is passing here on the highway. The emperor is with them. I want to see the emperor."

"The emperor?"

"Him."

"Well, the noble son can see him."

Gergely's eyes twinkled. "Really? How?"

"There is a rock by the side of the highway. Not just one. Two across from each other. You climb one of those rocks, cover yourself with branches, and you will be able to see the entire army pass by."

"Well then, Tulipán. Get dressed quickly and come with me. Your wife can put some food in a bag. You can bring a bottle."

Tulipán became lively at the sound of the word *bottle*. He threw on some clothes and shouted to the woman feeding the poultry, "Dear Juliska, my ducky. Come here quickly, my moonlight."

"What would you like?"

"The bottle, my precious," said Tulipán. "I need the flask."

"Thunder and lightning! So far you have drunk only in the afternoon. Now you are beginning at dawn?"

"No, no, my little lamb, my Istanbulu sweet," said Tulipán, stroking the woman's face. "The young nobleman wants it."

"Not true. That nobleman doesn't drink wine."

"I don't drink," said Gergely, "but we have to leave and probably we'll be away until dark. Well, I don't want Tulipán to get thirsty."

"You're leaving? Where are you going, young sir?"

"We are off to see the Turkish army, auntie Juli. They are crossing the Mecsek Hills today."

The woman was dumbfounded. "A Turkish army. My dear young sir, don't go there!"

"But definitely we shall go there. I have to see them."

"Oh dear, dear sir, what danger waits for you. What are you thinking?"

"One word is like a hundred," said Gergely impatiently. "We have to go!"

He stamped his foot and the woman ran into the house. However, she quickly returned. Her face was sulking. "I don't care. May the young sir go wherever he wants. I am not telling the young sir what to do. But don't make Tulipán go with you. I tell you that."

"Nothing doing," replied Tulipán.

"You stay at home, understand?"

"Tulipán has to come with me," said Gergely sharply.

"The servant has to carry the master's food. What is the point of a servant if not to serve?"

The other servant, János, was thinking the same thing. He had already packed the satchel and was watering the horses.

Tulipán, sensing his wife's uneasiness, rebelled, "And I am leaving, my dear. May I be blinded if I don't leave! I have to beg you to give me wine, and then only a bit here and a bit there. You are not a good woman."

The woman then whined, "If they see you, the Turks will take you. You would leave these two beautiful children and me here?"

"If you don't give me wine. You even beat me last Thursday."

"I'll give, my sweet husband, as much as you want, just don't leave me here …"

"Well then, good. Just don't forget what you promised in front of this young nobleman. I will accompany the young sir and return by nightfall. Don't think," he said embracing the woman, "that the sultan has a diamond big enough that I would swap it for you. I just have to drink a little. See, if you calmly let me drink, I don't get drunk. I only want to get drunk because I think you won't give me any the next day."

With this, the little wife calmed down a bit. She gathered together some food for them. She tearfully accompanied her husband as far as the gate, and from there she remained gazing after them, worrying, as Tulipán swelled with satisfaction.

— § —

János went with them as far as the thicket. There he dismounted. János led the three horses back to the village as the other two continued on foot to the rock.

To this day, that rock is still standing by the highway. It is as high as five men, and from its top one can see the entire highway as far as the old wild pear tree where the priest had already concealed himself.

The Turk tore off heaps of leafy branches and arranged them like walls around the top of the rock so the two of them could see everything, but from below no one would suspect that men were hidden there.

"Let's put some branches there, too," said Gergely, "to the north."

"What for?"

"Well, if the sultan has passed that far, we can turn around and see him."

The sun was rising. The forest was covered in dew. In the distance was the dust of the lead horsemen.

4

A paprika-red banner appeared on the highway, then two, then another five, then many more. Under the banners and following were soldiers with tall turbans riding Arab horses. The horses were so small that some of the soldiers feet almost reached the ground.

"These are the *gurebas*," explained Tulipán. "They always go first. They aren't Turks."

"Well?"

"Arabs, Persians, Egyptians. A mix of all kinds of people."

They looked like it. Even their clothes were a mix. One had an enormous copper feather dangling over his head and was missing his nose. He had already been to Hungary.

The next regiment following the *gurebas* had green stiped white banners dangling. Brown from the sun, they were dressed in baggy blue pants. Their faces showed that they had eaten and drunk well the previous night.

"These are the *ulufedjis*," said Tulipán. "They are mercenaries and camp police. They also guard the war treasury. See that fellow with the big belly and smashed forehead? He has big brass buttons on his chest ...""

"I see him."

"His name is Turna. In Hungarian, 'crane'. But I would call him 'pig' instead."

"Why?"

"Once I saw him eat a hedgehog."

Following in their footprints rode a regiment with yellow flags. Their weapons glistened. The horse of one agha lord wore a breastplate ornament studded with silver.

These are the *silhatars*," said Tulipán. "Hey you rogues worthy of a hanging tree! I served with you for two years!"

"They are mercenaries also?"

"Mercenaries."

Red banners followed, *sipahis* armed with bows and arrows, their officers in armor; wide, curved swords at their sides. Then the Tatars with their pointed hats, all with greasy faces, leather jerkins, and wooden saddles.

"Thousand ... two thousand ... five thousand ... ten thousand," counted Gergely.

"You can never count them all," waved Tulipán. "There are at least twenty thousand."

"Ugly, boney cheeked people."

"Even the Turks detest them. They eat horse heads."

"Horse heads?"

"Well, if there's not enough to go around, but certainly they put one in the middle of the table."

"Boiled or roasted?"

"Well, if it was boiled or roasted, that would be fine, but it's raw. Then these dogs have no mercy even on the newborn. Because look, he will cut out his spleen."

"Don't talk about such terrible, wretched things!"

"But that's how it is. Because look, they believe if they rub a man's spleen on their horse's tongue, no matter how tired the horse may be, it gets new strength."

Gergely buried his head in the foliage. "I won't look at them," he said. "I believe they are not men but wild animals."

Tulipán just continued watching. "Here comes the *nisandji bey*," he said a quarter of an hour later. He is the one who writes the name of the *padishah* on sealed papers.

Gergely looked below. He saw a pike-headed, stately looking plump Turk with a long mustache riding among the soldiers.

Then the *defterdar* followed, an old, stooped Arab who was the Turks' finance minister. Behind him, in another formation of soldiers, the *kazai asker* in a long yellow robe and a tall, towering white cap. He was the chief judge for the army. The *cheshnidjis* followed, the head servers and various stewards, then the palace bodyguards on whom much gold glittered.

Then the Turk army band played. Accompanied by blaring trumpets and clanging cymbals, the gaudy procession of soldiers advanced and passed: the palace hunters, their horses' manes painted red, holding falcons on their arms.

After the hunters came the imperial studs. Prancing, fiery stallions, some already saddled. *Solaks* and janissaries led the horses.

After the horses came tall standards, with horse tails hanging, being carried on the road. Three hundred *kapudjis* came, all wearing the same gold-embroidered white hats. They were the sultan's palace guards.

Through the clouds of dust came a long, white column of janissaries marching up the slope. Their tall white caps mingled with the red ones of their officers and the blue dress suits they wore.

"Is the sultan far behind?" asked Gergely.

"Definitely he is far behind," replied Tulipán. "There are at least ten thousand janissaries. After that come the *chavishes* and all sorts of court dignitaries."

"Well then, let's pull back," said Gergely, "and have a snack."

The south side of the rock hid them from the army. On the road that sloped down to the north they could see masses of soldiers descending into the valley.

"We could even take a nap," said Tulipán.

And he opened the satchel. Out of it rattled a chain.

"What's that?" asked Gergely.

"This is my good buddy," replied Tulipán. "I never leave the village without this."

As the scholar looked at him not understanding, he continued. "These are my leg irons. When I have to leave the village, I put them on. See, like this I do not fear the Turks. Because instead of making me prisoner, the Turks free me. Here is the key. Put it in your pocket. Whatever happens to us, we will say that we come from Bálint Török's household. I am a slave, you are a scholar. Lord Bálint is on the side of the Turks, so they won't treat us badly. I can free myself at night and we can escape home."

"You are a clever man!" recognized the scholar honestly.

"That I believe!" replied Tulipán. "I can even outwit my wife."

And he thought it appropriate to add, "When I am sober."

The satchel yielded a freshly baked brown loaf, ham, and bacon, even a few green peppers. The scholar took the ham. Tulipán grabbed the bacon and sprinkled it thick with salt and paprika.

"If only the army could see this," said Tulipán gesturing with his head in that direction.

"Then what?"

"The Turk will drink wine," replied Tulipán, "but he hates bacon as much as we Hungarians hate rat meat."

Gergely chuckled.

"But if they knew," continued Tulipán, "how divine is bacon with paprika! But I think Muhammad never tasted bacon with paprika."

"Accordingly, it's better to be Hungarian than Turkish."

"Everyone is a fool who isn't Hungarian!"

He smoothed his silky mustache apart and drank from the flask. Then he offered it to the scholar.

"Not necessary," replied the scholar. "Perhaps later."

He reached into his pocket and took out the pouch.

"Do you recognize this ring, Tulipán?"

"No," replied the man. "But I see that it's worth the price of a horse. What is this small thing? A diamond?"

"Yes."

"Then it's good to look at. I have often heard that to see a diamond is to clear the eyes."

"Well, can you read this writing?"

"Of course. I was a janissary. I attended all through janissary school."

And he read, "*Ila mashallah la hakk ve la kuvvet il a billah el ali el azim.* In Hungarian, 'Whatever God wishes. There is no truth or strength without the majestic and exalted God.'"

He nodded. "This is how it is. If God didn't want it, I would not have become a Hungarian."

There was a minute of thoughtful silence before Tulipán spoke again. "When you see the sultan you will see what a fine man he is. His people are gaudy, but he himself dresses up in splendor only when he is on holiday or when he receives a guest. After the sultan comes a forest of golden standards, most with horsetails. One hundred trumpets after them. Each man has a gold chain attached from his trumpet to his shoulder. After the trumpets, two hundred drummers come, then one hundred big drums, two hundred rattles, a hundred bell ringers and another hundred pipers."

"The sultan must have good ears if he has to listen to that noise all day."

"Yes, it's a hellish din. Only when they rest do they become quiet. But the Turks require this, especially in battle. If there's no music, the Turk doesn't fight."

"Is it true that they raise Christian boys to be janissaries?"

"More than half. But this much is true, that from the captured boys come the best janissaries. They have no fathers or mothers. It's glory for them if they fall in battle."

"What comes after the bands?"

"An army of rag-tag people: rope dancers, tricksters, jugglers, quack-doctors, merchants who buy plunder and sell little things. You'll also see a lot of water barrels. At least five hundred camels come in the rear. They have goatskin water bags, but the water is usually lukewarm."

"After that, is there anything more?"

"A hundred caravans with gypsies and dogs. They live off of whatever is thrown away. But they will get here only tomorrow or the next day."

"And then?"

Tulipán shrugged his shoulders. "Vultures."

"Eagle vultures?"

"All kinds. Eagles, ravens, crows. After every army there is a black army in the sky. Sometimes numbering more than the men."

The noon sun was hot. The scholar took off his jacket. They crawled back up to the rock ledge and looked at the janissaries with their tall white hats constantly filing away.

Tulipán named many of them.

"This brown one here went to school with me. He has a scar on his chest so deep a child's fist would fit inside. The man sweating over there who took off his turban for a minute, he killed at least a hundred people in the Persian war. He doesn't have a single scar, unless he's gotten one since. That thin, scraggly looking fellow is an amazing knife thrower. He can throw a dagger into his enemy's chest from twenty-five paces away. His name is Tyapken. There are more like him. There is a grass covered mound at the janissary school. That's where they teach how to throw a dagger. There are those who practice throwing two thousand times every day."

"What about that Saracen?"

"Well then, you are still around, old Keskin? He is a damned good swimmer! He puts his sword in his mouth and swims like that across a river no matter how wide."

"Even Hungarians can do that."

"Perhaps. But that guy doesn't tire. He can fetch money underwater. Even the sultan played with him one time by the Danube. He threw gold pieces into the water. Many dived after them, but that guy came up with the most. Well, there's old Kalen. He's that man with big arms and a trumpet nose! See that wide, brown broadsword at his side? It weighs fifty pounds! In a battle at Belgrade, he made a cut with that on a Hungarian that not only cut off his head, but that of his horse, too, even though both were in armor."

"And, of course, the Hungarian dismounted to pick up his own head."

"Well, I didn't see it myself, but I heard about it."

Suddenly he recoiled. "Am I dreaming?" he said coughing. "Yumurjak!"

Indeed, the tense, one-eyed Arab janissary was advancing with them on a short, strong bay mount. His dress was more ornate than the others. A long ostrich feather fluttered from his tall white hat.

"God strike him!" exclaimed Gergely in amazement.

"I believe they said that the priest hung him!"

"That's my understanding."

"Did the priest talk about it?"

"No."

"Well, this is incomprehensible," gasped Tulipán. He stared at the janissary.

Then the astonished Gergely and Tulipán turned their eyes to each other as if expecting the other to give an explanation. They listened.

After some five minutes the scholar spoke. "Tell me honestly, Tulipán. Don't you want to be back among them?"

"Not me," replied Tulipán emphatically. "If I didn't have a wife and kids, even then no. But my wife is a good woman and I wouldn't give up my two children for all the treasure in Istanbul. The little one is really a beautiful child. The older one is so smart that the head boss isn't any smarter. Just a few days ago he asked why horses don't have horns."

"Only a Tartar knows!" replied the scholar Gergely laughing.

They did not talk any more. The scholar became more and more serious as he gazed at the endless line of janissaries that flooded the steep highway.

The air had become an ocean of dust. The rattle of weapons and the sound of horses' hooves filled the silence punctuated by periodic sounds of military bands drifting up from all over the valley.

The scholar suddenly raised his head. "Tulipán, all these men are not coming for no purpose."

"Well, they never travel for no reason."

"These intend on taking Buda!"

"Could be," replied Tulipán indifferently.

The scholar, the color gone from his face, stared at Tulipán. "And if the sultan should accidently die along the way?"

"He won't die."

"But still, if ..."

Tulipán shrugged his shoulders. "He always carries his son with him."

"In that case, he is a seven-headed dragon."

"Say what?"

Instead of answering, the scholar asked, "What do you think? How long until they reach Buda?"

"That can't be known."

"Still, what do you think?"

"If it rains, they will rest for two or three days, or maybe a week."

The scholar moved uneasily where he lay. "Then I can overtake them," he muttered, "if I see that they are not turning around."

"What are you saying?"

"This. If these men are headed towards Buda, then I have to bring back the Ceceys. Either that, or I have to be with them."

The blaring of a military band drowned out their conversation. The long procession of janissaries had come to an end, followed by a magnificent regiment bearing yellow standards and ostrich feathers. A dignified, huge giant emerged from the regiment. In front of him were two long, red colored horsetails, and the poles on which the horsetails hung glittered with solid gold.

"That's the sultan!" the scholar said with disgust.

"Of course not," replied Tulipán. "He's only the agha [master] of the janissaries. The dressed-up men around him are all *yaya-bashis*."

"What in hell's name are *yaya-bashis*?"

"Janissary officers."

A glittering group followed with gold halberds. Two calm faced young men rode among them. Both were on grey horses.

"The sultan's sons," explained Tulipán in a respectful tone of voice. "Muhammad and Selim." Then he quickly shrugged. "The devil take them."

The sultan's sons were two brown haired young men. They did not resemble each other, but it showed that they liked each other.

"Look, there goes Yaya-oglu Muhammad!"

"The famous pasha?"

"Him."

A dignified gray-bearded man plodded after the young sultans. In front of him, men with lots of white turbans on their heads carried seven horsetail standards.

"That," said Tulipán, "is the father of Yumurjak."

"Impossible!"

"Definitely, he is. His other son, Arslan Bey, just passed us by."

"What kind of name is 'Yumurjak'?"

"A nickname," replied Tulipán. Bored, he tore off and chewed a blade of grass.

A group carrying silver and gold maces and wearing frighteningly tall turbans followed. The scholar's body trembled as he anticipated the sultan coming. "Almighty God," he prayed, "be with us Hungarians!"

Many gold and silver weapons and waves of shimmering robes passed in front of his eyes. He even shaded his eyes with his hands for a minute to see better.

Tulipán nudged him in the side. "Look!" he said in a trembling voice. "There, he's coming."

"Which one?"

"The one with the dervish whirling in front."

He was riding alone on a simply dressed horse. In front of him, a dervish was spinning mechanically at an even speed. The dervish wore a tall camel hair cap about an arm and a half tall. His two hands were held apart. One palm to the sky, the other to the earth. His skirt flared out like a bell from the whirling.

"Whirling dervish," explained Tulipán.

"It's a wonder he doesn't pass out, either he or his horse."

"Both have gotten used to it."

The horse was cantering freely. Another six dervishes wearing white skirts walked on both sides ready to relieve the one who was whirling.

"These seven dervishes will be whirling in front of the sultan from Istanbul all the way to Buda," shouted Tulipán into the scholar's ear. Because of the trumpets, pipes, cymbals and drums, there was no other way they could hear each other.

The sultan sat on a beautiful small Arab bay horse. Behind him, two half-naked Saracens with long peacock feather fans struggled to defend the splendid lord from the harsh rays of the sun. Even so, the air was blowing up from the bends of the valley making his majesty suck the dust the same as his most ragged soldier.

As he arrived by the rock, it was possible to see that he was wearing a blood-red robe with matching baggy pants. His turban was green. His face was lean and hollow. Under his long, thin, almost sloping nose he had a thin, grey mustache. His chin was covered by a curly beard cut short. The eyes protruded.

As Gergely was trying to get a better look, suddenly, a boom! An explosion shakes earth and sky. The rock shakes under them.

Horses gallop back. The sultan falls on the neck of his rearing horse. The music stops. Crazy running about. Dust and bits of stone, body parts, weapons and blood droplets fall from the sky like rain. Confusion and yelling in the army from the valley.

"We're done!" cried scholar Gergely slapping his hands together.

And he stared down at the valley with two scared eyes. A dark column of smoke was rising from the valley towards the clouds. The air was heavy with the smell of gunpowder.

"What happened?" asked a frightened Tulipán.

"That," answered the scholar, his head lowering, "the agha of the janissaries is not the sultan!"

5

The explosion was followed by a minute of stunned silence. Then thousands and thousands of mixed shouts and curses. An army of men was swarming around like ants from a disturbed anthill. Everyone was pushing towards where the column of smoke was rising.

That place was filled with dead and wounded.

Those who were father away were also confused. They did not know whether an old cannon of a hidden army had fired, or a cart loaded with gunpowder had exploded on the road.

However, the janissaries immediately knew that someone had exploded a mine against them. They disbursed into the forest like angry wasps. They were looking for the enemy.

But all they found in the woods were the priest, the scholar, and Tulipán.

The priest was half-dead, bloody foam on his lips. His clothes looked like they had been sprinkled with bran. It was the soft, decayed wood from the crack in the tree. The explosion felled the tree and threw him out of the cavity.

They pulled the three captives in front of the sultan.

He got off his horse. The soldiers put a large copper drum on the ground. A senior officer covered it with his own blue silk kaftan.

However, the sultan did not sit down. He looked at Tulipán. "Who are you people?"

He recognized him as a Turkish prisoner from his face and leg-irons.

"I am a prisoner," replied Tulipán on his knees. "You can see, oh father of all true believers, the chains on my legs. Otherwise, I would be a janissary. My name is Tulipán."

"And this kid?"

The scholar just stood confused, his face pale. His walnut-colored eyes just stared at the hazel-eyed, sheep-nosed man, the lord of millions who should have just flown to the Turkish heaven.

"He is the adopted son of Bálint Török," Tulipán replied.

"The dog of Enying?"

"Yes, your majesty."

"And this man?" asked the sultan pointing towards the priest.

The priest was held by two janissaries. His head drooped. Blood dripped from his mouth onto his chest. It was impossible to tell whether he had fainted, or was dead.

Tulipán looked at the priest.

A senior officer grabbed the priest's hair from behind and pulled up his head so Tulipán could see the face better. "I don't know him," replied Tulipán.

"Does the scholar know him?"

Gergely shook his head.

The sultan looked at the boy, then turned again to Tulipán. "What kind of explosion was this?" he continued. "They wanted to kill me?"

"Your Majesty," replied Tulipán. "The scholar and I were gathering mushrooms around here. We heard the music. We hurried here. I am unworthy dust at your feet. We were waiting for you to pass by. Then I would have stepped forward and asked to be freed."

"That means you know nothing."

"May I be welcomed by the faithful in paradise!"

"Release him!" replied the sultan, rubbing a loathsome drop of blood from his coat sleeve. "Use his chains to bind the scholar's legs."

Then he looked at the priest. "The doctors will have to care for this dog. I want to get a confession out of him!"

Then the sultan mounted his horse. His sons joined him and they rode off towards the site of the explosion accompanied by *bostanjis* and pashas.

While the chains were being was tethered on his legs, the scholar saw the priest being laid on his back on the ground. They splashed water from a leather water bag over his face and chest. They were washing blood off him.

Dressed in an ash colored kaftan, a serious looking Turk occasionally lifted up the priest's eyelids and watched carefully.

Meanwhile, the leg irons were fastened on the scholar's legs and he was taken to the other prisoners.

The boy was pale and shaking like a poplar leaf.

A quarter of an hour later, there was Tulipán. He was dressed in blue like the other janissaries. A tall white cap on his head and red boots on his feet.

He shook his fist in the scholar's face and shouted angrily, "You've fallen into my grip, infidel dog!" He pushed aside the janissary standing by Gergely. "This is my prisoner," he said. "Until now I was his prisoner. Allah is just and powerful."

He pushed the janissary away from Gergely's side. The janissary nodded and let Tulipán guard Gergely.

The boy stared at Tulipán with his pale face. Did the soul of Tulipán really change back?

Not even two minutes had passed before Tulipán secretly gestured not to worry.

6

Gergely was walking in a group of tired and dusty child prisoners accompanied by a single file of janissaries. Behind them rumbled the cannon carriages. One cannon was immensely huge. It was pulled by fifty pairs of oxen and escorted by an army of *topchis* wearing short red cloaks.

The blazing heat of the sun tormented the entire army. Even the white dust of the road was hot. An eight-year-old child whimpered with every tenth step, "Give me water! Water! ..."

Gergely said to Tulipán sadly, "Give him some."

"There's none," replied Tulipán in Hungarian. "The flask got left behind."

"You hear, boy? There's none," said Gergely turning back towards the boy. "I would happily give you some if there were any. Just be as patient as you can until evening."

With each step he used one hand to hold up the leg irons, then the other to be able to take the next step. The irons grew heavier. By dusk he felt as if he were carrying a load of a hundred pounds.

By then the army of children was sitting on cannons and camels. The *topchis* were picking them up because they had collapsed from fatigue.

"Are we still far away?" asked Gergely of the ragged soldier walking on his right.

"No" he replied, giving a look of surprise at Gergely addressing him in Turkish.

He was a giant Turk with a round face. He wore a torn leather vest from which his naked arms stuck out. What arms! Other men would gladly have thighs that thick. His weapons: two long *yataghan* daggers[16] stuck in a cloth wrapped like a belt around his waist. One had a handle made of deer-bone, the other handle was made from the yellow leg bone of an ox, complete with the two bony bumps on the end that nature had created. But his main weapon was a long spear with a rusty point that he rested on one shoulder. He was one of the irregulars, joined up only for the plunder. He took orders from everyone, but he obeyed only as long as it took to stuff his satchel. Well, this fellow had a big satchel and it was flat. It flopped around on his back and it looked home-made, as if he had sewn it together himself. The ox-skin still had hair on it, as well

---

16 *Yataghan* (Turkish: *yatağan*) is a curved long knife or short sabre used by some Turks instead of swords during the 16th to 19th Centuries.

as its brand. The ox had been branded with a circle the size of a hand and two lines cutting quarters.

"Are you Turkish?" asked the soldier.

"No," replied the scholar proudly. "I don't belong to any such people who go around stealing."

The giant either did not understand the insult or he wasn't sensitive. He just kept walking at the same pace.

The scholar looked him up and down then stared at the huge sandals on his feet. With each step, white dust from the road slipped in holes worn in the toes and puffed out at the heels.

"Can you read?" asked the Turk about a quarter of an hour later.

"I know," replied Gergely.

"And you know how to write?"

"Write also."

"But you don't want to be a Turk?"

"No."

The Turk lifted an eyebrow. "Pity."

"Why?"

"Suleiman Pasha also was a Hungarian. He could write and read. Now he is a pasha."

"And he wars against his home."

"He fights for the true faith."

"If that's his true faith, what your prophet preached, let him fight someplace else."

"He fights wherever Allah wishes."

They talked no more. Tulipán indicated with his eyes to Gergely to be quiet.

The giant was lost in thoughts as he continued to shoot dust from his sandals.

7

Nightfall. Stars twinkled in the sky. As the road curved on a hill, the darkness of the countryside seemed to become a part of the sky; a sky sprinkled with red stars where towards the east, five large red stars shone brightly among others.

"We've arrived," said the giant. But they walked another quarter of an hour through dry pastures, hills, and fields of stubble.

Every group found its own place without having to search. The red stars were campfires by which onion smelling mutton was steaming. The five big red stars were enormous wax torches burning in front of the sultan's tent. The fifth was a large gold ball and moon on the top of the tent that reflected the red light of the four torches.

Past a field of sunflowers a *topchi pasha* blew twice on his whistle. They stopped.

In that place the tents had been erected in a "U" formation. They prisoners were led into the middle of the "U".

The giant smelled the sunflowers and went into the field to collect seeds. The scholar collapsed on the grass.

The soldiers came and went, a noisy din all around them. Some of them were opening their bundles, others loitered around the cauldron. The camp was full of stirring and bustling.

Gergely was looking for Tulipán, but he could only see him for a moment before a janissary spoke to him. Tulipán shrugged his shoulders, then went with the janissary by the side of a beetroot colored tent. Probably they were assigning a place for him in one of the janissary tents.

But what if Tulipán had to leave only because he had to guard the prisoners there! In that case, he could not come back. Both of them would remain prisoners!

This thought slid like ice down his back.

Sometime later the guards changed, replaced by the soldiers who had set up camp. Completely strange fellows who never even bothered to look his way.

By then the camels carrying water arrived at the camp.

"*Sucu, sucu!* [water-man!]" sounded the cries of water carriers everywhere. In earthenware pots, drinking horns, lead cups, and hats, soldiers drank water from the Danube.

Gergely also was thirsty.

He pushed in the crown of his cap and held it out under the Turk camel driver's spout.

The water was warm and not that clean, but he drank eagerly. Then he thought of the child who cried for water all the way. He looked around. He saw some of the cannons in the gloom. He saw the oxen grazing beside them. *Topchi* artillerymen were sitting and lying next to the cannons. He didn't see the child.

He drank the rest of the water in his cap and put it back on his head.

"We drink better water at home, don't we?" he said to the new guard, a long necked smooth faced *azab* foot soldier.

Maybe he was trying to make friends.

"Shut up! Drop dead!" shouted back the *azab*. He gave his lance a jerk towards him, then continued his pacing among the prisoners.

He almost went crazy when he saw Yumurjak. He was organizing the new guards, a sword in his hand.

"Yumurjak!" he yelled to him like someone greeting an old acquaintance.

Because he wanted to escape from the torment of loneliness.

The Turk turned around. From where was he called? From the group of prisoners? He was amazed to see Gergely. "Who are you?"

The boy got up.

"I am a prisoner," he said tightening up. "I just wanted to ask what's …, how is it that you are alive?"

"Why wouldn't I be alive?" replied the Turk with a shrug. "Well, why wouldn't I be alive?"

As he sheathed his sword, his crippled left hand could be seen. His fingers stuck out as if he had taken a pinch of salt then couldn't separate them.

"I heard that they strung you up."

"Me?"

"Indeed, you. Nine years ago, a priest in the Mecsek woods."

At the sound of *priest*, the Turk's eyes opened wide.

"Where is that priest? What do you know about him? Where does he live?" He grabbed the scholar by the shirt.

"Perhaps you want to do him harm," stammered the scholar.

"Of course not," replied the Turk with a cooler voice. "Instead, I want to thank him for not harming me." He placed his hand on the scholar's shoulder to make his earlier grab seem like a friendly gesture.

"Well, didn't you thank him back then?" asked Gergely.

"The thing happened so quickly," said Yumurjak wringing his hands. "It never occurred to me to thank him. I thought he was joking."

"So, instead of hanging you, he freed you?"

"Yes, like a Christian. At that time I did not understand. Since then I heard that according to Christian religion, it's possible to forgive one's enemy."

"So now you want to do him some good?

"Yes. I do not like to be in debt, either with money or in favors."

"Well, the priest is also here," said the scholar confidently.

"Here? In the camp?"

"Indeed, here. He is the sultan's prisoner. They accuse him of being responsible for the explosion in the Mecsek."

"How do you know the priest?"

"We live nearby," replied the scholar carefully.

"Did the priest show you a ring?"

"Possible. Maybe he did."

"A Turkish ring? It has a moon and stars."

The scholar shook his head. "He might have shown something like that to others, but not to me." And he put his hand in his pocket.

Yumurjak scratched the back of his neck. The long ostrich feather hung here and there on his tall cap. He turned and stepped away.

The guards greeted him in turn. Soon only the movement of their spears indicated where he was passing.

— §

Gergely was again alone. He sat back down on the grass. They brought a cauldron of soup for the prisoners along with some crude wooden spoons. The Turk who brought it remained standing there while the prisoners ate. When one prisoner said something to another, the Turk gave him a kick.

Gergely tasted the soup. It was made with a flour paste. No salt. No fat. Morning and night that was the provision for the prisoners in the camp. Gergely had heard that several times.

He put his spoon down and turned away from the others still eating. He lay down in the grass. Slowly, the other prisoners also finished eating, laid down, and even fell asleep.

Only Gergely did not sleep. His eyes filled with tears that drizzled down his face.

The moon was just above the horizon, shining light on the gold knobs and horsetails on the tops of tents, on the points of spears, and on the cannons.

The long-necked guard looked at him each time he walked by.

Gergely was annoyed by those looks. His breathing became almost relieved when he saw the broad shoulders of the giant Turk walking towards them.

He was chewing on a plate full of sunflower seeds the same way a pig chews. He could wander around wherever he wanted. He was neither a guard nor a regular soldier.

"The guys who set up camp trampled them before we got here," he complained to the long neck. "It was all I could do to find this plate full."

"Or the infidels hid them," he replied angrily. "These people, if they sense a Turk, they hide everything, even if it's not ready to harvest." He continued pacing around the prisoners.

The giant was eating the seeds off a sunflower and bit into the stalk. He spat.

"You don't get food?" asked Gergely.

"I get," replied the Turk. "But first they give to the janissaries. I am new in the army."

"What were you before?"

"A herder. I herded elephants. In Teheran."

"What's your name?"

"Hussein."

Another janissary sat on the grass next to them. He had a boiled vertebra in his hand. He used his knife to pick pieces of meat off the bone. He also spoke up, "We just call him Hayvan because he is a blockhead."

"Why would he be a blockhead?" asked the scholar.

"Because," replied the janissary throwing the bone behind his back, "he is always dreaming that he is a janissary pasha."

8

The scholar was lying down on the grass, his arm under his head.

He was tired but only his eyes slept. His mind, like a wheel on the ocean, was turning on thoughts of escape.

He was down-hearted to see Hayvan returning again, and squatting down beside him chewing noisily. He had gotten a bone from one of the cauldrons.

"Infidel," said Hayvan nudging the scholar's knee. "If you want to eat, I can bring some for you, too."

"Thanks," replied the scholar. "I'm not hungry."

"You haven't eaten since we caught you."

It was truly unusual for the giant to hear that someone was not hungry. He shook his head. "I'm always hungry." And he continued chewing.

The scholar leaned back on his arm and stared at the moon with orange colored light rising in the east above the tents. A guard's head some thirty paces away was blocking half of the moon. It looked like the shadow of a bishop wearing a tall mitre hat, and the spear in his hand looked like a handle for the moon.

"Don't sleep," said Hayvan. "I want to tell you something."

"We'll have time tomorrow."

"No. I'd like to now."

"Well, but quickly."

"Let's wait a little until the moonlight is brighter."

There was some movement on one side of the area where they had been herded. Among the shadows of the armed guards five more shadows appeared.

They were new prisoners. Five men and a woman.

"Take me to the sultan!" one of them shouted in Hungarian with a thick, bear-like voice. "I'm not German! Germans are dogs! You can't take me. Turks are not fighting Hungarians now. How dare you take me?"

The soldiers didn't understand a word. When he stopped, they just pushed him on.

There was a clearing near Gergely big enough for a cart to turn around. They took the prisoners there.

The Hungarian saw that no one listened to his words, so he just started cursing to himself. "These pagan swine have no god if they say Hungarians are their friends. Friends indeed, like rotten hell, but not with Hungarians!"

After a little rest, he continued.

"The guy was stupid who first believed them, and the guy who first invited them in! May they fall together with their rascal emperor!"

During this time, the woman was taken away towards the cannon carriages and oxen. The other four men sat silently on the grass. They were German soldiers. One of them wore a shiny breastplate. He had nothing on his head, just his tussled long hair.

Gergely turned towards the Hungarian.

"Isn't it," he asked "that those Germans escaped from below Buda?"

"Likely," replied the Hungarian. "I just got mixed up with them here in a vineyard."

That was when Gergely saw that the deep voiced Hungarian was a thin little man with a round beard sitting in his shirt among the others.

"Why were you taken prisoner?" asked Gergely further.

"Me? Because I was hiding them in a cellar. Maybe the fools think I am a spy. A spy, the devil! I am an honest cobbler. I would be happy never to see a Turk, much less follow them around."

"Perhaps you come from Buda?"

"From there, yes. Wish I'd stayed at home."

"Do you know an old man there named Cecey?"

"With wooden legs? Of course I know him."

"What's the old man doing?"

"What's he doing? Fighting."

"Fighting?"

"That's him. He tied himself onto a horse, then rushed out with Lord Bálint after the Germans."

"But he only has one hand!"

"Still he attacked the Germans. I saw them when they got back. He was next to Lord Bálint. That's how he took him to the queen."

"Bálint Török?"

"Him. Hey, he is also one of these guys raised on dragon's milk. Every day he returned from battle with blood up to his shoulders."

"Then, was the old man hurt?"

"Of course," replied the cobbler laughing. "They cut off his wooden hand in battle."

"Do you know his daughter?" asked the scholar timidly.

"Of course I know her. Two weeks ago I sewed a pair of boots for her. Made with yellow and crimson with gold decorations low around the ankle. This is the style the noble women are now wearing, if they can afford it."

"She is a beautiful girl, isn't she?"

The cobbler shrugged his shoulders, "Dainty."

He was silent for a minute, then pulled on his beard. "May the good Lord keep her from the pagans." Then he said with a changed voice, "If they would just return my coat!"

"When did you leave Buda?" further interrogated the scholar.

"I escaped three days ago. Wish I hadn't escaped! I would not have had luck this bad. The Turk is a dog. They promised at Nándorfehérvár that they would not harm anyone, but still they cut down the entire population. Isn't that true?"

"Surely you don't think that the Turks will capture Buda?"

"It's certain."

"How can it be certain?"

"For more than a week now Turkish souls are at mass each night."

"What? What are you saying?"

"Each midnight the Church of Our Lady is lit up, then you can hear all the *ilallah* as the Turks shout and sing to their god."

"That can't be, my older brother!"

"God's holy truth, it is. Wasn't it the same at Nándorfehérvár? Then also you could hear Turks singing from the church each night, then a week later, the Turks captured the castle."

"That's just superstition," said Gergely grimly.

"Whatever it is, I myself saw and heard. Otherwise I would not have left the castle."

"So that's why you escaped!"

"Of course it is. Before the struggle with the Germans started, I sent my family to Sopron to be with their grandmother. I myself couldn't leave with them because I was making good money. You, young nobleman, must know that the lords, when they come to Buda, the first thing they do is order a new pair of boots for themselves. I made a pair for Bálint Török, and also for noble Werbőczy. And also for the great noble lord Perényi!"

The boot-maker was unable to complete what he wanted to say because Hayvan grabbed him by the collar of his waistcoat and lifted him up like a cat. He threw him away from the scholar some ten paces.

The boot-maker groaned as he fell on the grass. Hayvan sat in his place. "You said you could read and write. Well, I'll show you something."

He wiped his fingers on the ox skin bag and from inside pulled out a folded piece of parchment.

"Look," he said. "I found this under the robes of a dead dervish. Some wound had killed the dervish. Either he got speared or he got shot. It doesn't matter. He also had money on him, thirty-six pieces of gold. That's also in my bag. If you tell me what's in this writing, then two gold pieces are yours. But if you don't tell me, I will punch you so hard it will kill you."

The moon shone brightly. Everyone around them was sleeping. The boot-maker was also curled up on the grass, working at finding some comfort in his dreams.

The scholar opened the bundle of parchment. The pages were the size of a hand, with four, five and six sided drawings all over them.

"I can't see well," said the scholar. "Moonlight isn't enough to read this tiny writing."

The Turk got up, went to the fire and returned with a burning branch, thick as an arm. He held it up.

The scholar carefully studied the writing and drawings — sadly. The heat from the burning branch was hot on his face, but he did not mind.

Suddenly he raised his head. "Have you shown these writings to anyone else?"

"I showed them, but no one could read."

The branch went out. The Turk dropped it.

"I don't need your money," continued the scholar. "And I am not afraid of your punch because I am the sultan's prisoner. If you hit me, you will answer to the sultan. However, if you want me to translate this writing, then I want something from you."

"What?"

"This writing is worth a lot to you because it belonged to a holy dervish. It's your one in a thousand luck that you showed it to me because any Turk would have stolen it from you. However, I will explain it to you on one condition, that you go to the priest who made the explosion this afternoon, or if he didn't, they found him nearby."

"Definitely he did it."

"No matter. Look and see if he is dead or alive."

The Turk held his chin and looked at Gergely thoughtfully.

"While you are gone to look, I will study your papers," assured the scholar. "Now I don't need a torch. The moonlight is enough."

And he again studied the drawings carefully.

They were drawings of castles in Hungary. They were done in lead. Here, there erasures. An "X" shape and an "O" shape stood out in one of the drawings. At the bottom, an explanation in Latin: *X means the weakest point of the castle. O is a good place to dig mines.* In some places, the "O" mark had an arrow pointing from it; in others, none.

The scholar shook his head in despair. In his hands he held some spy's drawings. Drawings of some thirty fortresses in Hungary.

What should he do?

Steal it?

That was hopeless.

Burn it?

The Turk would strangle him.

Anxiety made his face pale as he held the papers. Then he reached into the pocket of his waistcoat and pulled out a small piece of lead. He rubbed out all the X's and O's and put similar marks in different places.

That was all he could do.

While the Turk was gone, he held the last drawing in his hand for a long time. It was a drawing of the fortress at Eger. It looked like a frog with a piece missing from every leg. What caught his attention were four underground passages, each tunnel radiating out from a four-sided water reservoir. What an unusual structure! It was as if whoever built it was anticipating continuing battle underground, and if that were unsuccessful, then escaping in four different directions from the castle while the besiegers drown in the reservoir.

He glanced up to see whether the Turk was coming.

He was coming. A tall, huge shadow by the cannons was moving closer.

Gergely quickly crumpled that one page into a small ball and stuffed it in the pocket of his waistcoat. With his finger, he tore a hole in the pocket so the paper could fall inside the lining. Then he again knelt and leaned over the drawings spread out in front of him.

"The priest is still living," said the Turk as he crouched. "But they say he won't make it to morning."

"You saw him?"

"I saw him. All the doctors are sitting around the tent. The priest is lying on a bed with pillows, a rattle in his throat like a horse speared in its stomach."

Gergely covered his eyes with his hands.

"You're his accomplice!" said the Turk twitching.

"And what if I am? Your good fortune in my hands."

The Turk blinked, then brightened up. "Do these papers come with good luck?"

"Not the papers but the secret. But only for Turks."

And he returned the papers.

"Well then, talk," said the giant in a deep whisper. "I did what you asked."

"But you also have to free me."

"Uh ah!" grumbled the Turk.

"This secret is worth more to you."

"I will learn it from someone else."

"A Turk will take it from you. A Christian? When are you going to find a Christian who understands Latin as well as Turkish, and who you can make serve to open the lock to your good fortune?"

The Turk gabbed the scholar by the neck. "I will strangle you if you don't tell me!"

"And I will scream that you have in your possession the blessings of a holy man!"

He couldn't say anything more. The Turk's fingers around his neck were like an iron vice.

He could not breathe.

Suddenly the Turk did not want to continue. Of what use was that?

If he strangles the scholar, perhaps he also strangles his good fortune with him. And Hayvan did not join the war in order to bash his own head. Like any other soldier, he wanted to become a lord.

His fingers loosened around the scholar's neck.

"Well then," he said grimly. "I could also beat you to death if you mix up with trouble. How do you reckon I can free you?"

The scholar could not immediately reply. He had to breathe after being choked.

"First," he said gasping, "You saw off my leg irons."

The giant smiled with contempt. He looked around, then a large red hand reached for one of the clamps. He broke it in two places. The leg irons clattered onto the grass.

"And then?" he asked with curiosity in his eyes.

"Get me a *sipahi* hat and a *sipahi* cloak."

"That's trouble."

"Just take it from one who's sleeping."

The Turk scratched his neck.

"That's not all," continued the scholar. "You also have to get a horse and a weapon. Any kind of weapon. I don't care."

"If I can't find something else, you can have my daggers."

"I'll take it."

The Turk looked around. Everywhere people were asleep. Only the sentries appeared here and there, walking silently in the shadows.

Long-neck was standing some twenty steps away. His spear was stuck down into the ground. He was leaning on it.

"Wait," said the giant.

He got up and trudged towards the south. He disappeared among the tents.

9

Gergely lay down on the grass as if he, too, were going asleep. But he did not want to sleep, no matter how tired he was. With eyes half open, he studied the sky to see if the moon would meet the long, raft-shaped grey cloud sitting motionless in the middle of the sky. (If it neared, a desirable darkness would cover the land.) With his other eye he studied the long necked, irascible janissary standing like a captive, bare-necked eagle. Definitely he was asleep while standing. A soldier having marched all day can sleep standing.

The night was mild, and the air trembled with the soft snoring of hundred thousand people, as if the earth itself was muttering with a deep, monotonous murmur, like a cat purring. Only occasionally did some dog bark, a sentry talk, and horses quietly crunch as they grazed.

Gergely slowly became sleepy. Fatigue had worn out his body. Anxiety exhausted his soul. (The condemned always sleep the night before they are to be executed.) But he did not want to sleep. He struggled against the heavy air of sleep that covered the camp. He fought, but finally, his eyes closed.

— § —

And, behold, he sees where he had set out: in the study of the Somogyvár Castle, beside the two children of Bálint Török.

They are sitting at the table, the unpainted oak table. Across from them Father Gábor is bent over a large book bound in parchment. The window is on the left, the sun shining through its leaded, round glass, the light covering the corners of the table. Two large maps on the wall. One is of Hungary; the other is of the three continents.

(At that time, scholars did not include the lands of Columbus. News of it had only recently been spreading, that the Portuguese had discovered an unknown continent. But whether the rumors were true, no one knew. They had not even dreamed there was an Australia.) The castles were drawn on the map of Hungary with tent-shaped figures, and the forests were drawn with trees. They were good maps, those. Even someone who could not read could understand them. And in those days, there was many a great lord with a coat of arms who could neither read nor write. Well, what good is it? That's why he has a secretary — to write. And if a letter arrives, the secretary reads it to the lord.

The priest raises his head and speaks. "Starting today, we will not study syntax, geography, history, or botany, but only the Turkish language and the German; and in chemistry, only enough to be able to make gunpowder."

Jancsi Török puts his goose quill into its holder. "It is a waste of time to learn, master, because we can already talk with any Turkish prisoner. And my lord father has turned his back on the Germans."

Little ten-year-old Feri slightly jerks his head to whisk his shoulder-length, walnut-colored hair behind him, and interjects, "What's the good of chemistry? My father has so much gunpowder, that it can never be used it up, just like the world!"

"Oh no, noble boy," replies the priest smiling. "You can't even read decently. Just yesterday you read 'Kikero' instead of 'Cicero'."

The dashing figure of Bálint Török enters the room. He wears the blue silk robe that he had inherited from King János [Zápolya]. A curved, light sword is tied on his waist, a sword he wears only on ceremonial occasions.

"We have a guest," he says to the priest. "Get dressed, sons, then come down to the yard." He strokes the hair of his son Feri, then disappears.

In the yard is a large ironmonger's cart from Vienna. By it stands a German with his servant. They take out shiny armor from the cart and pass them down to Turkish prisoners. The prisoners hang the armor on posts in the yard.

By the cart a distinguished looking nobleman is standing in the company of Bálint. He is a smaller, brown haired young man with short nose and fiery eyes. The boys are introduced to him. He lifts up Ferenc Török and kisses him. "Do you know who I am?"

"Uncle Miklós" replies the child.

"And my other name?"

Feri looks carefully at uncle Miklós' soft black beard. János speaks in his stead, "Zirinyi."

"Not Zirinyi, you," corrects his father. "Zrínyi."[17]

All this had happened at one time. Sometimes we repeat in dream what happened in the past, and the dream really makes no change. How things continued to happen on that day, that was how Gergely continued to dream.

When the six suits of armor are standing up on posts, the lords take guns and fire at them. A bullet passes through one breastplate. They return it to the Viennese merchant. The others that only get dented by the bullets, they buy and share among themselves.

Meanwhile it gets dark. They sit down for dinner. Lady Török sits at the head of the table, Lord Bálint on the other end. Over dinner the guests examine the boys to find out how much they know about what. They particularly ask a lot of questions about the bible and catechism.

Bálint Török just listens for a while, smiling at the pious questions, then shakes his head. "Do you think that my sons only study catechism? Tell them, Jancsi, how to cast a cannon."

"How many hundredweight, father?"

"A hundred hundredweight. That's an archangel!"

"For a hundred hundredweight cannon," starts the boy standing, "we need ninety hundredweight bronze and ten hundredweight lead, but if need be, we can cast using church bells and then we don't need lead. When the material is ready, we dig a pit as deep as we want the cannon to be long. First we make a rod out of clean and sticky clay. We mix the clay with tarred hemp and pierce its middle with an iron rod."

"What's the iron rod for?" asks Lord Bálint.

"To keep the clay straight. Otherwise it would lean or bend."

Then, with his clever eyes fixed upon his father, he continues. "The clay has to be kneaded hard and mixed with the oakum. Sometimes they knead it for two days continuously. When that's done, they stand it up on the middle of the pit and measure it carefully to make sure it's standing straight. Then the canon founder fashions a similar cleaned and kneaded clay mixture for the outside of the cannon and carefully builds it up around the iron rod core. He has to leave a gap of some five fingers wide, but if we have lots of bronze, then the cannon can be thicker. When

---

[17] Miklós Zrínyi (1507/1508 – 1566) was a Croatian-Hungarian nobleman and general, Ban (Governor) of Croatia from 1542 until 1556, and royal master of the treasury from 1557 until 1566. Zrinyi became well known across Europe for his role in the Siege of Szigetvár (1566) where he heroically died stopping the Ottoman advance towards Vienna.

that is done, they surround the clay with rocks and iron braces. By the side they pile ten cords of wood under two cauldrons and put the bronze inside. Then ..."

"You left something out."

"The lead," interjects little Feri.

"Well, because I was just about to say," the boy shoots back, "We also add the lead. Then we keep the fire going day and night until the alloy begins to melt."

"You also left out how big the cauldrons have to be," interjects his younger brother again.

"Well, big and thick. Anyone with brains knows that."

The guests laugh. Jancsi sits down petulantly. "Just wait," he grumbles making eye contact with his younger brother. "I'm counting."

"Well, that's good," replies the father. "If you can't describe it, your younger brother will. Tell them, little Feri, what's missing."

"What's missing?" replies the little boy with a shrug of his shoulders. "When the cannon cools, they take it out of the ground."

"Obviously," says Jancsi triumphantly. "What about the grinding? And the smoothing? What about the three test firings?"

Feri blushes.

And the two boys would start fighting right there by the table but the guests grab them and cover them with kisses.

"The best part," says Bálint Török chuckling, "is that both forgot about the hole for the firing."

After they talked at the table about all sorts of military business, and about Turks and Germans.

At one point they address Gergely.

"Out of this fellow will become an outstanding man," says Bálint Török stroking Gergely's head. "His mind is like fire. Only his arm is still a little weak."

"Ah," replies Zrínyi. "It's not the strength of the arm that is the most important, but the strength of the heart: courage. One greyhound can chase a hundred rabbits."

Dinner is finished. Only the silver cups remain on the table.

"Now, now say good night to our guests and go under your mother's wings," says Bálint Török to the boys.

"Well, isn't uncle Sebők going to sing?" asks little Feri.

Hearing that, a quiet little man with a hairy face sitting at the table moves and looks at Bálint.

"Indeed, good Tinódi," says Zrínyi with a warm glance. "Sing something nice for us."

Sebestyén Tinódi gets up, goes to a corner of the room, and pull down a lute.

"Well good," says the father. "You can hear one song, but then it's time to clear out."

Tinódi pushes his chair back a little and runs his fingers over the strings of the lute. "What should I sing?" he asks his master.

"Well, the best. The one you composed last week."

"The one about Mohács?"

"That one, unless my guests would like something else."

"No, no," say the guests. "Let's hear the best one!"

The hall gets quiet. Servants tidy up the ash from the wax candles on the table and sit in the doorway. Tinódi once more strums his strings. He takes a sip from the silver cup in front of him, then starts singing in a soft, deep bass voice:

> *Now I sing my tears for Hungary:*
> *About the blood soaked earth of Mohács Battle;*
> *Where died many thousands of our nation's flowers,*
> *And the wretched lost the young king on a horse.*[18]

There was something unusual about his singing. It was more like a narration than a melody. He would sing a line, then follow with a spoken line leaving his lute to carry the melody. Sometimes he would sing the melody of only the last line.

As he sang, his eyes sank into in indefinite gaze, so his performance became as if he was alone in the hall, singing to himself.

But his simple poems, as Father Gábor once observed, if only read seemed rough and without any artistic accomplishment, but on his lips, sounded heartfelt and beautiful. The words acquired deeper meaning on

---

[18] The battle lost, the twenty year old King Lajos (Louis) the Second fled on horseback only to fall into a river and drown, weighed down by his heavy armor.

his lips. If he said "mourning", then everything became dark before the eyes of his listeners. When he said "battle", they saw the murderous scuffle. When he said "God", they all felt God's glory shining on their heads.

By the end of the first verse the guests are already putting hands to eyes as they lean on the table, and the eyes of Bálint Török are tearing up.

He had fought at Mohács next to the king as one of his bodyguards. There were still some four thousand living witnesses to that battle, and all of Hungary felt discouraged and powerless after the defeat. It was as if a veil of mourning covered the entire country!

Tinódi sings the entire story of the battle and the audience listens with sad attention. Their eyes brighten at the descriptions of heroic deeds. They tear up hearing familiar names.

Finally Tinódi reaches the final verse, and his voice becomes more like a sigh than a song.

> *By Mohács is an untilled field,*
> *The largest cemetery in the world;*
> *There a shroud covers an entire nation ...*
> *Not even to be raised up, perhaps, by the Eternal Creator!*

"He will raise them up!" exclaims Zrínyi, slapping his sword.

And he raises his right hand, "A sacred oath, gentlemen, to devote every thought of our life to the restoration of our home! Until then, we will not sleep on a soft pillow, while the Turks can claim possession of a single footprint of our homeland!"

"What about the Germans?" replies Bálint Török bitterly. "Are twenty-four thousand Hungarians going to die again so that the Germans can defeat us? To hell with them. An honorable pagan is a hundred times more preferable than Germans stuffed with lies!"

"Your father-in-law is German," shoots back an angry Zrínyi. "At least the Germans are Christians."

"That's the truth," says an old man among the guests trying to appease. "Hungarians should not fight for at least fifty years. We have to multiply before we fight."

"Thank you!" replies Zrínyi banging the table. "But I don't want to lie in bed for fifty years."

And with that, he gets up from the table, his sword clattering.

— § —

With the clattering Gergely's eyes opened. He was surprised to see not Bálint Török sitting at the table, but to realize that he was lying under a starry night, and that standing before him was not Zrínyi, but a broad shouldered Turk.

It was Hayvan. He had kicked his leg to wake him up.

"Here are the clothes." He placed a cloak and a turban before the scholar. "We'll get a horse along the way."

The scholar wrapped himself with the *sipahi* cloak and pulled the tall cap over his head. Both were a little big, but the scholar was more happy with them than if he had been given the clothes of a prince.

The giant bent down and with one and two jerks broke the last clasp of the leg irons. Then he began walking in front towards the north.

The cloak was too long for the scholar. He had to pull it up at the waist. The giant continued walking ahead briskly.

People were sleeping everywhere inside and outside tents. A sentry stood in front of the occasional tent with a brass nob and a horsetail on top — fast asleep.

The camp seemed endlessly long, as if the entire world was made up of tents.

They reached a place where a large herd of camels were gathered. There were few tents there. People were sleeping on the grass everywhere.

Hayvan stopped in front of a tent patched with blue canvas. "Old man," he called. "Wake up."

A small, short old man peeked out from the tent. His head was bald, his beard thin and white. He stepped out barefoot wearing a shirt that reached his knees.

"What's this" he asked, frightened. "Is that you, Hayvan?"

"It's me," replied the Turk. "Last week I made you an offer for one of you grey horses." He pointed towards a big clumsy grey horse foraging among the camel herd. "Will you sell it for what I offered?"

"That's why you woke me up? Twenty kurush, that's what I said."

The Turk fumbled with the silver coins from his belt. First he read the marks on one, then another, and finally he counted them out into the merchant's hand.

"Spurs also are needed," said the scholar as the merchant was untying the horse.

"Add two spurs," said Hayvan.

"Tomorrow."

"Now, immediately."

The merchant went inside his tent where he could be heard rattling and searching in the dark. Then he came back out with two rusty spurs.

10

In that same hour Yumurjak was wandering around the tents where the sick were lying. He asked one sentry, "Where is the prisoner who wanted to blow up His Majesty, the great Padishah, to paradise?"

The sentry pointed to a four-sided white tent.

In front of the tent, five white turbaned old men wearing black kaftans squatted around a fire. They were the sultan's doctors. All five looked serious and sad.

Yumurjak stopped in front of the tent's sentry. "Can I speak with the captive?"

"Ask the doctors," replied the guard respectfully.

Yumurjak bowed towards the doctors. They nodded in return.

"*Efendim*, if I could have a word with the sick man, I could do some nice things for the Padishah."

One of them shrugged his shoulders. From the movement of his hand, one could understand either *not possible* or *go inside the tent*.

Yumurjak chose the latter meaning.

The tent's curtain was half drawn. Inside a large oil lamp was burning. The priest was lying on his back on the bed with eyes half open.

"*Gâvur* [infidel]," said the Turk stepping in front of him. "Do you recognize me?"

The priest did not reply.

"I am the Yumurjak with whom you were once entrusted to hang. For the price of my amulet, you freed me."

The priest did not reply. His eyelids did not move.

"Now you are the prisoner" continued the Turk, "and nothing is as certain as they will cut off your head."

The priest did not reply to this, either.

"I came for my amulet," said the Turk humbly. "It's nothing to you. All my strength is in it. Since it's not been with me, I am unlucky in everything. I had a house on the Bosporus, my beautiful little palace. I bought it to live there in my old age. The house burned down. The treasure I had there was stolen. My hand was pierced in battle. Look at my right hand. It's probably crippled for life."

And he showed his red scar, probably about three months old.

The priest listened without moving.

"*Gâvur,*" said the Turk in a softened, tearful voice. "You are a good man. I think of you often, and I always concluded that the goodness of your heart was unequaled. Give me back my amulet!"

The priest did not reply.

Only the lamp spluttered near them.

"I will do whatever you want," continued the Turk after a short break. "I can also try to save you from the hands of the executioner. My father is a very great pasha. My older brother is Arslan Bey. As long as a man lives, there is hope. Just tell me, where is my amulet?"

The priest was silent.

"My amulet!" repeated the Turk angrily.

And he grabbed the priest shoulders.

"My amulet!" he shouted shaking.

The priest's head slumped, so the Turk pulled him up making him sit.

The priest's chin dropped. He stared vacantly with glassy eyes and an open mouth.

11

When they had passed the outermost sentry, Hayvan stopped.

"See," he said, "I have done what you wanted. Now talk. What is that fortunate secret that I am carrying around with me?"

"Kabbalah," replied the scholar secretly.

"Kabbalah?" repeated the Turk murmuring. And he furrowed his eyebrows like one endeavoring to understand the meaning of an obscure word.

"If you look more closely," said the scholar with his shoulder leaning on the saddle, "you will see some stars in the drawings. The holy dervish wrote a prayer around every good star. You also promised a *yataghan*."

The Turk offered both his *yataghans* to the scholar. "Choose!"

The scholar took the smaller short sabre and stuffed it in his belt.

"These drawings," he continued, "are valuable to wear on your body. Cut each into seven pieces and sew them into the lining of your clothes. Put some in your turban. Not even bullets will pass through where this blessed parchment protects."

The Turks eyes sparkled.

"Bullets won't pierce?"

"No. Haven't you heard of those heroes whom bullets couldn't harm?"

"Of course."

"Well, not for money or a good word, don't give this to anyone. Don't even show it or they will take it from you, steal it from you, or they will cheat it from you."

"Oh no, I have brains!"

"But that's not all. One of the papers says that you mustn't touch a woman or a child with your hands or weapons until you become a great lord. Your every thought must be to become a hero."

"That will happen."

"Because you will become a great lord. You will become the greatest bey of Hungary."

The Turk's mouth fell open in astonishment. "The greatest bey?"

"Well, not tomorrow morning, that's for certain, but with time, when you get a chance to show your heroism. Then it's also written that you will live according to the words of the Koran. Be zealous in prayers and holy washing. And whoever does good to you, don't do bad to him."

The giant, stupid man looked at the scholar with awe. "I often dreamed," he said, "that I would become a lord. I dreamed that. So, into seven?"

"Seven. It doesn't matter if they are not the same size. It's more important what parts of your body you want to protect."

The Turk looked forward with increasing satisfaction. "Well," he said lifting his head, "if I become a lord I will hire you as my secretary."

Gergely bit his lip so he would not burst out laughing.

"Well then, get up!" said Hayvan happily. He held the horse while the scholar mounted.

The scholar reached into his pocket.

"Look, Hayvan, here's a ring. You know it's the custom with Hungarians to never accept something for nothing."

Hayvan took the ring and marveled at it.

The scholar continued. "You gave me freedom and a horse. I pay you with this ring. May Allah help you, baldy." And he slapped the horse.

Hayvan grabbed the bridle.

"Just wait! This is a Turkish ring, isn't it?"

"Yes."

"Where did you get it?"

"What's it to you? If you want to know, it belonged to a janissary."

For a minute, Hayvan stared blankly ahead, then gave the ring back. "I don't need it. You have already paid me for your freedom and the horse." And he stuffed the ring back into the scholar's pocket.

— § —

Gergely headed south so that if they managed to follow him, it would not be on the road to Buda.

The moon was lowering to the west behind some clouds. Dawn was beginning to show in the east.

At one place, the wide main highway was crossed by a narrow road. Gergely saw a horseman galloping quickly along that narrow road. If both kept going at the same pace, they would meet at the intersection.

Gergely immediately slowed the pace of his horse, but then, as the other slowed down, he again made his horse gallop. He could reach the crossing about a hundred paces ahead.

He kept his eye on the stranger. In the rising morning light, he was shocked to see a tall-capped janissary headed toward him.

He pulled the reins and stopped.

The other also stopped.

"Lucifer!" he mumbled. "This Turk will capture me!" He held his breath in fear.

Then the words of István Dobó rang in his mind, "The first thing, never be afraid!"

He had not seen Dobó since childhood. Ever since Bálint Török left Ferdinand and went over to King János' party, Dobó never visited Szigetvár, or Somogyvár, or Ozora. But still Gergely thought of him with gratitude, and that one thing he had said stuck in his mind. "That's the first thing, my boy, that a man should never be afraid."

The Turk, sitting on his small, short horse, started off again. He also spurred his horse on. Let it be: they would meet at the crossing. It could be that the Turk was not looking for him. He would call a "Good morning!" to him and continue on.

However, it just so happened that the road on which the Turk rode turned towards the north. They would have to meet.

And if the Turk pulls out his weapon?

Gergely had never fought anyone. Bálint Török taught even Father Gábor how to use a sword, practicing in Lord Bálint's yard. Gergely used to practice fencing every day with the Turkish slaves. But that was only a game. They were protected head to toe in armor. They could hardly hurt each other even with a pick-axe.

If only he had a lance or a sword like the janissary! But all he had was a pagan *yataghan* short sword.

The thought, "the first thing, never be afraid!" again calms his heart. He continues his pace in the same direction.

But the Turk does not continue. He stands.

Gergely turns onto the road where the Turk is idly sitting on his horse. He almost screams with joy when he sees the Turk turn around and likewise look at him.

He could not be anyone else, only Tulipán!

"Tulipán!" calls the scholar.

At the shout, the Turk slaps his horse and gallops away on the narrow cart track.

The little horse is good at running, but there are puddles on the clay road. The Turk wants to jump across a ditch and head off into the fields, but his horse slips.

The Turk falls on the ground in a heap.

When the scholar got there, the Turk was already standing on his feet and holding his lance in his hand.

"Tulipán!" called the scholar chuckling. "Don't be silly."

"Oh, hell!" said Tulipán, somewhat out of sorts. "But, is that you, young lord?"

"Well now, you are the fine hero soldier!" said the scholar laughing.

And he jumped off his horse.

"I thought they were after me," said Tulipán uneasily. "How did you escape?"

"With my brains, Tulipán. I waited for a while hoping you would help me escape."

"It was hopeless," said Tulipán making excuses. "The captives were held in the middle of the camp and there were so many sentries everywhere. I myself could hardly get away."

He gave his horse a tug and scratched his head. "May the crows eat this horse! How am I going to get home on this horse?"

"Well, by riding it."

"The young lord will not come with me?"

"No."

"Well?"

"I am going to Buda."

"Then you again will end up in the hands of the Turks."

"I will get there before them. Then, if there is any trouble, my lord is there. He is a very great man. He could be king if he wanted."

Tulipán got back onto his horse. The scholar also mounted his. Gergely held out his hand to Tulipán. "Give my respects to those at home."

"Thank you," replied Tulipán. "I also give respects to my lord. Don't tell anyone that you found me drunk. I drank the servants' wine."

"Very good, Tulipán. God bless you!"

Tulipán turned around once more. "Is the priest alive?"

The scholar's eyes watered. "The poor man is sick. I could not talk to him."

He wanted to say something else, but he could not, either because of his tears, or he thought twice. He gave the reins a jerk and headed towards the south. The scholar spent the day in the forest. Only at night did he circle around towards Buda.

— § —

The sun was rising when he arrived at the broad plain under Gellért Hill. That was where he threw off his turban and hung his cloak in the saddle of a tree.

Everywhere the land was sparkling with dew. Gergely dismounted. He stripped down to his waist, took some dew in his hand. That was how he washed off two days' worth of dust.

He was refreshed after the washing. Meanwhile, the horse was grazing. As the first rays of the sun began to heat up, he mounted and hurried further on the highway.

By then the area around the road was full of evidence of the fighting for Buda. Broken pikes, pieces of cannon carts, dented shoulder pads, dead horses, blood, swords, and black painted, pot-shaped, worthless German helmets all over.

And unburied corpses.

Five Germans were lying around a blackthorn bush. Two on their backs, one curled up, and two with heads torn apart. Perhaps bullets killed them. Two may have dragged themselves, mortally wounded, before breathing out their souls.

There was a heavy stink in the air.

As the rider approached, ravens flew off corpses and circled above the field. They settled farther away to resume their feast.

The sound of a trumpet made Gergely lift his head away from the sad sights. A group dressed in red was coming out from Buda at a steady pace led by five lords wearing ornate clothes. Behind them a long column of infantry in blue uniforms.

Among the men riding in front, Gergely spotted a priest wearing a white habit.

He thought to himself, "That's the famous Friar György."

His heart started beating faster. Since he was a child, he had heard so much about Friar György that he thought of him as even greater than the king.

Next to the monk was a horseman wearing a fur-lined, short velvet coat decorated with jewels that glittered in the distance.

Gergely recognized Bálint Török.

Should he run away?

Running might be suspicious. Bálint Török would send a rider after him and he would be carried like a criminal to his beloved lord.

Should he tell him what happened to the priest? Then Bálint Török would probably banish him from his sight. Because it was Bálint who invited the Turks to fight against the Germans. Would he want to hear how members of his own household wanted to wipe out the Turks?

Gergely's head was spinning. He did not like to lie. He considered it dishonorable to lie, particularly to the person who had raised him up.

He just stood by the side of the highway, head down and face red. Then he dismounted and held onto the reins of his old grey horse.

Come what must come!

The horse was very hungry. As soon as it realized it had a respite from work, the horse bit into the grass.

Hey, God bless this horse, but mainly its hunger! What a job it was having to pull the horse this way and that, as if the animal were stubborn! What good luck that he could turn his back to the lords having a heated discussion.

They were already trotting and talking close by. The old grey horse was turning here, then there. Now it circled its owner, then its owner circled it.

Then, not even the devil would have thought that a wind could help a man. From the south a faint breeze raised a curtain of yellow dust. The only thing seen through it was some young lad struggling on the grass with an ugly grey horse. Certainly the Germans had left it without an owner. Let the lad be happy with it!

Gergely breathed more easily when he saw the backs of the leading nobles passing away, and no one shouting, *Gergely, my son!*

He jumped on his horse again, at first leaning forward on his stomach, then swinging a leg over the saddle. He turned his face towards the oncoming march.

That was when he saw that the infantry in blue uniforms were all chained together. Their clothes were ragged, their hair muddy, and their faces pale. Not a single old man among them, but wounded were many. One tall prisoner in rags had a swollen face, all red and blue, with only one eye showing on his smashed face.

Was it Bálint Török who had smashed him on the nose?

12

This was the first time Gergely saw Buda.

The many towers, the high walls, the greenery and trees in the royal garden on the Pest side, everything appeared to him as if a dream.

So, this was where King Mátyás had his home? This is where King Lajos loved? And here is where his little Éva lives and where he will see her?

A sentry armed with a halberd stood by the gate, but he did not even look at Gergely.

Gergely was not questioned as he continued up the road. He looked up and marveled at the royal courtyard with its round water fountain made of marble. Then he stopped at St. George square. His attention focused on cannons scattered about. Smoky, crude cannons. The mud on their wheels showed that they had been captured from the Germans, probably just the day before.

"Good day, my warrior sir," he said to a sentry soldier standing there. "This is German booty, isn't it?"

"That's it," replied the soldier proudly.

Gergely stared again at the huge cannons.

Among them were three so huge that twenty oxen would have been unable to move them.

And the many cannons still smelled of gunpowder.

"My sir warrior," spoke Gergely again. "Do you know old Cecey, the one with a wooden hand?"

"Of course I know him."

"Where does he live?"

"Down that way," said the soldier gesturing north with his head. "In St. John Street."

"I don't know the streets by name here."

"Well kid, just go and ask around. He lives in a small green house. Above the gate hangs a bow. A bow-maker lives there."

"*Sagittarius?*" he asked in Latin.

"Yes."

Gergely gave another look at the cannons, then trotted off with the old grey.

— § —

After a lot of inquiries and directions, he finally found St. John Street and a little two-level house painted green.

Only five windows were visible on the house. Three on the upper level and two on the ground level. In the middle was an entrance gate about the size of a door to a room.

Above it hung a bow made of tin painted red.

The Ceceys lived on the upper floor. As Gergely opened the door, he found the old lord in his breakfast dressing gown and slippers, slapping the side of a cupboard with a long handled fly swatter.

"Ah, you dog," he exclaimed as he struck with a crack as loud as a gunshot.

Then, as he heard footsteps, he continued. "There isn't a braver animal in the world! Here they see me hitting and beating them to death, and instead of escaping, they sit on my beard. Ah, you dog!"

And he gave the air another swish with the fly swatter.

"My dear father," said Gergely smiling. "Good morning."

Only when he heard that voice did the old man turn around. "Look! Gergely, my son!" he exclaimed, his old eyes wide open. "Is that you, my soul?"

Even his chin dropped in his amazement.

Gergely himself felt wonderful to be there, but still he waited to be hugged and kissed like they used to at home, in the Christian manner.

Hearing the words, the lady of the house came out from the next room. She was just as amazed and stared just as much.

"How did you get here?" she asked. "What brought you here, my son?"

And she did kiss him and stroke his hair.

But it seemed like she would have kissed him more warmly at other times. This thought flashed across Gergely's mind like a shadow; more like a feeling than a thought.

"I come for no other reason," Gergely replied, "but to take you back to Kereszt."

"Oho!" said the old man.

It was as if he had said w*hat a stupid thing to say.*

"I saw the Turkish army," continued Gergely. "They are coming to occupy Buda."

"Oho!" repeated Cecey more loudly.

It was as if he had said *this is even more stupid.*

The woman looked at the boy with a look of pity on her face typically used for a simpleton who had thought up something stupid with his little brain.

"Are you hungry, my dear?" she asked, putting her arm on his shoulder. "Perhaps you haven't slept?"

Gergely nodded yes and no. He glanced at the open door with half an eye, then stared at the chessboard on the table.

"You're waiting for Vicus, right?" said the lady with a glance at her husband. "She's not at home, my son. She doesn't stay at home. She is with the queen. She only manages to get out every now and again. Even then she comes in a carriage accompanied by coachmen from the court."

And as she was spluttering, she clapped her hands. "Jesus Mary! My milk is boiling over!"

Gergely waited for Cecey to continue talking about Vica, but the old man just sat, blinking and listening.

"Where's the reverend priest?" Gergely asked with a heavy heart.

"Burying," Cecey replied, "He got together with some friend. They are burying."

"Germans?"

"Of course they're Germans. Since we've had fighting, every day he goes out to bury. It's worthwhile burying Germans!"

"They were not fired upon?"

"They are in white shirts. They don't shoot at them."

"I saw a lot of unburied bodies."

"I believe you, *young brother.* We cut them down considerably."

The *young brother* expression struck Gergely unpleasantly. But he could not wait any longer. He turned the conversation back to Vicus. "She is still with the queen?"

"There," replied the old man. He got up and walked across the room. The expression on his face became serious and dignified. Then he began unfolding the explanation how the other day Friar György had taken little Vicus to the castle garden to present her to the Queen. The infant royal son immediately smiled at Vicus and reached out to her with his hand. Vicus was not lazy. She took him in her lap, just like the peasant women do at home, and swung him in the air without any sense of having to be respectful. She even called him, "*You little fool!*" Since that day the queen has loved her and kept her by her side, hardly even allowing her to visit home.

Gergely started listening to this explanation only out of curiosity, but then his eyes sparkled as the old man went on.

It was a bit strange to Gergely that Cecey assumed such a dignified expression and looked at him with eyes coldly blinking. Finally, the old man got serious again. "Well, what happened?" the old man said. "Why are you looking so stupidly?

"I'm sleepy," replied Gergely.

He could hardly hold back his tears.

Because then he realized that little Éva would never be his wife.

13

Well, what had happened in Buda?

That the Germans would have liked to have sat inside it. The queen would have allowed it, but the idea was not at all to the liking of the Hungarian nobility, that a German would be landlord in the palace of King Mátyás.

They called the Turks for help and until then, they defended. When the Turkish advance guard began arriving, the Germans began to dwindle.

And when the sultan arrived with his huge army, Roggendorf's army broke apart.

The Friar (that is what they always called the famous György Martinuzzi[19]) took four hundred German prisoners with him to present to the sultan.

---

[19]   Friar György, (1482-1551), later a cardinal, was the guardian of John Zápolya's son, the infant "king". More on the historical Queen Isabella Jagiellon

Isabella Jagiellon (1519 –1559) was the oldest child of the King of Poland, Sigismund I, and his Italian wife, Bona Sforza.

In 1539 Isabella married John Zápolya, the voivode (governor) of Transylvania and King of Hungary. She became the queen consort of Hungary. She was twenty. John was fifty-two and suffered from gout. The marriage lasted only a year and a half and produced a male heir. John Sigismund Zápolya was born just two weeks before his father's death in July 1540. Isabella spent the rest of her life embroiled in succession disputes on behalf of her son.

John Zápolya and the Hapsburg Ferdinand, the two rival Kings of Hungary, warred against each other for the throne, then entered into the Treaty of Nagyvárad whereby Ferdinand would succeed to the throne upon John's death. George Martinuzzi (Friar György) and other Hungarian nobles refused to abide by the treaty and elected the infant John Sigismund as King John II and appointed Isabella as his regent. Sultan Suleiman also recognized Isabella as regent with authority over the eastern regions of Hungary, including Transylvania.

With him went Bálint Török and old Péter Petrovich as well.

The sultan and his army had stopped at Cserepes, one army camp away from Buda. The sultan graciously welcomed the lords in his silk tent with its towers and porch. He already knew all three by name. He knew about the Friar that the Hungarian people think through his head. He knew Bálint Török from when he tried to raise the crescent moon flag over Vienna. That was when Lord Bálint slaughtered Pasha Kason together with his army and earned the name "fiery devil" from the Turks.

Portrait of Isabella Jagiellon, painted a few years after her death

Gárdonyi's setting for Book II of *Egri Csillagok* is 1541 when Isabella was only twenty-two. She was noted for her beauty, scolded for her expensive tastes, and was known to have complained about financial troubles and the ruined state of her new domains. Then Sultan Suleiman took Buda by subterfuge and forced Isabella to leave for eastern Hungary.

Ferdinand conspired with Friar György to force Isabella to abdicate in 1551. She returned to her native Poland. Meanwhile, Sultan Suleiman retaliated and threatened to invade Hungary in 1555, thereby forcing the Transylvanian nobles to invite Isabella back. She returned in October of 1556 and again ruled as her son's regent until her death three years later.

Friar György (George Martinuzzi) after the end of the novel.

The sultan's advisors had told him that old Petrovich was related to the royal infant prince, and that it was he who, in 1514, had pulled György Dózsa off his horse and made him prisoner.

They led the three lords into the tent. All three bowed. After, as the sultan stepped before them and held out his hand, the Friar stepped forward and kissed it. Old Petrovich also kissed it.

Bálint Török, instead of kissing the sultan's hand, again bowed, then with a pale face, looked at the sultan proudly.

Well, that was an insult. The Friar felt ice in his bones. Had he known this would happen, he would never have pressured Bálint to join them.

The sultan did not even blink. He lifted the hand he had held out for the kiss and put it on Bálint's shoulder. He embraced him.

Everything happened in such a family, Hungarian manner as if it could not have happened any other way.

The sultan's two young sons were also standing in the tent. They gave the Hungarian lords a friendly handshake. Obviously they had been taught in advance how to behave. Then they stood behind their father again and fixed their eyes on Bálint Török.

Well, they could stare. Such a dignified, handsome Magyar man! Dressed in a red, silk cloak with cut sleeves, every other dignitary paled beside him.

The sultan's old, sheep's eyes also turned towards Bálint Török more often than towards the Friar bowing before him, talking in a cunning Latin oration, proclaiming that the German peril had been parried and how the Hungarian nation was happy to be under the protective wing of such a powerful patron.

The interpreter was Suleiman Pasha, a sickly, thin old lord who, when he was still a growing young lad, ended up away from Hungarian soil and among Turks. He spoke both languages faultlessly.

He translated the Friar's words sentence by sentence.

The sultan nodded. Then, as the talk ended in a deep silence, the sultan smiled. "You spoke well. I also came because King János was also my good friend. The welfare of his people is not the welfare of strangers to me. The nation has to be restored to peace. After this, the Hungarian people may sleep calmly. My sword will be above and protecting them forever."

The Friar bowed down to express his joy. Old Petrovich wiped a tear from his eye. Bálint Török just stared ahead, his brow furrowed.

"Well, let us see. What kind of people did you have to fight?" asked the sultan. He mounted his horse and accompanied by the Hungarian nobles slowly rode by the lines of prisoners. They were kneeling in two rows in the dust close by the Danube.

To the right of the sultan rode the Friar, Suleiman Pasha was on his left. The sultan would occasionally turn around towards Petrovich, or Bálint Török, or his two sons to say something.

The prisoners all prostrated themselves before the sultan. One or two raised their chained two hands and begged.

"Ragged, mercenary people," said the sultan in Turkish, "but their bodies are strongly built."

"There were some even stronger," added Bálint Török in Hungarian as the sultan turned towards him. "There were a few Swabians, but they aren't here."

And as the sultan had an inquisitive look, Lord Bálint was comfortable adding, "Those I cut down."

They returned to the tent. The sultan did not enter so attendants brought him a camp armchair, but none for the delegation or the sultan's sons.

"Your Majesty, what shall we do with the prisoners?" asked Ahmet Pasha.

"Cut off their heads," replied the sultan as calmly as if he had just asked to have his kaftan brushed.

He sat in front of the tent on a pillow embroidered with gold. Behind him stood two servants with peacock feather fly whisks, and not for the sake of splendor, but indeed for flies. Because it was already late August, and the camp attracted swarms of flies.

The two sons also stood next to the sultan. In front of him were the Hungarian lords with their caps off.

For a minute the sultan looked ahead, then turned towards Bálint Török. "Some priest was taken prisoner on the road. He belongs to your castle's county. Perhaps you know him?"

Bálint Török understood what the sultan asked, and for that reason he listened to the translation.

He replied in Hungarian, "I do not know all the priests in my castle's county. On my estates there are some hundred different religions. But it is possible that I know that prisoner."

"Bring him here," ordered the sultan, arching his eyebrows and gazing ahead as if bored.

The sound of beheadings could be heard from the bank of the Danube. Cries and begging for mercy mixed with the noise of the camp.

Two men hurried forward with a shape covered in a sheet. They laid it down before the sultan and removed the sheet from its head.

"You know him?" asked the sultan, turning halfway towards Bálint Török.

"Of course I know him," replied Bálint Török in shock, "because he is my priest!"

He looked around at those present as if waiting for an explanation. But the faces of the Turkish dignitaries were cold. All he saw was cold, staring, black eyes.

"Something bad happened to him," said the sultan. "He was already sick when they brought him into my camp." He turned towards the servants, "Bury him decently," he said, "according to Christian religion ceremony."

Then some refreshments were brought in silver cups on a silver tray. It was some drink made from oranges and rose water, iced and fragrant.

The sultan, with a friendly smile, offered it first to Bálint Török.

14

Lady Cecey provided Gergely with a bed in the little room by the yard. The boy was not as much pleased with the bed as being left alone with his sorrow.

He was not surprised that the queen took a liking to his little Éva. In his opinion, there was no creature in the world as loveable as Éva. But it still hurt in his heart that Cecey was so proud about it. Vicus had risen to be a part of the royal court where only princes and the country's higher nobility circulated. How could he even visit her? He was just a nothing little man who had no house, no coat of arms, not even a dog.

He leaned on a bench covered with a worn bearskin and rested his tear-soaked face on an arm.

Sorrow has one good quality: it makes a person sleepy and all kinds of pleasant dreams give encouragement.

Gergely slept for a good half a day on that bearskin and woke up smiling.

He looked around the walls of the small room with astonishment, a picture on the wall of Saint Imre[20] with a twisted leg, and then grinned. He rested his head in his hands, elbows on his knees. The events of the previous two days swirled around in his head like a dark whirlpool. The great Turkish camp, the capture, the death of the priest, the escape, Buda Castle, breaking up with his little wife, the change in tone of his stepparents — all these thoughts arose and swirled in his mind. Then he thought of the horse, the old gray, whether he had given him a drink. How will he go home to Somogyvár again? What if they ask what happened to the master? Who will be their teacher now? Certainly Sebestyén Tinódi, the lame, is a good lute player.

He got up and shook himself, like someone trying to rid himself of a bad dream.

He went across to the Ceceys.

"Dear mother," he said to the lady. "I only came here to bring news of the danger from the Turks. Now I will return."

The woman was sitting by the window, edging some piece of linen with gold thread. In those days women wore collars edged with gold. She was sewing it for her daughter.

"Where are you hurrying?" she replied. "Because we haven't even talked. My husband isn't at home. Perhaps he also wants to talk with you. Have you visited Lord Bálint yet?"

"No," answered the scholar. "And I am not going to him. I left his house so suddenly, I didn't tell him where I was going."

"Well, don't you want to talk with our old priest?"

"Where does he live?"

"Here, with us. Where else would he live? But he also isn't at home. He's burying."

"Are they still quarreling?"

"Even more now than before. Now he is in favor of the Ferdinand party and my husband is for János."

"*Dear lady*, give him my respects."

Deliberately, he did not address her as *mother*.

---

[20] Prince St. Imre (Saint Emeric), the son of King St. István (Stephen), was killed while hunting; tradition has it, gored in the leg by a boar.

The woman turned over her sewing, then after only a few short seconds of silence, she replied. "Well then, I won't hold you back, my son Gergely. I just want to offer you some lunch. I put some aside for you. I didn't want to disturb your rest."

Gergely lowered his head. He was thinking whether to accept the offer of lunch. Finally he thought he should not offend them. He accepted.

The woman covered the table with a yellow leather spread and laid out some cold roast with some wine.

Meanwhile, Father Bálint returned home. At other times, he got home from his charitable work only at night. This day he returned early because the heat and the work had tired him out.

In his footsteps limped Cecey.

Gergely kissed the priest's hand. Then, as the priest gestured to Gergely to sit back down at the table, he answered questions while the boy continued eating his lunch.

"How you have grown!" admired the priest. "You are a man's man now. It seems like you left us only yesterday."

He looked around. "Where is Vica?"

"At the palace," replied Cecey.

The priest's expression asked for an explanation. Cecey replied apologetically. "The queen has really taken a liking to her. She doesn't let her go,"

"Since when?"

"For some days now."

"But she is not with *the child*?" rattled the priest.

"She's with him," replied Cecey. "Surely you don't think she is a nanny! There are enough nannies already there. It's just that Vica is also there, see."

"Your daughter with Zápolya's son?" shouted the priest, the color draining from his face.

Cecey stumped back and forth in the room uneasily. "Well, what's the matter with that?" he replied turning around. "You yourself said better a Hungarian, even if a dog, than a German, even if an angel."

"But your daughter is rocking Zápolya's son," said the priest turning red from anger. Suddenly he snapped. He shouted at Cecey with infernal anger. "So this is how a man's brain grows soft as he grows old? Have you forgotten that we two together ate from György Dózsa's meat?"[21]

And he threw a chair on the ground so hard it broke into pieces.

A morsel of food fell from Gergely's mouth. He ran down the stairs and led his horse out. He galloped off without saying goodbye.

15

He dismounted in front of the royal palace and held onto the reins.

On the palace wall he saw a sundial the size of a cartwheel. The sun was just then behind a cloud, so only a faint shadow marked the Roman numeral IV among the gilded rods that marked the hours.

Gergely examined the windows. In turn he studied the rows on the ground level, the upper levels, and then the windows in the towers.

Soldiers passed in and out of the palace gate. A very old Hungarian nobleman with a white beard and bent back tottered through the gate with two secretaries. He must have been a very great lord because everyone greeted him, but he gave no greeting in return. His secretaries were carrying papers bundled in rolls. Goose quills were pinned to their cloth caps. Copper ink wells hung from their belts. As the sun shone on them, their shadows moved majestically across the palace walls.

Then Gergely spotted a fair-skinned soldier with thin legs. He saw only the legs wearing red boots and red pants, but even from that he could recognize that he was one of the guards from Szigetvár. His name was Bálint Nagy.

He turned around and hurried towards St. George Square with his horse. He did not want to be recognized by any of Bálint Török's men.

However, even there he ran into someone he knew. He was a limber, small, round bearded man: Imre Martonfalvai, Bálint Török's secretary, steward, and lieutenant, so very much the lord's useful agent.

Gergely moved to the other side of the horse to hide his face from the man. But the secretary Imre, ever curious and watchful, spotted him.

"What!" he shouted, "young Gergely!"

---

[21] It was János (John) Zápolya, the most powerful of the Hungarian lords, who led the brutal suppression of a peasants' revolt led by György Dózsa. After his defeat at Temesvár in 1514, Dózsa was horribly tortured. He was chained to an iron chair in a smoldering fire. Pieces of his living flesh were cut off. Eight of the other rebel leaders were forced to eat his flesh. Those who refused were killed. Those who ate were released.

Gergely raised his head, blushing red all the way to his ears.

"How did you get here? Have you come to see the master? Where did you get this ox with a horse's head? Because it's not one of our horses!"

Gergely would have loved to have sunk beneath the pavement together with his worthy beast that had been called an ox. But he quickly pulled himself together. "I came to see the master," he blinked with embarrassment. "Where is he?"

"I don't know whether he has come. He took the German prisoners to the sultan. Hey, what a heroic man is our master! You should have seen how he chopped up the Germans. Every day for a week he would return from battle with blood dripping from his right arm. The queen would sit at her window. As he passed by on his horse he would hold up his arm and sword. Say, is there any cattle disease at home?"

"No, there isn't" replied Gergely.

"Have the prisoners cleaned out the old well?"

"Yes."

"Are the threshers stealing?"

"No."

"The master's sons are healthy?"

"Healthy."

"And our women?"

"They, too."

"Have you been to Remeteudvar?"

"No."

"Do you know whether they have covered the hay?"

"No."

"Well," said the secretary as he used his cap to chase flies away. "Where are you off to? Do you have a place to stay?"

"None."

"Well come to my place. Did you come with some important news? Or are you carrying a letter for the master?"

"No. I just came here somewhat by accident."

"Well, stay here then. I'm headed to the palace. Or come with me here to the courtyard. Then we can go home and you can change your clothes.

Or don't you have any clothes? Well, you will get some. Then you can talk with the master."

He led the scholar into the yard and sat him down in some shade.

Gergely's eyes followed the lively chatterbox. He saw the man run up the wide, red marble steps. Then he wondered whether he should get away to keep from standing in front of Lord Bálint cursing him.

Hey, escape from him is not possible! He has eyes everywhere. He can hook and reel in a man from afar. The truth must be said. You have to admit that ... Oh, no way you can admit it!

He scratched his head. His thoughts were almost steaming inside his head. Then he again stared at the windows.

As he was looking, he saw an opening in the courtyard and through it the green of garden trees. What if he slipped through? Then he might be able to see his little Éva from a distance. Just from a distance, because a mere mortal rustic like him was forbidden to approach the queen.

Where are they? Probably somewhere on the far side where there is some shade, or in the garden, or by one of the windows. He could recognize Éva even from afar. He could recognize her gentle, fair face, and sweet smiling, cat-like eyes. He would wave to her with his cap. After, Éva would be wondering for a week whether Gergely had been walking there, or a similar looking tall boy, or perhaps only the ghost of Gergely.

There were large, heavy iron rings embedded in the walls around the courtyard. They were there for visitors to tie their horses.

Gergely tied his horse to one, then strolled quietly past soldiers. He slipped into the alley through which the foliage was visible.

— § —

Gergely thought it was an entrance to the garden. As if they used to construct such narrow alleys to serve as an entrance to gardens! There was no indication anywhere of a door. On one side of the alley was a high iron grate and a building on the other. Scholars and artists of King Mátyás once lived in that area, later in the time of King Ulászló, Polish priests and servants lived there. Later still, the women servants.

But Gergely knew nothing of that. He just looked at the grating. The iron was painted green and the ends of the bars were gilded. In some places, foliage leaned over the grating.

Gergely looked inside. Somewhere he saw a gravel path, and a small garden building covered with a green glazed tiled roof. Iron crows decorated the grating here and there, but some of them had only their feet remaining. Gergely saw some pink spots through the foliage. Women's clothes! Gergely's heart was beating like a hammermill.

He peered inside as he went down and father along the fence.

At last he saw a group of women under an old linden tree.

They were sitting around a cradle. They were dressed in pale pink dresses. Only one was dressed in black, a woman with a long face and thin hands. Her face was pale and sad. She only smiled when she bent down and looked at the cradle, but her smile was also sad.

Gergely could not see inside the cradle. His view was blocked by the back of a fat woman in a white dress. She was fanning the cradle with a branch from the linden tree.

Gergely peered here and there through the grating to get a better look. He could see that altogether there were four women around the cradle, and a fifth was leaning against a large chalice-shaped marble vase.

He ran down the grating. She really was his little Éva. But how had she grown! She was picking wild chestnuts from the ground and collecting them in a basket.

"Vicuska, Cicuska," he whispered softly through the grating.

The young girl was about twenty steps away. She was humming some tune. That was the reason she could not hear Gergely's words.

"Vicuska, Cicuska," Gergely repeated.

The girl lifted her head. She looked towards the grating with serious astonishment.

"Cicuska!" repeated Gergely almost laughing. "Cicus, Vicus, come over here!"

The girl could not see Gergely hidden behind some tamarisk branches, but she recognized his voice.

She came, like a young deer. Some steps, then standing, some more steps and standing, her eyes staring in amazement without blinking.

"It's me here, Vicuska," repeated Gergely.

Then the girl stood there. "Gergő!" she said clapping her hands. "How did you get here?"

A glow of joy spread over her. She put her face against an opening in the grating so Gergely could kiss her. Gergely smelled a pleasant fragrance, similar to the scent of honeysuckle blooming in April.

Then both of them grabbed the grating so their hands could touch. The iron was cold. Their hands were warm. Both of their faces were flushed.

As the boy briefly told the story of how he got there, he examined the girl's face, hands and clothes.

How she had grown! How she had become beautiful! Only her eyes, those open, innocent, beautiful eyes like those of a cat, only they were the same.

Perhaps another person might not have thought the girl was beautiful. Because she was at that age when her hands and feet were still developing, the face was immature, the breasts still boyish, and her hair was still short, but to Gergely, she was still beautiful. He liked her big hands. They were fair and felt velvety. And as she was wearing shapely shoes on her feet, he gave them an admiring look.

"I brought a ring," said Gergely.

He unbundled the large Turkish ring from his pocket. "My good master left this for me. I will give it to you, Vicuska."

Vicus took the ring in her hand and looked with pleasure at the topaz crescent moon and diamond stars. Then she put a finger through it and smiled. "Such a large ring! But beautiful!"

And because the ring was so loose on her finger, she put a second finger through it.

"It will be better if I grow into it," she said. "Meanwhile, just let it be with you." Then with child-like honesty she added, "You know, if I become your wife."

Gergely's face clouded over and his eyes got wet. "You will not be my wife, Vica."

"Why not?" asked the girl annoyed.

"Now you are living among only kings and princes. They won't give you to an ordinary man like I am."

"Oh, nothing of the sort!" relied the girl. "Do you think that I see them as something great? Even the queen said for me to just love the Crown Prince, and when I grow up, she will find me a proper fiancé. I replied that I already had one. I even told her your name and that Bálint Török was your guardian."

"You told her? Then what did she say?"

"She laughed so hard, she almost fell off her chair."

"Is she also in the garden?"

"Here. She is in the black dress."

"There?"

"There. Isn't she beautiful?"

"Beautiful, but I expected her to be even more beautiful."

"Even more beautiful? Isn't she beautiful enough?"

"I don't see any crown on her head."

"If you want, you can talk with her. She is really a very good lady. She doesn't understand Hungarian."

"Then?"

"She knows words in Polish, German, Latin, French and all sorts of languages, only not Hungarian. She pronounces your name as *Kerkő*."

"I don't want to talk with her," said Gergely shyly, "although I know a few words in German. But tell me, Vicuska, if I again come to Buda, how can I talk with you?"

"How? Well, I will tell the queen to let you in."

"And she will let me in?"

"Why not? She likes me so much, she allows me everything. She even gives me some of her perfume. Just smell my dress sleeves. Doesn't it smell nice? The royals all have such good smells! Then she also showed me her prayer book. There are all pretty pictures in it! There is one of Mary in a blue silk dress surrounded by roses. You should see that!"

From under the linden tree came the sound of a noise like when someone steps on the tail of a cat.

Éva winced.

"Oh dear! The Crown Prince has woken up. Wait here, Gergő!"

"Vicus, I can't stay, but I will come tomorrow."

"Good," replied the girl. "Be here every day at this hour!" And she ran off to the Crown Prince.

16

Nothing turns out the way we plan.

When Bálint Török returned home, no one could talk to him for several hours.

He shut himself in his room and paced back and forth. From the front rooms they could hear his heavy, even footsteps.

"The lord is angry," said Martonfalvai worried. "But perhaps not with me?"

"And what if he sees me," thought Gergely to himself. He gave his head a scratch.

Three times Martonfalvai climbed up the stairs before he dared open the door.

Bálint Török was standing by the window that looked out onto the Danube. He was still dressed the way he had stood before the Turkish emperor. He had not even taken the velvet decorated dress sword off of his waist.

"What's that?" he asked turning around. "What do you want, Imre? I don't want to talk about anything now."

Imre stood in the doorway and scratched his ear lobe, confused. Because there could be trouble if he said anything. Lord Bálint, when he was angry, was like storm clouds. Thunderbolts easily burst out from him. But it could also be trouble if he said nothing? If anyone comes from home, the lord was always happy to see them.

Bálint Török's house was by the Fehérvár Gate. On one side the windows opened towards Pest, on the other towards Gellért Hill. Martonfalvai was helped out of his dilemma when he looked down from the window and saw Werbőczy stepping into the front door of the house.

He went back, and again he opened the door. "My noble lord, Lord Werbőczy is coming."

"I'm at home," replied Bálint Török.

"Gergely is also here," said the secretary with a deep breath. "The little Bornemissza boy."

"Gergely? Alone?"

"Alone."

"Well how did he get here? Let him come in."

Gergely arrived at the door at the same time as the white bearded Werbőczy with his bent back.

As Martonfalvai bowed down low, Gergely did the same.

He had just met the old lord by the royal palace. He had been accompanied by the secretaries with quill pens and rolls of papers. (Hey, he is a very famous man! When he was a young man, he saw King Mátyas![22])

"God has brought you, my older brother," sounded the deep, masculine voice of Bálint Török from the room.

He saw Gergely. "Please permit me, my older brother, to first speak with my adopted son. Come in, Gergely!"

Gergely did not know whether he was dead or alive. He stood frozen in front of the two lords.

Bálint frowned as he looked at him. "Is there some trouble at home?"

"No," replied the scholar.

"You came with the priest!!!"

"With him," replied the pale boy.

"And how did you become prisoners? Because the priest is dead. Were my sons with you?"

"No."

"Well, how did you get mixed up with the Turks?"

Ancient Werbőczy spoke up. "No, no, my younger brother Bálint," he said with a kind, deeply resonant voice. "Don't shout like that at the poor boy. He is so frightened, he can't reply."

And he stroked the boy's face, then sat down in the middle of the room in a leather armchair.

At the sound of the word *frightened*, the boy regained his senses as if someone had splashed water on his face.

"How?" he replied suddenly bold. "Because we wanted to blow up the Turkish emperor."

"*Per amorem*," exclaimed a horrified Werbőczy.

Bálint Török himself was stunned.

---

[22] István Werbőczy (1458? – 1541) was Palatine of Hungary and a Hungarian legal theorist and statesman. He wrote the Hungarian Customary Law, portions of which remained in effect until 1848. He first became known as a legal scholar and theologian of such eminence that he was appointed to accompany alongside emperor Charles V to Worms, to take up the cudgels against Martin Luther.

The boy — come whatever has to come — explained how they took gunpowder to the highway and how the priest mistook a pasha for the emperor.

Werbőczy clapped his hands together. "What thoughtlessness! What a stupid idea, my boy!"

"The stupidity isn't there," replied Bálint Török tapping his sword on the floor. "But in the priest not knowing which was the sultan."

The two lords turned towards each other.

"The sultan is our friend!" said Werbőczy.

"He will destroy us!" replied Bálint Török.

"He is a noble thinking lord."

"He is a crowned bastard!"

"I know him, but you don't. I was with him in Constantinople …"

"The words of a Turk are not holy scripture. And even if they were scripture, their scriptures are not ours, and ours are not theirs. Their scriptures say that they have to trample over Christians."

"You are disappointed."

"God bless it, my older brother, but I feel an evil stench around this visit. I am going home from here. My son," he said to Gergely, "you could have saved Hungary!"

And that said, his voice became painful.

— § —

The next morning, Gergely was woken up by Martonfalvai who had laid out a red and blue silk page's uniform on the table that had been taken from a wardrobe.

"The lord orders you to dress up. Be ready standing in the yard at ten o'clock. You will go with him to the royal palace."

With that, he took care of Gergely like a caring mother. He washed and dressed him. He combed and parted his hair. He wiped his golden buttons with deerskin. He even wanted to pull the dark cherry red-colored shoes on his feet.

"But this I cannot allow," laughed Gergely. "I'm not such a helpless fellow that I can't even put on my own shoes."

"But, aren't you afraid?"

"What should I be afraid of, sir secretary? That I am going in front of the queen? My lady, even without a crown on her head, is greater than she!"

"There's truth in your words," replied the secretary looking over the boy, pleased. "But you know, still, she is the queen."

As they went with Bálint Török to the royal palace, a servant hurried before them in the courtyard.

"My noble lord," he said panting. "Her Majesty the Queen sent me to come immediately. Some pasha is arriving. They are bringing so much treasure, it's horrible!"

Bálint Török turned towards the warriors accompanying him. "They aren't bringing it for nothing. You will see!"

The soldiers stayed in the courtyard. Lord Bálint with Gergely walked up the wide red marble steps.

The guard by the door saluted with his halberd and pointed to the right. "Her Highness wishes to see you in the throne room."

"Then you can come with me," said Lord Bálint to Gergely. "Always stay behind me some four or five steps. And stand like a soldier! Speak to no one! Don't clear your throat, don't spit, don't yawn, but be well mannered."

High arched halls; colorful and carved walls; everywhere decorated with gold and gilded, crowned coats of arms; tall, wide doors; blue ceilings with silver stars; thick red carpets absorbing noises.

Gergely was stunned by the splendor.

He felt like there was a crowned ghost in every corner whispering, *You are walking on the footsteps of kings! The air here was breathed by kings!*

Five brilliantly dressed noblemen were already standing in the throne room. Behind them were officers and pages. A few halberdiers stood as guards by the throne. But as yet, no one was sitting on the throne.

The hall had a vaulted ceiling, like the others, and the stars depicted in the cyan blue silk covering the ceiling depicted the sky at the hour when the nation chose Mátyás as its king.

Behind the throne was a large crimson tapestry in which the country's coat of arms was woven in gold thread. Inside the national coat of arms was another, small coat of arms: A Polish eagle over a crowned snake and a leopard bearing three crowns. It was the coat of arms of the Zápolya family.

A lieutenant of the royal guards stepped in front of Bálint Török. "Her Majesty is calling you, noble lord."

Gergely stayed behind surrounded by pages and secretaries. He turned towards two pages who were talking nearby. "Gergely Bornemissza is my name. I am a page to Bálint Török."

One of the young men (cheerful, sun tanned, blond hair) held out his hand. "I am István Zoltay, in the army of my Lord Batthyány."

The other, a short-necked, dumpy lad, just folded his arms and stared over Gergely's shoulder. Gergely stared at him, shocked. (This bullheaded young noble obviously had contempt for him!) "I'm Gergely Bornemissza," he repeated with his chest puffed.

The bullhead looked at him sideways. "What do I have to do with you, little brother? The name of a page is *Silence*."

Gergely blushed. His eyes glared at the arrogant boy. "I am not your page! And as for whom I serve, he doesn't call me that, but as *Suffer no Insult!*"

The bullhead looked at Gergely up and down. "Well, once we are outside in the courtyard, I will show you your name." And he lifted his hand in an obvious gesture.

Zoltay stepped between them. "Now, now, Mekcsey. Surely you don't want to start something with this kid."

"I am not a kid if I am insulted," replied Gergely. "I was seven years old when István Dobó girded me with a sword and called me a warrior."

Zoltay turned around at the name of Dobó and put his hand on Gergely's shoulder. "Look," he said, "maybe you are the boy who stole the janissary's horse?"

"That's me," replied Gergely with proud joy.

"Some place by Pécs ?"

"In the Mecsek Hills."

"Well then, my buddy, give me your hand again!" He grasped and shook Gergely's hand, then embraced him.

While this was going on, Mekcsey had his back to them.

"Who is this ill-tempered guy?" shot Gergely.

"He's a good fellow," replied Zoltay, "just a little prickly."

"But I will not let him go," shot back Gergely. He hit Mekcsey on the shoulder. "Just listen, sir ...."

Mekcsey turned around. "Midnight at St. George Square, we can get acquainted." And he slapped his sword.

"I'll be there," replied Mekcsey curtly.

Zoltay just shook his head.

It was as if a breeze swept through the room. There was movement. Two halberdier guards — or, as they used to say in those days, *palotás* — entered the door, then some court dignitaries: the major-domo, chamberlain, a priest in black robe — certainly the royal chaplain; then four young pages, then the queen; followed by the Friar, Bálint Török, Werbőczy, Orbán Batthyány and old Petrovich.

Gergely blushed as he looked at the door. He was still waiting for someone to come. He must have thought that as the men have their boy pages, such a great lady should be surrounded by girl pages. But not even one girl page came out.

The queen was dressed in veiled mourning clothes. Except that on her head she wore a thin, moon-shaped crown studded with brilliant diamonds. She sat on the throne, two guard officers behind her, high ranking lords next to her.

The queen looked around the hall. She turned to quietly ask something from the Friar, then again arranged herself on the throne. The Friar gestured towards those standing by the door.

The envoy from the Turkish sultan entered, a well-built man dressed in white silk embroidered with gold thread.

Upon entering, he bowed down to the ground. Then with a hurried run, he advanced as far as the carpet in front of the throne. There he put his hands in front of him and lay down on his stomach.

With him came ten page-like, brown haired Circassians wearing lemon-colored clothes. They also hurried in, like their agha (master). Two by two they carried chests covered with violet-colored silk. They put the chests down on either side of the agha. Then they also prostrated on the carpet.

"God has brought you, Ali Agha," said the queen in Latin.

Her voice trembled weakly. One could not tell whether she had no strength in her chest, or, like many women, she had a soul that trembled like a poplar leaf.

The Turk got up. Only then could it be seen what a handsome faced Arab he was. He could have been about forty years of age.

"Most noble Queen," he said in Latin with a coarse morning voice, "I bring greetings from the great Padishah to your throne. He asks that you welcome them as warmly as he sends them to you."

Upon his gesture, the pages opened the chests and one by one the agha took out brilliant gold chains, bracelets, silk and velvet scarves, and a beautiful precious sword and mace.

He laid it on the carpet, in front of the queen's feet.

A weak flush of joy appeared on the queen's pale face.

The agha opened a small, filigreed, silver framed crystal box and held it out toward the queen. Rings sparkled in it. They were among the most beautiful treasures of the East. The queen looked at the rings with sincere pleasure.

"The sword and the mace, Your Majesty, are presents from my lord to the infant king," Ali Agha continued. "In addition, there are three thoroughbred Arabian horses down the yard. Two are gifts from the sultan's two sons. They also have come and they send their brotherly kisses to His Majesty, little János Zsigmond. If it please you to look, my majestic lady, I had them stand where you can see them from the window."

The queen got up and, accompanied by the great lords, hurried to the courtyard window. As she passed by, Gergely sensed the same delicate honeysuckle fragrance that Vica had worn. A guard opened the heavy tapestry curtains of the window. Sunlight flooded the room. The queen looked down at the courtyard, using her hand to shield her eyes.

There stood the three beautiful steeds outfitted with costly saddles, bridles and other gear in the eastern style, all decorated with gold, and around them stood a crowd of people staring at them.

The queen had a few words with the Friar.

The Friar turned towards the ambassador. "Her Majesty is deeply moved and sincerely thanks the gracious Sultan for his gifts and those of his two princes. Tell your lord, the gracious Sultan, to designate an hour when the emissaries of Her Majesty and the King may convey their thanks to the gracious Padishah."

The queen nodded and wanted to go back to her rooms, but the agha was not finished.

"All these gifts," he said with a subtle smile, "are sent by the great Padishah only as tokens, that he regards His Highness János Zsigmond as his son and Her Highness the Queen as his daughter. And it would be his greatest joy to see the son of his recently departed royal friend, so he may give His Highness the young king, a fatherly kiss."

The queen turned pale.

"For this reason," the ambassador continued, "the mighty Padishah asks Your Highness to send His Highness the Crown Prince, along with his nurse, in a carriage, to be accompanied by a worthy escort."

There was an emphasis on *worthy escort*. No one understood it then. Everyone understood the next day.

The queen was white as the wall. She leaned back on her throne to avoid fainting.

The hall was filled with murmurs and horror. Gergely was cold.

"What did he say?" Mekcsey whispered.

"I didn't understand it clearly," replied Zoltay. And he turned towards Gergely. "Did you understand? You must know Latin better than we."

"I understood, " replied Gergely, "and I will tell *you*."

Before he could say anything more, the Turk spoke again. "There is no reason for concern. The great Padishah is only feared by his enemies. To a good friend, he is just a good friend. Besides, he personally would have come to express his respect and good intentions, but Your Majesty, our religious laws prohibit this."

And he stopped speaking. He waited for a reply from either the Friar or the queen. However, no one replied.

"Moreover," continued the Turk, "my lord and emperor would like the gentlemen of His Highness János Zsigmond who were honored to defend Buda to accompany him. He desires to know these Hungarian heroes. He regards them all as his own heroes."

Because there was no reply to this either, he bowed. "With this I have completed what the great Padishah has entrusted to me, and I look forward to your gracious response."

"We shall be there at three in the afternoon," replied Friar György instead of the queen. "His Majesty, the Emperor, will be satisfied with our response."

The queen got up. She gestured to Bálint Török, and as he stepped towards the throne, he held her arm with his. She looked as though she could barely stand on her feet.

17

At noon, Ali Agha did the rounds visiting the most prominent Hungarian lords: Friar György, Bálint Török, and Péter Petrovich who was not only a relative of the Crown Prince but also his guardian. He also went to Werbőczy, Orbán Batthyány and János Podmaniczky.

He brought a precious kaftan for everyone and, with words of honey, he assured the gentlemen that the sultan was benevolent and generous.

The most valuable of the kaftans was given to Bálint Török. It was tough, heavy yellow silk that reached the ankles. The other kaftans were all of the same violet color lined inside with orange-yellow silk. His was made of sunflower-colored silk with a lining of foamy white silk. Its belt was so intricately woven with gold thread that it must have taken a lifetime to complete. It had gold buttons from the neck to the belt, the each gold button surrounded with diamonds.

As the household marveled at the wonderful gift, Bálint Török shook his head with a smile. "It will be useful as a quilt."

Then he got serious. "Pack up everything. We leave for home in the afternoon!"

At three o'clock he walked over to the palace. The main lords were waiting for him in the library room.

"The queen will not permit," said Friar György. "I ask you, speak with her."

Bálint Török shrugged his shoulders. "I came to say goodbye."

The lords were dumbfounded. "What's gotten into your mind?"

"I sense which way the wind is blowing. I don't want to be caught outside my own house."

Werbőczy told him, "You are playing with the fate of the country!"

"It revolves around me?"

"We mustn't anger the sultan," said Werbőczy shrugging his shoulders.

"So I should please him with my head?"

"You've gone crazy," said Werbőczy with another shrug of his shoulders. "Didn't he give you the finest kaftan? Didn't he go out of his way to embrace you the most?"

Bálint Török leaned his elbows on the rim of a large globe of the world and nodded, "The smart fowler whistles most beautifully to the bird for which he aches the most."

The servant by the door opened it to indicate that the queen was waiting for the lords.

What followed inside was a long and unpleasant argument. The queen feared for her child. The lords replied that if she refused the request, she risked the fate of the country and the nation.

Bálint Török stood silently and grimly, leaning against a wall. The queen turned to him, "And you say nothing?"

"I just came to say goodbye, Majesty," he replied, stepping forward to acknowledge the queen's words.

"Goodbye?" the queen asked, staring at him.

"I have to leave for home today. Such things have happened there that I cannot stay here for a minute longer. And I am also sick …"

The queen was wringing her hands nervously. "Wait. Sit down if you are feeling sick. Tell me, what should we do?"

Bálint Török shrugged. "I do not trust the Turks. The Turk sees every Christian as a dog. You should not deliver the royal child into their hands. Tell them he is sick."

Werbőczy became stern. "He will reply, 'I will wait,' and they will be here for weeks. We have to feed the army, the horses …"

The Friar angrily stamped his foot. "Think of the country! The sultan is here with a large army. We invited him. He was a friend to the dearly departed king. We have to honor his wishes. If he sees that we do not trust him, who will guarantee that he will not get angry? Then he will not be calling your son as Majesty, but as prisoner!"

The queen pressed her hand to her forehead and slumped back into her chair.

"Woe is me! I am a wretched woman! … They say I am a queen, but a beggar crawling on the ground has more power! … A tree feels no pain when a blossom is torn from it, but oh, the Creator kneaded a mother's heart with pain!"

18

As all this unfolded in the hall, Gergely was standing about in the anteroom.

As he stood by a tiled fireplace some six feet tall, he felt as if some kind of spider had landed on his face. He slapped at it. Well, he found a peacock feather in his hand.

The fireplace stove stood between two rooms, and through it one could see into the other room.

He heard a soft, "Gergely!"

With a happy thrill, Gergely turned around.

He saw Vica's face and her mischievous eyes as she peeped out from the other room.

"Come out to the hallway," whispered the girl.

Gergely slipped out. The girl was already waiting in a window alcove. They clasped hands. "Let's go to the garden!"

She led him. They went through four or five rooms. Some were covered with thick carpets, and some had heavy curtains hanging over the windows facing the sun. Paintings of kings and saints on the walls. In one place, that of a battle between cavalry. The furniture and walls were gilded. One room was lobster-red, another lily-colored, a third blue like lavender. Every one different with a different color, but each had little in the way of furniture.

They finally stepped out a door into the garden. Gergely relaxed.

"We're alone," said Vica.

She had on a white dress made of a veil-like, light fabric and cut low around her neck. Her hair fell in a single braid behind her back. Yellow saffian shoes on his feet. She stood on the shaded sandy path next to a group of bushes. She smiled as Gergely stared at her.

"Am I beautiful?" she asked with an innocent honesty that belongs to childhood.

"Beautiful," replied Gergely. "You are always beautiful. You are a white dove."

"The queen chose this dress for me." And she held onto Gergely's arm.

"Come, let's sit under those linden trees. There is much I want to tell you, and you must have a lot, too. I immediately recognized your voice when you called through the iron grating, but I didn't believe it could be you. I think of you often. I dreamed of you last night. I told the queen yesterday that you were here. She said she wants to see you once the Turk leaves."

They sat under a linden tree on a marble bench whose arms were two sitting lions. From there, one had a clear view of the Danube River and Pest on the other side. Pest was a dirty little city surrounded by a tall stone wall. Inside the walls were small houses. Outside the walls were yellow sandy fields. But Gergely looked at neither the Danube nor Pest but only at Vica. He admired the clear, marble-like complexion of the girl's face, her beautiful teeth, round chin, white velvety neck, and cheerful, innocent two eyes.

"Well, now you talk," said the girl. "How is life with the Török household? Are you still studying a lot? Did you know that I am taking painting lessons? Well, why are you staring? You haven't said a word."

"I am staring at you, at how you have grown, and how beautiful you are!"

"That's what the queen said. She said that I was growing up to be a young lady. My hands and feet are already as big as they will get, so I won't grow much more. Because with a girl, her hands and feet get bigger only until about age thirteen. You are also handsome, Gergely."

A redness blushed all over his face and he covered his eyes with a hand.

"Oh, what silly things I'm saying! Don't look at me! I am ashamed of myself."

But the boy was also embarrassed. He was blushing to the tips of his ears.

They were silent for one or two minutes. A swallow rested on the linden tree and twittered. Perhaps they were listening to it. They heard nicer music: the sound beating in their hearts.

"Give me your hand," said the boy.

The girl readily gave it.

The boy held the girl's hand. She waited to find out what Gergely wanted. Gergely just sat silently and gazed.

Then he slowly lifted the girl's hand and kissed it.

Éva blushed.

"This garden is nice," said Gergely just to break the silence.

They were quiet again. A leaf fell off a linden branch and landed in front of them. They both looked at it, then the boy spoke, "Everything comes to an end."

He said this so sadly that the girl looked at him almost frightened.

Gergely got up. "Let's go, Vica, in case my lord father comes."

Vica also got up.

She held Gergely's arm again and stroked it. Silently they took ten steps when the girl spoke up, "Why did you say everything comes to an end?"

"Because it's over," replied Gergely.

They took some more steps silently. Gergely shook his head, "I have a feeling that you will not be my wife." And he sighed.

"And I have a feeling that I will," replied the girl comforting.

The boy looked at her in the eyes. "Will you promise me?"

"I promise."

"Upon your soul?"

"On my soul."

"And if your parents want something else? And if the queen wants something else?"

"I will tell them that we have already agreed."

They walked back through the rooms. When they reached the door to the hallway, Vica spoke, "We cannot meet while the Turk is here; only if you come with Lord Bálint. Then just stand here by the stove and I will come out for you."

Gergely held the girl's hand. The girl felt his hand shaking. "Can I kiss you?" asked Gergely.

Until then they had always given each other kisses without asking. But Gergely felt that *this girl* is no longer *this girl* whom he had loved in Keresztes as a sister. It was more. The girl also felt something similar because she blushed at Gergely's question.

"Well, kiss me," she said both happily and seriously.

And she offered him not her face, but her lips.

19

The little infant king was dressed and ready to go by four in the afternoon. A gilded carriage waited in the courtyard to take him down to the Óbuda valley where the Turks had sent up their camp tents.

Until the last minutes the queen did not want to let her child go. She held his head in her two hands and cried. "You have no little children," she said. "You have none, Friar György, nor has Podmaniczky. Petrovich has none. You don't know what it's like to have your baby enter a tiger's lair. Who knows if he will return ever again? Bálint Török! You have no permission to leave me. I entrust my child to you! You are also a parent. You know what it means when a parent's heart trembles for her children. Protect him as your own!"

And when she said, *you have no permission to leave me*, she forgot all her dignity and fell on her knees on the carpet in front of Bálint Török. She stretched her hand out to him, pleading.

This scene affected everyone deeply.

"For the love of God, Majesty!" said Friar György. He lifted the queen up from the floor.

"Your Majesty," began Bálint Török with a deep voice, "I will accompany your little baby. But I give you my oath that if even one hair on his head is ruffled, then I will wash my sword with the sultan's blood!"

— § —

The sultan was camped below Óbuda. His three splendid tents were standing on what today is the Császár Fürdő, the Veli Bey hot baths. It was a tent only in name. In reality it was a palace constructed from fabric. Inside it was divided into rooms and niches. Outside it sparkled with gold.

At around five in the afternoon, the Hungarian delegation set off from the courtyard of the royal palace to render homage. In front was a company of hussars, followed by the mounted and armed nobility, and then the pages bearing treasure. (They were taking the treasures of Tamás Bornemissza, who had trafficked with the Germans and sold out his country, to the sultan as a gift.[23]) There followed a unit of royal palace guards, halberdiers, various court officers, and then the selected flowers of the remaining high nobility, among them Friar György wearing a white cassock. It was a beautiful and dignified cowl, made all the more white next to the summer uniform decorated with blue flowers that Bálint Török wore. Among the high nobility, the Crown Prince's gilded carriage was drawn by six horses. Two ladies of the court sat inside with a nanny. Dancing on the nanny's lap, dressed in white silk, was the ruddy-cheeked Crown Prince.

The horses were led by a long-haired page wearing a tall silk cap. Behind the carriage were the inner palace guards wearing silver helmets, followed by a long line of officers on horseback who had fought during the Hapsburg German siege of Buda.

---

[23] Tamás Bornemissza was a wealthy Buda merchant and counselor who tried to surrender Buda to Ferdinand earlier that same year, 1541.

Gergely, riding a small copper-colored horse, followed Bálint Török. His lord was uneasy, so he too rode his horse in a serious mood. He brightened up only when he glanced back and saw old Cecey. How strangely the old man sat on his horse! He was holding one of his legs, the one made of wood, firmly outstretched, and the other one, which was only wood below the knee, was pulled in. Then he held the reins with his right hand and his sword was tied on his right.

Gergely had never seen him on horse or armed. He chuckled.

Well, the old man did look odd the way he had dressed up. A big eagle feather in his cloth cap was pulled to one side of his head, and his mustache — a little white — had been waxed to a fine point, like those of a young man. He had already lost his teeth in front and his eyes had sunk deeply with age. The old Cecey could have been called a decorated scarecrow rather than a decorated Magyar.

Gergely laughed. But immediately he regretted it, and to make up for his slight, he waited for him. He greeted the man, "Good day, my lord father!" he said brightly. "How is it that I have not seen your grace until now?"

"I just joined up with this procession," the old man said, staring. "Well, what kind of angel skin are you wearing?"

He was referring to the beautiful page's uniform, made of red and blue satin, that Gergely was wearing, and his expensive sword with mother-of-pearl inlaid on its hilt.

"The lord made me his page," replied Gergely. "I go wherever he goes. I visit the royal palace. Now I am going with him to the sultan's tent."

He boasted. He wanted to show off that he was not such a common man as they had thought until then. He moved in the same circles as the young lady, Éva.

The crowd was bustling in St. George Square. Doors and windows were open in the streets. Lively kids were climbing and sitting on roofs and in trees. But everyone was looking only at the Crown Prince. He was only an infant, but he had already been chosen to be king!

"He holds his head the same way as his father," said one woman.

Assembled at the gate was a squadron of some three hundred of Bálint Török's men dressed in red. They were all men from Somogyi, and among them was one whose head stuck out from the others, like a stalk of rye in a wheat field.

As the procession reached them, Bálint Török turned his horse. He brandished his sword in the sky signaling for the procession to halt.

"My hero warriors! My sons!" he said in front of his soldiers with a deep resounding voice. "Do you remember that only a month ago, here, at this gate, all the great nobles and all the soldiers accepted my word that we would not give Buda Castle to either the Germans or the Turks?"

"We remember," the squadron shouted.

Lord Bálint continued, "We defeated the Germans. Now we go before the sultan in the Turkish camp. As God is my witness, and you also be my witnesses, I opposed this outcome in the council."

He had said this in a roaring voice. Then his voice lost its thunder. "My dear sons, I feel as if I will never see you again. As God is my witness, it is only for the sake of the country that I obey. May heaven bless you, my dear sons!"

He could not talk any more. His voice was choking. As his hand stretched out, the soldiers one by one clenched it. Their eyes were full of tears. Bálint Török bent down and kissed one of his soldiers on the cheek.

"That is my farewell kiss for all of you!"

And he turned his horse about and rode out the castle gates.

"There, there, my younger brother" said the old Werbőczy. "Of what good is such emotion?"

Bálint Török wrenched his reins and angrily replied, "I have shown, more than once, that I am not made out of lead."

"Well, whoever isn't cold shouldn't shiver."

"Oh no, my older brother. We shall see who can better predict the weather."

"Even if the emperor had not said," interjected Friar György, "this is how we should go to him. We cannot behave coldly towards him."

"Friar György," said Bálint Török with a grave expression, "You are an intelligent man, but you are not God. Even if a man were to wear his heart on his clothes, the emperor would still hide it from us."

The Friar calmly replied, "If the Germans were still here on our necks, you would talk differently."

Janissaries lined the road like a wall from the gate to the camp. They cheered the Hungarian nobles and the Crown Prince so loudly that it was impossible to continue the conversation.

They proceeded past a variety of soldiers and tents. A few minutes later, they saw a distinguished group of beys and pashas coming to receive the Crown Prince.

If someone could have watched those two processions from above, certainly it would have looked as if two large lines of tulips of all colors were approaching each other in a field covered with more flowers. When they met, they stopped and bowed, then they joined together to proceed further on the Danube shore northward, where a palace-like triple tent was growing out from among all the others.

20

The sultan was standing in front of his tent. He wore rouge on his cheeks, as always. He nodded with a smile when Friar György lifted the blue eyed, chubby little boy from the carriage.

They entered the tent. Gergely also entered behind his lord. He was struck by its comfortable cool air with the fragrance of roses. The strong horse stench of the camp, which was overpowering in the heat, could not enter inside. A guard by the entrance kept the others back.

The sultan was dressed in a cherry-red silk kaftan that reached down to his heels. A white cord around his waist held in the kaftan, but the kaftan was made of such fine and light silk that the shape of his arms could be seen through it. And in those times, Europe was shaking from those thin arms!

The sultan took the child in his hands and looked at him approvingly.

The child smiled at him and reached out to grab his beard. The sultan responded by giving the child a kiss.

The great lords breathe more easily. Because this is not the bloody Suleiman! He is a good-hearted family father! His gaze is clear, his smile is honest. Behold, the child reaches for the diamond star on the sultan's turban. He gives it to him as a toy. Then he speaks to his sons. Bálint understands, as does Gergely.

"Give a kiss to the little Hungarian king!"

And the two sons of the sultan each give a kiss. Both smile at the child, and the child giggles in return.

"Do you accept him as your brother?" asks the sultan.

"Of course," replies Selim. "Because this child is so dear, he could have been born in Istanbul."

Gergely glanced around inside the tent. What magnificent blueish silk! Thick, floral, blue carpets on the ground. Round, glassy windows on the tent walls. Margaret Island was visible through one of them. Next to the tent walls, thick cushions were lying about for sitting.

The only people in the tent were the three great lords, Friar György, Werbőczy and Bálint Török, then the nanny and Gergely, who in his page uniform might have been mistaken by the sentry as a page for the Crown Prince. Then there were the sultan's two sons, two pashas, and an interpreter.

The sultan gave the Crown Prince back to his nanny, but continued smiling at the child, tapping his cheek and stroking his hair. "How beautiful, how healthy!" he said, glancing at the interpreter.

Upon which the interpreter spoke Latin. "The merciful Sultan says the child is charming, like an angel, and as healthy as an Oriental rose that opened this morning."

"I'm glad I saw him," said the sultan. "Take him back to the queen and tell her that I will be his father in place of his real father, and that my sword will protect him and his country."

"His Majesty rejoices," the interpreter said, "as if he were seeing his own child. He receives him as his son, and he spreads the power of his world-dominating wings to protect over him. Say this to Her Majesty the Queen, and convey his most gracious greetings to her."

The sultan picked up a dark cherry-red silk purse from his pocket and gently slipped it into the hands of the nanny.

Then he kissed the child once more. He waved goodbye with his hand.

It was a sign for the others that the sultan was finished and that they could go.

Everyone breathed happily. The nanny carried the child out, almost running.

They stepped out from the tent. There, the pashas surrounded the great lords, and they bluntly said that the sultan had invited them to stay as his guests. The rest of the escort could turn back and return the Crown Prince.

"Go with the Crown Prince," said Bálint Török to Gergely standing behind him. And a pasha held him by the arm as he disappeared inside the tent.

The sun had already fallen behind the hills of Buda, and the reflection of its fire upon clouds lit the ground below.

The little Crown Prince was back in the carriage again. With his right hand, he waved to the pashas and the Hungarian great lords. Then the gilded carriage started off and headed back up to Buda Castle between two lines of cheering janissaries.

<h1 style="text-align:center">21</h1>

Gergely rode behind the carriage.

The wooden handed Cecey went ahead with the other old men; the young men behind. Gergely was riding behind Zoltay and Mekcsey and alongside the auburn haired boy, beginning to grow chubby, to whom he had introduced himself at the beginning of the procession.

"My older brother, Fűrjes," he said to the boy. "I just arrived in Buda so I know practically no one here."

"What would you like, my young brother? I will gladly give if I can."

He thought the boy needed money.

"I have a little work to do at St. George Square at midnight."

"What sort of work?" he asked with a smile.

Because he suspected that the boy was planning a romantic encounter at St. George Square. He shook his thick auburn hair and cheerfully added, "Well, well. What is it?"

"The thing is, it's not really something to laugh about," replied Gergely, "but it's also not that serious."

"In a word, heart."

"No. Sword."

"But surely you are not fighting?"

"I certainly am."

"With whom?"

Gergely pointed to the rider ahead wearing green satin, Mekcsey.

Fűrjes gave him a long, serious look.

"With Mekcsey?"

"Him."

"You've heard, haven't you, that he is a devil of a fellow."

"I'm no sheep."

"He has already cut down Germans."

"Well then, I will cut him down."

"You handle a sword well?"

"I started when I was seven."

"Well, that's different." He tapped the muscles of Gergely's arm and shook his head. "It would be better if you apologized."

"What, me apologize?"

"He will beat you," said Fűrjes anxiously.

"How can you know that ahead of time?" replied a cocky Gergely. He straightened up and threw his shoulders back to puff out his chest towards Mekcsey, then similarly turned towards Fűrjes. "Well, will you be my second, my older brother?"

Fűrjes shrugged. "Because if you need only a second, well, gladly. But if something bad happens …"

"What would that be?"

"Anything. But I will not stand in for you and fight on your account."

There was movement and loud commotion in the procession. Incomprehensible screaming, horses rearing. Necks seemed to stiffen as everyone stared at the castle.

Then Gergely looked up.

Well than, what is it? Hanging above the gate of Buda Castle were three large horsetail flags on the Buda gate. Other horsetail flags hung from churches and towers.

At the gate, turbaned Turkish halberdiers had replaced the Hungarian sentries.

"Buda is lost!" shouted a ghostly voice.

And from that, like wind passing through a forest, a shudder passed through the Hungarian crowd.

The wooden handed Cecey screamed.

No one replied. Faces were pale. And the mute silence was punctuated by the distant cry of a muezzin from the bell tower of the Church of Our Lady.

Allahu akbar... Ashadu anna la ilaha ill Allah.

— § —

Gergely, with some others in the procession, galloped back to the camp.

"Where are the lords?! There's been an atrocious treachery!"

Red capped *bostanji*[24] guards in front of the tent barred their way.

"We have to go inside," Mekcsey screamed, almost on fire, "or send out the lords!"

The *bostanjis* did not reply. They just held their spears close to their chests.

Gergely shouted at them in Turkish. "Send out Lord Bálint Török immediately!"

"Not possible!" replied the *bostanjis*.

The Hungarians stood there not knowing what to do.

"Lords!" shouted one thick necked Hungarian. "Come out. There's trouble!"

No response.

Gergely rode his horse to look around. He went up a hill towards the *sipahis* and around to see if he could locate the visiting Hungarian lords.

From one of the tents came a Hungarian voice, "Is that you, Gergely?"

Gergely recognized Lord Bálint's chatterbox secretary, Martonfalvai.

He was sitting with two Turks in front of a *sipahi* tent eating a cantaloupe melon.

"What are you doing here?" Martonfalvai shouted.

"I want to see my lord."

"You can't go there now! Come on, stay with us!" He sliced a piece of melon and offered it to Gergely.

Gergely shook his head. "I don't want it."

"Well, just come here," Martonfalvai said, "These two Turks are my good friends. Then when they light the torches, we also can go down and join the lords."

"Coom Hoongar brozer!" said one of the *sipahis* good naturedly, a full bodied, brown skinned man. He gestured to Gergely with a fleshy hand.

"Impossible," replied the boy grimly. And he moved on.

---

[24] The *bostanji*s were the sultan's personal guards and servants.

He rode down a tent street between sappers, hunters and janissaries to reach the sultan's tent again. There also he ran into *bostanji* sentries. From that side also he was unable to get to Bálint Török.

The other Hungarian lads were still waiting in the same place, shouting as before. Turkish music could be heard from inside the tent; the sounds of metal-stringed *kanun* zither and many *kemençe* lutes and shrill *zurna* pipes.

"Bastards!" Mekcsey shouted, gritting his teeth.

Fürjes almost cried in anger. "Had my lord remained in the castle, this wouldn't have happened." He was the Friar's page. To him, the Friar was almighty.

As the music paused, everyone shouted, "Lords inside! Come out lords! The Turks have occupied the castle."

However, no one came out. The sky was cloudy. All of a sudden, it began to rain. It rained for a half an hour, then stopped. Black clouds hurried towards the east like escaping armies.

Finally the lords straggled out towards midnight. With caps askew, they merrily staggered out the tent door. Torches were burning in the camp to give them light. A double row of torches lined the entire way to the gates of Buda Castle. The fresh air after the rain mingled with the smoke of the eastern torches.

Martonfalvai was already standing there, and the *bostanjis* allowed the lords who had been kept outside to mingle with the lords coming out.

Martonfalvai called the grooms by name.

The lords mounted their horses one by one.

In the light of the torches red faces could be seen frowning, then one by one becoming pale.

The Friar in his white habit looked like a ghost.

"Don't cry!" said Fürjes riding beside him. "It's not right for a grown man to cry!"

One by one, in pairs, and in triplets, the lords galloped by the torch-lit road to Buda Castle.

Gergely still did not see Lord Bálint.

Martonfalvai stood beside him and also looked with a worried face at the tent opening from where reddish light came out.

The last lord who came out was Podmaniczky. Two Turkish officers held him by the arms as he staggered out. He had to be lifted onto his horse.

Then came a motley group of Moors and Saracens: the servants.

Then no one.

The opening to the tent closed, covering the light from the tent.

"Well, what are you two waiting for?" asked an ostrich-feathered big bellied Turk.

"Our lord, Lord Bálint Török."

"Hasn't he gone already?"

"No."

"Then he is the one with whom the gracious Padishah speaks."

"We will wait," Martonfalvai said.

The Turk shrugged and left.

"I can't wait," Gergely said uneasily. "I have to be up there at midnight."

"Well, just go then, my younger brother," Martonfalvai replied. "Then if you find some Turk in my bed, just throw him out."

He said as a joke, but Gergely didn't laugh. He thanked Martonfalvai and left for Buda Castle at a full gallop.

— § —

By then the moon had emerged from behind clouds to shed light on the Buda road.

The Turks armed with pikes standing by the gate did not even bother to look at Gergely. People could come and go freely. Who knows whether tomorrow all Hungarians will be forced out of the castle?

The horse's hooves clattered on the cobblestones. Gergely saw janissaries armed with pikes in front of houses. A janissary in front of every house. Horsetail flags on every tower. Only the Church of Our Lady still had its gilded cross.

Gergely reached St. George Square. He was surprised to see no one there.

He rode around the fountain and the cannons. No one, no one. Only one Turk with a spear, probably a sentry by the cannons.

Gergely dismounted and tied his horse to the wheel of a cannon.

"What are you doing here?" the Turk shouted.

"I'm waiting," said Gergely in Turkish. "Surely you don't think I am going to steal the cannon."

"Oh no," the *topchi*[25] said in a friendly manner. "Are you Turkish?"

"Not me."

"Then go home."

"But I have some business here regarding honor. Be patient, please."

The Turk aimed his spear at the boy.

"Clear out of here!"

Gergely untied his horse and mounted.

Somebody was walking and running from the Fehérvár Gate. Gergely recognized Fűrjes, whose blond features almost lit up the night.

He stepped in front of him.

"Mekcsey is in Lord Bálint's house," said Fűrjes panting. "Come, because the janissaries don't allow any talking in the streets."

Gergely dismounted and walked with Fűrjes.

"How did this outrage happen?" Gergely asked.

He shrugged. "It was planned and cunning. While we went down to the camp with the little king, the janissaries slipped through the gates as if they were interested to look at the buildings. They just loitered and stared. But more and more of them. When all the streets were full of them, a horn sounded and they all drew their weapons and forced everyone into their houses."

"Bastards!"

"It's very easy to occupy a fortress like that."

"My lord had warned ..."

The windows of the palace were open. Two heads appeared in one of the upstairs windows.

Just then, the guards in front of the gate were changing, and a large janissary took up the position.

"What do you want?" he asked contemptuously.

---

[25] A *topchi* is an Ottoman artilleryman.

"We belong here," Gergely said dryly.

"I just got my orders," said the Turk. "No one out and no one in."

"I belong to the household of Bálint Török," insisted Gergely.

"Go home, boy," said the Turk looking down, "to Szigetvár."

"Let me in," Gergely shouted angrily as he slapped his sword.

The Turk pulled out his sword. "Get out of here!"

Gergely grabbed the bridle of his horse and in the same motion drew his sword. Maybe he trusted that he was not alone.

The giant Turk took a step and brandished his sword. He thrust at Gergely's head.

Gergely parried the thrust and swords sparkled in the gloom. At the same moment, he jumped forward like a cat and thrust. He cut his face.

"Allah!" bellowed the Turk. He staggered against the wall. The plaster crumbled under his back.

There was a cry from upstairs, "Stab him."

Gergely thrust his sword into the Turk all the way to the hilt.

He stared at the giant when he saw that he had dropped his sword and was leaning like a sack against the wall.

Gergely looked around for Fűrjes. He already was running away to the royal palace.

Instead, three janissaries with tall caps were rushing towards him, angry and cursing.

The boy saw that he had no time to lose. He jumped on the gate and pushed it open. Then he quickly locked it from inside.

Still excited from the fight, his shaking legs ran several more steps, then he heard someone rattling inside on wooden steps. He sat down on a bench beneath the gate and panted.

It was Zoltay, sword in his hand. In his footsteps, Mekcsey, also with sword in hand.

A lamp burning in the doorway lit up their two shocked faces when they saw him.

"Is that you?" Zoltay shouted. "Are you wounded?"

Gergely gestured with his head that he was not.

"Did you cut down the Turk?"

Gergely nodded that he had.

"Let me embrace you, my little hero," said Zoltay enthusiastically, and he embraced the fifteen-year-old boy who had just proved himself to be a warrior.

There was rattling at the gate.

"We have to leave," said Mekcsey. "Janissaries are running all around. But first, let's shake hands. Don't be angry with me because I insulted you."

Gergely held out his hand. He was stunned. He did not know what was happening to him. Without saying a word, he allowed himself to be dragged away. He only began to come to his senses when the two boys began twisting sheets and tying them together to make a rope. Mekcsey told him to climb down first from the window.

Gergely looked down.

Deep below the moonlight lit up the royal kitchen garden.

22

The next morning, Ali Agha again appeared before the queen. He said the following:

"His Majesty, the Padishah saw that it would be good to put Turkish soldiers into Buda Castle until your son is grown. The child cannot defend Buda Castle against the Germans. The gracious Padishah cannot come here every two or three months. Until then, you will have enough, Majesty: Transylvania and the silver and gold mines and the salt mines that are there."

The queen was already prepared for the worst. She listened to the envoy with calm contempt.

The ambassador continued. "So His Majesty the Padishah will protect Buda Castle and Hungary, and in a few days, he will deliver his written imperial promise to protect you and your son. Once the child is grown, he will return Buda and the country."

The lords were all present, only Bálint Török was missing, and Podmaniczky. The Friar was more colorless than usual. His face almost matched his white hood.

The ambassador continued. "Therefore Buda Castle, together with the Danube and the Tisza region, will be under the protection of the great Padishah, and Your Majesties will move to Lippó and from there rule Transylvania and the region east of the Tisza River. There will be two governors in Buda: one Turkish and the other Hungarian. For this latter honor, the lords will appoint Lord István Werbőczy and he will be the judge and governor of the Hungarian population of the province."

The lords, each with despair written on his face, stood sadly as though they were not standing beside a royal throne, but a coffin.

When the ambassador left, there was a minute of silence in the room.

Then the queen raised her head and looked at them.

Werbőczy blurted into tears.

The queen's eyes also teared up. She wiped them off. "Where is Podmaniczky?" she asked weakly.

"He left," replied Petrovich.

"Without taking leave?"

"He escaped, Your Highness. He disguised himself as a peasant carrying a hoe and left before dawn."

"And Bálint still has not returned home?"

"No."

— § —

The following day, the Turks threw out the bells from the Church of Our Lady. They tore down the pictures from the altar. They pulled down the statue of King St. István. Pieces of the gilded and embellished altars, broken angels carved from marble and wood, and prayer books were scattered in front of the church. The organ was also destroyed. Two carts took its tin pipes to the camp to be melted down into bullets.

Three more carts were loaded with silver pipes and masterpiece gold and silver candle holders, altar carpets and altar cloths. They were all taken to the sultan's treasurer. The church's beautiful frescoes were whitewashed. The cross was knocked off the tower and replaced with a large, gilded copper crescent.

On September 2, the sultan accompanied by pashas rode up to the castle. His two sons were with him.

The aghas, in ceremonial dress, waited for him at Szombat Gate, then, with trumpets blaring, they proceeded together to the church.

The sultan prostrated himself in the middle of the church and gave thanks to the god of the Turks for having taken Buda Castle.

23

On September 4, forty oxen carts wound their way down from the royal castle to the ship bridge over the Danube River.

The queen was moving.

Carriages were already waiting in the palace courtyard, and the great lords crowded around them. Everyone was ready for the journey. Only Werbőczy was to remain in Buda, together with his favorite officer, Mekcsey.

Gergely was also standing there with the lords when he spotted Fűrjes. "Well, Gergely," Fűrjes said in the patronizing manner, "aren't you coming with us?"

Gergely looked at him contemptuously. "*Thou* nothing.[26] I am not the brother of rabbits."

The blonde lad twitched. But then, when he met the piercing gaze of Mekcsey, he shrugged.

Old Cecey was also on horseback among the lords. Gergely put his hand on his saddle horn. "My lord father."

"Good day, son."

"Your grace is also leaving?"

"Only until Hatvan."

"Éva, also?"

"The queen is also taking her. Go to my wife for lunch and comfort her."

"Why are you letting Éva go?"

"Werbőczy told us to let her go. Next year, don't worry, we will return with many regiments ..."

They did not say anything more. The royal bodyguards appeared, so the queen was coming.

She came. She was dressed in mourning clothes. The fragrance of honeysuckle surrounded her.

Among her ladies was Éva.

---

[26] Gárdonyi italicized the familiar (and insulting) "you" to emphasize Gergely's contempt for Fűrjes who had run away when Gergely fought the janissary.

She was wearing a light silk, walnut-colored, hooded traveling cloak, but she had not pulled up the hood. She looked around as if searching for someone. Gergely made his way through the lords to be beside her.

"Aren't you coming with us?" the girl asked.

"I would go." Gergely replied, "But my lord has not returned."

"You will come after us?"

"I don't know."

The girl's face clouded. "If you're not coming with us, when will I see you?"

"I don't know."

The boy's eyes filled with tears.

The queen had already sat inside her spacious carriage with windows in its leather canopy.

Vica stretched out her had to Gergely. "You won't forget me, will you?"

Gergely wanted to say, "No, Vica, not even in the next world." But he could not speak. He just shook his head.

24

Ten days later the sultan also took to the road.

He took Bálint Török with him, in chains.

Part III
The Lion Prisoner

1

A mounted soldier stood on the bank of the Berettyó wearing the blue cloak and red cap of a royal soldier.

He waived with his cap from the shore and shouted over the willow bushes, "Hey! Water here!"

He rode down the sunbaked, swampy banks covered with yellow marsh marigold flowers.

The grass came up to the horse's knees, covering the water at the bottom. The horse bent its neck to drink.

However, it did not drink. As the horse lifted its head, water dripped from its nose and mouth. It snorted and shook its head.

"What's with this horse?" muttered the warrior. "Why don't you drink, rascal?"

The horse again lowered its head, and again shook the water from its mouth and nose.

Eighteen Hungarian horsemen wearing different kinds of outfits trotted across the field. Among them was a thread-thin man with an eagle feather pinned to his cap. Instead of a cloak, he wore a dark cherry-colored short cloth coat over his shoulder.

"Lieutenant sir," the warrior said from the water, "This water has worms or something. My horse won't drink it."

The man with the eagle feather galloped into the water and looked carefully at the waves. "The water is bloody," he said in astonishment.

The shore was covered with willow bushes. The bushes were full of yellow catkins. The earth was blue from violets. The afternoon breeze was an apron full of the sweet fragrances of spring.

The lieutenant slapped his horse and splashed a few steps upstream. He stumbled upon a young man dressed down to his shirt. The man was sitting on a willow stump, washing his head in the stream. His head was gnarly and big, like that of a bull. His eyes were similar: small, black and powerful. The tips of his mustache ended with points as sharp as iron. His hussar coat, two yellow boots, cap, and sword lay on the grass next to him.

It was from that washing that the Berettyó stream was bloody.

"Who are you, my young brother?" said the lieutenant to him.

The boy replied with ill humor, "My name is István Mekcsey."

"Mine is István Dobó," the lieutenant said. "What's the problem, brother?"

"I got a cut from a Turk, God damn him." He held his hand to his face.

"Turk," said Dobó, his eyes flashing. "All those pagan Turks, they can't be far away! How many of them are there? Hey, men! Grab your swords!" And he made his horse jump out of the water.

"Don't tire yourselves," Mekcsey said. "I've already cut him up into pieces. He's lying behind me."

"Where?"

"Somewhere, not far from here."

Dobó, sitting on his horse, called to an aide carrying his weapons. "Get the pack," he said. "Tear some bandages and bind this young lord's wound."

"There are some more further up," said Mekcsey, holding his palm to his head again.

"Turks?"

"No, an old nobleman and his wife." Blood covered his face. Again he leaned down to the water.

Dobó spurred on his horse and, after a few steps, he found more people. A red-haired, old man was sitting by the stream, also undressed down to his shirt. A stout old woman was crying as she washed red from the old man's head.

"My God!" exclaimed Dobó. "Is it a deep wound?"

The old man looked up and happily whispered, "Turk cut ..."

That was when Dobó noticed that the old man had only one hand. "Damn it, that's familiar!" he said as he dismounted.

The old man looked up again. "Possibly."

"I am István Dobó."

The old man mused, "Dobó? Say! Is that you, my young brother Pista? Well of course you know me! You've been to my place, old Cecey's."

And the two men shook hands warmly.

"What happened here, my older brother? How did you end up here in the Alföld Plain?"

"Ay!" the old man said, passing his head back to his wife. "The pagan dogs attacked my carriage. It was my good fortune that this young man had just reached us when the pagans fell upon us. Well, a good man! He cut up the Turks like pumpkins. I myself was able to hack from the carriage."

"How many were they?"

"Ten, the dogs. May the devil bury them! Luckily, they couldn't deal with us. I have some four hundred pieces of gold with me, if not more." He slapped his side.

The woman asked, "Did the boy die?"

"No, not even a little," replied Dobó. "Down below there, he also is washing himself."

He saw a reddened dead body of a Turk nearby. "I'll give him a look," he said, "and see what kind of people we are dealing with." He rode by the side of the stream and along the road.

He found seven corpses in the grass, two Hungarians and five Turks, and on the road, a three-horse carriage leaning into the ditch. A young driver was struggling to collect boxes and chests.

"Don't struggle, young brother," he said. "You'll get help soon."

He returned to Mekcsey. "There is not one Turk here, my young brother," he said, "but five. Nice cuts! They are to your credit."

"There has to be one more," replied Mekcsey. "Maybe he's in the water. Have you found my soldiers, older brother Dobó?"

"Poor lads. One had his head cut in two."

"There were only three of us."

"And the Turks?"

"There were ten dogs."

"Well then, four ran away."

"So they did."

Dobó dismounted and examined the boy's head wound. "The cut is long, but not deep," he said pressing the gash together. He himself bandaged the wound, tying a piece of linen tightly around his head.

"Well, where are you going, young brother?"

"To Debrecen."

"But surely not to the Turks?"

"But actually, yes."

"Well now, young brother. I have a nice man there, Gergely Bornemissza. He is still young. Do you know him?"

"I am going there for him. He wrote a letter that he would like to join me in the army."

"Has he already grown up?"

"He's eighteen."

"Of course, Lord Bálint's people have scattered."

"They've been blown about by the wind since the lord was taken prisoner."

"Tinódi has also gone?"

"He wanders here and there. But it's possible he also is in Debrecen."

"Well, give him my respect and greetings, and to the two Török sons."

As they were talking, Dobó rolled up his jacket sleeves and grabbed a rag. He washed Mekcsey's face while one of Dobó's soldiers wiped blood off his uniform.

"Is the old man there?" asked Mekcsey, pointing towards Cecey.

"He's there. He's alright. Aren't you hungry, young brother?"

"No, just thirsty."

Dobó gestured for a water bottle. He sent the other soldiers to help put the carriage back together. Then they went to Cecey. The old married couple were sitting on the grass by the carriage. Cecey had a turkey thigh in his hand. He was eating happily.

"Join us!" he called cheerfully. "Good thing you're alright, young brother!"

The soldiers collected the booty: five Turkish horses, the same number of cloaks, and all kinds of Turkish weapons.

Mekcsey looked at the horses, then the weapons lying on the ground. "Chose, older brother," he said to Cecey. "The booty belongs to all of us."

"Like I need it!" laughed Cecey. "I have enough horses and enough weapons."

"Well then, older brother Dobó. I offer you a weapon."

"Thank you," replied Dobó. "But how can I chose? I didn't earn any by fighting."

"But, just chose."

Dobó shook his head. "The booty is yours down to the last button. How can I take a present from you?"

"I don't give it for nothing."

"That's something else," said Dobó. His piercing glance rested on a finely wrought Turkish sword. "Well, what's the price?"

"That when you become the captain of a fortress and your boots are tight, you call me to join you."

Dobó smiled. "We can't plan on something uncertain."

"Well then, I'll offer another price. Come with me to Debrecen."

"It can't be right now, young brother. I have a royal commission now. I am collecting tithes from rascal estates. Unless I have time later ..."

"Well, just choose and you can pay with a gift of friendship."

"That's already yours. But don't be angry with me. I'll take one because I see you are kindly willing to offer it." And, looking at the swords, he continued, "These were Turkish nobility. One was a bey. I wonder where they are from."

"I would think from Fehérvár."

Dobó picked up the swords. One had a velvet scabbard and turquoise on its hilt. Its grip had a gilded snake head with two diamonds for its eyes.

"Well, this is yours, my young brother. I don't choose this because it's worth a fortune."

There were two cheaper, Turkish iron swords still lying there. Dobó picked up one and waved it in a circle. "Now this is steel!" he said cheerfully. "Well, if you give this to me, thank you."

"You're welcome," Mekcsey replied.

"But now, if you give this to me, do me a favor and take it to Debrecen and if Tinódi is there, tell him to inscribe some words on it. Whatever he wants. There are goldsmiths there who can engrave into the steel."

"With pleasure," Mekcsey replied. "I also will get something inscribed on this serpent sword." He swung the curved sword then tied it on next to the other.

"Did you find any money on this Turkish officer?" Dobó asked his soldiers.

"We haven't searched him yet."

"Well, just search him."

The man quickly dragged the Turk back with him, pulling him by the collar on the grass. Then he searched him.

There was no pocket in the red velvet pants, but they found gold and all sorts of silver coins in a pouch tied to his belt.

"This will be good for expenses," said Mekcsey cheerfully. "A soldier is always in need."

There was even a gold pin with a ruby in his turban, and a gold chain which the bey wore inside his shirt. On the chain hung coconut shavings wrapped in parchment.

Mekcsey put the two gold pieces on his palms and offered them to Cecey.

"You have to choose from this, my older brother sir."

"Put it away, my young brother," said the old man waving his hand. "I'm not going to start a fire in my old age."

"Let's take that chain to our daughter," said the lady. "We have a lovely young daughter," she said. "She is with the queen."

"Come to the wedding, young brother!" said Cecey shaking his leg. "I'll dance once more for my pleasure before I die."

Mekcsey put the chain in the woman's palm.

"Who's marrying her?"

"The queen's lieutenant, Ádám Fürjes. Perhaps you know him?"

Mekcsey became serious and indicated no.

"He's a fine boy," said the woman. "The queen is giving my daughter to him."

"May God bless them," said Dobó.

Mekcsey gave the Turkish clothes and the plain weapons to Dobó's soldiers. They got ready to leave.

Mekcsey picked up his cap and rolled it in his hands, annoyed. It had been cut and almost torn in two.

"Never be annoyed," Cecey said. "If it hadn't been cut, it wouldn't fit your head now."

Their clothes were still wet, but by evening, they will have dried in the breeze and the sun.

"Choose two of my soldiers to accompany you," said Dobó. "I'll also give two to my older brother Cecey."

"I don't know if we're going together," Mekcsey asked, turning to the Ceceys. "Are we going together?"

"Where?" said the old man.

"Debrecen."

"Together."

"Well then, three soldiers should be enough."

"As many as you want," Dobó said graciously.

While the old couple was getting settled in the carriage, the two surveyed the dead. Among them was the large body of a roughly thirty-year-old Turk lying on his back with his arms and legs spread out. He was wearing baggy pants made of blue cloth. His head had been slashed to his eyes.

"I know him," said Dobó. "I once fought with him."

The two Hungarian soldiers were severely cut apart. The head of one was covered with a cloth.

The Turks were stabbed in the stomach and Dobó's soldiers threw them in the Berettyó. They dug graves for the Hungarians in the soft soil of the shore under an old willow. They laid the bodies down in their clothes, covered them with their cloaks, covered them with soil and, instead of crosses, shoved their swords into the mounds.

2

On the south corner of Constantinople stands an old fortress. Its walls are high. Inside its walls are seven stocky towers, like seven huge windmills, arranged like this:

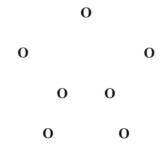

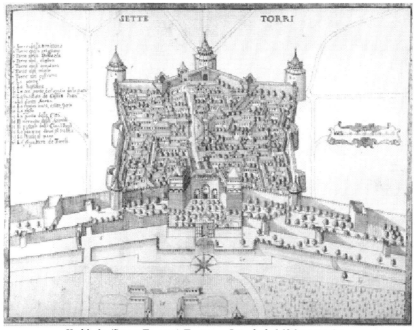

Yedikule (Seven Towers) Fortress, Istanbul. 1686 engraving.

Half of the walls is washed by the Sea of Marmara. The other half has wooden houses built around it.

This is the famous Yedikule, Seven Towers. All the sultan's treasures are packed and stuffed inside Seven Towers. In the middle two are ornaments made of gold and jewels. In the towers by the sea are siege weapons, hand guns, and silver treasure. In the other two are old weapons, old documents, and books.

Seven Towers also served as a dungeon where important prisoners were guarded. Each one differently. Some were kept in chains inside a dark stone pit. Others were allowed comforts and freedom, as if at home. They could enjoy the sun all day into the night, walking in the castle garden, in the vegetable garden, on the balconies of the towers, or in the bath. He may have three servants, write letters, receive visitors, play music, eat, and drink. It's just that he cannot leave.

— § —

On a spring day, two grey haired old men were sitting on a bench in the Yedikule garden. Both had a kind of light chain around their legs.

One had his elbows on his knees. The other had his arms stretched out on the back of the bench and was staring at the clouds.

The one who was looking at the sky was more white-haired than the other. His beard reached the middle of his chest, his hair hung like a mane around his head.

Hungarian clothes on both. Hey, Magyar clothes were wearing thin on many prisoners in Seven Towers!

They sat silently.

The spring day filled the garden with warm air. Tulips and peonies were already blooming among the cedar, thuya and laurel trees. Above their heads, the leaves of an old tree drank the sun rays.

The man staring at the clouds lowered his muscular arms from the back of the bench and crossed them on his chest. Then he looked at his companion. "What are you thinking about, my friend Maylád?"

"My walnut tree," replied the man leaning on his knees. "I have a walnut tree in Fogaras …"

The two men fell silent again. After a few minutes, Maylád spoke again. "One of its outer branches froze. Has it gotten new growth? That's what I am wondering."

"It's gotten new growth, certainly. If a tree freezes, it has new growth. Even grapes have new growth from its roots. Only men have no new growth."

Again they were silent for a while.

Then Maylád broke the silence again. "What about you, Bálint? What are you thinking about?"

"I'm thinking," replied Bálint Török sadly, "that Kapi Agha is just as good for nothing as the others."

"That I never doubted."

"They said that he was cunning. My wife sent him thirty thousand pieces of gold to get him to take these chains off my legs. It's been three months."

They fell silent again. Maylád reached down for a dandelion that was flowering yellow in the grass. He plucked it and rubbed it into pieces in his hands, then dropped it on the ground.

He spoke again. "Last night I thought that I still don't know why they made you a prisoner. You have often told me how they brought you down the Danube, how you shoved a guard against the wall of the boat, and how they drove you here. But the beginning, the real reason ..."

"As a practical matter, I don't know either."

"After all, you were satisfied with your own nest. No one could say that you had ambitions to be a king or a prince."

"I also have been speculating about this often. The Turks don't need much of a reason, but as to why they chose me from among so many others, that I would also like to know."

In the yard, a group of *kapıcı*, the sultan's guards of the palace gates, marched by to the beat of drums. Then they again were alone.

Bálint continued. "I think that after all, the main reason was the evening conversation. The sultan asked me why I had told the Germans about his coming. 'Told the Germans?' I asked in amazement. 'I did not tell the Germans, but only Perényi.' 'He's a dog,' the sultan said. 'Perényi was with the Germans.' The sultan looked at me with angry eyes. 'If you hadn't warned them, we would have overrun the German camp here. We would have captured all the nobles, and I would have broken Ferdinand's strength! I would have Vienna too!' As the ugly Turk shouted at me this way, the blood began to boil in me. I, as you know, have always been a gentleman throughout my entire life. I have never gotten used to hiding my thoughts from others."

"You got angry at him?"

"I wasn't rude. I just told him that I had informed them about the sultan coming because I wanted to save the Hungarians in the German camp."

"That was a big mistake!"

"I was still free at the time."

"Then what did he say?"

"Nothing. He walked up and down in front of me. Then he suddenly turned to one of his pashas. He told him to give me a good tent where I would be staying because he wanted to talk with me the next day."

"Well, and what did you talk about the next day?"

"Nothing. I never saw the sultan again. They gave me a big tent, but they didn't let me out. Each time I tried to leave, ten spears were pointed at my chest."

"When did they put you in irons?"

"Only when the sultan left to return home."

"They put me in irons immediately after I was captured. In my anger, I cried just like a child."

"I cannot cry. I have no tears. I didn't even cry when my father died."

"You don't even cry for your children?"

"No," replied Bálint Török turning pale. "But each time they come to my mind, I feel as if they are turning a sword inside my chest." He sighed painfully, his hand on his forehead.

"A prisoner comes to mind often," he sadly mused. "A thin, bad Turk whom I captured by the Danube. For years I kept him in the castle. He once looked me in the eyes and cursed me, face to face."

They didn't talk any more.

Trumpets blared in the distance. Sometimes they paid attention to that, only to again get lost in their own thoughts

When the sun was already turning the clouds red, the master of the castle walked through the garden and as he passed by, said to them over his shoulder, "Gentlemen, we're closing the gate."

They used to close the gate a half an hour before sunset, and then all prisoners were expected to be in their rooms.

"*Kapıcı effendim*," Bálint Török said, "What is the occasion for the trumpets?"

"It's tulip festival," replied the master of the castle. "They won't be sleeping in the *serayı* tonight." And he continued walking.

The prisoners already knew what that meant. There had been a similar festival the previous spring. On those occasions, all the sultan's women were in the garden of the *serayı*.

The sultan has women's tents set up around the tulip beds, and in the tents, the lower tier harem women sell all kinds of trinkets, beads, silk fabrics, gloves, stockings, shoes, veils and other items. His one hundred some women can never go out to the bazar, so once a year they are happy to spend money.

At those times, the garden is buzzing with joy. The cages of the palace parrots, thrushes, nightingales, and canary birds are suspended from trees and bushes, and their singing competes with the music.

In the evening, fragrant torches and multicolored paper lanterns light up one of the Bosporus ships on which the entire harem travels down to the Sea of Marmara.

The two prisoners shook hands at the bottom of Blood Tower.

"Good night, István Maylád."

"Good night, Bálint Török."

— § —

Because there was no other pleasure there but a good night. The sleeping prisoner dreams himself to be home.

That night Bálint Török did not feel sleepy. As was his custom, he took a nap after lunch so at night, he was not sleepy. He opened his window and sat there.

He looked at the starry sky.

The boat on the Sea of Marmara passed below Yedikule. The sky was filled with stars as there was no moonlight. The stars were almost floating as they flickered, and the sea mirrored back a second sky. The boat with its lanterns floated among the stars above and below.

Two high stone walls hid the boat from the prisoner's eyes, but he could hear the music. He could hear the strings of the Turkish cimbalom, the kanun, and the beat of cymbals. No matter how much he wanted to listen, his thoughts wandered elsewhere.

Around midnight the loud music became quiet. The women themselves were singing. Different tones and different instruments.

But Bálint Török heard little of that also. He looked at the sky which was slowly being covered by dark and ragged clouds. Where the clouds were thin, the light of some stars glistened. "How different is everything here," he thought. "Turkish sky, Turkish darkness."

Later, as there was a longer break in the music on the boat, he continued with his thoughts. "Even silence is different here. Turkish silence."

He thought that perhaps he would lie down, but he enjoyed the sleepy numbness he was feeling as he waited for time to pass and the members of his body to move. He was waiting for his body to move of its own accord and lie down to rest.

Then in the silence of the night, a harp began to play, and only Hungarian chords drifted through the foliage in the dark Turkish night:

A painful and sweet shiver ran through Bálint Török from his heart to his heels.

The harp was silent for a minute. Then the trembling chords were again played, rising up in the darkness of the night like gentle weeping:

Bálint Török raised his head the way a caged lion raises his head and with a measured gaze stares at the whispering wind.

The chords of the harp softened into a sigh in the night silence. Then the strings played again, this time accompanied by a thin, sad female voice in pure Hungarian:

> *Who has drunk the water of the Tisza,*
> *The heart longs to have again ...*
> *Hey! I have also drunk ... from it ...*

Bálint Török stopped breathing. His head raised, he looked with clear eyes towards the sound of the voice.

The curls of his grey hair almost wrinkled, his face similarly almost turned to stone.

As the old lion sat frozen listening to the song, two big tears dropped from his eyes onto his face and beard.

3

At night, around twelve o'clock, the servant knocked on the door on the door of the Török boys. "Gergely, sir."

"Well, what is it?" replied Gergely. "You can come in."

He had not yet gone to sleep. He was reading Horace by candlelight. The two Török boys woke up in the other beds.

"The watchman sent me," said the servant. "A gentleman-looking man is at the gate."

"What's his name?"

"Something like Kecske."[27]

"Kecske? Who on earth can this Kecske be?"

"He came from Győr and wants to stay here."

At hearing the word Győr, Gergely immediately jumped out of bed.

Jancsi Török spoke from under the covers, "Who is it, Gergely?"

"Mekcsey!" said Gergely happily. "Let the hero warrior in immediately!"

The servant ran off.

Gergely quickly pulled on some boots and threw a cloak around his shoulders. The two boys also got up out of bed. (Jancsi was sixteen and Feri already eleven.) They were curious about the visitor about whom all they knew was his name.

"Order some wine and food," said Gergely to them as he went out the door. He rushed downstairs.

When he got down, Mekcsey was already standing in the yard, the watchman and the castle commander by him with a lantern.

Another light also shone down from upstairs. For a while it swung back and forth, then stopped as the visitor arrived and said goodbye to Dobó's soldiers giving them a thaler each.

"Finally I have arrived," he said embracing Gergely. "I almost fell asleep on my horse."

"But older brother, Pista, what's on your head?"

"A turban, damn it! Can't you see that I have become a Turk?"

---

[27] The word *kecske* in Hungarian means goat. It rhymes somewhat with the name Mekcsey.

"Don't joke, brother! The cloth is bloody."

"Well brother, just give me a room and a washbasin, then I will tell you what the road from Győr to Debrecen is like."

A servant girl appeared on the stairs and looked at the newcomer curiously. Gergely indicated to her, "No." The maid disappeared.

Gergely turned to Mekcsey to explain. "Our noble lady is unable to sleep much. She lies awake waiting for her lord to arrive, or a letter from him."

— § —

For three days Mekcsey stayed in bed at the castle with a fever from his head wound. During that time, the Török boys and Gergely continued to sit by his bed. They gave him water mixed with red wine to drink. They listened to him speak with great interest.

The noble lady also came to see him.

Even as sick as he was, Mekcsey related that he came for Gergely to take him to the royal army.

The boys looked at Gergely with surprise. The lady reproached him with a sad face. "How can you leave us? Haven't I been like a mother to you? Haven't my sons been your brothers?"

Gergely replied discouraged. "I'm eighteen already. How can I be living here, idle and useless, when the country needs soldiers?"

He really appeared mature for his age. A light beard was beginning to grow on his fine, almost feminine brown face. His glittering black eyes were all intelligent and serious.

"But are you needed just at this moment?" said Lady Török. "Can't you wait for my sons? Everyone is turning away from us." The woman nodded, wiping her tears away. "Whom God has abandoned, people will also abandon."

Gergely knelt before her and kissed her hand:

"Dear good lady and mother, if this is how you understand me leaving, then nothing will come of it."

Tinódi was also sitting in the room. He had arrived from Érsekújvár that same day. He had come to ask for news about his lord, but of course, he choked back his inquiries when he saw the castle was not flying its flag and the lady was half dressed in mourning clothes.

He was sitting at a window on a chest covered with bearskin, drawing something on his sword. On hearing Gergely's words, he left off his work. "My noble lady, allow me to add something to this conversation."

"Well then, speak Sebők."[28]

"No matter where it goes, a bird always returns to its nest. Gergely also wants to fly around a little. I also will say that it would be good if he saw more of the world. Because, if you please, young lord János will soon become a man, and then it would also be good for him if he had a trained soldier with him."

There was nothing to smile about with these words, but still they smiled. Because scholar Sebők was always joking when he was not singing, and even if he spoke seriously, they would still think there was some humor underneath his words.

"Well, we will think about it," nodded the lady.

And the scholar returned to his work.

"Well, is the verse completed?"

"Yes, indeed. But I don't know if it will please the honorable lord." He held the snake-headed sword and read from it.

> *Who is brave, is strong.*
> *Who is strong can overcome easily*
> *And who overcomes goes forward,*
> *Even death runs away from him.*

"Write this on my sword, too!" said Jancsi Török.

"No," replied Tinódi shaking his head. "I will write something else on that."

Mekcsey spoke from bed. "You also have to write the king's name on Dobó's sword. Something like, 'For God, for Homeland, for King.'"

"That saying is obsolete," replied Tinódi. "It's out of fashion now that a German wears the crown. If he wanted this written on his sword, he would have taken it and written it himself."

"I have something in mind," said Gergely, thumb on his forehead. "When I was a child I heard a saying. That's what need to be inscribed."

"What's that?"

---

[28] Sebők is an old Hungarian nickname for Sebestyén (Sebastian), the first name of Sebestyén "Lántos" (Lutenist) Tinódi.

"*'The most important is, never be afraid.'* It's good this way!" pronounced Gergely.

Tinódi stuck his goose pen into the wooden inkwell at the edge of the window, then drew on his sword.

There was still an unwritten sword. It was a match to that of Dobó. Mekcsey had given it to Gergely.

"Well, what do we write on this?" Tinódi asked. "Will this be good: *'Gergely Bornemissza, saddle more quickly'*!"

They laughed. Gergely shook his head. "No. I don't need a poem, just one word. That one word contains all poems and every thought. Write this on it, older brother Sebők: *For Homeland!*"

— § —

Dobó showed up on the fifth day. They welcomed him with joy. With the lord of the house taken prisoner, it had been years since they had set the table with gold and silverware. The house shone with some unusual laughter.

However, the lady still wore her customary mourning clothes and no jewelry to the dinner table. She sat in her usual seat facing the door. Across from her they also laid a place. At first Dobó thought it was for the priest who was somehow late for the occasion, then he realized the setting was for Bálint Török. They set his place every day, morning, noon and night.

Baroness Török listened to the news that Dobó shared from Vienna and what he had learned from the Hungarian lords still living in the country.

In those days, there were no newspapers. One could only learn through letters and the occasional visitor about what was going on in the world, from which noble family tree a branch had broken off, and which had sprouted a new bud.

For a long time only one man's name was not mentioned in the conversation, that of the lord of the house. Gergely had warned Dobó not to mention or ask about him.

But when the servants had cleared the table and left the dining hall, it was the lady herself who raised the subject. "Well kind sir, have you heard anything about my beloved lord?"

And immediately she burst into tears.

Dobó shook his head. "Until this sultan is dead, he will not return home."

He said this with blunt honesty. In those days, men expressed their thoughts the same way in which they came to their minds.

The woman's head dropped.

Dobó angrily slammed the table. "But how long does he want to live? Such tyrants typically don't live to honorable old age!"

He continued earnestly. "If we can capture some pasha or the other, we can ransom him."

The woman shook her head sadly. "I don't think so, Dobó. They are keeping my lord not just locked up like a horde of treasure, but like they used to cage lions — because they are afraid of him. I have promised them everything," she continued sadly, "I have said, 'take all our property, take all our gold and silver.' The pashas pocket whatever money I send them and the sultan makes no reply."

"Or they don't dare mention the subject to him."

"Is there no other way he could get out?" asked Mekcsey.

Dobó replied, "From Seven Towers? Have you never heard about Seven Towers, my young brother?"

"Sure I have heard. But I have also heard that nothing is impossible if someone really wants."

"My dear young brother Mekcsey," spoke the lady. "Don't you think that my lord and his orphaned family have that strong desire? Haven't I been to the queen, to the Friar, and to the pasha in Buda? I even fell on my knees in front of King Ferdinand. I did not dare write about that to my grieving husband."

As the woman's words drowned in tears, they looked at her in sad silence.

The lady wiped her tears and turned towards Tinódi. "Scholar Sebők," she said with a forced smile on her face, "Do we welcome friends to our house with tears? Come then, take out the lute, and play what my lord liked to hear, just those. We shall close our eyes while your grace is singing and imagine that he is sitting among us."

It had been three years since scholar Sebők last played his lute. The boys became excited in anticipation of this concession.

Scholar Sebők went out to his room and fetched his guitar-like instrument. "The Story of Lady Judith," he said in a quiet, conversational tone as he plucked the melody.

It was good consolation. Everyone understood that Holofernes[29] represented the sultan. But hey, where is the woman Judith who would destroy him off the face of the earth!

As Tinódi reached the middle of the song, the melody his fingers were playing suddenly changed, and his voice changed to a deep, soft drone.

> *Poor Hungary is perishing in tears,*
> *Because lively loudness is leaving it*
> *From it are taken brilliant wealth*
> *And nobility have fallen captives.*

A painful shudder ran through those sitting at the table. Even Dobó's eyes shed tears.

"Shall I continue?" asked Tinódi softly.

The lady nodded.

Tinódi then sang how Lord Bálint was caught in the Turks' net, and how he was taken prisoner, first to Nándorfehérvár, then to Constantinople.

His voice became a painful whisper when he reached the end of his song:

> *Now praying with frequent crying*
> *Your lady wife with your two beautiful sons,*
> *Because they are now orphaned living with their great loss*
> *With their great sorrow, with their loss of their guardian.*
> *There is no joy among your good servants*
> *Who love you deeply with their hearts, and regularly pray,*
> *Some among them are confused exiles,*
> *If you should win your freedom, many still wait.*

Here even the lutenist drowned in tears. Because indeed, he was the confused exile, the servant who cried and prayed for his lord the most.

The two boys held onto their mother and cried, and the mother hugged both of them.

Some minutes passed silently in the sad house before Dobó spoke in a blunt, bitter voice. "Why am I not a free man! If it takes me a year, I will go down to that city, at least look at it, just to see if that prison is as strong as its reputation."

---

[29] A Biblical reference to the Book of Judith. The Neo-Babylonian (Assyrian) King Nebuchadnezzar II sent Holofernes with an army to wreak vengeance upon the Levant. Holofernes was laying siege to Bethulia. Judith, a beautiful Hebrew widow, entered Holofernes's camp, seduced him, then beheaded him while he was drunk.

Mekcsey jumped up. "I am a free man! I swear to the Almighty that I will go down! I will go down! And if I can, even at the cost of my life, I will free Bálint Török!"

Gergely also spoke up. "I am going with you. I will stay with you throughout all dangers for the sake of my lord and my father!"

"My mother," said the shaken boy János Török, "should I stay here when there are men setting off to free my father?"

"It's madness!" said the widow trembling.

"Whether madness or not," said a fired-up Mekcsey, "What I say, I will do."

"I will also go with you," said Tinódi. "My arm is lame, but perhaps my brains will be of use."

The widow spoke again. "What do you want? Something two kings and a king's ransom could not achieve, you think you can accomplish?"

"Our gracious lady speaks well," said Dobó regaining his composure. "Neither money nor cleverness is of any use. Only the sultan's goodwill can loosen his chains."

"But if that goodwill never comes?" snapped Mekcsey.

— § —

The next morning Dobó went on his way. They did not hold him back. They knew that all his time was tailored to be short. Mekcsey stayed with them.

He called Gergely into his room. "I waited so we could sleep on what we talked about last night. Not for my sake, because no matter how long I sleep on what I had said, I am going down to that Turkish land."

"I am with you," said Gergely firmly.

"For now there is no war at home. Then, who knows? Maybe we will find some mouse hole!"

"If we fail, there's no reason to be ashamed."

"Should we take Tinódi?"

"As you wish."

"Well, Janci?"

"Our lady will not let him go."

"Well, let just the two of us go. Let's leave Tinódi at home. The old man can't use a sword or ride a horse."

"As you wish."

"We will be risking our heads. It would be a shame to lead old Tinódi on the road to death. He is among the most worthy men in the country. Even God wants him to roam here and there to light a fire in hearts. This man sounds the pain out of the country's soul."

Jancsi Török opened the door. He had a riding whip in his hand and wore riding pants made of deerskin dyed yellow. On his head a wide brimmed, Debrecen-style cloth cap. Yellow boots on his feet.

Mekcsey, as if just continuing what he had been talking, just glanced at Jancsi and laughed, "That's it! The red rabbit is getting married!"

Then he explained to Jancsi. "You don't know who I am talking about, but perhaps Gergely can tell you."

"Who?" asked Jancsi disinterestedly.

"Ádám Fürjes."

"And who is he marrying?" asked Gergely with a smile.

"The daughter of an old man with a wooden hand."

The color immediately drained from Gergely's face. "Éva Cecey?" he asked, almost shouting.

"Her, her. You know her perhaps?"

Gergely stared at Mekcsey with a face of stone.

"No more comedy," said Jancsi, and he struck his boot with the riding whip. "This isn't what you were talking about. Do you think I am just a child? I am not a child any more. I did not sleep all night. There are some types of fruit that ripen overnight. I matured into a man last night."

"Well, will your mother give you leave?" asked Mekcsey.

"I haven't spoken to her, but it's all the same. There is some work to be done at Hunyad Castle. I will tell her to trust me to get it done."

Mekcsey shrugged. "Accordingly, we can leave."

"Preferably today. That's what I am dressed for."

"Hold on," said Gergely, still very pale. "You mentioned something just now, Pista. Is it true, or is it something you just made up?"

"What I said about Fürjes?"

"That."

"It's true. Her own mother was boasting how the queen herself was giving her to be married to a lieutenant."

Gergely's paleness turned red, the blood vessels in his forehead stood out.

"What's happened?" asked Jancsi. "Perhaps you know her?"

Gergely, his color draining, paced up and down in the room. "Of course I know her! Because she is my Éva!"

"They are taking your Éva away from you?" asked Jancsi astonished.

"That's it. But I don't think so." And he cried out angrily, almost scowling, "I'll kill the villain."

Mekcsey wanted to use his own calmness to appease. "You will kill him. But maybe that girl is in love with him?"

"She doesn't love him!"

"You think they are forcing her?"

"Certainly!"

"And you love her"

"Since childhood."

"Then," Mekcsey said, "we have to do something." Then, leaning on his elbows, he continued. "But even if we do something, you can't marry her. But what if they really have become friends?"

"How can you even think of such a thing!" replied Gergely.

Mekcsey shrugged. "Do you exchange letters?"

"How can we exchange letters? Do you think I have servants to run here and there?"

Mekcsey again shrugged his shoulders.

There was a quick knock on the porch. Jancsi Török jumped to the door and turned the lock slowly.

The next moment the door handle rattled. Jancsi gestured to stay quiet.

Because it was his younger brother who was knocking. He did not want him to know anything about their plans.

4

Queen Isabella wintered in Gyalu, and stayed there even through spring. The two young men, Gergely and Mekcsey, were in Gyalu within three days. Jancsi Török did not accompany them so his mother would not suspect what they had discussed.

Lady Török knew only that Gergely had gone with Mekcsey to join Ferdinand's army, and that he would spend the summer with the soldiers, and return around the feast of St. Demetrius in late October.

However, the plans of the young men had not yet been set. They had agreed that Gergely would find out whether the girl loved him or not. If she loved him, Gergely cannot do anything but say goodbye to his dreams. And if she doesn't love him, then Gergely, as if he had never been there, would disappear. Then Mekcsey would make such a fool of Fürjes that there was no girl in Transylvania who would ever entertain the notion of wanting to marry him.

Once they were finished in Gyalu, the three of them would meet in Hunyad and from there proceed to Constantinople.

They could ride as far as the frontier. Jancsi would keep the money intended for the work at the castle, and whatever other money he could gather because if money was needed, they would have some to work with. Then, from the frontier, they would disguise themselves as dervishes, or merchants, or beggars and proceed on foot so they could pass by without attracting attention from robbers or stray Turkish soldiers. Whether they have success freeing Lord Bálint or not, after two months they would turn back, perhaps sooner, so Lady Török would not worry about her son.

— § —

The two young men arrived in Gyalu in the evening. They were accompanied by only the one servant whom Mekcsey had hired in Debrecen. This lad was called Mátyás. He had been a *csikós* cowboy in the Hortobágy plains. He was sitting on a small, muscular Turkish horse that Mekcsey had kept from the five.

Right at the first house, they asked a Wallachian if he would provide lodging.

The Wallachian understood Hungarian. He shook his head in amazement, together with his tall black cap. "You didn't come for the wedding that you want lodging with me?"

"But indeed, that is why we came."

"If that's why you came, why aren't you staying at the castle?"

The two young me looked at each other.

"I," said Gergely, "will not stay there because I got sick on the road." And indeed, he looked pale, like someone who was sick. "Only my companion will stay there," he continued. "If your front room is vacant, I will pay you."

At the mention of pay, the amazement of the Wallachian softened. He was eager to open the gates to allow the horses to enter.

"Aren't we late for the wedding?" Mekcsey asked.

"How can you be late, gentlemen?" replied the Wallachian. "Don't you know that the wedding is tomorrow?"

When the two young men were left alone in the room, Gergely looked at Mekcsey in despair. "We're late."

"That's what I thought."

Gergely sat on a rough straw chair and stared ahead helplessly.

Mekcsey stood by the window and stared at the lilac bushes that were just beginning to turn green. Finally he turned around and said, "I think it best if we turn back. One dream less, one experience more."

Gergely got up. "No. I do not put my bliss behind me so easily. One day; big time. I was thinking that I would stay here. You should go up to the castle and join the guests."

"What if they ask?"

"Didn't Cecey invite you? The main thing is to find the girl and find out if she chose Fürjes because of her heart. But that is impossible! Impossible! Impossible!"

"Well, good. I will go up to the castle and stay there with Mátyás, if they accept me."

"Tell them Cecey invited you. After all, you saved the old man's life."

"That's for sure. I also think that no matter what expression is on his face when he greets me, the result will be that I get inside the castle and speak to the girl. If possible, today; if not, tomorrow. But couldn't you come with me somehow? Maybe you can be my apprentice."

"No. If the girl says she was forced, then it is better that they don't know that I am here."

"Then I'll punch up Fürjes!"

"Don't plan on anything until you talk to the girl. Then come back right away and we'll see ..."

The Wallachian woman made a soft bed for Gergely and offered him some medicine with a wet cloth. But the patient did not lie down, did not drink any flower-infused water, or put a wet cloth on his head. He just paced up and down in the room, banging the air with his fists.

Mekcsey returned in the morning. He found Gergely sitting at the table, a candle burning in front of him. He was leaned over, sleeping on his arms.

"Why didn't you lie down?"

"I thought I would not be able to sleep."

"Well, I talked to the girl. You guessed correctly. Her heart is not leading her to Fürjes."

Gergely shook as if water had been poured down his back. The fire returned to his eyes.

"Did you say that I'm here?"

"I said. She wanted to run to you, but I held her back."

"Why did you hold her back?" fired back Gergely.

"Oh, no. You jumping on me is a fine thank you."

"Don't be angry! For me, coals are burning under my feet."

"Well, the reason I didn't bring her to you is that the entire court would have followed. It would bring shame on her and trouble for us."

"What did you tell her?"

"That I will mock Fürjes, and that she can return his ring."

"How did she reply?" asked Gergely with fire in his eyes.

"That the queen had arranged for the wedding, that she could not get out of it, and that even her parents were forcing her into it. So the old queen in her great winter boredom is playing matchmaker. Fürjes, of course, gets the girl. Then the girl, to stay in the good favor of the queen, puts her own heart in the queen's hands, offered with fine virgin humility."

"But why is she offering it to her! Perhaps she has forgotten. She has forgotten."

"Of course she hasn't forgotten. What I said did not come out right, but I know how it was!"

"Well, what did she say! Did she very clearly say that she did not love Fürjes?"

"She did."

"And that she wants to speak with me?"

"With you. I told her that I would bring you to her tonight."

Gergely paced back and forth in the room, then slumped into the rough straw chair.

"What's the use even if we manage to get Fürjes out of the saddle? They wouldn't give her to me even if I could marry her. Who am I? No one. Neither my father nor my mother nor my little house. It is true that the Török family raised me as if I were their own son, but I was never such a son that I would dare to open my mouth for such a request. Especially now when their own nest has fallen apart!"

Mekcsey stood at the window with folded arms and looked at Gergely with pity.

"I don't know what you're saying, but I see you're confused. After all, if you want to marry a girl, you don't need a father or a mother, just a little home. If you want, I have a small house in Zemplén. It's empty. You can live there for ten years."

"You need an oven in the house, and bread in the oven!"

"Aren't you a scholar? You know more than any priest. Nowadays, people are looking for a good secretary."

Gergely was encouraged. "That's an idea."

"What's important now is that Éva doesn't marry. You will come to the army camp with me, and within a year you will have enough money to support her!"

Gergely put on his cloak, his sword, and his cap. "I'm going," he said, "to her father and her mother. I will tell them that what they are planning is against God's will! That ..."

Mekcsey pushed him back into the straw chair.

"You'll be going to a fiery hell! They will shut you in some prison until the wedding is completed. I tell you, no one will even see the tip of your nose!"

Horsemen rode by the front of the house. Guests were arriving from Kolozsvár.

— § —

When darkness descended in the valley, Gergely went up to the castle with Mekcsey.

No one asked who he was. The castle shook with guests. Windows shone with light. Torches threw light in the courtyard and wax candles lit up hallways. The only darkness was the dark sky.

People came and went like rabbits in the hallways. Gergely's heart tightened. With so many people about, how could he talk to Éva?

"Let's go to the kitchen yard," Mekcsey said.

They ended up in the area in back of the castle. There was even more light there. Kitchen servants wearing leather aprons were turning an ox on a six-foot long iron spit, and inside the kitchen, numerous kitchen workers dressed in white were fussing about and cooking.

"Wait here," Mekcsey said. "I'm going to accidently wander into the women's corridor and find out from Éva where you can meet."

Gergely mingled with the group that was watching the ox roast. Mostly the work had been entrusted to wagon driver people, but there were some pages among them.

Curiosity had attracted them there. People have all sorts of grandiose ideas about the royal kitchen, but even the rural gentry are eager to learn how things are prepared in the country's largest kitchen.

In Gyalu, the kitchen building stood between the castle and the garden. A grey haired roasting master was giving instructions to eleven cooks and twenty assistant cooks on how the turn the spit.

Not even one woman was there.

A large, fattened ox was turning on the spit in the kitchen yard and giving the air a delicious smell. The roasting master, just by pointing his stick, was indicating how to arrange the fire so it would give off heat evenly.

In the hell of fire and heat, pestles rang in mortars, chopping knives clattered, and mallets slammed meat, all the while porridge bubbled and roasts sizzled, smoked and steamed, their smells thick in the air.

One rabbit of a page yelled an explanation to the others, "I've been here from the beginning, but they don't roast fattened ox here like anywhere else."

The hot breath of fire flooded the small courtyard and reddened faces. Gergely, flushed from the heat like the others, listened with amusement to the boy's tale.

"But here," the boy continued, "they stitched an entire calf into the ox, a fattened male turkey inside the calf, and a game bird inside the turkey."

"What about the game bird?" asked a small page dressed in yellow.

"Inside that," he replied seriously, "the egg of a male goose. The youngest page has to eat it."

They laughed. The little page stepped backwards embarrassed, then left the area.

Half an hour later, the roasting master indeed went after the ox and pulled out a half-baked turkey

The smell of marjoram wafted under the noses of those watching, creating an appetite even among those not hungry. It was not fully roasted yet. The coals were pushed back under the ox and they kept turning the spit.

From the kitchen the sounds of pestles grinding mortars, grating, and mallets beating meat blocked further explanation.

But Gergely was not interested. There was a time when his lord had a larger kitchen, and this kind of ox roasting was more common in Lord Bálint's castles that at the Transylvanian court of the queen.

A servant in livery brought out a fresh, warm loaf from the kitchen. The pages grabbed it from him and tore it to pieces. Our rabbit of a page, the one who had just explained the roast, gave Gergely a piece. Gergely accepted it. He was hungry.

The roasting master, seeing that the pages were snacking, stopped the spit from turning, took the knife that was hanging off his belt, and sharpened its edge over the steel spit. He cut off the ox's two ears and gave them to the pages. They thanked him with shouts of "*Vivat.*"

Gergely ate with a good appetite. At the Wallachians, he had received nothing for lunch but porridge. Pages had also laid their hands on some cups of wine. Gergely also drank, then extended his hand to the page who had offered it to him without even knowing who he was. "I am Gergely Bornemissza," he said wiping his mustache.

The other fellow said his name, but neither understood the other. Meanwhile, the cup found its way back. Gergely was still thirsty. He took a big swallow.

As he took the cup from his mouth, he saw Mekcsey in front of him.

Mekcsey waved at him to follow.

They went down to the garden. There was a mist among the trees and bushes. The garden was sheltered from the noise in the kitchen yard.

Mekcsey stopped under an elder tree. "Well, I talked to the girl. Her eyes are red from constant crying. She pleaded with her mother and her father not to make her marry, except to you sometime in the future. They are, of course, blinded by the light, the goodness of the queen, and the generosity of the Friar. They tried to comfort their daughter by telling her that they were not in love when they were married, but they got used to each other."

Gergely listened with shallow breaths.

"That's why she cried," Mekcsey continued. "That she loves only you is certain."

"And she marries Fürjes."

"Not really. She says she wants to speak to you, and that she will also speak to the queen."

"Why hasn't she talked with her already?"

"No one asked for the girl's opinion. This kind of queen is accustomed to thinking that whatever she thinks up is a good idea, and no one dares contradict her. And then she didn't even take the slightest notice of you. She didn't even know if you were alive or dead."

"And if the queen won't allow?"

"Then she can say no at the altar tomorrow. She can say no to everything. It's going to be great confusion. But anyway, at worst, the queen gets angry and goes home to Buda. And with time, you can marry her."

"But then they won't give her to me."

"But of course they will. But let's not talk about what's going to happen in four years. The girl will come here at midnight, if not earlier. There's some sort of house here, a greenhouse. She said wait there. She won't go to bed until she has talked with you."

They soon found the greenhouse in the garden. A lantern was burning in it. Three gardeners were leaning over picking salad greens and leeks. One and the other looked up, but none said anything. They must have thought they were just curious strangers.

"Well, Gergely," Mekcsey said, "I'll leave you here. Say you're sick or pretend to be drunk. Lie down somewhere and wait for the bride. Maybe I'll come with her."

And he left.

Gergely really did feel like he was drunk. Did wine get into his head or was it his emotion? He felt a heat in his heart, as he did in his head, a kind of angry heat that made him clench his fists.

He walked through the greenhouse among lemon trees, banana trees, and fig trees. He paced up and down anxiously and faster. Suddenly he just emerged from the greenhouse. He pulled his hat over his eyes, squeezed his hand on his sword, and walked up to the castle.

"Which is the room of the bride's happy parents?" he asked in the hallways. Pages pointed him in the direction. It was a room with a white door. It had, like every door, a piece of dark slate on it with the guest's name written on it with chalk.

Gergely knocked.

The old man with his wood hand was sitting in front of the table dressed in shirt sleeves. His wife was rubbing rosemary oil on her husband's gray hair.

Gergely didn't kiss their hands. He just bowed curtly and stood in the frozen stares of the old couple.

"My lord father," Gergely began.

Then, finding the word *father* unsuitable, he started again. "Respected sir, don't be angry because I am here. I did not come here for the wedding, and I will not get in anyone's way. I did not even come here to remind you of your old promise when I freed little Éva from the Turks."

"What do you want!" growled old Cecey.

"I just want to ask," Gergely said firmly. "Do you know that Vica does not like her fiancé?"

"That's none of your business!" retorted the old man. "What are you blaring at me! Get out of here!"

Gergely folded his arms. "Do you want to make your daughter unhappy?"

"How dare you question us, you! You whelp! Peasant dog!" yelled the old man turning blue in the face. He grabbed the wooden hand lying on the table and was ready to throw it at Gergely.

"Go away, son, out of here! Don't ruin our daughter's luck! Since childhood you have been thinking you love each other, but you see, that young man is already a lieutenant ..."

"I also will be."

"He is not a *will be*, but an *is*. The queen wants this marriage. For the love of God I ask you, go away from here!"

"Fürjes is only a cowardly plate-licker. Vica loves me. Vica can only be happy with me! Don't break her heart! Wait for me to take it. I swear I will be worthy!" A tear glistened in his eyes. He knelt before them.

The old man screamed furiously, "Get out or I will kick you out!"

Gergely got up. He shook his head as if awakening from a bad dream.

"My lord Cecey," he said obstinately, grimly. "From this moment, I do not know your grace. All I want to know is, whether you have the gold on which my mother's blood was spilled."

"Three hundred fifteen," the old man shouted. "Pay him, woman. Even if nothing remains, pay him!"

That said, she reached for her waist. She pulled out a thin leather pouch and poured the gold in front of Gergely. The woman counted out Gergely's inheritance on the table, or rather, his military booty. Gergely put the gold pieces in his pockets.

He stood still for a moment. Perhaps he was wondering whether he should thank them for anything? That they had kept his money? But they did not keep it for him, but for their daughter.

He bowed silently and left them.

— § —

He was pale as he walked in the hallway. Here and there he encountered nobles dressed in fancy clothes, then he stood against the wall to give way to an approaching fat gentleman.

Meanwhile, his eyes glanced upon the opposite door and he read the name, Mekcsey.

He opened the door. There was no one in the room. Candles were burning on the table.

Gergely threw himself on the bed and wept. Why did he cry? He himself didn't know. His pockets were full of money. In that hour he had become a master and a free man. And yet he felt orphaned and abandoned. How many insults, how much contempt he had to endure!

"You pagan old man, even your heart is made of wood!"

The castle walls were shaken by a horn. It was the call for guests to gather for dinner.

In the hallway, doors swung open from all directions, and some were also slammed shut. Many boots were tramping down the marble squares of the corridor floors.

Then there was a pause, and the door to the room opened.

"Mekcsey," said a female voice softly.

Gergely jumped up.

Éva was standing in front of him wearing a pink silk dress.

A little shock, a slight scream, and then the two young people dissolved into each other's arms.

"My Évi! My Évi!"

"Gergely!"

"Will you come with me, Éva?"

"Even to the end of the world!"

— § —

About seventy people were sitting around the dinner table. More than half were from the royal court. The others were invited relatives of the groom.

The queen sat at the head of the table with her son. Both of them in green velvet. Behind them on the wall was a flower arrangement made to look like the crown. To the left of the queen sat Friar György. The bride and her happy mother sat beside the little king.

The groom sat opposite the bride.

Dinner started quietly. People were just here and there, whispering. After the third course, Friar György got up and congratulated the new couple. In his speech, he called the queen a lucky star, the bride a lily, and the groom favored by fortune. Here and there he showered verbal flowers and sugarcanes, and even those who were enemies were eager to listen.

By the time the best of the wines ended up on the table, the conversations began. Of course, they talked only softly and only to their neighbors.

"Why do they call this the night of crying?" asked one.

"The bride is mourning the loss of being a girl."

"But she isn't crying. She's as cheerful as if she's happy to be done with being a girl."

"I am surprised that the queen permits her to leave."

"She won't let her go. Until now she was a palace girl, and after she will be a palace woman."

After dinner, a new singer was introduced to the company. He came from somewhere in Italy and he had already demonstrated his abilities to the queen.

While he was singing, the bride, with a dreamy face, whispered softly to her mother. "Mother, what if I died today?"

The woman looked at her shocked, but when she smiled, she replied only with a reproach, "My daughter, how can you say such a thing!"

"But still ..."

"Come on, come on."

"Would you cry over me?"

"I would follow you and die, and your father also."

"But what if I were to be resurrected in a month, or maybe in two, and sneak into your house in Buda?"

The woman stared at her daughter.

Éva continued smiling. "Well, you see, you would regret it lying in the dirt for being in such a rush to follow my death."

And she got up. She moved behind the queen. She leaned over her ear and whispered something into it.

The girl hurried out of the room.

The guests listened to the singer. He had a nice baritone voice. They liked it. They applauded.

"Another one," said the queen.

And for more than half an hour, the singer entertained the crowd.

Only her mother saw Éva leave, and as her daughter's words echoed in her mind, she became more and more anxious.

— § —

When the Italian was finally done, the doorman shouted, "New singer! No name!"

All eyes turned to the door, but they saw only a slim, fifteen-year-old boy. He was dressed in cherry-colored satin; his robe reached halfway to his thigh. He wore a small, gold-plated sword around his waist. He came in with his head down. His long hair covered his face. He knelt before the queen.

Then he rose and shook his hair to expose his face.

The guests gasped in surprise. The singer was the bride herself.

One of the queen's pages followed her carrying a small harp. He handed it to her in the middle of the room. The bride plucked the strings.

She sang.

With her attention on the queen, she began with a Polish song which she had learned from the queen herself. She had a wonderful silver tone. Listeners even stopped breathing.

She sang a Hungarian song, a Wallachian lament, then Italian, French, Croatian and Serbian songs. After each song the guests applauded enthusiastically.

"She's a great devil!" said Mekcsey's neighbor, a court dignitary. "See, my young brother, she'll even dance."

"Is she always so happy?" Mekcsey asked.

"Always. The queen already would have died of grief if that girl hadn't been by her side."

"He's getting a good deal that ... Fürjes."

He wanted to say, bloody.[30]

The speaker shrugged. "He's a mommy's boy. You will see that she will go to war instead of him. Because she can fight better than he."

"She handles a weapon?"

"What? This last summer she was defeating Italians at fencing. Then with a horse, how she can ride! She has enough fire for seven men, and still have some left over for the devil."

The bride, praised in this fashion, began another Hungarian song, for which these were always its words:

---

[30] In Hungarian, Fürjes rhymes somewhat with *véres* (bloody).

Go, lad, quickly
On your crane-haired steed
To your sweetheart!

The guests were familiar with this song, but the words they were expecting sounded like this from the bride:

Go, lad, quickly
On your crane-haired steed
To your Gergely!

And as the bride sang this, her gaze slid down the row of guests and settled upon Mekcsey.

The guests laughed. They thought that *to your Gergely* was variation for a joke.

But Mekcsey was shaking. When the bride looked at him at the end of the second verse, he sipped his wine and slipped out.

He ran down the stairs and called to the stable, "Matyi! Matyi Balogh!"

Not a soul replied. He had to search for his servant among the wagoneers. They were in the kitchen yard drinking from cups, pots and even boots.

Somehow he could identify his servant from among them. But his disheveled hair, what condition! Matyi looked like a man sitting at the table, but as soon as he tried to stand up, he was no man.

Some ten men were already lying under the table and near the wall. The one lying under the table was left alone, but those who had fallen behind the bench had been dragged into a pile by the wall.

Matyi got up, that is, he just wanted to get up when he recognized his master, but he quickly sat down again because he felt that he would also fall behind the bench and would end up being pulled to the pile by the wall.

"Matyi!" yelled Mekcsey. "Damn your father! Where's my horse?!"

Matyi got up again and leaned on the table. "Over there."

"But where?"

"With the horses."

And holding his eyelids open, he continued, "Horse's place among horses."

Mekcsey grabbed him by the collar. "Speak smart, because I'm about to shake you so hard your soul will fall out."

He could shake the man all he wanted. Even the man's soul was drunk.

Mekcsey pushed him back among the others, then hurried to the stable to find his horse himself. The stable master was also drunk. Mekcsey could have taken as many horses from him as he wanted. He went through the dark barn and shouted: "Muszta!"

From one corner sounded the whinny that answered his call. It was the yellow horse, and next to it Matyi's horse. Mekcsey saddled them both with the help of a half-drunk servant and left before anyone could ask him why he was leaving so early, before dinner was over.

Gergely was waiting for him in the courtyard of the Wallachian house. His horse was neighing as it pawed the ground by the fence.

The night was cool. The clouds seemed to be standing still. But the moon, like a half of a silver plate, was slowly rising from cloud to cloud, filling the landscape with its pale light.

"I came," said Mekcsey. "I understood the bride as telling me to come here."

"You understood correctly," replied Gergely. "Tonight we are escaping."

In less than half an hour, the shadow of a man arrived in front of the house, quickly opened the gate, and came into the yard.

It was Vica.

She had escaped in the cherry-colored satin robe in which she had been singing.

5

The highway to Adrianople was just as dusty and as rutted as the highways to Gyöngyös or even Debrecen. But all the tears shed on that highway to Adrianople! If they were transformed into pearls, how many pearls there would be in the world! And perhaps they would be called Hungarian pearls!

Each of the inns at the end of the town was a little Babel. You could speak any of the world's languages in them. But whether they understood one other is another matter. And most of all, they do not understand when a man accustomed to a gentleman's life needs a private room, a clean bed and other such accommodations.

The inn, that is to say, the *caravanserai*, is the same in every place in the East. Large lead roof building; its courtyard surrounded by stone walls the height of a man. Next to and on the inside of the stone wall is another small low and wide stone structure.

I would describe it as a bed, but it is not a bed, because it is just a wide, flat wall. But if I say it is a wall, then it is more like a bed because that is where travelers stay the night so frogs do not jump into their pockets.

However, the Turks require such a resting place. On it he cooks his dinner, to it he ties his horse, and on it he sleeps. If it happens at night that the horse bumps its head on its owner, well, he slaps the horse's head, but then relaxes because his horse is still with him. He turns to the other side and goes back to sleep.

One May evening, two young Turkish horsemen arrived in the Adrianople caravanserai. They wore Hungarian clothes: tight blue trousers, blue *atilla* hussar's jackets, yellow cloth belts, and handkerchiefs in their belts; on their shoulders, generous rust-colored camelhair coats with their hoods pulled over their heads. At first glance, they looked like *deli* irregular cavalrymen serving under the flag of true faith only in war, and otherwise living off of theft. Hungarian clothing is actually Turkish clothing: both are eastern peoples. The *deli* were all Turkish.

No one in the caravanserai bothered with them. At most they were interested in their wagon because two handsome slave boys were sitting in it, and two handsome horses were pulling it.

The wagon driver was also a slave and young. The slaves were either Hungarian or Croatian, but that they were nobles was obvious from their faces and hands. Well, wherever those two *deli* had plundered them, they would fetch a good price in the slave market!

The caravanserai yard was crowded with all sort of people. Turks, Bulgarians, Serbs, Albanians, Greeks and Wallachians; women, children, merchants and soldiers, all in a noisy jumble. That highway was like the Danube: everything flowed into it. No wonder that every night and every morning caravanserais were a buzzing Babel of jumbled languages.

The sun was setting. People were watering, some horses, others camels. Everyone was hurrying to claim a space on the wall, covering it with a mat or a rug. He who had neither a mat nor a rug piled hay and straw so the stone would not break his waist.

As the two *deli* arrived in the courtyard, one of them, a young man with brave eyes and hardly eighteen, shouted for the innkeeper, "*Meyhaneci*!"

A stocky man in a turban stepped out of the porch and asked how he could be of help.

"Do you have a room, *meyhaneci*? I will pay you."

"It was taken an hour ago," replied the innkeeper.

"Who took it? I'll pay him too, if you allow."

"You will have some trouble paying for it. The noble Altin Agha is occupying it!" He gestured respectfully toward the porch, on which a raven-like black Turk was sitting on a small carpet. His legs were folded under him in Turkish fashion.

From his clothes, he certainly appeared to be a gentleman. His turban had two white ostrich feathers. Next to him was a servant fanning him. Another servant was mixing a drink for him. There were about twenty other servants in the courtyard dressed half-red, half-blue. They drank; they cooked. One was washing the agha's underwear at the well, another was pulling a bedroll down from a camel's back. It was a thick and expensive wool bedroll.

Well, it certainly appeared problematic to take his room away.

The two unhappy *deli* turned back to the wagon. The wagon driver soon unhitched the horses and untied the prisoners' hands. He watered the horses. Then he started a fire on the top of the stone wall and set up a pot to cook dinner.

The two young prisoners do not seem to be sad. It is true that their two Turk captors treated them with respect. They ate together from the same pot and drank from the same cup. Well, they must have been very distinguished prisoners.

The agha was already having his dinner. His cook had placed rice stew in a silver bowl in front of his carpet. He ate with his fingers, because eating with a knife and fork was not only unnecessary, but inappropriate. Only unclean infidels eat with tools at a table.

Next to the two *deli* was a one-eyed, barefoot dervish. He was wearing no clothes other than a rust-colored cloak made of hair that reached down to the ankles. The cloak was tied around the waist with a rope, and a worn coconut shell cup hung on the rope. There was no hat on his head. His long, unkempt hair was tied into a knot. That was his hat. He held a long stick capped with a copper moon. His cloak was gray from the dust of the road.

The dervish stumbled across the wall and looked over at the company having dinner next to him.

"Are you not disciples of the prophet?" he asked the two *deli* seriously.

They looked at him annoyed. "Maybe better than you," replied the younger, a brown-skinned and shiny black-eyed young man. "For there are many wandering dervishes who respect the prophet only with his belly."

"I ask," the dervish replied, rubbing his droopy eye, "because you are eating with the unclean."

"They are already true believers, janissary," answered the *deli* looking over his shoulder.

The dervish stared at the *deli*, then stood tall and stroked the thirteen whiskers of his beard with five fingers. "How do you know me?"

"How do I know you?" replied the young man with a smile. "I know you from when you were a warrior, when you were bearing the padishah's weapons."

"Have you been in camp for that long?"

"Five years."

"I do not remember you."

"But why did you abandon serving the flag of glory?"

Before the dervish could answer, there was a cruel scream from the porch, so terrible that it made the horses rear up.

It was the agha screaming. The young men looked to see what it was. All they could see was that the agha's face was red and he was drinking.

"What's happened to that man?" asked the *deli* from the dervish.

The dervish waved his hand in contempt. "Don't you see him drinking wine?"

"How can I see it? He's drinking from a flask."

"Perhaps you are not born a Muslim?"

"Certainly, my friend, I was born Dalmatian. It was only five years ago that I learned true faith."

"That's it," the dervish said calmly. "Well, know that the agha was screaming because his soul dribbles down from his head and stays in his feet as long as he is drinking. Because the soul resides in the head, and it leaves for the next world when we die. There, you know, the true believers are punished for drinking."

"But if the soul is not guilty?"

"Well, he also thinks that his soul won't be affected by sin if he scares it for a minute. But I just think that this kind of clever trickery is no good."

He sighed. "You just asked me why I left the holy flag."

"I did indeed. Because you were a brave soldier, and still young, probably only thirty-five."

The dervish looked pleased. But then his face became sad again. He waved it off.

"Bravery is nothing without luck. I was always a warrior while I had my amulet. I got it on the battlefield from a dying old bey. Some hero's soul is in it. That hero fought beside the prophet. But his soul is still fighting for the one who has that ring. Then I was captured and a priest took it from me. While that amulet was with me, no bullet or sword could touch me. As soon as it wasn't with me, one wound after another! My officers hated me. My father, the famous Pasha of Buda, Oglu Muhammad, chased me away. My brother, the famous Arslan Bey, quarreled with me. My companions stole from me. I was even taken prisoner twice. All luck has left me."

The *deli* looked at the left hand of the dervish, which had a large red wound along the index finger. It was as if at some point his index finger had been cut all the way to the wrist, then welded together. "You have a scar on your hand."

"Yes. I couldn't move it for a year. Finally a holy dervish recommended that I visit Mecca three times. Well, it healed with the first turn."

"In that case, you will remain a dervish."

"I don't know. I think my luck will come back, however, and if I take the holy pilgrimage twice more, I can rejoin the army. But hey, until I find my amulet, everything is uncertain."

"You still have hope that you will find it?"

"If I complete the thousand and one days, everything is possible."

"You are doing penance for a thousand and one days?"

"Thousand and one."

"And you visit mosques."

"No. I am just taking the road from Pécs to Mecca. And every day I read my beads and repeat the name of Allah a thousand and one times."

"It's amazing that a clever man like you ..."

"No one is clever before Allah. We are worms."

The dervish already held a long string of ninety-nine beads. He started praying. The wagon driver cleared his dinner and took out the rugs. He laid two on the wall. The third covered the wagon. The youngest prisoner took the car as his bed. The tongue of the wagon was lifted to the wall. One of the *deli* lay beside the tongue and put a saddle under his head.

He will be the sentry while the others sleep.

The moon flooded the caravanserai almost as if daylight. People were visible lying on the wall and getting ready for a night's rest. Only the mixed stench of horses and onions did not calm down, and bats hovered here and there over the courtyard.

A servant with red facings stepped across the yard and stopped in front of the *deli* who was about to settle in for sleep.

"The agha calls. He wants to talk to you."

The other *deli* rose uneasily from his bed, and as his companion silently responded to the invitation, he watched after him. He tied on his sword, which had been lying loose beside him.

The agha was still sitting on the porch. But he was no longer screaming. His red face was staring at the moonlight.

The *deli* bowed before him.

"Where are you coming from, son?" asked the agha.

"From Buda, sir," the *deli* replied. "For now, the pasha has no need for us."

"You brought such beautiful horses that I could not help but stare. You want to sell?"

"No, sir."

The agha gave the young man an angry look. "Have you seen my horses?"

"I haven't seen them, sir."

"Well, look at them tomorrow. If you like them, we can make an exchange."

"Possible, sir. Is there anything else you would like?"

"You can go."

And the agha's eyebrows were furrowed as he looked at the *deli* leave.

— § —

Everyone was already asleep. The agha entered his room and lay down behind the white curtained window. The inn was filled with snoring and horses crunching on oats. Every minute there was the sound of a horse stomping, but that did not bother the sleepers. Travelers are tired and sleep as if everything is silent and they are lying in a silk bed.

The moon rose slowly in the sky like part of a gold bowl that had been broken in half.

When no one seemed to be awake, the elder *deli* raised his head. He looked around. The young prisoner also moved.

And all three of them put their heads together.

"What did the agha want?" the older *deli* asked in Hungarian.

"He liked our horses. He wanted to buy them."

"And what did you say?"

"That they weren't for sale."

"Of course they're not for sale."

"We left it that we would exchange them tomorrow. We'll exchange our horses for some of his."

The carpet covering the wagon separated, and the beautifully engraved face of the youngest prisoner leaned out. "Gergely ..."

"Pssst," replied the third *deli*. "What do you want, Vicus? There is nothing wrong. Go to sleep."

"What did the agha want?"

"He was only asking about our horses. Sleep, dear." And as the two faces were close, they touched with a soft kiss.

The three young men exchanged a few more words.

"There's nothing to fear," Gergely encouraged. "We move on before dawn and leave the agha here with his horses."

"But I'm not going to be a prisoner tomorrow," said Jancsi Török. "Make Mekcsey the prisoner tomorrow. It's so boring to riding in a wagon with hands tied up. Then all that gold weighs terribly. Still, it would be wiser to hide it in the wagon."

"Okay, okay," said Gergely, "I'll gladly be the prisoner tomorrow, but when do we get changed? It's not possible at night because maybe the agha will wake up early."

"Well then, tomorrow, Gergely, while we are on the road. May the devil take this agha!"

Mekcsey shook his head. "I don't like this. These lords are not used to a *deli* dressed in rags denying them their wishes."

"Just you both be careful," said Gergely, "that when someone comes close, do not speak in Hungarian. That dervish understands Hungarian."

The dervish was lying next to them. He was curled up, like a hedgehog.

— § —

In the morning, when the sun was rising, the agha stepped out of the door to his room and released the remaining slumber in his head with a huge yawn. "Squinty," he said to the servant bowing before him. "Where are those two *deli*?"

The servant turned around to give the yard a good look.

The dervish was squatting next to the door. Upon hearing the agha talk, he got up. "They're gone, my lord."

"They are gone?" grumbled the agha. "They've gone?"

"Gone."

"How dare they leave?"

"That's why I was waiting for you, my lord. Those two *deli* are not regular people."

"How do you know?"

"I listened to them last night."

"What did they talk about?"

"This and that. But mostly, that it was not good for them to meet men like you."

The agha's eyes were staring.

"Then we have to take away their horses, their prisoners, their wagon, everything."

And as he said, his voice grew louder and louder with every word. By the last word, he was yelling.

"They also have money," the dervish continued. "One of the prisoners said he was unable to carry the gold."

"Gold? Hey *sipahis*! Everyone mount up! After those two *deli*! Bring them back here dead or alive! But mainly, bring back their wagon!"

Within the next minute twenty-two mounted *sipahis* galloped out the caravanserai gates.

The agha looked at them leave, then turned towards the dervish. "What else did you talk about?"

"I didn't understand everything. They spoke in whispers. This much is certain, that they spoke in Hungarian and that one of the prisoners is a woman."

"A woman? That I didn't see."

"They dressed her in men's clothing."

"Pretty?"

"Charming."

The agha's eyes opened wide and blinked. "You will get your share of the booty." And he went back inside his room.

"My lord," called the dervish after him, "I used to be a janissary. Would you allow me to ride one of your horses?"

"I also am going," said the fired-up agha. "So saddle me one, too!" He strapped on his sword and soon they were riding off.

They caught up with the twenty-two armed *sipahi* servants on the Constantinople highway. The servants saw their lord chasing after them. They stopped to look back. The agha gestured for them to keep going forward.

The horses' hooves kicked up white clouds of dust from the highway.

Within two hours, the agha heard howling and shouting indicating that his servants had spotted the wagon.

By then, the servants were already at the crest of a hill, and as the highway descended on the other side, they disappeared from the agha's sight. The agha could hardly wait to get to the crest of the hill.

He spurred his horse and galloped, driven by the thought of rich booty. Behind him was a dervish looking like a hairy devil on a horse. He squeezed and flogged his horse. His knotted hair had fallen apart making his head look like some large, disheveled broom. The agha had given him a sword so suddenly that he did not even have time to tie it around his waist so he held it in his hand and was using it to slap the horse, sometimes on its chest, sometimes on its rump.

When they reached the crest they saw that their quarry was still a long way ahead, but they had already sensed their danger.

Indeed, the two prisoners grabbed weapons from the wagon rack and lept upon horses. The driver fumbled and pulled out some things from the wagon and gave them to the riders. They put them in front of their saddles. Then the driver crawled under the wagon. White smoke rose up from under the wagon. Then the driver also got on a horse and rode off after the other four riders.

The agha was amazed. "What kind of prisoners are they," he called back to the dervish, "that they don't want to be released?"

"I told you they were dogs!" shouted the dervish.

The fire was already burning the wagon. The *sipahis* were standing around it confused.

"Put it out!" yelled the agha. "Break up the wagon! Tear it apart!" Then he shouted again, "Three of you stay here. The rest after the dogs!"

At that moment, the wagon exploded with a huge noise and an eruption of flames. There was no more wagon, no more men, only the horrible dervish, numbed and deafened by the concussion from the blast, like a witch's cat on top of a chimney.

— § —

"What was that?" scowled the agha lying in the dust of the highway where his horse had bucked him.

The dervish wanted to get off his horse, but the horse was terrified. It danced backwards and reared up on two hind legs. Then the horse took off into the fields in a frantic gallop. Foaming at the mouth, it bucked the dervish into the air, jumped over a ditch covered with bushes.

The agha got up. He spat out dust and angrily cursed pagans.

He looked around.

The highway looked like a battlefield: writhing horses and *sipahis* lying about. Where the wagon had stood was a big nothing. A wide, walnut-brown cloud hung over the highway where the wagon had been.

The agha's horse had also run away. The raven-faced lord did not even know where to turn. Finally he limped towards his soldiers.

Well, they had been scattered by the explosion. One man's head here, another man's foot there were lying in the dust, and those bodies that remained in one piece were not pretty to look at.

The agha saw that no one was moving. He sat down by the side of the ditch and stared stupidly in front of him. Perhaps he was wondering from where and why bells were ringing so loudly. Of course, no bells were ringing, only his ears.

He was still in that deaf chicken condition when the dervish found him half an hour later. He had managed to hang onto his wildly galloping horse and return, the horse dripping foam from its muzzle and covered in sweat.

He tied the trembling horse to a beech tree by the side of the road and hurried to the agha.

"Are you hurt, my lord?"

The agha shook his head. "Nothing."

"But you have been hit somewhere?"

"My buttocks."

"Blessed be Allah, who delivered me from this peril!"

"Be blessed!" the agha repeated automatically.

The dervish walked along the highway looking at the horses lying about to see if any was able to stand up. No, none. Some were still alive, but so badly injured that only the ravens could appreciate them for anything.

He returned to the agha. "My lord," he said, "can you stand on your feet? Or should I put you on this horse?"

The agha rubbed his leg and knee. "I will get my revenge. But where can I get horses and soldiers?" He looked stupidly at the dervish.

"Those damned dogs surely are headed for Istanbul. We can find them there," said the dervish expressing his opinion.

The agha struggled to get up. He groaned. He patted his buttocks. "Come. Help me get on the horse and lead me back to the inn. Stay with me as my servant. You're a good rider."

"Servant?" asked the dervish in shock. But then he bowed his head humbly. "As you command."

"What is your name?"

"Yumurjak."

6

Meanwhile the five Hungarian riders had galloped farther along the highway to Constantinople. The explosion had also frightened their horses, but that gave them little trouble. They flew that much more quickly. One passed the other in turns in their furious dash. Others on the road, seeing them coming from a distance, pulled off to the side to get out of the way.

But how did Éva Cecey end up with them?

That festive evening, before the wedding eve banquet when she met Gergely, old feelings arose inside her: that she and Gergely are one. She had these thoughts earlier, but because she was being pressured from all sides, she felt she could not escape. Gergely had no house, no land, not even his own table. He was tied to his guardian, still only a young boy. They could not even send each other letters. So she had begun to accept her fate.

But Gergely's appearance undermined every other power.

A woman thinks with her heart. Éva's heart told her: This is your true partner! Even if the entire world speaks against him, you are created for him! And she tore herself away from rational reasoning and followed her inner instinct, which was more powerful than the queen's word, and more powerful than her mother's.

They fled over the Gyalu Mountains, and by the morning light they were by the waters of the Aranyos.

The forest glistened in the pale green of new foliage. Violets were blooming everywhere, and the valley was carpeted in the yellows of cinquefoil, dandelions and lilies. The air was full of the fragrance of pine.

"Now I understand why this stream is called Aranyos[31]," said Gergely. "Look, Éva, it's as if the ground has been sprinkled with gold. But you are thinking. Do you regret having come with me?"

"No," Éva replied. "Just something sad." Her young, fresh face was sad, her eyes serious.

"It's," she continued, "that I'm a girl after all, and I think my actions are immoral. You are happy today that I am following my heart's desire, but maybe years later, maybe in our old age, it may come to your mind that you did not walk me down a church aisle, but led me from a banquet table."

---

[31] In Hungarian, *aranyos* means golden and darling.

Mekcsey rode ahead with the Wallachian peasant who guided them down the mountain road. The two of them rode side by side.

"You are young," Éva continued, "and there is no priest in the world who would agree to marry the two of us."

"Éva," Gergely said in a reproachful tone. "Have you not always felt like I was your brother? Don't you still feel the same next to me? Am I a stranger to you? And if you are overwhelmed by the lack of a priest, will you not trust me that until we can wed? I will protect you so much that even the dove-winged Holy Spirit couldn't protect you better. If this is what you want, I will not hold your hand or kiss your face until a priest gives us his holy blessing."

Éva smiled. "Hold my hand. It's yours. Kiss my face. It's yours!" And as they rode along side by side, she offered him her hand and her cheek.

"Catechism came out of you just now," Gergely said, relieved. "You see, I'm a papist, too, but my teacher did not teach me about God from any catechism, but from the stars in heaven."

"Father Gábor?"

"Him. He was a Lutheran, but he never wanted to convert anyone to Lutheranism. He told me that the true God is not in paintings and writings. He's not the old, bearded, threatening, hysterical, god of the Old Testament. We have no idea of the true nature of God. We can only see God's meaning and love. The true God is with us, Éva. The true God is not angry with anyone. He has no anger. If you lift your gaze to the sky and say, "God, Father, I choose this Gergely as my partner, and if I say so with your name, then, dear Éva, we are already married in the sight of God."

Éva looked at Gergely happily as he spoke softly, almost as if thinking out loud. He, a child growing up as an orphan, had matured and become serious early!

The boy continued. "The papist ceremony, Éva, is only for the world. The world has to document that we have intended to merge our hearts and souls as one, and not as an impulse and not for just an occasion, like animals. Our marriage, my dear soul, was already made when we were small children."

Mekcsey reached a grassy hill. He stopped and turned around and waited for them. "A little rest wouldn't hurt," he said.

"Good," said Gergely. "Let's dismount. I see there is water down there. The Wallachian can water the horses."

He jumped off his horse and helped Éva off hers.

He dropped his cloak on the grass and lay down.

Mekcsey opened the saddlebags and took out bread and salt. He cut off the dry parts of the bread and offered the rest to Éva.

"Let's wait," said Gergely. And he turned to Éva.

"Éva, before we take bread, shouldn't we speak the promises of our hearts in the sight of God?"

Éva got up. She didn't know what Gergely wanted, but she felt from the vibration of his voice that his thoughts were sacred and ceremonial. She held out her hand to Gergely.

And as they stood next to each other, holding each other's hands, Gergely took off his cap and looked at the sky. With a trembling voice, he reverently prayed.

"Our God, Father! We are in your temple. Not in a man-made stone building, but under your sky, among your trees! Out of the woods, your breath is coming to us! Your sun shines upon us from the mountains! And from the heights, they are your eyes that look upon us. This girl has been dear to me since I was little, the dearest of all the girls on earth. I love only her. I will love only her even to my grave, and even beyond. People did not allow us to come together in the usual way, so let her be my wife through your blessing."

And he turned his wet eyes towards the girl. "Let us kneel. Woman, I hereby declare before God that you are my wife!"

Éva, tears in her eyes, stammered, "And I that you are my husband ..." And she put her head on Gergely's shoulder.

Gergely lifted a finger. "I swear that I will never leave you, no matter what your troubles, no matter what your miseries! Until your death. Until my death. God help me so!"

"Amen!" said Mekcsey firmly.

Éva also raised her hand, "I swear what you swore. Until your death. Until my death. God help me!"

"Amen!" Mekcsey said again.

The young couple hugged. They kissed each other reverently as if they were feeling the blessing hand of God on their heads.

Mekcsey sat down next to the bread and wiped his eyes. "Now," he said, "I've never seen such a marriage. I feel that this is a more holy and a stronger marriage than had nine priests performed a ceremony before Her Majesty in Gyalu."

They smiled. They sat down and set about taking their food.

They reached Hunyad Castle by nightfall. Jancsi was waiting for them with dinner. (He had been waiting for them every day, both for lunch and dinner.)

The travelers changed clothes. They gathered some women's clothes for Éva. Then they sat down to dinner.

At dinner, they were joined by the parish priest of the castle, a sick old man with a long mustache who had aged in the silence of the castle like a linden tree. "I called the reverend," said Jancsi Török, "to marry you two.'

"We are beyond that," said Gergely.

"How is that?"

"We have taken the sacrament of marriage before God."

"How? When?" asked the priest.

"In the forest."

"In the forest?"

"There. Just like Adam and Eve. Perhaps you think it wasn't a legal marriage?"

The priest looked at them in horror.

"What's to wonder?" Mekcsey said with a chuckle. "God has no need of a priest if He wants to bless someone!"

The priest shook his head again.

"God may not need a priest, but man does. Then, from heaven, the Good Lord does not issue marriage certificates to anyone."

Gergely shrugged. "Even without a certificate we know that we are married."

"That's true," the priest muttered. "But your grandchildren won't know."

Éva blushed.

Gergely scratched his ear. He glanced at Éva. Then he turned to the priest. "Well reverend sir, would you marry us?"

"Marry you, yes."

"Without parental permission?"

"Without it. After all, the Bible does not say there is any need for parental permission for a marriage."

"Well then," said Gergely, "Let's do it, Éva, for the sake of the *certificate*."

They went to the chapel and the wedding took place in a few minutes. The priest wrote their names in the church book. The names of János Török and István Mekcsey were written down as witnesses.

"I will send written confirmation to your parents," the priest said as they sat back at the table. "Let us give them some peace."

"We want to," said Éva, "but it will take a month or two for their anger to subside." She turned to Gergely. "Where are we going to spend those two months, my dear husband?"

"Well, my dear wife, you will be here in Hunyad and I will be somewhere else." Having said this, he looked at his companions.

"We can tell her," said János Török. "After all, you are one, and from now on you are one, so there are no secrets. It's also better if the priest knows. At least if something goes wrong, he can notify my dear mother in two months."

"Then know, my sweet young mate," said Gergely, "that we were already to set off for Constantinople when I heard that you were engaged. The three of us resolved with sacred determination to free Lord Bálint, our noble father."

"If possible," János Török added.

The bride listened to her husband earnestly, then smiled. "To be sure, you have been cheating with me, my dear lord." — Sometimes she addressed Gergely familiarly, and because they were now married, sometimes formally — "I would happily take a two-month vacation here in this beautiful castle, but have I not promised today, in two places, that I will never leave your grace?"

"Surely you don't want to come with us?"

"Can't I ride as well as any of you?"

"But this isn't just riding, my angel, but a road full of dangers."

"I can fight with a sword. I learned from an Italian master. I can shoot a rabbit with a bow and arrow, or a swallow with a gun."

"A gem of a woman!" Mekcsey shouted, raising his cup. "I'm jealous, Gergely!"

"Okay, okay," Gergely said worriedly, "but this kind of woman is accustomed to sleeping in a bed covered in lace."

"I'm not going to be a woman on the road," Éva said. "I came here in men's clothes, I will go there in men's clothes. How quickly you have regretted taking me as wife, my lord! Reverend father, divorce us immediately because this man is mocking me. He wants to leave me on the first day!"

The priest, however, rather preferred to tear the capon's breast meat off the bone.

"But you don't even know any Turkish," said Gergely as a final objection.

"I will learn on the road."

"You speak well," Jancsi said. "I can also teach you, and it's not that difficult."

"Say a couple of words!" said the bride of one hour.

"Well, for example, *elma* [*alma*] means "apple"; *benim* [*enyém*] means "mine"; *baba* means "papa"; *papuç* [*papucs*] means slippers; *şarampol* [*sorompó*] means barrier; *daduk* [*duda*] means horn; *çapalamak* means ..."

"... Pick [*csákány*]!" said Éva, clapping. "I had no idea I could speak Turkish!"

The servant who had been waiting on them quietly told Mekcsey that a man definitely wanted to come in.

"What man?"

"He says Mátyás."

"Mátyás? Mátyás who?"

"He didn't give any other name."

"Lord or peasant?"

"Kind of servant-like."

Mekcsey broke out laughing. "It's Matyti, the devil. Well, let him in. What does he want?"

The Matyi who had turned into Mátyás appeared with a lobster-red blush on his face. He looked at Mekcsey. "I'm here, lieutenant, at your service."

"I see that. But where were you last night?"

"Last night I was ready at a moment's notice. But you left in such a hurry that I couldn't catch up with you on the road."

"Because you were drunk as a tap!"

"Not really, begging your pardon."

"So how did you get here? After all, I took your horse."

Matyi raised his shoulder and eyebrows. "There were more than enough horses there."

"You are a horse thief, suitable to be hung from a tree!"

"Not me. Just as the gentleman was leaving, I put myself on a horse. A steward helped me get up on the horse because I couldn't climb on myself. What can I do if they put me on a horse that isn't mine?"

The company livened up and laughed. Matyi was forgiven. His drunken escape was exactly what Gergely liked. "Where are you from, Matyi?" he asked, laughing.

"Keresztes," he replied.

"Where in hell is Keresztes?"

How strange it would have been if the wagon driver were to answer the question like this: *Hey, poor Gergely, there will come a time when you will learn, your grace, where Keresztes is. Then, when your grace has grown a nice beard and you have become a noble lord, there the evil Turks will trap you and slap irons on your feet and hands! And they will not remove those irons, only upon death ...*[32]

— § —

Three days later they set off for the journey. Matyi was the wagon driver. The four of them alternated playing prisoner and *deli*. At the same time, the wagon became Éva's nighttime resting place.

7

What is that in the woods? Is it a camp or a village? Is it a robbers' lair or a leper colony? Is there a funeral or a wedding?

Well, this is not a camp, a village, a robbers' lair, or a leper colony but a big Gypsy caravan.

---

[32] See the section on the historical **Error! Reference source not found.** after the end of the novel..

Tattered, sooty tents stand among the trees in the shade of some rocks. From one and the other some smoke snakes into the sky. A violin plays and a drum beats in the clearing: the girls are dancing.

An old Gypsy woman is teaching them. She is shouting at one or the other in an unknown language. As old companions watch, she grabs the tambourine from the hand of a fifteen-year-old girl and demonstrates the art of dance, how to move hands and feet gracefully.

Gypsy girls are almost born with this art, but among them you can find some who have inherited either big legs or laziness in their blood from their parents. They require some teaching.

Otherwise, the dancers are all dressed in veils. Without a veil there is no dance. Its movements extend the circular motions of the dancers. The main thing in dance is to make the dancer look supple.

Some of the Gypsies sit around the dancers. Naked Gypsy children imitate the dancers' motions. Even two or three-year-old little children are spinning like smoky angels and falling down on the grass. Instead of tambourine, they shake coconut shells, and instead of a veil, they wave a spider web.

All at once, like a flock of sparrows disturbed from a bush, all the children were alarmed and rushed toward an opening in the forest.

Our five riders arrived there tired, leading their horses by the bridles. An infernal swarm of Gypsy children surrounded them with loud, unintelligible chatter. They held out their hands for baksheesh.

"Where's the *voyvodası*?" asked Gergely in Turkish. "You will all get *bahşiş*, but I will only give it to the *voyvodası*."

They did not run to fetch the voivode chief, but kept pushing and screaming at the riders.

Éva had already reached into her pocket to give them some coppers, but Gergely urged her not to. "Voivode!" he shouted at them, raising his sword.

The frightened sparrows scattered.

The older Gypsies were also frightened. Some leaped into tents, others hid in bushes. Only the women stayed. They were waiting and staring at the strangers.

"Don't be afraid," said Gergely in Turkish. "We won't hurt you. I just scared the kids off so they wouldn't make a noise. Where's the voivode?"

An old Gypsy stepped out from one of the tents. He was wearing a Turkish kaftan and a tall Persian hat on his head. Big silver buttons on his cloak. A gold chain around his neck. He held the staff of the voivode chief in his hand.

"What language do you speak?" asked Gergely in Turkish.

"Well," said the voivode, "mainly Turkish. But if I can serve you I can speak Wallachian, Persian, Greek, Bosnian, Serbian, Croatian, Italian, Hungarian, German, Czech, French and Spanish. I also speak some Muscovy."

"Well, for now, let's just speak Turkish. What are you people so scared about?"

"A band of Greek robbers is ravaging around here. They say there are fifty of them. Last week they killed a merchant in this forest."

"We're not robbers, just lost travelers. We come from Albania. We also heard about those robbers, which is why we got off the highway. Well, all we want is a guide to lead us to Istanbul and stay with us for a few days."

"Even ten men," replied the voivode. "It's not far."

"We only need one. A kind of man who knows his way around the capital, who can also repair weapons and knows how to take care of horses."

The voivode looked at him thoughtfully, then turned towards a smoky tent and shouted, "Sárközi!"

The five horsemen almost trembled at the Hungarian name.

From the tent emerged a forty-five-year-old grimy Gypsy. He was wearing Wallachian pants and a blue shirt. The knees of his Wallachian pants were patched with red cloth. He had a Hungarian cloak under his arm. He was dressing himself as he came out. When he got near the voivode, he buttoned up, dusted off his pants, and even combed his hair with ten fingers. He was pock-marked.

"You will accompany the valiant gentlemen to the city and serve them there."

Gergely gave the voivode some silver money. "Distribute it among the children! Thank you for your kindness."

"What should I bring with me?" asked Sárközi humbly in Turkish.

"Just a couple of tools to repair a gun or to shoe a horse, and if you have any, a good balm for a wound, whether for a man or a horse."

"I will, gentlemen." He ran back to the tent.

"Aren't you tired, young gentlemen?" asked the voivode. "Come in and relax. Have you eaten today?" He started leading the strangers towards his own tent that stood out from the others because of its red color. It was set up under a broad beech tree.

The voivode laid three small mats on the grass. His daughter, veiled as she had been dancing earlier, turned to her mother for help. "Well, we have cottage cheese, eggs, rice, butter, bread," she said. "I can roast chicken if you wait, my handsome young warriors."

"We can wait," said Gergely, "because we are hungry. We are not in a rush, just now."

They were surrounded by Gypsy people. Every woman wanted to read their fortunes. Some were already squatting and shaking spotted beans in a screen.

"Please, have them leave us," Gergely asked the voivode. "We have no desire to have our fortunes read."

The voivode lifted his staff and shouted at his people.

It is unclear which they respected more: the staff or the voivode. But it is certain that the women quickly dispersed. The five travelers could rest assuredly on the grass next to a variety of food the voivode's wife had placed in front of them.

"You live very well," said Gergely chatting with the voivode, then took a large gulp of water from a jug. "Is it a holiday today, or do girls always dance like this?"

"Tomorrow is Friday," replied the voivode. "All the girls will be at Sweet Water."

Gergely struggled to translate every word. "We've never been to Constantinople," he said. "We're going to join the army now. What is Sweet Water?"

"The Turkish amusement place at the end of the Golden Horn. On Fridays, all Turkish families go boating. At that time, some piastres fall down for the Gypsies. The girls are dancing. The old ladies tell fortunes."

"Aren't you afraid for your daughters?"

"Why? If they are enslaved, they will only do well. But the Turks need a white woman, mainly Hungarian. Our daughters do visit the harem court sometimes. Even now they dance together because they want to train them in the seraglio."

Éva said to Gergely, "What's Turkish for water?"

"*Su*, my dear."

Éva went inside the tent and turned towards the voivode's daughter, "*Su, su*, my angel."

The Gypsy girl pulled aside a back flap of the tent to reveal a spacious and cool cave behind. Water dripped from walls and had carved a depression in the rock.

"Take a bath, if you like," said the Gypsy girl with a gesture of her hand. She handed a small rectangular piece of clay to Éva to serve as soap.

Éva looked at her. The Gypsy girl looked back with eyes half-closed. Her gaze said, "You boy, you are handsome!" Éva smiled and stroked the girl's face. It was smooth and hot. The Gypsy girl caught Éva's hand and kissed her, then she ran out.

— § —

When they were well into the woods, Gergely addressed the Gypsy blacksmith. "My friend Sárközi! Have you ever had ten gold pieces?"

The Gypsy looked surprised at being addressed in Hungarian. "I've had more, but only in my dreams, my lord."

"Really?"

"Actually, I had two once. I hung onto one for two nights. I wanted to give it to a little kid. Then I bought a horse. The horse died. Now I have neither horse nor gold."

"Well, if you serve us well, you can earn ten gold pieces in a few days."

The Gypsy body almost sparkled.

Gergely further asked, "Why did you come to Turkey?"

"Because I was so strong, they definitely wanted to make a soldier out of me."

"You were never strong."

"Well, I'm not talking about my body. I kiss your hands and feet, but I have a great ability to play the flute. Because I am a flautist, and a locksmith, kissing your hands and feet, and then the Turks captured me. They brought me down here and put me in a workshop. But trust me, I escaped."

"Do you have a wife?"

"Sometimes yes, sometimes no. Just now, I don't have."

"Well then, if you want, you can also come home with us."

"Why would I want to go home, my lord? I wouldn't be able to find my master, and once home, the Turks would again make me a prisoner."

"So, were you a servant to anyone?"

"Yes, indeed. I served a great lord, the biggest among the Hungarians. Every day he gave roast meat, then he would talk to me in a friendly manner and say, 'Fix this gun, you Smokey.'"

"Who was this lord?"

"Who else but noble Lord Bálint."

"Which Bálint?" asked Jancsi Török.

"Which Bálint? Well Bálint Török, my noble lord."

Gergely hastened to take over Jancsi's lead with the questions. "What do you know about him?" He gestured to Jancsi to be careful.

The Gypsy shrugged. "Only that he was taken prisoner. If he's alive or dead, I don't know. He's probably dead or I would have heard something."

"At which of his houses were you working?"

"Szigetvár."

The two boys looked at each other. Neither one could remember the Gypsy. But it was true that neither of them spent much time at Szigetvár. They had been here and there on Lord Bálint's estates, and they could not have known all of his many servants.

Gergely looked carefully at the Gypsy's face then smiled. "I remember you. Now I remember. You were once the prisoner of Yumurjak, and Dobó freed you from him."

The Gypsy's eyes opened wide. "Not Dobó. A seven-year-old boy. Gergely something." He sighed. "God bless him, wherever he is, that boy. I was given a horse and a cart. That's why I am saving my gold piece. But then I thought to myself, he must have been an angel."

"And what if that angel was me?"

The Gypsy squinted at Gergely in disbelief. "I have never seen an angel with a mustache."

"But it is me," said Gergely. "I also remember that you got married that day. Your wife's name was Böske. It happened in the forest. You also received some guns as your share."

The Gypsy's eyes almost fell out, he was so stunned.

"My God! God in paradise bless you, my young lord! May He make your dear progeny multiply like millet! My God! What a miraculous, lucky day this is!" And he fell to his knees, held Gergely's feet, and kissed them.

"The Good Lord brought us together again," said Gergely. "Now I trust that we did not come here for no reason."

He handed his horse's reins to Matyi so he could lead it out to graze on the grass. The others followed his example.

Gergely told the Gypsy why they had come and asked him what he thought. How could they get to Lord Bálint?

The Gypsy listened to Gergely sometimes with bright eyes and sometimes with disdain. He kissed Jancsi's hand. Then he nodded thoughtfully. "You can only enter Istanbul, maybe even into Seven Towers. But they are not guarding the lord with wooden swords ..."

He buried his head in his hands and lamented, "That poor Lord Bálint is there! Oh, if I had known, I would have shouted from the window to say good day, I kiss your hands and feet."

Gergely waited for the Gypsy's imagination to run its Gypsy course, and then drew his attention back to more serious thinking.

"Well, it's possible to enter the city," said the Gypsy, "particularly today. Because today is the Persian Day of Mourning,[33] and there are as many pilgrims there as at home on the feast day of Our Lady. But for Seven Towers, not even a bird dares to fly there."

"No matter," fired back Jancsi. "Let's just get inside the city. Then we will see."

---

[33] The Mourning of Muharram marks the anniversary of the Battle of Karbala (680 AD) where the caliph's army defeated and killed Hussein, a grandson of Muhammad. Hassan was his elder brother who had been forced to cede the caliphate after the death of their father, the fourth caliph, Ali, the cousin and son-in-law of Mohammed.

— § —

The Golden Horn is a wide, horn-shaped bay, as wide as the Danube, that extends from the sea at the center of Constantinople up into to the woods.

A large fishing boat carried our travelers along that bay. Gergely, whose clothes looked the most Turkish, sat on the bow of the boat, Mekcsey, whose reddened clothes also suggested Turkish, sat in the middle, and the rest sat inside the boat.

In the light of the setting sun, the minarets towered high like golden pillars, and the gilded domes of the churches shone. All this was reflected in the sea and made our passengers stare in astonishment.

"It's a dream world!" Éva said as she sat near Gergely's feet.

"It's nicer than a dream," said Gergely. "But dear, it's like a fairy tale castle. It's exquisite on the outside, but inside, it's inhabited by monsters and the cursed."

"Fairy town!" Mekcsey added.

Only Jancsi sat quietly in the boat. It was almost pleasing for him, among the many buildings and fantastic splendor, to see some blackness.

"What forest is that there?" he asked the Gypsy, pointing to the left. "I think it's all poplar trees. But how black those poplar trees are! Well, they've grown huge."

"They aren't poplars," said the Gypsy. "They're cypress trees. It's not a forest, but a cemetery. It's Pera where Turks are buried."

Jancsi closed his eyes. He wondered if his father was already lying under one of the cypress trees.

Gergely looked at him and wanted to distract Jancsi from thoughts of graveyards. "It is a city like Buda on the banks of the Danube. But here there are two Budas, or rather three."

"I didn't think it was such a hilly city," Mekcsey added. "I thought it would be flat, like Szeged or Debrecen."

"It was easy for them to build such a beautiful city," Éva said. "It's a city of thieves. They made this city from plunder stolen from all corners of the world. I wonder which house has our queen's furniture?"

"You wanted to say King Mátyás' furniture, dear," Gergely replied. Because he didn't like Queen Isabella. And indeed he spoke accurately because the furniture that was in Buda Castle did not come from Poland.

The sun had set when they arrived at the bridge. They could see an endless crowd of people milling around on the bridge.

"There will be many gathered today for the Day of Mourning," said the boatman.

"We also have come here for that," said Gergely.

Jancsi shivered. His face was pale as he stared at the teeming crowd that was flooding across the bridge to Istanbul.

— § —

The push of the crowd also helped them get inside.

The guards on the bridge did not look at anyone. A flood of people swept them into the streets of Istanbul.

They had no idea where they were going. The tide was flowing upwards through some three streets. Then it stopped. Soldiers pushed a gap in the crowd to make way for the Persian pilgrims.

Gergely held onto Éva tightly. The others clung to the wall of another building. They kept looking out for each other.

All of a sudden, the end of the street was lit up with a torch bigger than anything our travelers had ever seen.

Because it was not the kind of wax torch used to accompany the dead in Hungary, but a barrel-sized basket made of iron ribs.

The basket was held up by a strong Persian holding the end of a pole a fathom long. A bunch of logs, wood as thick as a man's arm, was burning in the basket.

That one torch lit up the whole street.

In front of it walked some ten brown men dressed in mourning clothes. Their short-cut, curly beards and small stature indicated that they were Persian.

Behind them paraded a white horse. A white sheet on the back. Saddle on the sheet. On the saddle were two crossed swords in the shape of an "X", and two white living doves. The legs of the two doves were tied to the saddle. The horse, the doves, the swords, and the sheet were all sprinkled with blood.

The horse was followed by another group of men in mourning clothes. They were singing some sort of bitter litany in which each line had the same two words — *Hussein! Hassan!* — and loud cries of *Hu!* mixed with an unusual drumming that sounded like thumping.

As the procession continued, the source of the unusual drumming became clear.

What followed were two long rows of bare-breasted Persian men. They wore black shirts that reached their heels. Their heads were tied with black cloths, the ends hanging over the backs of their necks. Only their chests were naked. As they moved sideways, they shook their right hands with each *Hussein! Hassan!* With each shout of *Hu!*, they punched their chests with their fists.

The thumping was the beating of their breasts. The blue-red marks on their chests proved that they were not beating themselves just in a papist manner.

There could have been about three hundred Persian chest-beaters. They walked sideways, taking only two or three steps after each punch in the chest.

Among them were triangular flags of various colors, mostly green, but also black, yellow and red. Here and there on the flag poles, and on the hats of Persian children, were silver figures of a hand. They represented the hand of a Turkish martyr named Abbas. They cut off Abbas' hand because he had offered water to Hussein after he was captured in the Battle of Karbala

And the singing grew louder:

Hassan! Hassein! Hussan! Hu![34]

More torches lit up a new group in black surrounding a camel covered with a green sheet. On the back of the camel was a small tent-like structure made from branches. From inside a child, with only his face visible in an opening, occasionally reached out with his hand to throw a handful of sawdust over the mourners.

They were followed by an occasional, strange rattling and rumbling.

Soon the other group of mourners arrived. They were also walking slowly sideways and dressed in mourning. But their shirts were open on their backs. They held whips made of chains thick as a thumb and so

---

[34] Gárdonyi's footnote: I myself noted this song in Istanbul where I witnessed this ceremony on May 19, 1899. I have recorded it as faithfully as possible.

heavy that each held it with both hands. At the end of each line of the chanting, they whipped their naked backs, sometimes over their right shoulders, sometimes over their left shoulders.

Éva, when she saw that the men's backs were bloody and blistered, clung to Gergely's arm. "Gergely, I'm going to faint."

"But it's going to get even more terrible," Gergely said. "A Turkish prisoner told me about this Day of Mourning. But I did not believe him, that men were actually whipping their backs bloody."

"They aren't going to kill that boy, are they?"

"Certainly not. Those two doves and that boy are only symbols. At midnight, they cut the cords tying the doves down. The two doves are the souls of Hassan and Hussein. A pious shout accompanies their ascension to heaven."

"And the boy?"

"He represents an orphaned Persian people."

"What comes next?"

"Men with swords who cut their heads."

And just then followed another bloody procession, an image that only a dream of hell could possibly bring to mind.

They too were dressed in white. Everyone's head was shaved. In their right hands, a scimitar. Each man's left hand was hanging onto the belt of the man next to him — to keep from falling due to loss of blood, and to hold up his companion should he collapse.

And they also walked sideways. The litany-type of songs on their lips was more like screaming. At the end of each line, each scimitar flashed in the light of the torches as each man touched his own bald head.

They were already bathed in blood.

For some, blood streamed out of nose and ears, staining the white sheets red. A breeze made the torches splutter causing sparks to fall on bloody heads.

The air was thick with a mist of blood.

Éva closed her eyes. "I'm horrified."

"I told you, didn't I, to stay home. This is no journey for a woman. Close your eyes, my little lamb."

Éva shook her head and opened her eyes. "Well, just for that I will look." Although she looked pale, she continued watching the bloody funereal procession.

— § —

Gergely was more calm. He got used to seeing blood in his childhood. It does not hurt very much. It was more surprising, he thought to himself, that these men were voluntarily spilling their own blood. And Hungarians had been fighting these kinds of men continuously for more than a hundred years!

He looked through the bloody crowd towards the other side of the street. How strange it is to feel strongly when he senses he is being keenly watched by someone else!

And someone was watching him.

In the light of the torches, within the teeming crowd, he saw the eyes of two men staring at him.

One was like an Armenian. It was the raven-black agha whose soldiers had been blown up into the sky.

The other was Yumurjak.

8

One summer morning in the prior year, Maylád greeted Bálint Török with the news that some new prisoners would be arriving that night.

"Hungarians?" asked Bálint with big eyes.

"I do not know yet. All I heard was that in the morning, when the gate was opened, chains were rattling all over the yard. I know the sound of every prisoner's chains. Even when I am in my bed, I always know who is passing in front of my door."

"Me too."

"I heard new rattles in the morning. But not just one man, but two, three, maybe four. They were ringing all through the courtyard. Maybe they were being led to the Tas Çukuru!"

Tas Çukuru[35] was a cave-like prison in Seven Towers. That was the cell at the bottom of Blood Tower for those condemned to death. Those who got there soon became acquainted with the secrets above the starry sky.

---

[35] In Turkish, *tas çukuru* means stone pit.

They wandered to the garden where they used to sit. But that day, they gazed neither at the growth of the bushes nor at the clouds traveling to Hungary. They waited anxiously to see the new prisoners.

Their legs were no longer bound in chains. The piles of gold that Lady Török had sent to the sultan and the pashas did not open the gates, but at least they dissolved the chains.

The two men were old anyway, and the castle was guarded by two hundred and fifty soldiers who had families. No one had ever escaped from there.

The inner sentries were being rotated. A big bellied bey appeared in the yard to command the sentries being relieved. "Three to go to the mill," he said, wiping his forehead. Because the heat always tormented that fat man.

"Three go to the mill and cut rocks." He named who would be the three.

Then he turned towards two short men. "You come back here in an hour. You will clean up the armory."

Bálint Török could not wait for the bey to finish. He walked in front of him. "Good morning, Veli Bey! How did you sleep?"

"Badly. They woke me up early this morning. Three new prisoners arrived from Hungary."

"Surely it's not *the Friar* who has been brought here?"

"Not the Friar. He is some violent noble. He may not be noble, only a beggar. He doesn't even have a decent shirt. It's written that he spied upon the Pasha of Buda and robbed him of everything."

"The Pasha of Buda?"

"That's it. They brought his two sons with him."

"What's his name?"

"I wrote it down, but I forget. You all have such peculiar names that the devil can't keep them all in mind." And without as much as a hello or goodbye, he turned around and walked away, perhaps to his bed.

Lord Bálint was confused as he sat down beside Maylád. "He robbed the Pasha of Buda?" he speculated. "Who could that be?"

"A beggar?" continued Maylád with the speculation. "If he were a beggar, they wouldn't bring him here."

"Whoever he may be, my first job will be to give him some clothes."

They continued speculating and pondering the entire morning. They went through a mental list of a thousand Hungarian and Transylvanian names, but they could not agree on any of them.

At noon, the new prisoner appeared at the common table which had been laid out in the shady side of the courtyard.

Both of them watched. They do not recognize the man. They saw a short, half bald, old brown man. He was dressed in tattered Hungarian linen. Next to him were two better dressed Hungarian youths, about twenty or twenty-five. Their features indicated that they were brothers and the old man's sons.

The old man's legs wore the same kind of light steel chains that Bálint Török wore for about two years. The chain was shiny from wear, almost like silver.

Maylád hurried to the prisoner. He didn't know who he was, he only saw that he was Hungarian. Bálint stood at the table staring with deep emotion at the old man.

Maylád couldn't say anything but hugged the old man. But Bálint became excited and shivered, almost screaming, "Who are you?"

The old man bowed his head and mumbled, barely audibly, "László Móré."

Bálint was like a man who had just been hit. He turned away. He sat down.

Maylád dropped his hand from the old man.

The two young men stood sadly behind their father.

"You will be eating here, gentlemen," Veli Bey said, pointing to the corner of the table opposite Bálint Török's place.

Bálint Török got up. "Well, if they eat here, then I won't eat here!" He turned to the servant behind him. "Bring my plate to my room."

Maylád hesitated for a moment, then said to his servant, "Bring my plate, too." And he went after Lord Bálint.

Veli Bey shrugged. But then he couldn't just stand there without saying a word. He looked at Móré. "Why do they hate you?"

Móré angrily glared at the two lords leaving. "Because they are Hungarians."

"Aren't you Hungarian?"

"It's for that reason. Two Hungarians can manage to get along, but three spell trouble."

— § —

Bálint Török did not leave his room for two weeks. He did not go down to the courtyard, nor did Maylád, who had become his shadow.

Maylád would listen to Lord Bálint's sermons on the new faith spread by the famous John Calvin and Martin Luther. Bálint Török would explain, "It's more the religion of Jesus than the Latin corruptions that have spread like weeds from Rome."

And slowly, Maylád became more and more convinced about the new beliefs. He wrote a letter to his son Gábor and encouraged him to think about it at home.

Finally, they grew bored with the four walls of the room, and one day Lord Bálint said, "Maybe we should go down to the garden."

"The brigand is there."

"What if he isn't there?

"But is he there?"

"If he's there, let's not say anything to him. We have every right to walk there, just like him.

Maylád smiled. "*Every right*. Well, we still have some *rights*."

"We have indeed, that of the Creator. How long have we been prisoners? That fellow has been here only two weeks."

So they went down to the garden.

A Persian prince was sitting under a sycamore tree. He, like them, had been a prisoner for a long time. Another Asian noble was also there who had almost grown moldy in his sorrow and boredom. They were playing chess. They had been playing chess from morning to night for years and never said anything to each other.

Bálint and Maylád were familiar with the two chess players, as much as they were familiar with the marble fountain that shone white between Blood Tower and Gold Tower; or even the gigantic old Kurdish dignitary who had cursed the emperor and was punished by having to wear chains so heavy that all he could do was sit or lie on his bench in Blood Tower until the end of the day. Only his eyes turned to where the prisoners were walking between the bushes.

Well, they were not looking at the chess players, but they were struck by a new figure sitting behind the players, watching their game.

"Who the devil can he be, that small, old Turk wearing the yellow kaftan? And why is he bare headed?"

Hearing their steps, the man turned around. It was Móré.

He got up and left the chess players. The drowsiness that had made him almost sick on the first day had disappeared from his face. His tiny black eyes blinked vigorously, and his gait was strong, almost youthful.

He stepped in front of the two lords and crossed his arms. "Why do you hate me? How are you different than me? Are you richer? Nobody's rich here. Are you nobler? I am old nobility like any of you."

"You were a robber!" growled Bálint Török.

"Weren't you robbers? Didn't you get your fortune from wherever you could reach? Have you not fought against each other? Did you not turn to János and then to Ferdinand seventy-seven times? You whistled the song of the one who gave you more."

"Let's get out of here," Maylád said, blushing. "Let's leave this man here!"

"I'm not leaving" Bálint Török replied. "I have never backed away from any man." He sat down on the bench. He contained his anger because he saw Veli Bey coming from the gate with a Turkish imam and the two Móré boys. The two boys were already dressed in Turkish clothes, but had no turban on their heads. They were bareheaded, like their father.

Maylád also sat beside Bálint Török.

Móré stood in front of them with his legs spread out and a hand on his hip and continued blustering. "I was in the battle where György Dozsa was cut down. I was at the Battle of Mohács, where the blood of twenty-four thousand Hungarians was spilled for their homeland."

"I was there, too," Maylád said, striking his chest.

"Well, if you were there at that blood baptism, you should know that those who survived value each other as brothers."

"Such a roadside bandit is no longer be my brother!" Maylád growled red in the face. "I know why your fortress was demolished."

"You may know. But you don't know why they demolished Nána?[36] You don't know that the entire Hungarian nation is bowing at the feet of

---

[36] Nána was a fortress across the Danube River opposite Esztergom.

the Pasha of Buda, and that I, László Móré, was the only one who cried out to him, '*Mangy dog lord!*' For years, I fought with my small force against the Turks. Neither Ferdinand nor the Hungarian nation but I, László Móré, smashed his army at Belgrade last year. I, László Móré, whom you call a robber and bandit!"

He sniffed. Then, waving his fist, he continued. "If I had as much money as István Maylád, or as many goods, castles and servants as Bálint Török, or as many soldiers as the one who wears the crown only as an ornament, then the name László Móré would be celebrated as the liberator of the nation. But because I didn't, the damned pagans surrounded me in Nána and razed my fortress to the ground."

Veli Bey arrived with the imam.

"I don't know what you're arguing about, but Selim's word is true. He lives closer to the source of truth than you unbelievers."

"What Selim?" Bálint Török chuckled.

"Selim," replied Veli Bey, "who a few days ago was called László Móré in the language of the unbelievers."

Bálint Török laughed bitterly: "Selim! And this fellow is preaching to us about patriotism! Get out, pagan, for the sake of your father's honor!"

Surely he would have punched the man had Veli Bey not jumped between them. "Infidel pig!" shouted the bey at Bálint. "I will have you in chains immediately!"

Lord Bálint jerked his head up like a horse that had been hit on the nose. His eyes were burning. God knows what would have happened had Maylád not pulled him away!

The bey looked at them contemptuously. Probably he was thinking about his purse because he stopped cursing Lord Bálint. Instead, he turned to Móré and spoke loudly enough so all could hear. "The gracious sultan was delighted to be informed that you are entering into the army of the true believers. He sent this venerable priest so that you may learn the light of the Prophet, whose name be blessed forever."

"Let's return to our room!" growled Bálint Török. "Come back Maylád, my dear friend!"

— § —

A few days later, the two Móré boys were released. They both received an official position in Constantinople.

Only old Móré remained between the walls.

Bálint did not speak to him anymore, but he heard more than once that he was pleading for his own freedom.

On one occasion Veli Bey replied to Móré this way. "I presented your case again at the Sublime Porte. The letter has already arrived from Hungary. The Pasha of Buda was very critical, I must say. He writes, among other things, that when Nána was besieged, you threw money at the Turks to save your skin."

He shook his head and laughed. "You are an old, old fox!"

Székesfehérvár and Esztergom already belonged to the Turks. The sultan himself had led his army to demolish the two bastions of western Hungary. It was winter when he returned home.

The prisoners at Seven Towers were informed week by week of the campaign, and also of the return. They waited for new prisoners. May God not hold it a sin, but they were happy to see new acquaintances, perhaps even good friends, in the giant prison. How much news would they hear! Maybe about their families, also.

One morning they just happened to be talking about this when the door opened and Veli Bey dropped in. His face was red from having to run. He placed his two hands on his chest and bowed to Lord Bálint. "The gracious Padishah calls, oh great lord. Please deign to dress immediately, and we will go."

Lord Bálint was shocked. His gaze was almost frozen.

"You are free!" Maylád chuckled.

They pulled some clothes out of the closet. Veli Bey ran away to get dressed herself.

"Remember me!" Maylád begged. "Remind him about me, Bálint. You will see him face to face. You will talk. You can remind him about me. You can ask him to forgive me along with you."

"I won't forget," Bálint said. His hands were shaking as he took out the floral design, blue satin coat that he had worn when he was made prisoner. His beautiful winter clothes were all worn. He had not worn the blue satin. He was keeping it. He was hoping that he would get to wear it when he went home.

It was just that he had no sword to wear.

"You will have one when you return," Maylád said. He accompanied him down the stairs. He watched with pleasure as he and Veli Bey sat in a carriage, wrapping themselves in loose fur coats.

The carriage set off. Two soldiers with lances rode behind him.

"My God, my God!" exclaimed Lord Bálint across the road.

It seemed like a hundred years passed until they finally turned into the gate of the serai. They walked on foot through the Court of the Janissaries to the palace.

Many stairs, but all in white marble; many splendid bodyguards, but all servants; large marble columns; soft carpets. With each step they passed gilded filigree masterpieces of Oriental art. But Bálint Török saw nothing but the middle of the back of the servant in front of him dressed in a white kaftan. Here and there the servant would pull aside a silk carpet to open a door to the next room, and each time Bálint expected to see the sultan on the other side.

He was led to a small hall. There was nothing in it but a carpet with a cushion on it. Beside the cushion was a giant copper basin, similar to the brass baptismal font in the church at Buda, except that this basin was not mounted on a pillar, but on a marble slab, and it did not contain water, but a charcoal fire.

Bálint Török was already familiar with that furniture: its name is *mangal*. It is the brazier used in the winters of Turkish lands.

There was no one in the room, only three Saracen doormen by its three doors. They stood like statues with large, shiny halberds. Next to them was Veli Bey.

Bálint looked out the window. He looked down over green waves of the sea towards Scutari, just as if he were looking through the window of his Buda palace towards the city of Pest.

He had been standing there for about five minutes when finally one of the Saracens pulled aside a hanging carpet. The next moment, the sultan stepped in.

No retinue before him; none behind; only a sixteen-year-old, thin Saracen boy who stopped and waited by the doorman.

The bey prostrated himself on the carpet. Bálint clicked his heels and bowed. When he raised his head, the sultan was standing by the brazier holding his two thin hands over the heat. He was wearing a walnut-colored kaftan bordered with ermine and so long that only two red slippers were visible underneath. He had a light, cambric linen turban on his head. His face was shaven. His thin, long white mustache drooped low, reaching past his shoulders. For a minute they just stood without saying a word.

The sultan looked at the bey. "Leave!"

The bey got up, bowed, and walked backwards to the door. There he bowed again, then disappeared.

"I have not seen you for a long time," began the sultan calmly. "You haven't changed at all. Except that you hair is more grey."

Bálint thought to himself, "But you have not grown any younger, Suleiman." Because the sultan had become thinner since he had last seen him, wrinkles all around his large, sheep eyes. His nose looked like it had grown longer. His cheeks had been shamelessly reddened.

But Bálint said nothing. He only waited, waited with an anxious heart, for what would follow.

The sultan folded his arms. "You know, perhaps, that Hungary is no more." (Lord Bálint grew pale. His breathing stopped.) "There are some holdouts here and there. It's just a matter of time. They will be subdued this year." (Lord Bálint took a deep breath.) "I need a good pasha in Buda. A pasha who is not a foreigner to the Hungarians, or to me. You are a worthy man. I would return your estates. Everything."

Bálint looked like he was considering. His lips moved. But before he could say anything, the sultan continued.

"Do you understand what I am saying? You understand Turkish?"

"*Evet*," replied Bálint in Turkish to say *yes*.

"Well, I would make you the Pasha of Buda."

Bálint's shoulders trembled for a moment. His face was serious and sad at the same time. His gaze dropped from the sultan to the brazier where the embers glowed red in an arabesque pattern.

The sultan was quiet for a minute. Perhaps he was waiting for Bálint to fall to his feet in the Turkish fashion, or to kiss his hand in the Hungarian fashion, or at least to say something. But Bálint just stood there. And as if he was not even standing before the sultan, he folded his arms.

The sultan became serious. He paced back and forth in the room twice. Then he stood and impatiently asked, "So you will not accept this position?"

Bálint was roused.

Where had his mind been vacationing during the previous minutes? It had been flying over all his castles, estates, forests, fields, hugging his wife, kissing his children, sitting on his favorite steed, and breathing the air of freedom.

He was roused, like waking from a dream.

"Gracious emperor," he began in a deep voice. "If I understood your words correctly, you are ordering me to replace Werbőczy."

"No. Werbőczy is dead. He died the same year you came here. We have not filled his position. I want you to be a proper pasha. I am making you pasha of the largest province and giving you complete freedom."

Lord Bálint stared at the emperor as if he were some sort of miraculous vision.

"But how, my gracious lord?" he finally said. "A Hungarian pasha?"

"No. A Turkish pasha."

"A Turkish pasha?"

"Turkish pasha. I said Hungary is no more, so there is no more Magyar."

"So I would be Turkish?"

"Pasha."

Bálint Török dropped his head. He sighed. He looked up at the sultan's face and spoke with a deep, sad voice. "Is there any other way?"

"No."

Bálint Török closed his eyes. His chest heaved from deep breathing. "Gracious lord," he finally said, "I know that you are not accustomed to hearing honest words, but I have grown old with them ... I cannot say anything except what I am thinking."

"Well, what are you thinking?" said the sultan coldly.

A pale Lord Bálint replied with a calm, determined voice. "That, even if the entire country is your possession, and even if every Hungarian becomes a Turk ... I will not ... I will not."

9

On the way back, Veli Bey was horrified to hear what the two had discussed in private. "What a fool you are!" he said shaking his head. "I bet my neck that you are going to die tonight in Blood Tower."

That night he stayed up walking in the yard waiting for the sultan's orders.

However, the order did not arrive that night or over the following days. No letter, no message, nothing, nothing.

A week later, the aged Sheikh ul-Islam, the head prince of the Turks' religious leaders, appeared at Seven Towers. "There is some famous infidel here," he told the bey. "His name is Bálint Török."

"*Evet*," the bey responded, leaning forward.

"The Padishah — may Allah grant him long life — is graciously thinking of making this man the governor of our Hungarian province, but the man does not want to convert from the infidel beliefs of dogs."

"Dog."

"I asked him — may Allah grant him long life — to allow me see the prisoner. Maybe I can do something. You know, my son, I am an old and experienced man."

"You are the wisest of the wise, sheikh, the Solomon of our times."

"I also think that every knot has its own way of being untied. Just patience and cleverness are required. Perhaps he will be changed if I myself bring him to the light of the Prophet? First he will only listen to what I say, and then he himself will not feel the first seed of the true faith being planted in his heart."

"He's quite an intelligent man."

"Then you will see, my son, if we convert this evil infidel, we will bring joy to the Padishah."

And they both said simultaneously, "May Allah grant him long life."

— § —

In the eighth hour of the day, or in the way we mark the time of day, at two o'clock in the afternoon, Lord Bálint was asleep in his room, when the bey opened his door and came in with the chief mufti.

Lord Bálint leaned up on his elbow from the couch and rubbed his eyes in confusion.

He just looked at the big bearded biblical figure, a person he had never before seen, but Bálint recognized his priest-like demeanor, black kaftan, and white turban.

"Wake up, Lord Bálint," the bey said. "You have earned a great honor. It is His Worship Sheikh ul-Islam himself who comes to educate you. Listen to him carefully."

He grabbed the mat rug from the wall and spread it in on the floor in the middle of the room. Then he took off his kaftan to lay it over the carpet, but the old man did not want it. He sat down and crossed his legs.

His beard reached the carpet. His sensitive, old eyes explored Lord Bálint. Then he leafed through the pages of a small, parchment bound copy of the Koran.

"What do you want?" muttered Lord Bálint. "Because I told the emperor that I would not turn Turkish."

The bey did not answer. He looked at the head mufti. Instead of making a reply, the head mufti raised the book to his heart, forehead and lips. Then he said, "In the name of Allah the Merciful and the Compassionate. Abul Kazem Muhammad, son of Abdullah, son of Abd el Motalleb, son of Hazem, son of Abd Menaf, son of Kasi, son of Kelab, son of Morra, son of Lova, son of Galeb ..."

Mr. Bálint just looked. He put on his cloak. He sat on the chair facing the old man. He was waiting for what would become of this.

The old man calmly continued, "The son of Fer, the son of Malek, the son of Madar, the son of Kenana, the son of Kazima ..."

Lord Bálint yawned.

The old man continued, "The son of Modreka, the son of Elias, the son of Modar, the son of Nazar, the son of Moad ..." And he recited a sea of names until he finally arrived back to Muhammad and his birth.

The bey was not in the room by then. He had left unseen in order to go about his business. In the hallway, he met Maylád, who also had woken up from sleep. He was going to Lord Bálint to wake him up.

"Don't disturb him," the bey said. "He is with a priest. He is being educated in the true religion."

"In the Turkish religion?"

"That's it," the bey replied, smiling. And he hopped down the stairs in a hurry.

Maylád stared after him in astonishment.

10

Before the Persian mourning procession had passed, Gergely grabbed Éva's hand and began walking. He mixed in with the crowd. As he passed the Gypsy and Mekcsey, he said, "Come on! There's trouble!"

Mekcsey stepped ahead. With his broad shoulders he pushed his way through the crowd. Yumurjak and the agha were anxious on the other side of the street. They could not pass through the sacred procession.

Nor would the soldiers maintaining order allow them. And all the many scimitars flashing with religious rage would have turned against them.

Moreover, Muslims and Shiites have a particular hatred for each other. The Shiites believe that today's Muslim priests have strayed from righteousness. The Turks believe that the Persian people are heretics.

Finally, after a lot of pressing and shoving, they emerged from the crowd and entered a narrow, dark street.

"Let's run!" said Gergely. "I saw Yumurjak and the agha. They came with soldiers."

They set off in the dark. They ran. The Gypsy ran first, even though he did not know why he had to run. He also tumbled into a sleeping pack of dogs. One dog whined. Others scattered in fright.

Because it is worth knowing that Constantinople is a paradise for dogs. The dog stays on the roof of the house even if the house has a courtyard. Well, the dog has no home anywhere. In some areas, hundreds of red-haired, fox-like dogs are living in packs on the streets. The Turks do not hurt them, and when a dog is having puppies, he throws a rag or matting outside his gate to help. Those dogs clean and tidy Constantinople. Even in our time, Turks empty their four-sided trash bins outside their gates. The dogs eat the garbage. They eat anything other than iron and glass. And those dogs are not bad or wild. Pet any one of them and it will wag its tail. There is none among them that cannot be petted.

The whole company stopped as the Gypsy fell. Gergely laughed. "The devil take you, Sárközi!" he said. "Why are you running so crazy?"

"If they're chasing," the Gypsy replied, getting up.

"No one's chasing here. Let's listen!"

The street was quiet. Only the Persian chanting could be heard in the distance. They listened.

They listened. They concentrated.

"I'm not running anymore," Mekcsey said resolutely. "If somebody attacks me, I'll thrust my dagger in him."

But no one showed up.

"We lost them," Gergely suggested. "Well, Sárközi my friend, where are we?"

"The moon is about to rise," replied the Gypsy. "I have someone I know where we can stay. But it's still a little far away, behind Yedikule."

Jancsi shivered. "We are going by Yedikule?"

"There," said the Gypsy. "It's only an arrow flight away from that inn."

"And you say that the moon will rise."

"It will rise. Don't you see, young masters, that the horizon is brightening? We need to hurry. That inn-keeper is Greek. He's our fence. For some good money, he can get us clothes."

"Can't we look around Yedikule?" Jancsi asked in a shaky voice.

"At night?"

"At night."

"Maybe, if you're in such a hurry," replied the Gypsy. "Just make sure they don't hear us." And he headed out in front of the boys. He carefully walked through a pack of dogs lying in the street. As the moon rose, he carefully walked in the shadows of the streets.

— § —

Sleeping houses and sleeping streets. Only the occasional yapping of a dog. Nowhere is there a human soul.

The moon illuminates tiny wooden houses. They are all the same. One upper floor. Two grated windows upstairs, but only wooden shutters. Those are the harem windows. Then here and there is a stone house, and then again an endless row of wooden houses.

The Gypsy stops at a house and gestures to the others to be quiet. Inside the house, a child cries and a man's voice is heard. Then an angry female voice. Of course there is never any glass in any window, so they could hear her shout. "*Sessiz ol! Hunyadi geliyor!*" (Be quiet! Hunyadi is coming!)[37]

The child becomes quiet. Our travelers hurry past.

It's not yet midnight when they turn a corner and see the reflection of moonlight and stars in the sea.

The Gypsy listens again, then whispers softly, "We need to take a boat, if we can find one, to get around Yedikule. The inn is on the other side of Yedikule."

"So Turks here also drink?" asked Gergely.

---

[37] Turks used the name Hunyadi to frighten children, much like an angry parent today would frighten a child by saying, "the boogie monster will get you." János (John) Hunyadi had wreaked havoc leading Hungarians to victories over the Turks between 1438 and 1456. His family became so powerful that his son, Mátyás (Mathias), was elected King of Hungary in 1458.

"In that inn, Turks also drink," replied the Gypsy. "There's a back room that's full of only Turks drinking."

He walked here and there on the sandy shore until he finally found a boat by a post.

At that moment, a small brown-haired female figure glided down the street like a bat. She headed down the shore towards the Gypsy.

The Gypsy looked at her in surprise. "Is that you, Cherhan?" She was the voivode's daughter.

"Where are the *deli*?" he asked, panting.

The Gypsy pointed to the shadow by the row of houses where the Gergely group stood listening.

The girl ran there. She grabbed Éva's arm. "Danger threatens! A raven-faced agha is on your trail with twenty soldiers."

Éva looked at Gergely. She didn't understand what the Gypsy girl was saying.

"The agha came to us," the girl continued, "just after you left. They searched and ransacked our tents. They hit my father with swords to make him say where you had gone. They even went into the cave."

"And you led them on our trail?"

She shook her head. "No. For two reasons. I won't say one." (She glanced at Éva.) "The other reason is that Sárközi came with you and he might have been killed."

"You're honest," Gergely said, smiling. "We have already met them."

"But they are coming! They're on your trail! Come, quickly! Run!"

"Let's sit in this boat," Sárközi said.

"The moon is shining on the sea," worried the girl.

"No matter," said Gergely. "There is just this one boat here. Even if they see us, it will take them time before they find another boat to chase us." He set off towards the boat.

The moon illuminated the sea and the tall bastion walls, in the center of which four huge, dark towers loomed over the sea. Their pointed roofs looked like gigantic hats.

As they reached the boat, they heard a rattling sound of weapons from the street. "They're coming!" said the frightened girl.

Frogs do not jump into water faster than our passengers jumped into that boat. "The boat is small!" cried Gergely. But his voice was lost in the sound of the sea on the shore.

The Gypsy girl also jumped into the boat. Mekcsey grabbed the two oars from the Gypsy and ripped off the straps in a single jerk. "Sit down!"

"Push the boat away!" said Gergely. Because the boat was lying on the shore.

"Not yet," Mekcsey replied. He waited with a raised shovel for the Turk who was running towards them, a hundred steps ahead of his companions. "Come on, dervish!" Mekcsey screamed angrily. "Come!"

However, seeing that raised shovel, Yumurjak recoiled. He held only a scimitar in his hand.

"Come on now!" Mekcsey called again.

Not only did he not push the boat, but he jumped out of it and ran with the shovel towards Yumujak.

The dervish froze, and as Mekcsey ran towards him, he turned back.

"Hurry!" said Gergely.

Mekcsey walked calmly back to the boat and shoved it off the shore with a single push.

Meanwhile, some ten more Turks arrived. Their loud shouting accompanied the sounds of the boat moving through the water.

But the load in the boat was really heavy. The sides of the boat were barely out of the water. They had to sit still so the boat would not rock.

Those on the shore ran up and down looking for a boat.

Mekcsey turned towards the Gypsy. "Which way?"

The Gypsy was crouching on the other end of the boat, and his teeth were shaking so hard that he could barely respond. "Avoid the castle."

"What's beyond the castle?"

"Nothing.

"Forest, fields?"

"Gardens. Bushy places."

The Gypsy girl groaned, "They found a boat!"

Just then a boat was pushed out into the water. It was full of soldiers. Six were seated, but they had only two oars. The other Turks must have been running in different directions looking for another boat.

"How many of us?" Mekcsey asked.

"Eight," replied the Gypsy.

"Only six. Because you and the girl are not warriors."

Listening, they continued to paddle east. The Turks' boat followed them.

"If more people don't come," Mekcsey thought, "I'll work on the oar, and you will do what you have to."

"We can hardly fight here," Gergely said. "If they catch us, both boats will capsize. I suggest you paddle towards Scutari."

"Well, who here can't swim?"

"I, my gracious lord," the Gypsy replied, shivering.

"Well, cling to the boat if it happens to capsize."

"That's not how it's going to be, Pista," Gergely said calmly. "Just row to the far shore where the water is only waist deep. We can get our feet wet."

"Then what?"

"I packed two pounds of gunpowder here. I'll wet it and light it. As soon as they get close, I'll throw it at them. Then jump out of the boat. After you, me, then Jancsi, and then Matyi. The Turks will be confused. We can take care of them one at a time."

And he handed the tinder and steel to the Gypsy. "Strike a light, Sárközi!"

Without a word, Mekcsey turned towards the Asian coast. But they were far away. They had to row for more than an hour. They were sitting quietly in the boat. Mekcsey and Matyi took turns rowing. Sometimes Mekcsey pushed his oar deep into the water. Even to the elbows. But he could not feel the bottom.

Meanwhile, the Turks followed them, shouting and shouting.

"*Perzevenk dinini sikeim!* [You pimp, I'll shit on your religion!]" cried one.

"*Perzevenk batakdji!* [You pimp of a man!]" cried another.

Gergely once shouted back. "*Perzevenk kenf oglu! Hersiz agha!*"[38]

He reached into the sea and kneaded the gunpowder on Sárközi's back into a black noodle the thickness of a thumb.

"Well, now, my Éva, a little dry in the middle."

Éva unscrewed the plug from the gunpowder horn and poured dry gunpowder into the middle of the pie.

Gergely folded the pie and shaped it like a mushroom. He twisted it into his scarf. He left only one opening for igniting the gunpowder.

"Earth," Mekcsey suddenly said. But they had hardly gone past the middle of the strait. The lad worked well. Since they had left shore, the Turks had hardly closed the distance. And there were many strong arms in the Turks' boat, enough to be able to throw flat stones.

"Is the tinder burning?"

"Burning," the Gypsy replied.

"Well, just hold it. Mekcsey, paddle slower. Turn the boat sideways. Just be careful they don't hit us. I'd rather they rush past us, should they happen to come after us."

"I'll get out of their way, don't fear."

"When they are only ten steps away, the Gypsy will slide off the boat's bow into the water. The Gypsy girl too. Maybe you too, Éva, but only the moment I light the fire. They must not realize that the water here is only waist deep. Let them swim!"

He gave another twist on his scarf and used his teeth to twist it tighter. Then he continued. "If the explosion throws them out of the boat, you, Mekcsey, still stay in the boat with the oar. Jancsi and I will jump into the water and take care of the swimmers. If their confusion is really great, then you, Matyi, work on grabbing hold of their boat, and whoever is hanging onto it, cut him down."

"Well, what about me?" the Gypsy asked.

"You three should hold onto our boat to prevent Mekcsey from tipping over."

He leaned over and whispered into Éva's ear. "You get into the water on the far side of the boat and stay low so the gunpowder doesn't get

---

[38] Roughly translated, but more delicately, "You pimp! I'll defecate on your religion!" and "You pimp of a man". Gergely's retort, "You dirty little pimp! You thief-agha! You scoundrel-agha!"

your face. Then, grab the other oar and hit any Turk who comes near you. After all, an oar is longer that a sword."

The Turks saw that the two boats were getting close. Triumphant shouting indicated they expected certain victory.

When the distance between them was only thirty steps, Mekcsey dropped his oar down into the water. "It's waist deep."

"Well then, let's stop," said Gergely. He got up from the bench.

"Give me the tinder," he told the Gypsy. Then he cried out to the Turks, "What do you want?"

"You will soon know!" they replied with the laugh of a wolf.

Gergely handed the tinder and the scarf to Éva, then picked up one of the boards that served as a boat seat.

The Turks held swords in hands and daggers between their teeth. They listened. Their rowers worked hard, oars making big splashes.

They were already close. Gergely threw the board in front of their boat. Big splash. The Turkish rower, as the water splashed the back of his neck, stopped rowing and looked back at what was splashing.

The boat floated closer by itself.

When it was hardly fifteen steps away, Gergely touched the tinder to the gunpowder. The dust sizzled with a red glow. Gergely held it for a moment. Then, with a well-directed motion, he threw it into the Turkish boat.

The Turks, as the fiery dragon flew over, moved aside. The next moment the boat turned into a fountain of fire, and then a flame three fathoms long exploded among them.

The Turkish boat capsized.

Six Turks splashed into the sea in six different directions.

"On them!" shouted Gergely.

However, their eyes were blinded by the sudden light from the explosion. None of them could see much of anything. It took a while before Gergely saw the first Turk hanging onto their boat, then pulling Mekcsey overboard with a big jerk.

Gergely struck with his sword. He felt his sword hit something hard. "Strike them!" he shouted.

But his companions also worked half-blindly. By the time they could see a little, they saw Mekcsey struggling in the water with a broad shouldered Turk.

Gergely also struck at him. He cut him on the head. The Turk turned to him. He punched Gergely on the shoulder, hoping to make him fall. But Mekcsey was hanging onto the Turk. He grabbed his neck from behind and pushed the man into the water. He held him until there was only bubbling.

11

One afternoon in May, three young Italian men dressed in velvet and two Italian girls in short skirts appeared in front of the gates of Seven Towers. One young man had a lute, a girl had another. The other girl held a tambourine under her arm.

A guard was standing around in the shade, half-asleep. Perhaps he would have fallen asleep if soldiers had not passed through the gate from time to time. When he saw the strangers, he pointed his lance at them. "What do you want?"

"We're Italian singers," said one. "We'd like to talk to the captain of the fortress."

"Not possible."

"But we must."

"Not possible!"

"Why not?"

"He told me not to let any foreigners in. He is busy. He is moving."

Some six soldiers stood and squatted in the shadows of the wall. An old Gypsy woman was telling fortunes by shaking some dried spotted beans.

One of the girls, the smaller one, stepped forward boldly and addressed the Gypsy woman. "Lalalka. The guard doesn't want to let us in. Send someone to Veli Bey to tell him that we're bringing a present."

The Gypsy woman was just about to make an interesting prediction She had divided the beans into five groups and was chatting with the soldiers. "I've just thrown to see about your luck, but I won't tell you before you go to the bey and tell him that some Italians are here. They have brought him a gift."

The customer's face was already red with curiosity. He scratched the back of his head, then got up and hurried inside.

It was not even ten minutes before he reappeared at the gate. He gestured to the Italians, "Follow me."

He set off before the Italians. He led them through a few corridors, then into a garden next to the mill and then into another garden full of giant leafy greens. The soldier pulled a head of lettuce and began to tear leaves off and eat them raw. He also offered it to the girls. "Eat some *marul*."

The Gypsy girl accepted a leaf and offered it to her partner.

"I do not need it. Thank you, Cherhan."

"But eat! It's good."

"I know it's good, but we don't eat it this way."

"Well, how then? With salt?

"Salt, but mostly with fried chicken."

One of the Italians was always translating what was being said, and because the two girls were always talking and the translator turned away a few times, the girl was always calling, "Gergely, what is Cherhan saying?"

The garden was between two high walls. Double castle. Two towers in the center were connected by a separate wall.

"The towers also have double walls inside," explained the Gypsy girl to Gergely. "A soldier was talking about it in the inn, when we were listening one night. He said that these towers are filled with gold and silver. He was sweeping there and looked through a keyhole."

"That's why it's guarded by so many soldiers," Jancsi said sadly. Otherwise, the boy was generally animated. Sometimes he blushed, otherwise he was pale, and he looked around everywhere and listened.

They reached the bey's quarters. There were no more houses inside the wall, just a lot of thick cannons, one every fifty steps. Next to them lay piles of rusty cannonballs.

The bey's yard was full of boxes and pieces of a tent made of red canvas. Weapons, camp furniture and rugs were strewn about, lying on cobbles and pebbles and in the well-kept flower beds. Whoever was moving away was certainly not planning on welcoming those who would be moving in.

Some ten or fifteen soldiers were loading boxes.

The bey was standing with them, and he was also eating raw lettuce — without fried chicken. He called the Italians aside by the bastion wall. He sat on the wheel of a large cannon facing out from the fortress, where he continued eating his salad. "Well, what do you want?" he asked good naturedly.

Gergely stood in front of him. With his cap in his hands, he spoke in Turkish. "My lord, we are Italian singers. We were fishing by the fortress at night. You know, my lord, that we are poor, so we have to be fishing at night. But at night, it wasn't just fish that we caught. As we pulled out a fish, something glittered. We look to see what it is. Well, it's a beautiful gold plate."

"What the devil!"

"Yes, my lord. Look. Here it is. Have you ever seen one more beautiful?"

He reached in his bag and pulled out a small gold plate. The figures of Greek gods had been beautifully hammered into its middle.

"*Mashallah!*" mumbled the bey. His eyes opened wide with delight.

"We also have never seen anything like this," continued Gergely. "We were thinking, what would we get with this. If we try to sell it, people will think we stole it. God only knows what trouble we'd be in! If we don't sell it, what's the plate worth to someone who has nothing to eat off it?"

The bey turned the plate over, looking at both sides, and feeling its weight. "Alright. So why are you bringing it to me?"

"I was just about to tell you, my noble lord. As we were pondering, it came to mind that there is a prisoner here in Seven Towers, someone who had been a good patron for us, some Hungarian lord. When my younger brother and I were small children, we were the slaves of that lord."

"And he treated you well?"

"He taught us, and he loved us just like his own sons. Well, we thought we would ask you. Let us sing some songs for him."

"That's why you brought me the plate?"

"Yes."

"And you can sing well? Sing something for me."

The five Italians stood together. Two of them strummed lutes, and they began:

> *Mamma,*
> *Mamma,*
> *Ora muoio,*

Ora muoio!
Desio tal cosa
Che all'orto ci sta. [39]

The two girls sang like violins. Gergely and Jancsi like two flutes. Mekcsek like some sort of cello.

The bey stopped eating his salad, and even staring at the gold plate, and you could almost see his ears growing bigger.

"Are you are angels, or jinns?" he said marveling.

Instead of replying, the singers started a lively dance. The Gypsy girl spun around into the middle and rattled the tambourine in front of the bey.

The bey got up.

"I will see you in three days; three nights. But I have to go to Hungary tomorrow morning. Join me. Either stay here with me, or join me on the road, but I will take good care of you. I'll give you money. You will never have a problem in life again."

The five Italians looked at each other a bit puzzled.

"My lord," said Gergely, "we need some advice. But first, if you will permit what we asked for ..."

"Willingly. But who is it that you want to see?"

"Lord Bálint Török."

The bey's expression turned unpleasant and he spread his hands out, palms down. "Török? Difficult. He is now in the *hundredweight*."

"What kind of *hundredweight*?" asked Gergely.

"Well," replied the bey angrily, "He was rude to the head mufti."

— § —

The bey nevertheless fulfilled the wish of the Italians. He entrusted them to a soldier and ordered the soldier to put Lord Bálint in the courtyard, whether he wanted to or not, because the Italians wanted to sing to him.

The gates of the inner castle also opened. Its courtyard was barely bigger than Elizabeth Square in Pest. The two chess players were still sitting

---

[39] Italian: "Mother, mother, now I am dying, now I am dying. I want that which is in the garden."

under the sycamore tree. Móré watched the players there, and Maylád was there commenting on the game to the prince's annoyance.

Only the hundredweight chains had changed owners.

The five Italians were stopped at the gate while Lord Bálint was led in. He was brought out of his cage. Two soldiers lifted his chains to allow him to walk. They put a hard wooden chair in the middle of the courtyard, and made Lord Bálint sit there. It was nice of them to put it in the shade. Then the old man could sit down. But he could not have moved in the iron chains thick as a man's arm.

Well, he was sitting. He did not know why he was made to sit there. He was wearing summer hemp linen clothes. He had no cap on his head, just his white hair that had overgrown into a mane. His hands were pulled down by the clamp on both sides of the chair. Those two clamps weighed fifty pounds. He was unable to lift his weak, old arms. His face was pale and he was suffering.

"You can come," the soldier told the singers.

And indeed they came through the gate. They stopped in a line next to each other, hardly five steps ahead of Lord Bálint.

The chess players stopped playing. What is going to happen here? It must be a fancy celebration: Italian singers at Seven Towers! They lined up behind Lord Bálint and waited for the song and, in particular, the dance of the two girls.

"The younger ones aren't Italian," says the prince.

"He can pick a Gypsy out of a hundred people," Maylád replied.

"But the rest are Italian."

By chance, they were all brown. Mekcsey has the broadest shoulders, Gergely the most slender, and Jancsi the blackest eyes. Éva was tanned with walnut oil. Her hair was hidden in a red Phrygian cap like the rest.

The five Italians stood.

"Well, sing," said the soldier.

But they were just standing, motionless and pale.

The youngest Italian's face flooded with tears. On the other, too.

"Well, sing it, comedian dogs!" said the Turk.

The youngest stumbled forward, collapsing in front of the prisoner in chains and hugging his leg. "Dad! My dear father!"

12

An arrow's flight distance from Yedikule, behind the Armenian hospital, standing by itself, is a small inn frequented by day laborers.

At one time it may have been a garden home, a beautiful marble holiday home when Constantinople was called Byzantium. But now, time and earthquakes have loosened the marble blocks, broken the alabaster balustrades of the terraces and the carved stone flowers framing the windows, moved the stairs aside, and planted weeds in the crevices of broken columns. The summer cottage turned into a inn.

All kinds of people frequented the place, and its owner, whose name was Miltiades, also dealt with stolen goods.

The Gypsy led our youths there. Miltiades gave them lodging, Italian clothes, gold plates — of course, for good money.

The production in Seven Towers didn't turn out as well as expected, so our youngsters ended up in trouble.

The soldier immediately told the bey that the Italians were some kind of relatives because they were crying so much about the prisoner. However, by then the bey did not have much interest in the affairs of Yedikule. His mind was engrossed with the Hungarian province (*vilayet* in Turkish). In Yedikule, he had been just another prisoner. He had to live inside the walls, and he could only step out once a year to pray in the Hagia Sophia mosque.

"You're an ass!" he scowled at the soldier. "Those Italians were prisoners of that master, and now my prisoners."

He was about to put his box of writing instruments in a crate. He removed a reed pen from the side of his box and pressed it into the ink-filled sponge. He wrote a few lines on a small piece of parchment, the size of a palm, and handed it to the dumbfounded soldier.

"Here you go. Give it to the Italians and escort them out the gate. No harm must come to them!"

Of course, when the paper was pressed into his hand, Gergely immediately read the writing. This is what was written:

These five Italian singers belong to my army. I gave them this temeşsük [safe conduct pass] *so that no one will cause them any harm while they were not with me. Veli Bey.*

Gergely happily put the letter away.

He looked at the soldier. Where did he see that owl face? Where?

Well, certainly, his honor was drinking at the Greek's place the night before with all kinds of day laborers and sailors. His red nose showed that he will be standing in the defendant's dock when he comes before the Prophet Muhammad.

"Will you be coming with the bey?" Gergely asked as they stepped outside the gate. And he shoved a silver thaler into the man's hand.

"No," replied the soldier, enlivened by the thaler. "The bey only takes sappers and *deli* soldiers. From tomorrow on, my lord will be Ismael Bey."

"But he doesn't live here yet?"

"No. He's living there in that house covered with vines."

He pointed to a house overrun by wild grape vines. Its back had been built against the wall of the old Byzantine castle. Perhaps it had even been built with the castle stones.

That night, owl-face had already drank a silver thaler's worth at the Greek's.

Our young people had dinner that night in a pretty little marble room. They had eaten a mutton rice stew, and they were already discussing whether they would return to their home country with the bey, or just by themselves.

Because it was certain that danger was nipping at their heels. It was even more certain that Lord Bálint could not be released.

"We have to go back with the bey," said Gergely. "This is the smartest thing we can do."

"Well, I'm not going to be singing for him," Mekcsey murmured. "Let's God's thunder sing for him."

"Well, then you can pretend you have a sore throat," said Gergely. "Why not sing for him? Doesn't the proverb say that if you sit in his carriage, you play his tune!"

"If they find out back home that we were entertaining Turks ..."

"Why not? We sang for him here. At home we'll make him dance."

Jancsi did not get involved in their conversation. He just stared blankly, tears rolling down his cheeks.

Gergely put a hand on his shoulder. "Don't cry, Jancsik. Because that big chain is not eternal. It could be that they will take it off tomorrow."

"I couldn't even talk to my dad. I just answered when he asked about Ferkó. I told him that he stayed at home so that if I were to die on this journey, mother would still have a child."

They listened and looked at him with pity.

"What a fool I am!" Jancsi continued. "I'm masquerading in costume sneaking in to see him when I could have visited him normally. After what's happened, can I go in? At least I should have given him some money."

The Gypsy girl picked up the dinner bowl and took it out. The moon shone in the room, making the candle light seem pale.

"There's one more thing we should try," said Gergely. "Because, pretty much we still have all of our money. Jancsi, you have a thousand gold pieces and I have three hundred. Mekcsey has enough for us to get home. Even Éva has money."

The Gypsy girl returned. "Won't you go see the owl-Turk? He is so drunk now that he fell off his chair. Sárközi is drinking at his expense, but he's not drunk yet. He and Matyi are toasting each other."

Then, realizing that she was the only one laughing, she dropped the subject. She sat down on the mat with the others, leaned on her elbows, and rested her chin on her hands. She stared at Éva.

"The new bey," said Gergely, "will surely get some money. He will get it the same way as the rest. What if he could do something? Money is a key that always fits in every lock."

"I'll give you everything I have," Jancsi replied. "I'd give my life, too!"

"Well, then. Let's give it one last try."

"How can you get to the bey at night?"

"He arrests you," Mekcsey volunteers. "He listens, he accepts the money, but you stay there."

Gergely smiled. "But I'm not such a fool. I'm not going to see him in my own skin."

"Well?"

"I'll dress up like a Turkish soldier."

Jancsi grabbed Gergely's hand. "Would you do it, Gergely? Would you?"

"I am already doing it," replied Gergely.

He got up and called for master Miltiades. "Master," he said, "I need a Turkish military uniform, the kind the guards at Seven Towers wear."

The Greek rubbed his bushy black beard. He had already gotten used to his customers wearing disguises, and also to getting two or three gold coins each day. Devil take them, whether robbers or thieves, the main thing is that they pay well. He had already advised them to stay in the cellar room.

"Well, I don't have such a uniform," he said, grinning. "But we have a drunk Turk here. You can take his turban and cloak."

"That'll be good enough. But I also need a beard."

"There's plenty."

"But I need a beard just like that of the soldier."

"There are some like that."

He turned around. In just five minutes, he returned with all kinds of beards, black hair and glue.

"Shall I stick it on?"

"Stick it on. Use your mastery to make me look like a picture of that Turk." He sat down. Miltiades got to work.

Meanwhile, they talked. "Do you know the new bey who is going to Seven Towers?"

"Of course I do," the Greek replied. "He was a *topchi*."

"What do you know about him?"

"Country bumpkin. Drinks water. His brain is water. He can't even write."

"The other officers don't know either. At most, they can read a little."

"But this fellow is stuck-up like a sultan's horse, though a horse knows more than he does. But when he sees a tree bigger than he, he bends like hemp in a breeze."

"Has he been to war?"

"He came with the emperor last year. He was caned in Esztergom."

"You mean he's a coward?"

"He's a coward and stupid. Can a man raised on water be any different?"

Gergely scrunched his face left and right feeling the glue. By then he had changed so much in appearance that Mekcsey almost fell over laughing.

The Greek fetched the turban, scimitar and cloak. "*Allaha emanet olun* [may God be with you]," said Gergely jokingly as he took a bow.

They wanted to accompany him but he allowed only Jancsi and Mekcsey. Jancsi handed him his gold on the way. Gergely thought, then sent Jancsi back. Only Mekcsey stayed with him.

"You too," he said to Mekcsey, "Keep a distance as you follow me. Don't let anyone suspect we are together."

Within a half hour, he was standing in front in front of the bey's house. He rattled the copper plates on its gates. An old, capon face appeared at the gate's spyhole.

"What do you want?"

"Send the bey immediately to Seven Towers! There's trouble!"

The capon disappeared. Gergely stepped back. He knew that the capon would reappear. But he also knew that if there was no one at the gate, he couldn't ask whatever questions the bey wanted answered. He would be compelled to return to the bey and tell him that the soldier had disappeared. The bey will wonder, get angry, and finally come out of his hiding and go to Seven Towers.

Gergely walked towards Seven Towers. He stopped at the Adrianople Gate. This was how they named the north gate of Seven Towers.

The gate was closed. The guard squatting by the gate was sleeping. Above his head burned a worthless oil lamp hanging from an iron rod protruding from the wall.

All around silence.

Mekcsey followed about thirty or forty steps behind Gergely, and when he stopped, he stopped. Perhaps Gergely was standing in the light of the lamp so Mekcsey could see him.

Minutes passed slowly. Gergely was silently cursing Turkish time for how sluggishly it passed.

And because in the dark, man and insect only look at what is lit up, Gergely turned his eyes towards the oil lamp. "I'll be an old man by the time this bey climbs out!" he muttered to himself.

Poor young hero, you beautiful star of Hungarian glory, you will never grow old! What kind of a face would you see in a mirror of the future if some hand from the sky would show it to you, and you would see yourself in fetters in this very same place, and you would see the Turkish executioner tying a rope from that rusty iron where the lamp now hangs. ...

In the silence of the street, a gate rumbled.

Gergely shuddered. He moved quickly toward the rumble.

The bey was coming. He came alone. He was wrapped in a cloak and wore a tall white turban on his head.

Gergely stopped for a minute. He listened to check if anyone was coming with the bey. No one came.

Then he hurried in front of the bey. "Sir," he addressed the bey with a Turkish military salutation, "It wasn't Veli Bey who called you. I cheated you because of a very important matter."

The bey drew back. He reached for his sword. "Who are you?"

Gergely also reached for his sword. He pulled it out and handed it to the bey. "Take it if you think you have to keep it from me." The bey pushed his sword back into its scabbard.

Gergely, too.

"I'm bringing you more good than you might think," said Gergely.

He pulled out a money bag from the inside pocket of his cloak. He jingled the gold. "Take it as an introduction."

The bey took the heavy bag in his palm, but then returned it. "First I need to know. Who are you and what do you want?"

He stepped into the shadow of the house. There was a stone bench there. He sat there and looked carefully into Gergely's face.

Gergely also sat on the bench. He folded his arms, and from time to time, scratched at his itchy false beard. He spoke softly and carefully. "My name is *Hundred Thousand Gold*. I think it's a pretty good-sounding name."

The bey smiled. But isn't it a nickname?"

"You can try it soon. But your name is *Poor Man*, though no doubt you are a great warrior. Everyone knows that you were in the triumphant campaign in Hungary."

"I see you know me."

"Well, let's make this short. As of tomorrow morning, you will be the governor of Yedikule. In other words, you will also become its prisoner, but a paid prisoner. You can go out to town once a year. And if Allah extends your life, you will see Constantinople twenty or thirty more times in your life.

"Go on."

"It's up to you whether you chose a greater and freer destiny."

"I'm listening."

"There is a prisoner in Yedikule, a rich Hungarian gentleman: Bálint Török."

"You want to free him?"

"As you say. Let's just say that's what I want."

"I'm listening."

"A few new soldiers are coming with you. If nothing else, they are your servants. What would happen if you brought out Lord Bálint tomorrow night, as if the sultan were calling for him?"

"No one can leave the fortress after sunset."

"He can come out if the sultan commands. But let's just say he comes out in while it's still daytime, with you and two soldiers. The streets around here are empty by then. You send the two soldiers back, and you with Lord Bálint continue strolling. But instead of going to the serai, you lead the so-called prisoner to a ship. A ship standing on the shore waving an orange flag. That ship could be a grain ship, a barge, or a boat. There's not very many around here. Well, I say, at most you change clothes and cloaks, and you both settle down in the boat."

"So simply"

"Not exactly. On the ship, before it starts, you find three hundred gold pieces, equivalent to three thousand Turkish gurus or piastres. Then, either on water or on land, we go to Tekirdağ. There our man is waiting for you with good horses and five hundred gold. That's five thousand gurus. We go down to Athens, and from there to Italy, as we enter the Italian coast, there are again five hundred gold pieces falling into your grasp."

"One thousand three hundred."

"So far. I guess that's about ten years of your salary. But think about it. He is the man who says he owns Debrecen, Szigetvár and Vajdahunyad castles, and who, after all, is in control of a royal estate, even almost all of Western Hungary. He would gladly pay you even ninety-nine thousand gold pieces, even if he had to sell half of his fortune."

"And if I don't even get the first thousand?"

"I'll give it to you now, if you like."

The bey looked at him thoughtfully.

Gergely shrugged. "If you ever see that we were cheating, even though you have yet to see a Hungarian who cheats, then you would always have time to blame Bálint Török for escaping and that you ran after him alone and caught him on the boat. Whether you bring him back from the ship or from the land, they will believe you because you brought him back."

The bey thought. "All right," he finally said. "One hour before sunset, that yellow flag ship should be within an arrow's flight from Seven Towers. You wait on the beach. How will I recognize you?"

"If you don't recognize my face, though, look at my face, for the moon is shining. My turban will also be yellow, sulfur-yellow. You will be able to recognize me."

"One hour before sunset."

"Exactly at eleven o'clock," replied Gergely.

Because as the Turks count time, the sun sets a twelve o'clock.

It was midnight when Gergely returned with Mekcsey.

"Is there an owl-faced Turk still here?" he asked as he entered the inn.

"He's sleeping," said Miltiades.

"Can you arrange it that he sleeps until eleven tomorrow?"

"I can," the innkeeper replied. He took out a glass. He poured water into it and mixed some powder in it. The powder dissolved like salt.

He shook the Turk. "Hey, Bayguk! Time to think about going home."

The Turk lifted his head and looked at him with confused eyes. He yawned.

"Well, drink this one glass of water, then wander off home."

The Turk did not even look at the glass, but held out his hand. He downed it. He looked vacant again. He moved to get up, but fell back again.

Gergely pressed five gold coins into the innkeeper's hand.

"Rest easy," said Miltiades. "He won't be moving from here, perhaps not even tomorrow night."

— § —

It was easy to hire a boat. They chose a four-oared Greek boat in the Golden Horn and took it as far as Tekirdağ, a day's journey from Constantinople. They gave them an orange flag and two gold pins. Gergely guided the boat to the meeting place by that afternoon, well ahead of time. Two hours before sunset they raised the orange flag.

Gergely then hurried to the inn. They woke up the Turk from his dreaming. He was told that the agha had ordered him to stand in front of the orange flagged ship. He was to stand there on the shore.

The Turk was still a little dopey. Sárközi had to lead him to the shore. The innocent fellow stumbled along wearing his yellow turban, not knowing whether it was morning or evening. All he knew was that the bey had ordered him to the shore by some ship.

Gergely and his companions were spread out, following him from a distance.

If the bey accepted the offer then, as soon as they step into the boat, they also would suddenly show up. And if the bey does not dare, or cannot make the arrangements, then they can come to an understanding with their friend in the yellow turban.

The first question was whether the bey would bring Bálint Török.

This was entrusted to Cherhan. They did not tell her that Lord Bálint was about to escape, only that he was being taken to the sultan who wanted to see him again. If she saw the bey, the two soldiers, and Lord Bálint, she would signal by reaching for the wild grape vines in the street corner, as if she were trying to tear off leaves. Mekcsey would be able to see this from about a thousand paces away and signal his associates. They in turn were about a thousand paces towards the shore. Gergely was dressed as a dervish, Éva as a Gypsy girl, Jancsi as a Persian merchant, Matyi as a Kurdish pretzel vendor, and Mekcsey as a fishmonger.

Éva squatted beside Matyi and ate pretzels.

At exactly the right time, Mekcsey lifted his wooden plate with fish over his head and headed for the shore.

That was the signal.

Jancsi was pale. Tears flooded his eyes. Gergely flushed. They both started walking towards the shore, staying a couple of hundred paces apart for each other.

The ship was waiting. The wind fluttered the orange flag. The ship's owner, a young Greek onion merchant, was by the ship's rudder counting his daily collections.

And standing in front of the ship was the stupid owl-faced Turk, a yellow turban on his head.

Behind him on the shore sat Sárközi, washing his feet in the green sea water.

"They're coming," Jancsi said, hurrying past Gergely. "God help us!" Even his legs were shaking.

Gergely looked back. He saw the bey on foot approaching with the white-haired Hungarian lord. Behind them were two soldiers in white turbans and armed with spears.

The bey turned around and said something to the soldiers. The soldiers turned back to Seven Towers.

Jancsi took quick steps towards the boat, but as he was about to pass Gergely, Gergely grabbed his cloak. "Wait!"

The bey calmly walked towards the shore with Lord Bálint.

They walked past the Kurdish pretzel vendor without looking either at him or at the Gypsy girl sitting next to him.

Lord Bálint looked as if he was just staring in wonder. The bey was lively. He kept chatting.

They stepped onto the shore. The yellow-turbaned Turk stood at attention.

At that moment, the bey turned around. His sword flashed. He signaled behind with it. Then he fell like an eagle on the yellow turbaned soldier, knocking him to the ground.

Some fifty soldiers rushed out of the bushes and houses.

First they tied up the yellow-turbaned soldier, then the Gypsy. Then they jumped on board the boat and pulled the young Greek off his feet. Everyone who was on the boat was tied up.

In all that noise and confusion, Cherhan appeared, screaming and begging for Sárközi. They grabbed her and tied her hands with a cord.

The sun was descending behind the Christian part of the city, when Gergely turned around towards the Constantine Column. His companions were all panting following his lead. They were dusty and pale.

Gergely wiped his forehead. He looked at Jancsi. "Well, isn't it good not to hurry for nothing?"

And they mingled among the people on the street.

13

By the middle of July, Veli Bey came to Mohács with his elite *silahdar* bodyguards and his fifty sappers.

Each time Turkish troops went to Buda or western Hungary, their first main camp was at Mohács. They loved that place. They called it the field of luck. Suleiman himself always preferred taking his rest there. He would have his tent pitched on the same hill where it had been pitched on that memorable day.

The bey's tent was ready when the army arrived in the evening, very tired.

The bey first bathed in the Danube, then tore into a roast capon. As the sun was going down, he sat down in front of his tent.

The field was still white from the many horse bones. Here and there, soldiers ate from their wooden bowls using a horse's skull as a table. They were lively.

Some fifteen aghas surrounded the bey giving him their daily reports. As each one finished his account, he sat down on the grass mat in front of the bey. Officers used to dine together at Mohács where even those angry with each other were reconciled.

A horseman arrived at the bey's camp that night with mail. He had been sent to the sultan with the news that Visegrád was now owned by the Turks. They did not gain it by fighting, but by ruining the aqueduct that provided water to the castle defenders. The castle died of thirst. People inside had been waiting for help from Ferdinand, but indeed he was a Hungarian king who entrusted the defense of his fortresses to God. So Amade surrendered the keys to the castle. He asked only to be allowed to retreat peacefully. The Pasha of Buda swore they would not be hurt. But his people had given no oath. As the Hungarians laid down their weapons in the middle of the castle and marched out unarmed, the Turks charged and massacred them.

"Well then, we can rest here for another two days," said Veli Bey to one of the aghas. "Tonight we sleep, tomorrow we will enjoy ourselves. The day after tomorrow, we'll leave for Nógrád."

Because after Visegrád, that was the next fortress they would besiege.

The Turkish post continued its journey towards Constantinople. Veli Bey's army laid down to sleep.

At noon the next day, the bey gave only one command to his officers. "Everyone is invited to have dinner with me tonight. There is wine, and it's good! The Italians are going to be singing."

He was a merry man. He loved to eat and drink. And every time he entered Turk-occupied Hungarian land, he immediately forgot Prophet Muhammad's prohibition of drinking wine.

"A common man has something secret to report. Will you hear him?" asked an agha.

"Let him come," the bey replied cheerfully.

A short *silahdar* with the eyes of a fox stepped forward. His clothes were tattered, like everyone else's. His turban was slightly larger than a child's handkerchief.

"Your servant has something to report about the Italians," he said.

"I'm listening," the bey replied.

"Those five people have long been suspicious dust at your feet. My first suspicion came when I saw one of the Italians using pieces of paper to wipe the others' swords."

"You're a donkey," the bey replied. "You must know that they are infidels. We pick up the papers in case the name of Allah may be written on it, but those pigs live without Allah. They have dark minds and are lower than animals."

The *silahdar* stood firmly in place. "My other suspicion arose around Sofia. You might remember, oh noble bey, when we encountered carts carrying plunder that one of the carts had fallen over by the side of the road."

"I remember."

"A cage full of chickens broke apart and the chickens scattered. An old lady kept calling them, '*Kotópoula, kotópoula!*' None of the chickens responded. She was a Greek woman. A Turk wanted to help and yelled, '*Gak-gak-gak!*' The hens didn't respond. Then one of the young Italians, a girl, takes her wheat basket and calls out to the poultry, '*Pi-pi-pi!, pityi-pityi-pity! Come my pityi!*' All the hens ran to her. She even caught a hen and kissed it."

"So, what about it?"

"This, sir, that the chickens understood Hungarian. But also, whoever called them!"

The bey mumbled. "Well, *pipi* means chicken in Italian. Do you understand Italian?"

"Italian? No."

"Then don't talk, you camel!"

The *silahdar* accepted the title of the camel with a humble bow. He continued calmly. "Well, what about when that *silahdar* was buying a foal near Belgrade? His name was Kerelece. Some peasant sold it to him for ten *aspers*. But the foal was so wild that no one could ride it. Then the broad shouldered Italian jumped on him like a leopard and rode him. The foal almost collapsed. Since when can an Italian singer break a horse?"

The bey shrugged his shoulders. "Maybe he was a groom in his childhood."

"Let me continue, sir."

"Continue."

"An agha came to us that evening, the largest agha I have ever seen in my life."

"Manda Agha."

"Yes. As he walks past the Italians, he stops in front of the thin one and says to him, 'Why, you're Bornemissza!' That fellow collects himself and replies, 'That's not me.' 'My God, you are he' says the agha, 'Gergely Bornemissza .' And he goes on to say, 'Don't you recognize me? Do you still have that nice ring? I took the advice you gave me. See, I'm already an agha. But not my name is Havan, but Manda. Bullets don't touch me.'"

"What did the Italian answer?"

"He said, 'I don't know what you're talking about. But I know there is another man who looks like me. How did you know the name of that Hungarian?' 'I learned it in Buda,' replied the agha, 'when they captured Bálint Török. He was one of his attendants. Well, pity it's not you! Yeah, you look like him. You lost ten gold because you aren't him.'"

"See there, he's not Hungarian, you elephant!"

"Oh yes he is!" answered the *silahdar* triumphantly. "I became convinced of that last night. Not just that he's a Hungarian, but all of them. When they set up a pot to cook dinner, one of them reached for a hemlock sapling and pulled it out by the roots to make room for the fire. With the roots there was a skull. All five looked at it and wondered whether it was a Turk or Hungarian. Your servant lay beside them and looked asleep. Your servant understands Hungarian."

The bey snorted, like a horse. "So they spoke Hungarian? What did the dogs talk about?"

"Our young thin one says, 'Certainly he was Hungarian because the Turks buried their own dead.' Then the other one took the skull and said this. 'Whoever you were in life, you died for your country. You are a saint to me!' And he kissed the skull. Then they buried it again in the ground."

The bey slapped his sword.

"Infidel dogs! But why didn't you report this right away, you ox?!"

"You were sleeping, sir."

"Chains for those treacherous spies! Bring them here!"

The *silahdar* ran away with a bright face. The bey looked from the hill with grim anticipation as *silahdars* ran in all directions among the tents.

It took two hours before the *silahdar* returned. Sweat ran from his forehead. "Sir, the Italians ..."

"Well, where are they?"

"The dogs escaped. They escaped!"

Part IV
Eger in Danger

1

If there is a book in heaven in which the history of Hungary is written, the following eight years would read as follows:

1545: The Turks have occupied Buda, Esztergom, Fehérvár, Szeged, Nógrád, Hatvan, Veszprém, Pécs – almost the entire country.

1546: The Turks have divided Hungary into fifteen *sanjak* districts. The Hungarians have kept only Upper Hungary[40] and one or two counties neighboring Austria.

1547: Not only are the Turks grinding down the Hungarians, but the Austrians, also.

1548: Luther's and Calvin's teachings are spreading throughout the country. Not only are Turks and Austrians enemies, but Hungarians themselves are their own enemies.

1549: Turks take everything as taxes, even children.

1550: A Wallachian and Turkish army attacks Transylvania. Friar György assembles an army of some fifty thousand within a few days. They defeat the Wallachians. The Turks pull back.

1551: Queen Isabella leaves Transylvania. Friar György is assassinated.

Then came the year 1552.

— § —

The plums of Sopron were already ripening blue, and the sunflowers were blooming when, on a sunny, windy afternoon, Éva was standing on the porch of a house in the city. She was choosing from her lord's clothes to give to a young man who was traveling abroad.

Since the last time we saw her, she has filled out and become a wife. Her thin, white velvet face is still feminine, but missing the old impish smile in her dear, cat-like eyes. There is a tame, intelligent calmness to her face.

"There are two suits here," she told the student scholar. She placed a worn, dark cherry-colored damask suit on the table and another casual

---

[40] Upper Hungary is Felvidék, *i.e.*, today's Slovakia.

suit made of hemp cloth. "This damask is a little big for you, but perhaps you will grow into it in a few months."

"Thank you, truly thank you, honorable lady," stammered the scholar. His face turned red from happiness.

"I'll adjust something here and there," she said further. "Well, you'll be resting until evening." Then she picked up the hemp suit. "This is just fine. My husband wore this when he was in Buda. When the Turks occupied Buda and we moved to Lippa with the queen."

"Thank you," said the happy scholar. "I will travel in this. The dust won't collect on this."

She reached into every pocket. They were all empty. But there was something hard in the top of the vest.

The pocket had a hole in it. Éva stuck a finger inside and found a folded, thin parchment paper in the lining.

She looked, unfolded, and opened the paper. Well, it had a drawing of a five-cornered shape with all sorts of lines and dots.

"What could this be, scholar Miklós? Some kind of tortoise, right?"

The scholar took the paper in his hand. He turned it over, and studied it at length. "It's not a tortoise," he said, "although it does look like one."

At that moment, a small, six-year-old black-eyed kid burst into the room. At his side he wore a splendid little sword with a gilded hilt. Its scabbard was made of worn red velvet.

"Mother," the child said, "you promised you would buy a trumpet, a gold trumpet."

"Don't worry now, my Jancsika," the mother replied. "Dear, go down into the garden, to Luca."

"Then you'll buy the gold trumpet?"

"Yes, yes."

The child held the sword between his legs and darted down into the yard to the garden.

"Well, it's certain," the scholar says, looking at the paper. "It's a drawing of a fortress, in particular, Eger fortress."

"Eger fortress?"

"That's it. Look, a double, frog-shaped line is drawn around it. That double line is the wall. The frog's head and four legs are the outer bastions. The thin square lines inside are the buildings."

"And that sickle-shape, here by the frog?"

"Outer fortress. There is no building inside as in other outer fortresses. Just the two bastions and two towers."

"And these two hooks connecting the sickle to the frog?"

"That is the Dark Gate."

"Why is it dark?"

"Because it's underground."

"Why is it underground?"

"Stable."

"A stable that big."

"It has to be big, honorable lady. Because it has a coach house and living quarters for the riders. The housekeeper also lives there."

"What about these dots by the gate?"

"That was a church. That was a church built by King St. István. They pulled down half of it not that long ago, about ten years back."

"What a pity!"

"Certainly a pity. But when they built this outer fortress, they put it a new moat that cut through the middle of the church. It was necessary because this was the weak point of its defenses."

"How do you know all this, Miklós?"

"Of course I recognize it. I went to school there for two years. Everyone there was talking about it. That was also when they were building the Dark Gate."

"But here there is another gate, on the west side beside the stream."

"And there is another in front on the south side. It has three gates."

"What are these red lines everywhere?"

The scholar looked carefully, following the lettering. He shook his head. "These are underground passages."

"So many underground passages?"

"There are many, but not all of them are passable now."

"And these rectangular room-like shapes?"

"Underground chambers. This one here is a water reservoir. That one is a cemetery."

"A cemetery among underground passageways?"

"It has to be because here by this passageway it's written, *road of the dead*."

The woman shuddered. "Strange," she said, "that they bury the dead there."

"Only when there was cholera," replied the scholar. "Now I remember that I had heard about this."

"It's a pity you didn't come earlier, Miklós, at least two weeks earlier."

"Why, honorable lady?"

"If you had come earlier, I would have given you these clothes earlier. Had I given you these clothes earlier, I would have discovered this drawing. My poor husband just left for Eger."

"I've heard that the Turks are turning towards there."

"That's why my husband went to Eger. If only my poor father hadn't gone with him. Just think. A seventy-year-old man. His hand and both legs are made of wood. And he left with my husband!"

"To fight?"

"Yes, that too. But also because he has an old, good friend, Father Bálint. About a year ago they had a quarrel over something. My mother was still living then. After that, the priest moved to Eger to be with Dobó. That's why my dear father left, to make peace. They really love each other."

Meanwhile the lady opened a chest painted green with flowers and took out a small book. It was her prayer book. She put the fortress drawing in it. She looked outside towards the garden at her son who was running around the servant watering the flowers.

"Someone will come from Eger," she said pensively. "The older brother of Gáspár Pető lives here. He is on the side of the king. He sent a wagon of gunpowder to the fortress, with bullets, because his brother is there. If a messenger comes from Eger, I will give him this drawing to take back to my husband."

She picked up needle and thread and put the hemp suit in her lap.

As they continued talking, a man wearing a dark blue cape stepped in, and as he closed the gate behind him, he greeted someone. "Don't trouble yourself anymore," he said, "I will straighten it inside."

Éva got up. The voice was unfamiliar, as was the man.

Three steps led up to the porch. The stranger's head appeared there. One-eyed, brown, muscular man. He had a mustache like the hussars. He held a staff like the village judges used to have.

"Good day!" he said to the woman. "They say that my honorable Lieutenant Gergely Bornemissza lives here."

"He lives here," replied the woman, "but he's not home."

"So he's already gone?"

"Gone, to Eger."

"Dear, dear." The man shakes his head, "I am very sorry. I had to talk with him ... but maybe his wife ...."

"I am his wife. Please come in."

The man walked up the stairs. He took off his cap and bowed with deep respect. "My name is Tamás Balogh," he said. "I am a nobleman from Révfalu." It was obvious from how he bowed that he was no peasant.

The lady, a smile on her face, pulled out a chair from table and introduced the scholar. "Miklós Réz is a scholar. He is traveling to a school abroad. His older brother is in the king's army and he knows my husband. He came here on a market cart and got off to stay here for a short rest."

"God bless you, young brother," said the one-eyed without bothering to shake hands with the scholar.

He sat down and continued lamenting. "Dear, dear. I came for the horse market," he said slapping his knee. "I would have had a lot of things to do with him. Among other things, I would have brought money for him."

"Money?" asked an amazed Éva.

"They said he had need of money, that he is going to Eger, and that he was selling some gold and silverware."

"We don't really have any."

"I really like rings," said the man raising his hand. He had ten of the most beautiful rings on his left hand. He might have worn more on his right hand, but it was covered by a grey leather glove.

He continued. "And how he has a beautiful ring, among other things."

"Yes, he has," replied the woman with a smile.

"With a moon."

"And stars."

"The moon is made of topaz."

"The stars are diamonds. But how do you know this, brother?

"May I see that ring?" asked the man. His voice was shaking.

"No," replied the woman. "He always carries it in his pocket. It's some kind of lucky ring. It had belonged to a Turk."

Little Jancsi was rattling his little sword in the yard again. With one leap he was up the stairs. When he saw the stranger, he stared in the way that children often do.

"Say hello to the man," said the lady.

"Is this the lieutenant's son?" the stranger asked. "But what am I asking, because he is an exact copy!" He pulled the child to himself. He kissed him.

The mother felt a wave of some discomfort. Oh, a mother's heart feels what kind of person is touching their child! But it was only a passing feeling. The next moment she had forgotten.

"Are we going to buy the trumpet yet?" the child asked.

"I'll have a look around at the fair," the scholar said. "I'll take Jancsi to my cart. I'll show him the little foal."

"Good," replied the woman, "Here's a penny. Give him a trumpet. But look after him, Miklós. You, too, Jancsi ... You know what your father said!"

And he turned to Mr. Tamás. She smiled sadly. "Yes, he told us to look after the child."

The child jumped with joy and left with the scholar.

The mother shouted after them, "Walk near the church, Miklós. We'll also be going out soon." She had already planned to go to the fair. She wanted to buy some small things from the Viennese merchants who had come to the fair.

During this time, Mr. Tamás Balogh was absent mindedly turning his cap with an unpleasant expression.

"What news do you have from Szolnok?" asked the woman anxiously. "It's true, isn't it, that the Turks can't deal with it?"

"That's also my opinion," Tamás Balogh replied absent mindedly.

"When my husband left, he told me the Turk will hardly get as far as Eger this year. Szolnok was really very strengthened last year. Stronger than Eger."

"Much stronger."

"And even if it falls, Eger is protected by the whole of Upper Hungary."

Mr. Tamás Balogh smiled wryly. He looked up and asked, "Does the honorable lieutenant here have any portrait here?"

"There is," replied the lady. "It was painted last year by a German painter."

"Would the honorable lady show it to me? I have heard many good things about the warrior. I would like to get to know him."

"Don't you already know each other?" Éva asked in amazement.

"There was time, but it's been very long time since I have spoken with him."

The woman led the guest into to the room. The room was dark and full of lavender scent. When she opened the windows, one could see that it was a guest room.

Turkish carpets on the floor. A bearskin covered couch by the wall. At the window, a writing desk and a bookcase. Many parchment-bound books, maybe a hundred. Portraits on the wall. A portrait of old Cecey in a helmet, when his hair was brown. Mrs. Cecey looking on, wearing a gold-embroidered headdress. Then framed in walnut wood, a yellow image of Christ; a mischievous portrait of a girl whose face resembled Mrs. Bornemissza next to a portrait of her husband. Young, thin-faced, brown haired man, almost Gypsy dark brown hair. Cheerful wisdom radiated from his open eyes. The mustache was curled. A small round, soft beard on his chin. His hair fell down to his shoulders.

Mr. Tamás looked at the picture carefully and nodded. "Good-looking person. How old was he?"

"Twenty-six."

"And you already have such a grown son!"

"We have been married for eight years," the young bride replied with a smile. "We were young children when we got together."

Mr. Tamás looked at the portrait again. "And is it true that the gentleman warrior was also in Constantinople?"

"He was. I was with him."

"I have a Turkish acquaintance who talked about it. Manda Bey. He's a huge man. The gentleman warrior was very kind to him once."

"Manda Bey? I've never heard that name."

"Of course," said Mr. Tamás, nodding. "Before that his name was Hayvan."

Éva smiled. "Hayvan? Of course I know him. I saw him, too!"

Mr. Tamás looked up at the portrait once more, looking at it with a long, silent frown, as if he never wanted to forget that face. He nodded his head to the picture as if to say goodbye, then nodded to the woman and walked backwards out the door.

Again, she felt the same shudder and bad feeling that she had when he touched her child. However, she escorted him to the porch stairs.

The man always kept to her right. That's what a peasant does. He bowed when he greeted her. That was what a nobleman does. He walked backwards out the door. That's what a Turk does.

The woman was uneasy. But she was soon rebuking himself. "I shouldn't feel badly about an unfortunate person," she said, sitting and getting back to her sewing. "He's a one-eyed man. It's unpleasant to look at him."

And to drive the unrest out of her mind, she sang a song. The maid was singing in the garden, so she also sang the same song. With quick fingers she sewed new buttons, one after the other, on the dark cherry-colored damask coat. There was some fraying in one place. She looked for some red silk thread to repair it.

But the visitor just would not get out of her mind.

"Who is that man?" she asked, putting the coat on her knees.

The ring, the staring at the portrait, the mention of Hayvan, the departure in the manner of the Turks.

Who is this man?

She stared at the closed gate with a pale face, forcing her brain to answer. She was already familiar with the face, even the voice. But she did not know from where. She kept thinking about the ring. Gergely said he would take it, but put it in his everyday vest. Did he take that vest?

She hurried to the wardrobe and went through it, pulling the clothes out. The vest was inside. She touched it. There was something hard inside. The ring! The ring! He did not even wrap it with paper.

And then, like lightning flashing through a cloud, the name flashed through her mind. She slapped her forehead. "Yumurjak!"

— § —

That was when the maid returned from the garden. She saw her mistress and the scattered clothes in front of the wardrobe. Her face was pale and her eyes were circled. "Honorable woman!"

No answer.

The maid looked around. She ran into the other room. She suspected robbery.

She finally got a bottle of vinegar and rubbed some on the woman and made her smell it.

"My husband is in danger!" Those were Éva's first words. "Where's the child? That's right. I sent him off. My cloak soon, Luca! Let's get Jancsi!"

"But you are so sick, honorable woman ..."

"I'm not sick," replied the woman. But she was deadly pale.

And like that, she got dressed and hurried out the gate. Her sense of danger steeled her nerves. She hurried straight towards the church.

Crowds of fair-going people were coming and going in the streets. Carts, cows, pigs led on ropes. Among the animals, villagers with loaded crates and barrels. All the sounds and noises of a town market. Dust and the smell of onions.

The maid caught up with her by the church. She covered her with a cloak.

Suddenly, the scholar emerged from the multitude.

Running and pushing people, he made his way to reach them and cried out, "The pagans have occupied Szolnok! The news was announced in front of the church. How can I go now ...?"

"My child!" cried Éva. "Where did you leave him?"

"Mr. Balogh took him to the church. He said that while he was praying, I could listen to the news. Oh my God, my God! The country is finished! If Szolnok is in Turkish hands, Eger cannot stand."

"The child ... the child!" Éva panted. She rushed up the stairs and went through the main doors into the multitude.

"My child!" she shouted, choking. "My child!"

Inside, just at this time, they were singing a litany, and German peasants from the surrounding area were singing a German litany loudly. *"Christus, höre uns! Christus, erhöre uns! Herr, erbarme Dich unser."*[41]

She screamed at them, screaming madly. "Jancsi!" she shouted. "Jancsi my son!"

But little Jancsi did not answer from any of the pews.

2

On the fifth day of September, Gergely greeted the rising sun under Sirok Castle. The sun shone in his eyes and those of his company of two hundred and fifty infantrymen. Actually, he did not greet the sun, but another brigade coming towards him, which is why he pulled his cap to shield his eyes.

He was in front of his soldiers, the only one ahead on horseback, so he was the first to see the disorganized band armed with swords and pikes coming like a snowstorm.

"What the hell could this be?" he muttered to himself. "They're not Turkish to be Turks. They can't be Hungarians if they're coming from Eger." Then the thought fluttered across his mind that Dobó had left Eger.

Because, well, that King Ferdinand always sends help only with his mouth. That was how Lippa and Temesvár were lost the previous year. And Szolnok. Who knows if Eger can stand its ground? Dobó is a smart and calculating man who can add two and two together and reckon that one Hungarian cannot withstand a hundred Turks.

On the road, they saw nothing but priests sitting in carriages. All from Eger! Carts all loaded with big crates and bags. At first, he greeted them, but then, having gotten fed up with their numbers, he did not bother to make way for them on the road.

Well, he was startled for a moment with the thought that Dobó might have left the castle in Eger. But only for a moment. The next moment, he chased the thought away. He is not that sort of man! Whoever is coming on the road, it is not Dobó. And if it is Dobó's army coming, then Dobó is not with them. He will stay there alone, and die there alone, but history cannot write that he left the castle that had been entrusted to him.

---

[41] Christ hear us. Lord have mercy on us.

There was no flag flying above the oncoming infantry, or, if there was one, it was folded up and being carried in a cart. About two hundred people, hurrying on foot in small groups.

Gergely gestured to Cecey. The old man was riding behind the company and talking to an old soldier. The old man always talked. As his son waved, he rushed forward on his horse.

"I'll go ahead a little," said Gergely.

He spurred his horse. He trotted in front of the unknown brigade.

His eyes searched for the leader. There were no feathered caps among them. He stood in front of them and raised his arm, gesturing to them to halt. "Are you from Kassa?"

None of them answered. They looked at him with confused eyes. Some of them turned red.

"Where are you coming from?"

None replied to this, either.

"Well," shouted Gergely angrily, "Perhaps you are soldiers of mute monks?"

Finally a tall man with a big chin lifted his head and talked. "Well, we're from Kassa, lieutenant sir, and we're coming from where the respected lieutenant is going."

"You're coming from Eger?"

"From there. But it's better if the honorable lieutenant doesn't head there. It's not worth it. You'll have to turn back anyway."

"Why? What's wrong?"

"What? Well, it's just that it's a foolish goat who jumps onto the knife!"

"What knife!"

"Do you happen to know what happened at the end in Temesvár?"

"I know."

"Do you like to know that Losonczi was cut down and his people slaughtered?"

"I said I know."

"Do you happen to know that there are two hundred thousand Turks?"

"I know that too."

"Do you happen to know that my Lord Dobó does not have even a thousand soldiers?"

"There can be that many."

"Well, do you happen to know that since yesterday, Szolnok belongs to the Turks?"

Gergely paled. "Now I know that, too. And I also know that if you all had been there, then it would have been taken a lot sooner. Well, just go back to your homes. And so you won't go empty handed, here you are, for your pleasure, you rats!" He punched the big man in the face so hard that he fell over the man next to him.

The next moment, he had drawn his sword, and he would certainly would have cut a path through them had they not jumped off the road.

"My respects to György Serédy!" he shouted after them. "I wish him soldiers different from you. You're all rats!" He spit after them.

The men from Kassa scattered across the field, and Gergely never looked back at them. He moved again, and his horse, feeling the pressure of the spurs, felt his master trembling with anger.

Good thing he found a Gypsy caravan on the road. Whether the men from Kassa had overturned one of their carts or it fell into the ditch by itself, the Gypsies were struggling with getting it back up.

Gergely looked back to see if his company was staying behind. After waiting for them, he stopped in front of the Gypsies. He watched them working in order to forget his anger.

"What, ho!" he suddenly shouted. "My friend, Sárközi!"

One of the shaggy Gypsies grinned at this friendly address and took off his hat. When his cunning eyes had probed over Gergely's face, he came forward bowing.

"Well, don't you recognize me?"

"Of course I recognize you, your greatness, my lord. I kiss your hands and feet. I immediately recognized you. It's just that your name did not come to my mind."

"Well, it will come to your mind. What are you doing here? I see you're ragged like a scarecrow."

The Gypsy was indeed ragged. He was just wearing a shirt with leather patches on patches, or maybe patches with patches on leather. His red legs poked through his pants. There was nothing on his feet.

"Well, do you have a horse yet?"

"Of course not. I kiss the mud of your boots, but no. I never will have one again!"

"Come with me to Eger, old man. You'll get a horse if you serve there for a month. On top of that, I will give you such a pair of red pants that every Gypsy will be sick from envy."

The Gypsy grinned. He glanced down at his ragged clothes, looked up again at the warrior's face, then scratched his head. "To Eger? It'll be hot there, my lord."

"Don't be afraid of that. You can work under the coolest bastion. I will give you wages. You'll be the manager of my armory. Then he continued in Turkish. "*Allah işinizde rast getirzün!*" (God help you in your work!)

The Gypsy jumped into the air. "Gergely Bornemissza, lieutenant warrior sir!" he shouted. "Oh, I even kiss your horse's legs! Oh, it's not for nothing I dreamed of a yellow thrush last night."

"Well, yet you recognized me."

"Yes! You! Of course I recognized you. I kiss your dear legs. I immediately recognized you. It's just that I didn't know who you were."

"Well, will you come with me?"

"I'd go, sure as God I would go ..."

"Then come!"

"If only those damned Turks weren't there!" By now he was using both hands to scratch his head.

"But they're not there yet."

"But the dogs will be there! With these soldiers coming and going, it's not a healthy pace to be."

"I'll be there, Sárközi. Don't be afraid as long as you can see me! Then, if it so happens that we're hemmed in, the castle has a mouse path to Miskolc."

Gergely just said it randomly. Because every castle has a tunnel. But he knew nothing about Eger Castle except that Dobó was the captain and that Mekcsey was his first lieutenant. These were two people he would follow until the ends of the world.

Did the mention of the underground tunnel affect the Gypsy, or the offer of a horse, or the red pants, or that he liked Gergely? He scratched a little more, then agreed. "Well, if I get paid, a soldier's uniform, yellow boots with spurs, and a good mount, it doesn't matter if the horse is blind, then I'll sign up!"

Gergely's company had already caught up. They were listening to this conversation, laughing. There was even greater confusion when Gergely extended his hand to the Gypsy and he grabbed it.

"Now," said Gergely reaching into his pocket, "Here's a penny for your enlistment. You can ride on my reserve horse all the way to Eger. Then, as soon as we get a blind horse, you'll be first in line."

The Gypsy happily jumped up on the horse and spurred its side with his bare heels.

The Gypsy caravan screamed good luck to him. He also shouted something back to the Gypsies. Then he flipped his cap on and, with his chest stuck out, he rode proudly alongside Gergely.

"Hey, how God has taken up my work!"

— § —

A few hours later, on the road to Bakta between branches and hills, the green glaze tiled towers of Eger Castle shone in front of them. National flags and the red and blue flags of the city fluttered on the towers.

Beautiful castle! And around it vineyards and forests turning red and yellow. Behind it, a short distance away, a tall, blue mountain six times larger than St. Gellert Hill in Buda.

Gergely lifted his cap and turned towards the company. "Look at it, boys. Because the good Lord is also now looking at it from heaven!" He spurred his horse and galloped forward.

The Gypsy wondered for a minute whether to remain at the head of the company or follow his lieutenant. Then he realized that he would look like a comedian if he were to lead the company. He gave the horse a good slap on its buttocks and hammered the horse's belly with his heels.

The horse bucked several times and tossed the Gypsy high. But not for nothing did he learn the ways of a horse trader. Each time he cleverly landed back in the saddle.

Clouds of warm dust rose from the wagon ruts. The dust was being kicked up by refugees. Women, old people and children were sitting on carts or walking next to carts full of furniture and poultry. Some of the carts had calves standing and mooing, some had pigs grunting.

A Turk will not eat pigs, but who knows when they would be able to return?! Some were driving cows. Beside one cart, a little girl in red boots carried her pet tit bird in a cage, and a woman carried a flowering, potted rosewood on her back. Many carts and carriages. Big hauling. Surely some of them will never again return. Especially those who, in the valley below, passing through the Cifra Gate, were headed towards Felnémet. The cotters and widows would stay in the more rugged terrain of Upper Hungary where the Turks' horses have not left their hoofprints. Especially Kassa. That was the main objective for the refugees.

However, Gergely was not interested in them. Within a quarter of a hour, he galloped through the Bakta Gate, the western entrance through the city walls. Then looking up, he rode through the market and wended his way up to the castle gates.

The wall there was white and almost smelled like lime, it was so new.

The bridge was lowered. Gergely flew like a bird into the castle, up among old trees. His eyes searched for the captain.

He was standing in the castle market wearing violet colored velvet, a sword, red boots, and an eagle feathered velvet cap in his hand. Next to him was a blonde page holding two flags on his arm: one with the national colors and the other blue-red. On the other side of the Dobó stood old Father Bálint wearing a white surplice over his black priest's clothes and a silver crucifix in his hand. With his long white beard, he looked like some sort of biblical prophet.

They had just finished swearing in soldiers. Dobó said something to them, put on his cap, then turned towards the galloping horse.

Gergely jumped down from his mount and presented his sword with sparkling eyes.

"Humbly reporting, warrior captain sir. I have arrived!"

Dobó just looked. He smoothed his round gray beard, his long, wavy mustache, and looked again.

"You don't recognize me, do you, captain sir? It's been eight years since we last saw each other. I am your grace's most devoted soldier, Gergely Bornemissza."

"Gergely son!" cried Dobó, spreading his arms wide. "On my heart, my soul! I knew you wouldn't abandon me!" He embraced and kissed the warrior.

"But did you come alone?"

At that moment, Sárközi's steed pranced in, tossing the ragged, barefoot Gypsy some three feet into the air.

Dobó also smiled. "Surely this isn't your army?"

"Not really," Gergely laughed. "He is just my gunsmith Gypsy. Did I do well to bring him in?"

"All people are worth gold here," replied Dobó. He pulled his hands away lest the Gypsy kiss them. But you can't cheat a Gypsy. He kissed the strap of his boots.

"But how many of you came?" Dobó asked anxiously.

"Not many," sighed Gergely. "Altogether only two hundred and fifty infantry were assigned under me."

Dobó's eyes sparkled. "Two hundred and fifty?! Son, if I had gathered that many soldiers from all around here, I would go out and meet the Turks on the fields of Maklár."

"Is there no help coming?"

Instead of a reply, Dobó waved into the air. Then he turned towards the officers around him. He introduced them to Gergely. From the king's army, Zoltay was already there, whom Gergely met in Buda eleven years before. He was still blonde and thin, a cheerful man, and he did not even have a beard, so he probably was single.

Then there was Gáspár Pető, a quick-handed, small man who was also from the king's army and bore the title of a noble family.

There was a slim faced, blue-eyed lad standing next to Pető. He also shook Gergely's hand warmly. "I am János Fügedy, the lieutenant of the church chapter."[42]

Gergely looked at him. "You look very familiar to me, dear younger brother!"

The other shrugged and smiled. "I don't remember."

"Didn't you give me some ox ear in Transylvania?"

"Ox ear?"

"That indeed. When Fürjes was to have his wedding, in the back in the kitchen yard."

"Maybe, because I did serve all kinds to the pages there."

"I hope I can serve something back to you now."

"How so?"

"I'll give you a pasha's ear in return."

---

[42] Chapter (*káptalan*): A governing group in a Catholic diocese that assists in the church administration. In those days, even the church maintained a military.

Then Gergely turned to Pető. "Well, why are you so quiet?"

"Naturally I'm quiet," replied Pető. "Twenty of my cavalrymen slipped away down the road. Certainly, if I ever come across any of them again! ..."

"Never mind," Dobó said. And he waved. "The gate is open. Go, whoever is afraid for his skin. I don't need any lizards on these walls!"

Only then did Gergely look at Father Bálint. He had not seen him in a year. He embraced and kissed the old man.

"How come you didn't leave with all the other priests, my reverend Father?"

"Someone needs to stay here," the old man grumbled. "What's Cecey doing?"

"He's on his way!" Gergely replied almost shouting. "Young people run away, elders come, and they bring swords. You will see how my father's wooden hand handles a sword!"

A dumpy man with a short neck stepped out from the church's shadows. A sword as wide as a man's hand was slapping the side of his leg. He walked briskly with an old man, and from a distance, he was already waving and laughing at Gergely.

It was Mekcsey.

Since Gergely had seen him, he had grown a beard and looked even more like a bull. The earth almost shook under his steps.

"Well, have you married?" asked Gergely after embracing him some three times.

"What?" Mekcsey replied. "I've gotten a dear Sári since then."

"Who did you marry?"

"The most blue-eyed angel in heaven!"

"Well, who?"

"Eszter Szúnyog"

"Long life! Well, and your pretty snake-headed sword?"

"I still have it. I just don't wear it on weekdays."

"And where is your dear family?"

"I sent them to Budetin Castle until the Turks are beaten to a pulp."

Looking at Dobó he continued. "I told the old man not to send our wives away, but he was so protective of his own Sára as if she were a child, so we sent them away. We'll have enough trouble with the Turks."

The steward's report interrupted their conversation. The old man spread an sheet of paper in front of Dobó and, holding the paper back from his spectacles, read. "Well, we have lamb, 8050; ox, cow, calf, that is, all beef cattle, 486; wheat, rye and flour altogether 11,671 bushes. Another 1540 bushes of barley and oats."

Dobó shook his head. "It's not enough, uncle Sukán."

"That's what I thought, my lord captain."

"If the Turks are besieging over winter, what do we give the horses?"

The old man shrugged. "Well, my noble lord captain, probably shoes, like for our soldiers."

"How much wine?"

"2215 barrels."[43]

"That also is not enough."

"But at least it's aged wine. This year's harvest went to the dogs. There is also some barrels of beer."

"Pigs?"

"139 live. Bacon, 215 sides."

Bornemissza would have been interested to listen to this report, but he thought of his company. He sat back on his horse and galloped out of the gate to lead them in.

He led them in and introduced them. Dobó shook hands with the flag-bearer. He handed them over to Mekcsey to give them the oath, show them their billets, and give them some breakfast.

"You also go into my house. That's the yellow, two-story over there. Have a bite of something."

Gergely started out, but he was more interested in the castle. He rode around on horseback. "Beautiful castle!" he shouted, returning to Dobó. "If I ever become a captain of a fortress, may God let me settle down here."

"You haven't seen anything," said Dobó. "Come, I'll show you."

---

[43] Gárdonyi's note: A barrel contained 22.5 litres.

And as Bornemissza dismounted, he gestured to the blonde page. "Kristóf, bring the horses after us."

He took Gergely by the arm and led him to the southern gate. "Well you see," he said, standing there. "To orient yourself quickly, imagine a large tortoise looking south. This is where we are now, this is the head. The four legs and the tail are the bastions. The two sides are two pedestrian gates.

Meanwhile he called out to the gate tower, "Are you looking out up there?"

The guard leaned over the tower window, pushing aside the horn that hung at his side. "We're looking out. Two of us, captain sir."

"Let's go up," Dobó said. "This is where the Turks will come today or tomorrow, so let's look at this also."

With the gesture of his hand he wanted to make Gergely go first, but he backed away. "I have already enlisted, captain sir."

Meaning that he was no guest. So Dobó went first.

There were four guards in the tower. They saluted.

"Meet Lieutenant Gergely Bornemissza!" Dobó said.

The guards saluted once more. Gergely similarly raised his hand and lifted his cap.

Two small villages and a mill were visible to the south from the balcony of the tower. Beyond them, a blue-green plain between two ranges of hills.

"This is where the Great Alföld Plain begins," Dobó explained.

"And these two small villages?"

"The innermost Almagyar, the farther, Tihamér."

"And this stream?"

"Eger Stream."

"Are these new walls here around the gate?"

"New. I built it."

"They're good and tall. The Turks would hardly make an attempt here."

"Well, that's why I built it. From the left, as you can see, a cannon defends the gate and guns from above."

"Every castle has defenses on the left. The attackers have no shields on their right arms."

"Here, it would not have been possible on the right. As you can see, the stream flows out here on the west side of the castle. I closed the locks at the mill so we have water."

They went to the west side of the castle, the side overlooking the city.

"A dizzying high wall. It must be at least ten fathoms."

"Perhaps more. On this side the Turks really can't try anything. Outside stone, inside earth. But now, let's mount up. On this side we are unlikely to have any trouble with the Turks."

They mounted and continued on horseback.

Down below, the city was quiet and deserted. Among the houses were the bishop's church and the bishop's palace. On the other side of the hill, to the west, the church of St. Nicholas that belonged to the Augustine monks. On the west, the city was surrounded with thick, even hills. Beyond were the blue of the Mátra Mountains.

There were two bastions on the west side and a small strong gate in the middle. Soldiers were driving horses down to the stream.

Beyond the stream, in the city market, some people were lounging around a herd of pigs.

"They're still here?" Gergely asked staring.

"Some are still here," Dobó replied. "Every day I tell them to clear out, but they all want to sell their pigs and young cattle."

In front of the gate, inside the castle, a broad-faced, lean lieutenant was training about fifty soldiers. They had swords, rusty helmets with visors lowered on their heads, and armor plates on their shoulders. Two stood in the middle. The lieutenant shouted, "Back! Back! I say, donkey! Pull your sword back as soon as you make a cut with it!"

From the instructions, it was obvious the trainee had never been a soldier. Markos was a small, strong peasant boy, and Dobó only added him to the Kassa team because young strength was needed to work the cannons.

"Who is this lieutenant?" asked Gergely.

"Hegedüs," Dobó replied, "a lieutenant from Kassa. A tough man."

And he said to the group, "If you don't understand, ask the lieutenant."

At this, the young man lowered his sword and looked at Dobó. "I don't understand, captain sir, why do I have to pull my sword back?"

"The lieutenant will explain."

"Because, you pair of Muscovy boots," said the lieutenant angrily, "you need to protect yourself with it. You need to be ready to strike again."

"But, my lord lieutenant," said the young man, spitting to one side, "If I have cut someone once, he won't be cutting at me again!"

Dobó tugged on his horse and smiled. "A child of Eger. He speaks well."

They lumbered under the wall towards the north. Two palaces stood there. The smaller one was more ornate and had glass windows. The larger one was a building that looked like a granary on a lord's estate. It was the monastery and it had only parchment windows. At some point in the time of Dobó, it belonged to the church chapter and served as the quarters for the chapter officers. Behind the smaller palace was a flower garden surrounded by iron grating painted green. Inside were benches and an arbor of grape vines.

A late butterfly was fluttering over the asters.

As Gergely forgot himself staring at the roses, Dobó also looked that way. "My poor wife planted all those flowers in vain."

"Where is the noble woman?"

"I sent her home to my brothers. A woman's eyes weaken a man."

They crossed the garden and reached the corner of the west side.

The wall there was also dreadfully high. A hill protruded underneath. It had been carved steeply down to the ground level of the city.

"Well, look," Dobó said. "This bastion is made of earth. Its purpose is just to protect this corner from being shot and to protect that other bastion there. That's Prison Bastion." He pointed to the tall tower in back of the castle: the tortoise's tail.

From there was a beautiful panoramic view of the city and the valley by the stream with a forest of poplar trees stretching to the north. At the end of the valley was a beautiful wooded village: Félnémet, a big village. Beyond that, forested mountains lined the wide valley on all sides.

But Gergely did not take much time to admire the view. His attention was attracted to the back of the castle. There, high hills rose behind the castle, and those hills were separated from the fortress by only a deep, hand-dug ditch.

"You can expect the attack from here," he said, looking at the hills.

"From here," Dobó replied, "but this is where the walls are the strongest, and four of our largest cannons are positioned here."

He dismounted by the Prison Bastion and handed the reins to his page, Kristóf. "You can lead him to the stable."

They went up inside the Prison Bastion, where four large cannons, four mortars, and some twenty bearded cannons yawned towards the hill.[44]

Next to the cannons, a curly-haired blond German artilleryman was training some peasants. "When I say *bor* [wine], then give me *bor*! When I say *düss* [fire] then give me *düss*!"

The peasants listened to the cannon master with serious faces. Dobó smiled, "*Venn Sie sangs* bor, *dann bekommen Sie keine Pulver, weil das* Bor *keine Pulver ist, sondern Wein.*"

He spoke German as badly as the artilleryman spoke Hungarian, but they understood each other. And the cannon master resumed. "When I say *por* [powder], then don't bring me *bor* [wine], but powder! *Krucifix Donnerwetter!*"

In the end, they had to explain to the peasants that when Master Joseph asked for wine, they would have to open a bag of gunpowder, and when he asked for powder, they should give him wine.

There were five such German artillerymen in the castle. Dobó brought them from Vienna. There were no other foreigners among the people of the castle.

"Look at this beautiful cannon," Dobó said, stroking its barrel. "Its name is Frog. When this croaks, the Turks will feel the rain!" The cannon was made of bronze polished to brilliance. And with its iron clad, strong oak bed, it truly did look like a sitting frog.

They walked eastward, where again a protruding strong bastion loomed high around the corner. That was the back left leg of the tortoise.

"This is Sándor Bastion," Dobó said.

Gergely stood and stared.

From Sándor Bastion, starting on the eastern side of the castle, a strong, high wall surrounded the eastern side of the castle as in the shape of three broken sickles:

---

[44] Bearded cannons (*szakállas ágyú*) were early small cannons consisting primarily of a barrel with a support at the muzzle, as if a beard. Hence the Hungarian name, "bearded" cannon. Probably the type of smaller cannon known in English as a falconet. The small cannon was placed on a wall to fire with the "beard" hanging over the wall. The beard served to absorb the recoil.

```
    \                    /


    _____/
```

There was a ditch outside and another ditch inside. Ten to twelve fathoms deep. In the middle was a narrow causeway obviously filled in so that soldiers could pass over it.

"This is the outer fortress," Dobó said. "You can see by the hill on the east there is a mound. That's the King's Seat. It's called that because King St. István used to sit there in front of his tent and look at the construction of his church. This hill down below had to be cut in two."

"I understand," said Gergely. "He was a clever man who constructed this."

"Perényi did it ten years ago. At the far end is another bastion, the Bebek Bastion. The tower on the corner serves to see and fire down on the enemy at the gate."

There too, the wall all around was heightened with wicker-fencing and mud. In places the mud was still damp. That palisade was necessary to keep the enemy from being able to see inside, and to allow the defenders to walk about on the wall without being seen.

"Now, let's go to the Church Bastion," Dobó said, again taking Gergely by the arm.

They had to walk only a few steps from the Sándor Bastion before Gergely could see a strange building in front of Gergely. It was about half the size of a huge church. It also had two towers in back. (Before, it had four towers.) There were carvings on the doorway, huge flowers carved in stone above the doorway, and worn stone faces of saints. But what a church! Instead of worshippers, it was filled with earth. Instead of bells, it had cannons sitting on top, and instead of the notes of organ pipes, they sounded explosions of cannon balls. It was the organ of death!

The sides of this church were packed with earth from left to right. Goats grazed on the hill. There was a vaulted entrance. Its stones were black from soot.

"Perhaps this is where the gunpowder is stored?" asked Gergely.

"That's it," Dobó replied. "Come and see how much powder has been gathered here!"

"Did this used to be the sacristy?"

"Yes. It's a good dry place for gunpowder."

"Well, it was a great sin to destroy this church."

"I also regret it, but rather it be like this than to have praises for Allah inside."

They entered. The place was more like a wine cellar than a sacristy. It was full of black barrels.

"How many are there?" asked Gergely astonished.

"A lot," Dobó replied. "More than two hundred barrels. I keep all my gunpowder here."

"In one place? What if it exploded?"

"That is impossible. There is a guard in front of the door. No one else has the key but me. No one can go inside except Mekcsey and old Sukán. After sunset, I won't give the key to anyone until sunrise."

Gergely looked up at the window. The window was made of small, round pieces of glass that was typical back then, protected by three layers of iron grating. Opposite the door, where the light came in at a slant, was a large, round tub. It was filled to the brim with gunpowder.

Gergely grabbed a handful and ran it through his fingers. "This belongs in a cannon. It's good and dry."

"I keep powder for the guns in small casks," Dobó explained.

"Did they make it here or in Vienna?"

"Both here and in Vienna."

"What's the mix here?"

"Three-quarters saltpeter, one-quarter sulfur and charcoal."

"Soft charcoal or hard?"

"Soft."

"That's the best. But I mix one or two more spoons of charcoal than others."

Above the tub, on the black wall, a large, dirty and tarnished painting was visible. Only two heads could be seen. One was of a bearded man with a sad face. The other one was that of a young man leaning on the man's chest. The two figures had a circle of light around their heads. From the neck down, the canvas was torn so that the wall was bleached beneath it.

"It must have been an altar painting of the church," Dobó said. "Maybe even St. István had it painted."

In front of the sacristy were two dry mills. Horses turned both millstones. By the side of the temple, under a vault, soldiers were making hand bombs. Two artillerymen were supervising their work.

Gergely stopped. He looked at the gunpowder and the wick and shook his head.

"Maybe not good?" Dobó asked.

"Good enough," Gergely replied, "but I ask permission to be allowed to make the bombs on the bastion where I will be stationed."

"Tell me honestly whether you can do better! You're a knowledgeable fellow, and here the most important thing is to protect the castle and not the bystanders."

"Well, I know better," said Gergely. "These old bombs bounce, jump, pop, then go out. I put seeds in them."

"What sort of seed?"

"In a small bomb, oakum mixed with oil and powdered copper, powdered iron and a piece of sulfur. My bomb only starts its work after it has exploded."

Dobó shouted back to the bomb makers. "Stop work! Lieutenant Bornemissza will come back and you will work as he orders."

They ascended to the top of the church converted into the bastion. It was surrounded by a wall of large wicker baskets filled with earth. Canons had been positioned between the baskets and stone work. In the middle was a stack of cannonballs and pit full of gunpowder.

From there could be seen the entire outer walls as it encircled the eastern side of the castle in the shape of a giant arm. There were two bastions and two round towers on the two bastions. Also visible beyond the outer walls was a large hill almost half as tall as the bastions.

"The attacks will come here, on the east side," said Gergely. "The sun will be in our eyes in the mornings. We need people here."

"I was thinking about you," Dobó replied.

"Thank you. I will stand my ground."

The two men shook hands.

Among the cannons was a large, thick bronze cannon. Its cavernous throat could take a cannonball the size of a man's head. Lettering and decorations glittered like gold.

"This is the *Baba*," Dobó said. "Read the writing."

On the waist of the cannon, between two leaning palm leaves, this sentence shone: *God is for our strong castle!*

3

The sun did not shine on the ninth of September. The sky was covered with gray clouds. Clouds also hung over the peaks of the Mátra Mountains. The whole day was like the face of a delicate child who wants to cry; all he has to do is figure out why.

Life in the castle was teeming. The carpenters in the lower market were flattening the ends of stakes a half a yard long. Next to them, some soldiers were drilling holes in the flattened ends and forming crosses. A third group of soldiers was tying oil-soaked oakum and pitch onto the crosses. The crosses are called *clubs*. There already was a large pile of them.

Next to the sacristy, old steward Sukán was measuring gunpowder by the bushel. Peasants were stuffing powder into small leather bags and carrying them to the artillerymen.

Also, next to the sacristy, gunner master János was stuffing gunpowder into spheres made of pottery. Those were the *balls*. Each had its gunpowder-wrapped wick sticking out. When they wanted to light and throw it, they put it in a wire-mesh tool much like today's English tennis rackets. But they also threw them by hand, and those with handles they could throw with pikes. About a thousand of them were ready.

Towards the Old Gate, which connects to the lower market, there were two long rows of houses that served as barracks. There grinders and locksmiths worked. Whoever brought them guns, they had to adjust and repair them.

Next to the Dark Gate, in beautifully constructed underground stables, stood the cattle. Butchers were at work near the wall. Blood dripped through a hole into the moat. Every day four or five cattle were slaughtered for the people of the castle.

Gergely was standing on Sándor Bastion. There was a platform made of beams and planks so that whole groups of men could step up from inside and onto the walls. Every bastion already had such a platform, but they had to rebuild the one at Sándor Bastion because they had not dug a post hole properly and the platform was shaky.

Dobó went up on that platform with his officers and shook the posts. "This needs to stand," he said, "so it can still support a hundred men even if all the supporting posts fail. Nail brackets to each post. And you need to put on a thick coat of lime wash."

From Church Tower came the long sound of a horn.

"Well, what's that?" exclaimed Mekcsey. "We're here!"

"Coming!"

From that one word, the officers completely understood. "The advance guard is coming!"

For about a week, a long line of sentries had been posted all the way to Maklár. It was a living telescope that reached as far as the fields of Abony, watching day and night for the arrival of the Turks. It were these sentries who announced, "*Coming!*"

Mekcsey jumped to the top of the wall and hurried towards Old Gate on the south. Dobó, also. The officers followed him. They stopped at the southern bastion and, shading their eyes from the sun, they gazed at the road that runs from the far fields through the small village of Almagyar then straight to the castle gate.

They saw a rider galloping at full speed on that Almagyar road. He had no cap. His red cloak was strapped and fluttering behind him.

"That's my soldier!" opined Gergely. "Bakocsai!" Because Bakocsai was an excellent rider, and although fate made him an infantryman, he always insisted that he should be riding a horse. That's why he had been assigned sentry duty on that day.

As he came closer, they could see that his face was covered in blood, and the flank of his horse had some lump on it the size of a melon.

"That's my man!" said Gergely, rejoicing, but now almost shouting. "Bakocsai!"

"He's been fighting!" said Dobó.

"A child of Eger," replied Mekcsey.

"But my soldier," responded Gergely. "My student!"

In the footsteps of the messenger, three more sentries were kicking up dust from the road. The rest may have been cut down.

Well, the Turks had arrived.

What could Dobó have been feeling upon hearing this news? The same Turkish army was coming which in that summer had destroyed two of the strongest castles in the country: Temesvár and Szolnok, and occupied Drégely, Hollókő, Salgó, Buják, Ság, Balassagyarmat … pretty much any place it wanted. Because the Turkish army had set out with instructions to invade what was left of Hungary and place it under the power of the sultan.

Well, they had arrived. One hundred and fifty thousand wild animals with human faces.[45] Most of them had been trained since tender childhood on how to shoot arrows, fire guns, climb walls, and live in camps. Their swords were forged in Damascus, their armor was made from Derbend steel, their lances were made by Hindu master craftsmen, their cannons were cast by the best founders in Europe, and they had unlimited supplies of gunpowder, bullets, and other weapons.

And against them?

There stood this little castle, barely two thousand people, and barely six old, worthless cannons and a few hollow iron pipes, cannons called bearded guns.

What could have Dobó been feeling?

The messenger István Bakocsai climbed up to the castle and jumped off his horse. He stopped sweaty and dusty in front of Dobó. Strapped to his saddle was the head of a brown Turk with a curly mustache. The left side of Bakocsai's own face was black from congealed blood. "I am reporting, captain sir," he said clicking his heels, "The God-forsaken Turks are here!"

"The whole army or just one group?"

"The beginning of the entire army, captain sir! We haven't seen them all because of the Abony forest, but they are coming quickly, those goddamned! As soon as we were spotted, they immediately caught two of us. They even chased me for a while. The last fellow was this goddamned stinky fellow!"

"Where are your companions?"

The warrior glanced toward the gate. "They are washing in the stream, goddamn them!"

"Well now," said Dobó. "From today on you are a corporal. Go and drink a quart of wine." He added with a smile, "Goddamn it!"

Everyone in the castle yard rushed in to see the severed head.

The otherwise shaved head had a long bunch of hair on top. That was how Bakocsai proudly held and displayed the head.

---

[45] The number of besieged defenders was about 2,000. The number of attacking Turks is now believed to have been about 40,000 and not the 200,000 or 80,000 in earlier estimates, or Gárdonyi's 150,000 number.

— § —

With the news of the arrival of the Turks, the castle became like a roaring beehive. Everyone gathered around Bakocsai to hear his account. Even the women ran up from the baking houses and kitchens and, standing on their toes, listened from back of the group to what the warrior had to say.

But, of course, this only happened after Dobó left the market and went up to the palace with the officers to discuss and organize.

The warrior hung the Turk's head on a linden tree and sat himself in a chair to offer his own head to the barber.

There were thirteen barber shops in the castle: four masters and nine apprentices. Well, not just to give shaves and haircuts. They will wash wounds, rub alum in them, then sew them. Doctor? In the entire country there was not as many as you would find in a country town today. The barber is a doctor everywhere … well, and the good Lord.

Well, thirteen barbers all fell on Bakocsai just to be close to him speaking. First of all, they pulled off his cloak, and then his shirt.

Master Péter was the oldest among them, so he was the first to begin washing. They had a large tile bowl, and a pot of water over it.

They washed.

The warrior put up with the washing and even the alum, but when they began to sew the long wound on his head, he kicked the chair, the bowl, the barber, and the barber apprentices and entered the barracks bearing horrible aches and pains.

"I'm not a pair of pants, goddamn it!" he said angrily.

He caught a large cobweb from the window edge and placed it on his head. He tied a bandage around his head. He sat down, ate bacon, drank wine, and then leaned over the straw sacks. He was asleep within five minutes.

— § —

Almost at the same time as the warrior, a peasant man on horseback arrived at the castle. He was wearing a *szűr*, the long embroidered felt coat worn by shepherds, and a black hat with a wide brim. He had a green staff in his hand, as tall as himself.

When Dobó was done with the warrior, the man on his horse spoke to a woman. "Which one is the captain?"

"There," she said, "the man with the long mustache walking in the middle."

The man dismounted and tied his horse to a tree. He reached into his satchel. He took out a large, sealed letter. He ran after Dobó. "I brought a letter, captain sir."

"From who?"

"From the Turks."

Dobó's face darkened. "How dare you bring it?!" he shouted at the man. "Or are you Turkish?"

"No," replied the man suddenly frightened. "I'm from Kál."

"Do you know that Hungarians are not allowed to carry letters of the enemy?" He turned towards the soldiers. "Get your weapons."

Two soldiers with pikes stepped beside the peasant.

"Sir!" the man cried out in astonishment. "They forced me!"

"They could only force you to take it. Not to deliver it." Again he turned to the soldiers. "Stand here!"

He had trumpets gather the people of the castle and, without opening the letter, stood with a folded arms by the linden tree on which the Turkish head hung. Within five minutes, the people of the castle were all together. The officers around Dobó. Soldiers in order. The peasants and women behind.

Then Dobó spoke.

"I called you all together because the Turks sent a letter. I don't correspond with the enemy. If the enemy writes a letter, I will throw it back. Or I will shove it down the throat of the person who dared deliver it to me. I will only read this first letter and then have it immediately sent to the king. He can see with his own eyes that the Turks are here and we need help. Without reading this, I know what's inside: a threat and a bargain. We are not scared of the threat. We do not enter into bargains. Our home is not for sale for any amount of money. But you should hear with your own ears how the enemy speaks, so I will read it."

He handed the letter to Gergely, who could read all kinds of writings at first glance and was the best educated among the people of the castle. "Read it out loud."

Gergely stood on a rock. He broke the seal and shook the fine sand out of the paper. He glanced at the bottom of the letter and read aloud:

Sent by Pasha Ahmed from Kál,

Greetings to István Dobó, Captain of Eger.

I am the chief adviser to Ahmed Pasha, the great, invincible emperor of Anatolia, the captain of his countless and irresistible army, and I write that the mighty emperor sent two armies to Hungary this spring. One of the armies occupied Lippa, Temesvár, Csanád and Szolnok and all the castles and castles in the regions of Körös, Maros, Tisza and Danube rivers. The other army captured Veszprém, Drégely, Szécsén and the whole of the Ipoly region, and, in addition, defeated two Hungarian armies. There is no force that can resist us.

And now these two victorious armies are uniting under Eger castle.

By the will of the mighty and invincible emperor I advise you not to dare to oppose His Majesty, but to willingly obey, and whichever pasha I send you, you will deliver the castle and city of Eger to him.

"Hell no!" was resounding everywhere. "Read no more! Let dogs listen!"

But Dobó gestured for them to be silent. "Just listen to Turkish music. It's quite pretty when it sounds so loud. Just continue reading!"

If you will be obedient, on my faith I say, you and your livestock will not be harmed. You will earn all good things from the emperor, and we will keep you in the same freedom as your kings of old.

"We need no Turkish freedoms!" interrupted Cecey with his wooden hand. "Hungarian is good enough for us!"

Everyone laughed.

Gergely continued:

And I will protect you from all trouble ...

"So that's why they are coming, to protect us!" shouted Gáspár Pető.

Everyone was laughing, including the letter reader. Only Dobó stood grimly.

Gergely read on:

I have my official seal on this. But if you do not obey, the anger of the mighty emperor will be brought down on your heads, and you and your children will all die. So answer me immediately!

The answer was an angry roar. "To hell with your mighty emperor! Just let him get here! ..."

Faces turned red. The eyes of even the most mild of men were burning.

Gergely handed the letter back to the captain. The noise calmed down.

Dobó did not need to stand on a rock to look out over the crowd. He was a tall man, over six feet. He stood out over everyone's head.

"Behold," he said in a stern and bitter voice, "This is the first and last letter that comes from the Turks to this castle, and we have all read it. You can understand from this why they are coming. They bring freedom with swords and cannons. The pagan emperor, bathed in Christian blood, brings this freedom to us. You don't want it? If you don't need freedom, then cut off our heads! Well, let's give them an answer. This is my answer!"

He crumpled the letter and threw it in the peasant's face.

"How dare you bring this to me, you scoundrel?!" He turned to the soldiers. "Iron on his feet! Throw him in the prison!"

4

After the Turkish letter had gotten everyone fired up, Dobó called his officers to the palace. "In half an hour. Everyone should be there."

The room was full sooner. Whoever arrived late, it was just because he was putting on his dress uniform. Everyone felt that the letter was the first peal of the alarm bell.

Dobó was waiting for the remaining garrison.

He stood at the window with his arms crossed, looking at the city below. Such beautiful buildings; such beautiful white houses! The city was deserted. Only below the palace, by the stream, were crowds from the castle teeming. Soldiers watering their horses. People carrying water. Farther down in the city a woman in a yellow scarf was stepping out a gate, a big bundle on the back. Dragging two small children, she hurried toward the castle.

"Such are also coming to the castle," Dobó muttered reluctantly.

A page was standing next to Dobó. He wore a velvet cape the color of flax flowers. With his long hair and girlish face, he looked like a girl in a boy's dress. But if someone glanced at his hand, he would see the strength in it. Every day the boy practiced throwing pikes.

Dobó turned to him. He stroked the boy's shoulder-length hair. "What did you dream, Kristóf? Haven't you dreamed of being home?"

"No," he replied, smiling. "I would be ashamed if I had such a dream, captain sir."

He was the only page remaining in the castle. He remained only because his father wrote to the captain not to send the boy home. He had a stepmother who did not look kindly upon the lad. Dobó regarded him as his son.

Dobó sent all the other pages home. They were fourteen to sixteen years of age. To be with Dobó was to attend warrior school. Dobó would not put them to the test.

There had been one another dear page among them. Balázs Balogh, the son of one of Friar György's lieutenants who had been killed the year before. Balázs was a year younger than Kristóf and an excellent rider. He left in August, in tears. It hurt Balázs that Kristóf could stay in the castle, but not him.

"Wait for me if I return," he said. "I will share a cup with you."

"You don't think that I am sending you away!" So Kristóf also begged Dobó, "Let Balázs stay here, captain sir."

"He can't stay," Dobó replied. "He is the son of a widow and an only child. He shouldn't even be allowed to climb a walnut tree. Get out!"

Dobó had sent Lukács Nagy to the king with a letter requesting help. Nagy took the boy along in order drop him off at his mother's on the way.

"Well, that Lukács is staying there a long time," Dobó said to Mekcsey, shaking his head. "I'm afraid he got mixed up in some trouble."

"I don't think so," Mekcsey replied. "I don't fear for short men. I have a peculiar superstition that short men are lucky in war."

"It's the other way around," said Gergely, who was tall rather than short. "A short man never sits as securely on his horse as a tall one. The horse will carry a short man to battle, a tall man takes the horse."

The soldier at the door reported that the guards had arrived.

"Let them in," Dobó replied grimly.

Seven young men stood in the middle of the hall wearing yellow boots and spurs. Two had wet hair. Well, they had been washing up.

One of the wet-haired men stepped forward. "Humbly reporting, captain sir, the enemy has arrived. They are below Abony."

"I know," Dobó replied. "The first Turk is already here. Bakocsai brought him here."

That was said in a reproachful voice. The warrior was wearing the blue and red colors of the city. He sighed, then gestured with his hand around his neck. "Captain, sir, I could have brought three."

"Well, why didn't you?"

"Only because I split the heads of all three."

There was a great cheer in the hall. Four of the seven soldiers were bandaged. Dobó himself smiled.

"Well, my son Komlósi," he said, "it's not the Turk's head that's missing here, but yours. It was not your responsibility to fight, but to bring news. The soldier of Lieutenant Bornemissza brought the news. However, your priority was to wash your clothes, to comb, to change your shirt, and powder your mustache. What kind of a soldier are you, Antal Komlósi?!"

Komlósi stared dejected. He felt that Dobó's words were right. However, he lifted his head. "Well, you will see, captain sir, what kind of a soldier I am."

The guards' reports confirmed that the Turks were marching towards Eger. Dobó ordered new guards with instructions not to engage the Turks, but only to report their approach hourly. Then he sent them out and sat down at the table.

By this time, all the lieutenants and all the officers of the garrison were assembled in the hall. The five German artillerymen, too. There was the priest and old Cecey.

"My friends," Dobó began in the festive silence, "you have heard that what we have been waiting for over many years is now upon us."

His voice was like a great bell. He paused for a minute. Maybe he was silent because he was thinking. Then, as if trying to shorten what he intended to say, he continued in his usual voice.

"My co-captain Mekcsey has just given me a full assessment of the castle's strength. You already know about it generally, but I still feel it is necessary to read and hear it. Please, my younger brother Gergely."

He handed the writing to Gergely, who was able to handle such things easier and faster than the steward, uncle Sukán. Gergely was happy to read.

"The strength of Eger Castle as of September 9, 1552 ..."

"That is today," Dobó added.

"The castle has two hundred garrison cavalry today. Its garrison infantry is the same number. 875 gunners conscripted from Eger and its surroundings. The noble Ferenc Perényi sent 25 men. Lord György Serédy sent some two hundred."

"Of them, there are no more than about fifty," said Mekcsey. He stared at a shifty-eyed, bony faced lieutenant.

"I can't help it," he replied. "I am here." And he slapped his sword.

Dobó said to the lieutenant in a reassuring voice, "My friend Hegedüs. Who is talking about you? Hunyadi also had worthless soldiers."

Gergely continued reading. "Two hundred and ten protestants came from Kassa. Well, here it is," he said, glancing at Hegedüs. "Even Kassa has warriors."

He continued. "The 'silent monks' sent four *drabant* infantrymen.[46] The chapter of Eger sent nine."

"Nine?" growled Tamás Bolyky, the lieutenant of the Borsod gunners. "They have more than a hundred soldiers!"

"They weren't paid," Dobó said tersely.

Fügedi, the lieutenant of the Eger chapter, got up. But Dobó waved, "Please, my brother, another time. Not even the devil will harm the chapter. Keep going, my young brother Gergely, just briefly and quickly."

Gergely read briskly in a friendly manner. The register of warriors was long. Sáros, Gömör, Szepes, Ung, and the free cities all sent small contingents of *drabant* infantry. The Provost of Jászó by himself sent forty men. He was cheered.

Finally, Gergely raised his voice again. "So we are perhaps two thousand less a hundred."

Dobó looked down the table and his gaze stopped at Hegedüs. Looking at the lieutenant from Kassa, he continued. "To this we can add the people I called to castle service: thirteen barbers, eight butchers, three locksmiths, four blacksmiths, five carpenters, nine millers, and thirty-four peasants who will help with the cannons. In times of siege, they all can bear weapons. Then, let's count on Lukács Nagy, whom I sent to

---

[46] *Drabant* is the Hungarian name for foot soldiers retained by the great lords in the 16th and 17th Centuries to garrison their fortresses and guard their castles.

Szolnok with twenty-four cavalry on the feast day of John the Baptist. They can be arriving at any hour," he added, glancing at Mekcsey.

Dobó continued. "We can make do with what we have, but I expect His Majesty the King to be of the greatest help."

Old Cecey beat into the air and muttered.

"No, my brother Cecey," Dobó said. "It's not like it used to be. The king knows that if Eger falls, he can put the Holy Crown into storage."

"And there will be no more Hungary," Mekcsey added, standing next to Dobó.

"It'll be German," the old man muttered.

"The king's forces are coming in two large armies," Dobó continued. "Fifty or sixty thousand, perhaps a hundred thousand well-nourished and well-paid soldiers. One is led by Prince Maurice of Saxony and the other by Prince Maximillian. The king surely urges them not to waste time but to hurry. And today the password for those two camps is Eger!"

"Only a baker in Miskolc believes that!" growled Cecey.

"Well, I believe so," growled back Dobó. "I kindly ask you not to interfere with what I am saying. My envoy, Miklós Vas, resumes his journey to Vienna today, and if he cannot find the king's army along the way, he will report the arrival of the Turks."

He turned to Gergely. "Immediately after this meeting, write a petition to His Majesty enclosing the Turk's letter. Write it so well that even the rocks will roll over here under Eger."

"I will write it," replied Gergely.

"We have no reason to wait for the Turks with a heavy heart. The walls are strong. We have plenty of gunpowder and food. We can hold out for a year. Even if the king sends only his Transylvanian army, all the Turks will move from Eger to Muhammad. But read the second list now," he said to Gergely.

Gergely read:

"One cannon that fires large bombs, another two big bomb cannons called Frog and Baba; three cannons from the king, four cannons from Gábor Perényi, and one cannon from Benedek Serédy."

"We didn't measure the gunpowder because we can't," interjected Dobó. "We still have some from last year, and we got some more from the king. Gunpowder is piled to the brim in the cellar of the sacristy. In addition, we have saltpeter and a mill to make gunpowder ourselves if needed. Continue."

Gergely read:

"An old copper howitzer; five battering rams; five of the same iron howitzers; four brass siege guns from His Majesty; cannonball casting mold for the siege guns and bearded cannons, twenty-five; two bearded cannons from Prague; bearded field cannon, five."

"We can answer the Turks, but that's nothing. Read on!"

"Copper and iron bearded cannons from Prague and Csetnek, three hundred; handguns, ninety-three; German handguns, one hundred ninety-four."

"Not worth anything!" Cecey yelled. "A good bow is worth more than any gun."

This caused a little chatter within the assembly. The older men agreed with Cecey. The younger people were on the side of guns.

Finally Dobó split the argument by saying that guns are good, bows are good, but cannons are the best.

The page Kristóf placed a superbly crafted, gilded helmet and a small silver crucifix on the table. He also had a robe-like cloak draped over his arm. He stood behind Dobó holding the robe without saying a word.

Gergely continued reading from the long inventory. It listed all the weapons: lances, javelins, shields, all kinds of bullets, halberds, pickaxes, maces, wicks, spears, and all the weapons of war that had not been brought by the soldiers themselves who had come to help with the defense.

Then Dobó got up.

He put the gilded helmet on his head, the red velvet captain's cape around his shoulders. He spoke calmly with his left hand resting on the hilt of his sword. "My dear friends and fellow defenders. You have seen the walls, and now you know the strength of what is inside the walls. The fate of the rest of the country now rests within the walls of this castle."

There was silence in the hall. All eyes were on Dobó.

"If Eger falls, neither Miskolc nor Kassa can stand. The Turks will shake those tiny castles like walnuts off a tree. There will be no more resistance. Then Hungary can be written into history's book of the dead."

He looked around with gloomy eyes and continued.

"The castle of Eger is strong, but the example of Szolnok is that the strength of the walls is not in the stone, but in the souls of its defenders. Szolnok was defended by hired, foreign mercenaries. They didn't go there to defend the castle, but to earn money. Here, all but five artillerymen are Hungarian. Everyone here is protecting his home. If blood is needed, then blood. If life is needed, then life. But let future generations not be able to say that those Hungarians who lived here in 1552 did not deserve the name Hungarian."

The sun shone through the window lighting up weapons hanging on the wall and the armor set on poles by the walls. The captain's gilded helmet sparkled as well. Gergely stood beside him. He glanced at the window, then shielded his eyes with his hands to be able to look at the commander.

"I called this honorable garrison together," Dobó continued, "so that everyone can count on each other. For those who value their skin more than the future of the nation, the gate is still open. I need men: a few lions rather than many rabbits. For those who tremble in a thunderstorm, leave this hall before I say any more. We must swear to protect the castle with such an oath that if someone breaks it, his dead soul will not be able to withstand the eyes of the eternal God."

He looked up and waited for someone to move.

There was silence in the hall.

No one moved.

Next to the crucifix stood two wax candles. The page lit them.

Dobó continued to speak. "We must take an oath for each other with the holy name of the eternal God as follows ..."

He picked up a sheet of paper from the table and read.

"First of all: whatever letter comes from the Turks, we will not accept it, but will burn it unread before everyone."

"So be it!" resounded in the hall. "We accept!"

"Second, when the Turks surround the castle, no one will yell. No matter what the Turks shout, no one will answer, whether good or bad."

"We accept!"

"Third, after the siege has begun, there will be no conversations in groups either outside or inside. There should not even be any whispering between two or three."

"We accept!"

"Fourth, subordinates shall not give orders to their soldiers without the knowledge of their lieutenants, and lieutenants shall take no action without the knowledge of the two captains."

"We accept!"

A harsh voice spoke from near Fügedy. "I want to say something here." He was Hegedüs, Serédy's lieutenant. He was blushing.

"Let's hear it," they said at the table.

"I suggest, however, that the two captains always act in consensus with the lieutenants, no matter what the decision, whether a matter raised by a lieutenant, or with regard to the defense or any other important measure."

"I accept that, but only during lulls in the siege," Dobó said.

"We accept!" they all shouted.

Dobó continued:

"Last point. Whoever talks about surrendering the castle, asks, answers, or wants to surrender the castle in any way, let him be the son of death!"

"Let him die!" they shouted enthusiastically. Everywhere came shouts of "We will not surrender the castle!" "We are not mercenaries!" "We are not from Szolnok!"

Dobó took off the gilded helmet. He stroked his long gray hair. He gestured to the priest.

Father Bálint got up. He took off his cap and lifted the small silver crucifix off the table.

"Swear to me," Dobó said.

Everyone in the room extended his hand to the crucifix.

"I swear to the one living God ..."

"I swear to the one living God," sounded solemn, muted voices.

"... that I dedicate my blood and my life for the country and the king, to protect the castle of Eger. I fear neither strength nor cunning. I will not waver for money or promises. I will neither speak nor listen to anything about surrendering the castle. I will not surrender myself whether inside or outside the castle. To defend the castle, from beginning to the end, I will submit my will to the orders of my superiors. So help me God!"

"So help me God!" they shouted with one voice.

"And now I will take an oath," Dobó said, lifting his two fingers to the crucifix. "I swear to use all my strength, every thought, every drop of blood to protect the castle and the country. I swear that I will be here with you in every danger! I swear I will not let the castle fall into pagan hands! I will not surrender the castle or myself alive! Earth accept my body, and the sky my soul! May the eternal God reject me if I do not keep my oath!"

No one doubted it. Everyone's face was on fire, for there was fire in everyone's heart. All of the swords flashed to Dobó's oath. With one soul they cried out: "We swear! We swear!"

Dobó put on his helmet again and sat down.

"Well, my brothers," he said, taking a sheet of paper in his hand. "Now we are going to discuss how to position guards on the walls. Defending the walls does not require an even distribution, because the side facing the city and the new bastion face flat land and a valley. The eastern and northern walls face hills and mountains. It is certain that they will place cannons on those high points and attempt to attack there after they have broken the walls."

"They will never break those walls," Cecey said.

"Not necessarily," replied Dobó. He continued, "I ordered a good number of carpenters and masons to stand by at night so whatever the Turks damage, they can repair at night. That will be the biggest job. If we assign guards now, it will change according to how the siege develops."

Shouts of "Just decide, captain sir," and "We will accept!" came from all sides.

"Well, I think we divide our defense into four groups. There should be one group at the main gate, another at Sándor Bastion, a third at the outer castle, and a fourth at Prison Bastion to the north. There will be a corresponding reserves for each group — four reserves. My fellow captain Mekcsey will command the reserve groups. During the siege, he will be in charge of rotating soldiers and protecting the inner castle."

"Well, what about the city side?" Hegedüs asked.

"We need only a few guards there. It's enough to have twenty people at that gate. It is a narrow pedestrian gate anyway, and from there the Turks can't force an attack."

He picked up another sheet of paper. "Accordingly, this is how I propose to allocate the men. At the Old Gate, that is, the new bastion by the main gate, there should always be a hundred *drabant* infantry. One hundred forty on Prison Bastion, together with an officer, a total of one hundred forty-one. One hundred and twenty along Sándor Bastion without a gate. From there back to the gate a hundred.

"That's four hundred sixty-six," said Gergely.

"On the two Church Towers, ten *drabant* infantry each. This is all to protect the inner castle."

"Four hundred eighty-six," said Gergely aloud.

Dobó continued. "Now we come to the outer castle. The Csabi Bastion should have ninety people, up to Bebek Bastion. From there to the corner tower, a hundred and thirty. From the Old Gate to the corner, fifty-eight. There is another narrow stone wall that connects the inner castle with the outer one. There, defense is more with the eyes than with weapons. Thirty-eight *drabant* infantry should be enough."

Looking at Mekcsey, he continued. "You can station the weaker men there, and after the siege begins, the walking wounded."

"Nearly eight hundred," said Gergely.

"So then, how do we station officers? To start with myself, I want to be everywhere."

Enthusiastic cheering.

"We already know what Mekcsey has to do. Of the four first lieutenants, one will be at the Old Gate. It needs strength and a fearless soul. Because it is predictable that the Turks will want to break through that gate. That is where soldiers will have to boldly stare death in the face."

Gáspár Pető got up and slapped his chest. "I want that assignment!"

Amidst the loud cheers, only Dobó's consenting head movement could be seen. Old Cecey's left hand shook Pető's right hand.

"After that," Dobó continued, "the next most dangerous side is the outer castle. The Turks will be trying to fill in that ditch. The defense of that side will also require courage, the patriotism and a contempt of death for its commanding officer."

There were three first lieutenants besides Pető. All three jumped up.

"I am here!" said Bornemissza.

"I'm here!" said Fügedy.

"I'm here!" said Zoltay.

"Well, so you won't get into a fight with each other," replied Dobó, "all three of you will be there."

The artillerymen had already received their assignments to cannons. At any rate, none of them could speak a word in Hungarian. But Dobó wanted another artilleryman. Who would he be?

No one else knew enough about cannons except Dobó. Well Dobó took it upon himself.

That there was another cheer in the room, and that they were looking at the artillerymen, and they asked anxiously, *"Was ist das? Was sagt er?"*[47]

Bornemissza turned to them and explained to the five Germans, *"Meine Herrn, Kapitany Dobó wird sein der Haupt Bum-bum! Verstanden?"*[48]

Dobro then called for trumpets to summon the soldiers. In the castle yard, he told them about the five oaths the officers had taken inside. He told them that whoever felt any fear, he preferred that he put his sword down, rather than weaken the rest. "Because," he said, "fear is as infectious as the plague. Even more infectious. Because in a moment, it spreads from one to the other. Well, here during the difficult days ahead of us, we need men with strong souls."

Then he unfurled the blue-red flag of the castle and held it together with the national colors.

"Take the oath!"

At those words, the bell of the cathedral in the city rang. It rang just once, no more.

Everyone looked towards the city. The peal was like a cry for help. Just one. Then a watchful silence descended upon the entire area.

5

That night, Dobó entertained everyone who had taken the oath in the hall that morning.

At one end of the table sat Dobó, and at the other end Mekcsey. Next to Dobó was Father Bálint on the right and Cecey on the left. Next to the priest was Pető. It was appropriate to give Pető that place of honor. His older brother, János Pető, was a dignitary in the king's court. It was because of his name that they had received gunpowder and the five artillerymen from Vienna.

---

[47] "What's that? What's he saying?"

[48] "My lords, Captain Dobó will be the chief Boom-boom. Understand?"

Only then was the seating arranged by age and rank, beginning with Mekcsey and Dobó: Zoltay, Bornemissza, Fügedy. Then Farkas Koron, the lieutenant of Abaúj County infantry, Bálint Kendy and István Hegedüs, lieutenants of György Serédy, who had brought fifty *drabant* infantrymen; Lőrinc Fekete who came from Regéc bringing another fifteen with him; Mihály Lőkös, sent by the free cities with a hundred on foot; Pál Nagy, lieutenant of György Báthory's thirty *drabant* infantry, a bold bull of a man; Márton Jászai, the lieutenant of the forty *drabant* infantry sent by the Provost of Jászay; Lieutenant Márton Szenczi from Szepes who brought forty infantry; Mihály Bor, an excellent shot with a gun, who had been from Sáros County with sixty-six foot soldiers; György Szalacskai and Imre Nagy were from Ugocsa. The latter was sent by Gábor Homonnay with eighteen foot soldiers. Antal Blaskó came from Eperjes. All these named were lieutenants.

After them sat Jób Paksy, the tallest officer in the royal army, and Tamás Bolyky, the lieutenant from Borsod in charge of fifty gunners. These were seated among the officers of the castle garrison. They were: János Sukán, the aged steward of the castle; Imre the clerk and manager of the wine cellar; Mihály the clerk in charge of food supplies or as they said, *loaf splitter*; Matthias Gyöngyösy, another clerk and dean of the bishop (the castle was the property of the bishop); Boldizsár, a scrivener; and several others. Dobó had invited not only the officers, but he also wanted the entire castle to be represented at the dinner. He made sure that his guests included a corporal, a common man, a noble of Eger, and a peasant of Eger.

Serving food would have been the job of Dobó's four or five servants. But in order to facilitate their work, the senior officers also provided their servants.

Behind Dobó was Kristóf Tarjáni, the page. He served Dobó. He placed the food in front of him, always filling his cup whenever it was empty.

It was Friday that day, so the dinner started with pike and horseradish, continued with fried pike-perch, catfish and sturgeon, and finished with thin pancakes stuffed with sweet cottage cheese and sour cream (*túrós csusza*) and steamed dried fruit with cinnamon. There were also grapes, apples, pears and melons on the table.

Why did the frugal Dobó give this dinner? To finish the oath ceremony? Or for the unknown officers to meet and warm up? Or perhaps for the wine to reveal the strength of souls? At first the air was calm, almost church-like. The snow-white tablecloths, the silverware engraved with Dobó's coat of arms, the carved barrel hanging by a chain over the table, and the arrangements made with autumn flowers all suggested a wedding feast rather than casual hospitality.

No one's hands became lively even after the pike was served and pomegranate-colored wine from the decorated barrel poured into cups. Dobó's lofty speech sat on the souls, just as silence had descended after the one peal of the church bell.

After the fried fish, the servants changed plates. Everyone was waiting for someone to talk.

Dobó sat in a brown leather armchair, lost in thought. He was watching.

And in the silence came the sound from the kitchen of women singing a cheerful song:

> *I just like to live at the end of the village,*
> *That's where my rose goes to water his horse.*
> *To water his horse, to show himself off,*
> *Kiss his red two cheeks with mine.*

The clouds suddenly disappeared. The sky cleared. Should men be serious when women wait for the coming of danger with a song?

Mekcsey picked up the silver cup in front of him and got up.

"Honorable friends!" he said. "We have big days ahead. The good Lord Himself is sitting in the window of heaven and watching how two thousand people here will fight two hundred thousand. And I have no despair. There is not one coward among us, not even among the women, as we can hear them singing cheerfully down there."

"But even if it wasn't like this, there are two men among us in whom fear is not possible. I know both from my early youth. One was created by God to be an example of Hungarian courage. He has the strength of iron. He is like a gold-encrusted sword. All strength and nobility. The other, whom I also know from my youth, is a master of cunning and all ingenuity. Wherever these two people are present, I feel confident in either power or cunning. Where they are, there is Hungarian courage, Hungarian intelligence, Hungarian glory!"

"We cannot fear danger. I wish you to know them as I do: István Dobó, our captain, and Gergely Bornemissza, our lieutenant."

Dobó stood up to accept the toasts, then kept standing. He replied like this.

"My dear blood brothers! If when it comes to the fate of my country, then even if I were as timid as a deer frightened by the yapping of any kind of old dog, I would fight and resist that fear."

"The example of Jurisics proves how strong even the most worthless castle can be when it is defended by men. Our castle is stronger than what Kőszeg was, and we also have to be stronger."

"I know the Turkish army. My mustache was barely sprouting when I stood on the field of Mohács and saw Suleiman's army. Believe you me, those twenty-eight thousand Hungarians could have wiped out that mob of a hundred thousand had there been only one man who could lead them in battle. Not even one man was a leader there; not even one man was directing and giving orders. The soldiers in their formations were not broken apart by enemy attacks, but by their own lack of discipline and direction."

"Tomory, the poor man whose memory is glorious, was a great hero, but he was no leader. He thought the science of leadership rested in the single command, 'Follow me!' Well, he said a prayer, and then he cursed, and then he ordered, 'Follow me!' Our army charged the center of the Turkish army like a flock of sparrows taking flight in autumn. The Turks scattered like a flock of geese. We rushed blindly into a line of cannons. Of course, the cannons, loaded with shot and chains, did what human power could not. Only four thousand remained of the twenty-eight thousand."

"But there are two great lessons to be learned from this terrible catastrophe. One is that the Turkish camp is not made up of warriors, but of all sorts of people and martyrs. They gather a multitude of any kind of men and animals just to scare the chicken-hearted with their numbers. The other lesson is that no matter how few the Hungarians may be, they can still confuse and defeat the Turks if, in addition to bravery, they use their intelligence like a friend."

Those sitting at the table listened intently to the captain.

Dobó continued. "In our situation, cleverness commands us to make our legs like iron until the king's army arrives. They will fire at this castle and damage it, and maybe they will destroy a wall that has protected us. Then we have to take a stand. Just as the walls protect us, so must we protect the walls. If any of the enemy pass through our walls, they will find us everywhere."

"We will never let the fate of the Hungarian nation get wrenched out of our hands!"

They all shouted, "No! No! They shall not pass!"

"Thank you for coming," Dobó continued. "Thank you for bringing your sword and heart to protect our home. I have a strong feeling that God is stretching out His hand over Eger Castle and saying to the sea of pagans,

'This far, no more!' This feeling should strengthen you, and then I am sure that we will be sitting in this very same place and celebrating our victory."

Shouts of "So be it!" came from all over as silver and tin cups banged against each other.

After Dobó, Pető stood up, the lieutenant who moved briskly and who was the best speaker in the castle. He pulled his neck left and right as if loosening up, then spoke. "Lord Mekcsey trusts Dobó and Bornemissza. They trust us with the walls. Well, I will tell you what I trust."

"Let's hear it! Let's hear it!"

"Two strong castles have fallen this year: Temesvár and Szolnok."

"Veszprém?"

"There was no garrison in Veszprém," responded Pető, then continued. "Why did those two strong castles fall? With time they will say that they fell because the Turks were stronger. But that's not what happened. Temesvár fell because it was defended by Spanish mercenaries. Szolnok was defended by Spaniards, Czechs and Germans. So, I will tell you what I trust. I trust in the fact that Eger is not protected by Spaniards, Germans or Czechs. With the exception of the five artillerymen, everyone here is Hungarian and mainly from Eger. Lions protecting their own lairs! I trust in Hungarian blood!"

By now all faces had warmed up and cups raised. Pető could have finished his speech at this point, but he went on with the exuberance of a public speaker. "The Hungarian is like flint. The more he is struck, the more he sparks. Well, pity the riff-raff, water drinking Turks, fallen out of fig trees and pulled from Muhammad's hovels, because surely they can be handled by two thousand warriors born of Hungarian mothers, raised on horses, and raised on Hungarian wheat and Egri Bikavér wine!"

He was drowned out by cheering, clattering of swords, and laughter, but gave his mustache another twist, took a glance to the side, then finished. "Until now, Eger has been only a good city, the city of the Hungarians of Heves County. God willing, from now on it will be the city of Hungarian glory! Let's write on its walls with pagan blood, '*Do not cross the Hungarians!*' And if, in the centuries to come, the moss of eternal earthly peace glazes green over the remains of this castle, the sons of those future generations will come here and say with pride, 'Our fathers fought there, blessed be their ashes!'"

A huge commotion ensued as people embraced and kissed the speaker. He could not continue talking even if he tried, but he needed to add nothing more. He sat down and extended his hand to Tamás Bolyky, the lieutenant of the men from Borsod. "Tamás," he said, "wherever we two stand, let Turkish heads fall!"

"You spoke so well," Tamás replied, nodding his head, "that I could take on a hundred Turks now!"

After Pető, no one felt strongly enough to address the hall. They prodded Gergely, but he, being the scholar-type, was uncomfortable giving public speeches. So everyone ended up talking to his neighbor, and the lively hustle and bustle of dinner filled the room.

Dobó was also warming up, toasting and clinking wine cups with one neighbor, then another. Once he reached forward to Gergely with his cup, and seeing that the priest had sat beside Pető to talk, gestured for Gergely to come close. "Wander over here, my son," he said. After Gergely had sat next to him, Dobó told him, "I want to talk to you about the Török boys. I wrote to them too, but was it in vain?"

"Yes," said Gergely, putting his cup down in front of him, "I don't think we will see them. Jancsi doesn't want to defend the castle. He prefers to fight with the Turks in the open field. Feri doesn't come this far. He won't leave Western Hungary."

"Is it true that Lord Bálint is dead?"

"Yes, it's certain, the poor man. It's been a few months. Only his death released him from his shackles."

"How long did he survive his widow?"

"For a good few years. The lady, as you may know, died when we returned from Constantinople. She had just been buried when we arrived in Debrecen."

"She was a good woman," Dobó said thoughtfully. He reached for his cup as if he wanted to drink to her.

"Certainly there are few like her created on this earth," said Gergely. He also reached for his cup. They clinked in silence. Perhaps both had the idea that the good woman could see from above that the cups were raised in her honor.

"What about Zrínyi?" Dobó asked after a pause. "I also wrote to him to come to Eger."

"And he would have come, but for months now he has been getting reports that the Pasha of Bosnia was preparing to attack him. In February, I spoke with uncle Miklós in Csáktoryna. He already knew that the Turks were coming to Temesvár, Szolnok, and Eger with large army. He had me write a letter for him to the king." As he spoke, he stroked the page's hair.

A group stood in front of the door with pipes and trumpets.

> *Miska in yellow boots walks in mud,*
> *Panni waits for him by the stream.*

It was as if new blood had been poured into everyone. At Dobó's gesture, the page led the group in. Three pipes and two trumpets. Among them also the Gypsy wearing a large, rusty helmet with three cock's feathers, a sleek sword strapped to his side, and giant spurs on his naked feet. His cheeks were puffed as he played his pipe.

Everyone was pleased to pay attention. When they recognized the song, a deep baritone voice could be heard from among the lieutenants.

> *Heavens quickly sprout the willows green!*
> *Let me again saddle my chestnut steed,*
> *Let me again test my rested weapons,*
> *May the Turks remember my name with tears.*

The lieutenant was a bulky, mustached guy. His mustache was forever stretching out from under his nose so that he could be recognized even from behind.

"Who is that lieutenant?" asked Gergely leaning over to Dobó.

"Jób Paksy, the younger brother of the Komárom captain."

"Good song."

"And certainly a valiant boy. All men who enjoy singing make good warriors."

The lieutenant wanted to sing another verse to the song, but he could not remember it. The pipe players also waited for him to start.

During this one-minute break, somebody gave loud shout, "Long live our priest!"

"Long live the elders of our army!" Zoltay shouted.

Cecey cheerfully replied, "Your grandfathers are old!"

"Long live the youngest defender of the castle!" cried Pető. Kristóf Tarjáni had already reached for a cup. Blushing, he clinked his cup with the guests.

"Long live the Turk," shouted Gergely, "whose teeth we first knock out!" He had no one to clink cups with over this as everyone was laughing and clinking with his neighbor.

The red-faced nobleman from Eger got up from his seat. He threw his collared, blue cloak back over his right shoulder. He wiped his mustache left and right, then brushed his hair back. He spoke. "Long live the man who is the first to die for Eger!"

He looked around with serious pride, and, without clinking his cup with anyone, he emptied his cup to the bottom. He hardly realized that he was drinking to himself.

— § —

The clock with big feet was at eleven when a guard entered and stood in the doorway. "Captain, sir, the Turks are already in Maklár."

"The advance guard or the beginning of the army?"

"More than an advance guard. In the moonlight they came like a flood. We can see many tents and many fires."

"Then they'll be here tomorrow," Dobó nodded.

And he dismissed the guard and told him not to have to report until the morning. Then he got up. It was a sign for others to leave.

Mekcsey pulled Gergely, Fügedy, Pető and Zoltay into a corner of the hall. He said a few words to them, then hurried to Dobó. "Captain sir," he said clicking his spurs, "some or two hundred could raid at night."

"Where the hell?"

"To Maklár."

"To Maklár?"

"To wish the Turks a good night."

Dobó cheerfully smoothed his mustache. Then he stepped into the window alcove. Mekcsey had to go after him. "Well," Dobó said, "I don't mind. It will be an encouragement for the people in the castle."

"That's what I was thinking."

"If there's a strong desire to fight, the sword cuts better. But I won't let you go."

Mekcsey jerked.

Dad looked at him calmly. "You're like a bull. You charge at every tree and sooner or later you will get your horns stuck. You have to take care of your head so that if I fall, you can immediately take command. I'm only telling you this. But Bornemissza and the rest can go. Gergely is a smart boy. It's hard to lead him into a trap. Call him here."

Gergely reported. "You can go out, Gergely," Dobó said, "but not with two hundred men but one hundred. That's enough. Charge them. You shake them up a little. Then you turn around. Do not risk the lives of your men."

"Captain sir," asked little Tarjáni, the page. "Let me go with them, too!"

Dobó smoothed his mustache again. "Well, I don't mind," he said. "But always stay close behind Lieutenant Gergely. If they hit you on the brain, don't ever stand before me again. This I tell you!"

6

Gergely rushed to where the cavalry was quartered. Instead of a trumpet, he fired a pistol in the room. The men jumped out of their bunks all at once.

"Come here!" shouted Gergely.

He chose the most nimble to make up his hundred. "One, two! Get dressed! When I say three, be downstairs with swords and mounted up. You there. Run to the second captain and ask for a man-trap. Bring it with you. Every man is to have a small gun in his saddle!"

Because back in those days, they called a pistol a "small gun."

Gergely ran down the stairs and hurried toward the stables. In the red light emanating from the kitchen, he saw a man in a yellow hussar's jacket wearing a helmet. The man was sitting on an upside down bucket and holding a watermelon on his knee. He was eating it with a spoon. He was barefoot.

"This can't be anyone other than my Gypsy," Gergely said. He shouted, "Sárközi!"

"At your command," the Gypsy replied, half standing.

"If you come with me, you can get a horse today. A good one."

The Gypsy jumped up. "I'm going. Where?"

"To the Turks," Gergely replied cheerfully. "They are asleep now. We'll surprise them."

The Gypsy scratched his head. He looked at the ground. He sat back down on the bucket. "But it's not possible" he said seriously.

"Why not?"

"Today I gave my oath that I would not leave the castle.

"That wasn't our oath. We swore to protect the castle."

"Maybe others swore to that," the Gypsy replied, shrugging his shoulders until they almost reached his ears. "I swore that I would die before I would leave the castle. So help me God!" He picked up the watermelon and continued eating.

Ten minutes later, Gergely was leading his soldiers in the moonlight on the road to Maklár.

In front of him were two men: István Fekete, a corporal, and Péter Bódogfalvi, a private. Past the hot springs they turned towards the meadow. There, the sound of the horses' hooves were absorbed by the soft ground. The hundred horsemen looked like a hundred swinging shadows.

They saw the first campfires by the willows at Andornak.

Péter stopped. The rest stopped.

The light through the clouds from the half-moon was enough to see the dark shapes of trees and men.

Gergely rode up to Bódogfalvi. "Dismount. Crawl like a snake to the first sentry. If he has a dog and it barks at you, return as quietly as you went. But if he has no dog, get behind him and stab him. Then look at the campfire. If there is no other sentry, throw half a handful of gunpowder on the fire. But at that moment, be sure to drop down so no one can see you!"

"And my horse?"

"Tie your horse to this tree. You will find it here when we return."

"And if there are more sentries by the fire?"

"Look around carefully and make a note where and how they are lying, and where most of them are. Then hurry back."

They waited for a good half an hour by the banks of the creek where the willows grew. During that time, Gergely was telling them the plan. "As long as you see them running, hit and cut them down. Everyone is to stay within a hundred steps of his companion or you risk being separated and cut down. As soon as you hear the horn, we immediately turn back and head home. As long as the horn does not sound, you may have fun."

The men stood in a circle and listened to every word.

Gergely continued. "They will be frightened and will not be thinking about organized resistance. If that's the case, attack where they are closest together until they scatter. Learn this once and remember it always: who fights on horseback must lunge and cut quickly so the enemy has no time to strike back. Your cuts must fall as quickly as rain from a sudden downpour."

Gergely stopped. He listened towards the direction of the Turks. Then he turned back to the men again. "Where's the man-trap?"

"It's here, lieutenant sir," replied a tall man in the line.

"Do you have the tool?"

"With me," the lad replied, lifting up a long, fork-shaped device.

"Can you handle it?"

"The captain taught me."

"Well, just grab anyone of their necks with it and squeeze the dog down. It would be glorious, men, if we could catch a higher officer. Those kind are in the nicest tents, and probably dressed only in their shirts. We should grab them, if you can."

He listened again, then continued. "Prisoners must be tied, but only their hands. Hands behind the back. If we catch horses, we can make them mount. In that case, you, Kristóf, and you there also, one on each side, tie the reins to your saddles and gallop back. If they try to escape in any way, or if they talk or shout, or if try to slip off the horse, immediately cut them down!"

"And if we don't capture horses?" asked Kristóf.

"Then he has to run by your horse, and you both hurry back home. Don't wait for us."

Péter's shape appeared by a bush. He was running.

"I killed the sentry," he said panting. "He didn't make a sound. Just fell over like a sack. The fire is within a circle of tents. One servant-looking Turk is sitting by the fire. He has yellow slippers in his hands and yellow paint on his knees."

"Officer's servant," said Gergely. "What else?"

"The rest are lying on blankets on the grass. Hundreds. To the left of the fire, all in a circle."

"Are they sleeping?"

"Like bears."

"Good," replied Gergely. "Well now, men. Spread out ten steps from each other. As soon as I fire my gun, fire all your guns at them and charge, like wolves. Yell, shout, strike and cut as hard as you can."

They waited until Bódogfalvi mounted. They spread out in a line facing east.

Pető was at the end of one side. The three eagle feathers pinned to his helmet made him recognizable from a distance. He led the line of cavalry in a semi-circle formation, following the pace of Gergely's trot.

Then Gergely took command. For a while they trotted quietly by the side of the bushes, then they suddenly took off at a gallop.

— § —

The first wild shout of a Turk fills the night. He fires his gun at Gergely. Gergely shoots back. The next moment, all the guns fire, and a hundred cavalry charge the sleeping Turkish army like a storm from hell.

In that same moment the forest of tents becomes alive with crunching and rolling. Turkish and Magyar yelling mingle in a storm of noise. Those sleeping on the ground lose their minds, jump up in alarm, crash into tents and into each other.

"On them! On them!" shouts Gergely.

"*Allah! Allahu akbar!*" scream the Turks.

"Slash the dogs!" roars Gáspár Pető from somewhere among the tents.

Turkish yelling, Hungarian cursing. Swords flashing, poleaxes showering, horses neighing, tents shaking, dogs howling. The ground shakes under the hooves of a hundred cavalry.

Gergely jumps between a tent and a flock of hemmed-in pagans. He slashes at them right and left. He feels his sword always cutting into flesh, bodies leaning and falling on all sides, like a hound running through a wheat field in June.

In the moonlight, he sees that all the Turks' horses are grazing in one herd, and that Turks were trying to escape by cutting their tethers with their *yataghan* short swords, then climbing on the horses.

"After me, boys!" cries Pető, who has already arrived there.

They charge the riders. They cut men and horses equally. Swords ring, spears crunch, maces crush. Terrified Turks are jumping on horseback. Some of them, two to a horse. Whoever can flees on horseback. Anyone who cannot find a horse scampers away in the dark on foot.

Gergely does not pursue them. He stops and has the trumpet sound the call to re-group.

"The Turks are running!" shouts Gergely. "Grab everything you can, but don't let your reins out of your hands! If there is a fire in front of the tent, kick some embers on the tent!"

The men disperse again. Gergely shakes the blood off his sword and stabs it three times through the canvas of a tent to clean it. "Ugh, what a hateful job this is!" he says to Fekete, who similarly wipes his sword.

Then, because no Turks were jumping, he calls for Kristóf. "Let's look at the tents."

In the weak light of the moon, it was impossible to see which tent belonged to the commanding officer. The tents were not the same. One was round, another rectangular. And even if one tent was more ornate than the others, it was still the tent of the vanguard. Regular soldiers died in them.

Gergely grabbed a horsetail flag off of a tent. When he saw Kristóf, he shouted, "Well, lad, have you cut anyone?"

"Two," said the page, panting.

"Only two?"

"The rest ran away from me."

Meanwhile, the men rounded up a couple of wagons and carts. They tossed in whatever they could not carry on their horses: carpets, gilded horsetails, horse collars decorated with gemstones, horse tack, helmets, weapons, cooking pots and everything else they could carry. They even took two tents apart and threw them in the cart.

It was dawn when they returned to the castle.

Dobó already was anxiously waiting for them at the bastion. If the raid was unsuccessful, then people in the castle will be discouraged.

Then, as soon as he saw the horses, carts and wagons loaded down with booty, and Gergely waving the Turkish horsehair flag in the distance, his face lit up with joy.

When the warriors rode through the gate, the people of the castle were already waiting, cheering with joy.

The number of warriors had not lessened, If anything, they had multiplied. The tall man brought along a fat cheeked Turk and took him straight to Dobó. There he pulled the turban knot out of his mouth.

"Humbly reporting," he said proudly, "We also brought a tongue."

"Fathead!" yelled the Turk with the anger of a tiger, staring at the warrior.

Dobó ordinarily did not laugh, but this time he laughed so hard that tears flowed out of his eyes.

"Varsányi," he said to the prisoner, "You play the role of a Turk well."

He turned to the warrior. "Untie him! Because this is our own spy."

"I wanted to tell the dumb ox that I'm Hungarian," Varsányi lamented, "but each time I spoke he'd hit me on the head. Then he stuffed my mouth."

He lifted his hand to slap the warrior, who pulled back embarrassed.

— § —

Dobó gestured to Gergely and Mekcsey. And he also called the spy, "Come."

He walked into the tower by the inner gate and entered the sentry's room. He sat in an armchair made from tree roots and gestured to Varsányi that he should speak.

"Well, captain sir," began the spy rubbing his hands, "the whole army is coming. Ahmed Pasha comes in front. That night their camp was in Abony. Its vanguard, with Manda Bey in charge, made it as far as Maklár. Damnation! ..." he added in a changed voice.

This *damnation* was directed at the warrior who had dragged him to Eger. There were deep welts in his wrists from where they had been tied, and he had a couple of bruises on his head from where he had been punched. Obviously he had struggled against being roughed up.

"There was a bey with you?" asked Gergely with a start. "We could have captured that bey!"

"Hardly," the spy said. "He is a fat man, as fat as a monk's pig. He must weigh three hundredweight, if not more."

"What name did you say?"

"Manda. He won't catch a bullet. He hasn't been a bey for long. He only got appointed bey after the siege of Temesvár. Otherwise the soldiers just call him Hayvan."

Gergely smiled. "That's him," he said to the two captains, "the one I told you about a few nights ago. Ho, ho. He'll catch a bullet here!"

"Keep talking," Dobó said to the spy.

"Then comes Mehmet Sokolovich Beylerbeyi. He's a good shooter. He is the one who sets up and first fires the cannons. They say he has eyes that can see through walls. I don't think so."

"How many cannons do they have?"

"They have sixteen old siege cannons. They have another eighty-five large cannons. They have another hundred and fifty cannon that fire smaller balls. Mortars they have plenty. Some hundred forty carts are loaded with cannonballs. I saw about two hundred camels carrying gunpowder. One four-oxen cart is loaded with marble cannonballs, each as large as the largest watermelon."

"Is the army well supplied with food?"

"There's not enough rice. By now only officers get rice. But they have plundered huge amounts of flour and meat from everywhere."

"Is there any sickness in the camps?"

"No. Only Kason Bey was sick in Hatvan, and that was from cucumbers."

"Who else is coming?"

"Arslan Bey."

"The son of a former Pasha of Buda?"

"Him."

"Who else?"

"Mustafa Bey, Kamber Bey, Veli Bey."

"Damn that Veli Bey," Mekcsey growled, "I will cut him down!"

"But we'll make him dance first," Gergely said.

"Well, what about that dervish bey?" asked Dobó asked. "What's he like"

Varsányi shook his head. "Very strange. He's a regular bull like the rest, but when he fights, he takes off his bey's clothes and wears a shirt made of hair. That's why they call him dervish bey." He looked at Dobó a little disappointed, because his question about the dervish bey implied that another of Dobó's spies had gotten back earlier.

"What kind of a man?" Dobó continued. "In which army is he?"

"I saw him with some cavalry. The one-eyed man. He used to be a janissary. His real name is Yumurjak."

At this name Gergely's hand moved to grasp the hilt of his sword. "Yumurjak," he said. "Don't you remember, captain sir? Because it was from him that I escaped when I was a child."

Dobó shook his head. "So many Turks have given me trouble throughout my life. It's no surprise if I have forgotten one or the other."

Then he slapped his forehead. "Of course I know him. He is Arslan Bey's younger brother. That dog is a cruel man."

He turned again towards his spy. "What was in the camp?"

"I was already a servant of the Manda Bey. The devil take that calf who caught me. I could have learned all their plans."

"How did you get to the bey?"

"I made friends with his servants and I always loitered around his tent. Near Hatvan, the bey got angry at his servant and had him beaten. He had seen me so often, he called me over, because I also knew how to cook ink."

"What?"

"Ink. He drinks ink like we do wine. In the morning, at noon, in the evening, he drinks only ink."

"That's not ink."

"It certainly is ink, authentic, good and black ink. They make it from some kind of bean. It's so bitter that the day after I tasted it I was still spitting. They call the bean *kahve*."

The officers looked at each other. None of them had ever heard of coffee.

"Well, it's good you got there," Dobó said, looking forward. "What is the army saying about Eger? Are they saying it's strong, or do they think it will be easy work?"

"Since the fall of Szolnok," the spy replied, "they think the entire world is theirs. There is talk throughout the camp that Ali Pasha wrote to Ahmed that Eger is just a dilapidated sheep pen."

"So the two armies haven't joined yet?"

"Not yet."

Dobó looked at Mekcsey. Mekcsey smiled and shrugged. "Well, they will find out what kind of biting sheep are inside this dilapidated sheep pen."

The spy continued. "There are many different rabbles in the camp. They have all kinds of camp followers: Greek merchants, rope dancers,

Armenians, horse traders and Gypsies. There are also a few hundred prisoners. Mostly women from Temesvár. They have been distributed among the officers."

"Bastards!" growled Mekcsey.

The spy continued. "Among the male prisoners I saw only boys. Oh, and the cart drivers hauling the cannonballs. At least ten times every day Arslan Bey says that as soon as the people in Eger see their immense army, they will run away like they did in Szolnok."

"What's the main strength of their army?"

"The many janissaries, and the even greater number of *műsellem* Cavalry. They also have sappers. They are called *lagundjis*. They also have *kumbarajis* who throw pottery bombs over the walls using spears and slingS."

Dobó got up. "Well, you can go and rest. At night you will return to the camp. If you have something to report, just come here under the city walls and wave a white cloth."

7

The auction was about to begin in the market. Five loaded carts and eight small Turkish horses.

They pulled the provisions clerk out of bed. A table in front, a drum next to him. They made Bódogfalvi the auctioneer.

"Let's start with the horses," said Pető.

"A beautiful Arabian horse," Bódogfalvi began.

"Put the two together," Mekcsey said. There were two similar small bay horses among the plunder.

Well, nobody offered to bid for them, but they sold anyway. Dobó had instructed Mekcsey to buy the two beautiful horses for the page. Mekcsey waited to see if anyone bid.

Everyone was keeping their money for the weapons and clothes. Mekcsey bought all eight horses for four forint and brought them into the stable.

The carts followed. Many beautiful weapons were pulled out of them. One or two pennies would buy a sword with semi-precious stones, or a gun with an ivory stock. Women competed for the clothes. Fügedy bought a twenty-pound mace, Jób Paksya a velvet saddle-cloth, Zoltay a silver helmet with a nose guard. The money piled up on the table in front of Mihály the clerk as he dutifully wrote down who bought what for how much.

When they reached the bottom of the first cart, Bódogfalvi shouted cheerfully, "Now comes the treasure chest of that famous King Darius!"

And with the help of a soldier, he placed a beautiful calfskin covered chest on the back of the cart. The chest would not open, but it had no lock or catch. They needed an axe to break it open.

The castle's people were pushing and shoving to get a good look. Even if the chest did not contain Darius' treasure, certainly there was something valuable inside.

"I'd like to buy a couple of silver cups," said one of the tavern keepers at the castle.

"I'd like a nice silk scarf," said a young woman wearing red boots.

A bunch of women's clothes and a few flower pots were taken out from the wagon. It was obvious that some Turkish officers had brought their wives.

"I just want a pair of slippers," said an old woman. "I've always heard the Turks sew good slippers."

The chest broke open. To everyone's surprise, out popped a little boy some six or seven years of age. A white-faced, roe-eyed, scared Turkish child. His hair was short. He wore only a shirt and a gold coin hung from his neck.

Bódogfalvi cursed. "Damn that ugly, frog-headed creature of a daddy raised on a fig tree!" He scrunched his face with mock disgust.

They laughed.

"Kill the brat!" yelled a soldier from the other cart.

"Even their seeds have to be destroyed!" shouted another.

The child was crying.

"So jump out, damn your father's spurs!" shouted Bódogfalvi. He grabbed the boy by the shoulders and lifted him out of the chest and threw him on the grass so roughly, he fell. The child screamed.

Everyone looked at him with hatred.

"Oh so ugly!" said a woman.

"Not ugly," replied another.

The child stood on the ground with teary, scared eyes and quivering lips. Every moment he wiped his eyes. He looked around hopelessly, here and there. He did not dare to cry out loud, so he just whimpered.

"Kill him!" shouted the soldier again as he took out one of the tents.

The child was frightened by the sound and clung to a woman's skirt, burying his face. It just so happened she was the same woman who had said the child was ugly. She was one of the cooks, a thin, hawk-nosed old woman. Her sleeves were still rolled up and her hair tied back with a blue scarf.

"Oh, sure!" she said, putting her hand on the child's head. "Maybe he's not even Turkish. You are not Turkish, my son, are you?"

The child lifted his face but did not reply.

"What then?" said Bódogfalvi. "His clothes are here, too. Here's his cap, red; here's his coat, also red! Who has ever seen pants like these? There's a rope on the bottoms. They can be pulled tight just like a sack." He tossed the clothes to the child.

"*Annem*," the child said, "*nerede?*"

"Well, he's Hungarian after all!" said the woman triumphantly. "He's saying, 'Mama, come here!'"

"No, not Hungarian, Mrs. Vas," Pető said, laughing. "He's not saying 'come here', but *nerede*. He's asking for his mother." He turned to the child. "*Yok burada annen!*" (Your mother is not here.)

The child started crying again:

"*Meded, meded!*" (Help, help!)

Mrs. Vas knelt down and dressed the child without saying a word. Red pants, red cap, red coat with purple velvet lining. His coat was patched and his red sandals faded. She wiped the boy's face with her apron. "We have to send him back," she said emphatically.

Pető himself didn't know what to do.

"Ach!" Bódogfalvi yelled rattling his sword, "Don't those dogs kill our own children? They don't even have mercy for nursing babies!"

"Kill him!" yelled the soldier working on the tent.

Mrs. Vas pulled the child away and held his arm so the soldier could not harm him. "Don't touch him!" By then, three other women had also grabbed the child.

By the time the soldier sheathed his sword, the child disappeared among skirts and aprons so that not even a bloodhound could find him.

— § —

After the night's fighting, Gergely jumped into the hot springs and bathed. Then he returned quickly.

In front of the palace, he ran into a thick waisted young man in a blue waistcoat. He was carrying an iron ramrod on his shoulder, or, as they said in those times, a *thunderer*. The end of the ramrod was covered in black soot. He greeted Gergely.

As he turned his face, Gergely stopped in shock.

This blonde man in a blue waistcoat, his child-like nose and two brave eyes ...

There are faces that remain with us like oil paintings on a wall. They do not change. Gergely had lived with this face and this figure. When he was a prisoner in his childhood and sat in the cart on the peasant girl's lap, he saw this face. The lad was chained and cursed the Turks.

Gergely shouted, "Gáspár!"

"That's my name," he replied with a smile. "How do you know me, lieutenant?" He took off his hat.

Gergely couldn't speak. "This is something crazy," he thought to himself, "because *this* cannot be *that*. It's been twenty years."

"What's your father's name?"

"Same as mine, lieutenant. Gáspár Kocsis."

"Your mother's name is some form of Margit, right?"

"That's it."

"Didn't they get together in Baranya?"

"Yes, certainly."

"They had been Turkish captives."

"They had taken them."

"But they escaped."

"That's how it happened. Dobó freed them."

"And a little boy." Heat ran over Gergely's face. "Is your mother here?"

"She came here. Because my father is here, lieutenant sir. My father is with me. We work on the same cannon."

"Where's your mother?"

"There. She's coming."

A round faced, stout woman was walking from the gate. She was carrying two cups of milk. A basket on the back. Her apron was full of carrots.

Gergely hurried over. "Dear Margit, this is me! Dear good aunt Margit! Let me kiss your face." And before the woman could react, he planted kisses on both her cheeks.

Dumfounded, she just stared at him.

"I am, my dear, that little boy," said Gergely, "whom you carried on your lap on the road to Pécs."

"No," says the woman, still startled, "would that have been your grace, sir warrior?" Her voice was as thick as a wooden trumpet.

"Me, my dear," replied Gergely happily. "I often remember the kind image of you as that girl! And how you mothered and nursed us on top of that cart."

The Margit woman's eyes were wet with joy. "Hold this cup," she said to her son, "because God knows I am going to drop it. Well that wisp of a little girl. Is she still living?"

"Yes, she lives! She's my wife now. She's at home in Sopron. I have a young son also. His name is Jancsi. I'll write to them that I've seen the good aunt Margit. I'll write to them."

— § —

Hey, warrior Gergely, where is your little boy? Where is your beautiful wife?

8

That day Gergely slept on his bear skin. He was woken up by some infernal cracking noise coming from the castle, as if a thousand doors were being slammed shut at the same time.

He stretched and got up. He opened the window shutters. Well, the city was in flames. The beautiful large cathedral, the episcopal palace, Nicholas Church, the canon's house, the Cifra mill, and houses everywhere were in flames and smoke. The shower of ashes over his head and throughout the castle was like hell.

He opened the inner window and a roof tile flew in front of his nose. The roof of the monastery was torn, as was the beautiful new roof of the church. Many green tile shingles, wood shingles, slats, and roof beams were flying around.

He opened a third window and saw nothing but flying pieces of roof. There was no one in the courtyard or among the houses. The walls were crowded with people.

He looked where the sun was. It was past noon. He called his servant. Not there. He got some water. He washed quickly. The next minute he put on clothes, sword and feathered cap. He ran down the stairs. He picked up a shield and covered himself from falling shingles as he hurried to the bastion.

Well, like a many colored antediluvian flood of water, Turks were pouring out from the valley. They came with great ringing, banging, drumming and trumpet blaring. Waves of red, white and blue colors weaved together in enormous knots.

Almagyar, the beautiful little village by the hot springs, was on fire. All of its houses were burning.

A long, endless black line of oxen and buffalo on the Maklár road, all pulling cannons.

The armor of *jebeji* gunsmiths shone on the hillside, and the red caps of mounted *akinji* flooded the game reserve. What else was coming after them?

"Where's the captain?"

"On Church Tower."

Gergely glanced up. The top of the tower was flat. Dobó was standing there wearing his every day, pigeon-colored cloth cap. Next to him were Mekcsey, Zoltay, Pető, the priest, Cecey and old steward Sukán.

Gergely hurried there, up the tower's wooden staircase, jumping three steps at a time. At one turn, he ran into Fügedy. "Why is the city burning?" he asked breathlessly.

"The captain set it on fire."

"What sort of destruction is this?"

"We destroy the roofs so the Turks have nothing to burn."

"Where are you going?"

"I'm carrying water to the reservoir. Come on, Dobó has already asked for you."

From the tower you could see the Turkish army even better. The army stretched all the way to Maklár, like a moving forest.

"Well, Gergely," said Mekcsey on the tower, "I was just asking Kristóf if this is how you slaughtered the Turks last night."

"The dogs have risen again!" replied Gergely. "There he comes, the one whose head Bakocsai brought here."

He turned to Dobó. "Shouldn't we shoot a volley in front as a greeting?"

"No," replied Dobó, smiling.

Gergely looked at him puzzled, gesturing with his head towards the Turks. "Whoever comes first should have to say good day."

Below the city, the army scattered around the reserve, just like a flood when it reaches a rock and flows around it.

9

That night, some men from Upper Hungary disappeared. Others came to replace them. Some thirty peasants came from Felnémet. They came with straightened scythes. One of them brought a flail. Of course, the flail had been studded with nails. They were led by a chubby man in a leather apron. A sledge hammer on his shoulder.

When they stopped in front of Dobó, he lifted the hammer and lowered it to the ground. He took off his cap. "We're from Felnémet. We came in. My name is Gergely. I'm a blacksmith. If need be, I beat iron. If need be, I beat Turks."

Dobó shook his hand.

After that came Hungarians from Almagyar, Tihamér, and even Abony. Mostly married peasants. The women in baggy pants. The men were well-stocked, bringing horses and wagons.

An ox cart also curved up into the castle. There was a bell on the cart, a bell so big that the wheels were rubbing on both sides.

An old gentleman was walking in front of the cart. Next to him were two gentlemen in blue cloth jackets and red boots. One was about twenty years of age with a turned-up mustache. The other was sixteen — still a child.

Their faces were similarly round and brown. Their necks were equally short. The old man wore a broad sword in a velvet sheath on his side. The two younger boys wore thin swords in their red velvet sheathes.

The old man was wearing black clothes. His boots were also black.

Dobó was remotely aware of his mourning dress, but he was preoccupied with the people from Felnémet. Only when the old man got close did Dobó get a good look.

He was the mayor of Eger.

"Well there, Mayor András!" said Dobó stretching out his hand.

"I am," the Eger mayor said. "Here I'm bringing the old bell. I buried the rest."

"And these two good boys?"

"My sons."

Dobó shook their hands also. Then he turned towards the driver of the ox-cart. "Put the bell next to Church Bastion. Kristóf," he said to his page, tell lord Mekcsey to bury the bell to prevent it from being hit by a bullet.

His eyes noticed the mayor's black boots. "For whom are you mourning, older brother?"

The mayor of Eger looked down. "My city." He lifted his head. His eyes were full of tears.

Then came a man in an ash-grey cloth together with two women, each woman leading a child.

Dobó looked at the man with a friendly eye and said, "The miller, correct?"

"I am the miller of Maklár," he replied, almost cheered up by the friendly word. "I was here last night in the Cifra mill."

"Well, these two women?"

"One is my wife, the other is my daughter. Those two are my little sons. They didn't want to leave me, so, I told them perhaps they could get little place to stay here."

"There's space here, no question, but we already have many women here." He turned to Sukán, "How many women are in the castle?

"Forty-five so far," Sukán replied.

Dobó shook his head.

Then another three people arrived accompanied by a priest, a thin priest with a sunken face. He did not have a sword, just a stick and a haversack made from fox skin.

Well, Dobó was overjoyed with them. By all means they needed more priests in the castle. They were needed to make the fighters feel closer to God, and also for sermons. And also to give the final sacraments to the dying and the dead. And to help bury.

"God brought you," said Dobó. "I won't even ask for your name because I know you came from God and God sent you to us."

"Is there a priest in the castle?" asked the church's man. "How many priests here?"

"Just one," replied Dobó sadly. Because from the priest's pronunciation, he could tell that he was not going to give any sermon.

— § —

And as the Turks poured in from the south and spread like a horseshoe around the city, the remaining population of the city pulled themselves into the castle. They were mostly peasants and craftsmen together with their women and even children.

In every town about to be besieged, skeptics remain who tell themselves, "It's not true that the Turks are coming. Every year they scare the world with it, and then we grow old and die. The Turks don't even bother us as much as the May bugs."

These are the ones who get destroyed by floods, and the ones most likely to be the casualties of war. The descendants of the *we-have-time* family never die out.

Dobó did not mind them coming. The more people, the better. Women and children were less welcome in the castle, but it was not possible to chase them away. And so many soldiers need a woman's hand.

Well, just let them come.

The women were divided between the kitchens and the ovens. Uncle Sukán found space for every family. Some rooms had to provide quarters for ten or twenty people. After all, all they needed was a place to sleep and put their belongings.

Mekcsey drove the men into the corner of the gatehouse, and they were not allowed to go father inside until they were sworn in as soldiers. "Ay," said an Eger vineyard owner after taking the oath, "because that's the reason we came here, to defend the castle."

At which another tacked on, "The reason the castle is here is to defend us."

Mekcsey immediately distributed weapons to them. There were piles of swords, spears, shields and helmets in the arches of the bastion. Of course, not Damascus, Hindustan, or Derbend masterpieces, just rusty, everyday weapons that had collected in the fortress over centuries. Each man could chose whatever he wanted.

A cobbler with a thick mustache, and eyebrows that could have served as a mustache, spoke confidently. "All these weapons are good, captain sir, but I brought my shoe knife." He pulled a bright shoe knife out of his apron pocket. "If a Turkish man comes at me, I'll use this to disembowel him!"

They also tried on one or two helmets, but because an iron hat is a heavy item, and they looked more like a cooking pot than the nice, shiny helmets the warriors wore, they just left them there.

"What good are these?"

Well, you will find out what they are good for.

At dusk, the sentries on the tower reported that a four-horse gentleman's carriage was coming fast from Felnémet. They could not figure out who it could be. Bishops often went about in a four-horse carriage. Any other gentleman would only ride inside such a carriage if he was sick.

But sick people do not come here.

"You will see, your graces, that the bishop is coming," said Fügedy, the lieutenant of the church chapter.

Because no one believed him, he gave examples from history. "Weren't they in every battle so far? Were there not many at Mohács? After all, the bishopric is not only an ecclesiastical function, but also a military one. Each bishop has his own army. Every bishop is a captain at the same time."

"Any captain could also be a bishop," Dobó replied. Maybe he thought if he were bishop, he could have fielded more soldiers against the Turks.

"Maybe it's some courier from the king, but he got sick along the way," suggested Mekcsey.

Dobó's face brightened. "The king can't abandon us here," he said with confidence. Impatient, he set off down the stairs, across the market to the Old Gate, the castle entrance for wheeled vehicles.

The gentleman's carriage was covered with leather and painted yellow. It turned towards the south gate and drove in to the castle market. Then out climbed a tall figure in black clothes: a lady.

"The captain?" were her first words

When she saw Dobó, she raised her veil. A woman in her forties. Her dress indicated she was a widow.

"Lady Balogh," Dobó said, shocked. He lifted his cap and bowed.

She was the mother of the page Dobó had sent home with Lukács Nagy. "My son ..." she said, her lips trembling. "Where is Balázs?"

"I sent him home," Dobó replied in amazement. "I sent him home over a month ago."

"I know. But he came back here."

"He didn't come back."

"He left a letter saying he was coming here."

"He hasn't come."

"He followed Lukács Nagy."

"He hasn't come back either."

The widow pressed her hand over her forehead. "He! My only son ... Well, he's also lost!"

"That's not certain."

"I swore at my lord's death bed that I wouldn't put him in danger until he got married. He's the last of the family."

"I know, honorable lady," Dobó said, sighing. "That's why I sent him home. Now, just turn back before the Turkish army closes the ring around us." He ordered a hundred cavalry to escort her.

She was wringing her hands, looking at Dobó as if begging. "If he were to come back ..."

"By now he can't come back. The city should be surrounded by nightfall. Only the king's army can break in here."

"But what if he comes before ..."

"I'll lock the urchin in my house!"

The woman sat in her carriage. Fifty riders before and another fifty after. The four horses set off with the carriage as if it were a feather and headed back to the Eger town's Cifra (Felnémet) Gate.

Only one of the four gates was still open. It was only possible to leave towards Szarvaskő or Turkány.

A quarter of a hour later the tower sentries reported that the upper wing of the Turkish army had reached Cifra Gate.

A rider came racing back from her escort. "Lieutenant Fekete is asking if they should cut through the Turkish lines with the lady?"

Dobó climbed up to the bastion. He saw a horde of Turkish armored cavalry around the gate, and behind them long lines of *azab* irregular infantry.

"No!"

He stayed at the bastion. He looked north, his hands shielding his eyes from the sun. "Lads," he said to the soldiers on the bastion. "Which one of you has good eyes? Just look towards Felnémet!"

"Some riders are coming from there," one of the lads replied.

"Twenty," said another.

"Twenty-five," the first said again.

"Lukács Nagy is coming!" shouted Mekcsey from Church Bastion.

Indeed, it was Lukács Nagy, the lieutenant who had been trailing the Turks. Where the hell had he been for so long? And how will he come inside? As if they were blown by a strong wind, they were galloping. It was already late, Lukács Nagy! The Turks have blocked the gate!

Lukács Nagy does not know anything about it yet. He turns down the hill towards Cifra Gate. There he sees the Turkish cavalry. He pulls on the reins of his horse and wheels with his group towards Bakta Gate.

There are even more Turkish soldiers there.

"You can scratch it now, Lukács, where it's not itching!" Zoltay says with a laugh.

"If only they didn't have cavalry at the gates," Dobó says with a sparkle in his eye. "Lukács would cut through them."

Lukács stands and looks towards the castle. He is scratching.

The men on the wall are waving to him with their caps. "Come on, Lukács, if you dare!"

Turkish horses in the distance are suddenly gathering. One hundred *akinji* mount horses. They chase Lukács Nagy.

Lukács Nagy is not resting. He takes off with his twenty-one horsemen and the race begins. At first the horses were visible, later only two clouds of dust rising above the poplar trees and moving rapidly away towards Felnémet.

10

The next day was Sunday, but the bells of Eger did not ring. The area around the castle and the city was inundated with Turks.

Mountains, hills and fields were covered with thousands of colorful tents. Crimson and white tents, sometimes green, blue, yellow and red tents. Ordinary soldiers' tents were like a card folded in the middle. Officers' tents were eight-sided, tall, ornately decorated, and flying golden horsetails and crescent moon flags. Thousands of horses grazed in the meadow of Felnémet, in the fields of Kistálya, and every other place where there was grass. All along the stream buffalo and humans were bathing. From the flood of banging-clanging folk, here and there a camel raised its neck, and mounted officers' turbans flashed white.

Standing like an island in the midst of this surging tide of colors was Eger Castle, the lawn in front of the castle, and King's Chair where Eger Castle's tallest walls had been constructed facing its eastern slope.

Dobó and his officers stood on the roof again. It was good of King St. István to have built those two towers. They could see how the Turks were setting up cannons.

Behind the castle lay a large grassy area, half the size of Vérmező Field in Buda. Beyond that was a beautiful vineyard. There, the Turkish pulled up three old cannons.

They did not even bother to set up gabion walls to protect the cannon. Nor did they bother to drive the thirty buffaloes far, just under the hill, onto the lawn. There they grazed. Now only the camels were next to the cannons. Their backs were loaded with black bags.

"Leather bags," Dobó explained. "They keep gunpowder in them."

Spinning around there in full view of the castle were small, red-turbaned *topchi* gunners. The black mouths of the cannons were silently pointing toward the castle. The *topchi pasha* crouched down and looked at them. Directed it left and right, up and down.

One of the cannons will be for the two towers, the other for the central north bastion, which covers the palace.

"Do you see how he is aiming?" said Dobó. "He's not aiming with the front of the cannon, but from the back."

The head of a gunner lad appeared at the tower door and said, "Captain, sir!"

"Come here," Dobó replied.

The lad climbed up. He took an anxious glance at the Turkish cannons, then stood at a military attention.

"Captain, sir," he said, "Master Balázs asks if he should shoot back."

"Tell him not to shoot until I order. Then you come back here."

The *topchis* continued to stuff the three *zarbuzan* siege cannons. They stuffed gunpowder into the stomachs of the cannons with club-headed, iron ramrods.

"I have a desire to drop a few shots among them" Mekcsey said fervently. "By the time they're ready, they would be scattered."

"Let them have some fun," Dobó replied calmly.

"At least we could raid them!" Gergely suggested.

"Not now," Dobó replied. "Let's see how they shoot."

The *topchis* continued to stuff the throats of the *zarbuzans*. Four people held the ramrod and with each word signal pushed it down the barrel.

Cecey also spoke up, "Pagan's mercy! Captain brother, why do we have guns?"

"My dear old man, even your grace is angry with me! Well, tomorrow you'll find out why I'm not shooting."

The topchis picked up skins from a bag. Two held the skin while a third smeared it with tallow. Then they turned it over and covered the cannonball with tallow smeared side.

"Maybe they're shooting eggs!" Zoltay asked mockingly.

That's when the gunner lad came back.

"Stand in front of me," Dobó said. "I just saw earlier that you were scared. Well, look, they will shoot here, at me. You stand in front of me!"

The lad blushed and stood in front of Dobó.

Dobó looked down from the tower. When he saw Pető, he called out, "Gáspár, my son! You have a good throat. Shout that the Turks are about to shoot and no one should be scared. The women, should they be afraid, should stay away from the shade of the walls."

The *topchis* had already pushed cannonballs into all three guns. Their three gunners held a flaming wick. A *topchi* behind them spit on his palm and stroking his neck, looked up at the castle.

The gunpowder ignited, the cannon smoked and flamed, and nine boombooms in succession shook the ground.

The castle trembled with the roar. Then there was silence.

"Nothing," Dobó said, smiling. Then he sent the gunner lad back down.

Smoke puffed out from the cannons.

But how the devil can three cannons make nine explosions? The mountains around Eger immediately echo the sound of gunfire; each cannon three times.

Well, there will be music here if the Turks fire three or four hundred cannons at once!

After a quarter of an hour, Pető ran up to the tower. A butcher's boy came after him. On his two strong arms he carried a stinking bullet toward Dobó.

"I humbly report, here's the ball," Pető said. "It fell into the stream. The water carriers brought it up in a basket."

"Tell them to continue fetching water. Do not close the gate."

"Don't we shoot?" Pető also asked.

"It's Sunday," replied Dobó smiling. "How can we shoot?"

And he continued watching how the *topchis* cooled the cannons and reloaded them.

11

The next morning, three siege cannons were already squatting in the middle of the grass.

They multiplied with another three.

The previous day nine shots were wasted. There was no return fire from the castle. Well, the cannons were set closer, so close that an ordinary arrow could hit them from the castle.

Dobó knew that would be the case. Why would you have them distracted? Why risk the confidence of the castle defenders with some useless puffs in return?

Already at dawn, he was on his feet making preparations for his cannon to answer back. Of course, he did not wrap his cannonballs in skins, only greased them a little. He himself carefully measured the gunpowder with a measuring spoon.

"Well, let's get on with it. Beat it in well, lad, with the ramrod! Get that ball in! ..."

And he took his time carefully aiming it.

He waited for the Turks to be finished behind the gabions. Then, when the first Turkish cannon thundered, he cried out, "In God's name, *fire!*"

Flames were raised to twelve Hungarian cannons at the same time, and all twelve touched the powder simultaneously.

The Turkish gabions and gun carriages leaned and shattered. Two Turkish cannons turned upside down. One was torn to pieces. The angry shouting and running of the *topchis* behind the gabions made people inside the castle laugh.

"Well, brother," Dobó said to old Cecey cheerfully, "now do you understand why we didn't shoot yesterday?"

He stood on the wall with his feet spread, smoothing his mustache with both hands.

— § —

The people inside the castle were not as frightened as Dobó had feared. Eger, since the introduction of gunpowder, is the world capital of gunshots. Even today, you can't imagine a picnic, firefighter dinner, song festival, garden party, or play without a cannon firing first. The cannon fire serves as advertising. Sometimes there is advertising, but it never replaces cannon fire. The castle always has some mortars lying about in the grass. Whoever wants can fire them. So how could the Eger be scared?

There was only one man in the castle who had fallen from his chair with the first cannon shot and yelled for help.

I need not identify him because it is easy to figure out who he is.

Soldiers got him and pulled his grace out of the nook. They dragged him to the bastion, yellow coat, red pants, helmet, bare feet and all.

There, two held him by his arms, two by his feet and another behind him. They shouted to the Turks, "Shoot here!"

The Gypsy just stood there while the cannons were being re-loading, but when they fired again, he pulled himself out of the soldier's arms and made a hair-raising, twelve foot leap down from the platform. There he first tapped himself all over to see if a cannonball had nicked him somewhere, then ran like a greyhound to the Old Gate.

"Oh, oh, oh!" he shouted, holding his head in both hands, "if only my legs had cramped up before I walked towards here. Oh dear, oh dear! If only that stinking horse had gone blind bringing me here!"

— § —

That day Dobó destroyed all the cannons set up on King's Seat hill. The *topchis* screamed, yelled and ran all over. Two *topchi* aghas died. A third officer was taken away on a canvas.

There was nothing left in the area except fallen and broken gabions, three dead camels, crippled cannons, boxes, and the cannon wheels lying in pieces.

As if that was not enough, Gergely even raided them at midnight and carried away twenty horses and a mule that followed the horses.

But the Turks had so many horses, and so many men, and so many cannons, that by dawn, gabion walls filled with pounds of pounds of earth were standing again. Of course, they pushed the guns back a little, and they built up a wall of dirt in front. Twelve new cannon were placed in the spaces between the gabion walls. There were new *topchis* and new aghas around the cannons.

Even before sunrise, the castle was shaken by dreadful thunder and the dull blows of cannonballs hitting the walls.

Dobó fired his own cannons again, and once more damaging the gabions and cannons, but a new line of gabions and new cannons was being set up in back of the damaged ones.

And this time the *topchis* did not run off in all directions. Sitting close behind them was a brigade of *jebeji* soldiers with nail-studded whips.[49] "Here you can only fire and die!"

"Well, let them fire," Dobó said. "We need to be careful with our supply of gunpowder." And only the bearded cannons sometimes popped up to disrupt their work.

---

[49] The *jebeji* soldiers (Turkish, *cebeci*) were part of a small, privileged unit within the janissary corps responsible for keeping, maintaining and transporting weapons — and maintaining discipline.

That day the Turks had not yet occupied the city. Hungarian infantry guarded the castle gates and the cavalry guarded the city gates.

The Turks had yet to fight them. For what do they need the city! It is the castle they need! Whoever holds the castle also has the city.

For two days now, Turkish senior officers had been riding horses over higher terrain and hills to see inside the castle. But they could not see over the walls; only the birds could. Only the towers stuck out. The tops of the walls and bastions were covered with planks and woven wicker stuffed with earth that hid what was inside.

So where do they shoot?

They aimed at the walls and the wood and earth stockade.

Inside the castle were some beautiful buildings. Many remaining great churches were masterpieces of architecture. The church next to the old monastery was made of carved stone. (Since then, Hungarian soldiers have not had such nice barracks!) The castle palace was decorated by Dobó when he got married. It was carved, assembled, and had glass windows installed by a master Italian builder. Below in the city, the bishop himself had only windows made with parchment.

So the Turks just shot and shot. From dawn to dusk their cannons burped and bellowed. They broke the walls and tore into the wood, wicker and earth palisades. After, when the sun went down behind Bakta Mountain, all of their cannons were fired at once, and from all sides throughout the camp you could hear imams calling and chanting "*Allahu Akbar ...*".

The entire Turkish camp was saying their prayers. The *topchis* also.

Dobó's stonemasons pulled out their trowels and, with what light remained, began the work to fill in the gaps with new stone.

12

The two pashas shook their heads. Both men had aged over many wars. Wherever they went, they left rubble behind, and the sultan's empire expanded.

"You have to break into the city! You also have to fire cannons at the walls from there!"

On the fourth day, they entered the city. It was a child's play for the army. A thousand ladders and a thousand young fighters ...

Our gatekeepers were allowed to retreat as soon as the Turks appeared on the wall. Well, they indeed left the gates. In good order with drumbeats, they returned to the castle.

Then Arslan Bey had four large siege cannons pulled near the Church of the Blessed Virgin and aimed them at the bastions where the Hungarians' silent cannons were positioned.

Arslan Bey was beginning to aim better.

His cannonballs broke the walls and palisade above the city. Most of the balls missed, but the ones that found their targets broke down the walls.

That day, the Turkish removed the crosses from the towers of the churches in the city and installed crescent moons in their places. Altars were broken down. Pictures were burned. And at noon, muezzins sang from the windows of the towers, the long yelling of:

> *Allahu Akbar! Allahu Akbar! Allahu Akbar! Allahu Akbar!*
> *Ashhadu an la ilaha illa Allah. Ashhadu an la ilaha illa Allah.*
> *Ashadu anna Muhammadan Rasool Allah. Ashadu anna*
> *Muhammadan Rasool Allah.*
> *Hayya 'ala-s-Salah. Hayya 'ala-s-Salah.*
> *Hayya 'ala-l-Falah. Hayya 'ala-l-Falah.*
> *Allahu Akbar! Allahu Akbar!*[50]

At noon, having lunch together, Dobó was silent and serious.

No message from the king yet. The spy returned from the bishop of Eger at night. The bishop replied that he had no money or soldiers, but he would pray for the people in the castle.

None of the muscles on Dobó's face twitched at this message. Only his eyebrows knitted closer.

He was saddened by the report from Lukács Nagy. That man was a brave officer and warrior. He always liked lurking around the Turks. He had been captured in the great Turkish war and disappeared. Now, indeed, how could he come back when the castle was surrounded and tents were pitched all the way to Felnémet! Or maybe he was already lost ...

It was reported at lunch that Antal Nagy had been hit by a cannonball.

Bornemissza popped up: "Captain sir, let me lead a raid the Turks! I regret that we left the city gates without a fight."

---

[50] God is Great! God is Great! God is Great! God is Great! I bear witness that there is no god except the One God. I bear witness that there is no god except the One God. I bear witness that Mohammed is the messenger of God. I bear witness that Mohammed is the messenger of God. Hurry to the prayer. Hurry to the prayer. Hurry to salvation. Hurry to salvation. God is Great! God is Great! There is no god except the One God.

Budaházi, an officer with strong shoulders and chest, added, "Let the Turks see, captain sir, that not only do we dare to raid them at night, but also in the daytime!"

Pető also growled. "Even if we are few, we're going to cut a hundred, a hundred thousand."

"All right," Dobó replied with brightened eyes. "But it's not worth it for you to leave this lunch."

Then he did not say anything about the Turks until just after lunch. "You will attack the infantry next to the big church. You cut through them with one charge then turn back immediately. Fight only those who get in your way. You shall not line up, re-group, or wait for orders, or else you will leave your teeth behind. One hundred can go."

So then, the officers grabbed their guns and armored shirts. Mount up! The lads all want to join, but scholar Gergely choose only the strongest.

The *azab*, *lagumji*, and *piyad* soldiers were having their lunch sitting on the lawn in front of the church. Today they had just finished soup for lunch, and they had already put their spoons back in their belts. After the soup they were eating onions with bread. Some had melons, some had cucumbers, some greens. All this could be seen from the castle. Only the stream and the city market separated them from unoccupied land. A company of janissaries had settled next to the houses by the market. Just then they were relaxing. A clever fellow threw a scimitar and a melon up high. First he caught the scimitar, then the melon with the tip of the scimitar.

It was obvious he was playing a bet. Because, see, another janissary brought him a watermelon. They talked for a while, then the janissary tossed up the watermelon, and another tossed a sword.

A third Janissary pulled the clever fellow back. The melon fell to the ground and splattered, all to the general amusement of the soldiers.

The gate of the castle was still open. Peasants from the castle were watering horses and carrying water back to the castle. What would the Turks gain if they rushed the gate? A couple of bullets in their sides. The Turks knew that the gate, even when open, had teeth in it like the open mouth of a lion.

While the janissaries are distracted, the watering stops at the stream.

Only two or three minutes pass, so how would anyone notice? They do not even notice the men multiplying on the walls, particularly those armed with bows and guns. But they do twitch at the approaching, thundering sound of hooves. As their eyes turn towards the castle, the mortars on the walls thunder and spew all manner of nails, shot, and pieces of iron into their faces. A long line of horses and riders gallop through the castle gate.

They jump over the stream like a storm. Their swords slash — chi-puhi! — cutting and chopping. They ride through the Turkish lines and reach the large grassy market plaza where the bishop's church casts its afternoon shadow.

Turkish infantry are running and jumping from fear and looking towards the market. Some run, some stand and draw swords.

See, the galloping cavalry is there in the market, their spurred steeds like fiery dragons. Many hundreds of Turks are running, like a flock frightened by wolves. Hungarians on their backs.

But help is gathering from the streets: *akinji* riders, *gönüllü* garrison infantry, and janissaries armed with spears and guns.

There, a white-capped janissary lunges his spear at Gergely. Gergely's sword flashes twice. With one flash, the spear is cut in two. With the other, the Turk's back is cut.

"Jesus! Jesus!" come shouts from the bastion.

"Allah! Allah!" roar the Turks.

More and more Hungarians are wheeling around on both sides. Their swords glitter and flash. However, a janissary stabs Mihály Horváth's horse in the rump. The horse falls. Horváth jumps off and cuts the janissary to pieces, and then another until his sword breaks. Left only with his fists, he punches the third in the nose, then starts running, then walking back to the castle in the empty space cleared by the riders.

The rest are still ahead. Horses' legs trample men. Budaházi is raising his sword for a terrible cut when the janissaries fire a gun at him. The sword falls out of Budaházy's hand. He turns his horse and leaning against the back of its neck, he rides back.

At this, the rest also turn around.

A thousand *akinji* come to help, galloping and storming down the main street. Gergely avoids them just in time. He rides in an "S" pattern towards Káptalan Street. That street is also swarming with Turks, but more infantry than cavalry, and the foot soldiers fleeing in disorder serve to disrupt the Turkish riders who have to avoid their own soldiers. Even so, a frightening number of Persian *gureba* cavalry scramble to confront the raiders. But their rush is in vain as our enraged squadron turns on them! A blood drenched street opens up as Persians stagger left and right like stacks of grain in a hurricane.

Now it shows how weak the little eastern horse is beside the full-bodied, strong Hungarian horse. Ten Hungarian horsemen can charge and scatter a hundred Turkish horse. And if any Hungarian goes after a Turk, well, that Turk will not become any noble lord in Eger Castle.

They are already galloping to return.

"Get away from the gate!" Shouting and cheering from the castle walls mingle with the din of the fighters riding back.

Dobó is worried to see how the *akinji* riders and *jebeji* soldiers are rushing out from the small streets to help the other Turks. He orders his men to fire. Guns on the wall thunder and bows twang. The leading Turkish groups stop and jam up.

At this minute, there is a horrible, animal-like roar on the castle wall — horrible like the bray of a donkey. Everybody looks up. Well the Gypsy is shouting. He is angrily jumping and shaking his sword at the Turks. "Stop, wretched Turk dogs! You die!"

Our horsemen, fired up from the turmoil they caused among the Turks, scamper back through the castle gates on their foamy, bloody, and sweaty horses.

It didn't last a quarter of an hour. But Church Square, the market, and Káptalan Street were full of dead and wounded men and limping horses. The rattled Turks cleared out backwards, foaming with rage. From a safe distance, they turned and angrily shook their fists.

— § —

Dobó did not close the gate to the stream that day. He allowed the people of the castle to come and go from morning till evening. Let the Turks see that Eger was calmly facing the siege.

The gate was wide open. Armed guards were nowhere to be seen. It is true that garrison *drabant* soldiers stood inside, a hundred and twenty strong. It is also true that a sentry sat in the tower window, and in one movement he could lower the *organ*, that is, the iron bars that, like organ pipes, protect the bottom of the gate. A mortar also pokes out from inside the gate. The bridge can also be raised even when it is crowded with people.

Well, mounted soldiers and people carrying water just came and went. Cavalrymen watered their horses. People carried water to fill the stone pools in the castle. There was also a well in the castle, but a well was not enough to satisfy two thousand people and as many horses. So it was necessary to fetch as much water as possible!

Turks watered their horses from the other side of the stream. Some of the Turkish foot soldiers also drank from the stream.

There was plenty of water in the creek because the sluice gate had been closed. It was waist deep in the middle. The Turks also had left the sluice closed. The water was needed not only for the many, many animals, but for their many people. There was no well in the city, just a couple of springs running out of spouts in the sides of the hills.

So the peasants from Eger fetching water had become used to the Turks. They also had seen how the castle soldiers had attacked and routed them.

So as one fellow is dipping and carrying water to the wagon, he cannot resist taunting the Turks. "Come on over, buddy, if you dare!"

The Turks, even if they do not understand the words, can understand movements of the head. Well, one Turk also gestures, "You come over!"

Another Turk smiles. He also gestures an invitation. In the next minute, five or six Turks and as many Hungarians are inviting each other.

A giant Kurd wearing a dirty turban is washing his injured leg on the far side. He is knee deep in the stream. He gets up and wades across the stream. He shoves his big, blonde mustache in the face of a Hungarian. "Well, here I am. What do you want?"

Our peasants do not jump away. They also are standing in the water with pant legs rolled up. One, like lightning, grabs the Kurd's arm and drags him towards the other peasants.

By the time the other Turks realize what had happened, four peasants are already pushing and dragging the Kurd towards the wagons. The rest point spears at the pagans jumping into the water.

The Kurd is screaming. Shaking. But strong hands hold him. Coat, buttons and cords are torn off. His turban falls off his head. His nose is bleeding. He yells, "*Yetishin!*" [Help!] and throws himself on the ground. Help is not coming. He is pulled by his feet so fast that he cannot get up until he has slid through the castle gate.

They stand him up in front of Dobó.

The Kurd is no longer so proud. He shakes off the dust and folds his hands across his chest. He bows deeply.

Dobó leads him to the castle guardroom. He calls Bornemissza to interpret. He is sitting beside a suit of armor hanging on a pole. He does not even bother to chain the Kurd.

"What is your name?"

"Chekan," replies the Kurd, trembling with anger and fear.

"In whose army do you serve?"

"Ahmed Pasha."

"What are you?"

"*Piyad*"

"So you are a foot soldier?"

"Yes, sir."

"Were you at the siege of Temesvár?"

The Kurd points to his leg showing a red, four-inch wound on his calf. "I was there, sir."

"Why was the castle lost?"

"It was the will of Allah."

"Talk to me clearly, and if I hear one false word, you are dead." He raises his pistol.

The Kurd bows. His eyes reveal that he will not lie.

Dobó did not know any of the details about the siege of Temesvár. All he knew was that Temesvár was more fortified than Eger, and that it was besieged by only half of the army surrounding Eger, and yet it was occupied.

There were some officers in the room during the interrogation. They happened to be off duty at the time. They were Pető, Zoltay, Hegedüs, Tamás Bolyky, Kristóf the page, and András, the mayor of Eger.

They were sitting around Dobó. Only the page stood behind Dobó, leaning with his elbows on the back of Dobó's armchair. The prisoner stood barefoot, bare-headed, four steps in front of Dobó.

Behind the prisoner, two guards armed with spears.

"When did your army arrive at Temesvár?"

"The fifth day in the month of Redjep." (on June 27th)

"How many siege cannons did your army have?"

"The noble pasha brought twelve *zarbuzan*."

Bolyky grumbled, "He's lying!"

"He's not lying," Dobó replied, "because Ali was in Upper Hungary with the others."

Then he continued interrogating the pagan. "How many *zarbuzan* did Ali Pasha bring with him?"

"Four," the Kurd replied.

"My spy also said sixteen siege guns." He turned back to the Kurd. "Tell me how the siege of that castle was conducted. I'm not hiding from you that I am asking for our own protection. If you want to deceive me with even one word, you will be killed. If you speak the truth, I will release you peacefully after the siege."

He spoke in such a deliberate voice that every word could have been cast into iron.

"Noble lord!" said the Kurd in a grateful voice. "Let my tongue be the salvation of my soul."

From then on he spoke boldly and fluently. "The noble pasha there, just like here, looked for the weakest walls and parts of the castle, and fired and ruined them until they were fit to be attacked."

"What was the weakest part there?"

"The water tower, sir. We could only take it with great struggle. Man fell like grass under a sickle. For me, there was an arrow in my leg. After the fall of the water tower, the Germans and Spaniards sent a message from the castle that they would surrender if they could leave peacefully. Well, the pasha gave them his word of honor that they would not be hurt."

While the Kurd was talking, cannons fired without interruption, and as the Kurd got to this point, the palace's ceiling crashed with a terrible bang. A cannonball the size of a man's head, together with lime and plaster, fell near Dobó and the Kurd.

It was still spinning. The Kurd backed away, but Dobó glanced at the cannonball that smelled of gunpowder and, as if nothing had happened, calmly gestured, "Continue!"

"The people of the city," the Kurd continued, "the people of the city ..." His breathing got stuck. He was unable to continue.

The page Kristóf pulled a tiny embroidered scarf out of his pocket and wiped the lime powder from the captain's face, hat and dress. During this time the Kurd managed to regain his breath.

"Continue!" Dobó said.

"The people wanted to take everything with them. That was the mistake. Losonczy asked for a day to prepare. The soldiers saw themselves being deprived of their plunder, and the next morning, when the infidels began to leave, they looked angry. 'This is why we fought here for twenty-five days,' they said, 'to allow them to take everything?' And they climbed onto their carts. The Christians did not defend themselves, so the grabbing became more and more greedy. They grabbed children, in particular, and the young women. They don't sell nicer girls in Istanbul, sir, than the ones that were in that group."

"But didn't the pasha provide protection?"

"He sent, but to no avail. When the line of Christian soldiers followed, one of them was also pulled out. One of Losonczy's beautiful young pages. The page screamed. Losonczy got angry. The Hungarians all rebelled. They drew their swords and charged us. We were lucky enough to have *jebejis* standing nearby, otherwise they would have cut through the whole army."

Dobó shrugged. "*Jebejis*? You think someone wearing a little tin can becomes invincible? It was not the tin, but that the Hungarians were few."

A second cannonball crashed into the room. It tore through the old, faded flags that adorned the wall and into the floor.

All those sitting got up. Hegedüs left. The rest, because Dobó remained sitting, waited.

"Where's Pasha Ahmed's tent?" he asked the Kurd.

"Next to the hot springs in the game preserve."

"I thought so," said Dobó looking at his officers.

Again he turned to the Kurd. "Tell me, what is the greatest strength of this army?" He looked sternly into the man's eyes.

"The janissaries, the artillery, the numbers. Noble Ali Pasha is an experienced commander. In one hand he holds out rich rewards. The other holds a nailed whip. Whoever does not advance on his command, the *yasauls* whip them on the back."

"And what's your weakness?"

The Kurd shrugged thoughtfully. Dobó's eyes stared at him like two daggers.

"Well," said the Kurd, "I can give no other answer even if I bare my soul to you like an open book at your feet, my noble lord. I can only say that this army was strong when it was divided. Some thirty fortresses were destroyed by this army, my noble lord, and they have never been defeated, so what can I say?"

Dobó gestured to the two men behind the prisoner. "Tie it up and take him to the dungeon."

Then he stood up. A third cannonball crashed into where he had been sitting. It crushed the beautiful carved armchair and continued spinning.

Dobó didn't turn around. He took his everyday steel helmet from Kristóf and put it on his head.

He went to the top of Prison Bastion and looked around to see which cannon was firing balls into his palace. He quickly spotted it. He aimed three of his cannons. They fired together.

The gabions fell over. The *topchis* were running in confusion. The cannon became quiet. Dobó did not waste gunpowder.

"Glorious shot!" Gergely said cheerfully. As they went back down the stairs of the bastion, he smiled at Dobó and pulled him aside in a corner of the stairs. "Captain sir, you made the Kurd swear to tell the truth, but you forgot to take the same oath from the interpreter."

"Surely you didn't alter his testimony?"

"I did indeed. When the captain sir asked what was the Turks' greatest strength, I missed something. The Kurd said that Ali, with his four cannons, could do more damage than Ahmed with his twelve. Well, it is foreseeable that Ali will bombard the castle until all its walls have fallen."

"Let him," Dobó said calmly.

"Well, this was all I didn't translate," Bornemissza finished. "If you think it's good, captain, please tell the other officers."

"You did well," Dobó said, holding out his hand. "We must not make the people of the castle anxious. But now I'm telling you what your Kurdish boy didn't know: the weakness of the army."

He leaned back against the wall of the bastion and folded his arms.

"The sixteen *zarbuzas*," he continued, "may work tomorrow all together. They are firing one or two hundred cannons at a time. Gates in the walls are broken and towers are knocked down. But it takes time; weeks. In the meantime, you have to feed this huge army. Do you think they carry enough food with them to feed themselves? Do you think that they can produce whatever they need? And if they are hit by October frost, do you think these people raised in warm climates will climb walls with hungry stomachs and cold skins?"

A cannonball slammed past them and blew a hole in the ground. Dobó glanced up at the gunners, then continued. "The people are brave as long as they see us as brave. The main thing is to hold the castle until they run out of food, until the weather worsens, or until the king's army arrives."

"What if they have something to eat? And if there is no freeze in October? What if the king's army remains at Győr?"

Had Gergely asked these questions earnestly, then before he could have thought of a fourth, Dobó probably would have immediately slapped him in irons. But Gergely spoke with a bright face, almost smiling. Perhaps he spoke not to get any answer from Dobó to answer, but as they were talking confidentially, there was no other reply to Dobó's words.

Dobó shrugged. "Didn't the Bishop of Eger send word he would say masses for us?"

— § —

That day as dusk approached, a woman wearing a black *hijab* hurried across the city market square. She was alone except for a boy of about fifteen and a big, mongrel camp dog.

The dog ran to the water at the creek, and the woman walked up and down the bank wringing her hands. She looked towards the gate. At dusk, the gate was shut and locked with nine padlocks. Maybe that was why the woman was waiting. And as the gate was being closed, she waded across the stream without lifting her dress.

"Son!" she shouted in front of the gate, almost screaming. "*Benim* son!"

They reported to Dobó that the mother of the little Turkish boy was at the gate. "Let her in if she wants to come in," said Dobó.

The draw bridge, which also served as a gate, had a narrow iron door. They opened it for the woman, but she backed away frightened.

The dog barked.

"*Benim* son!" she cried again. She held up some sort of purse. She poured pieces of gold from it into her other hand.

The door closed again.

She approached again. She again paced in front of the gate, still wringing her hands. She lifted her veil and wiped her tears with a white cloth. Meanwhile, she continued crying, "Selim! *Benim* son!"

Finally she rattled the iron door. The door opened, but again she backed away.

Then Gergely appeared on the bastion above the gate, and holding the child by the arm, lifted him up.

"Selim!" screamed the Turkish woman, stretching her arms towards the child.

The child also shouted. "*Anne!*" he cried, stretching his free arm to his mother.

The dog jumped whimpering and let out an occasional loud bark.

Gergely might not be allowed to shout from the castle, but the child could. The child cried out to his mother, "You can exchange me for a Christian prisoner, mother, after the siege."

She knelt down and, as if trying to hug him through the air, she stretched out her two arms and kissed him as the child disappeared.

— § —

That night, darkness covered the castle, the city, the mountains, the sky, and the whole world.

Dobó went to bed late, but at midnight he roamed over the bastions again. He wore a thick, long fur overcoat, and a black velvet cap on his head. In his hand he held a roster of the sentries.

The on-duty lieutenant that hour was Zoltay. He also wore a fur overcoat because the night was cool. As soon as he saw Dobó at Sándor Bastion, he saluted him with his sword.

"Do you have anything to report?" Dobó asked.

"I just looked around earlier," Zoltay said. "All man are at their stations."

"The masons?"

"They are working."

"Come with me. I trust you, but the sentries must see that I am also on guard."

He hands the roster over to Zoltay, and they walk in a line along the bastions. Zoltay reads the names in each station. The cannons on each bastion are covered in darkness. The cannon guards are black shadows. By each guard station, a fire is burning in front of the bastion vaults. Those waiting to relieve the guards are keeping themselves warm.

The castle is quiet, only the occasional silent clatter of the stone masons as they plaster.

Dobó stands on the edge of the bastion. Every five minutes, a lantern is pushed through the firing slots. The lantern hangs from a spear. It spreads light a hundred feet over the wall and beyond the moat. Then the spear is drawn in, and taken to another part of the bastion where its light shoots out into the dark night.

Dobó stops at the west gate. The sentry salutes. Dobó takes his spear and sends him to fetch the gatekeeper.

The guard runs up the stairs. His call to the gatekeeper can be heard below. "Mihály uncle!"

"What?"

"Come down quick!"

"Why?"

"The captain is here."

A rumble sound. (He is jumping out of bed.) Two thuds. (He is pulling on his boots.) A rattle. (He is buckling on his sword.) Footsteps. (He is running down the wooden stairs.)

And a man with a big mustache stops in front of Dobó. He is wearing an embroidered shepherd's *szűr* overcoat from Szikszó. One side of his mustache is turned up, the other down.

"First of all," Dobó tells the sentry, returning his spear, "if you're a soldier, don't call your corporal *Mihály uncle!* Or even say, 'Come down quick!' Instead, you say, '*Corporal, sir, the captain sir is calling you.*' That is the proper way. During a siege, even more so."

"Worse still, your words are actually quite accurate. Whoever is sleeping in his shirt and drawers is no *corporal*, only an *uncle Mihály*. That kind of a gatekeeper guard deserves to be lying under a seventy-seven pound cannonball. Is it permitted in a castle under siege to go to sleep undressed?!"

As if in response to this question, Mihály's up-turned mustache drooped down, but no one answered. Dobó continued. "From today on, you will sleep here every night on the floor under the gate. You understand?"

"I understand."

"One more thing. No longer are we going to lower the gate in the mornings. Instead, we will lower the *organ* all the way except for one iron bar. If there is any assault, you will lower that all the way without waiting for any order."

"I understand."

It didn't take five minutes for the thick, sharp-pointed iron bars inside of the gate to be lowered one by one, blocking the gate like a row of organ pipes. Only one bar remained hanging. Just enough for a man to go in and out.

Dobó stepped up to Church Bastion. He also looked at the cannons and the sleeping sentries and those on watch. Then he crossed his arms and looked around the night.

The sky was dark, but as far as the eye could see, thousands of red stars twinkled on the land. They were Turkish camp fires.

He stood and looked.

Then, in the silence of the night, there is a sharp cry from the east, near the castle, from the depths of darkness. "Gergely Bornemissza! You royal lieutenant! Can you hear?"

Silence, long silence.

The same voice shouts again. "You have a Turkish ring. I have a Hungarian child. That ring is mine. This child is yours."

Silence.

The voice shouts again. "If you want your child, come to the market gate. Give me my ring. I'll give you your child. Answer me, Gergely Bornemissza!"

Dobó sees the sentries' faces all turn towards the voice, though nothing can be seen in the darkness.

"Nobody dares answer!" the voice mutters, his sword ringing.

Nobody answers.

The voice continues. "If you don't believe my word, then you will believe it if I throw your child's head at you."

Dobó looks to his right and left, then slaps his sword, "Don't you dare say anything to Lieutenant Bornemissza! Whoever dares to speak a word about it, either to him or to anyone else, by God I will cut him twenty-five times."

"Thanks, captain sir," a hoarse voice replies behind Dobó's back.

It is Bornemissza.

He was tying black oakum onto an arrow head and dipping it in pitch as he continued, "Every night they shout such stupid nonsense. Last night they shouted to Mecskey that his wife was being entertained in Arslan Bey's tent."

He dipped the arrow in a pot of oil and continued. "My wife and child are in Sopron. They don't leave there either in winter or summer."

The voice shouted again. "Can you hear me, Bornemissza! Your son is here with me. Come to the gate in an hour and you can see him."

Gergely placed the arrow on his bow. He touched the arrowhead to fire, pulled the bowstring, and shot it toward the voice.

The fiery arrow passed through the darkness like a blazing comet, illuminating for a moment the hill where the sun rose each morning.

Standing on the hill were two Turks wearing kaftans. One had a voice horn in his hand. The other had an eye covered with a white cloth.

There was no child with them.

— § —

Something else happened that night.

Varsányi rushed through the gate and ran straight to Dobó.

Dobó was still standing on Church Bastion, warming his hands at the fire.

"Sir," said the spy, "I've come to report that all the siege cannons have been set up. They also will be firing from Hécey's yard. In addition, all bearded cannons and howitzers will be firing. The siege guns will be firing at the walls from two places in the city and three places on the hills. The other guns will be pouring cannonballs from some fifty locations. During the noon prayers, the *kumbarajis*[51] will run out and launch fire-bombs with slings and catapults. Ay, ay, ay!" he added, almost crying.

"According to this," Dobó said calmly, "they will be aiming at Prison Bastion, the outer castle and the Old Gate. What else?"

"That's all, captain sir!"

"Do you have anything else to say?"

"Nothing, sir, nothing else, but wouldn't it be better ... if we are already so few ... and such a danger ..."

He couldn't finish because Zoltay slapped his face so that blood from his nose splashed on the wall.

Dobó stretched out his arm between them. "Leave him alone."

---

[51] *Kumbaradji*: Soldiers who manufacture and throw bombs.

"Don't you know that anyone who dares mention surrendering the castle is a dead man?"

"I'm a spy," Varsányi growled. "I'm paid to tell you everything."

"Enough," Dobó said. "You will be sworn in tonight. Then I'll have a problem wiping your nose with gold. Come with me."

They passed the wall where Gergely, the Gypsy, and four peasants were packing bombs. Five people were making bombs from night to dawn. Gergely had taught them, and they had to work at night so there would be no risk of explosion from enemy cannon fire.

Dobó called Gergely. All three went up to the palace. There Dobó pulled out his desk drawer and turned to Gergely. "Write a letter to Szalkay that so far we have received no help from the king or the bishop, and for him to request urgent assistance from counties and cities."

While Gergely was writing the letter, Dobó made Varsányi take the oath in the next room.

"Sir," Varsányi said after the oath, "I know whom I serve. If this castle remains, I will no longer need to wear this Turkish disguise."

"You speak well," replied Dobó. "But even if you weren't expecting any reward, you should still serve your homeland."

There was a jug of wine on the table. He put it in front of the spy. "Drink, Imre."

The spy was thirsty. He lifted the jug. As he wiped his mustache, he could see in his eyes that he was about to say thank you, but Dobó spoke. "You don't have to go back to the Turks. You must take this letter to Szarvaskő this very night. Then wait until Miklós Vas returns from the king and the bishop. If possible, you can bring him in as well. If it is not possible, then return alone. Do the Turks uses passwords in their camps?"

"No, sir. If someone is dressed in Turkish clothes and knows a word or two in Turkish, he can walk among them as if he had come with them. And they don't slap me in the face like this! ..."

Gergely's spurs rattled in the next room. Dobó got up to hear him read the letter.

13

And on the next day, September 16th, the sun rose from behind the mountains to the roar of cannons.

The ground shook. The gunfire made brown puffs of smoke climb up to the clouds in the sky. By the first hour, they blocked the sun and covered the blue ocean of the sky.

Bastions and walls rumbled and crackled. Heavy and tiny balls struck the inner castle. Fiery arrows and fiery bombs fell. Cannonballs fell and struck in all directions. Human and animal life was no longer safe.

But this plague had been anticipated by the castle defenders. Dobó had sounded the alarm to his soldiers the night before.

Some of them raised the palisades facing the area where they expected the cannon fire to come from Hécey's yard. Others collected animal skins remaining in attics and carried them to tubs filled with water. Still others carried beams, barrels, and earth-filled bags to the outer castle, Prison Bastion, and the gates, to be ready should there be any breach in the defenses.

As many empty cups and pots as there were in the castle, they all had to be filled with water. All surplus items were removed from downstairs and underground rooms and replaced with beds. Carrots, pumpkins, cabbage, salt — everything that cannonballs would not damage — were carried up from below and repacked by working and resting men.

The stables were also dug out so horses and cows would be standing that much deeper.

Earth was piled on the north and east sides of houses. Where cannonballs would fall in the market square, they dug a ditch and raised the ground in front of it. The balls fell into the ditch.

There was nothing left to burn in the castle except the roof of the livestock stable, a few haystacks in front of the barn, a small heap of wheat, and some straw for bedding.

Dobó had the stable roof taken down. He had the haystacks and wheat covered with wet cowhide and the straw covered with earth.

What was still flammable, like the roofs of houses and wooden defense works, also had to be covered with wet skins.

This work was still going on when a cannonball crashed into the castle. The first half a hundredweight ball smashed into the kitchen and broke several pots.

The women just happened to be starting a fire and were preparing flour, fat, and bacon to cook for the soldiers.

The cannonball terrified them. They pushed and shoved each other to rush out of the kitchen. Who couldn't reach the door jumped out a window.

The cannonball was still spinning there among a pile of broken pots, a wooden bowl and crushed tiles.

Mekcsey saw the strike from the stables. He ran over.

"What's that?" he yelled at them holding his arms wide to hold them together.

"Cannonball!"

"Back! Back! Follow me!"

He hurried into the kitchen. He grabbed a bucket by its two handles and poured water on the ball.

"Now," he said, kicking the ball into a corner, "keep cooking. The ball came from the left, so work in the left half of the kitchen. All pots should be gathered from the other side and moved over. No one should walk in that area. There's no danger on the left side of the kitchen."

"Oh," a woman worried, "my hen was crowing the night before. This is the end!"

"That was a cock," said Mekcsey.

"But sure it was a hen, captain sir."

"Well, if it was a chicken, cook it for me by noon, then it won't crow!"

For several minutes the women made signs of the cross. But then, when another cannonball burst through the roof, they poured water on it and rolled it over next to the other one.

Well, the downpour of cannonballs had all of the people in the castle confused. Until then, the cannons had been firing from only one location, so even if some balls fell inside the castle, they knew they could avoid being hit by staying close to the walls that get only morning light or are always in shade. Now, however, with cannonballs whistling, crashing and rolling from everywhere, and alternating between watermelon and walnut sizes, they did not know where they could be safe.

All the old helmets and armor would have been useful! Until now, only the Gypsy wore a helmet and breastplates, even if he was barefoot, but now that balls were bouncing, knocking, snarling everywhere, and the barbers had to clean and sew-up ten wounded in the first hour, everyone rushed to the armory to find the thickest armor they could wear.

The two captains and the six first lieutenants walked and surveyed all parts of the castle during the first quarter of an hour.

"Do not be afraid!" thundered Dobó.

And the words of the first lieutenants echoed everywhere. "Do not be afraid! The aim of the cannons doesn't change. If a ball falls somewhere, don't go there!"

But they themselves went everywhere.

A full hour did not pass before the balls themselves showed which buildings and which walls were dangerous. The balls tore down plaster, and where a building was made of sandstone, so many balls had lodged in them that the wall looked black.

However, some walls remained intact and white. Even if the ball had struck such a place, it just bounced onto another wall. Those walls served as protection where the craftsmen could work and soldiers could rest.

It is true that not many walls in the castle were that strong.

— § —

Amidst this maelstrom and thunderstorm of death, Dobó appeared at one bastion after the other. He had a shiny steel helmet on his head, blood on his chest, and protective armor on his arms and legs. He wore iron gloves on his hands.

Here he adjusted the gabions protecting cannons, there he adjusted the cannon itself. "Aim only at targets that are certain. Men, we need to preserve our gunpowder!"

This was one order the castle defenders did not understand.

"Damn his gunpowder," complained the peasants roared. "What's it good for if not to shot back?"

There was no man in the castle who was not itching to shoot at targets. After all, it was obvious that the Turks were under their noses. They had to destroy the evil brigands, or at least scare them away. However, they did not dare speak to Dobó. The more violent the siege, the more he took every arrangement into his own hands.

At that time, the Turks also had swarmed over King's Seat. Tents, horsetail flags, bustling and thronging crowds of soldiers spread in a riot of colors in every direction around the castle. Turkish camp music could be heard from here and there as the sounds of pipes, trumpets and copper cymbals accompanied the uninterrupted thunder of cannons.

Where the walls had not been broken by cannon fire, the *kumbarajis* launched bombs and janissaries fired flaming arrows. A deluge of cannonballs and fire.

Of course, the arrows and exploding bombs caused more confusion than the cannonballs. However, the experienced lieutenants also taught the defenders what to do.

As soon as the first bombs dropped and sputtered, jumping and bouncing red sparks, Dobó himself grabbed a wet skin and slammed into onto the bomb. People stared. The bomb did not tear the captain to pieces. Instead, it made small noises then fell asleep.

Those bombs were made of pottery and glass.

"We'll show the Turks how bombs really work!" shouted Gergely. He brought out some of his bombs that they had been making over the previous week.

Dobó put his hand on Gergely's shoulder, "Not yet!"

— § —

From morning to night without break the cannons roared and rained death. The half-hundredweight balls of the *zarbuzans* broke gaps in the walls the size of gates. Small and heavy balls fired by bearded canons and howitzers broke the beautiful church carvings and tore into the back wall of the castle.

In the morning when the guards assembled behind the palisade on Sándor Bastion, balls from the Turkish bearded guns fell like a hailstorm.

"Get down!" yelled Gergely. One hundred and fifty soldiers fell to the ground. Gergely pressed himself against the wall. The balls whistled above their heads and slammed into the castle wall. A plank on the wall became like a sieve.

There was a pause. The Turks had fired all their cannons, so they had to reload.

"Up!" yelled Gergely.

Five people remained lying down.

"Take them to the church," Gergely said sadly. "Are any of you also wounded?"

Fifteen bloody men silently stepped forward from the line.

"Well, go see the barber." He shook his head. He got an idea.

"Men," he said, "we can't stay here all day. Bring shovels and let's dig a ditch."

Some ten men ran to get shovels, and soon all the soldiers were digging. Within an hour they had dug a trench chest deep.

Gergely waited for the Turks to fire again, then jumped out of the trench and hurried to the inner castle to report the trench to Dobó.

He found the little Turkish boy next to the monastery, casually playing under the eaves. He was using a spoon to dig cannonballs, still smoking, out from the wall. The child must have escaped from the kitchen and was standing in a place where balls were falling.

"*Haydi!*" (Get out of here!) shouted Gergely. The child was frightened and turned towards Gergely. Leaning against the wall, he looked at him, face pale and eyes full of fear. He placed his two palms against the wall as if looking for his mother's skirt.

New balls hit the wall and smashed the plaster. A fist-sized black ball slammed into the wall over the child's shoulder, leaving a dirty ring around him.

Gergely jumped, pulled the child away, and carried him to the palace.

— § —

That evening, the sun descended toward Bakta behind dark, ashen clouds. Just for just a moment, it shone streaks of golden light in the middle of the sky, then disappeared behind blood-colored clouds to bring its fading light to people in happier parts of the world, who, on this evening, would be resting their heads on pillows and sleeping to the peaceful sounds of autumn beetles.

Work in Eger Castle was just beginning.

As the last shots from the *topchis* fell, masons grabbed trowels, peasants carried stones, earth, wood planks, water, and sand to fill the broken gaps. Gunners lay on their stomachs by the sides of the walls while workers labored in the gaps.

From time to time, a mortar shot sounds from one or the other bastion. Its shot flies into the air and briefly throws some red light in open ground in front of the castle. They are light bulbs; flares. They need them now. They serve to keep an eye on Turkish trickery.

"Work, men, work!" can be heard here and there as officers urge the laborers.

One stonemason is lowered with ropes down the outside of a wall. He uses iron to fasten a beam over the outside of a large gap torn in the wall.

Some gun shots are fired from below. Bullets shower on the workers. Then many more gun shots flare and crack. The flames of the Turkish guns throw light on two companies of prone janissaries. A volley replies from the walls.

But the stonemason falls into the darkness.

"Work inside only!" resound Pető's words. The workers continue to labor as the *tüfekchi* snipers take an occasional shot.

At midnight the gatekeeper's horn blows.

Dobó sits on a box full of gunpowder. He raises his head. Pető says, "Well, here's the letter from the king."

Indeed, within five minutes, two panting, bloody men stand in front of Dobó.

Both of them are dressed in Turkish clothes. They hold bloody swords in their hands suggesting that it is not easy to get into Eger Castle.

"Well," says Dobó.

Varsányi is one of those who left the previous night. The other is Miklós Vas, who had delivered the letter from Ahmed Pasha to the king.

Varsányi gasps, "They almost killed us!"

Miklós Vas pushes his bloody sword into his scabbard and sits down on the ground covered with stone dust. He has yellow boots on his feet. He pulls them off. He takes out a knife. He cuts open the sole of his boot. Inside is a letter. He gives it to Dobó.

Only then is he able to speak. "I saw the bishop. He sends his respects to the noble captain sir. The bishop himself delivered the letter to the king. This is the reply."

Varsányi adds, "They killed our third man."

"What third man?" growls Pető.

"István Szűrszabó, one of our soldiers. He also sneaked out of the castle. He wanted to return with us. He was speared in front of the gate here."

He breathes heavily and continued. "We didn't think we would find any Turks here by the gate. As we got here, I blew my whistle. As I blow my whistle, ten Turks attack us, here beside the gate. There was a brawl! Luckily, it was dark and the gate was about to open. István was stabbed in front of me, I could barely jump inside."

Meanwhile, Dobó has broken the seal, which had been ground to dust in the boot anyway, takes the letter to a nearby lantern, and reads it.

His face is getting darker. His two eyebrows almost touch. When he finishes reading, he jerks his head once and shoves the letter into his pocket.

Pető wants to ask what the king had written. However, Dobó gives a dark look around him and turns to Varsányi. "You handed the letter to Lord Szalkay?"

"I gave it to him, sir. He sends his respects. He was writing all morning, and as many letters as he wrote, as many messengers he dispatched that same morning."

"Anything else you have to say?"

"Not me," says Miklós Vas. "The lord bishop received me very graciously. His Majesty the King also welcomed everyone kindly. But I have a cut on my head. I'd like to see the barber."

"Pető, my son," says Dobó, "do not forget this tomorrow. Tell Sukán to write the names of these two men on the list of those for whom we ask the king for a reward after the siege."

"Sir," Varsányi says, scratching his head, "I still have something to report."

Dobó looks at him.

"Well," Varsányi continues, "Lukács Nagy asks your lordship to keep a few torches at the main gate. He may come home tonight ..."

"I will put him in chains!" growls Dobó angrily. "I'll teach him what delay means!"

A pudgy man hurries past them with water for the stonemasons. Dobó steps aside and shouts to the stonemasons, "Crossways with that harrow, not upright!"

Back then they called a beam a harrow.

Dobó turns to Varsányi again, "Perhaps that Lukács thinks ... Well, just let him get in my sight!"

Varsányi scratches his chin and looks at Dobó. "He really is very sorry, sir, for having slipped out. He doesn't even know where to hide."

Dobó restlessly paces under the lantern. "It would be stupid! What is that man thinking? Otherwise, whatever he says, he will not escape the penalty. You all have to go back tonight. You will carry another letter to the bishop and the king. Are you able to go back, Miklós?"

Miklós has a scarf tied around his head. Blood drips from the left side of his young face and the scarf is already red with blood.

"Back," he says willingly. "Then I can get my head sewn up in Szarvaskő."

14

Walls were crumbling day after day. More and more people were working with the stonemasons. More guards were posted each night. The next day, when the Turkish cannons again began firing, mortars fired cannonballs some eighty feet up on the walls where they became permanently embedded.

"Just shoot!" shouted the aged Cecey. "Strengthen our village with iron."

But on the tenth day the Turks awoke to see gaps that had not been filled. They had been unable to repair all the breaches the previous night.

At the end of the second week, an old peasant shepherd came to the gate. He was not wearing a *szűr* coat embroidered in the style of Heves County. But they let him inside anyway.

Dobó met him in the market square. He knew they had sent another letter.

"Where are you from?" he asked angrily.

"I live in Csábrág, sir."

"What do you want here?"

"Well ... I brought flour, sir, for the Turks."

"How much?"

"Well ... sixteen carts."

"Who sent you?"

"The steward."

"That's no steward, but a disgusting assistant executioner!"

"Well, sir ... we had to bow. We didn't want to end up like the neighbor."

"What neighbor?"

"Drégely's castle, sir."

"You brought a letter, didn't you?"

"Well ... I would have brought that ..."

"From the Turks?"

"Yes, sir."

"Did your conscience tell you that you engaging in a crime bringing that letter?"

"Well ... I know what's in the letter."

"Can there be any good in anything that comes from the Turks?"

The man did not answer.

"Can you read?"

"No."

Dobó turned towards the women. "Bring out a pot of embers." They brought some out and emptied the pot onto the ground. Dobó threw the letter on the glowing embers.

"Grab this old traitor and hold him in the smoke. Smell it, worthless, if you can't read!"

Then he had the man clapped in stocks and left him there in the market square. Let the castle defenders see what happens to anyone who accepts a letter from the Turks.

— § —

Lieutenants also witnessed the scene. The people also gathered around. They laughed and stared at the man whose eyes were tearing from the smoke and his despair.

"See you stupid!" said the Gypsy to him. "What made you become a postman?"

The letter burned red and black on the embers. When it was red, the writing appeared as black lines. When the pages were charred, the letters curled up in a glowing red for a minute.

Gergely also stood there.

When the peasant had entered the gate, all the cannons stopped firing.

The Turks were waiting for the answer.

"Captain sir," said Gergely as they left the group, "I unintentionally read a line from the letter."

"Why did you read that?" Dobó replied shrugging. "I didn't read it, but I know what it says."

"Well, it wouldn't be worth talking about," Gergely continued, "but because that one line was so really pagan, I can't hold back from telling your grace."

Dobó said neither say nor don't say.

Gergely continued. "This was the line: *Or is your coffin ready, István Dobó?*"

Dobó grunted. "Well, it's ready. And if by this he wants to ask me if I am prepared for death, then I will give him one reply."

A quarter of an hour later, a black coffin appeared on the castle wall. It was held by hooks and iron chains on each end. The warriors pinned the two hooks to firing slots in the stone wall.

The Turkish cannons began thundering again.

15

By the eve of St. Michael's Day [September 29], there were already about fifteen large gaps in the walls.

Most were in the outer castle walls. There was a second large gap by the southeast rampart tower. A third and fourth were on the south wall, where the gate was broken. The tall watchtower was so damaged, especially at its waist, that it was impossible to understand what kept it from collapsing.

The people of the castle were no longer able to keep up with the filling and repairs. It was obvious that even if they were all working, not even half of the damage could be filled.

But let's just work, men!

At midnight, Dobó called his officers to Church Bastion and had some flares shot high up.

"Look," he said, "those mounds of earth coming in this direction are like what moles dig underground. Those ditches are all filled with Turks."

Indeed, that night the Turks were all nearing the walls. Yellow-red janissary flags, siege ladders stretched among tents, and sackcloth janissary tents, each hiding ten or twenty men could be seen everywhere getting closer and closer. It was the inner line of the siege ring.

"My sons," Dobó said, "that means there will be an assault tomorrow. Everybody is to sleep outside here."

He set up guns and howitzers in the ruins. He also aimed cannons in the direction of the breaches in the walls. All hooks, spears, bombs, pickaxes, scythes, and any other weapon in the castle were set out by the walls.

He shook hands with all his officers.

"My sons," he said, "you all know what to do. Sleep as much as you can. We have to repel the assault."

There is a strange commotion from the city.

Varsányi's whistle sounds sharply from the gate above the stream.

"Open the gate!" yells Dobó.

The noise from the city grows louder. The pounding of horses' hoofs. Gunshots, snapping. Hungarian shouts, "Open the gate! Lukács is coming!"

The sentry at the gate is Lieutenant János Vajda. He immediately lights a torch and holds it out. Well, racing through the city marketplace is a long line of Lukács Nagy's cavalry, galloping past and over slumbering *jebeji* infantry to get to the castle.

"Down the torch!" shouts Vajda. "Under the gate!"

Because he immediately realizes it is better for them to come in the dark. The bridge is immediately lowered and the organ is lifted.

"Gunners, spears, all around the gate!" Our warriors ride in one after another. On their heels, a shrieking crowd of Turks. A bloody brawl begins under the gate.

A barefoot *piyad* runs like a cat up the bridge chain, a scimitar in his mouth. That is what the sentry holding the torch sees. They look at his wolf-eyes for a minute. The sentry then shoves the fiery end of the torch into his face. The Turk falls back into the darkness.

Meanwhile, other Turks endlessly yelling *Allahu Akbar*, crowd together below the gate.

"Bridge up!" orders Dobó. Gun shots drown out his voice.

"We can't raise the bridge!" cries the gate keeper. And indeed, it is all crowded with Turks.

That is when Gergely gets there. He grabs the torch from a guard and uses it to light a mortar fuse.

The next moment, the mortar bursts into flames and sweeps the bridge swarming with Turks.

The bridge groans and creaks as it is raised up with winches the size of wheelbarrows. Turks are raised up with it. Then the iron bars of the organ are lowered. Inside, the gate closes shut.

Some fifty Turks are trapped between the organ and the gate. They spin furiously, trying to escape anywhere until they fall in heaps from gunshots and spear thrusts. After a few minutes, only a writhing mound of men remains under the dark gate.

Dobó is already standing in the square in front of the gate.

Twenty-two cap-less riders line up in front of him in the light of torches.

A broad shouldered small man steps forward and stands in front of Dobó. "Humbly reporting," he says panting. "I've arrived."

"Lukács, my son!" replies Dobó emotionally. "You deserve chains on your legs, you rascal tramp! Gold chain around your neck, my brave good man!" And he embraces and kisses his soldier on the cheeks.

"How did you make it?"

"We had to wait, captain sir, until we could cut down enough Turks so that each of us would have a turban and a cape. We kept raiding from Szarvaskő, and by tonight we needed only two more turbans. Varsányi gave us his whistle. And we could have come in easily had there been cavalry in the market. But the infantry thought we didn't belong to them, so they attacked us."

"Who is missing?"

The soldiers look at each other. The night torches light only half of their faces. They all are bleeding, blood on clothes and horses.

"Gábor." The word is said quietly.

"Bicskei," he says again.

"Balkányi ..."

"Gyuri Soós ..."

Dobó's eyes notice a small lad with hair like a little girl. He is standing in the line, but holding back, his face almost hidden by the neck of his horse. "Balázs!" he exclaims in shock. "Is that you?"

The boy steps forward. Half kneels. He puts his bloody sword at Dobó's feet and looks down without saying a word.

It was Balázs Balogh, his youngest page.

16

That night, every soldier could sleep except eighty gunners. They lay beside the walls on straw and in ditches. On them and next to them were their weapons: swords and spears.

Above by the palisades, next to the gunners, guns rested against the walls, loaded and covered with rags, and oakum to protect the powder from dew.

Every ten or twenty steps a sentry stood between the sleepers. Other sentries stood by cannons and on the towers. There were only a few on the walls that faced the city.

And all who were not soldiers were awake and working.

Dobó had ordered all the peasants in the castle, the butchers, millers, locksmiths, carpenters, the four blacksmiths, the two dog-catchers, and even the Gypsy to work with the stone masons.

They set the longest timbers in the breaches. In hurried confusion, they piled earth, planks and sand in the gaps of the broken walls. The collapsed gate had to be covered with earth, stone, sand, and filled barrels. Mortars in front and above; howitzers and bearded canons on the sides; as many as could fit.

Below the walls, *tüfekchi* stood in deep ditches. They fired up each time one of the workers appeared in a breach. No matter how the workers tried to labor unseen behind defenses, inevitably some would be exposed.

At the corner tower, Tamás Bolyky stuffs rubble into the breaches. There, the debris is piled over twenty feet high with timber bound by ropes and chains. The lieutenant from Borsod tightens the chains. Difficult work. You also have to move outside sometimes, and the janissaries below always take a shot.

It is useless to shoot back, or throw bombs at them. They are protected by mounds of earth and wicker fencing so that only the barrels of their guns stick out.

But the lanterns burning inside the castle walls give light for the snipers to see the workers.

"Lift the beam!" shouts Tamás Bolyky. The peasants stand by the beam, but three of them had already been wounded that night.

"Lift the beam!" repeats Tamás Bolyky.

The peasants hesitate.

The lieutenant steps into the middle of the breach and shouts again, "Move it! Here! Here!"

And the beams rise up fast. Turkish guns crackle below. Above hammers work. The chain rattles and clangs as it is fastened to the beam.

"Don't be afraid!" shouts the lieutenant from Borsod. And no one dares to fear.

A bullet grazes the lieutenant's helmet and knocks off the silver clasp that holds the feather plume. "Hurry, hurry!" He grabs a spruce limb and chains it to the timber.

"Tamás" shouts exclaims Mekcsey. "Get out!"

Because a hail of bullets hit the tower, and below the Turkish guns crackle.

"Right away," replies Tamás Bolyky. And he leans down to lift up another beam.

He stays in that leaning position, as if turned to stone.

"Tamás!" Mekcsey shouts, shaken.

Tamás is on his knees. The helmet falls off his head, his long gray hair falls forward.

Mekcsey rushes up and pulls Tamás from the breach. He lays him down in the inner corner of the bastion wall. "Lantern here!"

Tamás Bolyky's face is wax-white. Blood runs through his beard and drips onto lime dust on the ground.

"Tamás!" cries Mekcsey. "Can you speak?" He looks at him with a tear.

"I can," groans Tamás. "Fight ... for your country ..."

— § —

Lanterns and tar torches hanging from nails were scattered about inside the castle. Dobó rode a horse to inspect one tower after the other.

He worried most about the tower above the old gate. Turkish guns had smashed the gate and damaged the tower. On the south side, the spiral staircase was blackened and four steps were broken.

The gate could be filled, but there was no time to strengthen the tower. What if they fired at the tower the next day? That tower served as a lookout and a firing position towards the south. If it collapsed, the castle would lose much of its strength.

He ordered forty *drabant* soldiers, each a good shot, to the tower. They had to stay there with loaded guns, ready to fight. "Sleep!" he told them. "It's enough if two people stand watch by the outside windows!"

He turned his horse around and galloped to the corner tower. "What's this?" he shouted. "Why aren't you working?"

"Sir," said a trembling worker, "just now my Lieutenant Bolyky was shot."

They were carrying him down the stairs in a rack used to carry stones. His legs were hanging out. His two hands, gloves removed, were clasped over his breastplate. Mekcsey carried his helmet.

"Is he dead?" asked Dobó.

"Yes," replied Mekcsey sadly.

"Keep working!" shouted Dobó up to the bastion. Then he dismounted and took off his helmet. He stepped over to the body and silently looked at it sadly. "God be with you, Tamás Bolyky. Stand in front of God and show Him your bleeding wound, and show Him this castle."

Bareheaded, he looked at them sadly until the lantern disappeared by the corner of the stables. Then he mounted and hurried to the other tower behind the palace.

There, Zoltay struggled with a large coil of rope, tying beams to beams to cover a gap on the wall. He was helping to pull the rope and shouted to the workers from time to time. "Don't be afraid of the rope, It's not a sausage! Hold it, Jancsi, for mercy's sake. Pull it like you're dragging the Turkish emperor to a hanging tree!"

The beams crunched against each other. The carpenters hammered in iron clamps, and earth, stone and sand were piled up to fill the gap that the Turkish cannons had torn.

Dobó called up to Zoltay, "Come down!"

Zoltay lowered the rope, but shouted up again, "Iron clips in it, many more!"

Dobó put his hand on the man's shoulder. "Go to bed, son. Tomorrow needs strength!"

"Just a couple more barrels ..."

"Clear out! Sleep!" growled Dobó. "One! Two!"

Zoltay raised his hand to his cap and stepped away without a word. Dobó did not put up with any argument.

Dobó chased even Fügedy and Pető away before dismounting in front of the palace. He handed his horse to the sentry at the door. He went into his room.

The small ground-level room where he had relocated since the cannon-fire was lit with a hanging, green ceramic lamp. There was cold meat, wine and bread on the table. Dobó just stood, picked up the bread and tore off a piece.

From the neighboring room, a gray-haired woman in mourning clothes opened Dobó's door, a candle in her hand. When she saw Dobó, she entered the room.

She was Lady Balogh, the mother of page Balázs.

The brave little noblewoman, trapped inside the fortress, had quickly accepted her situation. She took over the work of the steward's wife, cooked for Dobó, and took care of everything.

"How is your son?" Dobó asked.

"He's fallen asleep," replied the woman. He has some wounds. On his chest, head and arm. But, captain sir, you don't eat by day or sleep by night. You can't stay this way for long. If you don't eat lunch tomorrow, I will carry it after you myself until you do."

"I have no time," replied Dobó raising the cup to his lips. "Is my bed ready?"

"It's been ready for three days and three nights."

"Well, then. I'll lie down." And indeed, he did. "There's no deep wound on the boy?"

"Sure, the cut on his forehead is long. His leather jacket gave some protection from the other cuts, thank God. He can easily move all his limbs."

"You also go and sleep, honorable woman. I am also headed there now. I have to rest. Good night."

He gazed up into the air, then jumped off his bed and hurried out the room.

His heavy overcoat was hanging in the anteroom. He grabbed it and hurried to Prison Bastion. He found Gergely there with another lad, carrying large leather bags upstairs.

"What's going on?" he asked angrily, "Are you awake? Didn't I order you to sleep?!"

"I was sleeping," replied Gergely. "But I remembered that dew would collect on the cannons. I'm carrying dry powder everywhere."

Dobó called down to a flare-loaded mortar, "Fire!"

The mortar sizzled and rolled. The mortar tossed a flame a hundred fathoms high and lit up the area around the castle.

The Turkish camp around the castle was still. Only sentries were seated here and there in front of the troops, collars pulled up to their ears.

Dobó followed Bornemissza to Church Bastion, watching as he wiped wet powder out of the burner holes and carefully sprinkled dry powder, checking to make sure the wick, the ramrod, the powder spoon, and the cannonballs were all in place.

Dobó remained there. He stood with his arms crossed on the bastion next to the Baba cannon. He listened to the surrounding great silence and lifted his eyes to the sky.

Moonless, cloudy sky. Just a few stars glistened in a small clearing.

Dobó took off his hat and dropped to his knees. He raised his eyes to the sky. "My God!" he murmured, holding his hands in prayer. "You see our little ruined castle and this handful of determined people ... In your great universe, this earthly world is small. Oh, but what is this universe to us! If you need our lives, Lord, take it from us. Let us fall like a blade of grass during harvest! Just let this country remain ... this little Hungary ..."

His face was pale. Tears streamed from his eyes. And with a tearful face he continued. "Mary, Mother of Jesus, Protector of Hungary! We carry your image on our flags! Your name is sung in Hungarian by millions of lips! Pray for us!"

Then again, he continued. "King St. István! Look down from the sky! Look at your ruined country, your lost nation! Look at Eger, where the walls of your church are still standing, and where, in your language, your religion, the people praise the Almighty. Move in your heavenly tent, King St. István. Oh, fall at the feet of God! My God, my God! Let your heart be with us!"

That little clearing in the sky is like a window in the sky, and the stars in it are white candles ...

Dobó wiped his eyes and sat on the wood carriage of the cannon. Motionless, he looked gravely into the darkness of the castle below.

The Turkish camp was asleep with a low murmur. Hundreds of thousands of people were breathing the air.

Dobó leaned back, his elbow on the cannon barrel. His head slumped lower and lower. At last he leaned on his arm and fell asleep.

17

From the area of the stables comes the first, faint cackle of hens, followed by the loud crow of a cock. A thin line of grey separates the black sky from the hills to the east.

Dawn is breaking.

It is as if the rocks of the earth are moving down. There is a low rumble from far away. The surface of the earth moves like black waves, and rattling and roaring becomes louder. There is already a ringing tone and a faint beeping sound. The gray ribbon at the bottom of the sky is getting wider, and the black sky is getting more transparent.

The movement of the flags below is already visible, as are companies of turbans, thin ladders here and there held up into the sky and approaching the castle.

The eastern sky is brightening fast. Pink is replacing grey, and the rampart towers and ruined walls of the castle stand out from the chilling cold haze.

"Sir," Bornemissza said. He put his hand on Dobó's shoulder.

Dobó woke up.

"Is that you, Gergely?" He looked down at the moving ocean of Turks.

"Sound the alarm!"

The bell tower sounded. Eight horns answered immediately. Guns rolled. A pounding and humming noise sounded everywhere. The trenches of the outer castle also came to life. Soldiers took their positions on bastions and walls lined.

Dobó jumped on a horse and in the early light of dawn, watched where the Turks were taking position. Most of them were gathered by the palaces.

"As soon as they rush the walls, throw down the fire bombs!" Dobó ordered everywhere.

The page Kristóf met the captain in the market square. He sat on a small, grey Turkish horse wearing a warm, dark blue overcoat.

"Sir," he asked, "should I bring the armor?"

"No," Dobó replied, "I'll go in immediately."

But he didn't go in. As the light increased every minute, he roamed from one bastion to another to see how they were prepared.

"Fire only where they are massed together," he instructed the gunners. "What's most important now are fire bombs and lances."

Then he shouted again, "Don't get up on the walls until the Turks have stopped firing their cannons."

The fire bombs were stacked in pyramids in the rubble behind the breaches. They had been making them for weeks.

Gergely Bornemissza had placed an inner charge in each bomb that made it twice as powerful. They first exploded when they were thrown down; the second time when the inner charge ignited. It would smolder for a few minutes, throwing out large white sparks that burned clothes and faces of these who did not jump out of the way.

The Turks were unable to manufacture these.

For a while Kristóf waited by the palace for his master, and when he saw him speeding from one bastion to another, he went into the hall and brought out breastplate, arm plates, and greaves and piled them on his horse. He grabbed the helmet and held it under his arm, and galloped to the corner tower to intercept Dobó.

Dobó remained mounted as he strapped on the armor. Kristóf was also mounted as he handed him breastplate, arm plates, and gauntlets. Then he jumped down and strapped the iron greaves on his lord. Finally he gave him the gilded helmet.

"Bring the other one," Dobó replied, "the steel helmet."

By then it was already so light that the Turkish troops below were clearly visible. Thousands of turbans and helmets gathered beneath the walls and in the trenches. But they were still standing. They were waiting for the signal to begin the assault.

They did not have to wait long. As the daylight increased to where the ruined walls, protruding rocks and beams were visible, a hundred muezzins began their mournful singing all over the surrounding Turkish camps. With a great clatter, the vast throngs of the army fell on their faces and rose to their knees.

Like an approaching thunderstorm, the vast pagan horde muttered their prayers.

... Allah ... our Prophet Muhammad ... strengthen our hearts ... expand your invincible arms ... stuff the throats of their fire-spewing devices ... turn the infidels into dogs that slaughter each other ... send a whirlwind to their earth, that their eyes may be filled with dust, and their strikes hit the ground ... break the bones of their feet so they cannot stand before us ... make them ashamed, our glorious Prophet, that your people may be glorified forever!

Then with a great rumble they sprang up. *"Bismillah!"* (In the name of God!)

Turkish cannons and guns explode simultaneously. Castle walls shake and embankments are torn up from the explosive cannonballs. Arrows and bullets fall on the bastions palisades. The air is filled with gunpowder. The heavens and the earth shake from the noise of drums, horns, trumpets, and howls to Allah from hundreds of thousands of Turks.

From the trenches jump *azabs,* janissaries, *delis, jebejis*, and all other kinds of Turkish foot soldiers, like a dense cloud of locusts. A forest of siege ladders rushes toward the ruined walls and bastions, and from behind the ladders, a rain of arrows fly in high arcs towards the walls.

And the Turkish military bands blare.

But the reply also falls from above. Downward-facing cannons fire flame, iron, lead and glass pots where the Turks are most crowded together. Hundreds are covered in blood, waver, then fall. But in the same minute, more hundreds follow, trampling over bodies.

The smell of sulfur spreads with the smoke billowing from the castle.

Siege ladders slam into the stone, iron, and beams, and the surge of soldiers rises up almost to the walls. Shields on heads. Barbed spear in one hand, curved swords in mouths.

Twenty-seven Turkish flags are fluttering on the ruins, leading the army up the ladders from behind the palaces.

Continuous, endless, furious shouts of *"Allah akbar! La illah il Allah! Ya kerim! Ya rahim! Ya fettah!"*

Shouting everywhere. "To the walls! To the walls!"

And the walls are filled with soldiers. The bombing is just starting. Using only hands, they just drop the sizzling, then flaming, and finally exploding bombs. Thousands of falling-thundering-bouncing streaks of lightning. Shrieks, yells, smoke, thunder, stink of sulfur. Hatchets, pick-axes, and axes smash the hooks of ladders. On some, twenty people are still holding onto ladders as they crash into each other and cut swathes in the swarms below. Within a minute, a new wave of armed soldiers rush and take their place, and new ladders rise connected to each other. *Allah!*

The defense of the corner bastion, which since the previous night had been renamed Bolyky Bastion, is organized by scholar Gergely and Zoltay.

The storm of the assault is greater at that tower than the other three. Because the breach is bigger. And the numbers of the army that had caused that damage were also greater there.

Hundreds of bombs are dropped on the climbers, and gunners fire on them from either side. But when there are so many, no life is worth much for the Turks. If only ten could force their way inside! Then with the force of the army in their footsteps, pushing each other forward, the entire army could flood inside.

Well, men are needed for the dam!

For an hour already, bombs beat back the endless waves of climbing men forcing their way up, but the ladders remain, and men on the ladders, and once the first big ladder is fixed on the stone, others hoist up smaller ladders to reach the top ledge.

"Pull that ladder up!" shouts Gergely.

And to the great astonishment of the Turks, the ladders are not smashed but nicely caught and pulled up.

Some five ladders have already been pulled up and away when a Turk dressed in brass hangs on a ladder and is pulled up with it.

"Pull it!" shouts Gergely. He pushes his pike into the rungs of the ladder and forces it out. "Help me."

The ladder is held so it sticks out from the top of the wall like a bridge. Hanging on the end is the brass-clad Turk. He has a tasseled, long lance in his hand. But as he is suspended in the air, he drops his shield and lance in order to use both hands to hang onto the bottom rung of the ladder.

He is hanging in the air.

Below, the army is screaming.

Gergely wants to drag the Turk inside, but there was no time for that. An *azab* with a fur cap jumps up on the other ladder and Gergely has to deal with him. "Turn it over!" he yells to the four men pulling and holding the castle end of the ladder.

He grabs his lance and stabs the *azab* in the shoulder. The *azab* wavers as blood gushes over his arm. Then he falls backwards, taking some ten others down with him.

Meanwhile, the men follow instructions. They flip the ladder over. The bronze-clad Turk has to make a quick decision: a sprained arm or flying some eighty feet through the air. He chooses the latter.

A Turkish drummer who was beating a drum shaped like a loaf of bread, some twenty yards from the wall, happens to get the bronze-clad man land on his head. Together they join piles of dead bodies.

But what is that among these thousands!

A crocodile skin shield rises up and runs upwards. A Turk is hidden underneath. The tips of lances slide off the smooth, hard shield. The cunning Turk must have fastened the center of the shield to the tip of his helmet. No matter from what side they lunge and cut, the edge of the weapon slides off the shield and hits air.

With one jump, Gergely is there. "This is how you do it!" He turns his lance around so the thick end is pointing out and pushes against the edge of the crocodile Turk. The Turk falls back head first.

All the while the shrieking and screaming continues. "*Allah! Ya kerim! Ya fetih!*" Sometimes also in Hungarian. "Give me the castle!"

"Here!" says Zoltay, and wielding a pickaxe, he delivers a terrible blow that tears through shield, helmet and skull. He is working on the other side of the breach using only a pickaxe

The wall protects him up to the waist. His men allow him to work with the pickaxe, and he allows his men to do the work of lances. He is standing on a beam where it is easy to hang a ladder, and where ladders stand next to ladders and crowds of armed men are climbing.

He breaks a ladder or two, but then gives a great shout, "Just the heads, men!" He himself is standing the farthest forward, so he is the first to greet the arrivals. His armor is made of steel. The handle of his pick-axe is a long as a tall walking stick.

He taunts a black-faced Saracen climbing his way up, his white eyes peering out from behind a light wicker shield. "Come on, smoky, come on. Let this eat your pretty thick-lipped face."

As the Saracen gets within three yards, he crouches into a ball and pushes up. His intention is to suddenly uncurl on the top rung of the ladder and throw his spear into Zoltay, then climb on top of the wall.

The position of Pasha of Eger had been promised to the first man to plant the flag of triumph. The castle defenders also know this.

Well, the black panther continues climbing upwards. In his footsteps is a *jebeji* with a big beard, his mouth foaming from continuously shouting,

"*Allahu akbar.*" Stuck behind in his belt is a short stick with a horsetail flag on its end. Crosswise in his mouth is a naked scimitar.

"*Allahu akbar! Ya kerim! Ya Rahim!*"

Zoltay pulls down his visor. Just in time. The Saracen throws his spear straight up and breaks its tip on the visor.

At that same moment the pickaxe strikes and the Saracen falls head first from the ladder through the air.

Then there is the bearded man underneath. He has no spear in his hands, but a nail-studded mace hanging on the end of a chain. Zoltay moves his head away from the blow and strikes back with the pick so that the bearded Turk's hand breaks and hangs to one side.

The Turk screams for a while, half-handed, but is silenced by a second blow. His big body falls, sweeping the living down with him off the ladder.

"Give my respects to your prophet," yells Zoltay after him.

Speaking to the Turks is forbidden, but Zoltay forgets in the heat of a fight. He surely cannot fight without accompanying each blow with some sort of comment. The men fighting with him are fired up with laughter.

"Hit him, János my son," he shouts to the man next to him, "Hit him like a thunderbolt from heaven. Poof! Here's another guy who won't make it to Pasha of Eger!"

"What are you waiting for?" he shouts to another man. "Perhaps you're waiting for him to kiss you? Poof! Your father, for mercy's sake!"

Then, as a turbaned *gureba* in a steel shirt makes his way towards him, he yells out to his men standing by his side, "This is how you should tap him." He gets him in the neck. Blood spurts on the wall and the *gureba* falls sideways and down. "Fall to the bottom of hell!" he yells after him.

The sun has come out, as much as can be seen from the smoke of the castle's cannons. But sometimes the breeze catches the smoke to reveal the blinding reflections of flocks of steel-shielded, gold-buttoned, flag-carrying enemies.

Dobó is riding his horse from one besieged place to another. Here he aims a cannon; there he directs the wounded to be carried away. He hurries loading and firing. He carries spears and lances to where weapons are lacking. He encourages, praises, and chides. He runs his two pages to the reserves that Mekcsey is commanding in the inner castle. "One hundred to the palaces!" "Fifty to Bolyky Bastion!" "Fifty to the Old Gate!"

Companies fight for a half an hour, then fall back to rest as replacements relieve them. Sweaty, bloody, and smelling of gunpowder, they enter the castle's two taverns and boast of their heroic acts to those who have yet to be sent forward.

And they burn with a desire to fight. Mekcsey is secretly furious that he cannot fight, but must wait in the castle courtyard and be content with organizing squads as Dobó commands and giving them encouraging words. "The fate of your homeland lies with your weapons!"

With flushed faces, they rush into the roaring thunderstorm.

Siege ladders are drenched in blood. The walls around the ladders are stained purple. Down below, the dead and dying writhe in bloody heaps. But farther below, fresh thousands and thousands shout at the dead. Horns blasting, drums beating, the racket of military bands, and the endless yells of *Allah* mingle with the din of battle, mounted *yasaul* officers shouting orders, the cannonballs firing, guns shooting, bombs exploding, horses neighing, the dying screaming, and ladders smashing.

"Come on, pasha, come on! Poof! ..."

"Tell your prophet that Zoltay gave you this cut!" The shouts can be heard through the smoke of the bastion.

The howling of animals and the explosions from mortars drown out the warrior's shouts. But the swarming shapes and quick flashes of weapons around him indicate that his men are hard at work.

Smoke and ash blot out the sun. Smoke also curls around the fortress, through which every now and again glimpses can be seen of Turkish regiments in helmets, camels carrying gunpowder, and flags and horsetails fluttering.

Men are rotated most often at Old Gate Bastion. Gáspár Pető is in command there. The Turks use mortars to fire stone balls to break the wall and palisade every time the forest of ladders diminishes.

Turks use axes and shovels to dig out the rubble that fills the gate. They have already broken three of the thick iron poles of the organ gate.

"Five hundred!" shouts Dobó to Kristóf. And Kristóf turns his horse and runs to fetch five hundred men.

That is almost the entire reserve.

Mekcsey straps on his helmet and runs to the Old Gate with nine others. If they break in, his work begins: protecting the inner castle.

Turks fall like flies under the gate and on the gate's bastion. From the tower, our gunners briskly shoot and waste the attackers in heaps. The thunderous words of Gáspár Pető sound everywhere. "After me, men! Don't back away! Use both hands, for God's sake!"

He is already in blood up to his waist, cutting, sometimes with a sword, sometimes with a pick, sometimes with a spear.

"Jesus, help me!"

"Allah! Allah!"

When the people climbing up the ladders get scarce, cries of "Water, water! water!" come from everywhere.

Women bring water in jugs and cups from under the bastions.

Pető picks up a wooden cup. He pushes up the visor of his helmet. He drinks so eagerly that water flows over his armor on both sides. It trickles farther inside his armor and flows out like a spring at his elbows, knees, and ankles. But in his anger and thirst, he cares little.

As he takes the cup away his mouth, he sees a Turk jumping on the wall. He holds a horsetail in one hand. With the other, he slashes with his sword about like a madman. Then the other Turkish head pops up, and the third.

"Hey, I'll be damned!" He pulls the Turk by the ankle. Together they roll down the stairs. When they stop, he grabs him by the neck and punches his face with his iron gloved fist.

Then he jumps up and lets the peasants below finish off the half-strangled Turk. He runs back up onto the bastion. In seconds, his agile hands swiftly hit and cut in six directions.

"*Allahu akbar!*"

The wall is teeming with Turks. An *akinji* has already reached the tower. He sets the flag. Down below the flag is welcomed with horrendous shouts of victory. Jesus, help! Well, it does not hang there even two minutes. Our warriors rush at the climbing intruders and smash heads. A Hungarian warrior wearing a rusty helmet is creeping like a cat after the *akinji*. He anchors his heel on a stone and strikes a terrible blow on him. He cuts off the Turk's arm holding the ensign so that the arm, together with the flag, falls from the height.

"Who you are?" yells a pleased Pető from below.

The warrior turns around and proudly calls back, "Antal Komlósi."

The page Balázs gallops down from the palaces. The side of his head is bandaged with a white cloth. But he flies as if he has nothing wrong. "The repairs by the palace. They have been smashed!"

"One hundred men!" replies Dobó. And while the boy gallops off to Mekcsey, Dobó himself heads towards the palaces.

The Turks have broken down the barriers. Beams protrude from walls like the backbone of a fried fish. Turks are crawling over the walls like a swarm of red ants. Dobó jumps to the top of the wall. He cleaves a Turk's head in two. He kicks another off the wall. He shouts down, "Push the beam out!"

Until then, they were holding it in with pickaxes. At Dobó's command, they immediately push it out.

The beams themselves sweep the shrieking pagans off ladders, leaving behind a large breach in the wall. It makes little difference. Three or five yards higher or lower, you still have to fight the attackers.

A bullet hits the Hungarian flag and it falls off the wall. It lands among the Turks. See how useful the breach in the wall can be! A Hungarian soldier jumps over it, slashes a Turk, and grabs the flag before they can get him.

"I see you, my son, László Török!" shouts Dobó with pride.

A cannonball hits the wall and throws up a cloud of grit that gets into the soldiers' eyes. A stout man standing in front of Dobó leans against the wall and falls along it. His helmet falls off and rolls towards Dobó's leg.

Dobó rubs his eyes and looks at him. It is András lying there, the mayor of Eger. The hand clutching his sword spasms. Blood flows from his neck as if he is wearing a loose scarf.

But look! Both pages are running from the Old Gate. A glance at the tower by the Old Gate: a horsetail Turkish flag hangs there — one, two, five, even ten.

From around the tower gun shots fire inside. Janissaries are climbing up the outside of the tower. One has a large red flag hanging from a pole between his teeth that he intends to plant on top of the tower.

Terror spreads inside the castle. The din of a hundred thousand Turks victoriously shouting shakes the castle. "*Allah! Ya kerim!*"

Hungarian faces are pale.

Dobó jumps on a horse and gallops to Church Bastion. He aims the cannons at the center of the tower. And while some three hundred janissaries triumphantly gather on the tower, they fire three cannons at once.

The tower shakes. It collapses with a great crash. Clouds of lime dust rise from the debris. Turkish blood trickles from rocks like wine from a press.

The sky falls and the earth tears apart. Those who have gotten inside the gate and on the walls are horrified and turn their backs. Within five minutes, the siege ladders are empty.

Only bloody piles of dead and dying cover inside and outside the Old Gate and its surroundings.

In other places on the south, the assault is gradually receding. Thousands of sooty and bloody Turks, dead and wounded, lay beneath the walls. The air shakes with the moans and cries of the wounded. "*Ey va!*" and "*meded!*" Like sheep bleating.

The *jasavuls* no longer have the strength to force the soldiers to continue the assault that day.

But the market square in the castle is also full of wounded.

The barber and the women all attend the wounded with bowls of water, linen, bandages, alum, and arnica herbs.

Those with wounds to hands or feet are treated first. They bandage the wounds as best they can. For the time being, the rest must be content with women washing their wounds. Most are silent and wait for it to happen. But some moan bitterly.

"My God, my God," cries a young soldier, a gunner from Eger named Mihály Arany. "They shot my eye out." He presses the cuff of his burned shirt against his bloody face.

Pető sits with the other wounded on a straw chair covered with a peasant *szűr* coat. The wound on his ankle is so deep that his blood has collected in a puddle under the chair. "Don't cry, Miska," he tells the young soldier. "Better to live in Eger Castle with one eye rather than the Turks hanging you with two eyes!"

And clenching his teeth, the barber washes the horrible wound on his ankle with arnica.

The dead are gathered and lying in a neat row by the church door. They are bloody, ragged, sooty, and motionless.

Dobó dismounts and takes off his helmet. He walks like that among them, tears streaming down his cheeks.

The mayor from Eger is also lying there. His gray hair is red with blood. His dust-covered black boots show a bloodstained wound. His two sons kneel beside him.

Some of the soldiers are sitting around the market square smoky, ragged, sweaty, and bloody. The two flagpoles stand on both sides.

Dobó calls to the page Balázs. "Bring the city's flag here."

He takes the blue and red flag off its mast and uses it as a shroud to cover the mayor of Eger.

Part V
The Waning Moon

1

The captain of Szarvaskő stood in the tower of his castle day and night listening to the roar of cannon fire coming from Eger.

Autumn sun shined nicely on Szarvaskő. A few days earlier the forest had started to turn yellow, and as it had rained every day, and every night the sky cleared, green growth appeared under trees and by the banks of streams. It was not like autumn, but like spring.

Szarvaskő is about seven miles north of Eger, about the same distance as Isaszeg from Gödöllő, or Siófok across the water from Füred. But mountains stand between Eger and Szarvaskő. Through those mountains, only a narrow, winding road connects Felnémet to Gömör.

When the cannons began firing in the morning, clouds gathered and darkened the sky, and an hour later, rain fell. Sometimes the rain was dirty. Wind mixed smoke with clouds and carried it to Szarvaskő where the rain was like the chimneys of heaven being rinsed and dirty water being dumped. The ash-laden rain sometimes smudged the walls of Szarvaskő Castle, its courtyard, stones, and the captain's roses.

Szarvaskő was a small castle like what Drégely had been. It was built on top of a tall cliff of slate. At first glance, it looked like a fort carved into the tops of the slate. But it was very small. It had only three houses, and its courtyard was barely large enough for a carriage to turn around. Well, it was more like a hunting lodge. It could only be used for defense at a time when cannons were not yet known. At the time of our story, it was only useful as a place for soldiers heading to Eger to rest, and it could serve as a station for messengers when Eger was attacked by the enemy.

If Eger falls, Lord Balázs Szalkay could sit on his horse with his forty-nine soldiers and go to the northern counties to his relatives — unless he wanted to make like the angry Szondi, or like Lőrinc Nyáry, the captain of Szolnok who, on the fourth of that same month, had stood alone at the gates of his castle to face hundreds of thousands of Turks.[52]

---

[52] Lőrinc Nyáry was captain of the strategically important Szolnok Castle that was besieged by a large Ottoman army in September of 1552. Its garrison of largely foreign mercenaries escaped under cover of night, but Nyáry stayed and resisted with a handful of men. He was captured by the Turks and imprisoned in Seven Towers. He was released by a Hungarian who had become a Muslim.

Well, there was the good Balázs Szalkay standing in the tower. He wore a mushroom-colored, fur-collared cloak that reached his ankles, and a cap made of fox-fur. Worried, he strained his blue, watering eyes to see the tall hill that blocked the sight of Eger. He could not see Eger, so he looked at the hill. If he had looked elsewhere, he still would have seen mountains. The mountains were so close that he could use a good musket to shoot a deer grazing on the side of any of them.

Below the castle were a few small houses and the Eger stream. There was a rocky cart trail running along the stream.

Well, Lord Balázs was standing in the tower looking at nothing.

He was surrounded by silence. No wonder Lord Balázs almost fell over when the sentry behind him blew his horn.

"They're coming," said the sentry apologetically when he saw that his master had been frightened by the sudden blast and was raising his hand to slap him.

"Mule!" shouted Lord Balázs. "Why blast that horn in my ear when I'm standing here! Ox!"

He glanced down at the winding, rocky path and saw two riders. They looked like gentlemen. The smaller one might be a page. They could be coming from far away because behind them, their saddles were loaded with belongings. They had guns slung over their shoulders. Both wore coats that reached their stirrups.

"These aren't coming from Eger," Szalkay mumbled.

"Maybe it's Miklós Vas," said the sentry. He hoped to add something intelligent to his master's words so his earlier stupidity would be forgotten. However, it was not his day. Lord Balázs again erupted in anger.

"Miklós Vas is coming? You turkey! You buffalo! You think Vienna is as far away as Apátfalva! Your father's ass!"

Ever since the Turks had attacked Eger, the good man had always been irritated. Now that he had been embarrassed by being scared from the bugle blast, he almost devoured the man.

The guard had turned completely red. He didn't dare say another word. Lord Szalkay gripped the hilt of his sword and headed down the spiral staircase to see what kind of birds were flying towards him. Because for two days the only people they had seen traveling were leaving. Nobody was coming.

In the courtyard of the castle stood a young, bold-looking, pale-faced man. He had neither mustache nor beard. Behind the two horses was a small boy. Upon seeing the landlord, the man approached. He took off his cap with great flourish and bowed. "I am the younger brother of Lieutenant Bornemissza of Eger. My name is János. This boy is Miklós Réz, a scholar. His brother is also in Eger Castle.

Szalkay offered János Bornemissza a hand, but not to the other. His trained eyes recognized that he was not a gentleman.

"God has brought you," he said. "I don't know your older brother. But if I meet him, I will embrace him. You are my dear guest."

He kindly gestured towards the door.

"Thank you," replied the young man. "But I didn't come here to be a guest, only to ask a couple of questions. I want to know, what's the news from Eger?"

Szalkay shrugged and gestured toward Eger. "You can hear it!"

"I hear they are bombarding."

"It's the nineteenth day."

"Is the castle strong?"

Szalkay shrugged again. "The Turks are also strong."

"Are there enough soldiers?"

"There were one thousand, nine hundred thirty-five on the tenth. Since then they are constantly being shot."

"The king hasn't sent help?"

"Not yet."

"The bishop?"

"He neither."

"So they're waiting?"

"Waiting, they're waiting. But let's not talk so much, young brother. Come, and rest your fatigue. I see from your horse that you left early at dawn."

It was obvious that Lord Balázs was irritated having to answer the visitor's increasing number of questions while standing in the castle courtyard. For some time he had been longing to sit at a table himself. Only the roar of the siege kept him out. It was almost noon and he had not even had his breakfast.

"Sir," said the newcomer at the gate, "this boy who came with me is a theology student."

"Student? Well then ... Hey, student!" he shouted over his shoulder.

He showed his guests to a room and provided them with fragrant bathing water. (Varsányi had brought him some rose oil from the Turkish camp. He wanted to boast about it.)

By the time his guests entered the dining room, the table was already set, and even the roast rabbit was steaming on the table.

"Rabbit again?" Lord Balázs growled at the cook. When the two youngsters entered, he apologized. "By now we are living off of rabbits only. The rabbits around Eger all scampered up here to get away from the noise."

Bornemissza, having taken off his coat, appeared in the dining room wearing a close fitting, dark cherry-colored, shaggy damask coat. The scholar was wearing hemp cloth. Both wore similar belts around their waists, a Hungarian sword strapped to their sides.

There was no eating utensil on the table other than spoons. At that time, everyone ate using their own knives. Forks were only used in the kitchen.

The two guests pulled small knives from their belts. The young man's knife had a gilded, mother-of-pearl handle. The student's was a knife from Fehérvár with a carved wooden handle.

"I like rabbit," said János Bornemissza. "And this looks very well prepared. We cook ours differently at home. Do you know anything about my older brother, captain sir?"

"Differently?" asked Szalkay. He was more interested in rabbit.

"Otherwise," János Bornemissza replied. "We marinade the rabbit in wine and put it on the fire in some water. They also add slices of bread and cook it together. But they are careful not to let it dry out. When the liquid boils, it is taken off the heat, the meat is taken out, and the liquid is strained. Then they add pepper, saffron and ginger. ... But do we know what happened in the castle today? Has my poor brother been killed?" His eyes teared.

"Try it with some vinegar," said Szalkay without looking up.

"Of course, but only at the end, when the rabbit is put back into the sauce. ... We need to get to Eger today."

Szalkay sucked the bone of the rabbit's thigh, then lifted his cup as a toast to his guests.

They didn't drink wine.

"Hmm," Szalkay said. He wiped his mustache with the tablecloth, looked at them, then repeated, "Hmmm."

He was silent for a moment. Then he put his elbows on the table and said, "To Eger Castle?"

"There, there," replied János Bornemissza with a pale face. "Tonight."

"Hmm. I'd like to know how. Like a bird? Or like ghosts through a keyhole?"

"Like moles, my dear brother."

"Moles?"

"The castle has underground passages."

"Underground passages?" He shook his head.

János Bornemissza reached inside his coat and took out a sheet of parchment. He put it down in front of Szalkay. "Here they are, these red lines."

"I know," Szalkay nodded, glancing at the drawing. "They are here, but they are not there. They were all filled in Perényi's time."

"They filled them in?"

"Indeed they did. When Perényi tore down half of the King St. István church, they stumbled upon the tunnels and filled them all. They all collapsed. Those tunnels weren't made by Hungarians. Hungarians don't think about escape when they build a castle."

"Is this certain?" asked the guest.

"As sure as we're sitting here."

"But you are absolutely certain? How does your grace know for certain?"

Szalkay shrugged. "Dobó's messengers came to me. They come and go through the Turkish camp. One of them was stabbed the other day. Even if there were only one passageway, don't you think they would be using it?"

Young Bornemissza listened thoughtfully. He finally lifted his head. "When does the messenger come and when does he leave?"

"Well, there are two out now! Miklós Vas is one and Imre Szabó the other. Dobó sent them to Vienna, to the king."

"When will they return? When do they enter the castle?"

"Miklós Vas, maybe in a week. Szabó, maybe two weeks. Every week a messenger leaves here."

The questioner's eyes filled with tears. He stared ahead, pale.

Szalkay sipped his cup. He mumbled another hmm. Then he leaned back in his armchair and, looking from the corner of his eye, quietly said, "Do you hear that, János Bornemissza! You are no more a János than I am an Abraham. And you're not the brother of Bornemissza any more than I am the Bishop of Eger. You are a woman, dear sister. No matter what kind of coat you wear, my eyes do not deceive me!"

"Forgive me, Lord Szalkay," the newcomer replied, getting up. "I did not hide from your grace to deceive you, but so you would not keep me from my journey. I am the wife of Gergely Bornemissza."

Szalkay stood up and bowed. "At your service, my younger sister."

"Thank you. Well, now I'll tell you why I came. My good husband has a Turkish talisman. The one who owned it stole our little boy and brought him to Eger. He thought the talisman was with my lord. Look, this is it."

She reached into her bosom and took out a fine Turkish ring on a string.

Szalkay stared at the ring.

She continued. "For a while I searched for the Turk with soldiers in Sopron, but because they couldn't find him, I came after him. The Turks are superstitious. That talisman is everything to him. If possible, he will kill my husband. If he can't, he will kill my son. But if my husband has the ring, maybe they could talk to each other. My lord can return the ring, and the Turk would deliver the child."

Szalkay shook his head. "Dear young sister, the people in Eger swore an oath that they would not speak to the Turks, nor accept any message from them. Anyone who speaks or exchanges messages with the Turks, whether an officer or a common man, is a dead man."

He scratched his head, continuing. "If only you had come here yesterday, sister. But who knows if they have gotten inside?" The captain was thinking of Lukács Nagy.

"It doesn't matter now," she replied. "I need to get in today! I took no oath not to talk to Turks."

"But how do you think you can enter? After all, you two can't fight your way through the camps."

"We're in disguise."

"If you go in disguise, you will be shot from the castle."

"We will shout to them."

"Then you will fall into the hands of the Turks outside the castle. The gates are blocked. They may already be filled with masonry."

"So, how will Dobó's messenger get inside five days from now?"

"At risk of his life. He certainly knows which gate to use, where they are waiting for his return. He has a whistle and a password. He can speak Turkish. They must wait patiently if they are to avoid running into danger."

"And if I go with a white flag? If I say I'm looking for an officer called Yumurjak?"

"Your grace is beautiful and young. If you look like a boy, you are just as valuable as being recognized as a woman. The first soldier to grab you will tie you to his tent."

"But if I ask for an officer?"

"There are two hundred thousand people there. He won't know officers by name. They don't even speak the same language. Persians, Arabs, Egyptians, Kurds, Tatars, Serbs, Albanians, Croatians, Greeks, Armenians — a thousand different peoples. Officers are known by name only in their own commands. But that name is not the officer's real name, but a nickname. For example, if the officer is big-nosed, whether Ahmed is his name or Hassan, they call him Big Nose or the Elephant. If he has red hair, they call him Squirrel or Copper. If he is lean and long-legged, he is called Stork. And in other ways. Everyone has a name that can easily be recognized from his physical features."

She lowered her head. "Well then, give me some advice, brother Szalkay."

"My advice is to wait for a messenger who is going in. Whether it be Miklós Vas or anyone else, your grace will give him the ring and it will be taken. Then Lord Bornemissza will figure out how to talk to the Turk."

In reality, it was good advice. But hey, the pounding heart of a mother doesn't know the word *wait*. She sees only a killer hovering over her loved one. She has to hold a shield to protect as soon as possible!

Éva stretched out the drawing of the castle and remained absorbed studying it for a long time.

"If the castle was built before the Hungarians came in," she said, raising her head, then those there now do not know what is underneath. See, here is the church, and here are three underground tunnels branching out. These could indeed have been filled. But here's a fourth tunnel. This one takes you to this palace, and it's far from the rest. They could not have been able to find it when Sándor Bastion was built. They either knew it or not. Where is its entrance, Miklós?"

She pushed the paper in front of the boy. "At the brick kilns," he replied after a minute's study.

"Is there such a thing?" she asked Szalkay.

"Yes," Szalkay replied. "It's northeast from the castle."

The boy read the tiny, poppyseed writing.

Northeast brick kiln. Flat, round stone; ten steps south of the walnut tree. This is the entrance.

"Is there a walnut tree there?" she asked again.

"I don't remember," Szalkay said. "I've been there only once in my life, in Perényi's time."

"And the brick kiln is far from the castle?"

"Not far. Quarter of an hour, maybe."

"Then there are Turks there, too."

"Certainly there are. If no one else, the camp followers; shepherds and other types."

"Can you give me some Turkish clothes?"

"Yes."

"Do you have a *deli*'s cloak?"

"I also have that, but only one. But it has been cut all the way through."

"I'll sew it together," she said. "I once traveled dressed as a *deli*. I never thought it would ever be useful."

She rested her forehead on her hand while she calmly thought. Suddenly, she looked up. "No," she said, "I won't stay to sew the cape. It will be even better as it is. Thank you for your kind hospitality."

She held out her hand to the captain.

"But, surely not ..."

"We're leaving immediately."

The captain got up stood in the doorway. "I can't let you! To go blindly into such danger ... I'd be blamed forever."

Éva slid back into her chair. "You speak well," she said with a sigh. "We have to go a different way. We have to figure out some way so we don't get caught."

"That's it," said Lord Balázs, also sitting down. "Even if there is only one plausible scheme, then I'll let you leave."

2

To the north-east of Eger Castle is a high mountain called the Eged. In truth, Saint Egid or Saint Egyed would have been its real name, but since the Hungarian could not stomach the name Egyed, today they use only the name Eged for that mountain. It is some seven miles from Eger, about as far as St. Gellert Hill is from Kőbánya. But much taller and more massive.

If a man with strong arms were to pull a bow and shoot a goose-feathered arrow from Eger Castle in the direction of that mountain, that arrow would fly over a hill where one of the batteries of Turkish cannons were firing, and fall behind in a valley where the camp followers had settled. Merchants, blacksmith harriers, barbers, dervishes, charlatan healers, grinders, sorbet and halva vendors, rope dancers, slave traders, rag-and-bone men, gypsies, and many other people were in that valley. From there, they went to the camps day and night to squat, swap, rummage, entertain, steal, and cheat — in other words, *live* — among the soldiers.

On the second of October, the third day after the assault on St. Michael's Day, a young *deli* arrives on horseback from Tárkány Forest. He wears a short *atilla*-style coat, tight pants, yellow boots and camelhair cap. Instead of a turban, the hood of his cape is drawn over his head the way *delis* typically dress. A scimitar girds his waist. Bow and quiver on his shoulder. He is driving a Hungarian boy, chains on his legs, in front of him. The boy and an ox. The boy and the ox are obviously plunder belonging to the *deli*.

There are vineyards in that area. The Hungarians did not harvest this year. The vineyards are full of Turks. Wherever one looks, Turks in turbans or fur hats stumble among the vines.

Some shout at the young *deli*. "Where did you find that beautiful booty?"

But at that moment they drive the ox furiously. They do not reply.

The *deli*: Éva.

The prisoner: Miklós.

There are no sentries there. Or if there are, they are wandering about the vineyard. What's the point of guarding if there is no enemy? Mrs.

Bornemissza reaches the brick kiln valley without being challenged. There she finds a confusion of dirty tents and ornate tents, and she attracts noisy crowds of dogs and Gypsy children. Merchants break their way through the crowds.

"How much do you want for the boy?"

"I'll give you fifty piastres."

"I'll pay sixty kurush."

"I'll give seventy."

"I'll give you twenty piastres for the ox!"

"Thirty."

"Forty."

The *deli* does not talk to them. He uses his spear to control the prisoner and the ox. The chained prisoner holds a small whip to handle the ox.

They wander down from the vineyard to the brick kiln. That world is an even more colorful scene. Gypsies have used the bricks to build make-shift housing. Instead of a roof, they covered it with twigs or a tarpaulin. Some Gypsy families have even set themselves up inside the kilns. They are baking, cooking, and sleeping on that autumn day.

The old walnut tree is still standing and living. Some sort of horse trader has settled under the tree. Éva is only interested in what is ten steps to the south. Horses are tethered there. Next to it is the dealer's four-pole tent, with the quotation from the Koran written in Turkish:

Fakri fakhiri. (My poverty, my pride.)

Because a Turkish merchant never writes his name on his shop, but only a few words from the Koran.

Éva saw the stone. It was once a millstone. It had been there for a very long time. It had sunken into the ground with only a half visible. Grass grew tall through its center, and moss and sempervivum plants had grown over it.

Éva drove her ox and her prisoner between the horses. She stabbed her spear in the middle of the millstone.

The merchant came forward bowing.

"How much for the prisoner?" he asked, stroking his beard.

Éva played with silence. She pointed to her lips and gestured no.

A mute soldier is not a rarity. Even if one is mute and has no beard or mustache, Turks immediately understand when faced with one of God's creations who, when he is not a *deli* living off of plunder, would still be earning his bread from what he does not have.

Well the Greek spoke. "*Otuz kurush.*" (thirty piastres.)

Éva gestured that only the ox was for sale.

The Greek looked at the ox front and back. He appreciated the lifting motion of its shoulders and offered a another price, "*Yirmi kurush.*" (twenty piastres.)

Éva shook her head. The merchant promised thirty, thirty-five piastres.

As the bargaining was going on, Éva sat down on the stone and felt her ankle as if painful. It had raw meat tied to it. Its juice had seeped through the blue cloth.

When the Greek promised thirty-five piastres, Éva gestured with signs and a spear point that she needed a tent at that place.

The Greek saw that the *deli* was wounded, faint, and dead tired. He understood that the *deli* wanted to rest for the remainder of the siege. He had his servant bring out three, four ragged and even more ragged tents. "Here, you chose."

Éva picked the biggest one, the one with the most patches, and gestured that he could take the ox. The merchant was not satisfied with the ox. Éva gave him her horse, too, but she made herself understood that she wanted to take the tent.

The merchant agreed. With the help of his two Saracen servants, they set up the tent for Éva.

Well, that worked out smoothly.

"God help us!" Éva whispered as she and Miklós remained alone inside the tent.

Now the only question was: how and when to lift the stone? All they have to do is somehow get a pole, push it into the hole in the middle of the millstone, then tip over the stone.

And getting a pole was not that difficult. All they had to do was take one of the railings from the horse corral. They arranged it that night.

Cannons continuously thundered on the other side of the hill, and the castle's thin bearded cannons returned heavy fire. Sometimes the smell of smoke was blown their way. They could see one of the castle towers through some of the tree branches. It was already ruined, like a candle gnawed by a mouse, but they were happy to see it. The tower marked the direction where they were headed that night.

All kinds of people were buzzing around them. Sometimes soldiers also appeared among them. Mostly they were buying horses or were looking for quack healers. Gypsy talismans were also favorites of those from the East. They did not really trust them, but they bought them anyway. One *azab* wore a garland of talismans hanging on his hairy chest.

Éva was lying on her cloak. "What do you think, Miklós? Is it possible for me to find my son? I got this far. I can get further inside."

"Honorable lady, are you worrying about this again?"

"No one will stop me in these clothes. I can find him, even if I have to search the army. I will stand in front of Yumurjak and tell him, here is the ring, give me my son!"

"He takes the ring and doesn't give up the boy."

"Oh godless beast!"

"Because if he weren't ... But even if he were honorable, what would happen if an officer in the camp gave an order to your grace? There may be companies where *delis* are not permitted. Certainly, the areas around cannons are restricted. They would immediately suspect that your grace is an intruder and not part of the camp."

"They would take me prisoner ..."

"And even if they don't take you prisoner, Yumurjak would never let you out of his hands."

Éva sighed. She opened her satchel. She took out bread and cold chicken. She put it on the millstone. "Let's eat, Miklós."

It was finally dusk. The gunfire ceased. In the darkness, everyone soon fell asleep.

Éva took out a candle from her satchel. They used flint to light it.

Around midnight, Miklós crept out of the tent. After a few minutes he returned with a pole as thick as an arm.

They put it in the millstone. They moved the stone.

Under the stone was nothing but wet black clay and a few black beetles.

Éva stomped on the exposed area with her foot.

The stomping was a question for the ground: Are you empty?

The ground thumped hollow: I'm empty.

Éva took the head of a shovel from her satchel. They forced it onto the butt of the spear and used it to dig. Miklós used his hands to scrape the ground.

At a depth of about two shovels, the metal knocked on a board.

It was a strong and thick oak board, but it was rotting. They dug it out. Below that, there was a dark hole the width of a man's waist.

They had to go down some ten small stairs. The hole widened there. It was braced like a cellar. They could walk in it standing.

The air was heavy. The tunnel dark. Here and there on the walls were white patches, like flowers, of saltpeter. The stones breathed a damp cold.

Miklós went ahead. He carried the candle. At times they walked ankle deep in water, and sometimes they stumbled on stones that had fallen from the vaulting. Then Miklós would say, "Careful, there's a stone in the way."

In some places, the ground thumped from their steps. There must be other tunnels. What kind of people could have built them? There was no history written, not even when the castle was built. Who knows what kinds of people have lived on this land before us?

Miklós again warned, "Careful. We have to bend low here!"

The tunnel had been sloping down for quite some time. Its vaulted roof was getting lower. Then the tunnel went up, but the vault did not.

Miklós was already on all fours. Éva stopped. "Go ahead, Miklós," she said. "If the tunnel is blocked, we'll have to go back for the shovel."

Miklós climbed on. The candlelight got narrower, then finally disappeared. Éva was left alone in the darkness.

She knelt down and prayed. "Oh my God ... father of my poor wandering soul! Do you see me here, blind in this depth? ... Just a few steps away from my Gergely ... Did you join us together just to tear us apart in such misfortune? ... I turn my face to you, my trembling heart … My God, here under enemy feet, in the black depths of the earth, please let me reach him!"

The light reappeared. Soon, Miklós also appeared. He slid down his belly, then crouched as he emerged from the darkness. "The tunnel narrows in about twenty steps, then after another ten steps, widens again. There the tunnel splits in two. But both are caved in."

"Go back for the spade, Miklós. We have to dig until morning. But, Miklós, every hour you have to stand in front of the tent, so as not to raise suspicion."

The boy obeyed without saying a word.

"If I get to my husband, Miklós," said Éva, "we will be indebted to you for your kindness. Dobó loves my husband like a brother. He will also make you Dobó's secretary, like him."

"I wouldn't accept it," replied Miklós. "The child was lost because of my mistake. I have to help you find him. As soon as he's found, I'll take a walking stick and leave for school."

You poor, good Miklós! You are never going to school again!

3

The assault on St. Michael's Day lasted until noon. Cannons on both sides cooled that afternoon. In the castle they sang the Psalm *Circumdederunt*, "They Surrounded." Down below the castle, camp dervishes and priests loaded carts with the dead and the wounded who were unable to walk.

The insides and outsides of the castle were black from dried blood. At the bastions and at the four sites of the assault, women sprinkled ash and stone dust on the blood. The castle executioner tossed down the bodies of the janissaries who were killed when the corner tower collapsed. They carried their flags into the stables. Weapons were distributed among the soldiers. People could take whatever they wanted for free.

They found money in every janissary's clothing, belt or cap. Silver, copper, sometimes gold. Not much. Whatever was valuable was placed in a sealed bag in the castle chest. It would all be distributed after the siege.

Immediately after lunch, Dobó ordered the soldiers who had fought for the least amount of time to repair the walls. First they gathered stones from the fallen tower. They were pulling dead Turks from the rubble until the evening.

Dobó even gave children work to do, "Children, collect all the cannonballs lying around. Carry the big ones under the big guns, and the smaller ones to the bottom of the bastions."

That night, Lieutenant Hegedüs slept with Gergely at Sándor Bastion.

The night was cool. The broad crescent of the moon shone white among the stars. Gergely brought bags stuffed with straw to set up places for himself and his two lieutenants to sleep under a vault. There was a fire before the vault.

And as they lay there, warmed by the fire, Hegedüs spoke up. "You are a knowledgeable man, Gergely. I was studying to be a priest, but I was thrown out. I killed forty Turks today with my own hands. One of them cut at me twice. Well, you can't say I don't have courage."

Gergely was tired and sleepy. But Hegedüs' voice was so unusually shaky. He looked at him.

The lieutenant was sitting on a straw bag. The fire lit his face, his blue cloak reaching his ankles.

He continued. "Yet I often wonder. A man is only a man, whether his face is shaved or not. And that we actually are killing."

"Well, yes ..." Gergely muttered sleepily.

"And they kill us too."

"Of course they kill. If they were climbing the wall with wine flasks instead of weapons, we would be welcoming them with wine flasks. Wine would be flowing instead of blood."

"That's clear enough," replied Hegedüs. He swallowed and looked sideways into the fire, as if hesitating whether or not to speak. Finally he said, "What is courage?"

"You just said that you killed forty Turks, and you ask what is courage? Lie down, sleep! You're tired too."

Hegedüs shrugged. "If there was a smart person among us who had as much wisdom as all of us here, or, say, as much wisdom as could be gathered from everyone in the world, I think he would not be brave."

He looked at Gergely. The firelight shone on Gergely's face, revealing only the bulging bones of his face.

What did he mean by that?

Gergely closed his eyes and said sleepily, "He would be the bravest. Why do you think he wouldn't be brave?"

"Because he could better appreciate the value of life. That we are here on this earth, that is certain. But if the Turks have our heads, it's not clear that we will live much longer. A man with such great wisdom would not readily risk what he has just so people will say that he was a brave man."

Gergely yawned. He replied, "Only an average mind clings to life. The weak-minded man is brave because he does not understand death. A strong-minded person is brave because he understands."

"Death?"

Gergely leaned on his elbow. "That's it. The weak-minded man lives the life of an animal. An animal does not know death. Look at the hen, for example. How much effort the hen takes to protect her chickens! But should one chicken roll over and die, she leaves it with no regret. But if that chicken understood death like the average man, then wouldn't she feel sorry and cry? She would know that her child has died. But those who have no idea of death have no idea of life. Consider the strong-minded man. He is brave because he understands that his body is not everything. He feels that he is more soul than body. The more spiritual a person, the less value for the body. The heroes, the great heroes of world history, were all spiritual people. All to the last hero. Well, but now, let's sleep."

But still, to reassure Hegedüs, he continued thoughtfully. "Where we were before we lived, or where we will be when we are no longer living, we cannot know in this earthly body. But what would become of us if we could? Because we would not be thinking about whatever is going on now, but instead, what this or that acquaintance is doing in the next world, or the work we had been doing here and how it is continuing after we left."

"Good, good," replied Hegedüs. "I've heard this kind of speech from priests many times. But this earthly life certainly has value, and its purpose isn't to provide a tormented pagan with someone to cut down."

The fire was crackling, casting a golden hue on the armor and swords lying by the straw sacks. Gergely used a leather shield for his pillow. He leaned back and said sleepily, "You're talking nonsense, my good Hegedüs. The animal man sometimes does good, the intelligent man always knowing. You know that protecting a home is a great and sacred thing, just like children protecting their mother."

And he pulled his cape over his ears.

"Where is it written, in what law, that someone has to protect his mother; if need be, at the cost of his life? The animal certainly does not protect. But man, the most stupid as well as the most intelligent, runs up to his mother's attacker, and when he is killed, he feels that he could not have done otherwise."

Gergely replied in a sleepy voice. "Divine law sometimes moves the will. Love is the divine law. Love of mother, love of home, are one. The soul cannot be killed by the Turks. Well but, for the sake of your Pontius, let me sleep already! You are philosophizing at a time like this? I'm about ready to hit you with this shield."

Hegedüs said nothing more. He also lay down on his bed. There was no sound in the castle other than the sentries walking with even paces, the quiet grinding of one of the gunpowder mills, and the steps of the horse turning the mill.

— § —

The cannons did not speak the following next morning. However, behind the Turkish earthworks, the camp was buzzing.

"The Turks are writing another letter," Dobó said.

A sheet of white paper was in his hand. He had the horn call assembly. Two minutes later, the resting soldiers were standing in order.

Dobó spoke. "Warriors! I called you together to praise you. You beat back the first assault on the castle fiercely, as is fitting for Hungarian soldiers. I did not see any cowardice among you, not even once. You deserve the name of hero warriors! After the Turks clear out, I myself will go to his Majesty the King to ask him to reward you. But until then, until I can do that, there are four men among you whom I have to reward from the castle treasury. Step forward István Bakocsai, László Török, Antal Komlósi, Szaniszló Soncy."

The four warriors stepped forward from the line and stood before Dobó. All four had bandages on their heads.

Dobó continued. "The enemy reached the top of the outer castle walls and managed to set their first flag. Soldier warrior István Bakocsai single handedly attacked the company of janissaries. He wrenched the flag from the Turks and threw it down. Even before he receives his reward from the king, I promote him to corporal and reward him with fifty silver pennies and new clothes."

Steward Sukán counted fifty pennies into the warrior's hands.

Dobó continued. "The castle flag was shot down along with the wall by a cannonball. It fell among the Turks. László Török, by himself, jumped out of the breach and brought it back. Even before he receives his reward from the king, he will receive one forint from the castle treasury and a Bergamo-cloth suit."

The warrior glanced around triumphantly. Sukán pressed the reward into his grip.

Dobó continued. "They also planted a flag by the Old Gate. Antal Komlósi ran to the wall and cut it down along with the Turk's right hand. Even before he receives his reward from the king, he receives two forint and a dress suit."

The fourth man remained.

Dobó called out, "Szaniszló Soncy! When the repairs to the breach were broken and hundreds of Turks were about to enter, you jumped alone into the breach and, without regard to the enemy numbers, you attacked and held them back until help came. Even before he receives his reward from the king, he is now rewarded with two yards of fine cloth and one forint."

In those days, cloth was very expensive, and because soldiers did not wear uniforms, the cloth from which their clothes were made often had to last a lifetime. As for the money, Dobó's entire salary as captain was six hundred forints, and we should understand that what he refers to as the castle treasury means his own purse.[53]

Dobó added, "The amounts given as rewards are not a measure of your bravery, but a measure of the castle treasury. There are many others here who have acted with similar heroism. I myself have seen some of you cut down some fifty Turks. To mention only one example, here is Lukács Nagy and his company. You know what he did! Now, understand. I wanted only to praise the most exceptionally outstanding, those who risked certain death for their homeland."

A horn sounded from above the gate, and within a minute, a stranger, a peasant, walked across the market square towards Dobó. He had a letter in his hand.

"Go about your business," Dobó said to his soldiers.

He spoke a second word to Mekcsey, and when the peasant reached him, he looked him up and down with contempt. He mounted a horse. He rode away.

The peasant was received by the officers. The letter, without having been read, was torn in two. Half was thrown into a fire, the other half stuffed into the peasant's mouth. "Eat what you brought, dog!"

Then he ended up in the prison, probably thinking that it was not a good idea to serve the Turks in any way.

---

[53] Gárdonyi's note: In those days cloth was very expensive and available only in Vienna. As far as money was concerned, Dobó's annual salary as commander was 600 forint, Sukán's 50 forint, the clerk Boldizsár got only 20 forint, and Dobó's gardener got 6 forint.

He was called András Sári. The Turks brought him with them from Fehérvár.

The pagan army waited an hour to see whether the man would come out of the gate again. When they saw that the Eger defenders would not write letters, all their cannons around the walls fired again. And the trenches dug below the castle were filled with Turkish warriors.

So far only cries of Allah and mocking comments had been heard from the Turkish camp. Now from all sides came Hungarian words: "Surrender! You will have a miserable end if you don't!"

Another voice: "Do you think you can continue to defend the siege? That was just a test! We have no mercy even for babies!"

Another one again: "Leave Dobó! Dobó is a fool! If you want to die, die yourself! Whoever comes out of the castle gates will not be hurt! You can take your money and your weapons with you!"

"Whoever comes out, just put a white scarf on his spear!" shouted a *sipahi* with a pointy helmet from a trench.

"Whoever lets us in will get a reward of a thousand gold pieces!" yelled an ostrich-feathered janissary. Hearing that, some three shot at him, but he ducked down in time.

"Dobó has gone crazy!" came the cry from the other side again. "Don't be a fool! The first one to come out of the castle will get a hundred gold pieces, and the next twenty will get ten each. You can go in peace!"

Old soldiers who knew Hungarian shouted like this from the enemy camp. But they also shouted in Slovak, German, Spanish, and even Italian.

The castle defenders did not respond in Hungarian, or in Slovak, German, Spanish, or even Italian.

The shouting continued more and more. The promises became increasingly encouraging and the threats more terrible. Finally Gergely gathered his drums, trumpets, and horns on his part of the walls. Every time a Turk started shouting, the drum beat, the horn blared, and the trumpet blew.

The people of the castle were amused. Drummers and buglers got up on the other wall, even three castle pipers did their work. Those warriors who had iron shields beat them loudly. Each shout from the Turks was drowned out by a hellish din.

Cavalry Lieutenant Jób Paksy asked Dobó for permission to sortie against the shouters.

That lieutenant was a tall young man with Herculean strength. His mustache, when he pulled it out in the morning, reached his two ears. During the assault, he had fought with a broadsword. With a single cut, he had split a Turk's helmeted head in two. Even the strong helmet fell in two pieces.

He asked for only a hundred people.

"Don't play clever, young brother Jób," Dobó replied, "because you might run into trouble!"

But Jób Paksy was burning with anger. He bargained down like Abraham on the road to Sodom.

"Only fifty. Only twenty!"

Finally he asked for only ten men with which to make one charge.

Dobó probably would not have allowed that either, but by then several other itchy-handed soldiers had gathered around Paksy. Faces flushed with angry determination, they asked, "Noble captain, sir! ..."

Dobó began to fear that if he continued to oppose them, they would not understand that he was motivated by clever caution. They would suspect that he was concerned that the castle defenders were getting weak. He shrugged.

"Well, if you feel like you want to get your heads bashed, just go."

"How many?" Paksy asked, almost screaming in pleasure.

"Two hundred," replied Dobó.

The gate to the stream was still intact. Paksy picked his two hundred people and they stormed out the gate.

It happened around noon.

The creek was full of Turkish peoples watering horses and camels. Mainly *akinjis* were watering in front of the gate.

Two hundred soldiers hit them like lightning. *Akinjis* fell like carrots. Paksy, as he went in front, carved a road out of them. The right side of his armor and horse were red with blood.

Others followed his example, and the *akinji* company, terrified and shouting, turned their backs on each other, while from two sides, janissaries by the thousands rushed towards them.

Dobó ordered the trumpet to signal retreat.

But they do not hear it below. Fighting fuels their rage. They charge the janissaries, cutting and killing them.

A camel frightens Paksy's horse. It rears and jumps to the side. At that moment, Paksy is making a terrible cut into a mail-shirted *sipahi*. He falls off the side of his veering horse. The horse was stabbed in the chest. The horse rolls over Paksy. He remains beside it.

The other men, seeing this, gather around to protect Paksy, waving swords to give the lieutenant time to get up.

But Paksy does not get up. His leg is dislocated. Even lying there he swings his sword wildly. He cuts and thrusts around him. His helmet falls off his head.

A janissary cuts his head.

Trumpets blare loudly from the walls: *back! back!* The squadron turns around and cuts its way through the Turkish crowd. Only ten men remain around Paksy. They are immediately surrounded by forest of spears.

"Surrender!" shout the Turks.

The ten men drop their swords one after another.

Angry shouts of "Cowards!" come from the castle.

Mekcsey could hardly be held back from rushing out.

— § —

An hour later, a tall plate-shaped platform was laid on King's Seat.

A Turkish hangman, there on the hill, before the eyes of castle defenders, on that platform, smashed the bodies of the wounded warriors from Eger with an iron wheel. All of them, save only Paksy.

4

Until then, the Eger defenders had only hated the Turks. From then on, they loathed them. The women were crying. The soldiers wanted to rush out and attack. But Dobó had the gate closed.

After the display of vicious cruelty, Ali Pasha shouted at the castle. "Know that we have destroyed the king's army sent to help you. No more mercy! If you do not surrender, you will all suffer like these here."

The people listened with pale faces. The words of the wicked Turk shocked the drummers so much that they forgot to drown out his shouting.

"Those miscreants are lying!" Gergely told the soldiers around him. "They are lying, just like when they shout to us every night, that they hold our wives, brides, and children as prisoners. The king's army is coming. We can expect them at any hour."

"But what if they aren't lying?" asked a raw voice from behind his back.

Even before, Gergely was pale. At these words, his face became so white with anger that each hair on his beard and mustache was clearly outlined like a thread.

The voice belonged to Lieutenant Hegedüs. Gergely looked at him. Grasping the hilt of his sword, he said, "Lieutenant, sir. You should know the custom that the flags and armor of a defeated army are stripped. If they had been beaten, wouldn't the flags have been displayed?"

And he looked at him up and down.

This happened at Church Bastion. Further along the bastion was Dobó. Next to him was Cecey leaning on his cane. Zoltay stood there, and Fügedy, and Márton the priest. The priest in a white shirt and stole. (He has just completed the funeral of a person who had been seriously injured.)

Dobó heard only Gergely's words. He looked at Hegedüs in amazement.

Cecey also turned around. "Stupid words!" he shouted to Hegedüs. "Do you want to scare our people?"

Hegedüs looked back at Gergely angrily. "I have been a soldier longer than you, kid! How dare you teach me! How dare you look at me like that!" His sword suddenly slipped out of its scabbard.

Gergely also drew his sword.

Dobó stepped between them. "You can finish this after the siege. While the castle is defended, don't even dare to draw swords with each other!"

The two angry lieutenants sheathed their swords. Dobó coldly ordered Hegedüs to report to Mekcsey's company by the Old Gate, and that Gergely was forbidden to leave the outer castle without good reason.

"After the siege ...!" Hegedüs repeated with a threatening twinkle.

"I'm not hiding," Gergely said coldly.

— § —

Dobó was discouraged by this altercation. As the two officers departed in two different directions, he turned to Cecey. "What will happen to us," he said, "if officers see each other as enemies? How they fight each other! They must be reconciled!"

"The devil with these men from Kassa!" Cecey replied. "My son spoke well."

They crossed the market square on foot. They could hear a song from the tavern, and as they got there, three soldiers stumbled out the door, clinging to each other's neck. With Laocoön's gestures, they scrambled towards the barracks. [54]

Bakocsai was in the middle. As the song ended, he let out a loud yell. "We'll never die!"

When these celebrators saw Dobó, they released each other and stood like the tower of Pisa. They were silent.

Dobó passed by them without saying a word and stopped in front of the tavern door.

They were singing inside. László Török was waving around the bandage that should have been binding his wound. Komlósi was beating the table with a tin cup. Szaniszló Soncy was shouting for the pipers. Alongside them, three other soldiers were helping them drink away the rewards for their bravery.

Dobó turned to his page. "Call the two innkeepers here."

A minute later, the two men stood there: György Debrőy with his shirt-sleeves rolled-up, and László Nagy in a blue apron. The two men stood confused in front of the captain's angry eyes.

"Innkeepers!" shouted Dobó. "If I see another drunk soldier in this castle, I will hang the innkeeper who helped him get drunk!"

He turned and left.

— § —

That night they again barricaded and filled the breaches blasted by cannons in the walls that day. Dobó slept only an hour or two. Day and night you could see him here and there, and you could hear his calm, deep voice as he directed action.

On the third night after the assault, a loud cry was heard from the eastern hill:

---

[54] Laocoön is a character in the Iliad. He was the Trojan high priest who suspected that the Greek's "Trojan" horse was a trap, which angered Goddess Athena who sent two sea-serpents to strangle Laocoön and his two sons.

"Do you hear, István Dobó! Your old opponent greets you, Arslan Bey. My honor is pure like my sword. You've never heard anything bad about my name."

After a minute's break: "Do not make good István Losonczy's death as your example! He caused his own death! But if you don't believe us, I offer myself as your hostage! I'm not afraid to come in alone if you fly a white flag! Hold me hostage until you leave the castle, and kill me immediately if any of those who come out loses even one strand of hair. I tell you this: Arslan Bey, the son of that famous *yahya pasha* Oglu Muhammad."

There was silence, as if the shouter was waiting for reply.

But at the first words being shouted, Dobó mounted and rode to the other bastion. This was how he showed how deaf he was to someone speaking Turkish.

Only the soldiers heard the speech continue. "I know my person is enough assurance for you. But if your people do not have enough, we will do so by withdrawing the entire army three miles back. No Turks will come out until you are three miles in the opposite direction. Answer me, warrior István Dobó!"

The castle was silent.

5

Around midnight, Dobó spotted a man by the door leading to the gunpowder magazine. He was carrying a few large bowls on his head. "What's that?"

"Lieutenant Gergely ordered me to bring bowls from the kitchen."

"Where's the lieutenant?"

"On Prison Bastion."

Dobó rode over there and dismounted. He hurried up the stairs. He found Gergely under the walls where a lantern was burning. He was kneeling and leaning over a bowl of water, motionless, faint, and grim.

"Gergely!"

Gergely got up.

"I didn't know you were still up, captain sir. In the meantime, I reported to Mekcsey that he should be watching bowls."

"For mines?"

"Certainly. With the assault having being repelled, it is foreseeable that they will be digging mines."

"Good," Dobó replied. "The drummers should also put their drums on the ground with beans on them."

"And small shot."

Dobó shouted down from the bastion to page Kristóf, "Go around and visit the sentries. Tell them to keep an eye on the drums and bowls at every turn. As soon as the water trembles or the beans or shot on the drums vibrate, report it immediately."

He took Gergely by the arm and pulled him inside the inner castle.

"My dear son, Gergely," he said in a fatherly voice, which he ordinarily used to address only his pages. "I've been watching you for a week. What is wrong? You never used to be like this."

"Sir," Gergely with a trembling voice, "I didn't want to burden your grace with this. But if you ask me, I will tell you. Ever since the castle was surrounded, every night they have been shouting that they have my little boy."

"It's just lies!"

"That's what I thought. At first, I didn't even pay attention. But a week ago they threw a small sword into the castle. That belonged to my son." That said, he pulled out a small sword from a velvet sheath under his cloak.

"This is it, sir. I know you don't remember this. Your grace gave me this sword when we first met. Then I gave it to my son when I left home. How did this get into the hands of the Turks?"

Dobó stared at the sword.

Gergely continued. "I left my wife and son in Sopron. No Turks wander around there. If they did, they would be killed. And my wife would not leave because she has no one else to stay with."

"Unbelievable," Dobó replied, shaking his head. "Maybe the sword was stolen? Maybe it ended up in the hands of a trader, or some soldiers."

"Then how would they know it belonged to my son? And there is some connection in this case that makes my heart feel like it is being strangled by a snake. This Yumurjak, the one also known as the dervish bey, had a talisman. That ring was taken from him by the priest who was my teacher, Father Gábor, now departed with God. He left it to me. Since then, that fool of a Turk has always been looking for it. I have no idea how he found out that I had it. But it's certain he found out because he has been asking me for it."

"And you think he has your son? Well, the devil take that ring. Throw it at him!"

Gergely took off his helmet and wiped his forehead. "The strange thing is, I don't have that ring. I left it at home!"

"My mind boggles!" said Dobó shaking his head. "If I think some Turks were adventuring in Sopron ... hmm ... the bey would have grabbed the ring and not the child."

"This is driving me crazy, too," replied Gergely.

"But you think your child is here?"

"As the little sword came from Sopron to here, I have to think that my son has also come here."

They reached the palace. Dobó sat on the marble bench under a lantern in front of the palace. "You also sit down," he said. He rested both elbows on his knees and stared straight ahead. Finally, he slapped a knee and said:

"Well, we'll find out tonight whether or not what the Turk says is true."

He called to the sentry in front of the palace. "Miska, go to the dungeon. Bring out the Kurd who was captured by the stream."

Lady Balogh's voice sounded from the window. "Captain sir, your long cape ..." Because Dobó was wearing only a short grey, deerskin coat and the night air was cold.

"Thank you," replied Dobó. "I'll go to bed soon. How's Pető?"

"Talking deliriously and groaning."

"Who is staying up with him?"

"I called the wife of Gáspár Kocsis. But until he is resting silently, I am also staying up with him."

"There's no reason," Dobó replied. "I saw the wound. He will heal. Rest assured, your grace!"

The sentry was jogging with the Kurd.

"Take the chains off him!" Dobó commanded.

The Kurd folded his arms across his chest, bowed deeply, and waited.

"Can you hear, pagan?" Dobó said. Gergely translated every sentence. "Do you know the dervish bey?"

"I know him."

"What does he look like?"

"One-eyed. He wears a dervish dress but wears armor underneath."

"That's him. Where are you from?"

"Bitlis, my lord."

"Is your mother alive?"

"She's alive, my lord."

"Your family?"

"I have two children." He burst into tears.

Dobó continued. "I will let you out of the castle, but you have to do one thing for me very carefully."

"I am your slave, my lord, until I'm dead."

"You go to the dervish bey. That bey has a little boy prisoner. You tell the bey that if he brings that little boy to the gate overlooking the creek tomorrow morning, he'll get what he wants. Both of you come with a white cloth."

"I understand, my lord."

"A man will come out from the gate for the boy. He will have the bey's talisman with him. You lead the boy away from the bey and hand it over to our man. But you have to swear that you will do what I ask."

"I swear, sir," answered the Kurd.

Kristóf was already standing next to them. Dobó turned to him. "Go inside Knight's Hall. There's a bunch of Turkish stuff in the corner, and somewhere there is a little Turkish book. Bring that book here."

The book was a Koran that used to belong to some soldiers who knew how to read. It was bound in parchment and had a steel ring attached to its corner. There was a string in that ring. That was how Turks who could read carried their Koran on their chests. The Kurd put his finger on the Qur'an and swore. Then he fell to Dobó's feet. He kissed the ground and happily left.

"But sir," said Gergely, trembling, "if the Turks see us cheating ..."

Dobo replied calmly. "If he had the child, he would have shown him already. Every Turk is a liar. I just want to reassure you."

— § —

Gergely rushes up to the bastion with a beating heart hoping to catch some sleep before dawn.

As he walks past the mill, he hears the word *pst* from the shadows, or rather the sound *pst*.

Gergely looks at the shadow and sees the Gypsy kneeling on some straw and waving to him.

"Well, what do you want?" asks Gergely reluctantly.

The Gypsy gets up and whispers, "There's a dog in the garden, your greatness my lord Gergely!"

"So?"

"This evening, by the Old Gate, I was repairing the visor of a Kassa soldier's helmet. Lieutenant Hegedüs was talking about how if there is a siege, the pay should be double. The soldiers were grumbling about noble Lord Dobó. They were saying that the Turks are promising everything, but he is offering nothing. They said you have to choose."

Gergely gasps. "They spoke like that in front of you?"

"In front of all the soldiers. I wouldn't have told you. But if I have to be afraid, I'm more afraid of the Turks than the lieutenant from Kassa."

"Come with me," says Gergely.

He finds Mekcsey. He is with the men making bombs. "Pista," he says, "listen to Sárközi."

And he leaves them there.

6

In the morning, when Dobó stepped out from the palace, Hegedüs was waiting at the door.

"Sir," he said, raising his hand, "I have a report."

"Urgent?"

"Not exactly."

"Come with me. Tell me at the gate."

Gergely was already standing above the gate, Mekcsey and Fügedy with him. Planks protected them from being seen by the Turks swarming by the stream.

Dobó looked through a hole in the planks towards the city, then turned to Gergely. "No one, so far?"

"Nobody," said Gergely. He glanced at Hegedüs. Hegedüs lifted his finger to his helmet. Gergely similarly saluted. But they looked at each other coldly.

Dobó looked at Hegedüs. He was waiting for his report.

"Sir," Hegedüs said, "I have to report that I see some discontent among the soldiers."

Dobós eyes widened.

"Unfortunately," Hegedüs continued, avoiding Dobó's eyes, "there are some old soldiers among them who know the taste of ... the siege money. Yesterday, they were expecting it all day, as is usual elsewhere. By the evening they were complaining. I thought the trouble would get worse if I scolded them. Well, I let them talk. They asked me to tell the captain what they wanted."

"Well, first of all," Dobó replied, "you should not have forgotten, lieutenant, that there is no room for sneaking or whispering in the castle. Secondly, with regard to siege money, who is not fighting for the homeland, but for the siege money, let him just apply. He'll get it."

He stepped away from the lieutenant. He leaned over the planks.

"He's coming," said Gergely.

The Kurd was leading the Turks. He was already armed. He led two Hungarian children. Both were barefoot peasants dressed in waistcoats and loose pants. Because the Kurd took long steps, the two children had to run to keep up with him.

They could see the one-eyed dervish riding a horse following a hundred steps behind the Kurd. He stopped a short distance away, standing on his stirrups looking straight up at the castle.

"Those children are not mine!" Gergely said with alarm.

Indeed, the two children were older than his Jancsika. One child was about ten years of age and the other twelve.

The Kurd stopped in front of the gate and shouted. "The bey sends two instead of one child. Give out the ring, then he will send out the third child."

Dobó said to the tower sentry, "Lean out! Wave your hand to tell the Kurd he can go."

— § —

That day, as before, the Turks fired and damaged the walls. The big-throated *zarbuzan* siege guns worked slowly but with tremendous power. The walls all shook and cracked with each burst, and sometimes with the sound of crumbling rubble.

But there was a change that day, which the guards reported early in the morning.

The cavalry pulled away from the castle. Nowhere could you see red-faced *akinjis*, *sipahis* in their shining armor, the helter-skelter clothed *beshlis*, the hooded *delis*, or the *gönüllüs*, *müsellems* and *silahdars* on their small horses. Even the nine hundred camels of the camp were missing.

What happened?

People inside the castle awoke and walked about with joy on their faces. The Gypsy showed up among a group of peasants grinding and polishing a long, rusty sword. The sound of women singing could be heard from the ovens. The children were playing on the grassy knoll by the ovens. Boys played war. The girls in a circle danced.

> *Katóká of Ujvár,*
> *Her skirt embroidered with gold*
> *Oats and oats for her horse*
> *Jingle and jangle for her mother*
> *Garland of pearls for her daughter!*

Lady Balogh's servant led the little Turkish boy there. He stared at the game amazed.

"Let him play with you," the maid asked the boys.

"We won't let him," the boys replied.

The girls took him.

The little Turkish boy did not understand what they were singing, but he joined their circle and danced so intently with them as if, God only knows, he was participating in a sacred ceremony.

But what was the reason for the happiness, the joy?

The Turkish cavalry had disappeared. Certainly, the relief army was approaching. The king's army! Where would the Turkish cavalry have gone if not to face them?

Drummers beat their drums with even more energy to drown out the Turkish taunts. The drummer of the castle's largest drum jumped up on the wall where he drummed. The Turks' shouts were lost in the noise.

But papers also fell into the castle. They were tied to arrows and shot inside the walls. Nobody read what was written on them. Whoever got one threw it into a fire. The arrows were taken to Cecey.

Day and night the old man sat in the dungeon bastion. Each time he saw a Turk pop up, he fired an arrow at him.

Only Dobó's face remained serious.

He climbed one tower, then the next, to spy on the enemy. He looked toward Mount Eged for a long time, shaking his head.

Suddenly he called Mekcsey to the palace.

"My dear young brother," he said, sitting down. "I don't like that Hegedüs. Keep an eye on him."

"I am already taking care of it."

"Watch who he talks to, where he looks, where he goes. I need to know every hour."

"We will know."

"But don't let him know he's being watched or he will pull some sort of surprise."

"He won't know."

"If there is an uprising in the castle, we're done. I could have him locked up, but we need to know who and how many people are with him. We have to cut out the rotten part so that nothing remains. Who do you have watching him?"

"The Gypsy."

"Reliable?"

"Reliable. Yesterday he was working next to the Kassa people. Today he will find things to do there. I told him he would get a completely outfitted, gorgeous horse if his service in this matter is helpful. He should pretend to be with them. We'll know when the time comes."

"Do you have anyone else who can be trusted?"

"I do, but the Kassa people would not trust him. They think so little of gypsies, they don't worry about talking in front of him."

"You have to find out who the ringleaders are!"

"That's what I told him."

"Then good. We can go."

"Captain sir," Mekcsey said in a different voice. "There are signs that the king's army is coming."

He shrugged. "They may be coming," he said sadly. "But the signs that you all interpret this way ... I don't see them as signs the king's army is coming."

Mekcsey looked at Dobó in astonishment.

Dobó wrung his hands. "The *yasauls* are all here. I saw their two commanders on horseback together in Almagyar. Not one of their cannons has been moved. Their two bands are also still here."

"What then?" Mekcsey asked with a frown.

Dobó shrugged again. "It can't be anything else, my young brother, except that they went into the woods."

"To the forest?"

"There and into the vineyards. I think the two commanders want to shorten the height of the walls. They are carrying brushwood and earth. They will fill our trenches and raise mounds over the rubble. But, my dear Pista, I am only telling you this. Let the people of the castle be happy with the idea that the relief army is on its way."

He reached out and shook his junior captain's hand, looking at him affectionately. Then he turned to the room where Pető was lying.

— § —

As the sun set, the Turkish cavalry rumbled back.

A flare cast light showing that every rider was leading his horse by the bridle, and every horse was laden with brushwood. Camels in a long line were loaded with stuffed bags. They made their way down Bajusz Hill, one by one, one after the other.

Dobó turned the barrels of the bearded cannons and mortars and fired at them.

But the night was getting darker, and the number of riders was not diminishing. Dobó stopped the cannon fire and had gunners take the occasional musket shot at them.

The Turks were bustling at work. They piled and smashed brushwood and vine cuttings. Here and there *yasauls* shouted orders.

Dobó had most of the lanterns in the castle placed in the gaps of the walls in such a manner as to illuminate the wall outside, but not cast light inside to reveal targets for arrows and bullets from below.

The castle was dark on the inside. Very few lanterns burned here and there. The area inside around the Old Gate was illuminated by light from the ovens. The women were still singing as they worked.

"Just let them sing," Dobó said. "Wherever there is singing, good luck doesn't leave."

At midnight, Mekcsey watched from the tower of Bolyky Bastion to keep track of how the Turks were organizing at night for the siege.

A small number of officers stationed here and there also kept a lookout.

Mekcsey leaned on his elbows, both hands by his ears, his gaze penetrating through the darkness.

Someone jerked his cloak from behind. It was the Gypsy.

He was dressed up like a janissary. A cock's feather was stuck in his helmet. On one side, a sword, and on the other, a Turkish scimitar with a white grip.

"Psst ..." he said mysteriously. "Psst! ..."

"What do you want?"

"I can already feel the bridle of a good horse in my hands."

"You know something?"

"Oh, yes!"

"Do you have any evidence?"

"Yes, you just have to grab it."

"Well, grab it then, you rascal."

"Me grab it? Come with me and you'll grab it right away!"

"Where?"

"The water tank. Hegedüs climbed down there. Ha, ha!"

"Alone?"

"Three of his soldiers are standing guard at the door to the tank."

Mekcsey hurried down the stairs, almost stumbling.

At the bottom of the tower he summoned six soldiers. "Come unarmed! Take off your boots. Bring straps or rope!" The soldiers silently obeyed.

When they got to the bottom of the bastion, Mekcsey gave further instructions. "We're going to the water tank. There are three soldiers sitting there, either standing or lying down. You rush them from behind and tie them. Take them to the dungeon and hand them over to the jail keeper to lock them up. No shouting! No noise!"

The area around the water tank was dark. The light from above reached only as far as the top of a broken pillar. From there, the soldiers went on all fours. The Gypsy kept making the sign of the cross.

After a few minutes, the sounds of rumbling, humping, and cursing came from around the tank, making Mecskey go see what was going on.

The three guards were held down.

Both trapdoors to the tank stood wide open. Mekcsey leaned in. There was only silent darkness below.

He turned around. "He's here?" he quietly asked the Gypsy.

"I myself saw him go down."

"Lieutenant Hegedüs? Did you make a mistake?"

"It was him."

"Run to the captain. Look for him on the new bastion. Tell him I am asking him to please come here! On the way, tell Lieutenant Gergely to send five *drabant* garrison soldiers immediately!"

The Gypsy galloped away.

Mekcsey pulled his sword out and sat down on the stairs leading up from the tank. He heard what sounded like voices from downstairs. Mekcsey got up and lowered one side of the trapdoors that covered the stairs.

From above he heard the sound of the five *drabant* arrive, and, almost at the same time, Dobó and the page Kristóf arriving.

The page held a small lantern and lit it for Dobó.

Mekcsey gestured to hurry. The voices below in the reservoir were already getting louder.

"This way, this way!" a dull voice sounded from the depths.

Dobó gestured to the *drabants* to cock their guns. They had to hold them on the edge of the water tank, barrels pointed down.

"Kristóf," he said, "bring twenty more men from lord Geregely!" He took the lantern from the page and placed it next to the pillar, but without it shining any light down towards the tank.

In the depths, the rattle of weapons and the sound of footsteps.

"This way, this way!" The voice sounded louder.

One big splash ... followed by another splash ... shouts of "*Ey va! Meded!*" ... more splashes ...

The trapdoor over the staircase opens. Someone pops up. Dobó picks up the lantern. He shines a light on his face.

It is Lieutenant Hegedüs, his face pale as lead. Mekcsey grabs him by the collar.

"Grab him!" says Dobó.

Strong hands grab the lieutenant and wrench him up from below.

"Take his gun."

The sounds of rattling and yelling continue from below. "*Yetishin, yetishin!*" (Help, help!)

For a moment, Dobó shines some light down below. Well, numerous armed, turbaned Turks were fumbling and floundering around in the big black water tank. They were flooding in on the heels of each other through a hole near the side of the tank.

"Fire!" shouts Dobó.

The five gunners fire into the hole.

The cavern of the water tank make a sound as loud as that of a cannon had been fired. The answer was furious screaming.

"Stay here," Dobó tells Mekcsey. "We have to explore the holes. Go as far as you can. If the tunnels extend beyond the castle, we have to fill it and build a brick wall. There should be a sentry stationed here at all times."

He turned to the soldiers. He pointed to Hegedüs and his associates:

"Put them in irons! Lock them up separately!"

He returned to the bastion.

From the depths, Mekcsey heard a Hungarian voice. "Help! Men!"

He shone light from the lantern. Among the drowning men, a Turkish man in a leather cap was calling. "Drop down a rope," he said. "Maybe this fellow is also from the castle."

The rope used to lower the bucket was lying about. They lowered the bucket. The floundering man held the bucket and three soldiers pulled him up.

When he got up, he was gasping like a hooked catfish pulled on a river bank.

Mekcsey held the lantern to his face. He was a mustachioed *akinji*. Water dripped from his mustache and clothes.

"Are you Hungarian?" Mekcsey asked.

The man fell on his knees. "Thee have mercy, my lord!" That he addressed Mekcsey so familiarly, something obviously insulting, made it clear he was a Turk.

Mekcsey almost pushed him back. But then he thought he might make a useful witness. "Take his gun," he told the soldiers, "and lock him up with the letter carrying peasants."

7

Around the castle the next day, the fourth of October, the rising sun shone light on the fresh fill. In various places, the deep ditch that surrounded the castle from the north had been filled. A ditch had become a hill.

The fresh mounds of fill had been placed in front of the breaches in the walls. At the bottom was the brush and branches from the woods. Earth packed on top. The Turks will surely continue with this work until just here and there, the mound is still low enough so that cannons can fire over it, but tall enough to attack the castle without need for ladders.

Dobó looked at their work. He calmly studied the fill without saying a word. Then he sent for the officers. He summoned the four first lieutenants to the Knight's Hall and summoned a lieutenant, a sergeant, a corporal, and a private. He also summoned scholar Mihály, the *loaf splitter* clerk in charge of food supplies.

The table was covered with green cloth. On it a crucifix and two burning candles. In the corner of the room, dressed in a red robe, stood the executioner. Next to him was a pan of burning charcoal. Bellows in his hands. Next to the pan were pieces of lead and pincers.

Dobó was dressed in black, his helmet topped with the captain's eagle feather. In front of him was a blank sheet of paper.

"My comrades," he said with a serious, almost grim face. "We come together to investigate the case of Lieutenant Hegedüs and his associates. Their actions suggest them to be traitors. We will honestly judge them."

He gestured for the prisoners to be brought forward.

Gergely got up. "Gentlemen," he said, "I cannot be a judge in this matter. I am angry with the accused. Excuse me from this of court."

Mekcsey also stood up. "I can only be a witness," he said. "No one can be a judge and a witness."

"Be a witness," replied those sitting at the table.

Gergely left. Mekcsey went out into the hallway.

The guards introduced Hegedüs and his three accomplices. And also the Turk.

Hegedüs was pale. His eyes were surrounded by blue rings. He dared not look up.

Dobó allowed only him to remain. He sent the rest out.

"Let's hear it," he said. "What was this business leading the Turks inside?"

Hegedüs tried to pull himself together and stuttered excuses. "I just wanted to lure the Turkish into the water tank. I didn't want to give up the castle. The water tank is big. We found a narrow entrance. I thought it would be to my credit to kill thousands of Turks myself."

Dobó listened quietly. The officers did not ask him anything. When he no longer spoke, Dobó set him aside and summoned his accomplices one by one.

"We," said the first, "could do nothing but what the lieutenant sir commands. We must obey when they command."

"What did he command?"

"He ordered us to stand by the side of the tank, that he was bringing in a couple of Turks."

"What did he say as to why?"

"To discuss surrendering the castle."

Dobó looked at the lieutenant.

Hegedüs shook his head. "Not true. He is lying!"

"Am I?" said the man, offended. "Didn't the lieutenant say that the Turks always say good things? 'My Lord Dobó never says anything good. He doesn't even want to pay siege money.'"

"He's lying," Hegedüs repeated.

The second man was brought in.

"Why were you at the tank?"

"We were waiting for the Turks," he said sadly. "The lieutenant sir said that sooner or later, the castle would fall into Turkish hands; that it would be better for money than blood. Certainly we would die if we do not surrender the castle."

Dobó had the third man brought in.

"I don't know anything," he stammered. "I was only assigned to the well, but why I don't know."

"Didn't Lieutenant Hegedüs say that it would be good to come to an understanding with the Turks?"

"Yes, he said that."

"When did he first say that?"

"The evening after the great assault."

"And how did he say that?"

"Well, he said it like, well, oh hell ... we're few, they are many, and that, well, the other castles couldn't hold out, even though the Turks were split in two."

"Did Lieutenant Hegedüs say something about bribes?"

"He spoke. He said we should get double mercenary pay."

"What did he say about surrendering the castle?"

"What the hell ... what the hell. He says the Turks will get it anyway, so it is better if they pay us instead of hanging our necks."

"And what did his company say back to him?"

"Nothing. We were only talking by the fire while the Turks were shouting."

"No one shouted anything back to them?"

"No. Only the lieutenant spoke to them at night."

"How did he talk with them?"

"Through a crack in the Old Gate. He went there three times to talk with them."

"With Turks?"

"With Turks."

"What did he say when he returned?"

"That the Turks would allow everyone to leave without harm. No one would be cut down. Those from Kassa would get ten gold pieces each. And that the two pashas would send a sealed letter with the promises."

"How many among you men heard this?"

"Maybe ten."

"Why didn't you report this to me? Didn't you take an oath not to discuss anything about surrender?"

The man was silent.

Dobó continued. "Wasn't it your duty to immediately report what the lieutenant said?!"

"We didn't dare."

"So. You decided to play the castle into Turkish hands. Who else agreed to this?"

The man said seven more names. Then he began making excuses. "We, my noble captain sir, we did not agree. We only obeyed. Only the lieutenant spoke and he gave us orders."

The wall crashed from the impact of a cannonball. The armor hanging on bars rattled. Patches of plaster fell from the walls onto the floor.

Dobo looked at the judges. "Anyone have any questions?"

The judges sat at the table almost frozen. Finally the judge who was a regular soldier asked, "Did the ten men agree that the Turks should have the castle?"

The man, pale, shrugged his shoulders. "A private can only do what his officer wants."

There were no more questions.

"There's still the Turk," Dobó said. "Bring him in."

The Turk bowed three times before reaching the table. There he remained bowed. Arms folded over his chest.

"What's your name?" Dobó asked.

"Yusuf."

"Yusuf, or József in Hungarian. Stand up straight!"

The Turk straightened up. He was an *akinji* about thirty years old. Squat, muscular man. His nose was flat and a scar on his head showed that he had already been in battle.

Replying to questions, he said that he had lived in Hungary for ten years and that he had been by the wall when Hegedüs spoke through the gap: "Hey, Turks! Who knows Hungarian?"

"He's lying," Hegedüs growled. "Zoltay was always talking with the Turks."

"Me?!" Zoltay growled.

"You certainly did. Whenever there is an assault, you always yell at them."

Zoltay jumped up from his chair furious. "I'm asking for an investigation," he said. "I can't sit as a judge here anymore. It's true that I always curse when I strike. But that's just cursing. That's not a crime! What slander is this?!"

Dobó hushed him. "We all know your habit, and no one has any issue with you about it. But because you were angry with the accused, we excuse you from being a judge."

Zoltay bowed and left.

Dobo looked at the Turk again.

In broken Hungarian, the Turk described how Hegedüs talked to an agha by the Old Gate and then to Arslan Bey. He asked the bey for his word of honor and a hundred gold coins. He said he would let the entire army into the castle at night. They only had to dig in front of the gate where they used to beat on the big copper drum. He (pointing to Hegedüs) said he had been walking by the water tank one night and discovered a tunnel, which had collapsed by the gate. Standing by the collapse, he heard the copper drum above his head, and he heard the soldiers stepping, so there was no need to dig much. He would be waiting for them at twelve o'clock at night. But they also have to agree not to harm the Kassa soldiers at the Old Gate. They agreed. At midnight, Hegedüs was leading them with a lantern. There was a mixed group of janissaries, *azabs* and *piyads*. Three thousand set out for the tunnel. The rest of the army, God knows how many thousands were waiting for the two gates to open. But what happened was that Hegedüs's lantern hit the wall by the corner of the tank and went out. He continued to lead in the dark. He knew the way, but the edge of the big tank was narrow. He managed well in the darkness, but the lead soldiers, following on the heels of each other, began falling into the water.

"Do you know anything," asked Dobó, "about a dervish having kidnapped one of our lieutenants' sons?"

"I know," the Turk replied. "For the last two weeks they've been looking for the child in every tent. The bey is looking for him. He was stolen from him, or he escaped on the third day after arriving here."

Dobó looked at Hegedüs. "Miserable traitor!" he said.

Hegedüs fell to his knees. "Have mercy! Have mercy on me!" he shouted. "I was wrong, I lost my mind."

"Do you admit that you wanted to deliver the castle into the hands of the enemy?"

"I confess."

The trial did not last more than an hour.

By the next hour, Lieutenant Hegedüs was already in the market square of the castle, hanging by the neck. Fügedy announced to the people of the castle. "This is how every man dies, whether an ordinary man or an officer, who breaks his oath and wants to deliver the castle into the hands of the Turks!"

The three accomplices were made to stand under the gallows. Their ears were cut off. The other seven were put in chains and made to work.

The Turk was thrown out of the castle from the high western wall, falling on his neck among his comrades.

The people of the castle could see that Dobó was not someone to trifle with.

8

You are a force stronger than all other forces: motherly love! Sunlight dressed in a human body! You are a holy flame coming from the heart of God, a strong weakness unafraid of death!

You have left your secure shelter, your soft pillows, and all your treasures in order to disguise yourself and cross a forest of death to find your lost loved ones! You who have descended into the depths of the earth, you who with your weak arms want to break through walls that have resisted a hundred thousand armed, shrieking beasts! You who do not know the meaning of impossible when it comes to the ones you love, when you have to suffer together, when you may have to die together. You, the heart of a mother, I admire!

— § —

For two nights and two days they dug through collapsed sections of the tunnel in the damp cold under weakened vaults. In some places, only a few steps of fill had to be dug out. They worked their way through in about an hour's work. But in some places they had to move and pile large stones, and neither a weak female arm nor the underdeveloped arms of a fifteen-year-old young man were accustomed to such work.

On the evening of the third of October, when the camp had fallen asleep, they gathered together all their food.

By their calculations, they were only a hundred steps away from the castle. They hoped they wouldn't have to return. And they worked all night.

Underground they did not know when the sun rose or set. All night long they could hear a rumbling noise. It was the horses carrying earth and brush. They heard the sounds of cannons and mortars being fired from the castle. They thought, digging underground, that there was a night assault, which made them even more eager to get inside.

However, it was dawn, and the sun was rising behind Borsod Hill. The servants of the Turkish horse-trader, seeing no one around the tent, looked inside. They were surprised to see that the millstone had been moved, its wide hole facing them. As the cavalry once again was gathering brush and branches everywhere, the trader rushed to a *deli* agha and reported, almost shaking with joy. "Sir! I will deliver the castle into the hands of the army. I discovered a tunnel last night!"

Numerous *delis, akinjis, beshlis, gönüllüs* and *gurebas* dropped underbrush and let their horses roam free. Whistles and trumpets ordered assembly. All kinds of soldiers mixed, shuffled, rumbled, shuddered, and pushed into the entrance, the throat of the abyss.

The trader led them with a torch.

— § —

Meanwhile, the two poor souls were struggling forward, crouching soaked, and moving stones and rubble.

In one place, the tunnel again began sloping. The stones were dry there and the tunnel widened. They reached a large damp triangular shaped underground room.

"We have to be under the castle moat," said Miklós.

However, the two corners of the room were blocked with rubble. Which of the two is the way?

One pile of rubble was saddle shaped. On its top was a small opening, the size of a fist. The other pile had a narrow opening on the side.

"Here the tunnels split," said Miklós. "Now the question is, where to dig."

He stepped over the stones and held his candle to the hole. The flame fluttered. He also tried the other opening on the side. The flame just stood there.

He pinned the candle to the side of his cap and grabbed the large rock on top. Éva helped. The rock rolled over the other stones.

"One more!" said Miklós. They both strained again. That rock would not give way.

"We need to pull out the smaller stones from under it."

He took the spade and used it to loosen the rubble under the rock. Then they grabbed it again. The rock moved a little.

Miklós breathed heavily and wiped his face. "I'm tired," he said wearily.

"Let's rest," Éva said.

They sat down on a rock. Miklós lay down and in that same moment, fell asleep.

Éva herself was dazed and dead tired. Her clothes were wet, she was covered with mud up to her knees, and her hands were bloody. Her hair had become disheveled; some hung over her cloak; some stuck to the perspiration on her neck.

She grabbed the candle and looked into the two cavities. Both showed an open tunnel.

"We'll rest a little," she said, fixing the candle to a stone, "but I'm not going to sleep, no. I'll just rest."

And as she leaned back, she heard a low rattling sound. Her eyebrows frowned in the darkness. Was the rattling coming from above or below?

She saw a red beam of light in the depths of the tunnel.

"Miklós!" screamed Éva. She shook the boy awake. "They're coming!" The boy opened his eyelids sleepily. "They're coming!" Éva repeated desperately.

He reached for his sword. He found only the scabbard. He had left it by an earlier pile of rubble. He had been using it as a lever to move rocks.

The short *yataghan* swords in his belt, even his pocket knife, had all been broken from digging. They had nothing.

The light was getting closer and closer.

Éva summoned all her strength to move that rock. Miklós did the same. Their candle had gone out. The rock moved but did not let go.

They watched with frightened terror as the trader holding the torch emerged from the darkness, beside him the large agha with long, drooping mustache, scimitars glittering in his belt.

In the following minutes, hands held them and they were captives.

But the agha looked at the work they had begun and made a quick decision. "Take the torch, kid," he told Miklós. "You already know the way here."

Miklós did not understand the words, but he understood the torch pressed into his hand.

It took only a minute for the soldiers to pull down the heavy rocks. The tunnel was wide enough for two people. By now, the chamber was full of armed soldiers.

"You're going to lead," said the agha to Miklós. "And the other one," he continued looking at Éva, "stays here. If you lead us badly, I'll give that woman to the soldiers."

A janissary translated his words.

Éva closed her eyes.

The agha looked back. "A *deli* to guard her." And he pushed Miklós to go ahead.

The *deli* stood next to Éva. The rest took off. However, as the agha has not said which *deli* to guard her, the *deli* quickly passed on the job to the next *deli*. "You guard her!"

He also around for a while, but perhaps it occurred to him that the first soldiers to enter the castle would become immensely noble lords. He offered the prisoner to a *müsellem*.

"I'm not guarding her," replied the *müsellem*. He stepped aside.

The *deli* was poisoned with anger.

"I'll guard her, just go," said a small *azab* in a fur cap.

He pulled out his scimitar. The woman stood beside him.

Éva leaned back against the wall, dead tired. Large numbers of soldiers filed by her headed towards the castle. They were filthy, dressed in all sorts of uniforms, and smelling of gunpowder and onions. Everyone carried a naked sword in his hand, and their eyes all filled with hopes of victory.

Sometimes a torch came and lit in front of a group. Sometimes they only came in the dark. Weapons on them rattled and clanged. One of them carried a wide red flag on his shoulder.

Suddenly, a deep, thundering sound is heard, as if the sky was crashing into the earth. From the entrance of the chamber backwards, the long tunnel collapses. The rumbling sound continues for minutes, stones rolling and falling. No one else can follow those who had already rushed ahead.

From the direction of the fall, dull wails and screaming. In the other direction, the receding sounds of weapons rattling.

The woman's guard speaks Hungarian. "Don't be afraid!" He held her hand. "Who are you?"

She couldn't speak.

"Hungarian?"

She nodded.

"Come on," said the *azab*. "The tunnels here go in two directions. If I can open the other tunnel, we'll be free. But if it also collapses here ..."

Éva felt the flow of life return in her veins. "Who are you, your grace?" she asked as she regained her senses.

"My name is Varsányi. I'm on your side." He pulled steel and flint out of his belt and a little tinder. The tinder was soon burning. Fragrant smoke mingled in the stifling air of the tunnel. He held it to a wax candle and blew on it. The candle burst into flames. The room was again flooded with light.

"Hold this candle, young sister."

He stepped over to the rubble on the left and loosened the stones with a couple of jerks.

He was a small man, but strong. The big rocks rolled one after another, outward and inward. Soon enough, he had made an opening big enough for a man to pass through.

He took the candle from the lady and went ahead. He held the candle in front. He moved so quickly that she could barely keep up.

The tunnel was more open, but they were still heading downhill.

Once Varsányi turned around. "Who are you, your grace? Perhaps you come from the king?"

"That's it," Éva replied, as if she were talking in a dream.

"Are we getting an army?"

"I don't know."

"Well, it doesn't matter. If only I knew where we were. We must hurry to overtake the Turks."

The tunnel headed upwards. They could see niches here and there in the sides. The stones there were brown, and moisture collected on them glistened in the light.

"We're are inside the castle," Varsányi said. "We're probably almost near the water tank."

The passage was blocked by pile of white plaster. They could smell lime from it.

Varsányi swore. "Puh! A purgatory in this miserable world!"

"What's that?"

"Nothing, maybe. I'll climb ahead. Hold the candle."

He crawled onto the pile. He climbed over. Éva passed him the candle.

Varsányi was inside. He took the candle and hummed. Then he helped Éva slip through the opening and stand up.

They were inside a wide and whitened chamber. From above, they heard a funereal chant: *In paradisum deducant te angeli* (May angels lead you to paradise). From high above, they could see faint daylight.

The chamber was filled with white coffins stacked on top of each other, wet lime spread all around. Lime had dried on the edges of the coffins. Off to one side, beside the coffins, a half-leaning, shirtless, thin, dead body with a mustache stared out from the limestone. Daylight from above illuminated his face. A rope hung around his neck.

Varsányi stared at that dead body. Then he looked back.

Éva was lying on the ground behind him, passed out.

— § —

During this time, the boy was leading the Turkish army.

At first he was frozen in fear, but then he thought that if they snuck out inside the castle, he would shout.

This thought encouraged him. He carried the torch without hesitation, either before or next to the agha.

Soon they were also moving upwards. There were no obstructions until they reached a wall made of the same sandstone used everywhere in Eger. The fresh plaster indicated it had been built recently.

"Tear it down!" ordered the agha.

The plaster soon fell under the iron of scimitars and spears. Only the first two or three rocks were difficult to move, the rest followed more easily, moved by the power of strong hands.

But still, they had to work for over an hour.

By the time the opening had become large enough for a man to pass through, the agha made Miklós go ahead.

They reached a spacious cellar. Barrels and barrels everywhere. The strange thing was that the place was more like a room than a cellar. There was a large, tattered painting on the wall and a round tub underneath. Two heads could be seen in the painting. One with a bearded, sad face. The other, the face of a sad young man leaning on the bearded man's chest. A circle of light above their heads. Under the young man's head, the wall was white behind the torn canvas.

"Weapons ready!" said the agha softly to those behind him. "Gather quietly. Silence! Silence ... When we open the doors, you must not yell! If we don't see anybody, we will wait for those coming behind us! The flag bearers should immediately jump on the walls."

As more and more men gathered around him, he continued. "We'll be rushing towards the gate. No mercy! First we have to get the guards and open the gates. Do you understand?"

"We understand," the soldiers murmured in response.

The agha stepped forward and saw the big tub of gunpowder in front of the iron door. He was astonished.

They were in the gunpowder chamber. There was no wine in the barrels, only gunpowder.

But Miklós already knew where they were.

As the agha stood by the large tub, Miklós turned back. He glanced across the mass of armed soldiers. His face was pale and exalted. He lifted the burning torch and slammed it into the gunpowder.

9

When the coffin was lowered, Varsányi shouted up to the people, "Hey, people!"

Crying faces appeared in the doorway of the crypt. One with a head of hair, the other in a rusty, ornate helmet, strapped to his chin.

Varsányi shouted again. "I'm here, Varsányi! Pull me up!"

He lifted and carried Éva in his arms and stepped over coffins and coffins to reach the ropes. He pulled the two ropes together and sat on the knot. People pulled them up.

Only two priests and two peasants with ropes were by the entrance to the crypt. They stared at Éva, lying as if dead on the grass where Varsányi had let her down.

"Bring water," Varsányi told the peasants.

At that moment, a red flame shot out from Church Tower. It soared up into the sky, and black planks, beams, stones, pieces of wood, and people were flying in it.

The castle was shaken in such a way that everyone was deaf and threw themselves to the ground.

— § —

Rocks, blood, weapons, wood and stone powder fell from the air. The explosion was followed by a silence like the dead that lasted for minutes.

Dead silence in the castle and outside the castle, including in the Turkish camp.

Everyone looked dazed.

Has the sky fallen? Has the earth opened up to engulf the world in a terrible, hellfire of doom? Nobody understood.

"Turkish trick!" That was all anyone in the castle could think.

"The castle is lost!" That was the only feeling inside hearts, already stunned from the explosion, that froze like stone.

Gergely was tying up pots filled with gunpowder below Sándor Bastion. The blast of air from the explosion threw him against the shields that had been leaning against the wall.

As he looked up, the red pillar of fire erupted upwards into the sky, in it a black millstone surrounded by men on their backs falling down, and a human leg.

He had enough presence to jump under a bastion vault, but for a minute, he too was also deafened and stunned, staring vacantly.

The people of the castle began stirring over the next moments. People running here and there, soldiers waving their weapons, wailing women, dresses torn, and maddened horses everywhere.

Down in the Turkish camp there was triumphant shouting, lifting of siege ladders, and waves of thousands of armed men running towards the castle.

Cries of "We're finished!" sounded everywhere in the castle.

Women grabbed their children and ran on the soot covered cobblestones, fallen beams, and smoldering embers. Everyone fled, and no one knew where.

Dense black snow was falling from the air. It was so dense that one could not see ten feet through it. It was ash. It covered everything in the castle, as if it was in mourning.

Corpses and bleeding bodies lay here and there on the scattered rubble and beams.

Dobó, bareheaded, pulled his horse, galloped towards the blast and ordered the soldiers to the wall. "Nothing happened!" he shouted right and left. "There were only twenty-four tons of gunpowder in the sacristy!"

The officers all mounted horses, and repeated the words of the Dobó to calm the people everywhere. "Everyone back in place! Just twenty-four tons of gunpowder ..."

Mekcsey was furious. He picked up a broken spear shaft and used it to hit stunned and disobedient soldiers. "Hold your weapons, damn you! On the walls!" He jumped off his horse, grabbed an eight-foot lance, and ran to the top of the wall. "After me, men! Follow me whoever is a man!"

Turks climbing the wall were greeted with long line of fire. Soldiers without any leaders ran from the inner square to the top of the wall and worked with mace, sword, lance, and pickaxe.

The Turks were similarly disorganized, pushing each other back and forth. There was just as much confusion outside the walls as inside the castle. Most of them ran towards the site of the explosion.

Gergely saw from his bastion how the mixed colors of Turks flowed in waves over gray ash towards Church Tower. "Stay here!" he shouted to Zoltay, and sword drawn, he ran to Church Tower.

On the way he ran past eight cauldrons cooking soup. It was lunch for the soldiers to be relieved at noon. Meat chopped into small pieces was steaming and rolling in its juices. Gergely pushed a carrying pole through the handles of one of the cauldrons and shouted to a peasant carrying bowls. "Grab this! You there, bring the rest to up to the bastion!"

When they got to the top of the wall, he poured the boiling soup onto the Turks climbing up on their ladders.

— § —

When Varsányi recovered after the explosion, he saw Éva lying on the ground before him. The two shirtless priests rushed to the walls and the two peasants, presumably, to the cannons.

Varsányi lifted the lady over his shoulder like a sack and carried her to the palace. He was thinking that if she was a royal courier, that was where she belonged. He left her in the care of Land Balogh who sprinkled water over her.

— § —

Only after the assault had been beaten back could the defenders assess the damage caused by the explosion.

The right side of Church Bastion, together with the sacristy, was a black, open cavern. The castle wall there, with its night-time construction, had collapsed. Only wreckage remained of the two dry mills that had worked there. Thirty beef cattle, ready for the butcher, had been standing on one the side of the sacristy. They lay dead in their blood.

Eight men on watch were found torn to pieces. A lieutenant had also been killed: Pál Nagy who had been sent by György Báthory from Erdőd Castle.

Many soldiers in the vicinity were wounded. Some flying debris had stuck a warrior named Gergely Horváth, severing his arm from his shoulder. That same day he died and his body was lowered into the crypt with the other coffins.

People in the castle only really began to regain their senses after it became obvious that the Turks had been beaten back and would not be breaking into the castle.

"God is with us!" shouted Dobó, stroking his hair back and looking at the sky. "Trust in God, Oh warriors!"

In fact, the assault had been beaten back by the soup. The Turks were accustomed to fire, swords, and lances, but not boiling soup.

As soon as the boiling paprika juice poured down the first ladder, men were swept off as if by a broom. At the bottom of the ladder, the swarm of soldiers also jumped. Some got their hands scalded, others their necks or faces. With shields over their heads, they cleared out and ran away from under the walls.

People inside the castle breathed more easily.

Dobó called the millers and carpenters. "Use what's left of the two mills and quickly piece one together so we can crush powder. If you need any wood part, the carpenters have to carve it immediately!"

He looked around. "Where's the steward?"

A sooty black figure emerged from the walls of the monastery. Blowing soot off his mustache and tapping it off his beard, he stood in front of Dobó. It was old Sukán.

"Uncle Sukán," Dobó said, "bring me some saltpeter, sulfur and charcoal from the cellar. As soon as the mill is completed, the millers will break the gunpowder."

It was only then that he thought that maybe he should wash himself. He looked like a chimney sweep.

— § —

A sooty man sat by the palace door. He was half dressed in Turkish clothes. He had a large piece of baked pumpkin in his hand. He was eating it with a spoon.

As soon as he saw Dobó, he got up.

"Is that you, Varsányi?"

"It's me, my lord."

"What news did you bring?"

"I brought a royal messenger, my lord, to the castle. She is a woman type."

Dobó immediately ran inside to Lady Balogh. "Where's the messenger?" he asked.

The lady was sitting beside Pető's bed. She was lining a helmet with red silk, her son's helmet.

"Messenger?" she asked staring. "Only one woman came."

"Well then, where's that woman?"

Lady Balogh opened the door to the next room and closed the door again. "She's asleep," she said, "so don't bother her. She really is exhausted, poor thing."

Dobó opened the door. Éva was lying in bed — a white, clean bed. Only her head was visible, her pale face was half buried in a pillow, her hair all in disarray. Dobó stared at the suffering, deathly pale woman's face. He did not know her. He pulled back and closed the door.

"Did she bring any kind of letter?"

"No."

"I'd like to see this woman's clothes. Who is this woman?"

Lady Balogh shrugged, then gave Dobó an imploring look. She asked us not to ask for her name. She is afraid that your grace may not be happy to see her."

"I want that woman's clothes!"

Lady Balogh lifted a muddy, lime-stained Turkish military outfit from the hallway. Small, sulfur-yellow boots with spurs on them. In her belt were fifty some Hungarian gold pieces, a scabbard, and two broken Turkish *yataghan* long knives.

"Feel the pockets." There was paper in one of his pockets.

"That's it," said Dobó. Using his sooty hands, he opened the folded parchment paper. It was the drawing of the castle.

There was nothing else in the pockets except a handkerchief and a pair of crumpled gloves. They also felt and cut open the seams of her clothes. The boots were also cut open.

Nothing.

"Does she have anything with her in bed?"

"No," replied Lady Balogh. "I gave the poor little one the shirt she's wearing. Oh, how she was worn out ... She must not have had any sleep for a very long time. She came underground, through the Way of the Dead.

Dobó called Varsányi inside.

"You said messenger."

"That's what I think."

"Didn't she say clearly?"

"We didn't talk, my lord. We came through the tunnel, all but running."

"What tunnel?"

"Through the cemetery."

"So there's a tunnel there?"

"Not any more, my lord."

"Do the Turks have food?"

"There are some ten or twenty carts of flour and one or two flocks of sheep. God knows where they get it! Their rice is long gone."

"So they are not hungry yet?"

"So far, not really."

"What else do you know about the camp?"

"Only that they are digging a mine from the top of King's Seat."

"To the castle?"

"Certainly, because they have the sappers working."

"Why hadn't you come in? You should have brought news of the brush gathering."

"It wasn't possible. They stationed the strongest janissaries in front of the gates, and I had no janissary outfit. It would have been suspicious had I tried to walk through them."

"Well, for now, stay in the castle. Report to lord Gergely Bornemissza and tell him where the mine is being dug. Then come back and remain near the palace."

The writing was still in his hands.

He called Mekcsey. "Take this drawing," he said to him. "It shows underground tunnels. I had no idea there was such a drawing anywhere in this world. Immediately call the stone masons and block them if any is still in place. But first, you have to erect a brick wall at the tunnel by the cemetery pit."

He handed a few assignments to the two pages, then went for a bath. After his bath, he put on fresh clothes, buckled on his greaves, and lay down on a bench covered with bear skin.

This was how he always slept, whether in daylight or at night, when fatigue compelled him, for an hour or two. Soldiers in the castle claimed he never slept.

10

Dobó could only talk to Éva in the evening.

Lady Bornemissza had already risen. She was dressed in a light housecoat. She must have picked something to wear from the women's clothes that had been plundered by her husband in that first raid. There were no buyers for those women's clothes at the auction, so they were hung in an empty room in the palace. They could be given to the poor after the siege.

Dobó talked with her over dinner. "Who are you, your grace?" Those were his first words to her. Because he saw that she was a lady.

Page Balázs stood behind Dobó. Lady Balogh was also walking about the room. She added red wine to the sheep roast. She lit one more candle beside the two wax candles already burning.

"I don't know if I can tell you any other way than among only four eyes," Éva replied. "Not because of Lady Balogh, but because I don't know if the lord captain would allow my name to be known by others."

Dobó waved the pages away. Lady Balogh also left.

Éva said, "I am the wife of Gergely Bornemissza."

The knife dropped out of Dobó's hand.

Éva continued, worried. " I know that in such a place, in such work, it is not good to have a woman present. But believe me, your grace, I am not going to try to pull my husband away from this battle."

"Please sit down," Dobó said. "Forgive me for receiving you while eating. Please join me."

But these were only cold words.

"Thank you," replied Éva.

She sat down wearily. They were quiet for a few minutes. Then Dobó spoke. "Does Gergely know that you are here?"

"No. And surely it's good that he doesn't know."

"Well, my young sister," Dobó said a little more warmly, "it was good for your grace to keep quiet about your name. Gergely must not know that your grace is here. In this I am adamant. The siege cannot last long. The rescue army must arrive. Why did your grace come here?"

Tears in Éva's eyes. "My child ..."

"Was he really kidnapped?"

"Yes."

"And the ring?"

"Here it is," Éva replied, pulling a cord hanging around her neck.

Dobó looked at the ring. He drank a sip of wine and got up. "How can your grace assure me that you will not talk to Gergely?"

"I will obey all your orders, my captain sir. I know that ..."

"Your grace, do you understand why it's forbidden to talk to Gergely?"

"I can imagine."

"Gergely is the intellect of this castle. His mind should not be distracted from defending the castle, even for a minute. Who else here can recognize you?"

"Mekcsey, Fügedy, Zoltay. My father is here. Uncle Bálint, and our priest."

"You must not show yourself outside Lady Balogh's rooms. Promise me this on your honor."

"I promise."

"Swear!"

"I swear!"

"In turn, I promise I will do everything I can to find your child. Give me the talisman."

Éva held it out.

Dobó strapped on his helmet, and, before he pulled on his gloves, he held out his hand to the lady. "Forgive me for being so blunt. It can't be any other way. Look around here in my wife's rooms. What she left here is yours."

"One more word," said Éva. "What should I tell Lady Balogh about who I am?"

"Tell her what you want, just make sure Gergely doesn't find out."

"He won't know."

Dobó said his goodbye, stepped out the door, and called for his horse.

— § —

Towards evening a strong wind picked up. It blew ash and soot away from the castle.

Dobó called the stone masons and peasants to the rubble that the explosion had left behind. "Gather the stones lying around. Build a wall in such a way that you are always protected from shots."

He went up to the Baba cannon, sat down on the cannon, and wrote with lead on a piece of paper:

Hear me, dervish bey! As soon as you find the Bornemissza child, fly the blue-red flag on the fir tree by the stream to the north of the castle. An imprint of your ring is on this letter. The child can be brought under a white flag. Not only will I give you the ring for the boy, but also the captive Turkish boy with us.

He called Mekcsey. He covered the writing with his hand and said to him, "Sign your name, please."

Mekcsey signed it without saying a word. Balázs was ready with the wax and candle. Dobó leaned against the cannon and melted a drop of wax by Mekcsey's signature. Mekcsey stamped his ring on the seal, then without asking who or why, hurried back to his work.

Dobó folded the letter and sealed it with the Ottoman ring. The crescent moon and stars were clearly visible on the seal.

He called Varsányi. "My friend Varsányi," he said bluntly. "Now I know why you're not coming to the castle. Why should you come when we always send you back? Do you know the dervish bey?"

"Like the heel of my boots," Varsányi replied cheerfully.

"Well, take this letter. Put it in his tent, his clothes, or his drinking cup. Just leave it however you can so he can find it."

"It will be done, my lord."

"Then go to Szarvaskő and wait for Miklós Vas. He has to be coming by now."

"And how do I get back inside the castle?"

"There will be a string hanging on the right side of the gate every night. Pull it out. Jerk it. The sentries will respond to the bell and let you in."

Varsányi wrapped the letter in a cloth and tucked it by his chest.

Cannonballs crashed into Sándor Bastion. Dobó saw that there was confusion. Soldiers were in disorder and jumping down from the bastion.

The Turks somehow became aware of a small gate that connected the outer castle wall with the inner. (The passage between the two walls was like the pin of a buckle.) Two tall ladders were set up on King's Seat: an upside-down letter "V." A Turkish man ran up to the top. He could see warriors coming in and out of the small gate. They aimed the cannons positioned on King's Seat and bombarded the gate heavily.

In just under an hour, there were numerous Hungarian casualties around the gate area; some five fell down dead.

"Planks up!" cried Dobó. "Put up the planks!"

But they lifted the planks in vain. The Turkish cannons were already aimed and the boards did little to fend off the cannonballs.

"This will cost me a hundredweight of gunpowder!" grumbled Dobó. "And at a bad time!"

Gergely came running from the corner tower. "Captain sir," he said, "the gate can't withstand this. My best soldiers are being hit!"

"We will do something," Dobó replied. He continued quietly. "Wait until they begin reloading."

Cannonballs fell on the gate like a downpour.

"Give me permission to open a gap in the wall, or dig underneath."

"You don't have to ask for special permission, Gergely. Do it!"

Gergely had a hole cut into the wall next to the gate and passed his soldiers through it.

And the Turks continued to fire so many cannonballs into the empty gate that they looked like they could have been swept aside with a broom.

— § —

At night the Turks once again piled earth and branches.

The moon lit them to some extent. Shots were fired at them from the castle.

"Don't shoot!" Dobó said.

As the noise from inside the castle grew quiet, the sound of Turks roaring, beating and crackling grew. They were multiplying.

Dobó assigned all of his soldiers with guns to the four breaches. One row lying prone, another behind kneeling. Behind, a third row standing, leaning forward. They put out the lanterns.

The Turks were gathering in greater numbers. They carried small hand lamps to do their work. They were more and more exposed. They continued building up the mound. Their turbans got higher and closer.

They were still piling fill by the breach when Dobó shouted the command to fire.

Screaming and confusion followed the shots. Companies running in a frenzy proved that the shots did not fall in vain. A few *tüfekchis* shot back, but hit no one. They continued their work only at the bottom of the wall, carefully and always covering themselves.

11

The mill rumbled day and night. Fresh gunpowder sparkled black in the tub. The confidence of the people in the castle returned.

The Turks fired a new barrage, and it had barely begun when shots from three *zarbuza* siege guns knocked down the provost's house. The new target was the northwest tower. An assault on that side would be difficult, but perhaps they simply wanted to generally weaken the castle.

Big black cannonballs flew towards the tower like eagles.

The soldiers' barracks were in the line of fire. A row of low houses. Everybody had their backs leaning against the castle wall. Cannonballs fell on the barracks from the cannons that were not loaded with enough gunpowder.

The western side of the palace began to break. A terrified Lady Balogh rushed into the room where she had made Dobó's bed.

The captain sat beside the bed. Dressed in iron, just as he was when he walked around the castle. Only this time, he was not wearing his helmet. His hands resting on the arms of his chair, he was sleeping sweetly. A candle burned before him. Above his head hung an oil painting, dull from age: King St. István offering his crown to Mother Mary. It had been salvaged from the church when it had been converted into a bastion, and it had become so dull and brown that the eyes of the figures looked like brown spots.

Dobó used to sleep there.

He had just returned home at dawn that day. Perhaps he was waiting for a surprise assault that morning because he had not undressed.

They were firing at the side of the castle where he was sleeping. The cannonballs shook the house so the beams cracked. One wall of the room had a crack four fingers wide. You could see through it to the palisade beyond.

"Captain sir!" screamed Lady Balogh. Plaster fell on his head from another shot. She ran to the captain and shook him.

"Well, what is it?" said Dobó with a shiver.

"They're firing at the palace! Wake up, for God's sake."

Dobó looked around. He saw the crack. He got up.

"Please have my bed taken down," he said, "to one of the lower rooms close to the door. I'll be back soon."

The *I'll be back soon* was such a frequent but never fulfilled statement from Dobó that Lady Balogh smiled, even in the middle of that danger. "At least give me enough time for me to make some mulled wine."

"That will be good. Thank you," Dobó replied, shaking plaster powder from his hair. "My stomach is a little faint. I'd like it with a few cloves."

"Where should I send it?"

"I'll jump in for it."

"You won't jump in, captain sir. I will send it out with my son."

There was always a horse saddled in front of the door, and beside that horse, one or the other page with his little horse. Dobó pivoted on a stirrup, mounted, and set off to inspect around the castle.

On the city side of the castle, some undressed soldiers were running out from the small houses that served as barracks. They carried outer-clothes and weapons over their shoulders or under their arms. Some had their trousers around their necks. They were cursing like a hailstorm.

"Go to the monastery," Dobó said. "They aren't firing there."

Mekcsey was running through the market square with another group of men. The soldiers carried shovels, hoes and pickaxes. Mekcsey was carrying a big musket. When he saw Dobó, he lifted up his gun and gestured. Dobó galloped over.

"They're digging a mine from King's Seat," Mekcsey reported. "We're going against them."

"Good," Dobó replied. "Well, just lead them to their work. Let them dig. Then find me immediately."

He went to Bolyky Bastion. At the bottom of it, beside the stables, were five people. Helmets on their heads. Their faces reflected red from the fire. They were making small straw wreaths. Next to them, pitch was cooking in cauldrons.

On the bastion, he saw Gergely leaning over a drum. He was watching peas. He saw Dobó and stood up. "The Turks are mining. We've already noticed one today. Mekcsey went after them himself."

"I know," Dobó replied.

"The skins of the drums are all limp and useless, but the movement of the water gives them away."

Dobó stood at the palisade and looked out an opening. The Turks had raised the mound in front of the breach by about another eight feet. Just then some dervishes were using two lances to carry a dead *akinji* from the brushwood. He had been killed during the previous night's volleys.

Ditches, planks and palisades facing the walls could be seen everywhere. The Turks also covered themselves.

"They're planning something again," Dobó said. "The *yasauls* and janissaries are nowhere to be seen."

That was when Mekcsey reached the bastion. "They're digging," he reported briefly.

It was obvious on his face that he had not slept that night. He was red-eyed, colorless and disheveled. The shoulders of his coat were covered with lime and mud. Certainly he had been helping the masons set up beams and pilings.

"My fellow captain," Dobó said in a cold, reproachful tone, "you again want to go into the mine by yourself! Go to sleep immediately!"

The page Balázs climbed up the stairs. He carried a silver tray with a silver cup on it. The cup steamed white in the cold air of dawn.

Mekcsey saluted and headed down. Dobó spoke in a changed, more gentle tone. "Pista!"

Mekcsey turned.

"Take this cup from Balazs and drink it, my dear young brother."

12

The next night they learned what the janissaries had been doing that day.

Well, they were constructing something like the canopies that priests use over their holy things in processions. But the tops of the Turks' canopies were made of strong boards, held up by four poles that were four lances.

Under such moving roofs, the earth and branches were carried from day to night.

In those days, these kinds of protective canopies were called *targets* in Hungarian.

By afternoon, sleep had relieved the fatigue of the senior officers. Most of them slept in the afternoon, because assaults could only be expected in the mornings, and that morning the Turkish intentions for that day had become known. At night they were on their feet again, and half of the garrison rested. Dobó and Mekcsey agreed not to set a specific time for each to sleep, but as soon as one felt awake, the other immediately rested.

Actually, neither really slept except an hour here and there on a bastion or in a trench, sometimes two in the afternoon.

Hey, the gunners were being driven crazy because the *targets* covered and hid the many Turks underneath. The Turks had collected whatever planks had remained in the city's houses and courtyards. They realized that they could not succeed unless they also raised a wall.

The fill by Sándor Bastion had gotten so high that it was near the breach, that is, it nearly reached the bottom of the castle wall where it had been destroyed by cannonballs.

The *targets* covered the Turks, the branches and brush covered the heads pushing their way up. Twenty gunners and a loaded mortar were stationed at all times to guard the breach. More weapons were ready on the walls. But in vain. The gloom of darkness, like a blanket, also covered the Turks as they worked at night.

Gergely himself spent most of his guard duty time at that breach.

Suddenly some twenty Turks appeared moving forward. Each had a bundle of vines on his head.

Gergely called down from the wall. "Gasparics!"

"Here," replies a man's voice.

"Aren't your fingers itchy?"

"And how, bless it! Let's let one loose on them, lieutenant sir."

"Let these pagan creations have it! Just make sure you jump back inside as soon as you cut one down."

"I understand, lieutenant sir."

The mason and other workers were laboring on the breach, but the gap was so big that even a cart could pass through.

Upon Gergely's word, Gasparics jumps out and spears a Turk armed with *yataghans*. He jumps back inside.

The Turk collapses. The rest carry on.

Seeing Gasparics' heroic act, three men jump out the gap. Their spears take out the same number of Turks. They jump back again.

The Turks curse for a moment, confused. But more Turks are moving up from below.

Now ten men are jumping into the gap, some with swords, some with spears. They cut and spear the Turks as they carry fill. Then they jump back inside and others jump into the gap, one after the other.

The Turks drop the fill, and thirty go after three men left in the gap.

Gergely has a volley fired from the wall. The Turks fall over each other, but a corporal named Kálmán returns with a deep lance wound in his chest.

"You also shoot" shouts Gergely.

Gunners stationed by the side of the breach fire like lightning. The remaining Turks fall dead.

The flash from the volley reveals some forty Turks lying in blood before the gap. A new company of Turks jump up and rush into the gap with swords and lances.

"Shoot!" Gergely shouts to those standing on the wall.

That is when Dobó arrives.

Kálmán is lying on his back, bleeding in front of the gap. A janissary penetrates the gap. Finding no one, he jumps inside with a loud scream.

Dobó is standing next to the gap. He uses his bare fist to punch the janissary on the nose. Blood splatters. At the same moment, Gasparics throws a spear at him.

Other Turks dare not follow. They turn their backs and jump back down onto the fill.

"Throw the dog out!" Dobó tells the stone masons. He goes up onto the wall.

"The Turks have stopped mining," he says to Gergely.

"I thought so," says Gergely.

"Do you have anything to say?"

"Please take a look at our mugs."

There were five men working by the side of the bastion in the light of an oil lamp, including the Gypsy.

They were surrounded by hundreds of pottery mugs. They were stuffing them.

One man was pouring a handful of gunpowder into each mug. Another was stuffing rocks and a rag. The third stuffed another handful of gunpowder. The fourth sat next to a pile of old, rusty gun barrels that had been cut into small pieces. He was filling them with gunpowder and stuffing pieces of wood in each end. The fifth was using wire to fix the two wood plugs on each loaded barrel. The Gypsy was tightening the wire.

"We have three hundred mugs ready," Gergely said.

"Put some sulphur in them," Dobó said. "Nice big pieces."

"That will be very nice," said Gergely.

Balázs ran to get the sulphur.

For short time, Dobó looked at this craftsmanship with a satisfied face, then turned around. "Is Gasparics here?"

"I'm here," he replied from below.

"Come up."

The man jumped up and clicked his heels in front of Dobó.

"Were you the first to jump out of the gap?"

"I, my captain sir."

"From today you are a corporal!"

— § —

The *targets* had provided good protection on that first night. The next day the people inside the castle saw a great mound extending from the provost's house to the southwestern wall of the castle, what today is the gate.

Turks hidden by trenches were quickly carrying barrels towards the wall. Thousands and thousands of hands were carrying and placing empty barrels against the bottom of the wall.

The Turks had broken into the city's cellars. They drained the wine and carried the barrels and the wine-making vats to the walls of the castle. Well, indeed, they were making a large barrel wall. Barrels were handed from man to man and stood on end.

That same day, the large mound of barrels was completed. Barrels stacked in stepped tiers leaned up against the castle wall.

Gunners shot from the castle until dark, but the barrels also provided cover for the Turks. They worked stubbornly. Even at night, many barrels and vats rolled and rumbled.

By then, most of the gunners had been positioned on that side. Mortars were also squatting on top of the wall. Two bearded cannons were aimed at the side of the barrel mound.

"Crazy Turks," said Fügedy.

But they are not crazy. Well, at dawn, two large, wide *targets* moved at the bottom of the barrels. Eight lances held them up. Twenty or thirty Turks could fit under each *target*.

"Fire and water!" ordered Dobó. "Bring straw, grappling irons, hooks and pickaxes. Lots of them!"

Because he saw not only the movement of *targets* but also that the Turks were lighting torches in the ditch.

Babek Bastion had also been fired upon the day before, and sacks full of earth had been piled on its steps.

Dobó looked around there also. He found Gergely ready with all kinds of grappling irons and pickaxes attached to lances with chain. There was a fire on the bastion. Fat was rendering in the cauldron on the fire. The prickly straw circles, black from pitch, were neatly arranged in piles around the fire. The Turks were also pressing forward there under the cover of more large *targets*.

Mekcsey was working to heap fill by the Old Gate. They also were waiting for the assault.

The danger was more threatening on the southwest corner where Fügedy was standing. Dobó pushed up the visor of his steel helmet and galloped over there accompanied by page Balázs.

Well, our planks in the palisade there were burning.

This time the Turks were not screaming. Carefully staying under cover of the *targets*, they shot at the castle defenders.

They could not be shot from above, so the defenders returned fire from the bottom of the burning planks and punched holes in the stones below the palisade to shoot through the gaps.

"Straw on them!" shouted Dobó.

On the one side and above, water was thrown on the burning planks, while on the other, burning straw wreaths drenched in oil and pitch were thrown onto the *targets*.

Whichever *target* reached the wall was flipped upside down or pushed away with pickaxes. Whichever *target* had been set on file, they left to its own fate. The Turks soon threw it away, screaming as they escaped from the flames.

The barrels were rocking underneath, and some of them were carrying flaming fire on their backs.

"Straw! Only straw!" shouted Dobó.

A new barrage of burning, oil-dipped straw flew like flaming rags over the *targets*. The Turks holding them up with lances threw away their tools and ran, stumbling and falling to escape the rain of bullets.

But it was just a pause. As the first attackers were repulsed, Turkish cannons tore into the palisade of planks.

Dobó ordered his men to drop to the ground to avoid being hit. Of the columns holding up the palisade structure, two were successfully destroyed by Turkish cannons. One column swayed, creaked, then dropped over the side to fall with a crash some three hundred feet below.

One more column hit, and the entire palisade would fall apart.

"Get the hooks!" cried Fügedy. "And chains!"

Fifty hooks grabbed the palisade wall that was leaning out from the wall. Iron chains and ropes, new posts and stakes were set. Our palisade soon returned to its former position.

Dobó was already at Bolyky Tower where Gergely was welcoming the assault in the stench of pitch, gunpowder, and burnt tallow.

The Turks were greatly encouraged by the damage to the middle of the corner tower. They knew that Temesvár fell after its tower was brought down, so they thought bringing down a tower was a sign of good fortune even though they had been unsuccessful in the first assault trying to force their way inside the castle.

They had piled so much earth on the north side that those standing on the walls could not fire upon them.

The Turks pushed each other up under the wide *targets*. Burning wreaths of tar and fat rained on them, but still some managed to reach the tower.

"*Allahu akbar!*" "Hit, cut!" Thousands and thousands of armed Turks rushed toward the castle from King's Seat side.

Shovels and pickaxes stuck out from the bottom of the wall. They pushed, scraped, cut, and pulled.

But the Turks also worked. *Tüfekchiks* shot their guns from under the *targets*. Lances, grenades and arrows flew from below towards the defenders.

One *sipahi* in armor scorned death and jumped on the wall, his two iron-clad hands smashed pickaxes and shovels. A second and a third followed his tracks.

While those three were cut down with maces, the rest climbed over their backs. Within a minute, a *target* covered with cowhide reached the top of the tower. From underneath, some thirty or forty janissaries knelt and fired at the soldiers defending the tower.

"*Allah! Allah!*" screamed a thousand throats below.

"Victory is at hand!" shouted the *yasauls*.

Dobo's helmet fell off. He rushed to the cannons bareheaded.

The Hungarian soldiers inside the tower had no way to shoot the janissaries that had climbed above them. The top of the tower was floored with boards and the janissaries were standing on them.

"Get out!" Gergely shouted as he saw Dobó aim the cannons.

Ignoring the janissaries' gunfire, he picked up a pickaxe and hooked it on one of the lances holding up the *target* and pulled it away.

The soldiers on the bastion were also shocked to see the tower occupied. They were all given fire wreaths which they threw upon the janissaries pressing upwards on the wall. They were covered in fire.

Dobó saw that the janissary formation was breaking up. Suddenly, he aimed the two cannons down and fired at the janissaries that were crowding on the earth rampart.

The janissary soldier is not afraid of cannons. Two balls from the cannons do not do much. They have gotten used to the sound of cannon fire. But Dobó's cannons were filled with tiny shot. Some ten or twenty Turk fall.

The janissaries retreated in horror.

"Fire on them! Fire!" shouted Gergely from above.

And the pitch wreathes flew on the janissaries trapped on the tower roof. The Turks rushed back and forth. They had fired their guns and had no time to reload. The fire and flames suddenly increases. They screamed as they jumped from the tower. And the ones who jumped outside were lucky. Their necks broke with a single crunch. Those who jumped inside the castle, they did not dance too much. They were beaten so badly that not a bone was left intact.

The Turks continued their fighting from their earth rampart that evening and into the night.

That earth bastion on the northwest corner of the city was an extension of the stone bastion. The Turks had dug all over under the wall hoping to dig a gap under the bastion, but that castle wall was not built on earth. It was walls built on walls to a height of some hundred and sixty feet, as if, during an unknown time, the castle had been built up from the valley, and people from each age had filled the old castle with earth and built a new castle on top until, finally, the people of King St. István constructed the castle as it is today.

Dobó soon realized that the yelling and commotion of the Turks continuing their attack into the night was a distraction to take attention away from their work building the wood and earth rampart.

He ordered a lieutenant with two hundred men to the earth bastion, and left the other men in the usual number in the guard positions.

The Turkish cavalry did not appear for the barrel hill or the assault on the tower. It was foreseeable that they would continue to gather and carry wood at night.

Now they could see that instead of brushwood and sticks, they were carrying thick timbers. At dusk, all the camels, horses, oxen, buffaloes and mules available in the camp returned loaded with logs and thick limbs.

First, they threw the timber at random from the earth ramparts facing the walls, then, once the wood was piled high enough to provide cover, they were put in order.

Thousands and thousands of hands moved and threw logs and thick branches over each other. Instead of the silent work of the previous nights, loud sounds of hustle and bustle could be heard everywhere.

The wood was fastened with iron clips and chains.

The big wooden bastion was erected in front of Gergely's bastion, with its top just three yards away.

The Turkish worked skillfully, always staying protected as they placed the trees. They threw large branches over the eight foot high rampart to fill the ditch in front of the wall.

The ditch appeared to be filled and the top of the wood rampart grew taller next to the stone wall.

And also getting closer to the castle wall!

Gergely looked through one firing hole and then another to see what the enemy was doing. Finally he went up to the palisade. There he found Dobó.

The captain stood in his usual knee-length cape. Light black steel helmet on his head.

"My lord," said Gergely, "I would like to use the wood shingles that we pulled off the roofs."

"You can take them."

"And then I would like to take some tallow, pitch and oil."

"Take as much as you need. There is not much fat."

"Well, whatever there is. If there is no fat, I request bacon. Lots of bacon."

"Bacon?"

"Twenty or thirty sides. As many as possible."

Dobó said to Kristóf standing behind him. "Go wake Sukán. Have him take fat and forty sides of bacon from the food stores. Get it here right away!"

Only then did he ask, "Why?"

Well sure. What Gergely has figured out was that while the Turks were piling up wood, he could be piling up bacon, tallow, shingles and oil between the logs and sticks.

The Turks took no notice. Stuff was always being thrown at them from the walls. Stones, bones, cracked pots, dead cats and whatever were always flying at them every minute. Pieces of bacon a few inches thick among all the other stuff hardly stood out. If someone actually noticed, either he did not recognize what it was and what it could do, or if he recognized it as bacon, he was just disgusted.

Gergely had the bacon cut into wide slices and tossed it occasionally in the wood. Meanwhile, oiled shingles, tallow, and straw fell. From time to time, he tossed a pottery mug wrapped in straw.

The mugs were covered with mud and wrapped in wire. Inside was gunpowder, bits of stuffed barrels, and finger-sized pieces of sulfur.

Dobó inspected. "By the time they are done," he said, "it will be morning. Kristóf, look for Mekcsey and see if he is awake. If he's awake, tell him I'm going to bed. If he's not awake, let him sleep. Then go to all the sentries. Tell them that as soon as they see any movement towards an assault, they should report to the corner tower. Aren't you going to lie down, Gergely?"

"Not today," said Gergely. "I'm waiting for morning."

"And Zoltay?"

"I sent him to go get some sleep so that come morning, there would be strength in the bastion."

"As soon as the wooden bastion is built, wake me!" He went up to the corner tower and leaned on a military armchair. Page Kristóf stood in front of the tower door with a drawn sword.

It was the duty of a page. He guarded the sleeping lion.

13

By dawn the Turkish wooden bastion was almost as tall as the castle wall. It was short by only about twelve feet.

Gergely had two large pieces of gun barrel filled. He hammered wood in either end.

"Well, this cannon didn't think that it would ever shoot again!" said the Gypsy.

"New cannon from an old," replied one of the soldiers.

"Well, if it's new, let's give it a name," the Gypsy said. Make one *Gypsy Child* and the other *Pigeon*.

Because each cannon had its own name.

Gergely took a lead bullet out of his pocket and used it to scratch on the smaller piece of cannon: *János*. For the bigger one: *Éva*. He took the two pieces and climbed up to the bastion.

Dawn quickly poured light over the sky. Down below the camp began to stir: the rattling sounds of companies organizing everywhere.

Gergely woke Dobó.

Men with pikes and pickaxes were already standing on the wall. Gunners had their freshly loaded muskets leaning against rocks white from frost. The three cannons on the bastion were aimed downward, and the two cannons by Dark Gate were pointed up at the wall.

"Light the pitch wreaths and the mugs," Gergely ordered, "and throw them out!" The men immediately went to work.

By the time Dobó got there, the Turks had already flooded onto the hills like ants. They were still piling and stacking wood. It was already as tall as the inner bastion. From time to time they pushed a log over to fill the gaps between the two walls. There was a huge amount of trees there. An entire forest. And the tree fortress was strong. Loose stacks on the top were carefully covered with raw cowhides.

Burning wreaths do not harm raw cowhide, and wherever else they fall, the Turks kick them aside.

A sharp whistle shook the air. Then the sound of thousands of thousands yelling *Bismallah* shook the air. Turkish martial music roared. And the giant wooden structure thundered from running feet.

"*Allah! Allah!*"

"Jesus! Mary!"

Short siege ladders move out quickly from under the *targets* to bridge between the wooden and stone bastions.

But the castle defenders are already standing on the stone bastion. All at once, fiery wreathes by the hundreds fly at the Turks. Burning straw and sulfur fall on the ladders, and shingles soaked in pitch fall on straw.

The first Turkish group to run through the burning fire meets the tips of lances and pickaxes. The rest are welcomed by swords, pickaxes, fiery clubs and chained maces.

A full-bodied Turkish man carrying a huge log pops up from the wood pile some three inches away from Gergely. As he shouts Allah, his entire face turns into a mouth, and Gergely takes the smaller piece of cannon barrel and shoves it into the Turk's face. He throws the larger cannon piece into the burning fire below.

The Turks had built the great wooden structure, and they certainly would have run through burning fires, had not the worst also happened. Guns and cannons fired from underneath.

The pottery mugs began to explode and spray their burning sulfur. It was as if a fire-spouting mountain had opened under them.

"*Ya kerim! Ya rahim! Meded! Ey va! Yetishin!*" they screamed in confusion.

But the *yasauls* would not allow them to come down. "*Victory is ours! Now is the hour of triumph!*" they shouted. Those remaining below were ordered to bring water.

And with water, weapons, and cloth, they tried to save the wooden construction they had been working on day and night.

But by then the fat and the bacon had started to drip between the logs, and the mugs were exploding more and more sulfur, setting fire to the logs.

"*Ya kerim! Ya rahim!* Through the fire! Inside the castle!"

They did not want to believe that those large pieces of wood would burn.

Water has already been brought in abundance in leather pouches and buckets and in all kinds of pots. They ran with water all over the place, wherever they saw a flame within the wood pile. Frightened and terrified, they doused flames furiously.

But the platform had become a huge bonfire. Only then did the gun barrels begin burning, and the fires spit scalding fat in blue flames into the faces of the fire fighters. One after the other, the two pieces of gun barrel ignited with huge explosions that tore apart the wood pile and the Turks.

A raging hell of horror, anger and screaming! The janissaries, trapped from retreating by the inferno, tried to push forward through smoke and flames onto the ladders bridging the wood and stone walls. One, then another made a desperate leap and hung onto the stone wall and, at the same moment, fell down with a bloody head. The rest angrily danced on the top of the bonfire, using their weapons to try to knock down burning logs.

But what hopeless work! The wood pile by the wall was a sea of flames with a maelstrom of explosions within. Turks ran in all directions trying escape the fires, screaming and jumping through flames like demon shadows. Their clothes were on fire, their beards were on fire, their turbans were on fire. They passed through the fires of hell to Muhammad's paradise.

The heat on the castle wall was so great that the cannons had to be pulled away, and warriors had to water the gun carriages so the wood would not catch fire.

And in the inferno of that fire, wounded Turks, impossible to save, screamed in agony, and *yasauls* angrily shouted as soldiers made their last attempts throwing water on the fires that spurted up in scalding columns of steam.

The two armies were separated by flame and smoke.

14

If we can't prosper with wood, we'll prosper with earth! — That is what the Turks thought.

They fired their siege guns at the outer fortress which was the most vulnerable from the Turks' earth works. The walls were pounded by day; by night the Turks piled branches and earth.

They also watered it.

Gergely watched with concern as the new, non-flammable route to the bastion grew day by day. That will be the road for hundreds, thousands, and the entire camp.

He walked and paced inside the castle, thinking.

He looked at all the ruins, the piles of stones, the stables, the rubble, the cannonballs in the mounds. He scratched and shook his head.

He also walked around among the ruined sacristy. Finally he stopped by a corner where the locksmiths were. There, among piles of dumped Hungarian and Turkish weapons, lay a large black wheel. Gergely recognized it. It was one of the mill stones from one of the ruined dry mills.

The Gypsy was sitting on the wheel eating cooked meat out of a large pottery bowl. He was terribly armed. Crimson-red janissary boots on his feet. In his belt were shiny *yataghans*. On his head a brass helmet with holes in it, which may have been Turkish.

The Gypsy, feeling himself to be one of the soldiers, got up. He held the bowl under his left arm. He saluted with his right. Then he started eating meat again.

"Just get up, dear fellow," said Gergely. "Let me see that wheel." The Gypsy stood up.

The wheel was quite intact. Only two of its spokes were broken. Gergely stood on it and pressed the spokes one by one. Only one moved.

"Hmm," said Gergely, putting his finger on his chin.

The Gypsy said: "Are we grinding, your greatness my lord lieutenant?"

"Indeed," said Gergely. "Nail it where it's loose."

The locksmiths put down their bowls and picked up hammers.

Gergely asked for Dobó's whereabouts. "Where did you last see him?"

"He's been by this way at least ten times today," replied one of the locksmiths, "but it's been a half an hour since we last saw him."

Gergely set out to find him.

He went to Church Bastion. He was not there. Maybe he was at the earth bastion.

As he walked looking around everywhere, he noticed a female eye in one of the open windows of the palace. From the darkness in that room, a pair of eyes were looking at him.

He is shocked. He stops. He blinks as if he wanted to see better. But the female eyes are gone.

Gergely was frozen as he stared at the window opening. There was a strange, warm feeling running through him when he saw those two eyes, a feeling strong enough that he was unable to move for a minute.

"Eh, foolish!" he muttered, shaking his head. "How can I think this!" But he looked up again. He saw the face of the little Turkish boy in the window.

Dobó came from the earth bastion.

Gergely hurried to see him. "That mill wheel, captain sir." He raised his hand to his helmet.

"Take it," Dobó said curtly. He turned to go inside the palace.

Greg went to the area in front of the kitchens where the soldiers were sitting in a long line on the ground having their lunch: vinegar-flavored lentil stew.

He called for ten of them. He had the wheel rolled to the front of his bastion.

— § —

There were plenty of rusty and broken guns in the castle. He loaded them. He tied them with wire to the wheel so that they were pointing outwards. He filled the middle of the barrels with shot, sulfur, tallow, and pitch. He nailed boards to the sides. Finally, he fashioned a wide plank around the wheel so that it would not tip over.

All the people in the castle marveled at the machine from hell.

Dobó himself looked at it several times. He had a mortar put in the middle.

"Make this, Gergely, so it's the last to fire."

"It will be done, captain sir."

"Do you need anything else, my son Gergely?"

"Well, if I can, I'd like to ask for the empty barrels."

"From the cellar?"

"From there."

"We have enough. Just take them."

Below, the pile of earth and stick was growing. Inside, the barrels were being worked on.

The barrels were also filled masterfully, just like the wheel. They also put rocks in them, below, above, and to the sides. They were stuffed hard. Only a fuse was left poking out of the hole.

Dobó had many bearded cannons — some three hundred. A bearded cannon was, in fact, an oversized musket that rested on a wall. It could not fire a bullet larger than a walnut. It was called bearded because it had a piece of iron at the muzzle of the barrel protruding down. That iron projection served to hold the gun when it recoiled from firing.

Well, Dobó made the rusty bearded guns available for the barrels.

Some fifty barrels were made to welcome the Turks. Each was well packed, tightly wired, and nailed.

Meanwhile, each night the Turks eagerly built their beautiful road to march up to the bastion.

15

Gergely was sleeping with his men in the morning when Zoltay got reports that the water and the peas in the corner of the stables were shaking.

Well, the evil Turks not only fill holes, but dig them too!

Zoltay did not allow them to wake Gergely. He sent for Mekcsey.

Mekcsey was soon there. He put bowls of water and drums with peas here and there until, finally, by where the carriages were standing, he found the place where they had to dig. Ten men began digging. They paused from time to time to rest and set down the dish to watch it.

Gergely woke up around noon and ran to the dig. The men had already dug some three fathoms deep. They could feel the *lagumji* sappers' drums beating so they knew they were getting close.

"Ho, ho, captain sir!" Gergely said to Mekcsey. "This is my bastion! You're not giving me orders here."

"Well, perhaps you think I didn't do well?"

"We'll stop digging."

"And put up a wall!"

"To avoid keeping us from doing our job."

"Do what you want," Mekcsey replied shrugging. And he left.

Gergely had a big blunderbuss gun brought. He himself loaded the gunpowder and primed it. He called for ten gunners. The lanterns were blown out.

They are in the dark.

The rumble is getting louder. They can make out the words of the commanding officer.

From time to time, Gergely presses his palm against the wall. He is feeling for where the ground is moving the most. "Pst," he says softly to the men. "They're about to break inside."

At that moment one of the pickaxes breaks through, and the ground crumbles at Gergely's feet.

A hole big enough for a man opens. The *lagumji* stops and looks inside the stables. It's dark. He can't see anything. As he turns around, their lanterns are visible, and among the lanterns a white turbaned, gold-braided, fat bellied agha.

The *lagumji* cries out that he has reached the hole. The agha turns in that direction.

Gergely aims. The blunderbuss sizzles and explodes. The agha is hit in the stomach. He collapses.

Gergely jumps back. "Fire!"

Ten men point their guns inside the hole. Crack! Crack! They shoot the backs of the *lagumjis* running away.

The men return with thirty pickaxes and the agha's body. One man is left as a sentry with a loaded gun and a lantern illuminating the mouth of the tunnel.

— § —

The agha was laid down in the castle's market square. He was not laid down nicely because his head hit the cobblestones and his turban rolled off when they put his body down.

But for him, it was good anyway.

He was a fat man with a gray beard. Three long scars on his bald head showed that he deserved to be promoted to agha. Gergely's shot went into his belly. A smaller bullet had hit his chest, probably when the men were firing their guns.

Steward Sukán dutifully recorded his turban, his belt, his pocket and noted how much money, rings and weapons he had. These were given as rewards to the soldiers who had been doing the digging.

Then he allowed the curious to stare at the dead body. The first ones to surround the body, of course, were the women.

"They walk around with these red slippers?"

"They tie a string around the bottoms of their pant legs."

"He must have been a rich lord."

"A lieutenant or a captain."

"Did he have a wife?"

"Maybe ten."

"He wasn't an ugly man," says the miller's wife from Maklár. "Too bad he was Turkish."

Zoltay walked over to look at the body. "This one agha got inside the castle after all!"

Suddenly, a small Turkish child slips past a woman's skirt and with a cry of joy leans over the dead body.

"*Baba! Babadjizim! Baba! Babatatli baba dizi!*" (Dad! Dear Dad! Dad! Sweet Dead Dad!)

He falls on his chest. Hugs, kisses. He lays his face on his face. He shakes him. He laughs at him. "*Baba! Babadjizim!*"

The women's eyes fill with tears. Lady Balogh holds the child's hand. "Come, Selim. Baba is sleeping."

16

Dawn, as the Turkish troops again assemble in the valley for another assault, the castle defenders watch their movements with the angry delight of the well-prepared. The excitement of vengeance tenses like a spring in their muscles. They can hardly wait anymore. A small, stocky man jumps out of the breach onto the earth mound and faces a wave of yelling Turks, threatening them with his sword.

Of course, the men on the wall laugh.

"Who's that?" Zoltay asks, laughing himself.

"The little Varga," they say. "János Varga."

The man jumps back, but as he sees the big laugh he got, he pops out of the breach a second time and threatens the Turkish army.

The *tüfekchi* gunners start firing at him and Varga jumps back inside even faster than before. The men laugh even more.

Dobó watches this happen. He nods his head in praise.

János Varga, upon seeing Dobó's approval, gets stirred up. He pops out a third time, ignoring bullets and threatening shouts from angry Turks looking up.

Bullets, bombs and spears fly at him. Not one can find him. He jumps with laughter and pokes his tongue out at them. In fact, he turns suddenly and, something really very indecent, but then he does a proper pat on his own. Then he jumps out from the breach again.

And that's right there under the Turkish noses! In front of hundreds of thousands of armed Turks!

"You are a man!" shouts Dobó. "You'll get a reward!"

And seeing that everything is in order, he mounts his horse. He gallops to the Old Gate. Because the Turks are pushing towards the east and south sides of the castle. The assault is directed at two places.

Gergely is dressed in armor on his bastion surrounded by barrels and the monstrous wheel. He stands there calmly, like a rock on the shore of a turbulent sea.

And they come, they flood. Screaming hellfire: *Bismillah! Bismillah!* For a few minutes, the war cries overwhelm the sounds of the military band, but then the band stops in front of the castle and plays continuously.

"Soon you all will be dancing, too," shouts Zoltay. Because the music was lively, jumping music.

The Turkish army is busy. The horsetail and crescent moon flags are flying. In front is the yellow-red flag of the janissaries. Further back, the white-green flag of the *ulufedji* household cavalry. Protected by long shields that reach their knees, *sipahis* clad in iron roar forward.

"*Allah! Allah!*"

They have spears and lances in their hands. They have naked swords hanging by cords tied to their wrists. They have another sword strapped on their waists. They start running from the trenches towards the bastion.

"*Allahu akra! La illah! Il Allah! Ya fettah!*"

In response, a black barrel crashes towards them, spouting flame, bouncing and rolling. One of the *sipahis* plants his spear in the ground in front of the barrel, another, and a third do the same.

"*Allah! Allah.*"

The fourth grabs the barrel and is about to throw it down into the ditch. At that moment, the barrel explodes, spraying flames and rocks onto the leading companies.

"*Allahu akbar!*"

By the time they can look back up, another barrel is among them. It spits and sprays fire at hundreds. It comes to a halt among the men dressed in iron and blows them to pieces.

"*Allah! Allah!*"

But they cannot turn back. Thousands upon thousands of men follow and push from below. All that can be seen is men jumping, men pressing themselves against the wall, shocked men trying to hold back, and fire shooting out eighty feet.

Forward, pagans, forward! Through the fire! And the densely packed companies of *sipahis* flow upwards.

But behold, the palisade on the bastion opens and a giant, smoky wheel with boards appears on the heights.

The center of the wheel smokes; smokes and groans. It turns and rolls off the stone wall. It rolls towards the crowded army of thousands.

"*Ileri, ileri!*" (forward!) shout aghas and *yasauls* everywhere. But the appearance of the wheel says something very different to those who have wildly charged ahead.

The wheel does not even reach them when the first lightning bursts out of it, shooting burning particles four hundred feet out, each drop of which continues to burn with a blue flame, falling on the living and the dead equally.

"*Gözünü aç! Sakin!*" (Look out! Quiet!)

Terrified soldiers in front of the Turkish army fall on their faces hoping the devil's wheel would roll over their backs. But, in the midst of them, the wheel is transformed into a sparkling circle of fire. It shoots flames, spits burning oil, and sprinkles violet-colored tulips of burning tar on their heads and battle clothes. The wheel continues rolling, jumping, bouncing, spitting and rumbling over them. Its spokes spray, spit, shoot and spread serpentine rays of red, blue and yellow stars.

"*Meded Allah!*"

Even the bravest companies of Turks hold back in fear, trampling each other as they try to escape from the demonic wonder.

And the wheel, as if it had the wit and the will, follows the runners, knocking them off their feet and spitting them with a lively fire: burning oil and burning sulfur. Its heat explodes the power in their guns so they end up shooting at each other. It spits fire into their eyes, mouths, ears, and necks catapaulting even the dead head over heels. Long fiery meteors shoot out from it, knocking down the *yasauls* together with their horses. Long flames burn flesh down to the bone and the smoke suffocates. The explosions deafen. The soldiers it passes are covered with flames as they try to escape. No one is left behind in its tracks, only the burning bodies of the dead, and the jumping, screaming, crazed bodies of the burning living.

And now, dressed in the cloud, the wheel rolls on, sprinkling hundreds of shafts of lightning.

"*Yetişin! Yetişin! Allah!*"

The *yasauls* continue shouting angrily, whipping with their nailed whips, punching fleeing men in the face. But their furious violence is useless. There are no more men left to assault the outer fortress.

And the Hungarians come out through the breach, and those who have been lying flat in the path of the wheel or frozen in terror are beaten, stabbed, and ruthlessly cut.

"Back! Back!" sounds the horn.

Gergely can barely get his men to respond and return to the ramparts.

"Barrel on the wall! Barrel!"

They roll and station the barrel. But what is left of the Turks is dispersing with great rustle and roar. Only the cannons remain in position together with their stunned *topchis*.

— § —

It was good for Mekcsey to have stayed by the digging

because the Turks would have broken through underground in three different places near the Old Gate.

While this fiery wheel was working, the underground struggle continued.

There the wall was so ruined there that the Turks poked spears through the holes in the stones, while the Hungarians thrust their spears out. Meanwhile Mekcsey had tunnels dug toward the Turkish mines in three places in succession, chasing the Turks back.

Finally the Turks set fire to the gate and tried to force their way inside, only to find a strong, thick wall behind the gate. Mekcsey had it constructed earlier.

Gergely, after his men returned from attacking and ransacking like madmen, covered the cannons and gunpowder boxes with wet skins, left ten men as a guard, and took the rest to help Mekcsey at the Old Gate.

— § —

There was nothing to help. The terror gripping the Turkish army had also reached the gate. Of the brigades led there, only the *topchis* stood their ground. They were positioned around the gate, steadily loading and firing.

Guards stood on top of the walls, beneath the palisade. A group of soldiers stood below under the vaults. They were spying through cracks in the wall.

Gergely runs up onto the wall. He looks down under the protection of a shield. He sees a company of Turks moving at the base of the wall where they cannot be fired upon, either from above or from the side.

Hungarians stab at them through holes in the wall. But they either lie flat or squat. Some have a bag, some have a stone. The bags and the stones are used to stuff the firing holes so the Hungarians cannot shoot.

Well, that kind of fill is pushed out from the inside. Lances are poked out at the Turks. The Turks, as a Hungarian lance pokes out, grabs the shaft. Two or three of them hold onto it. They try cutting on it for a while, then pull out the lance.

The Hungarian curses.

"Damn it!" shouts Gergely to the men. "The fire is there! Hold your lances in it!"

A fire is burning near the wall. Twenty soldiers jump up and hold the point of their lances over the coals. The metal glows red.

The Turks are on hands and knees, grinning as they wait for new lances.

Well, twenty spears poke out of the wall all at once.

The Turks are emboldened! But to be sure, their palms burn! And the reply to their angry cursing was the laughter from the Hungarian soldiers.

17

Wednesday, October 12th.

On this day, the castle is like a sieve.

Thirty-two days of shooting cannonballs without interruption, sometimes front, sometimes back, sometimes on one side or on the other.

The Turkish cannonballs are so many in the castle that people stumble on them trying to get around. The peasants use a birch broom to sweep the smaller bullets out of the way, lest they stumble upon them during an assault. Most of the larger ones are carried to the cannons and to the walls.

Between the new bastion and the earth bastion there is a V-shaped breach in the wall. One side of Prison Bastion has collapsed into its depth. The earth bastion is full of holes like a wasp's nest. Bolyky Tower has only two walls. The corner tower is like hollow tree from top to bottom. Palisade only here and there. The interior buildings also have walls fallen out or collapsed within; roofless walls. There are only three habitable rooms in the palace, and they are also exposed to the rain. The market square is also ruined with sharp eight foot trenches cutting through it. You have to walk in the trenches when the Turks are firing. Other times, they walk over planks placed on them as bridges.

Outside, angry wolves are howling.

The wall plastering work is now being done even during daylight. Beams and boards are used to fill holes. As much as possible.

The stones merely serve as support behind them.

At the Old Gate, Mekcsey himself is carrying stones. He encourages those who are tired and calls upon God for help. It is predictable that the assault will be angry there. Dobó, Gergely and Mekcsey examine the wall. All three see that the corner tower no longer protects the gate. They need hand bombs. They are carried to the wooden scaffolds. Skilled gunners are positioned at firing holes.

Gargely makes pitch wreaths, fire balls, and mugs and carries them everywhere.

Zoltay is building at Sándor Bastion.

Fügedy uses chains to tie the breaches in the new bastion.

Dobó rides on horseback here and there. There is room for his horse all around inside the castle wall, under the wooden platforms. But often he is exposed to flying bullets. He examines and organizes to make sure the work proceeds evenly everywhere. Page Balázs follows, riding the last little Turkish horse, carrying the captain's orders. The other seven horses have already been shot from under the two pages.

That day even Pető is riding a horse. His legs are bandaged to his knees. He is pale, but his mustache is stretched out. Mekcsey has replaced him at the Old Gate, so now he replaces Mekcsey with the inner company of reserves.

He speaks in a sonorous, deep voice to people here and there. "The Turks have been here for thirty-two days. But even if they were all here, we'll throw every last one into hell! The king's army is late, but it won't stay away! The whole world is talking about our bravery! A hundred years from now, instead of using the word *brave* they will be saying *He's from Eger*."

A large crowd gathers around the speaker, so Dobó pauses for a minute to listen to what is going on.

He smiles at the last sentence. He says thoughtfully to Cecey standing next to him. "A hundred years from now? Sure the world will be thinking of us, as if they want to know what our noses looked like!"

He said it to himself rather than to Cecey. And as if he regretted having spoken out loud, he shrugs. "No matter. It is not the nose that's important, but the soul. It's not the reward, but the duty!"

He gallops towards Sándor Bastion.

The warriors continue to soak up the many tasty words. They would have stood their ground without them. But nice words are like good wine.

Pető takes off his helmet and continues. "The king himself will come here. He has the Eger warriors stand in line and shakes hands with everyone. 'What's your name?' he says. 'My name is János Nagy, your majesty.' 'My name is Mihály Szabó Nagy, your majesty.' 'God bless you, my son.' That's how the king speaks with praise, with gratitude. But you also deserve it. I also have heard that from here on, he will be choosing all his officers from the brave ordinary soldiers here! Every ordinary soldier here will be promoted to lieutenant after the siege, so I heard. He could become a captain! After all, the best soldier for the king is the one who can stand his ground."

He looks to the side and sees the Gypsy jumping in the air like a bullet had hit him in the air. "Well, Gypsy," he says, "you won't get nobility. You haven't even cut down a single Turk."

"What can I do about that?" replies the Gypsy. "No one dares come where I stand, may the devil thrash him!"

— § —

In the evening, a Turkish man with a white cloth appeared at one of the breaches. They recognized him to be Miklós Vas. They pulled him in immediately and took him to Dobó.

On the way, a hundred and another hundred lips asked him, "What's the news?"

"The army is coming!" Miklós replied everywhere.

The good news spread like a roar throughout the castle. "The king's army is coming!"

But Dobó had ordered Miklós Vas to say this when he arrived. Well, maybe the army is coming! Maybe Lieutenant Pető was telling the truth!

Miklós Vas took off his turban in front of Dobó and pulled out the letter from his shirt. He handed it over.

Dobó looked at the seal. It had come from the bishop. He tore off the seal and calmly opened the letter.

He was sitting horseback. People had gathered around. As he read the letter, people strained to interpret the expression on his face to understand what was written. But his face was like iron. It was exactly the same from when he began to read to when he had finished.

He folded the letter and put it in his pocket, then glanced around as if he were surprised that so many people were standing around.

Of the lieutenants, only Pető was standing there. Dobó spoke to him loudly enough for others to hear. "I am inviting the lieutenants tonight. I want to share welcome news with them."

He went into his room.

He pulled the door shut behind him.

He sat down in the chair. His iron-like features turned sad. He stared ahead bitterly and hopelessly.

— § —

That day, Dobó received another letter. It was brought by a peasant man. He was carrying white paper in his hand, so it was obvious that it had come from the Turks.

That was Ali Pasha's fourth courier.

People inside the castle already knew that Dobó was treating Turkish postmen curtly, so they let him receive the man in the market square. The man was held there.

The evenings were cool and the resting soldiers were warming themselves by fires in the market square. They were toasting bacon, washing it down with a little wine mixed with water.

"You'd do better to burn that letter before the captain sees it," said a well-intentioned man. "Or else God help you!"

"How can I burn it?" the man replied, "It's not mine."

"But you bring it from the enemy."

"I bring it from whoever sent it."

"They will hang you."

"Hang me?"

"You indeed. Our captain had one of our lieutenants strung up. And he was a gentleman, a noble, not a greasy peasant like you."

The gallows were still standing in the market square. The soldier pointed to it. "There. The gallows are still standing."

The man got frightened. He suddenly started sweating all over. He scratched his head. He reached into his satchel.

Then Dobó arrived at a gallop. "What is that?" he asked. "Who is this man? What does he want?"

The peasant pushed the satchel under his heavy *szűr* coat.

"I'm Esvány Kovács. I kiss your hand," he replied, nervously fumbling with his cap.

"What do you want?"

"Me? Why nothing."

"Then why did you come inside?"

"Well ... I was just coming inside ... how do you say? ... so see ... how you are managing in this danger."

"You brought a letter!"

"No, not me. I haven't brought a single drop of a letter." Dobó stare pierced through him. As he wiped his forehead he repeated, "God damn me, I didn't bring any!"

"Search him!"

The man, pale like death, did not resist. A large sealed parchment letter came out of his satchel.

"Into the fire!" shouted Dobó.

The soldier threw the letter into the fire.

The man was shaking.

"I don't know how that got to me," he hemmed and hawed, scratching his head. "Somebody must have put it in ..."

"Shackle him!" said Dobó. "Then put this scoundrel with the others!"

18

It rained that day, October 12, during the heavy cannon fire, . Only in the evening did the clouds part as a strong autumn breeze blew over the land.

People inside the castle saw Turks gathering on their earth ramparts. Dobó allowed only three hundred soldiers to rest. The others had to stand ready around the breaches.

By eleven o'clock, the last cloud had blown from the sky. The full moon flooded Eger with near daylight.

Suddenly the cry "To arms, men!" was heard all over the castle at once. "Gather arms even those who aren't soldiers!"

And the alarm sounded on the drums.

So, there will be a night assault. On your feet everyone, whoever is alive!

The moonlight shone on the rubble surrounding the castle revealing helmeted, lance-armed shapes crouching everywhere.

Father Bálint, also dressed and armed for battle, walked into the market square to join the company of reserves. He carried a pike big enough to serve as a tongue shaft for a large cart. The two innkeepers also reported. Millers, carpenters, butchers, and peasants working inside the castle were all armed and waiting for the command.

People inside the castle felt that the final test coming.

Outside, the Turkish copper drums rang. Turkish troops poured into the ditches of the fortresses like a flash flood after a cloud burst. Horsetail flags floated above the human flood. Beyond the ramparts, Turkish officers wearing their pointed caps could be seen mounted on their horses, moonlight flashing on the jewel-studded silver trappings of their horses. Many wore their turban cloths wrapped around their gleaming helmets.

Yasauls with their towering turbans were galloping here and there organizing the attacking companies.

At midnight, Turkish cannons around the castle explode. For five minutes they continuously fire cannonballs at the castle. Then, hundreds of thousands of throats shout *Bismillah* and *Allah*, and the horsetail flags almost fly towards the walls.

Some thirty fires burn in front of the Old Gate and on the top of the wall. Bombs and wreaths are sizzling. Hundreds and hundreds fall in large arcs like fiery rainbows.

But the attackers are determined to move forward, hold on, strive, and push themselves against the walls. Siege ladders are quickly connected. Janissaries, *azabs* and cavalry working as foot soldiers climb the ladders.

Pickaxes clang on ladder hooks. Fire and stones are falling.

"Allahu akbar! Ya kerim! Ya fettah!"

Horsetail flags keep getting pushed back, but they are seized by new hands, and new flags follow. Ladders that have been broken are replaced with new ones. Fresh soldiers climb over the bodies of the dead and wounded to hoist more ladders.

They are packed so densely against the wall that the wall cannot be seen. Where a Hungarian lance strikes through a gap, the Turk falls off the ladder, but immediately another takes his place. He does not bother avoiding the ladder rung that is exposed to the gap and the lance. He leaves it to luck whether the lance cuts into his stomach or strikes by his arm to hit only the air.

The castle no longer has any gate. Turks on ladders with axes are chopping, breaking, and pulling apart the timber filling the breaches. Sometimes men falling from the tops of ladders fall on those below working with axes, and both fall into fire and blood. The next minute they are trampled upon by the next wave of attackers.

"Allahu akbar! Ya kerim! Ya fettah!"

"Jesus!"

Fiery projectiles fall, pickaxes strike, bombs explode, ladders shake, and axes chop in a bloody storm of battle.

Some fifty attackers reach a palisade. The palisade starts to groan as it leans outwards. Mekcsey grabs a battle-axe from a soldier and cuts a rope holding the palisade.

The palisade, with Turks wearing armor clinging to it, turns, falls, and sweeps hundreds off the wall.

"On the wall! To the wall!" shouts Mekcsey, jumping on the wall carrying a twelve-foot lance.

Zarbuzan siege guns rain huge squared stones and iron cannonballs weighing a half a hundredweight. They hit the castle and fall back onto the Turks writhing on the ground. But from underneath, arrows, bullets and even rocks fly up towards the defenders.

Mekcsey's helmet is splashed with red. "Captain sir!" they caution him.

"Fire! Fire!" Mekcsey screams. And with his iron boot he sweeps smoldering embers from a fire over the wall onto the men writhing on the ground below.

Hungarians are also falling from the wall. One out, the other in. But they are not looking to see who is dead. In his place, a new warrior jumps to the wall to drop a rock or a cannonball by hand, until the siege ladders are again full, and the Turks on the wall have to be repelled with pickaxe and mace.

The fighting at the earth bastion is just as fierce. There Dobó leads the defense. When the Turkish army pushes through the hell of bombs and flaming straw, he orders timbers to the walls. They use them to sweep Turks off the walls.

There is a short lull in the fighting that Dobó uses to mount his horse, ride to the Old Gate, and see how the defense is holding out. Then, as he returns to the top of Prison Bastion, he sees that the assault there has stopped. He orders the men stationed on Prison Bastion to the earth bastion.

The men on Prison Bastion were already looking in that direction. They were all anxiously waiting for the chance to use their weapons. Standing by our palisades, leaning against the wall, standing up on cannons, they look nervously at the struggle on the neighboring bastion. Well, at Dobó's words, they rush, almost jumping, to the earth bastion.

However, it happens that the Turks push up more ladders under Prison Bastion. First only two, three, then ten, fifteen. They climb up quickly because no one there is throwing down fire or stones. By the time old

Sukán, left to watch that bastion, turns around to see, a helmeted Turkish head pokes out over the top.

"Hey! Damn you!" screams the old man. He rushes over there with his lance, and swinging its stubby end, hits the man. He along with ten others on that ladder fall down.

"Here, here! Hey! Men!" screams Sukán, stabbing Turks on the other ladder.

János Pribék is the first to run beside him. He is carrying a bootmaker's stool that one of the cannon-masters was using. He smashes the stool between the eyes of a Turk climbing over the wall with a flag.

A soldier stationed below runs to the market square for help from the reserves. Two minutes later, Pető and a group of rested men are on Prison Bastion, hurling burning wreathes, timber, stones and bombs on the Turks.

Dobó also turns his attention there. He sees that bullets have snapped the flagpole flying the national flag. He has the flag of the standing army brought out. He gives it to István Nagy.

By then, dawn is beginning to break.

In the red light of dawn, István Nagy runs up with the flag. He has no armor or helmet, yet he climbs to the top of the bastion and looks for the iron clamps that hold the flagpole.

"Don't show it!" shouts Dobó. "They could take it!"

At that moment István Nagy clasps his chest. He turns, and slumps on the wall next to the cannon.

Dobó catches the flag flying towards him and gives it to Bakocsa. "Hold on, son."

As dawn gets brighter, the siege of Bolyky Bastion also begins. There they advance with eight flags. The light of the crimson sun turns the gold ornaments of the horsetail flags into burning rubies.

They have attacked that bastion so often that only the janissaries dare another attempt. These are the veteran and most tested tigers in the army. They have helmets on their heads, steel wire veils on their faces and necks, iron on their breasts and arms, and lightweight boots on their feet.

Both Gergely and Zoltay are stationed there. All night they had to stand awake without moving and listen to the fiery, turbulent fighting on the other bastions.

Well, but now, with some daylight, things are better.

There are some two hundred *azabs* in front of the bastion. They carry skins filled with water. No matter. They have to spread it before fire reaches their heads.

The Turks there do not start with siege ladders. As the defenders pile up on the wall, thousands of hands move together below, and the defenders are covered with showers of stones and arrows.

One stone finds Zoltay's head. Luckily, he is wearing his helmet. It only breaks the hinge of his visor. Zoltay taunts. "Well, stop, dogs!" he screams, breaking off his broken visor. "For this I will hit a hundred of your noses today!" Even a quarter of an hour later, he can still be heard shouting, "Here, pagan, for my helmet!" And to another, "Here, a taste of Eger!"

A huge *target* covered with cowhides is lifted from the Turkish camp. It is a wonder to watch. It takes fifty *azabs* just to lift it. There is room underneath to shield two hundred janissaries.

Gergely shouts for a fiery barrel and lights the oil-soaked fuse wrapped around its iron rod core.

The giant *target* approaches the wall like a tortoise. Even if the defenders strip off the cowhides with pickaxes, the Turks can still push it up and reach the top of the wall. It is also questionable whether they could set it afire. Not only are the cowhides dripping water, but also its wood frame. The Turks are learning.

The sun comes out from behind the eastern mountains, and shines in the faces of the defenders of Sándor Bastion. Daylight also helps the Turks.

As the advance reaches the slope of the bastion, Gergely gives a great shout, "On your stomachs!"

The men cannot understand why. The loud cracks of gunfire educate them.

The Turks have figured out how to line the top of the huge *target* with gun barrels. They point towards the defenders like organ pipes. That is what Gergely has seen.

"On your feet!" he shouts after the line of guns had fired. "Barrel!"

He rolls down a fiery barrel.

The Turks no longer fall to the ground in front of the barrel, but either jump aside or over and continue advancing forward.

"Two barrels!" orders Gergely.

He adjusts the direction of the third and he himself lifts the wick and lights it.

Two fiery barrels again sweep a path through the crowded Turks below. A thick waisted janissary catches the third and throws it into the pit. He covers it with earth. As he tramples dirt on it, the barrel explodes, throwing the janissary and dirt into the sky and killing another twenty men standing around.

This horrifies the advancing soldiers. But *yasauls* behind them shout "*ileri*" (forward) and "*savul*" (careful), and waterskins are emptied on the flames with loud hisses of steam.

"Only rocks on them now!" shouts Gergely. He wants to wait for the attackers to crowd together under the wall.

Screams of *Allah*, like hundreds of thousands of tigers roaring. Trumpet blasts and drum beating resume. A forest of ladders approaches the wall.

A janissary throws a grappling hook on a rope over the wall. Like a monkey, he climbs up the rope with a *yataghan* short sabre between his teeth. A stone falls on his head and knocks off his helmet. Scars of sword cuts on his bald head made it look like a cantaloupe melon.

He climbs on.

Gergely grabs a lance to stab him.

When the Turk is within eight feet of Gergely, he lifts his face.

His face is sweaty and his mouth is panting.

Gergely, as if struck in the chest, is shocked. That's the face! This is Father Gábor, his late teacher! Same gray eyes; the same thin mustache; the same protruding eyebrows!

"You're the younger brother of Father Gábor!" he shouts to the Turk.

The Turk just stares and does not understand.

"Kill him" orders Gergely turning away. "He doesn't even know Hungarian!"

— § —

The great assault lasted until dusk. Then tired Turks retreated on all sides from under the walls.

Thousands of Turkish corpses and wounded were lying around the castle walls. Everywhere men with broken bones writhed and groaned *ey va*, *yetishin*, and *Allah yardım* (woe, help me God).

But the castle was also full of dead and wounded, and the walls and platforms were red with blood. Warriors, dead tired and weary, gathered the wounded and the bodies of the dead.

The officers went for a wash. Dobó himself was so sooty, his beard and mustache covered with grime, that had he not been wearing his captain's helmet, no one would have recognized his face. And sooty as he was, he listened to reports sitting by the Baba cannon.

"I have sixty-five dead and seventy-eight badly wounded. Five hundredweight of gunpowder has been used up," reported Mekcsey.

"Thirty dead and one hundred and ten wounded. Eight hundredweight of gunpowder used," reported Gergely Bornemissza. "We still have to work all night repairing the breach."

"Three hundredweight of gunpowder used, twenty-five dead, some fifty wounded," reported Fügedy. He put his hand on his face.

"You have also been wounded?" asked Dobó.

"No," Fügedy replied. "But I have such a toothache, as if someone was turning a fiery spear in my face."

Among those reporting, Dobó saw Varsányi as well. The spy was dressed in a dervish robe. Blood on his chest down to his ankles looked like he was wearing a red apron. "Varsányi," Dobó said, interrupting the reports. "Come here! Are you hurt?"

"No," Varsányi replied, "I had to carry the dead Turks until I got a chance to get away."

"What's the news?"

"Lord Szalkay has written a second time to counties and cities everywhere."

"And no one has come yet?"

"Some came from here and there," Varsányi said slowly. "But they are waiting for each other before they go against the Turks."

Dobó understood that Szalkay got no answer from anywhere. "What do you know about the Turks?"

"I've been wandering around them for four days, so I know they're terribly demoralized."

"Louder!" said Dobó with bright eyes.

The spy repeated so loudly that those around him could hear. "The Turkish are terribly demoralized. The weather is cold for them. They have no food. I saw it with my own eyes when a man from Nógrád brought five carts of flour yesterday. It was carried away in bowls and caps. They didn't even bother to make it into noodles. They ate the flour by the handful, raw, just as they took them out of the bags. But what was that for so many men?"

"Kristóf," Dobó said to his page. "Go to the butchers. Have them butcher the finest cattle for the men. Every man is to eat roast meat today and tomorrow." He turned back to the spy.

"The janissaries were already grumbling yesterday," continued the spy.

"Loudly!"

"The janissaries are grumbling," Varsányi continued, shouting. "They said God was with the Hungarians. They also complained that they are used to all sorts of weapons, but they are not used to hellfire. They have never seen such fiery wonders as they have been fighting here."

Dobó stared ahead silently for a minute.

"In an hour," he said, "be in front of the palace. You will accompany Miklós Vas to Szarvaskő again."

Then he turned to Sukán.

The old man had his head and nose bandaged so that only his glasses and mustache could be seen of his face. However, he said in a loud, crackling voice, "Today we've used up of twenty hundredweight of powder."

19

The rising sun saw the Eger warriors on the wall again. But there were still so many corpses around the castle that the dervishes could not carry away.

The cannons were silent. The sky itself was shivering in the cold. The city and surrounding valleys were covered in fog that reached up to the towers. The fog only dissipated around eight o'clock. Then the sun seemed to lighten the blue sky slightly, as if it were trying to bring spring back.

People inside the castle also gathered their dead. Peasants and women collected them from the Old Gate on carts and stretchers. Father Bálint priest buried. Father Márton administered the last sacraments to the dying.

In the light of the rising sun, one could see the various Turkish companies gathering from the distant hills towards the castle. The entire army was being assembled. As soon as they are collected, they will rush the ruined castle with full force.

The warriors had a deep and long sleep after a long night and day of fighting. Dobó allowed them to sleep, but they had to lie around the bastions. Only a few sentries were posted here and there on the bastions. And the officers slept that night as if they were dead. Bornemissza was still sleeping at eight o'clock, lying under the Frog cannon, not stirring from the sound of a trumpet or the sound of the repairs being made to the breaches. He was wrapped in a blanket, his long brown hair white with frost. Mekcsey laid a scarf on his head and covered him with his own cloak.

Dobó filled the bellies of cannons and mortars with tiny iron nails. He had carts loaded with rocks dragged in front of some of the breaches. Others he had filled with barrels, timber, leather, and rubble. Stone masons cut off the cornices of the castle walls in some places to prevent siege ladders from anchoring easily. Walls were topped with stone. All the cauldrons and pots were removed from the kitchen and filled with water. All the pitch that could be found in the castle was collected and carried to bastions next to cauldrons. The lead gutters on the palace were stripped, broken up, and distributed among the cannons. Butchers had to roast an ox on a spit near the south side. Bread was brought to the market square, where waiting and resting people gathered. They were stacked in piles. Mihály, who was in charge of distributing bread, no longer minded. Everyone could eat as much as they wanted. He reported to the market square by the ovens dressed in a fine brown cloak and yellow boots and simply wrote in his papers: *Oct. 14. Seven hundred loaves.*

During this time, the Turks were angrily gathering. A multitude of people descended from the mountains and hills.

At ten o'clock the castle trumpet sounded assembly. The people of the castle came together, seemingly all with bandages on head and arms. If nothing else, a finger on the right hand is bandaged. But whoever is able to walk can defend on the wall.

Silk flags from the church fluttered in the middle of the market square. One bore the image of Mary, another that of King St. István, and the third with Saint John. Worn, faded flags. They were from the church that had been converted to Church Bastion. The priests were standing by a table that had been set up to serve as an altar. They wore violet-colored vestments. A monstrance to display the Holy Eucharist was on the table-altar.

The people of the castle knew that they would be saying a mass. They should have said mass before the earlier assaults, but Dobó did not allow it out of respect for the dead. "They are just testing!" he would typically say. "By the time they make a full blown assault, the king's army will be here."

But now it was obvious that this was the end.

Everyone was washed, combed, and dressed in their best clothes for worship. Officers in all colors of flowers, red boots, spurs; their mustaches curled up, their helmets feathered. Mekcsey's shiny new steel armor glittered. He wore two swords by his side. One was the serpent sword which he wore only on ceremonial occasions.

Gergely Bornemissza appeared in a pointed steel helmet, three white crane feathers attached to its visor. A silver clamp, fashioned like a bird's foot, held those three feathers. He wore a steel breastplate, red leather on his arms, and silk gloves on his hands covered with small steel chain links. His broad, turned-out collar was embroidered with gold thread.

Zoltay could not resist making a comment. "Your collar looks like you're dressed for your wedding!"

"It's my wife's work," said Gergely seriously. "I'm not wearing it for the Turks' honor, but for their death."

Zoltay was also dressed in military leather with two swords on his side. His helmet had no visor, only a steel bar that covered his nose. A short curtain of iron mail covered his neck. That helmet must have been belonged to a *sipahi*. He picked it up at the castle auction after the first sortie.

Függedy appeared covered in iron down to his feet. His eyes were agitated. He complained of toothache.

"You'll be that much more angry at the Turks!" encouraged Zoltay. "It's good for a warrior to be angry."

"I'm angry without it!" growled Függedy.

Pető wore only a helmet and deerskin robe. He was on horseback because he still could not walk. He stood behind the congregation and waved his sword to greet the senior officers.

The rest were dressed in their best clothes. They were not necessarily dressed for the mass because not all of them knew there would be one. They dressed because they all felt that day was the last. And death, no matter how ugly it is, is a master to be honored! Who had no other clothes, just the everyday ones, also straightened what they had and twirled out their mustaches.

Only Dobó was missing.

He stepped forward in brilliant armor. Gilded helmet on his head. A long crane feather streaming from the top of his helmet. A broad sword at his side, its hilt encrusted with gemstones. He wore gloves made of iron plates and silver chain links. He carried a gold-tipped lance with a velvet covered shaft.

Behind him the two pages were similarly dressed in iron armor. They had short swords at their sides. Their hair fell from their helmets to their shoulders.

Dobó stopped in front of the altar and removed his helmet.

Because the two priests were poor speakers, Mekcsey spoke to the people.

"My brothers," he said, holding his helmet under his arm. "After yesterday's siege, we see that the entire Turkish army is gathering. Today, every enemy force is going to test our power. But wherever God is, it's useless to test His will even if every pagan in the world tries. In this sacrament we see here, we know that the living Jesus is present. He's with us! Let us get down and pray!"

The people of the castle all knelt together.

Mekcsey started the prayer instead of the priest. "Our Father, Who art in heaven ..." They rumbled softly, reciting the prayer.

When the amen was said, there was a long, ceremonial silence. Father Martin leaned over to Mekcsey and told him what to do next.

Mekcsey got up and spoke. "These two faithful servants of God are now lifting up the eucharist in order to forgive and absolve everyone of all faults. Time is too short to permit confessions. At such an hour, the Church will grant absolution without confession. Only repent of your sins within yourself."

And he knelt again.

An altar boy rang bells. Father Bálint raised the sacrament. The people bowed and listened as the old priest shouted the words of absolution. When they raised their faces again, the monstrance had been put back on the table, and the priest extended his hands in a blessing, his teary eyes looking up to the clear sky.

At the end of the ceremony, Dobó put his helmet back on. He stood on a stone and said, "After God's words, I have some words for you! Thirty-four days ago, we took an oath not to surrender the castle. We have kept our oath. The castle has defied the siege so far, like a rock in a stormy sea. Now comes the final test. We called on God for help. With souls cleansed of our sins, we must fight to the death for the survival of the castle and our country! No one anywhere has ever fought so heroically as we have fought to defend this castle. No one has suffered as much as the shameless Turks. I trust in our weapons. I trust in the power of our souls. I place my trust in the Virgin Mary, the patron of Hungary. I trust King St. István, whose soul is always with the Hungarian nation. Above all, I trust in God! Let's go, my brothers!"

The drum beat and the trumpet blared.

Warriors with the strength of steel in their hands, took up their lances and dispersed in groups. Dobó mounted his horse. His two pages followed him on horseback.

Dobó looked around everywhere. He saw Turkish horses grazing in large herds on the hills around Eger — without soldiers. A forest of spears moved forward. The castle was surrounded by sea of Turks.

He saw two pashas on King's Seat. Ali Pasha had the pale face of an old woman and wore a huge cantaloupe-like turban. The other pasha was a big man with a long grey beard. Both wore blue silk kaftans, but Ali's was a lighter shade. The diamonds in their belts threw white sparkles with each movement.

Beys on horseback led the armies. Aghas and *yasauls* were also mounted. All the rest were on foot. A large black flag was prominent among all the Turkish war flags. The people of the castle had not yet seen that black flag. Only the officers understood the significance of flying that black flag: *No mercy! Death to every living being in the castle!*

The Turkish cannons began firing around noon, and the two Turkish army bands began playing.

The air was full of smoke. The castle trembled with the cries of *Allahu akbar*.

The fires inside were lit.

Dobó ordered peasants, women, and other people who had taken refuge in the castle to stand by the cauldrons and walls. Even the sick came out to help. Whoever was able to stand on his feet also left his bed, if only to relay shouts of orders and calls for help. There were those with both arms bandaged, yet they still came out to help. He could tend a fire by using his feet to push a piece of wood to keep the flames under the cauldrons burning.

There was no one left in the houses except the children and the two women in the palace.

Lady Balogh ... Poor Lady Balogh ... She gave her son to a warrior's school. She did not dare ask Dobó to not have her son serve him during the siege. The boy was still weak. How could he face the weapons of wild pagan beasts? But she never gave any suggestion that she was worried for her son. Dobó's iron will had put a clamp on her worries. She did not even dare to breathe when Dobó looked at her. It was like with the soldiers: Everyone moved with mechanical obedience to Dobó's words. People had lost their independent wills. It was his will that motivated everyone. He did not even need to use words. A gesture was enough to make people move.

What would have happened to the castle if Dobó had even just a single hair's worth of fear in his body? He warned everyone to be careful. He made people wear armor, breastplate, and helmet, but when death appeared on the wall, he guided the people of the castle against it without regard to his own protection.

No one is more precious than the homeland!

The days of the siege were agonizing for the poor woman. She was shaking every morning when her son joined Dobó. She was worried every hour whether he was hit by a bullet. What a joy it had been for her each time Kristóf relieved him, and her son Balázs returned to the palace tired and dirty!

She always welcomed him with open arms and kisses as if he had come home from a long journey. She washed and bathed him. She combed and brushed his silky long hair. And she gave him everything good that she could find in the kitchen.

"Who died? Who are wounded *among the officers*?" These were always the first questions from the two women.

The boy didn't know who Éva was. He thought she was just another lady from Eger, like many others, and that his mother had called her to the palace to help. Well, he would just report on the news. The news always began with a list of the dead and ended with the praise of uncle Gergely. What that uncle Gergely could come up with! His soul was filled with admiration for uncle Gergely. He explained how many Turks he had seen in the fight, and what tricks uncle Gergely had used to defeat the Turks.

Éva held her breath, pale and proud, but always with tears in her eyes. She only smiled when the boy came to the part about how the Turks could not bear that wonderful uncle Gergely.

During the assaults, the two women stood by the window crying. All they could see through the small opening was people running back and forth, smoke, burning fire, and the barber carrying linen bandages, piling them up, carrying them, and fetching clean water. Then, the wounded being brought in, one by one, then more and more of them, more and more bloody.

And then all their attention turned towards the wounded. Oh, they are bringing someone else! Not Balázs. Not Gergely. Thank God. They bring another wounded man ... But, what if they did not bring either one because they took him to the cemetery pit ...

And they were unable to even say, *God be with you!*

And Éva's worried, half-crippled father was there. Many times she saw him walking by the palace, a bow over his shoulder as long as he is tall. His quiver was sometimes empty, sometimes full of arrows. She so wanted to shout, "My dad! My father! Take care, your grace!"

As the cannons began to roar that day, the two women held each other and cried.

"Let's pray, young sister."

"Let's pray, elder sister."

And they knelt down, bending over to place their faces on the ground. They prayed.

And every night, every day, in the distance, here and there all over Upper Hungary, a thousand and more women prayed with them. Little children's hands were clasped together in prayer in their remote shelters, praying for their innocent fathers in Eger.

"Dear God, save the life for our dear father. Bring our dear father back to us!"

Hellish thunder of roaring cannons, trumpets, the cries of Jesus, the shouts of Allah. Heavy smoke clouds flowing in.

The first wounded is already being brought, carried on a wheelbarrow covered with dark, dry blood. A young, pale soldier. His leg is shot away at the knee. The barbers pretty much bind up the wound. There is not much reason to spend time on him. They can bind the wound for maybe one or two hours before he bleeds to death.

And they bring the second, third, and fourth. One man's face is a bloody wreck. His two eyes are missing. His teeth stand out from his face. Another has an arrow in his neck. It has to be cut out. The third is holding his hands against his right side. His hands are covered in blood streaming through his fingers. He sits down on the ground and waits silently for death to close his eyes.

Dobó speeding on his horse gallops by the front of the palace. Kristóf is running after him, unable to keep up.

"Where's the other one?" asks the suffering mother when she sees him.

He is running toward Sándor Bastion, surely carrying a message. *Thank God!* and *ay!*

There are so many wounded that all thirteen barbers have work. Three Turkish flags have already been brought with the wounded. The Turkish yelling is getting louder. Gunpowder smoke covers the eastern and northern bastions, and it descends upon the palace like a fog in winter so thick that it is impossible to see three steps ahead.

"Merciful God," asks Lady Balogh, "what will happen to us if the Turks break through?!"

"Then I will die!" replies Éva, pale. She goes into the weapons room. She finds a sword there, Dobó's everyday sword. She places it on the table carefully.

Through the open window they can hear the groaning and wailing of the wounded. "Oh my eyes, my eyes!" cries one. "I will never see God's beautiful world again!"

Another moans, "I'm a beggar! They cut off both of my hands!"

There are so many wounded around the barbers that they cannot keep up bandaging them to slow the bleeding.

Lady Balogh's entire body is shaking. "We have to go outside!" she says, her face anguished. "We must help the barbers!"

"Should I go out too? I *am* going out! I feel that caring for the wounded cannot be forbidden by honor or command."

Wind clears the gunpowder smoke. Lady Balogh opens the door and looks towards Prison Bastion. She sees Dobó there in a cloud of smoke as he strikes a terrible sword cut on the head of a Turk, then kicks the dead body back off the wall.

Page Balázs is standing behind him, wearing a steel helmet with visor lowered. He holds his lord's spear, mace, and another sword under his arm.

The sun shines through gaps in clouds and smoke. The weather should be horribly cold, a cold autumn day, but those fighting feel heat! Dobó unhooks his helmet with a jerk and throws it to Balázs. Then he pulls out a handkerchief from his belt and wipes his sweaty forehead. He continues fighting bareheaded.

Page Balázs does not know where to place the gilded helmet. He puts it on his head.

Smoke covers them. Go away, smoke, go away!

The cloud of smoke, as if it heard the mother's cry, clears. Balázs stands. He is standing on the wall. His mother wants to scream for him to get down, but he would never be able to hear it in that hellish rampage.

And as she raises her hand to wave to her son, the boy drops Dobó's weapons and reaches for his neck in a weak gesture. At the same time he stumbles and falls. The gilded helmet falls off its head and rolls away. The boy collapses on the ground without moving his hand to break his fall.

His mother slams the door with a marrow-shaking scream. She runs to the bastion. She hugs her son. She wails. She falls on him. She hugs him. She shouts his name.

Dobó glances at them and picks up the gilded helmet. He gestures to two soldiers and points to the boy. The two soldiers grab the boy, one by the shoulder and the other by the knees, and take him to the palace, to his mother's room.

The boy is lying with a bloody neck like a shot pigeon, lifeless.

"Oh, I no longer have a son!" cries the grey-haired widow.

"Maybe he just fainted," says one of the soldiers. He unfastens the helmet with visor and removes it from the page's head, then roves his breastplate and other armor.

But there was a large gunshot wound on his neck. The bullet did not enter his neck, but through his waist. It just came out through his neck.

The widow's face is distorted by pain. Her eyes are bloodshot. She grabs the sword on the table that Éva had just brought out of the weapons room, and rushes with it to the thunderstorm of men on Prison Bastion.

Several women there have already been at work below the bastion. They cook water and boil pitch and lead. When ready, they briskly carry it up to the soldiers.

"Bring some cold water to drink!" shout soldiers during a pause in the assault.

"To the cellar, ladies!" shouts Dobó. "Tap every barrel! Carry it in cups for the soldiers!"

Some of the women who heard the cry run for wine with skirts flying.

Imre the clerk is armed and pacing back and forth in front of the cellar. As the many women run there, he pushes the key on the cellar door lock. "For the officers, right?" he asks Mrs. Kocsis.

"The captain sir said for everyone, clerk sir, everyone!"

Imre clerk pushes the cellar door open. "The best is in back!" he shouts. He lowers his visor and draws his sword. He also rushes to Prison Bastion.

More and more Turks are forcing their way up the bastion. Some are already jumping on it. They engage the defender warriors in murderous hand to hand combat. Dobó himself grabs one by the throat, a giant whose bones alone weigh a hundredweight. He tries to push him back. The Turk plants his legs. For a minute, both stare at each other, panting. Then Dobó gathers his strength, pivots, and pulls the man over with a twist. The Turk drops from the platform to the yard below.

The Turk's helmet falls off as he rolls on the cobblestones. He gets up and turns his head to see if his companions are coming.

That is when Lady Balogh gets there. With a blood curdling scream, she swings her sword in the air and separates the Turk's head from his neck.

Other women are already up on top of the bastion. The soldiers are busy fighting Turks one-on-one. They can no longer take the burning pitch, stones, or molten lead to the fight, so the women themselves carry it all up and, in the smoke, dust, and flames, they throw it down on the climbing Turks.

The dead fall and the living multiply. The falling stones, pitch and lead clear a path on the wall, but the mounds of dead only make it easier for companies that follow to climb up. The living catch the horsetail flags from the falling dead bodies, and the horsetail flag dances again on the ladder.

"Allah! Allah! We are winning! Now we're winning!"

Dobó glances with amazement at Lady Balogh fighting next to him, but there is no time to talk. He himself is fighting. Blood is dripping from the shoulders to the ankles of his shining armor.

The lady strikes blow after blow on Turks trying to climb up until finally, a lance from below pierces her. She falls from the bastion to the platform below.

"The Women of Eger" (1867)
Oil painting by Bertalan Székely

There is no one to pull her away. The fighting has reached the top of the wall. The living trample over dead and wounded. Dobó jumps on a projection from the wall and looks down.

The aghas are already at the base of the wall. Veli Bey carries a large red velvet flag on horseback. Seeing the flag, the Turkish fighters break out in a new roar.

"Allah help! The time of triumph is here!"

The flag is Ali Pasha's victory flag. Already that summer, that flag has flown over thirty castles and forts to proclaim Turkish victory. It has never known anything but a symbol of glory!

Veli Bey rides towards the earth bastion with the flagpole. The defenses there seem to be the most worn out because the women there have already joined the fighting.

Dobó glances at the large ceremonial flag with its glittering gold letters. He sends a message to Pető and runs to the earth bastion.

Men are fighting men there. A figure carrying a flag appears here and there, then is lost below. Warriors struggle in clouds of rising dust and smoke. Pitch soaked wreaths and fiery mugs fly like comet stars among the clouds of smoke.

"Jesus, help me!" screams a woman.

Dobó reaches there at the same moment a Turk climbs onto the rampart and plunges his *yataghan* to the hilt in Mátyás Szőr, the miller from Maklár.

"On him! On him!" Dobó's voice shouts on the bastion.

Soldiers are propelled by the force of his words. They attack and kill the intruders on the ramparts with a vengeance, shouting Hungarian curses for which they ought not be thought sinful.

Dobó turns towards the miller's murderer. He sees that the Turk is dressed in Derbend steel from head to toe. Swords glance off of such steel. With a quick decision, he hurls himself at the Turk, pressing him down on the miller's body.

But the Turk is a strong, muscular man. He struggles to take down Dobó. Furiously helpless, he bites iron off Dobó's arm, then suddenly hits the ground and turns upside down. This is his death. Dobó has found his naked neck and mercilessly squeezes the soul out of him.

Dobó barely gets up when a Turkish spear thrown from above slams into his leg, slitting its leather strap, stopping in his calf.

Dobó cries out in pain like a lion. Crouching on his knees, he grabs his leg, his eyes wet with tears of pain.

"My lord!" shouts page Kristóf, frightened. "Are you wounded?"

Dobó does not answer. He pulls the spear from his leg and throws it away. He stands with a clenched fist for a minute and sucks through his teeth while the first poison of agony subsides. Then he kicks with his leg, testing to see if his leg is broken. Not broken, just bleeding. As the pain becomes bearable, he grabs his sword and throws himself like a tiger at the Turks pushing through the breach. Woe to him who comes before him!

While they are fighting each other, almost with their teeth, hardly eighty feet away, enemy troops have overwhelmed another breach. The timber holding the breach breaks from the pressure of hundreds. Turks shout of victory without having to climb a wall.

One pushes and tosses the other. Weapons in the right hand, horsetails in the left. Those in front jump on the bastion with horsetails. Those following attack the wounded and women under the platforms.

Meanwhile, one of them kicks the fire with his iron clad feet pushing the burning logs over the side of the wall onto the platform below. The fire begins to burn the timbers with tall flames.

The Turks can easily deal with the wounded, but the women grab cauldrons and pots with angry screams. Thick-waisted Mrs. Gáspár Kocsis throws boiling water over one of the big bearded aghas so that if that agha were to pull on his ornate beard, it will stay in his grip.

Another woman picks up a blazing log from another fire and uses it to hit Turks, sparks from the wood fluttering like stars. The other women are already attacking the pagans with weapons.

"Hit them! Hit them!" roars the blacksmith from Felnémet. He runs with his sledge hammer among the women. Three pagans are back to back with one another fighting the women. He hits the first one on the head so hard that his brains splatter out his ears and nose. A *yataghan* flashes in the hand of the second Turk and is buried up to the hilt in the blacksmith's stomach.

"You're coming to the next world with me, dog!" yells the blacksmith. Once more, he lifts his half-hundredweight sledge hammer over his head, and only sits down on the ground and holds his stomach after he sees his opponent fall face down with helmet pancaked from a terrible blow.

By then, the enraged women have all picked up weapons lying about and were furiously fighting the Turks. Their shawls fall. Their hair unravels. Their skirts flutter back and forth in the fight. But they no longer think of themselves as feminine. They savagely attack the Turks. Their swords do not parry any blows. What falls on them is theirs. But what they give belongs to the Turks.

"Long live the women!" Pető shouts from behind. And when he sees the platform posts on fire, he gets a bucket and pours water over the post.

The first lieutenant brings up the reserves. He himself flashes his sword and jumps at an *akinji* climbing up the breach like a cat. He drops the man among the timbers. Meanwhile, the Turks that have forced their way past the breach are cut up by his soldiers like rags. The soldiers even advance out into the breach hole.

Dobó is on the wall, kneeling on one knee, chest panting and staring down as blood drips from his sword and beard. More and more furious Eger defenders rush through the breaches to attack Turks among the dead below the bastion.

"Back!" screams Dobó as loudly as he can. But in that thunderstorm of battle, they cannot even hear their own voices.

A regular warrior named László Tóth sees the bey carrying the red velvet flag. He goes for him. He is carrying a blunderbuss. He fires it at the bey's chest. He makes a grab for the flag. His other move is to smash the empty blunderbuss between the eyes of another Turk. Then he jumps back with his plunder, while janissaries chase back his five companions.

Dobó sees only Veli Bey turning and falling off his horse and that a Hungarian has captured the pasha's victory flag. He gestures where the reserve troops should fight. He twists a bloody rag on his left arm and rushes down into the gap of the breach. Pető is already standing there and raises a flaming stick to the mortar positioned in front of the breach.

The janissaries chasing after the flag are kicked back by this shot.

"Load it!" shouts Dobó to one of the soldiers. "Four of you stay here. Pile stones and timber here, if there's time!"

And the fiery storm rages on the bastion with renewed force.

20

Éva was left alone with the dead boy.

She stared at him for a minute, petrified, then moved. She strapped his helmet on her head and his armor around her waist and arms. The boy was as big as she was. She dressed in his dress.

She thought his sword was too short. She entered Dobó's room and took a straight, long Italian rapier displayed on a wall and tied its strap to her wrist.

She left the scabbard behind.

She rushed out the door with the naked rapier. She ran. She herself did not know where. All she knew was that her husband and Zoltay were defending the outer castle. But she did not know how to get from the palace to the outer castle.

The sun was getting lower by then, but through the clouds of smoke everywhere, it looked like a fiery cannonball that was suspended in the air.

She remembered the drawing of Eger Castle. It showed the outer castle curved like a sickle around the east side of the tortoise. The sun was setting on her right side, so the outer castle must be on her left.

Ten sweaty, smoky garrison soldiers rattled towards her. They came running. A corporal in front. The soldiers' right arm and side were black with blood. They carried lances over their shoulders. They were running towards Prison Bastion. Then came a soldier staggering ... blood flowing from his face. Surely he wanted to go to the barber. He managed a few more uncertain steps, then collapsed on the ground.

For a moment, Éva hesitated wondering whether she should pick him up. But she saw a second and a third soldier lying around, either dead or unconscious. The third soldier was the older son of the mayor of Eger. She recognized him from looking out the window. An arrow was stuck in his chest.

Panting women running from the cellars. They carry wooden bowls on their heads and empty pots and cheese pails in their hands. They also head east. Éva joins them. As they run past the stables, they disappear inside a small downward sloping tunnel. Two lanterns are burning in the tunnel.

That is the Dark Gate which connects the outer castle to the upper walls.

When they get past there, they enter a hell of dust and smoke.

Dead bodies are lying all about on the ground, on the stairs, on the platforms. Éva recognizes the body of Father Bálint. The priest is lying face down. No helmet on his head. Long white beard red with blood. He is still holding his sword in his hand.

Éva picks up a mace from the ground and rushes up the stairs. The fighting there is mostly hand-to-hand. Soldiers standing on the wall are shoving Turks back. A woman is throwing a burning log down on the Turks. Another is swinging a burning stick and hits a Turk's neck. Cursing, cries of Jesus, shouts of Allah, feet pounding, rumbling, smashing everywhere.

Two cannons in the bastion fire, one after another.

Éva looks towards the sound. She sees her husband holding a smoking taper, eying down the barrel to see the aim of his shot.

The remaining five or six Turks on the platform are dispatched, then there is a one-minute break. The soldiers all turn around and shout, "Water! Water!"

An old soldier wearing a helmet is standing on a wall projection near Éva, shouting. His face is covered with bloody sweat, like pearly dew. His eyes are almost hidden by all the blood on his face.

Éva recognizes her father.

She grabs a cup from one of the women and hands it to him. She holds him, helps him.

The old man drinks eagerly. There is aged red Eger wine in the cup, not water. As he takes the cup from his mouth, wine dribbles down his mustache and he gulps a deep breath.

Éva sees the old man's right hand is burning. No wonder. It is wood is up to his wrist. Surely it caught fire from the burning, tarred straw. The old man didn't see it.

Éva drops the cup and the mace and holds onto the old man's arm. She knows where the wood is attached. She quickly releases the buckle and the wooden hand flies towards the Turks.

The old man grabs his sword with his left hand, then leaning over the bastion he strikes a reed shield decorated with copper moons.

Éva rushes towards her husband. Here and there she has to jump over a dead body. Here and there a burning plume flies in front of her eyes. Here and there a bullet hits the wall in front and behind her. But the warriors all drink. They just asked for water, and it would have been nectar for them. The wine? As if they were invoking divine power!

Zoltay's curses mingle with the din of Turks struggling below. "Come on now, dogs! Take some messages to Muhammad in paradise!"

And a minute later, a simple, "Good night!" The Turk to whom he was talking certainly must have forgotten to reply with a goodbye.

"*Ileri! Ileri!*" shout the *jasavuls* endlessly. "We've won! We've won!"

And new swarms, new ladders, new shields hover over the hills of the dead.

"*Allah! Allah!*"

Éva finally reaches Gergely just as he ignites a barrel loaded with gunpowder and throws it down from the wall. Then he throws off his helmet, jumps in front of a woman, grabs a cup and drinks so eagerly that the red wine splashes on both sides.

Éva gives her wine to another soldier, leaving the cup in his hand. She turns to her husband's helmet, but as she leans over to pick it up, pitch smoke hits her eyes. When she tears out the smoke, she sees Gergely nowhere. As she looks left and right, soldiers suddenly crouch around her.

Down below, just thirty feet from the wall, *tüfekchis* fire a volley of bullets. A bullet hits Éva's helmet, cracking it. Éva staggers. Several minutes pass before she recovers her senses.

Down below, infernal martial music, drumming and trumpet blares. A long-necked *yasaul* screams with a sharp voice from under the wall, "*Ya *ayuha!*" (Here!) The army has gotten all mixed up down there. Janissaries were replaced by leather-skinned *azabs* and red-caped *akinjis*.

A dervish dressed in white, wearing a helmet instead of the typical dervish camel-hair cap, holding a flag in his hand and surrounded by ten veteran janissaries, shouts "*Ileri! Ileri!*" and pushes his way towards the wall.

Our men ordinarily do not fire at dervishes, but seeing him with a helmet on his head and a sword in his hand, they fire at him. He also attracts Éva's attention.

There is a gust of wind. It blows smoke away and flutters the horsetail flag dangling from the three-button pole in the dervish's hand. As he turns toward the castle, Éva sees that one of the dervish's eyes is bandaged.

"Yumurjak!" she screams like a tiger.

And she throws her mace from the height like a yellow streak of lightning. The mace flies over the dervish's head and strikes a janissary in the chest. The dervish hears the scream and looks up. At the same time, the cannon on the bastion fires into the besiegers. The dervish and his group of janissaries are covered with flames and smoke.

By the time the smoke disappears from the ditch, there is no trace of the dervish. But the walls are crowded with men climbing up ladders and into the breaches.

They are no longer just climbing ladders. A janissary in a white cap begins climbing the wall itself; no ladder, only gripping stones and crevasses in the wall. From stone to stone! He finds a handholds and toeholds everywhere. And it is easy to climb up among the timber. He is followed by another, a third, then ten, twenty, and hundred more intrepid men, like the red chinch bug beetles of spring that swarm over the sunny sides of walls. Here, the besiegers hang on to the outer wall of the castle, climbing upwards. Some of them also carry rope ladders. He hooks it on a suitable stone, and the ones below immediately start climbing on it.

Gergely runs from the bastion to the rubble of the breach. He is bare headed, lance in his hand, face black from gunpowder. "Sukán," he yells to a man fighting with a blood-stained pike, "is there any pitch in the cellar?"

His voice is hoarse. The old man leans with his ear towards the question. "No!" replies Sukán replies. "But there's still a barrel of resin."

"Bring it to the Perényi cannon right now."

Fighting beside the old man is the clerk Imre. He puts his pike down and rushes away.

"Warriors!" shouts Gergely. "Let's gather our strength!"

Zoltaj's words echo the sentiment: "If we repel them now, they dare not come again!"

Shout of "Fire! Fire!" come from the other side. Women use poles to carry cauldrons full of hot lead and boiling oil.

Mrs. Ferenc Vas runs up to the wall with a large iron shovel full of glowing embers and turns it over onto the Turks. But at the same time, the shovel drops out of her hands. A bullet hit the stone wall smashing a large piece of rock against her forehead. She falls back against a post and slumps down.

A sturdy woman, black from smoke, leans over her. She quickly sees that she is done for. A second glance falls on the bastion stone next to Mrs. Ferenc Vas. She picks up the stone and hurries with it to the wall. A bullet hits her in the chest. She falls.

"My mother!" screams a young woman in a red skirt. But she does not lean over her mother, but picks up the stone she had dropped and throws it down from the wall as her mother had wanted.

The stone strikes and takes out two Turks. Only when she sees this does she turn back to her mother, lift her up, and carry her down the steps below the platform.

In the sea of smoke below, a company of besiegers are advancing under shields in a tortoise formation. The *akinjis* are packed so tightly under the shields, they cannot be seen.

"Watch out, warriors!" sound Gergely's words.

"Water! Fire!" shouts Zoltay. "Over there! Over there! They're climbing the wall without ladders!"

A tin-plated *target* rises from the moat. Four *piyads* run to the wall with it. Those on a ladder grab it and pull it over their heads. Then come the rest of the *targets*, each covered with tin, to prevent the defenders from using pickaxes to tear off the roof.

"Hot water!" shouts Gergely. "Lots of it!"

Éva jumps next to him and presses the helmet over his head. "Thank you, Balázs!" says Gergely. "Did Dobó send you?"

Éva does not reply. She runs down from the bastion to fetch boiling water. "Water! Boiling water, ladies!" he shouts with his hoarse throat.

During this time, the tin-plated *targets* are joined together. Lightly dressed wall-climbers jump underneath. Some are half-naked, but even so sweat drips off their bodies. Their heads are not weighed down by helmets. They have thrown down all their heavy weapons from their belts. They have only curved, sharp swords dangling from straps tied to their arms.

The many connected *targets* become a wide-spread metal roof. The aghas also jump underneath. Dervish bey also crosses the moat carrying crescent moon horsetails.

By the time Éva returns to be with Gergely, she could not make anyone out in the dense smoke, only explosions of red flames and the white flashes of swords.

"*Allah! Allah!*"

Bum! Bum! Bum! sound the cannons.

The smoke becomes even more dense, but suddenly it rises above the defenders' heads, like a white canopy waving over a bed. Suddenly flashing Turkish weapons are clearly visible, as are the Hungarian weapons flashing down.

"Water, water!" shouts Gergely.

The metal roof is rising from below. Stones weighing a half a hundredweight are flung down from the wall. The metal roof opens and swallows the stone. Then it closes again.

"Boiling water" shouts Zoltay as he rushes over.

Gergely, as he sees Zoltay coming, jumps down to the cannon.

The resin is already waiting in a half barrel. Gergely tilts the barrel and tells the artillerymen, "Put it in the cannon, over the gunpowder! As much as they can fit! Pound it in to crush it! Only a little wadding on top!"

Then the boiling water is poured off the wall.

Where the stone could not reach, the boiling water reaches. The *targets* all flutter and separate. Turks jumped out from underneath shouting *ey va* and *meded*.

The red chinch bugs still cover the wall. Gergely shoots at them with a mortar. But they still cling onto the wall. Gergely rushes at them with the ramrod.

"Gergely!" shouts Pető.

"I'm here," Gergely says hoarsely.

"I brought fifty people. Enough?"

"Bring more! As many as you can! Lay a fire below and have ten men constantly bringing up boiling water."

A new volley from the *tüfekchis* creates smoke that mixes with the smoke from mortar and obscures the wall for a minute. This minute is used by lightly clothed climbers to run up the ladders.

Gergely rushes back to the cannon. "Is it loaded yet?" he asks.

"It's loaded" replies the old Gáspár Kocsis.

"Fire!"

The cannon throws a flame, then explodes. Flaming resin shoots out in a column a hundred and fifty feet long. Even those Turks jump off the wall who feel only the wind from the explosion.

The wall is cleared. The *yasauls* and Turkish officers shout angrily.

From the bastion they can see that every soldier is running away from the wall. *Azabs, piyads, müsellems, delis, sipahis, gurebas*, and *akinjis* — all mixed up and terrified, running to their trenches. And they can see what the *yasauls* and aghas are using to try to control them. They are no longer using nail-studded whips to lash at the men running away in droves. They are using swords. The soldiers, their heads bloodied, filled with rage, pick up the siege ladders and run straight to the wall under the Hungarian cannon.

The dervish leads them. He is running in front. His white robe is red with blood. The precious horsetail flag is clenched between his teeth. He runs without a shield.

A giant agha is leading the neighboring ladder. His turban is the size of a stork's nest. His sword is the size of an executioner's.

Gergely glances around and again sees the rock-throwing page next to him. The page is lifting the great stones from the wall and throwing them down from the rampart!

"Balázs," says Gergely with his hoarse voice, which voice turns a little less gruff as he continues, "get out of here!"

Balázs does not answer. She is holding the Italian rapier she brought out of the room. She stumbles with it towards the ladder that the dervish is climbing.

Gergely looks down. "Hayvan!" he shouts to the giant climbing the ladder. "You beast! You ox!" he continued, in Turkish. "So you think weapons can't touch you!"

The Turk is surprised. His wide, huge figure stares at Gergely, petrified.

Gergely uses that pause. He lunges with the lance in his hand and pierces the Turk's chest.

The Turk grabs the spear with one hand and aims a horrible blow at Gergely with the other. But the blow finds only air, and his big body falls backward onto a tin covered *target* below.

Meanwhile, the dervish has gotten to the top of the wall.

Éva ducks to avoid the lance point striking her head. The next moment she cuts the dervish on his left arm holding onto the wall.

The dervish's arm is covered with wool cloth, but the cut reveals glittering wire mail underneath. He leaps onto the wall. With a sword hanging on a strap, he goes after Éva.

Éva jumps back two steps. She holds her rapier firmly in front of her. Her eyes are wide open as she waits for the rush.

But the Turks have long attended the school of death. He sees that he is facing a rapier and not a sword. He know it's not a good idea to run into a long rapier pointed at him. He stops abruptly and strikes the rapier to hit it aside, hoping with a second cut to send this page of a boy to the world of spirits.

But Éva also is familiar with parries and thrusts. With a swift circular movement, she cuts from underneath and hits the Turk's sword aside. By the time the Turk is ready to strike again, Éva's rapier slips under his arm.

The mail saves the Turk. The steel wire cracks, but at the same time the dervish makes his own cut, and his sword strikes Éva on the head.

Éva feels as if her head would split apart. The world darkens before her eyes. She feels the ground being pulled out from under feet. She raises her arm in front of her eyes and leans against a cannon like a sack.

21

When Éva regains consciousness, all is silent around her. Where is she? She did not know. She looks around. Slowly awakening from her stupor. A collapsed timber building ... Between the roof beams a clear moonlit sky with white stars is visible ... Something hard squeezing her waist. Her head is lying in something cold and wet ...

She reaches under her waist with a weak hand. She feels stone powder and a cold, apple-like iron ball.

Then at once everything clears up in front of her.

There is silence. So perhaps the fighting is over. Who is the master of the castle? Is he a Turk or a Magyar? She hears the even steps of a sentry on a platform: one, two, three, four ...

Éva wants to get up, but her head feels like it is made of lead. Yet from this gesture she is able to see that she is near the bastion, there is a woman lying on her belly next to her, and a soldier with no head.

God of mercy, if the Turks are lord ...

Through the beams, a lantern burns with a reddish light. Human steps approach. She hears a trembling male voice. "Shall we take the page first or the woman?"

Thank God! They are talking in Hungarian!

"Both of them," replies the other man.

"But still, the page ..."

"Well, let's take the page. The captain sir is still up."

And they stand by Éva.

"Should we take him to the palace or put him with the rest?"

"Among the rest. He is as dead as they are."

One grabbed legs, the other under the arms, and they lifted the body onto a stretcher.

Éva said, "Men."

"What, is this young noble still alive? Thank God, Young lord Balázs! Then let's take him to the palace."

"Men," groans Éva, "is my lord alive?"

"Is he alive? Of course he's alive! Just now the barber is bandaging the captain sir's leg."

"I'm asking about First Lieutenant Gergely."

"Lord Gergely, the scholar?"

And he pokes his companion. "He's delirious."

The man spits in his fist. They grasp the two ends of the stretcher and lift it up.

"Men," says Éva, almost crying. "Answer me: is First Lieutenant Gergely Bornemissza alive?"

She speaks with such authority that the two men reply almost simultaneously, "Yes, he's alive."

"Wounded?"

"Hand, leg."

"Take me to him."

The two peasants stop. "To him?"

One shouts to the sentry. "Hey, warrior! Where is Lieutenant Gergely?"

"What do you want?" It is Gergely's voice.

"Young Balázs is here, sir. He wants to say something."

The sound of slow steps approaching on the stairs. Gergely walks limping. He holds a lantern in his hand. A candle burns inside the lantern. He stops at the bottom of the stairs and says to someone, "Another assault tomorrow is impossible. They have so many dead it will take them at least two days to collect them all."

The lantern approaches.

"Take off my helmet," says Éva.

The peasant reaches for the buckle under her chin as Gergely gets there.

"My poor Balázs," he says. "Well, but you're alive."

The peasant unhooks the helmet and removes it. Éva feels a burning pain in her head. "Oh!" she gasps almost screaming.

Because the lining of the helmet had stuck to blood and hair, and the peasant certainly did not know that the page had a head wound.

Gergely puts down the lantern and leans over her. She can see that Gergely's face is still covered with soot as before. His mustache, beard, and eyebrows are all singed. His right hand is wrapped in a thick bandage.

But her face is also almost unrecognizable, covered with so much blood and so much soot. Only her eyes stand out white in her bloody, sooty face.

The same warm glow runs through Gergely's nerves as when he walked towards the mill wheel and saw the same eyes staring out the palace window.

And for a moment the two eyes face each other.

"Gergely!" said the woman.

"Éva, Éva! How did you get here!"

In that same moment, his mind understood everything he had heard about his son, and everything he had seen in the behavior of the page fighting by his side, and he came to the most bitter realization. Tears flowed from both of his eyes and down his gunpowder covered cheeks.

22

That terrible siege was followed by three-days of gathering corpses. Dervishes and unarmed *azabs* carried away the dead.

Bodies of men lay on each other at the bottom of the walls. The mud in the ditches was so deep from blood that sometimes they had to throw logs over them to walk across. Shields, maces, swords, spears, and guns were scattered and broken around the bodies.

Day and night the Turks collected their dead. Eight thousand dead had to be removed from under the walls of the outer castle alone. It was only on the third day that the last body was cleared. By then flocks of ravens had to be scared off with gunshots.

But the losses inside were also great. The morning after the assault, Father Martin sang the *Absolve Domine* over three hundred dead.

The three hundred dead lay in long rows around the common burial pit. Father Bálint was lying in the middle wearing a church shirt, a crucifix and a stole. Next to him, headless Cecey. Eight lieutenants. Page Balázs with his mother. Máté Szőr, the miller from Maklár. Gergely, the blacksmith from Felnémat. Gasparics. Ferenc Vas. Lady Balogh. Women, girls, unrecognizable faces, bones and blood of the dead in their silent multitude. Sometimes only one head. Sometimes only an arm. Sometimes only some bloody clothes with a leg wearing boot and spur.

The remaining officers were there for the funeral. Dobó himself, with his uncovered head, holding the castle flag in his hand.

When the priest had blessed the dead, Dobó spoke in a muffled voice, struggling to keep from bursting into tears. "I stand in front of you, helmet off, my fellow warriors who have died a holy death in blood and fire. Your souls are already beyond the stars in the land of eternity. The dust of your bodies blesses now and forever."

"I fly the castle flag before you, glorified heroes. You died for the homeland. Expect your reward from God. God be with you! In the light of eternity, we will meet again before the face of our King St. István!"

They said farewell using a sliding board to lower the dead into a common grave. No coffins.

The first signs of early winter appeared as white flakes from the sky.

— § —

On Sunday, October 16, Dobó slept an hour in the afternoon, and as soon as he rubbed dreams from his eyes, he mounted a horse and rode to Sándor Bastion.

By then the people of the castle were not building but only stacking to fill the breaches.

Cold autumn, cloudy weather.

The Turkish cannons roared continuously.

"Go, my son Kristóf," Dobó said to his page. "Look around Bolyky Bastion. What are they doing there? I am on my way to the Old Gate."

Kristóf, a white bandage covering one of his eyes, mounted a horse. When he reached the Dark Gate, he tethered his horse to a post and ran on foot. Then along the wall to Bornemissza.

A cannon ball struck him through one of the breaches. He just turned and fell from the wall onto the rubble on the platform.

The sentry shouted at Zoltay. "Lieutenant sir! The page has fallen!"

Zoltay climbed up to the wall in shock. He could see the big, bloody dent in the boy's chest. The sentry knelt beside him, and as the boy's head slumped to his chest, he unhooked his helmet.

"Go immediately to the captain," Zoltay said, embracing the boy. "Report to him."

The boy was still alive. His face was white as wax. He looked sadly at Zoltay and muttered, "Report that I am dead." He sighed and then he died.

— § —

The next day they did not awake to the sound of cannon fire. The tents spread white over the hills, but the Turks could not be seen.

"Take care," Dobó said, "so we don't get tricked!" He posted guards in the underground cellars and in the breaches above ground. Because it was difficult to stand anywhere on the walls. The castle was like a mouse-chewed almond cake. The walls would crumble should anyone step on them.

As they watched and stared at the unusually silent and empty tents, suddenly someone simply expressed an opinion.

"They're gone ..."

Like a fire racing through dry grass, the words were repeated throughout the castle. "They're gone! They're gone!"

Then louder and with increasing jubilation: "They're gone! They're gone!"

The officers would not allow anyone to go outside the walls.

A quarter of an hour after sunrise, the sentries reported the appearance of a woman. The black silk *feradje* cloak over her head showed her to be Turkish.

She came from Maklár direction. She was sitting on a mule. Sitting in front of her on the tall saddle was a small Hungarian child. A fifteen-year-old Serbian boy led the mule by a bridle.

They did not open a gate for the woman. But how indeed could they have opened a gate when there was none?

She rode inside through a breach near a gate. She could not speak Hungarian, so she just shouted the one word: "Dobó! Dobó!"

Dobó was standing on top of rubble that used to be a gate. He was staring out at the city. He saw the Turkish woman coming. He immediately suspected that she was the mother of little Selim. Still, when she called out his name, he limped off the rubble.

She fell to her knees at his feet. Then she lifted her head and, still on her knees, pointed towards the Hungarian child. "Selim! Selim!" she begged, both palms pressed together in prayer.

The Hungarian child was six years old. A brown-faced little boy with smart eyes. He held a carved wooden horse in his hand.

Dobó put his hand on the boy's head. "What do they call you, son?"

"Jancsi."

"What's your other name?"

"Bojnemissza."

Dobó, excited with joy, turned towards Sándor Bastion and shouted "Gergely! Gergely!" Then turned to the sentries, "Run quickly to Lieutenant Gergely."

But by then Gergely was already rushing down from the bastion, tears in his eyes, calling, "My Jancsi! My dear Jancsi!" Then he almost ate the child he was so happy. "Come. Let's see your mother!"

The Turkish woman grabbed the little boy with ten fingernails. She held onto him like an eagle clutching a lamb. "Selim!" she cried out, her black lined eyes flared open. "Selim!" She looked ready to tear the child apart if she did not get hers.

A minute later, Éva rushed out from the palace, her petticoat flying about. Her forehead was bandaged with white cloth, but her face was flushed with joy. She was bringing the little Turkish child, holding him by the hand. Little Selim was in his usual Turkish outfit, running beside Éva holding a big piece of *kalács* bread in his free hand.

Both mothers flew to their children with open arms.

One cried, "Selim!"

The other cried, "My Jancsi!"

They knelt before their children, hugging and kissing.

As the two women knelt facing each other, they looked up at each other. Each reached out a hand to the other.

23

The Turks had indeed left.

Varsányi, who appeared in the castle an hour after the Turkish woman, said that the pashas wanted another assault, but the janissaries, when they were informed, flung their weapons down by the pashas' tents. And they shouted angrily, "We won't fight anymore! Even if you hang all of us, we still won't fight! Allah is not with us! Allah is with the Hungarians! We are not fighting against God!"

Ahmed Pasha, standing in front of the army, tears in his eyes and tearing his beard, cursed Ali Pasha to his face. "Miserable lowlife!" he screamed looking him in the eye. "You said Eger Castle was a broken down sheep pen! And the people inside just sheep! Now you report this disgrace before the emperor!"

And it was only the beys who kept the two pashas from attacking each other in front of the army.

There was also a shortage of officers. They took Veli Bey off the battlefield on a bed. They discovered the dervish bey at night lying under the walls, beaten half dead.

The Turkish army had become so demoralized, they had suffered so many casualties from fire and weapons, that when the pashas gave the *topchis* the order to retreat, the rest did not wait for morning. They left tents and baggage and left that night.

The people of the castle listened to Varsányi's report. Heavenly joy filled the castle. Men and women were dancing. Their caps were fluttering to the ground. They put Turkish horsetail flags out on display. They fired cannons.

Father Márton lifted the crucifix that he always wore by his side. He held it up towards the sky and shouted in a frenzied voice of joy, "*Te Deum laudamus!*"[55] He fell on his knees, prostrated himself on the ground, kissed the crucifix, and cried.

They lifted the bell out from the ground. The beam on which it was hanging was placed on two posts. They rang the bell. Bim-bom, bim-bom! ... the bell joyfully rang, and as Father Márton stood in the center of market square singing *Te Deum*, holding his crucifix up towards heaven, people fell on their knees around him, as did Dobó himself.

Even the wounded limped or crawled out from corners and cellars in order to kneel down with the others.

Then suddenly Lukács Nagy gave out a great shout, "After them! No mercy for those dog Muhammadans!"

Dobó's eyes widened seeing the armed men. He nodded in agreement.

Well, as many horses remained in the castle, as many soldiers mounted up. Out of the castle. They rumbled towards Maklár after the Turks.

The foot soldiers also ran out from the castle to the abandoned tents and carried them back loaded on carts.

The cavalry returned to the castle that evening, their horses loaded with plunder.

Of the people of the castle, three hundred dead rested below in the common grave, and another eight hundred wounded lay still on hay and straw inside the castle.

The senior officers were all wounded. Dobó, Bornemissza in his hand and leg, Zoltay lying on his back, Mekcsey covered in wounds from head to toe, Fügedy having sacrificed three of his teeth to Muhammad. They had been knocked out by a Turk. But he boldly put up with the pain because one of the missing teeth had been giving him the toothache.

---

[55] *Te Deum laudamus*, Latin for "God, We Praise You". The *Te Deum* hymn is traditionally sung on occasions of public rejoicing.

There was no man or woman in the castle who did not bear a wound. With one exception. The Gypsy.

Sukán's final report was like this. "Noble captain sir, I can report that the larger cannonballs that have been fired into the castle have been gathered and counted."

"How many?"

"Well, not counting those embedded in the walls here and there, it's five short of twelve thousand."

— § —

Epilogue

Before the siege, when Dobó asked the assembly in Szikszó for reinforcements, they told him, actually, to Mekcsey who was representing Dobo, "If you are not enough, then don't remain in command! If you've eaten the bones, then drink its juice, too!"

After the siege, the two captains had a response. They both resigned.

All of Europe applauded and cheered the news of the victory. In Rome, the Pope said a *Te Deum* mass. The king received letters of praise from all sides. The flags captured from the Turks were delivered to Vienna where the Viennese marveled at them. (To this day, Ali Pasha's velvet victory flag must still be among the other Hapsburg victory trophies.)

The king sent Captain Mátyás Sforzia to Eger to persuade Dobó and Mekcsey to stay. But they remained unshakeable.

"We've done our duty," Dobó said. "Although *anyone* should have been able to do it! Please convey our respects to His Majesty."

The king then appointed Gergely Bornemissza to replace Dobó as Captain of Eger Castle.

List of Heroic Warriors Defending Eger

Dr. József Gárdonyi had this list published with the 1923 edition, as the author had requested in his will. The list is taken from the manuscript that was part of the author's estate, although that list was not in alphabetical order.

— § —

Abádi Varga Imre (Emory Varga Abádi) — Cannonball hit him during wall repairs.

Alfra Jakab (Jacob Alfra) — Suffered serious burns from gunpowder.

András deák (scholar Andrew, Mayor of Eger) — Died from cannonball on September 30; leaving two orphans.

Arany Mihály (Michael Arany, gunner soldier from Eger) — he suffered many wounds, one to the head so severe that his mind was disturbed.

Aradi Nagy Antal (Anthony Nagy Aradi, lieutenant) — Tinódi writes about him with great praise.)

Bakocsai István (Stephen Bakocsai, corporal). On September 17, he tore down the Turkish flag that had been raised during the assault, for which Dobó singled him out for a reward.

Baksa Benedek (Benedict Baksa) — Killed by a rock.

Baksay Tamás (Thomas Baksay, cavalry squad officer) — his leg was wounded by a piece of wood blown away by a bomb.

Balázs deák (scholar Balázs, clerk from Eger) — he was always armed, zealous about wall repairs at night.

Bálint pap (Father Valentine) — Fell in battle on October 13.

Balogh András (Andrew Balogh) — Fought with Paul Szirmai (see Szirmai). Lost an eye.

Balogh Antal (Anthony Balogh, gunner from Eger) — Crippled by a cannonball.

Balogh Bálint (Valentine Balogh)

Balogh Dénes (Dennis Balogh, corporal in Bornemissza's company) — Both legs injured.

Balogh György (George Balogh) — Leg injured in a collapse of stones.

Balogh György (George Balogh, another, from Eger) — Injured in his side from a cannonball; injured on his arm and face from rocks.

Balogh Mihály (Michael Balogh, from Eger) — An arrow and a lance pierced through his arm.

Baranyai György (George Baranyai, cavalry squad officer) — A bomb broke his arm.

Baranyai György (George Baranyai, non-commissioned officer).

Baranyai István (Stephen Baranyai) — His arm was broken apart by a bullet; bullets were left in his body.

Barát Miklós (Nicholas Barát)

Bartha Pál (Paul Bartha, garrison corporal) — Got a bullet in his hip.

Bay András (Andrew Bay, non-commissioned officer)

Bay Ferenc (Francis Bay, cavalry squad officer) — He fought fiercely when, after lunch on September 14, they raided the city crowded with Turks ; his leg was later broken by a rock collapse.

Benedek (Benedict) — Blacksmith of Eger Castle.

Benedek Istók (Istók Benedek from Felnémet) — While he was fighting in the castle, the Turks razed his home and took his wife captive.

Bereczky György (George Bereczky) — Aide to John Vajda; Killed by gunfire.

... Bertalan (Bartholomew ____, garrison gunner) — Killed by gunfire.

Blaskó Antal (Anthony Blaskó, lieutenant from Eperjes)

Bodó Demeter (Demetrius Blaskó, from Felnémat) — head wound from a bomb.

Bádogfalvi Péter (Peter Bádogfalvi, from Eger, garrison gunner) — shot in the chest and arm by two arrows.

Bódy János (John Bódy, miller from Maklár)

Bolyky Tamás (Thomas Bolyky, lieutenant of the fifty gunners from Borsod) — shot dead by janissaries on the night of September 28.

Borbély János (John Borbély, lieutenant)

Borbély Péter (Peter Borbély, aide to John Borbély) — Blinded in one eye.

Bordács Bálint (Valentine Bordács, from Cegléd) Wounded by a bullet in the face knocking out two teeth.

Bornemissza Gergely deák, királyi hadnagy (Gregory Bornemissza, scholar, royal lieutenant) — Sent by the king with 250 infantry.

Bor Mihály (Michael Bor) — Lieutenant of the seventy-six infantry sent from Sáros.

Bozy Tamás (Thomas Bozi, from Felsőtárkány) — Lost his right hand.

Brum János, mester (John Brum, master, artilleryman from Vienna)

Budaházi István (Stephen Budaházi, cavalry squad officer) — During the sortie on September 12, the Turks shot him in the shoulder. His shoulder bones were taken out in five pieces.

Csapy Mihály (Michael Csapy, garrison corporal) Severely wounded. *"Pixide sanciatus ambos testiculos amisit et est perpetuus castratus"* (Bad Medieval Latin, although the first two words are correct. The meaning of the text is: "After being injured by a gun, he lost both his testicles and is incapacitated forever.") He carried a letter from Dobó through a large Turkish camp surrounding Szolnok and made it back again. One can imagine the danger!

Czeredy Lénárd (Leonard Czeredy, gunner from Eger) — Injured by bullets. One remained lodged in his knee.

Cserney Benedek (Benedict Cserney, artilleryman) — He was standing by a cannon when a Turkish ball hit wood, shooting pieces into his throat and arm.

Cses Péter (Peter Cses, garrison gunner) — His heroism was written up separately. He was shot and killed by janissaries. He left three orphans behind.

Cseh János (John Cseh, artilleryman from Kisbeszterce)

Czirják Mihály (Michael Czirják, from Eger) — Cannonball shot off his arm.

Dobó István (Stephen Dobó, the head captain of the castle)

Deli Balázs (Blaise Deli, lance corporal)

Dormán György (George Dormán, lance corporal)

Döngelegi Gáspár (Gaspar Döngelegi)

Debrői György (George Debrői, castle innkeeper)

Dersy Ferenc, püspöki ügyész (Francis Dersy, bishop's prosecutor)

... Dömötör (Demeter ____, master butcher from Eger)

Deli Pál (Paul Deli, garrison gunner) — Killed by gunfire.

Eperjesi Janicskó (Johnny from Eper)

Enderfer Lajos (Louis Enderfer, artilleryman from Innsbruck)

Erdélyi Jakab (Jacob Erdélyi, gunner from Eger) — Shot by bullets in the face and neck. Bullets in his neck remained.

Erdélyi Mihály (Michael Erdély) — bullet passed through his chest.

Egres Mátyás (Mathias Egres, from Felnémet) — Injured in both knees by a bomb.

Fügedy János (John Fügedy, cavalry lieutenant)

Fülöp Dömötör (Demeter Fülöp, lance corporal)

Farkas János (John Farkas, lance corporal)

Fekete István (Stephen Fekete, cavalry squad officer) — Participated in the first sortie when Pető, Zoltay, and Bornemissza rode out at night and attacked the Turks before Abony. When the Turks cleared out on October 17, he was with a small group of cavalry that rode out against them and cut up the Turkish rear guard. Injured from bombs and swords.

Fayrich mester (Fayrich, master artilleryman from Laibach)

Fejérvári Pál (Paul Fejérvári, corporal) — Injured in the leg.

Fürjes Dömötör (Demeter Fürjes, garrison soldier) — Shot in the knee. His leg had to be amputated.

... Ferenc, egri mészároslegény (Francis _____, apprentice butcher from Eger)

... Ferenc, egri molnár (Francis _____, miller from Eger)

Garay Farkas (Wolf Garay, lance corporal)

Gusztovics György (George Gusztovics, lance corporal)

Gyulai György (George Gyulai, cavalry squad officer) — One of the severely wounded in the assault on Saint Michael's Day. Shot in the right hand and leg. Bullets in his body remained.

Gyulai György (George Gyulai, another) — Killed by a cannonball on the Bolyky Bastion during the September 29 assault.

Gasparics Mihály (Michael Gasparics, lance corporal) — Killed.

Gersei Benedek (Benedict Gersei, lance corporal)

Gálházi Miklós (Nicholas Gálházi, cavalry squad officer) — Shot through the face by an arrow.

Gallus, Galyas? vagy Kallós? (Gallusor Galyas or Kallós, miller from Tihamér)

Gyurkovics (Gyurkovics, aide to Mekcsey) — Killed, leaving a widow and orphans.

... *György* (George ____, blacksmith) — Came to the castle from Felnémet of his own accord and fought bavely.

... *György* (George ____, miller and master carpenter) — Worked night and day. He was the one who after the gunpowder magazine exploded, fashioned a gunpowder mill from the wreckage.

... *György* (George ____, blacksmith from Eger)

... *György* kovács, nagytállyai (George ____, blacksmith from Nagytállya) —

György mester (George, master, artilleryman from Trencsén)

Guthay Péter (Peter Guthay, inspector)

... *Gáspár* (Gaspar ____, master barber)

... *Gáspár* (Gaspar ____, apprentice barber)

Görgey Péter (Peter Görgey, worker and soldier from Eger) — Injured so severely on a collapse of stones that he was bedridden until his death.

Gyöngyösi Mátyás deák (Mathias Gyöngyösi) — He was in charge of the artillery tools. Fought bravely and was wounded many time.

... *Gáspár* (Gaspar ____, apprentice butcher from Eger)

Haranghy Miklós (Nicholas Haranghy, gunner soldier from Eger) — Cannon ball hit his knee. He was also injured when a wall collapsed.

Harsányi Ferenc (Francis Harsányi, from Eger). Killed by gunfire.

Halmai Miklós (Nicholas Halmai)

Hős Péter (Peter Hős)

Horváth Gergely (Gregory Horváth) — One of the victims of the October 4 explosion. He died from his arm being broken off.

Horváth György (George Horváth, castle garrison cavalry) — Killed.

Horváth Mihály (Michael Horváth, no-commissioned officer) — Participated in the sortie on September 21. His horse was shot out from underneath him.

Iváni György (George Iváni)

Istenmezei Sándor (Alexander Istenmezei)

... *Imre* (Emory ____, steward) — With four servants, he faithfully guarded stores day and night.

... *Imre* (Emory ____, aide to Stephen Budházy) — Injured by rocks.

... *István* (Stephen ____, butcher apprentice)

... *János* (John ____, blacksmith)

... *József mester* (Joseph, master, artilleryman from Prague)

János mester (Joseph, master, artilleryman from Szepes)

... *János* (John ____, master barber)

... *János* (John ____, aide to Emory Kamonyay) — A bullet tore his chin.

... *Jakab* (Jacob ____, barber apprentice)

... *Jakab* (Jacob ____, gunsmith from Eger)

... *Jakab* (Jacob ____, master blacksmith from Felnémet) — His heroism was singled out for praise and presented to the king as meriting a reward. "Each time there was an assault, he ran to the walls and he shot many Turks dead."

... *Jakab* (Jacob ____, blacksmith from Eger)

... *Jakab* (Jacob ____, apprentice butcher from Eger)

Janicskó (____ Jancsikó, lieutenant)

Jászai Márton (Martin Jászai) — Lieutenant of the forty-one infantry from the Jász provost.

... *János* (John ____, bailiff)

Józsa János (John Józsa)

... *Józsa* (Josephine ____, apprentice barber)

Kassika Tamás (Thomas Kassika, from Felnémet) — Killed, leaving a widow behind.

Koron vagy *Choron Farkas* (Wolf Koron or Choran) — Lieutenant of the fifty infantry from Abaúj.

Kendi Bálint (Valentine Kendi) — Lieutenant of the fifty *drabant* infantry sent by George Serédy.

Kispéter Antal (Anthony Kispéter) — Lieutenant of the fifty gunners from Gömör.

Kusztovics Horváth György (George Kusztovics Horváth, non-commissioned officer)

Kis Dénes (Dennis Kis, lance corporal)

Kis Jakab (Jacob Kis, gunner from Kassa) — Crippled from a rock hitting his right hand.

Kovács Antal (Anthony Kovács) — Killed.

Kovács Ferenc (Francis Kovács, from Eger) — Probably during the gunpowder magazine explosion, his face and arms were burned, losing one eye.

Komlósi Antal (Anthony Komlósi) — During the assault on September 29, he cut down a Turk as he was hoisting a flag, severing the Turk's right arm that was holding the flag, arm and flag falling down into the moat. Dobó rewarded him with two forint.

Kassay György (George Kassay) — died in a stone collapse.

Kassay Lukács (Lucas Kassay, corporal from Eger) — Crippled.

Korcsolás Máté (Matthew Korcsolás, corporal from Eger) — wounds to the head and elsewhere, and he became deaf.

Kocsis Gáspár (Gaspar Kocsis) — Wounded by bullets and rocks.

Kusztos Balázs (Blaise Kusztos, lance corporal)

Kóródi Máté (Matthew Kóródi, lance corporal)

Kamuthy Balázs (Blaise Kamuthy, cavalry squad officer) — Injured by rocks.

Kamonyay Imre (Emory Kamonyay) — A nobleman who came with his servants.

Körmendi Máté (Matthew Körmendi)

Kamorai Gábor (Gabriel Kamorai)

Kádas Péter (Peter Kádas) — Leader of the four soldiers from the Carthusian brothers. He suffered a serious wound to his head.

Kulcsár Imre (Emory Kulcsár)

Kálmán porkoláb (Coloman the jailer) — Tinódi wrote about him like this: "Poor Coloman the jailor; he was wounded by the entrance dug out by the Dark Gate and died."

Kőszegi Albert (Albert Kőszegi)

Lőkös Mihály (Michael Lőkös) — Lieutenant of the hundred infantry sent by the free towns [*i.e.*, towns that had received royal charters granting them self-rule].

Liszkai (Horváth) György (George Liszkai Horváth, non-commissioned officer)

... *Lőrinc* (Laurence ____, blacksmith)

... *Lőrinc* (Laurence ____, apprentice barber)

... *Lőrinc* (Laurence ____, another apprentice barber)

Landó Benedek (Benedict Landó, from Felnémet) — Severely injured by rocks.

Liptói János (John Liptói, gunner from Eger) — Shot in the leg.

... *László* (Leslie ____, apprentice butcher from Eger)

Lengyel Miklós (Nicholas Lengyel, from Tihamér) — Killed by gunfire.

Lengyel István (Stephen Lengyel, gunner from Eger) — Lost half of an arm.

Miskolczy László (Leslie Miskolczy, gunner from Eger) — Shot through the chest, but survived.

Máday György (George Máday, Eger garrison) — Seriously wounded in the arm, and shot through the side of his body.

Margit asszony, *Kocsis Gáspárné* (a woman named Margaret and Mrs. Gaspar Kocsis) — Wounded by bullets and rocks. Their names are listed among the seriously wounded soldiers. The list was in a report prepared in January, less than three months after the siege.

Major Ferenc (Francis Major, gunner from Eger) — Face and hands burned by gunpowder.

... *Máté* (Matthew ____, apprentice butcher from Eger).

... *Márton* (Martin ____, priest)

... *Mátyás* (Mathias ____, locksmith and gunsmith from Eger)

... *Mátyás* (Mathias ____, miller from Felnémet)

... *Márton* (Martin ____, apprentice barber)

... *Márton* (Martin ____, apprentice butcher from Eger)

Molnár János (John Molnár, from Eger) — Killed by a cannon, leaving orphans behind.

Molnár Ambrus (Ambrose Molnár, carpenter) — Killed, leaving three orphans behind.

Mekcsey István (Stephen Mekcsey, second captain)

Nágoli Urbán (Urban Nágoli, lance corporal)

Nagy András (Andrew Nagy) — A gunner in Bornemissza's company. His arm was paralyzed.

Nagy Antal (Anthony Nagy, lieutenant) — Bullets tore up a knee and some ribs. One bullet remained inside.

Nagy Antal (Anthony Nagy, lance corporal) — Among the first to be killed.

Nagy Bereck (Beresk Nagy, corporal from Eger) — Shot through the right shoulder.

Nagy Barnabás (Barnaby Nagy, corporal from Eger) — a bearded cannon tore off his hand.

Nagy Barnabás (Barnaby Nagy) — In Bornemissza's company. A cannonball shattered his shoulder blade.

Nagy Barnabás (Barnaby Nagy) — Commander of the twenty-five soldiers sent by Perényi.

Nagy Pál (Paul Nagy) — Lieutenant of the thirty infantry from George Báthory. Died on October 4 in the explosion of the gunpowder magazine.

Nagy Pál (Paul Nagy from Felnémet) — While fighting in the castle, the Turks raised his home and took his wife prisoner.

Nagy Pál (Paul Nagy, gunner from Eger) — wounded by rocks.

Nagy Imre (Emory Nagy) — The commander of the eighteen infantry from Ung County.

Nagy Imre (Emory Nagy, another) — One of the commanders of the infantry from Lady Gabriel Homonnay. He was killed during the St. Michael's Day assault.

Nagy Tamás (Thomas Nagy, lance corporal) — his right hand was shattered by a bomb.

Nagy Bálint (Valentine Nagy, lance corporal)

Nagy János (John Nagy, lance corporal)

Nagy Mihály (Michael Nagy, lance corporal)

Nagy Balázs (Blaise Nagy, infantry lieutenant) — Killed by a cannonball on September 16, as he was stacking earth-filled barrels and wicker baskets for protection against artillery fire.

Nagy Bertalan (Bartholomew Nagy, *viceporkoláb* ¿jailor?)

Nagy Gábor (Gabriel Nagy)

Nagy László (Leslie Nagy, the other castle innkeeper)

Nagy Lukács (Lucas Nagy, infantry corporal from Eger) — With twenty-four others, he left the castle toward Vác, plundering. When the Turks had surrounded the castle, he became enraged at Szarvaskő. "He fears for his honor. He takes and oath that either he dies or he goes in." And indeed, he rode through the massive Turkish camps and into the surrounded castle. He suffered a serious wound to the head.

Nagy Lukács (Lucas Nagy, civilian from the castle) — Killed by gunfire.

Nagy István (Stephen Nagy, Dobó's standard bearer) — Fell during the assault of October 12.

Nagy Péter (Peter Nagy, corporal from Eger) — Wounded in the forehead and both legs during the first assault. He lost one leg and the bullet remained in the other.

Nagy Miklós (Nicholas Nagy, corporal from Eger) — Wounded on the head and back in a stone collapse.

Naszádos János (John Naszádos) — a corporal in the company of Gergely scholar. Wounded in the shoulder by a bearded cannon.

Orbonáz (Orgonás) *György*, főlegény (George Orbonáz or Orgonás, lance corporal)

Onori Gábor (Gabriel Onori, cavalry warrior from Eger) — Killed.

Oroszi Gábor (Gabriel Oroszi) — Killed in the sortie on September 12, while trying to protect Budaházi who had been wounded.

Ormándy János (John Ormándy) — Participated in the daylight sortie of September 14 and fought valiantly. Later a bomb tore off his hand.

Országh Imre (Emory Országh) — Killed

Paksy Jób (Job Paksy, officer) — The younger brother of the captain from Komárom.

Pestyéni János (John Pestyéni, lieutenant)

Pozsgai János (John Pozsgai, lance corporal) — Killed during the assault on St Michael's Day.

Pozsgai Miklós (Nicholas Pozsgai)

Pribék Imre (Emory Pribék) — Commander of the forty soldiers sent by George Serédy. After the traitor Lieutenant Hegedüs was hung, Dobó promoted him to command the soldiers from Kassa. Tinódi remembers him with praise.

Pribék Józsa (Joseph Pribék)

Pribék János (John Pribék, see Sukán)

Paksi Borbás, viceudvarbíró (Borbas Paksi, ¿vice mayor?) — Wounded in three places by gun and cannon fire.

Papa vagy *Pápay Valentin* (Valentine Papa or Pápay) — Killed during the fighting; he fell to his death.

Platkó Antal (Anthony Platkó) — One of the commanders of the two hundred independents from Kassa.

... *Péter* (Peter ____, master barber)

... *Péte* (Peter ____, apprentice barber)

Puska Pál (Paul Puska, gunner from Eger) — Shot through the right hand; crippled.

Putnoky Tamás (Thomas Putnoky, from Eger) — Head wound from a rock.

Pap Máté (Matthew Pap, from Felnémet) — Severely wounded from rocks.

Porkoláb Kálmán (Coloman Porkoláb, cavalry squad officer) — smashed hip bones.

... *Pál* (Paul ____, master butcher from Eger)

... *Pál* (Paul ____, castle blacksmith)

Prini Ferenc (Francis Prini)

Prini Mihály (Michael Prini)

Pető Gáspár (Gaspar Pető, royal army first lieutenant) — Was sent with forty cavalry warriors to defend Eger. Participated in the first sortie on September 9. Wounded in the leg during the St. Michael's Day assault and collapsed from the pain.

Rhédey Ferenc (Francis Rhédy, lance corporal) — Ancestor to the Count Rhédey family, which was related to the English royal family.

Rácz Farkas (Wolf Rácz)

Ráskai Péter (Peter Ráskai)

Rahóy Miklós, (Michael Rahóy) — Bullet shot through his hand; crippled.

Rigó János (John Rigó, man from upper Felnémet) — Shoulder injury from rock collapse.

Somogyi András (Andrew Somogy) — Lieutenant under Pető.

Sukán János (John Sukán, castle steward and accountant) — Distinguished himself individually when with John Pribék, they fought back Turks that had forced their way through a breach.

Sáfár István (Stephen Sáfár)

Sánta Márton (Martin Sánta, miller)

Sáray András (Andrew Sáray)

Sárközi Balázs (Blaise Sárközi, gunner) — Both legs were shot.

Sipos Dénes (Dennis Sipos from Eger, garrison gunner) — Lost an eye from flying rock fragments.

Somogyi Ferenc (Francis Somogy) — Commander of the twenty-one *drabant* (garrison) infantry sent by Lady Gabriel Homonnay.

Soklyosi Nagy Albert (Albert Nagy Soklyosi, lieutenant) — Tinódi praises him as a hero warrior.

Soncy Szaniszló (Stanislaus Soncy) — Dobó singled him out for praise and reward for his bravery on the earth bastion.

Szabó Tamás (Thomas Szabó, man from Felnémet) — Injured by rocks.

Szabó Ádám (Adam Szabó) — Killed.

Szabó Imre (Emory Szabó) — Dobó's third courier who slipped through the Turkish camps from the castle to deliver a letter, then returned afterwards.

Szabó Márton (Martin Szabó)

Szirmai Pál (Paul Szirmai) — Tinódi remembers him as a hero warrior. In the first days of October, he rushed out of the castle through a small door to attack the Turks. "They cut down many Turks under the stone wall."

Szatai Imre (Emory Szirmai)

Szakács Balázs (Blaise Szakács)

Szalay Mihály (Michael Szalay, artilleryman from Pelsőc in Upper Hungary) — Wounded in the face, head, hands and back.

Szalay Tamás (Thomas Szalay, from Eger) — Severely wounded in the leg from rocks blasted by cannonfire; crippled.

Szaniszló (de Craccovia) (Stanislaus de Craccovia, gunner soldier from Kassa) — Leg shot off by a cannonball.

Szilágyi Pál (Paul Szilágyi, gunner soldier from Eger) — Head injury from a rock.

Szalánky György (George Szalánky) — The commander of the eighteen Chapter men and nine *drabant* garrison infantry from Ung County.

Szücs János, vagy Szőcs (John Szücs or Szőcs, from Eger) — Wounded in the arm.

Székely Tamás (Thomas Székely, gunner soldier from Eger) — Shot through both scapula.

Szőr Mátyás (Mathias Szőr, miller from Maklár) — Killed by a rock, leaving a widow and three orphans.

Szőr Katalin (Catherine Szőr, the miller's wife)

Szenczi Márton (Martin Szenczi) — Lieutenant in command of the forty *drabant* garrison infantry from Szepes.

Szalacskai György (George Szalacskai) — One of the commanders of the eighteen infantry sent by Lady George Homonnay.

Szólláti György (George Szólláti, lance corporal)

Szabolcska Mihály (Michael Szabolcska, lance corporal)

Szőke András (Andrew Szőke, lance corporal)

Székely Mihály (Michael Székely, lance corporal)

Székely György (George Székely)

Szikszay Deák János (John Deák Szikszay, Eger *provizor*) — Was rewarded with nobility for his defense of the castle. He adopted a coat of arms showing his own portrait, holding a Turk by the neck and spearing him in the side.

Tamás (Thomas, gunsmith from Eger)

Trencsényi Péter (Peter Trencsényi)

Tarjáni Kristóf (Christopher Tarjáni, Dobó's page) — Shot by Turks on October 16, when Dobó sent him to the Bolyky Bastion to bring back a report.

Tegnyei Péter (Peter Tegnyei, lance corporal)

Tardi Péter (Peter Tardi, lance corporal)

Tetétleni Pál (Paul Tetétleni, lance corporal)

Török János (John Török) — Killed.

Török János (John Török, lance corporal) — Shot in the back by a cannonball.

Török Dömötör (Demetrius Török) — Tinódi remembers him as a hero warrior.

Török László, (Leslie Török) — He distinguished himself when a cannonball made the Hungarian flag flying over the Old Gate fall down outside the walls. He leapt out the breach and brought it back. Dobó commended him and rewarded him with a Bergamo-cloth suit.

Török Imre (Emory Török, gunner from Eger) — his hands were all burned from gunpowder.

Tátorján György (George Tátorján, gunner from Ager) — Wounded by rocks as well as suffering many other injuries.

Temesváry Gáspár (Gaspar Temesváry) — A bomb broke his sword and the sword seriously wounded his leg.

Tóth Máté (Matthew Tóth, aide to Gaspar Pető) — Bullet lodged in his hip and remained there.

Tóth Endre (Andrew Tóth) — Travel companion to Nicholas Vas (see him); Dobó rewarded him with one forint.

Tóth László (Leslie Tóth) — This hero warrior captured Ali Pasha's velvet flag during the last assault.

Tamási Lőrinc (Lawrence Tamási, from Eger) — Half his leg crippled.

Urbán György (George Urbán, gunner from Eger) — Shot through the shoulder.

Vince (Vince, apprentice barber)

Vámos Mihály deák (Michael Varga, scholar) — The *loaf splitter* in charge of distributing bread. He joined the fighting during each assault.

Varga János (John Varga) — Was a member of Thomas Bolyky's company. Three times he jumped out from the walls ruined by cannon fire, in part as a hero warrior joke, to wave his sword at the besieging Turk army. Dobó rewarded him with one forint.

Vitéz György (George Vitéz) — rewarded for heroism, but as for who, when, and for what, the records do not state.

Vitéz István (Stephen Vitéz, lance corporal)

Vitéz János (John Vitéz, lance corporal) — Fought with Gaspar Pető's company on September 30.

... *Vince* (Vince ____, bailiff)

Vajda János (John Vajda, lieutenant of the garrison cavalry) Tinódi remembers him as a hero warrior. It was he, together with George Iványi, Andrew Somogyi and Albert Kőszegi, who, after the siege, carried Ali Pasha's velvet, horsetail flag and the recorded list of those deserving rewards to Vienna.

Vitéz Ferenc (Francis Vitéz, *viceporkoláb* jailor?)

Varsányi Imre (Emory Varsányi) — Dobó's spy and courier.

Vas Miklós (Nicholas Vas) — One of Dobó's trusted men. He carried a letter to the bishop, passing through the Turkish camps, then back again. He risked his life on three such missions. On one occasion, Turks attacked him and his companion, killing his companion. He was wounded in the face.

Vas Ferenc anyósa (mother-in-law of Francis Vas) — Killed.

Zádornik Ambrus (Ambrose Zádornik, infantry lieutenant) — One of the commanders of the Kassa independent company.

Zirkó Jakab (Jacob Zirkó) — Killed by a cannonball.

Zoltay István (Stephen Zoltay, first lieutenant) — Commander of the forty-strong royal army cavalry squadron. One of the hero warriors of the September 9th sortie.

Zsigmond Benedek (Benedict Zsigmond, carpenter) — Dobó entrusted him with the responsibility of directing the repairs to the walls after each Turkish bombardment.

— § —

Two hundred eighty-nine names. The others have been forgotten.

Some Nameless

A document dated February 20 was delivered to the king. It contained the list of names of men, and some women, [probably originally maintained by John Sukán, the aged castle steward and accountant, at Dobó's instructions] being recommended for bravery in the defense of Eger Castle.

The novelist, Géza Gárdonyi, did considerable historical research in order to write his novel, *Egri Csillagok*. The origin of this list of names appended to his manuscript is probably that February 20, 1553, document.

Among the names of wounded noblemen, there is an entry for a soldier from the castle. It states that he went out from the castle with Lucas Nagy and returned to the castle. Instead of his name, the entry is: *cuius nomen non succurrit* (his name is not remembered).

The manuscript ends here.

Appendix: The Context

by T. László Palotás

Egri Csillagok is set in the two decades between 1533 and 1552. By then, Hungarians had been fighting the Ottoman Turks for some hundred and forty years.

An Ottoman army defeated the Serbs at the Battle of Kosovo in 1389. After that, the Balkan peninsula was drawn into the Ottoman empire and the sultan's attention focused on Hungary, the major Christian power that stood in the way of Central Europe and Western Europe beyond.

King Louis the Great (Nagy Lajos) ruled Hungary from 1342 to 1382, expanded the kingdom temporarily into Moldavia, Wallachia, Serbia, Bosnia, and even the House of Anjou holdings of the Kingdom of Naples and Sicily. Louis was crowned King of Poland in 1370 after the death of his uncle, Casimir III. His Balkan conquests were directed at drawing their Orthodox Christian population into the Catholic fold to present a united front against the pressure of the Ottoman Muslims.

By 1396, Sigismund (Zsigmond) was King of Hungary and led an allied Christian army that originally had set out from France, gathered in Buda, and proceeded down the Danube River into Bulgaria. The invasion is counted as one of the minor Crusades: the Crusade of Nicopolis. The Christians besieged the Ottoman stronghold of Nicopolis. After some weeks of boredom, they were attacked by an Ottoman relief army. Few Christians escaped the Battle of Nicopolis with their lives, but one of them was Sigismund. This battle in 1396 may have been the first between Hungarian and Ottoman soldiers.

In the middle of the following century, John Hunyadi (Hunyadi János) emerged as the greatest Hungarian hero among the Turk-fighters. Hunyadi, born in Transylvania to a noble family with Romanian ancestry, successfully led Hungarians in pitched battles against the Turks in Transylvania, Wallachia, and Bulgaria. Following a truce, a Catholic cardinal talked Hunyadi into breaking the treaty and again attacking the Turks. Hunyadi's forces were already depleted. The King of both Hungary and Poland, Ladislas (Úlászló I of Hungary), charged the Turks, was killed, and his head was paraded on a spear. The effect was an Ottoman victory at the Battle of Varna in 1444.

Hunyadi's greatest victory was in 1456 at Nándorfehérvár (Belgrade), the strategic fortress in what was then southern Hungary near the confluence of the Sava and Danube River. Three years after his Ottoman armies conquered Constantinople, Mehmet II, "the Conqueror" advanced into southern Hungary with an army of some sixty or seventy thousand. He laid siege to Nándorfehérvár which was defended by a garrison of some five or seven thousand. Hunyadi quickly assembled an army and managed to join the defenders. The day after a fierce, all-out Ottoman assault was repulsed with great loss of life on both sides, some irregular Hungarian defenders, against orders, began to pillage the damaged Ottoman positions. What began as scattered looting turned into fighting. More defenders joined from behind the walls. The Turks panicked. The sultan's five thousand janissary bodyguards unsuccessfully tried to regain order, but Hunyadi took advantage of the spontaneous melee and his own forces joined the attack. That was July 22, 1456. The following day, the Ottomans retreated with their wounded sultan.

Nándorfehérvár is one of the very rare examples in which a siege was broken from the inside. The Christian victory was celebrated as far away as England. Pope Callixtus III ordered the bells of every European church to be rung every day at noon to commemorate the victory, as they still are today. The victory delayed the Ottoman invasion of Hungary for another seventy years.

John Hunyadi did not live long to savor his victory. He died the following month in a plague epidemic. He was buried in Gyulafehérvár, today's Alba Iulia in Romania.

John Hunyadi's son Matthias (Mátyás) Corvinus was fifteen when he was elected and crowned King of Hungary in 1458. He reigned forty-seven years, from 1443 to 1490. Like his father, Matthias successfully warred against the Turks as well as involving himself in wars against Czechs, Germans, Serbs and Poles. The Renaissance was in full swing and Hungary was among the first to embrace the new ideas from Italy. Matthias was a great patron of the arts and his royal library, the Bibliotheca Corviniana, was among the largest in Europe. He was Matthias the Just (*Mátyás az igazságos*), the popular Hungarian king who disguised himself to wander among his subjects.

The reign of Matthias is one of the great high points in a thousand years of Hungarian history. In Book II of *Egri Csillagok*, Géza Gárdonyi describes the royal palace in Buda that King Matthias rebuilt with Italian artists and craftsmen. Today, in its foundations, there are only fragments of the red marble and fireplace stove tiles that Matthias had constructed, much of it unearthed during excavations after the destruction of the Soviet siege in 1943-44.

The history of Hungary, indeed, in all history among all nations in all epochs, is riddled with stories of exploitation. Hungary was plagued by rulers who taxed their subjects mercilessly to finance their power-grabbing dynastic wars, and by nobility more comfortable with their foreign counterparts than their own folk. Serfs, peasants, and tradesmen were treated as property to be exploited.

Peasant rebellions broke out throughout Europe in the late Middle Ages. The one most immediate to the story of *Egri Csillagok* is the rebellion led by György Dózsa in the summer of 1514. He was from Transylvania, a soldier of fortune who earned a reputation fighting the Turks. He became in charge of organizing a peasant army to fight a crusade instigated by Pope Leo X. By harvest time, some forty thousand had gathered, peasants armed mainly with farming implements, cattlemen (*hajdú*) who served as light cavalry, and others from the lower classes. They received no food, clothing, pay or supplies from the nobility. Anger erupted. The crusade turned into a riot against landowners and the rebellion spread throughout Hungary.

Dózsa had some early successes in skirmishes, but his ill-equipped army was pursued by heavily armed nobles and their soldiers. They were led by John Zápolya and István Báthory. At the time, Zápolya was the most powerful noble in Hungary. Dózsa was captured and brutally tortured to death.

In *Egri Csillagok*, Gárdonyi creates two characters from among Dózsa's lieutenants: the old Lord Cecey with his wooden legs and hand, courtesy of John Zápolya, and the equally old priest with whom he argued, Father Bálint, whose tongue was cut, also courtesy of John Zápolya.

The significance of the 1514 peasant rebellion explains some of the character of both Cecey and Father Bálint in the novel. More historically, it helps explain the collapse of the Hungarian kingdom twelve years later. The repression of the rebellion was brutal, as the severed hand of Cecey and the mutilated tongue of Father Bálint suggest. By some counts, 70,000 peasants were tortured. The divisions and mistrust between the nobility and the common people in Hungary are some of the reasons why the country collapsed after the Battle of Mohács.

Seventy years after John Hunyadi's unlikely victory at Nándorfehérvár, an Ottoman army some fifty thousand strong led by Sultan Suleiman the Magnificent invaded Hungary in 1526, almost unopposed. A hastily organized, obsolete medieval army of about half that number confronted the Turks at Mohács, an ill-chosen, somewhat soggy place near the Danube River. Within about an hour, the Hungarian army was overwhelmed. Some 14,000 were killed including a thousand nobles. The King of Hungary, young Louis II, fled the battlefield and accidentally drowned in his armor.

Mohács marked the end of an independent Kingdom of Hungary. A divided Hungarian nobility elected John Zápolya king in November of 1526, then the following month another group elected the Austrian Hapsburg Ferdinand king. Historically, the nobility elected the kings of Hungary. With the death of so many Hungarian nobles at Mohács, Zápolya had few Hungarian rivals. Ferdinand was the brother-in-law of the late king and those who elected him hoped that he would muster Hapsburg armies to defend Hungary. That hope was sadly misplaced. As Gárdonyi quips in his novel, "he was a Hungarian king who entrusted the defense of his fortresses to God."

Transylvania, helped by its rugged terrain, maintained a semi-independence as a principality. Upper (northern) Hungary and Hungary west of the Danube were ruled by the Hapsburgs. The rest of Hungary, including Buda, Pest, and most of the Alföld, the Great Hungarian Plain, became a province of the Ottoman empire. For some two hundred years, Hapsburgs and Ottomans fought over Hungary. Its cities were ruined and its population decimated in almost constant warfare.

Ottoman occupation of Hungary through 1541.

The story of *Egri Csillagok* is set in the decades after the Battle of Mohács and reaches its climax with the successful defense of Eger Castle in 1552. Forty-four years later, the fortress, by then defended mostly with mercenaries, surrendered to the Ottomans and remained in Turkish hands for almost a century.

Appendix: The Historical Characters

Many, but not all, of the events and characters in *Egri Csillagok* are historical. Gárdonyi invented many details in his novel and modeled its characters after friends and acquaintances whom he knew, but the main events, including the details of the 1552 siege, actually occurred and the characters had actually existed.

Perhaps the most important character is Sebestyén Tinódi, the minstrel who chronicled the Siege of Eger. Without such records, Gárdonyi would not have known many of the details of the siege.

János Zápolya, Friar György Martinuzzi, the dowager queen Isabella Jagiełło, the infant king John Sigismund Zápolya, and, of course, Sultan Suleiman the Magnificent, are all well known historical figures. We also know about Bálint Török, István Dobó, István Mekcsey, and Gergely Bornemissza.

Contrary to Gárdonyi's romantic characterization of the Hungarian nobles who figure in his novel, actual histories reveal Bálint Török and István Dobó to be rather crass — much like the novelist's depiction of the Hungarian villain in the novel, László Moré. Bálint Török regularly switched allegiances when it served his thirst for property and power. By the time he was imprisoned by the Turks in Seven Towers, he had made so many enemies that none bothered to help ransom him. No one questions the courage or leadership of István Dobó at Eger, but otherwise he and his brothers were thieves and smugglers. His primary interest, like Bálint Török, was acquiring property and power.

Sebestyén Tinódi

Sebestyén "Lantos" (Lutenist) Tinódi was born around 1510 and died in 1556. He was a Hungarian lyricist, epic poet, political historian, and minstrel.

Sebestyén Tinódi, 18th Century painting

Little is known about Tinódi's childhood. He attended various schools, studied Latin, and excelled at sheet music. He joined the military service in 1535 and in 1539 was wounded in a battle, which rendered him ineligible for further military service. The Turkish invasion of 1541 made a big impression on him. He became a political poet, his works expressing the need to resist the Turks.

Tinódi began his career in Szigetvár in the service of Bálint (Valentine) Török, another character in *Egri Csillagok* who is also a historical figure.

Tinódi visited the scenes of battles and wrote poems about them. He began to put his poems to music and performed them to the accompaniment of a lute, which led to his nickname, "Lantos" — the lutenist. His songs became recognized as important chronicles of the events of the day.

From 1546 to 1551 there was a general period of peace, but in 1552 a new Ottoman military campaign began which culminated in the unsuccessful Ottoman siege of Eger.

Tinódi visited Eger almost immediately after the Turks retreated. He saw the places in Eger that played a part in its defense and gathered eyewitness accounts of the sorties, assaults, and bravery of the defenders, down to the smallest detail. Many interesting moments can be learned only from his songs. Géza Gárdonyi drew much detail from Tinódi's chronicles.

Before the Siege of Eger, in 1545, the Hungarian parliament had appointed Tinódi as an official historical chronicler with a stipend. After the siege, Tinódi's fame came to the court of King Ferdinand, who, on August 23, 1553, conferred on him the title of "nobleman" in recognition of his achievements in "the art of singing and the articulation of histories in Hungarian."

Tinódi was in good contact with István Dobó and when the captain of Eger became a Transylvanian voivode (governor), he followed Dobó to Transylvania. That is where he finished his song *Transylvanian History*, which tells the history of Transylvania from the death of King John to 1551. A collection of his works was published in Kolozsvár (Cluj-Napoca in today's Transylvania) in 1554 under the title *Cronica*. He returned from Transylvania in 1555 and died shortly afterwards.

János Zápolya

János (John) Zápolya (1490 or 1491 – 1540) was voivode (governor) of Transylvania 1510-1526, then King of Hungary (as John I) 1526-1540. His rule was disputed by the Hapsburg Archduke Ferdinand I, who also claimed the Hungarian throne.

John Zápolya, King John I of Hungary

After the Battle of Mohács and the death of King Louis II, and with the Ottoman failure to assert rule, there was a collapse of authority and a power vacuum in Hungary. Two candidates claimed the crown: John Zápolya, Hungary's most prominent aristocrat, the voivode of Transylvania who had led the nobles' brutal suppression of the 1514 Peasant Revolt led by György Dózsa; and the Austrian Hapsburg Ferdinand, the brother-in-law of the late King Louis II.

In November of 1526, Zápolya had himself proclaimed king by an assembly of nobles at Székesfehérvár, and he was duly crowned the next day (although not with the actual crown) under the name King John I of Hungary. Ferdinand had himself elected king by a rump gathering in Pozsony (Slovak Bratislava, German Pressburg) in December of that same year, 1526. What followed were fourteen years of intermittent warfare between the rival parties.

In 1527, Ferdinand sent an army of German mercenaries into Hungary and defeated Zápolya who fled to Poland the next year. Zápolya approached the Ottomans and agreed to make Hungary a vassal state in return for recognition and support. Sultan Suleiman the Magnificent accepted, and sent Ottoman armies to invade Austria and besiege Vienna, a war which lasted till 1533. This allowed Zápolya to regain his position in Hungary with the help of Friar György (George Martinuzzi) who became royal treasurer and Zápolya's most trusted minister.

In 1539, Zápolya married Princess Isabella Jagiellon of Poland, and in 1540 they had a son, John Sigismund. Zápolya died nine days later in Szászsebes (today's Sebeş in Transylvania). Apparently, the celebrations of begetting an heir proved too much for him.

Queen Isabella Jagiellon

Isabella Jagiellon (1519 –1559) was the oldest child of the King of Poland, Sigismund I, and his Italian wife, Bona Sforza.

In 1539 Isabella married John Zápolya, the voivode (governor) of Transylvania and King of Hungary. She became the queen consort of Hungary. She was twenty. John was fifty-two and suffered from gout. The marriage lasted only a year and a half and produced a male heir. John Sigismund Zápolya was born just two weeks before his father's death in July 1540. Isabella spent the rest of her life embroiled in succession disputes on behalf of her son.

John Zápolya and the Hapsburg Ferdinand, the two rival Kings of Hungary, warred against each other for the throne, then entered into the Treaty of Nagyvárad whereby Ferdinand would succeed to the throne upon John's death. George Martinuzzi (Friar György) and other Hungarian nobles refused to abide by the treaty and elected the infant John Sigismund as King John II and appointed Isabella as his regent. Sultan Suleiman also recognized Isabella as regent with authority over the eastern regions of Hungary, including Transylvania.

Portrait of Isabella Jagiellon, painted a few years after her death

Gárdonyi's setting for Book II of *Egri Csillagok* is 1541 when Isabella was only twenty-two. She was noted for her beauty, scolded for her expensive tastes, and was known to have complained about financial troubles and the ruined state of her new domains. Then Sultan Suleiman took Buda by subterfuge and forced Isabella to leave for eastern Hungary.

Ferdinand conspired with Friar György to force Isabella to abdicate in 1551. She returned to her native Poland. Meanwhile, Sultan Suleiman retaliated and threatened to invade Hungary in 1555, thereby forcing the Transylvanian nobles to invite Isabella back. She returned in October of 1556 and again ruled as her son's regent until her death three years later.

Friar György (George Martinuzzi)

Friar György (Fráter György, better known in English as George Martinuzzi, 1482 – 1551) was a Croatian nobleman, monk, and Hungarian statesman who supported King John Zápolya and his son, King John Sigismund Zápolya. He was Bishop of Nagyvárad (now Oradea in Transylvania), Archbishop of Esztergom, and became a cardinal.

Portrait of Friar György

John Zápolya named Friar György and Péter Petrovics guardians of his infant son John II Sigismund, who was elected King of Hungary by the Záploya faction of the Hungarian nobles. Ferdinand, contending that John II's election had violated his treaty with John Zápolya, invaded Hungary and laid siege to Buda in 1541.

Although Ferdinand became recognized as the sole King of Hungary, Ferdinand's inability to defend it against the Ottomans forced Friar György to resume the payment of tribute to the Ottoman sultan in

December 1551. However, the Ottomans no longer trusted a diplomat whose behavior they could not understand, and Ferdinand suspected him of wanting to secure Hungary for himself.

Friar György was assassinated on 17 December 1551. Ferdinand accepted responsibility, and the pope excommunicated him. The pope exonerated Ferdinand and lifted the excommunication in 1555.

István Dobó

István (Stephen) Dobó (c.1502-1572), the captain who successfully defended Eger Castle in 1552 from a vastly superior Ottoman army, is regarded as one of the great heroes of Hungarian history. He was praised for his leadership and bravery in contemporary accounts of the siege. Three and a half centuries later, Géza Gárdonyi has Dobó play the role of hero in this historical novel. However, his contemporaries also knew him as an avaricious fraud.

DOBÓ VEZÉR,
Egervárának hős védője, 1552.

István Dobó

Dobó came from a noble family with estates in Carpathian Ruthenia, a region in the northeast of the Carpathian Basin that was absorbed by Czecho-Slovakia after the First World War, then the Soviet Union (now Ukraine) after the Second World War. In the rivalry between the two competing Hungarian kings — the Hungarian noble John Zápolya and the Hapsburg King Ferdinand — Dobó consistently backed Ferdinand.

Dobó was appointed Captain of Eger Castle in 1548 and immediately commenced work improving its fortifications. István Mekcsey was named his co-Captain in 1551.

That same year, 1551, István Dobó and his two brothers were sentenced to loss of capital and livestock for previous violence against one of their neighbors, Tamás Tegenyei. The sentence was in effect at the time of the 1552 siege, but suspended for one year.

Dobó made his name during the Turkish siege of 1552. The number of besieged defenders was about 2,000 and the number of attacking Turks was 40,000 (not the 200,000 or 80,000 as in earlier estimates). During the siege, Dobó himself was injured.

Sebestyén Tinódi recorded the heroic acts of Dobó and the castle defenders in two historical songs. Another contemporary, Mátyás Csabai, wrote two glorious poems in Latin about the siege.

Dobó and his co-captain at Eger, István Mekcsey, both resigned after the siege. Among other reasons, no doubt, they were angry that King Ferdinand had not sent an army to break the siege of 1552.

King Ferdinand rewarded Dobó with castles at Déva and Szamosújvár, both in Transylvania, and in 1553, Dobó was named a voivode (governer) of Transylvania and raised to the rank of baron. In 1556, Turkish, Moldavian, and Wallachian troops marched into Transylvania and Dobó held out in Szamosújvár for more than ten months. Ferdinand sent no help, so Dobó was forced to surrender.

Meanwhile, the Transylvanian nobles had invited King John Zápolya's widow, Queen Isabella Jagiellon, and her six-year-old son, John Sigismund Zápolya, to return to Transylvania from her native Poland. Isabella served as regent for her young son. Dobó, who supported Ferdinand, the rival claimant to the throne, was imprisoned by Isabella in Szamosújvár, but he escaped in 1557.

In 1558, when Transylvania broke away from the Hapsburgs, King Ferdinand gave Dobó the castle of Léva (Levice) in Upper Hungary as compensation for his lost Transylvanian estates. Later that year, he was again promoted to baron and appointed Chief Governor of the County of Bars. By the 1560's he had become one of the largest landowners in the country.

Dobó, though known to the public today primarily as the heroic defender of Eger Castle, had less laudable traits. His stupidity and his craving for money, for example, were well known in the 16th century. Peter Bornemisza mentions Dobó as one of the insatiable fraudsters in his book *The Devil's Ghosts* (1578). If the situation so desired, the Dobó brothers, who dealt with farming and trading, took advantage of their neighbors and competitors, and did their utmost to acquire new estates. Because the family estates of Ung and Bereg counties bordered the

Kingdom of Poland, Dobó often smuggled goods bypassing royal customs offices.

The Tegenyei case dogged Dobó all his life and caused his 1568 arrest in Pozsony (Bratislava). Dobó escaped and fled to his Léva Castle in western Slovakia. The following year, Dobó was lured back to Pozsony where he was captured, imprisoned on suspicion of treason, and deprived of his rank as chief governor (*főispán*). He spent the last years of his life as a prisoner in Pozsony Castle.

By the time he was set free in 1572, his health had deteriorated considerably. He returned to his beloved Szerednye Castle in Carpathian Ruthenia, where he died shortly afterwards, at the age of seventy. His body was buried on the family estate in Russkan (now Dobóruszka).

Bálint Török

Bálint (Valentine) Török de Enying (c.1502-1550) was a Hungarian colonel, warlord, and governor (*bán*) of Nándorfehérvár (Belgrade).

For two previous generations, the Török family had rapidly risen in status, wealth and estates as supporters of the Hunyadi family. In 1507, his father and brother received the title of baron from King Úlászlo. In the mid-1520's, despite his young age, Bálint Török was one of the most prestigious and influential landlords in the country.

After the death of his father, Bálint at the age of nineteen inherited his father's post as governor of Nándorfehérvár. That fortress, successfully defended by John Hunyadi sixty-five years earlier, was again besieged by the Ottomans in 1521. Bálint Török was incapable of defending it. The garrison had been unpaid for years. The young lord's guardians complained to the Hungarian parliament about the deplorable situation, but they never received any substantial support. Thus, in 1521 Balázs Oláh, who heroically defended the castle for 66 days against a far superior force, was finally forced to give up. Parliament declared Bálint Török responsible and sentenced him to loss of property. The young aristocrat fled and, far from his estates, entered into the service of János Zápolya in Transylvania.

Bálint Török regained royal favor several years later, consolidated his position of power at the court in 1524, became an officer in the bodyguard of King Lajos II, and married Baroness Katalin Pemfflinger, the favorite lady-in-waiting of Queen Mária who was building her family base. They had two sons, János Török in 1529 and Ferenc Török in the early 1530's.

Bálint Török fought in the Battle of Mohács (1526) as one of the commanders of the Royal Guard. King Lajos II died fleeing the battlefield and — as with the fall of Nándorfehérvár five years earlier — the question of Bálint Török's personal responsibility arose. According to István Brodarics who prepared a report of the battle the following year, the king's death was caused by a tactical mistake of the commander-in-chief, Pál Tomori, who ordered the Royal Guard to attack a Turkish group that had unexpectedly appeared. Bálint Török had executed the order only after repeated urging.

After Mohács, Bálint Török supported the claims of John Zápolya and, as a member of the Székesfehérvár Parliament in 1526, helped Zápolya get elected king. King John was anxious to retain the support of the young members of the nobility, and Bálint Török was rewarded with the governorship of southern Hungary, making him powerful with estates in Temesvár (today's Timişoara in Romania).

Bálint Török turned against King John and attacked his troops in Subotica (Serbia, a part of Hungary during Hunyadi times), then expelled a Serbian insurgent, a vassal of King John who had occupied part of Török's estates.

Such lack of support for King John Zápolya certainly contributed to the fact that the Hungarian nobility grouped around Lajos II's widow, Queen Mary of Austria, and elected Ferdinand Hapsburg (Mary's younger brother) King of Hungary.

Bálint Török served the Hapsburg king faithfully for many years, though exacting a great price for that service. During more than a decade of internal wars (1526-1538) between John and Ferdinand, the two competing Kings of Hungary, Bálint Török acted as true robber, acquiring estates indiscriminately and becoming the most powerful landlord of Transdanubia (Hungary west of the Danube River) with his center at Szigetvár.

In the first half of the 1530's, King Ferdinand increasingly denied him new requests, and their relationship became increasingly tense. Bálint Török decided to leave Ferdinand and become a supporter of Zápolya again. The result was a royal order for his assassination, which attempt was botched.

In 1536, Zápolya rewarded Bálint Török with estates in several counties including governor of Hunyad County, its four castles and estates, and a gift of the city of Debrecen. Bálint Török became the country's largest, most powerful, and richest landowner. Taking advantage of the spread of the Reformation, he confiscated the treasures of the bishopric of Pécs and Nyitra. Not since the days of the Hunyadis had any one person amassed such vast estates in Hungary.

His power was at its peak when King John Zápolya died in 1540. That year, Friar György and Bálint Török defended Buda against an unsuccessful siege by one of Ferdinand's commanders, Leonhard Vels. The following year, under the command of Wilhelm Roggendorf, Ferdinand made another attempt to recapture Buda from the Zápolya party that supported King John's widow, Queen Isabella, and the infant king János Zsigmond. Roggendorf's troops were severely defeated, trapped between the garrison led by Bálint Török and an Ottoman force commanded by Mehmed Bey.

Sultan Suleiman arrived with his own army shortly after Roggendorf's defeat. Bálint Török and the other nobles guarding the infant king were invited to Suleiman's camp while janissaries occupied Buda without resistance. Bálint Török was taken prisoner and held captive in Istanbul, including in the infamous Seven Towers.

Bálint Török had repeatedly angered and crossed his fellow lords in order to gain new possessions, so nobody was interested in his return. The efforts made by his wife, Katalin Pemfflinger, to free him did not succeed. Sultan Suleiman saw a personal opponent in a charismatic military leader with considerable financial resources whose loyalty could not be trusted. Finally, in 1544, in return for his liberation, Bálint Török renounced all his castles in favor of the Turks. His final resting place is still unknown.

Gergely Bornemissza

Gergely (Gregory) Bornemissza (1526 – 1555), the hero of Géza Gárdonyi's novel, was a Hungarian soldier and is a national hero. Not much is known of his early life, but apparently he was the son of a blacksmith in Pécs and we know that he married twice and had six children. He is believed to have been an educated man and a Lutheran. Records from the siege of Eger refer to him as *deák*, a scholar.

According to Tinódi, he was particularly distinguished by his ingenious inventions and his clever ideas, which contributed significantly to the victory of the defenders in the 1552 Siege of Eger.

His first wife, Erzse Fighedi Oláh (Erzsébet Fügedi) died in January 1554. He married Dorottya Sygher (Sigér) in Eger Castle.

After the siege and following resignations by István Dobó and István Mekcsey, he was given command of Eger Castle. Bornemissza took over its administration, rebuilt its defenses, and designed and constructed Gergely Bastion.

Two years after the siege, in 1554, Bornemissza was riding through Keresztes (the village is mentioned in the novel) and was captured by a Turkish raiding party. No doubt, there was a bit of revenge on the part of the Turks. The Turks held him prisoner in Buda. Dobó, then a voivode of Transylvania, had it in his power to get Bornemissza exchanged for a prominent Turkish prisoner, but refused. It is hard to imagine how Dobó, who fought shoulder to shoulder with Bornemissza, could have abandoned him so easily.

Bornemissza was taken to Istanbul where he refused to betray secrets about the defenses at Eger. He was executed by hanging in Istanbul. His body is buried in a tomb located at the Bebek Bastion of Eger Castle.

István Mekcsey

István (Stephen) Mekcsey (? – 1553) was a Hungarian landowner and lieutenant of noble origin. He first appears in historical sources in 1542 as the owner of Baranya County. He held several diplomatic missions, and from 1551 he served as Co-Captain of Eger Castle with István Dobó.

After the 1552 siege, Ferdinand I rewarded him with 50 forints and donated land to him. On November 25, 1552, he and Dobó resigned as captains of Eger Castle. On March 13, 1555, he set off to join his wife in Ungvár (today's Uzhhorod in Ukrainian Carpathia). On the way he tried to take hay from travelers in the courtyard of an inn. He was struck with an axe and died on the spot. He was buried in St. Martin's church in Szepesség (today's Spiš in Slovakia).

Turkish Words

akinji (Turkish *akıncı*) — irregular light cavalry raiders that served as scouts and an advance party for the Ottomans. They were not paid. They lived off of looting. Their task was to lay waste to an area to be conquered by the main army.

agha (Turkish *ağa*, sometimes spelled aya) — Turkish officer or court official of middle rank.

azab — irregular Ottoman infantryman.

bey — senior Ottoman officer; the administrator of a province.

bismallah — in the name of Allah.

bostanji — (Turkish *bostancı*) personal guard and servant to the sultan.

deli – irregular cavalry fighting for the Ottomans.

feredje — a long outer robe worn by Muslim women.

gönüllü — an independent garrison soldier.

gureba — mercenary Arab, Egyptian or Persian cavalry serving the Ottoman court.

janissary — (Turkish *yeñiçeri*) elite Ottoman infantry mostly recruited from slaves captured in their youth.

jebeji — (Turkish, *cebeci*) were part of a small unit within the janissary corps responsible for keeping, maintaining and transporting weapons.

kapudji — the sultan's palace guards

kumbaraji — soldiers who manufacture and throw bombs.

lagumji — sappers.

müsellem — cavalry in military service for tax relief.

padishah — the shah of shahs, *i.e.*, the sultan as emperor.

piyad — Ottoman infantry.

serai — (Turkish *sarayı*) a palace, including Topkapi, the sultan's palace in Istanbul; also refers to a caravanserai, in inn for travelers

silahdar — bodyguard cavalry assigned to the sultan's court.

sipahi — Ottoman cavalry

topchi — (Turkish: *topçu*) Ottoman artilleryman.

topchi pasha — Ottoman artillery officer.

tüfekchis — Ottoman musket gunners

ulufedji — mercenary Turks serving in the cavalry.

yasaul — Ottoman soldiers charged with maintaining discipline.

yataghan — (Turkish *yatağan*) a curved short sword, like a long knife, with a single blade edge commonly used by Ottoman Turks.

zarbuza — Turkish siege cannon

Made in the USA
Columbia, SC
20 December 2024

50237203R00300